L. Sassaman

The English
Comedie Humaine

T̶̶ ̶̶NS OF

̶̶ ̶̶UER

468-BAB-416

O̶̶ ̶̶ER

The English
Comédie Humaine

Masterpieces of the great
English novelists in which
are portrayed the varying
aspects of English life from
the time of Addison to the
present day: a series analogous to that in which
Balzac depicted the man-
ners and morals of his
French contemporaries.

The Supper at Father Malachi's.

The English Comédie Humaine

THE CONFESSIONS OF
HARRY LORREQUER

BY

CHARLES LEVER

" We talked of pipe-clay, regulation caps,
    Long twenty-fours, short culverins and mortars;
Condemned the ' Horse Guards ' for a set of raps,
    And cursed our fate at being in such quarters.
Some smoked, some sighed, and some were heard to snore;
    Some wished themselves five fathoms 'neath the Solway;
And some did pray — who never prayed before —
    That they might get the ' route ' for Cork or Galway."

NEW YORK
The Century Co.
1905

PUBLISHERS' NOTE

CHARLES JAMES LEVER was born in Dublin in 1806. His ancestry was wholly English, and his keen sympathy with Irish life and character, and accurate understanding of it, were accordingly due not to racial inheritance, but to the accident of his Hibernian birth and residence. He was graduated at Trinity College, Dublin, in 1827; traveled on the Continent, and made a voyage to Canada (the latter in 1829); was a practising physician for several years; and held the position of secretary to the British embassy in Belgium 1840–42, and of consul at Spezzia and later at Trieste 1857–72. His death occurred at Trieste in 1872.

As has been the case with many other writers, his first novel, "Harry Lorrequer," not only made him famous, but is the one upon which his reputation still chiefly rests. It was published serially from February, 1837, in the "Dublin University Magazine," and exhibits Lever's rollicking humor, power of graphic and sustained narration, and vigorous style at their best. As a story-teller pure and simple, he ranks with Marryat and Collins—that is, with the best that English literature produced in the nineteenth century. Nor was he lacking in the higher qualities of the novelist. If his delineation of character is deficient in subtlety and fineness of imagination, it is conspicuous for fidelity to actual experience— namely, his own. His works are very largely accurate records of his own observation, "Harry Lorrequer," in particular, being professedly little more than an amplified note-book of the men he had met, the good stories he had heard, and the amusing scenes he saw. It has accordingly a distinct value as a record of manners, aside from its fascination as a story.

CONTENTS

CONTENTS

CONTENTS

LIST OF ILLUSTRATIONS

From drawings by "Phiz"

PREFACE.

THAT some thirty years after the sketches which form this volume were written I should be called on to revise and re-edit them, is strange enough to me, well remembering, as I do, with what little hope of permanence they were penned, how lightly they were undertaken, and how carelessly thrown together. But there is something still stranger in the retrospect, and that is that these same papers—for originally they were contributed as articles to the "Dublin University Magazine"—should mainly have directed the course of my future life and decided my entire career.

I may quote from a former preface that I was living in a very secluded spot when I formed the idea of jotting down these stories, many of them heard in boyhood, others constructed out of real incidents that had occurred to my friends in travel, and some, again,—as the adventures of Trevanion and the French duellist, for instance,—actual facts well known to many who had formed part of the army of occupation in France.

To give what consistency I might to a mass of incongruous adventure, to such a variety of strange situations befalling one individual, I was obliged to imagine a character which probably my experiences (and they were not very mature at the time) assured me as being perfectly possible,—one of a strong will and a certain energy, rarely persistent in purpose, and perpetually the sport of accident, with a hearty enjoyment of the pleasure of the hour and a very reckless indifference as to the price to be paid for it. If I looked out on my acquaintances, I believed I saw many of the traits I was bent on depicting, and for others I am half afraid I had only to take a peep into myself. If it is an error, then, to believe that in these "Confessions" I have ever recorded any incidents of my own life, there is no mistake in supposing that—without being in the least aware of it—in sketching Harry Lorrequer I was in a great measure depicting myself, and becoming, allegorically, an autobiographist.

Here is a confession which, if thirty odd years had not rolled over, I might be indisposed to make; but time has enabled me to look back on my work, and even on myself as I wrote it, with a certain degree of impartiality, and to feel, as regards both, as the great Paley said a man feels after he has finished his dinner, "that he might have done better."

It is perfectly unnecessary that I should say when and where I wrote these sketches; no thought of future authorship of any kind occurred to me, far less did I dream of abandoning my profession as a physician for the precarious livelihood of the pen. Indeed, their success, such as it was, only became known to me after I had left Ireland and gone to live abroad; and it was there—at Brussels—my publishers wrote to me to request a continuance of my "Confessions," with the assurance they had found favor with the world and flattering notice from the Press. Though I have been what the sarcastic French moralist called "blessed with a bad memory" all my life, I can still recall the delight—I cannot call it less—with which I heard my attempt at authorship was successful. I did not awake, indeed, "to find myself famous," but I well remember the thrill of triumphant joy with which I read the letter that said "Go on," and the entrancing ecstasy I felt at the bare possibility of my one day becoming known as a writer. I have had, since then, some moments in which a partial success has made me very happy and very grateful; but I do not believe that all these put together, or indeed any possible favor the world might mete to me, would impart a tithe of the enjoyment I felt on hearing that Harry

Lorrequer had been liked by the public, and that they had asked for more of him.

"If this sort of thing amuses them," thought I, "I can go on forever;" and believing this to be true, I launched forth with all that prodigal waste of material which, if it forms one of the reasons of the success, is, strictly speaking, one among the many demerits of this story. That I neither husbanded my resources nor imagined that they ever could fail me, were not my only mistakes; and I am tempted to show how little I understood of the responsibilities of authorship by repeating, what I have told elsewhere, an incident of the last number of "Harry Lorrequer." The MS. which contained the conclusion of the story had been sent through the Foreign Office bag from Brussels, and possibly had been mistaken for a despatch. At all events, like King Theodore's letter, it had been thrown to one side and forgotten. In this strait my publishers wrote to me in a strain that the trade alone knows how to employ towards an unknown author.

Stung by the reproaches—and they were not mild—of my correspondent, I wrote back, enclosing another conclusion, and telling him to print either, or both, as he pleased. Years after, I saw the first-sent MS., which came to hand at last, bound in my publisher's library, and lettered, "Another ending to H. L."

When the great master of fiction condescended to inform the world on what small fragments of tradition or local anecdote the Waverley Novels were founded, he best exalted the marvellous skill of his own handiwork in showing how genius could develop the veriest incident of a life into a story of surpassing power and interest. I have no such secrets to reveal, nor have I the faintest pretension to suppose the public would care to hear about the sources from which I drew either my characters or my incidents. I have seen, however, such references to supposed portraiture of individuals in this story that I am forced to declare that there is but one character in the book of which the original had any existence, and to which I contributed nothing of exaggeration. This is Father Malachi Brennan. The pleasant priest was alive when I wrote the tale, and saw himself in print, and—worse still—in picture,—not, I believe, without a certain mock indignation, for he was too racy a humorist and too genuine a lover of fun to be really angry at this caricature of him.

The amusing author of the "Wild Sports of the West," Hamilton Maxwell, was my neighbor in the little watering-place where I was living, and our intimacy was not the less close from the graver character of the society around us. We often exchanged our experiences of Irish character and life, and in our gossipings, stories were told, added to, and amplified in such a way between us that I believe neither of us could have pronounced at last who gave the initiative of an incident, or on which side lay the authorship of any particular event.

It would have been well had our intercourse stopped with these confidences; but unfortunately it did not. We often indulged in little practical jokes on our more well-conducted neighbors, and I remember that the old soldier from whom I drew some of the features I have given to Colonel Kamworth was especially the mark of these harmless pleasantries. Our colonel was an excellent fellow, kind-hearted and hospitable, but so infatuated with a propensity to meddle with every one and to be a partner in the joys, the afflictions, the failures, or the successes of all around him, that, with the best possible intentions and the most sincere desire to be useful to his neighbors, he became the cause of daily misconceptions and mistakes, sowed discord where he meant unity, and, in fact, originated more trouble and more distrust than the most malevolent mischief-maker of the whole country side.

I am forced to own that the small persecutions with which

my friend Maxwell and myself followed the worthy colonel, the wrong intelligence with which we supplied him, particularly as regarded the rank and station of the various visitors who came down during the bathing season, the false scents on which we sent him, and the absurd enterprises on which we embarked him, even to the extent of a mock address which induced him to stand for the "borough" (the address to the constituency being our joint production),—all these follies, I say, more or less disposed me, I feel sure, to that incessant flow of absurd incident which runs through this volume, and which, after all, was really little other than the reflex of our daily plottings and contrivings.

I believe my old friend the colonel is still living; if he be, and if he should read these lines, let him also read that I have other memories of him than those of mere jest and pleasantry,—memories of his cordial hospitality and genial good-nature,—and that there are few things I would like better than to meet and talk with him over bygones, knowing no one more likely to relish a pleasant reminiscence than himself, nor more certain to forgive a long-past liberty taken with him.

If there are many faults and blunders in this tale which I would willingly correct, if there be much that I would curtail or cut out altogether, and if there be also occasionally incidents of which I could improve the telling, I am held back from any attempts of this kind by the thought that it was by these sketches, such as they are, I first won that hearing from the public which for more than thirty years has never deserted me, and that the favor which has given the chief pride and interest to my life dates from the day I was known as Harry Lorrequer. Having given up the profession for which, I believe, I had some aptitude, to follow the precarious life of a writer, I suppose I am only admitting what many others under like circumstances might declare, that I have had my

moments, and more than mere moments, of doubt and mis-
giving that I made the wiser choice; and bating the intense
pleasure an occasional success has afforded, I have been led
to think that the career I had abandoned would have been
more rewarding, more safe from reverses, and less exposed
to those variations of public taste which are the terrors of
all who live on the world's favor.

Strangely enough, it is only my old doctorial instinct which
should suggest the consolation to this passing regret. The
life of the physician has nothing so thoroughly rewarding,
nothing so cheering, so full of hearty encouragement, as in
the occasional friendships to which it opens the way. The
doctor attains to a degree of intimacy and stands on a footing
of confidence so totally exceptional that if personal qualities
lend aid to the position, his intercourse becomes friendship.
Whether, therefore, my old career gave me any assistance
in new roads, whether it imparted to me any habits of inves-
tigation as applicable to the full in morals as to matter, it
certainly imparted to me the happy accident of standing on
good terms with—I was going to say—my patient,—and perhaps no better word could be found for him who has heard
me so long, trusted me so much, given me so large a share
of his favor, and come to look on me with such friendliness.
It would be the worst of ingratitude in me if I did not own
that I owe to my books, not only the pleasant intimacies of my
life, but some of my closest friendships. A chance expression,
a fairly shadowed thought, a mere chord struck at random
by a passing hand, as it were, has now and then placed me,
as mesmerists call it, *en rapport* with some one who may have
thought long and deeply on what I had but skimmed over; and
straightway there was a bond between us.

No small satisfaction has it been to me occasionally to hear
that out of the over-abundance of my own buoyancy and
light-heartedness—and I had a great deal of both long ago

PREFACE

—I have been able to share with my neighbor and given him part of my sunshine, and only felt the warmer myself. A great writer—one of the most eloquent historians who ever illustrated the military achievements of his country—once told me that as he lay sick and care-worn after a fever, it was in my reckless stories of soldier life he found the cheeriest moments of his solitude; and now let me hasten to say that I tell this in no spirit of boastfulness, but with the heartfelt gratitude of one who gained more by hearing that confession than Harry Lorrequer ever acquired by all his own.

One word now as regards the task I am immediately engaged in, and I have done.

My publishers propose to bring out in this edition a carefully revised version of all my books, in the order in which they were written, each story to be accompanied by some brief notice explaining the circumstances under which it was written, and to what extent fact or fiction had their share in the construction.

If such notices may occasionally be but leaves of an autobiography, I must ask my reader to pardon me, and to believe that I shall not impose my egotism upon him when it be possible to avoid it, while at the same time he shall know all that I myself know of the history of these volumes.

If to go over again the pages I wrote so many years ago is in a measure to revisit in age the loved scenes of boyhood, and to ponder over passages the very spirit of whose dictation is dead and gone,—if all this has its sadness, I am cheered by remembering that I am still addressing many old and dear friends, and have also for my audience the sons and grandsons, and, what I like better, the daughters and granddaughters, of those who once listened to Harry Lorrequer.

CHARLES LEVER.

TRIESTE, 1872.

HARRY LORREQUER

HARRY LORREQUER

CHAPTER I.

IT was on a splendid morning in the autumn of the year
181— that the *Howard* transport, with four hundred of
his Majesty's 4—th Regiment, dropped anchor in the picturesque harbor of Cove. The sea shone under the purple
light of the rising sun with a rich rosy hue, beautifully in
contrast with the different tints of the foliage of the deep
woods already tinged with the brown of autumn. Spike
Island lay "sleeping upon its broad shadow," and the large
ensign which crowns the battery was wrapped around the
flagstaff, there not being even air enough to stir it. It
was still so early that but few persons were abroad; and
as we leaned over the bulwarks, and looked now, for the
first time for eight long years, upon British ground, many
an eye filled, and many a heaving breast told how full of
recollections that short moment was, and how different our
feelings from the gay buoyancy with which we had sailed
from that same harbor for the Peninsula. Many of our
best and bravest had we left behind us, and more than one
native to the land we were approaching had found his last
rest in the soil of the stranger. It was, then, with a mingled sense of pain and pleasure we gazed upon that peaceful little village, whose white cottages lay dotted along the
edge of the harbor. The moody silence our thoughts had
shed over us was soon broken; the preparations for disem-
barking had begun, and I recollect well to this hour how,
shaking off the load that oppressed my heart, I descended
the gangway, humming poor Wolfe's well-known song,—

"Why, soldiers, why
Should we be melancholy, boys?"

And to this elasticity of spirits, whether the result of my profession, or the gift of God—as Dogberry has it—I know not, I owe the greater portion of the happiness I have enjoyed in a life whose changes and vicissitudes have equalled most men's.

Drawn up in a line along the shore, I could scarce refrain from a smile at our appearance. Four weeks on board a transport will certainly not contribute much to the *personnel* of any unfortunate therein confined; but when, in addition to this, you take into account that we had not received new clothes for three years,—if I except caps for our grenadiers, originally intended for a Scotch regiment, but found to be all too small for the long-headed generation. Many a patch of brown and gray variegated the faded scarlet of our uniform, and scarcely a pair of knees in the entire regiment did not confess their obligations to a blanket. But with all this, we showed a stout, weather-beaten front, that, disposed as the passer-by might feel to laugh at our expense, very little caution would teach him it were fully as safe to indulge it in his sleeve.

The bells from every steeple and tower rang gayly out a peal of welcome as we marched into "that beautiful city called Cork," our band playing "Garryowen,"—for we had been originally raised in Ireland, and still among our officers maintained a strong majority for that land of punch, priests, and potatoes,—the tattered flag of the regiment proudly waving over our heads, and not a man among us whose warm heart did not bound behind a Waterloo medal. Well, well! I am now—alas that I should say it!—somewhat in the "sere and yellow"; and I confess, after the experience of some moments of high, triumphant feeling, that I never before felt within me the same animating, spirit-filling glow of delight as rose within my heart that day as I marched at the head of my company down George's Street.

We were soon settled in barracks; and then began a series of entertainments on the side of the civic dignities of Cork which led most of us to believe that we had only escaped shot and shell to fall less gloriously beneath champagne and claret. I do not believe there is a coroner in the island who would have pronounced but the one verdict over the regi-

ment, "Killed by the mayor and corporation," had we so
fallen.

First of all, we were dined by the citizens of Cork; and
to do them justice, a harder-drinking set of gentlemen no
city need boast. Then we were feasted by the corporation;
then by the sheriffs; then came the mayor, solus; then an
address, with a cold collation, that left eight of us on the
sick-list for a fortnight. But the climax of all was a grand
entertainment given in the Mansion House, and to which
upwards of two thousand were invited. It was a species
of fancy ball, beginning by a *déjeûner* at three o'clock in
the afternoon, and ending—I never yet met the man who
could tell when it ended! As for myself, my *finale* partook a little of the adventurous, and I may as well
relate it.

After waltzing for about an hour with one of the preti-
est girls I ever set eyes upon, and getting a tender squeeze
of the hand as I restored her to a most affable-looking old
lady in a blue turban and a red velvet gown, who smiled
benignly at me and called me *"Meejor,"* I retired, to recruit
for a new attack, to a small table where three of ours were
quaffing *ponche à la Romaine,* with a crowd of Corkagians
about them eagerly inquiring after some heroes of their own
city whose deeds of arms they were surprised did not obtain
special mention from "the Duke." I soon ingratiated myself
into this well-occupied clique, and dosed them with glory to
their hearts' content. I resolved at once to enter into their
humor; and as the "ponche" mounted up to my brain, I
gradually found my acquaintanceship extend to every family
and connection in the country.

"Did ye know Phil Beamish, of the 3—th, sir?" said a
tall, red-faced, red-whiskered, well-looking gentleman, who
bore no slight resemblance to Feargus O'Connor.

"Phil Beamish!" said I. "Indeed I did, sir, and do still;
and there is not a man in the British army I am prouder
of knowing." Here, by the way, I may mention that I never
heard the name till that moment.

"You don't say so, sir?" said Feargus, for so I must call
him, for shortness' sake. "Has he any chance of the company yet, sir?"

5

"Company!" said I, in astonishment. "He obtained his majority three months since. You cannot possibly have heard from him lately, or you would have known that?"

"That's true, sir. I never heard since he quitted the 3—th to go to Versailles, I think they call it, for his health. But how did he get the step, sir?"

"Why, as to the company, that was remarkable enough!" said I, quaffing off a tumbler of champagne to assist my invention. "You know it was about four o'clock in the afternoon of the 18th that Napoleon ordered Grouchy to advance with the first and second brigade of the Old Guard and two regiments of chasseurs and attack the position occupied by Picton and the regiments under his command. Well, sir, on they came, masked by the smoke of a terrific discharge of artillery, stationed on a small eminence to our left, and which did tremendous execution among our poor fellows; on they came, sir, and as the smoke cleared partially away, we got a glimpse of them, and a more dangerous-looking set I should not desire to see,—grizzly-bearded, hard-featured, bronzed fellows, about five and thirty or forty years of age; their beauty not a whit improved by the red glare thrown upon their faces and along the whole line by each flash of the long twenty-fours that were playing away to the right. Just at this moment Picton rode down the line with his staff, and stopping within a few paces of me, said, 'They're coming up! Steady, boys; steady now! We shall have something to do soon!' And then turning sharply round, he looked in the direction of the French battery, that was thundering away again in full force. 'Ah! that must be silenced,' said he. 'Where's Beamish?'"

"Says Picton!" interrupted Feargus, his eyes starting from their sockets, and his mouth growing wider every moment, as he listened with the most intense interest.

"Yes," said I, slowly. And then, with all the provoking nonchalance of an Italian improvisatore, who always halts at the most exciting point of his narrative, I begged a listener near me to fill my glass from the iced punch beside him. Not a sound was heard as I lifted the bumper to my lips; all were breathless in their wound-up anxiety to hear of their countryman who had been selected by Picton—

for what, too, they knew not yet, and, indeed, at that instant I did not know myself, and nearly laughed outright, for the two of ours who had remained at the table had so well employed their interval of ease as to become very pleasantly drunk, and were listening to my confounded story with all the gravity and seriousness in the world. " 'Where's Beamish?' said Picton. 'Here, sir,' said Phil, stepping out from the line, and touching his cap to the general, who, taking him apart for a few minutes, spoke to him with great animation. We did not know what he said; but before five minutes were over, there was Phil with three companies of light-bobs drawn up at our left; their muskets at the charge, they set off at a round trot down the little steep which closed our flank. We had not much time to follow their movements, for our own amusement began soon; but I well remember, after repelling the French attack and standing in square against two heavy charges of cuirassiers, the first thing I saw, where the French battery had stood, was Phil Beamish and about a handful of brave fellows, all that remained from the skirmish. He captured two of the enemy's field-pieces, and was 'Captain Beamish' on the day after."

"Long life to him!" said at least a dozen voices behind and about me, while a general clinking of decanters and smacking of lips betokened that Phil's health, with all the honors, was being celebrated. For myself, I was really so engrossed by my narrative, and so excited by the "ponche," that I saw or heard very little of what was passing around, and have only a kind of dim recollection of being seized by the hand by "Feargus," who was Beamish's brother, and who, in the fullness of his heart, would have hugged me to his breast, if I had not opportunely been so overpowered as to fall senseless under the table.

When I first returned to consciousness, I found myself lying exactly where I had fallen. Around me lay heaps of slain, the two of "ours" among the number. One of them—I remember he was the Adjutant—held in his hand a wax candle (two to the pound). Whether he had himself seized it in the enthusiasm of my narrative of flood and field, or it had been put there by another, I know not; but he certainly cut a droll figure. The room we were in was a small one off the great saloon, and through the half-open folding-door I could clearly perceive that the festivities were still continued. The crash of fiddles and French horns and the tramp of feet, which had lost much of their elasticity since the entertainment began, rang through my ears, mingled with the sounds, "Down the middle," "Hands across," "Here's your partner, captain." What hour of the night or morning it then was, I could not guess; but certainly the vigor of the party seemed little abated, if I might judge from the specimen before me, and the testimony of a short, plethoric gentleman who stood wiping his bald head, after conducting his partner down twenty-eight couple, and who, turning to his friend, said, "Oh, the distance is nothing; but it is the pace that kills!"

The first evidence I showed of any return to reason was a strong anxiety to be at my quarters; but how to get there I knew not. The faint glimmering of sense I possessed told me that "to stand was to fall," and I was ashamed to go on all-fours, which prudence suggested.

At this moment I remembered I had brought with me my cane, which, from a perhaps pardonable vanity, I was fond of parading. It was a present from the officers of my regiment (many of them, alas! since dead), and had a most splendid gold head, with a stag at the top,—the arms of the regiment. This I would not have lost for any consideration I can mention; and this now was gone! I looked around me on every side; I groped beneath the table; I turned the sleeping sots who lay about me in no very gentle fashion: but, alas! it was gone. I sprang to my feet, and only then remembered how unfit I was to follow up the search, as tables, chairs, lights, and people seemed all rocking and waving before me. However, I succeeded in making my way through one room into another, sometimes guiding my steps along the walls; and once, as I recollect, striking the diagonal of a room, I bisected a quadrille with such ill-directed speed as to run foul of a Cork dandy and his partner who were just performing the *en avant;* but though I saw them lie tumbled in the dust by the shock of my encounter,—for I had upset them,—I still held on the even tenor of my way. In fact, I had feeling for but one loss; and, still in pursuit of my cane, I reached the hall-door. Now, be it known that the architecture of the Cork Mansion House has but one fault; but that fault is a grand one, and a strong evidence of how unsuited English architects are to provide buildings for a people whose tastes and habits they but imperfectly understand. Be it known, then, that the descent from the hall-door to the street was by a flight of twelve stone steps. How I should ever get down these was now my difficulty. If Falstaff deplored "eight yards of uneven ground as being three score and ten miles a foot," with equal truth did I feel that these twelve awful steps were worse to me than would be M'Gillicuddy's Reeks in the daylight and with a head clear from champagne.

While I yet hesitated, the problem resolved itself; for gazing down upon the bright gravel, brilliantly lighted by the surrounding lamps, I lost my balance and came tumbling and rolling from top to bottom, where I fell upon a large mass of some soft substance to which, in all probability, I owe my life. In a few seconds I recovered my senses; and what was my surprise to find that the downy cushion beneath snored most audibly! I moved a little to one side, and then discovered that in reality it was nothing less than an alderman of Cork, who, from his position, I concluded had shared the same fate with myself. There he lay, "like a warrior taking his rest," but not with his "martial cloak around him," but a much more comfortable and far more costly robe,—a scarlet gown of office,—with huge velvet cuffs and a great cape of the same material. True courage consists in presence of mind; and here mine came to my aid at once. Recollecting the loss I had just sustained, and perceiving that all was still about me, with that right Peninsular maxim that reprisals are fair in an enemy's camp, I proceeded to strip the slain; and with some little difficulty,—partly, indeed, owing to my own unsteadiness on my legs,—I succeeded in denuding the worthy alderman, who gave no other sign of life during the operation than an abortive effort to *"hip, hip, hurrah,"* in which I left him, having put on the spoil, and set out on my way to the barrack with as much dignity of manner as I could assume in honor of my costume. And here I may mention (in a parenthesis) that a more comfortable morning-gown no man ever possessed, and in its wide, luxuriant folds I revel while I write these lines.

When I awoke on the following day I had considerable difficulty in tracing the events of the past evening. The great scarlet cloak, however, unravelled much of the mystery, and gradually the whole of my career became clear before me, with the single exception of the episode of Phil Beamish, about which my memory was subsequently refreshed. But I anticipate. Only five appeared that day at mess; and, Lord! what spectres they were!—yellow as guineas. They called for soda-water without ceasing, and scarcely spoke a word to each other. It was plain that the corporation of Cork was committing more havoc among us than Corunna or Waterloo, and that if we did not change our quarters, there would be quick promotion in the corps for such as were "seasoned gentlemen." After a day or two we met again together, and then, what adventures were told!—each man had his own story to narrate; and from the occurrences detailed, one would have supposed years had been passing instead of the short hours of an evening party. Mine were, indeed, among the least remarkable; but I confess that the air of *vraisemblance* produced by my production of the aldermanic gown gave me the palm above all competitors.

Such was our life in Cork,—dining, drinking, dancing, riding, steeple-chasing, pigeon-shooting, and tandem-driving, filling up any little interval that was found to exist between a late breakfast and the time to dress for dinner; and here I hope I shall not be accused of a tendency to boasting while I add that among all ranks and degrees of men, and women too, there never was a regiment more highly in estimation than the 4—th. We felt the full value of all the attentions we were receiving, and we endeavored, as best we might, to repay them. We got up Garrison Balls and Garrison Plays, and usually performed once or twice a week during the winter. Here I shone conspicuously. In the morning I was employed painting scenery and arranging the properties; as it grew later, I regulated the lamps and looked after the footlights, mediating occasionally between angry litigants, whose jealousies abound to the full as much in private theatricals as in the regular *corps dramatique*. Then I was also leader in the orchestra, and had scarcely given the last scrape in the overture before I was obliged to appear to speak the prologue. Such are the cares of greatness. To do myself justice, I did not dislike them; though, to be sure, my taste for the drama did cost me a little dear, as will be seen in the sequel.

We were then in the full career of popularity,—our balls pronounced the very pleasantest, our plays far superior to any regular corps that had ever honored Cork with their talents,—when an event occurred which threw a gloom over all our proceedings, and finally put a stop to every project for amusement we had so completely given ourselves up to. This was no less than the removal of our Lieutenant-Colonel. After thirty years of active service in the regiment he then commanded, his age and infirmities, increased by some severe wounds, demanded ease and repose; he retired from us bearing along with him the love and regard of every man in the regiment. To the old officers he was endeared by long companionship and undeviating friendship; to the young, he was in every respect as a father, assisting by his advice and guiding by his counsel; while to the men, the best estimate of his worth appeared in the fact that corporal punishment was unknown in the corps. Such was the man we lost; and it may well be supposed that his successor, who or whatever he might be, came under circumstances of no common difficulty amongst us: but when I tell that our new Lieutenant-Colonel was in every respect his opposite, it may be believed how little cordiality he met with.

Lieutenant-Colonel Carden—for so I shall call him, although not his real name—had not been a month at quarters when he proved himself a regular martinet. Everlasting drills, continual reports, fatigue parties, and ball practice, and Heaven knows what besides, superseded our former morning's occupation; and at the end of the time I have mentioned, we, who had fought our way from Albuera to Waterloo, under some of the severest generals of division, were pronounced a most disorderly and ill-disciplined regiment by a colonel who had never seen a shot fired but at a review at Hounslow, or a sham battle in the Fifteen Acres. The

winter was now drawing to a close—already some little touch
of spring was appearing—as our last play for the season was
announced, and every effort to close with some little additional *éclat* was made; and each performer in the expected
piece was nerving himself for an effort beyond his wont.
The Colonel had most unequivocally condemned these plays;
but that mattered not, they came not within his jurisdiction,
and we took no notice of his displeasure further than sending him tickets, which were as immediately returned as received. From being the chief offender, I had become particularly obnoxious, and he had upon more than one occasion
expressed his desire for an opportunity to visit me with his
vengeance; but being aware of his kind intentions towards
me, I took particular care to let no such opportunity occur.

On the morning in question, then, I had scarcely left my
quarters when one of my brother officers informed me that
the Colonel had made a great uproar, that one of the bills
of the play had been put up on his door, which, with his
avowed dislike to such representations, he considered as intended to insult him: he added, too, that the Colonel attributed it to me. In this, however, he was wrong; and to this
hour I never knew who did it. I had little time, and still
less inclination, to meditate upon the Colonel's wrath,—the
theatre had all my thoughts; and indeed it was a day of no
common exertion, for our amusements were to conclude with
a grand supper on the stage, to which all the *élite* of Cork
were invited. Wherever I went through the city,—and many
were my peregrinations,—the great placard of the play stared
me in the face; and every gate and shuttered window in Cork
proclaimed "THE PART OF OTHELLO BY MR. LORREQUER."

As evening drew near, my cares and occupations were redoubled. My Iago I had fears for; 't is true he was an admirable Lord Grizzle in "Tom Thumb"—but then—then I
had to paint the whole company, and bear all their abuse
besides, for not making some of the most ill-looking wretches
perfect Apollos; but, last of all, I was sent for, at a quarter
to seven, to lace Desdemona's stays. Start not, gentle reader,
my fair Desdemona—she "who might lie by an emperor's
side and command him tasks"—was no other than the senior
lieutenant of the regiment, and who was as great a votary

of the jolly god as honest Cassio himself. But I must hasten on; I cannot delay to recount our successes in detail. Let it suffice to say, that, by universal consent, I was preferred to Kean; and the only fault the most critical observer could find to the representative of Desdemona was a rather unlady-like fondness for snuff. But whatever little demerits our acting might have displayed, were speedily forgotten in a champagne supper. There I took the head of the table; and in the costume of the noble Moor toasted, made speeches, returned thanks, and sang songs, till I might have exclaimed with Othello himself, "Chaos is come again;" and I believe I owe my ever reaching the barrack that night to the kind offices of Desdemona, who carried me the greater part of the way on her back.

The first waking thoughts of him who has indulged overnight are not among the most blissful of existence; and certainly the pleasure is not increased by the consciousness that he is called on to the discharge of duties to which a fevered pulse and throbbing temples are but ill suited. My sleep was suddenly broken in upon the morning after the play by a "row-dow-dow" beat beneath my window. I jumped hastily from my bed and looked out, and there, to my horror, perceived the regiment under arms. It was one of our confounded Colonel's morning drills; and there he stood himself, with the poor Adjutant, who had been up all night, shivering beside him. Some two or three of the officers had descended; and the drum was now summoning the others as it beat round the barrack-square. I saw there was not a moment to lose, and proceeded to dress with all despatch; but, to my misery, I discovered everywhere nothing but theatrical robes and decorations. There lay a splendid turban; here a pair of buskins. A spangled jacket glittered on one table, and a jewelled scimitar on the other. At last I detected my "regimental small-clothes," most ignominiously thrust into a corner in my ardor for my Moorish robes the preceding evening.

I dressed myself with the speed of lightning; but as I proceeded in my occupation, guess my annoyance to find that the toilet-table and glass, ay, and even the basin-stand, had been removed to the dressing-room of the theatre. And my servant, I suppose, following his master's example, was too tipsy to remember to bring them back, so that I was unable to procure the luxury of cold water; for now not a moment more remained, the drum had ceased, and the men had all fallen in. Hastily drawing on my coat, I put on my shako, and buckling on my belt as dandy-like as might be, hurried down the stairs to the barrack-yard. By the time I got down, the men were all drawn up in line along the square, while the Adjutant was proceeding to examine their accoutrements as he passed down. The Colonel and the officers were standing in a group, but not conversing. The anger of the commanding officer appeared still to continue, and there was a dead silence maintained on both sides. To reach the spot where they stood, I had to pass along part of the line. In doing so, how shall I convey my amazement at the faces that met me,—a general titter ran along the entire rank, which not even their fears for consequences seemed able to repress; for an effort on the part of many to stifle the laugh only ended in a still louder burst of merriment. I looked to the far side of the yard for an explanation, but there was nothing there to account for it. I now crossed over to where the officers were standing, determining in my own mind to investigate the occurrence thoroughly when free from the presence of the Colonel, to whom any representation of ill conduct always brought a punishment far exceeding the merits of the case.

Scarcely had I formed this resolve, when I reached the group of officers; but the moment I came near, one general roar of laughter saluted me, the like of which I never before heard. I looked down at my costume, expecting to discover that in my hurry to dress I had put on some of the garments of Othello. No, all was perfectly correct. I waited for a moment till, the first burst of their merriment over, I should obtain a clew to the jest. But there seemed no prospect of this, for as I stood patiently before them, their mirth appeared to increase. Indeed, poor G——, the senior major, one of the gravest men in Europe, laughed till the tears ran down his cheeks; and such was the effect upon me that I was induced to laugh too,—as men will sometimes, from the infectious nature of that strange emotion; but no sooner did I do this, than their fun knew no bounds, and some almost screamed aloud in the excess of their merriment. Just at this instant the Colonel, who had been examining some of the men, approached our group, advancing with an air of evident displeasure, as the shouts of laughter continued. As he came up, I turned hastily round, and touching my cap, wished him good morning. Never shall I forget the look he gave me. If a glance could have annihilated any man, his would have finished me. For a moment his face became purple with rage, his eye was almost hid beneath his bent brow, and he absolutely shook with passion.

"Go, sir," said he at length, as soon as he was able to find utterance for his words, "go, sir, to your quarters; and before you leave them a court-martial shall decide if such continued insult to your commanding officer warrants your name being in the Army List."

"What the devil can all this mean?" I said, in a half-whisper, turning to the others. But there they stood, their handkerchiefs to their mouths, and evidently choking with suppressed laughter.

"May I beg, Colonel Carden," said I—

"To your quarters, sir," roared the little man in the voice of a lion; and with a haughty wave of his hand, prevented all further attempt on my part to seek explanation.

"They're all mad, every man of them," I muttered, as I betook myself slowly back to my rooms, amid the same evidences of mirth my first appearance had excited, which even the Colonel's presence, feared as he was, could not entirely subdue.

With the air of a martyr I trod heavily up the stairs and entered my quarters, meditating within myself awful schemes for vengeance on the now open tyranny of my Colonel, upon whom I, too, in my honest rectitude of heart, vowed to have a "court-martial." I threw myself upon a chair, and endeavored to recollect what circumstances of the past evening could have possibly suggested all the mirth in which both officers and men seemed to participate equally; but nothing could I remember capable of solving the mystery. Surely the cruel wrongs of the manly Othello were no laughter-moving subject.

I rang the bell hastily for my servant. The door opened.

"Stubbes," said I, "are you aware—"

I had only got so far in my question when my servant, one of the most discreet of men, put on a broad grin, and turned away towards the door to hide his face.

"What the devil does this mean?" said I, stamping with passion; "he is as bad as the rest. Stubbes"—and this I spoke with the most grave and severe tone—"what is the meaning of this insolence?"

"Oh, sir," said the man, "oh, sir, surely you did not appear on parade with that face?" And then he burst into a fit of the most uncontrollable laughter.

Like lightning a horrid doubt shot across my mind. I sprang over to the dressing-glass, which had been replaced, and oh, horror of horrors! there I stood as black as the king of Ashantee. The cursed dye which I had put on for Othello, I had never washed off; and there, with a huge bearskin shako and a pair of dark bushy whiskers, shone my huge, black, and polished visage, glowering at itself in the looking-glass.

My first impulse, after amazement had a little subsided, was to laugh immoderately; in this I was joined by Stubbes, who, feeling that his mirth was participated in, gave full vent to his risibility. And, indeed, as I stood before the glass, grinning from ear to ear, I felt very little surprise that my joining in the laughter of my brother officers, a short time before, had caused an increase of their merriment. I threw myself upon a sofa, and absolutely laughed till my sides ached, when, the door opening, the Adjutant made his appearance. He looked for a moment at me, then at Stubbes, and then burst out himself as loud as either of us. When he had at length recovered himself, he wiped his face with his handkerchief, and said, with a tone of much gravity,—

"But, my dear Lorrequer, this will be a serious, a devilish serious affair. You know what kind of man Colonel Carden is; and you are aware, too, you are not one of his prime favorites. He is firmly persuaded that you intended to insult him, and nothing will convince him to the contrary. We told him how it must have occurred, but he will listen to no explanation."

I thought for one second before I replied. My mind, with the practised rapidity of an old campaigner, took in all the *pros* and *cons* of the case; I saw at a glance it were better to brave the anger of the Colonel, come in what shape it might, than be the laughing-stock of the mess for life, and with a face of the greatest gravity and self-possession, said,—

"Well, Adjutant, the Colonel is right. It was no mistake. You know I sent him tickets yesterday for the theatre. Well, he returned them; this did not annoy me, but on one account: I had made a wager with Alderman Gullable that the Colonel should see me in Othello. What was to be done? Don't you see, now, there was only one course, and I took it, old boy, and have won my bet!"

"And lost your commission for a dozen of champagne, I suppose," said the Adjutant.

"Never mind, my dear fellow," I replied; "I shall get out of this scrape, as I have done many others."

"But what do you intend doing?"

"Oh! as to that," said I, "I shall, of course, wait on the Colonel immediately; pretend to him that it was a mere blunder from the inattention of my servant, hand over Stubbes to the powers that punish" (here the poor fellow winced a little), "and make my peace as well as I can. But, Adjutant, mind," said I, "and give the real version to all our fellows, and tell them to make it public as much as they please."

"Never fear," said he, as he left the room still laughing, "they shall all know the true story; but I wish with all my heart you were well out of it."

I now lost no time in making my toilet, and presented myself at the Colonel's quarters. It is no pleasure for me to recount these passages in my life in which I have had to bear the "proud man's contumely." I shall therefore merely observe that after a very long interview the Colonel accepted my apologies and we parted.

Before a week elapsed, the story had gone far and near; every dinner-table in Cork had laughed at it. As for me, I attained immortal honor for my tact and courage. Poor Gullable readily agreed to favor the story, and gave us a dinner as the lost wager; and the Colonel was so unmercifully quizzed on the subject, and such broad allusions to his being humbugged were given in the Cork papers, that he was obliged to negotiate a change of quarters with another regiment, to get out of the continual jesting; and in less than a month we marched to Limerick, to relieve, as it was reported, the 9th, ordered for foreign service, but in reality only to relieve Lieutenant-Colonel Carden, quizzed beyond endurance.

However, if the Colonel had seemed to forgive, he did not forget; for the very second week after our arrival in Limerick, I received one morning at my breakfast-table the following brief note from our Adjutant:—

MY DEAR LORREQUER,—The Colonel has received orders to despatch two companies to some remote part of the County Clare; and as you have "done the state some service," you are selected for the beautiful town of Kilrush, where, to use the eulogistic language of the geography books, "there is a good harbor and a market plentifully supplied with fish." I have just heard of the kind intention in store for you, and lose no time in letting you know.

God give you a good deliverance from the *garçons blancs,* as the "Moniteur" calls the Whiteboys, and believe me ever yours, CHARLES CURZON.

I had scarcely twice read over the Adjutant's epistle when I received an official notification from the Colonel directing me to proceed to Kilrush, then and there to afford all aid and assistance in suppressing illicit distillation, when called on for that purpose; and other similar duties too agreeable to recapitulate. Alas! alas! "Othello's occupation" was indeed gone! The next morning at sunrise saw me on my march, with what appearance of gayety I could muster, but in reality very much chapfallen at my banishment, and invoking sundry things upon the devoted head of the Colonel which he would by no means consider as "blessings."

How short-sighted are we mortals, whether enjoying all the pomp and state of royalty, or marching, like myself, at the head of a detachment of his Majesty's 4—th.

Little, indeed, did I anticipate that the Siberia to which I fancied I was condemned should turn out the happiest quar-

ters my fate ever threw me into. But this, including as it
does one of the most important events of my life, I reserve for
another chapter.

"What is that place called, Sergeant?"

"Bunratty Castle, sir."

"Where do we breakfast?"

"At Clare Island, sir."

"March away, boys!"

CHAPTER II.

DETACHMENT DUTY.—THE BURTON ARMS.—CALLONBY.

FOR a week after my arrival at Kilrush, my life was one
of the most dreary monotony. The rain, which had begun to fall as I left Limerick, continued to descend in torrents,
and I found myself a close prisoner in the sanded parlor of
"mine inn." At no time would such "durance vile" have
been agreeable; but now, when I contrasted it with all I
had left behind at headquarters, it was absolutely maddening. The pleasant lounge in the morning, the social mess,
and the agreeable evening party were all exchanged for a
short promenade of fourteen feet in one direction, and twelve
in the other, such being the accurate measurement of my
salle à manger; a chicken, with legs as blue as a Highlander's
in winter, for my dinner; and the hours that all Christian man-
kind were devoting to pleasant intercourse and agreeable
chit-chat, spent in beating that dead-march to time, "the
Devil's Tattoo," upon my rickety table; and forming, between
whiles, sundry valorous resolutions to reform my life and
"eschew sack and loose company."

My front window looked out upon a long, straggling, ill-
paved street, with its due proportion of mud-heaps and duck-
pools; the houses on either side were for the most part dingy-
looking edifices with half-doors and such pretension to being
shops as a quart of meal or salt displayed in the window con-
fers; or sometimes two tobacco-pipes, placed "saltier-wise,"
would appear the only vendible article in the establishment.

A more wretched, gloomy-looking picture of woe-begone poverty I never beheld.

If I turned for consolation to the back of the house, my eyes fell upon the dirty yard of a dirty inn,—the half-thatched cow-shed, where two famished animals mourned their hard fate, "chewing the cud of sweet and bitter fancy;" the chaise, the yellow post-chaise, once the pride and glory of the establishment, now stood reduced from its wheels, and ignominiously degraded to a hen-house. On the grass-grown roof a cock had taken his stand, with an air of protective patronage to the feathered inhabitants beneath,—

"To what base uses must we come at last!"

That chaise, which once had conveyed the blooming bride, all blushes and tenderness, and the happy groom on their honeymoon visit to Ballybunnion and its romantic caves or to the gigantic cliffs and sea-girt shores of Moher, or, with more steady pace and becoming gravity, had borne along the "going judge of assize," was now become a lying-in hospital for fowls and a nursery for chickens. Fallen as I was from my high estate, it afforded me a species of malicious satisfaction to contemplate these sad reverses of fortune; and I verily believe—for on such slight foundation our greatest resolves are built—that if the rain had continued a week longer, I should have become a misanthropist for life. I made many inquiries from my landlady as to the society of the place, but the answers I received only led to greater despondence. My predecessor here, it seemed, had been an officer of a veteran battalion, with a wife and that amount of children which is algebraically expressed by an x,—meaning an unknown quantity. He, good man, in his two years' sojourn here had been much more solicitous about his own affairs than making acquaintance with his neighbors; and at last the few persons who had been in the habit of calling on "the officer" gave up the practice; and as there were no young ladies to refresh Pa's memory on the matter, they soon forgot completely that such a person existed. And to this happy oblivion I, Harry Lorrequer, succeeded, and was thus left, without benefit of clergy, to the tender mercies of Mrs. Healy, of the Burton Arms.

As during the inundation which deluged the whole country around I was unable to stir from the house, I enjoyed
abundant opportunity of cultivating the acquaintance of my
hostess; and it is but fair that my reader, who has journeyed
so far with me, should have an introduction.

Mrs. Healy, the sole proprietor of the Burton Arms, was
of some five-and-fifty—"or, by 'r lady," threescore—years,
of a rubicund and hale complexion; and though her short
neck and corpulent figure might have set her down as "doubly
hazardous," she looked a good life for many years to come.
In height and breadth she most nearly resembled a sugar-
hogshead, whose rolling, pitching motion, when trundled
along on edge, she emulated in her gait. To the ungainli-
ness of her figure her mode of dressing not a little contributed.
She usually wore a thick linsey-wolsey gown, with enormous
pockets on either side, and, like Nora Creina's, it certainly
inflicted no undue restriction upon her charms, but left

> " Every beauty free,
> To sink or swell as Heaven pleases."

Her feet—ye gods! such feet—were apparelled in listing
slippers, over which the upholstery of her ankles descended,
and completely relieved the mind of the spectator as to the
superincumbent weight being disproportioned to the support.
I remember well my first impression on seeing those feet and
ankles reposing upon a straw footstool, while she took her
afternoon doze, and I wondered within myself if elephants
were liable to the gout. There are few countenances in the
world that, if wishing to convey an idea of, we cannot refer
to some well-known standard, and thus nothing is more common than to hear comparisons with "Vulcan, Venus, Nicode-
mus," and the like; but in the present case I am totally at a
loss for anything resembling the face of the worthy Mrs.
Healy, except it be, perhaps, that most ancient and sour visage
we used to see upon old circular iron rappers formerly,—they
make none of them now,—the only difference being that Mrs.
Healy's nose had no ring through it; I am almost tempted
to add, "more's the pity."

Such was she in "the flesh;" would that I could say she

was more fascinating in the "spirit!" But alas! truth, from which I never may depart in these my "Confessions," constrains me to acknowledge the reverse. Most persons, in this miserable world of ours, have some prevailing, predominating characteristic, which usually gives the tone and color to all their thoughts and actions, forming what we denominate temperament; this we see actuating them, now more, now less. But rarely, however, is this great spring of action without its moments of repose. Not so with her of whom I have been speaking. She had but one passion,—but, like Aaron's rod, it had a most consuming tendency,—and that was to scold and abuse all whom hard fate had brought within the unfortunate limits of her tyranny. The English language, comprehensive as it is, afforded no epithets strong enough for her wrath, and she sought among the more classic beauties of her native Irish such additional ones as served her need; and with this holy alliance of tongues she had been for years long, the dread and terror of the entire village.

"The dawning of morn, the daylight sinking,"

ay, and even the "night's dull hours," it was said, too, found her laboring in her congenial occupation; and while thus she continued to "scold and grow fat," her inn, once a popular and frequented one, became gradually less and less frequented, and the dragon of the Rhine-fells did not more effectually lay waste the territory about him than did the evil influence of her tongue spread desolation and ruin around her. Her inn, at the time of my visit, had not been troubled with even a passing traveller for many months; and, indeed, had I had any, even the least, foreknowledge of the character of my hostess, its privacy should have still remained uninvaded for some time longer.

I had not been many hours installed, when I got a specimen of her powers; and before the first week was over, so constant and unremitting were her labors in this way that I have, upon the occasion of a slight lull in the storm, occasioned by her falling asleep, actually left my room to inquire if anything had gone wrong, in the same way as the miller is said to awake when the mill stops. I trust I have said enough to move the reader's pity and compassion for my situation; one more miserable it is difficult to conceive. It may be thought that much might be done by management, and that a slight exercise of the favorite Whig plan might avail. Nothing of the kind. She was proof against all such arts; and what was still worse, there was no subject, no possible circumstance, no matter, past, present, or to come, that she could not wind, by her diabolical ingenuity, into some cause of offence; and then came the quick transition to instant punishment. Thus, my apparently harmless inquiry as to the society of the neighborhood suggested to her—a wish on my part to make acquaintance; therefore to dine out; therefore not to dine at home; consequently to escape paying half-a-crown and devouring a chicken; therefore to defraud her, and behave, as she would herself observe, "like a beggarly scullion, with his four shillings a day, setting up for a gentleman," etc.

By a quiet and Job-like endurance of all manner of taunting suspicions and unmerited sarcasms, to which I daily became more reconciled, I absolutely rose into something like favor; and before the first month of my banishment expired, had got the length of an invitation to tea in her own snuggery, —an honor never known to be bestowed on any before, with the exception of Father Malachi Brennan, her ghostly adviser; and even he, it is said, never ventured on such an approximation to intimacy until he was, in Kilrush phrase, "half screwed," thereby meaning more than half tipsy. From time to time, thus, I learned from my hostess such particulars of the country and its inhabitants as I was desirous of hearing; and among other matters, she gave me an account of the great landed proprietor himself, Lord Callonby, who was daily expected at his seat within some miles of Kilrush, at the same time assuring me that I need not be looking so "pleased and curling out my whiskers; that they'd never take the trouble of asking even the name of me." This, though neither very courteous, nor altogether flattering to listen to, was no more than I had already learned from some brother officers who knew this quarter, and who informed me that the Earl of Callonby, though only visiting his Irish estates every three or four years, never took the slightest notice of any of the military in his neighborhood; nor, indeed, did he mix with the country gentry, confining himself to his own family or the guests who usually accompanied him from England and remained during his few weeks' stay. My impression of his lordship was therefore not calculated to cheer my solitude by any prospect of his rendering it lighter.

The Earl's family consisted of her ladyship, an only son, nearly of age, and two daughters,—the eldest, Lady Jane, had the reputation of being extremely beautiful; and I remembered when she came out in London, only the year before, hearing nothing but praises of the grace and elegance of her manner, united to the most classic beauty of her face and figure. The second daughter was some years younger, and said to be also very handsome; but as yet she had not been brought into society. Of the son, Lord Kilkee, I only heard that he had been a very gay fellow at Oxford, where he was much liked, and although not particularly studious, had given evidence of talent.

Such were the few particulars I obtained of my neighbors, and thus little did I know of those who were so soon to exercise a most important influence upon my future life.

After some weeks' close confinement, which, judging from my feelings alone, I should have counted as many years, I eagerly seized the opportunity of the first glimpse of sunshine to make a short excursion along the coast; I started early in the morning, and after a long stroll along the bold headlands of Kilkee, was returning late in the evening to my lodgings. My path lay across a wild, bleak moor, dotted with low clumps of furze, and not presenting on any side the least trace of habitation. In wading through the tangled bushes, my dog Mouche started a hare; and after a run "sharp, short, and decisive," killed her at the bottom of a little glen some hundred yards off.

I was just patting my dog and examining the prize, when I heard a crackling among the low bushes near me, and on looking up, perceived, about twenty paces distant, a short, thickset man, whose fustian jacket and leathern gaiters at once pronounced him the gamekeeper; he stood leaning upon his gun, quietly awaiting, as it seemed, for any movement on my part, before he interfered. With one glance I detected how matters stood, and immediately adopting my usual policy of "taking the bull by the horns," called out, in a tone of very sufficient authority,—

"I say, my man, are you his Lordship's gamekeeper?"

Taking off his hat, the man approached me, and very respectfully informed me that he was.

"Well, then," said I, "present this hare to his lordship with my respects,—here is my card,—and say I shall be most happy to wait on him in the morning and explain the circumstance."

The man took the card, and seemed for some moments undecided how to act; he seemed to think that probably he might be ill-treating a friend of his lordship's if he refused, and on the other hand might be merely "jockeyed" by some bold-faced poacher. Meanwhile I whistled my dog close up, and humming an air, with great appearance of indifference stepped out homeward. By this piece of presence of mind I saved poor Mouche; for I saw at a glance that, with true gamekeeper's law, he had been destined to death the moment he had committed the offence.

The following morning, as I sat at breakfast meditating upon the events of the preceding day, and not exactly determined how to act, whether to write to his lordship explaining how the matter occurred, or call personally, a loud rattling on the pavement drew me to the window. As the house stood at the end of a street, I could not see in the direction the noise came; but as I listened, a very handsome tandem turned the corner of the narrow street, and came along towards the hotel at a long sling trot; the horses were dark chestnuts, well matched, and showing a deal of blood. The carriage was a dark drab, with black wheels, the harness all of the same color. The whole turnout—and I was an amateur of that sort of thing—was perfect; the driver—for I come to him last, as he was the last I looked at—was a fashionable-looking young fellow, plainly but knowingly dressed, and evidently handling the "ribbons" like an experienced whip.

After bringing his nags up to the inn-door in very pretty style, he gave the reins to his servant and got down. Before I was well aware of it, the door of my room opened, and the gentleman entered with a certain easy air of good-breeding, and saying,—

"Mr. Lorrequer, I presume," introduced himself as Lord Kilkee.

I immediately opened the conversation by an apology for my dog's misconduct on the day before, and assured his lordship that I knew the value of a hare in a hunting country, and was really sorry for the circumstance.

"Then I must say," replied his lordship, "Mr. Lorrequer is the only person who regrets the matter; for had it not been for this, it is more than probable we should never have known we were so near neighbors,—in fact, nothing could equal our amazement at hearing *you* were playing the Solitaire down here. You must have found it dreadfully heavy, 'and have thought us downright savages.' But then I must explain to you that my father has made some 'rule absolute' about visiting when down here; and though I know you'll not consider it a compliment, yet I can assure you there is not another man I know of he would pay attention to but yourself. He made two efforts to get here this morning, but the gout 'would not be denied,' and so he deputed a most inferior 'diplomate;' and now will you let me return with some character from my first mission, and inform my friends that you will dine with us to-day at seven,—a mere family party; but make your arrangements to stop all night and to-morrow. We shall find some work for my friend there on the hearth,— what do you call him, Mr. Lorrequer?"

"Mouche. Come here, Mouche."

"Ah! Mouche, come here, my fine fellow. A splendid dog indeed; very tall for a thoroughbred. And now you'll not forget,—seven, *temps militaire;* and, so *sans adieu.*"

And with these words his lordship shook me heartily by the hand; and before two minutes had elapsed had wrapped his box-coat once more across him, and was round the corner.

I looked for a few moments on the again silent street, and was almost tempted to believe I was in a dream, so rapidly had the preceding moments passed over, and so surprised was I to find that the proud Earl of Callonby, who never did the "civil thing" anywhere, should think proper to pay attention to a poor sub in a marching regiment, whose only claim on his acquaintance was the suspicion of poaching on his manor. I repeated over and over all his lordship's most polite speeches, trying to solve the mystery of them, but in vain; a thousand explanations occurred, but none of them I felt at all satisfactory. That there was some mystery somewhere I had no doubt; for I remarked all through that Lord Kilkee laid some stress upon my identity, and even seemed surprised at *my* being in such banishment. "Oh!" thought I at last, "his lordship is about to get up private theatricals, and has seen my Captain Absolute, or perhaps my Hamlet," —I could not say "Othello" even to myself,—"and is anxious to get 'such unrivalled talent' even 'for one night only.' "

After many guesses this seemed the nearest I could think of; and by the time I had finished my dressing for dinner, it was quite clear to me I had solved all the secret of his lordship's attentions.

The road to "Callonby" was beautiful beyond anything I had ever seen in Ireland. For upwards of two miles it led along the margin of some lofty cliffs, now jutting out into bold promontories, and again retreating and forming small bays and mimic harbors, into which the heavy swell of the broad Atlantic was rolling its deep blue tide. The evening was perfectly calm, and at a little distance from the shore the surface of the sea was without a ripple. The only sound breaking the solemn stillness of the hour was the heavy plash of the waves as in minute peals they rolled in upon the pebbly beach and brought back with them, at each retreat, some of the larger and smoother stones, whose noise, as they fell back into old Ocean's bed, mingled with the din of the breaking surf. In one of the many little bays I passed, lay three or four fishing-smacks. The sails were drying, and flapped lazily against the mast. I could see the figures of the men as they passed backwards and forwards upon the decks, and although the height was nearly eight hundred feet, could hear their voices quite distinctly. Upon the golden strand, which was still marked with a deeper tint, where the tide had washed, stood a little white cottage of some fishermen,— at least so the net before the door bespoke it. Around it stood some children, whose merry voices and laughing tones sometimes reached me where I was standing. I could not but think, as I looked down from my lofty eyrie upon that little group of boats and that lone hut, how much of the "world," to the humble dwellers beneath, lay in that secluded and narrow bay. There the deep sea, where their days were passed in "storm or sunshine;" there the humble home where at night they rested, and around whose hearth lay all their cares and all their joys. How far, how very far removed from the busy haunts of men and all the struggles and contentions of the ambitious world; and yet, how short-sighted to suppose that even they had not their griefs and sorrows, and that their humble lot was devoid of the inheritance of those woes which all are heirs to!

I turned reluctantly from the sea-shore to enter the gate of the park, and my path in a few moments was as completely screened from all prospect of the sea as though it had lain miles inland. An avenue of tall and ancient lime-trees, so dense in their shadows as nearly to conceal the road beneath, led for above a mile through a beautiful lawn, whose surface, gently undulating, and studded with young clumps, was dotted over with sheep. At length, descending by a very steep road, I reached a beautiful little stream, over which a rustic bridge was thrown. As I looked down upon the rippling stream beneath, on the surface of which the dusky evening flies were dipping, I made a resolve, if I prospered in his lordship's good graces, to devote a day to the "angle" there before I left the country. It was now growing late; and remembering Lord Kilkee's intimation of "sharp seven," I threw my reins over my cob Sir Roger's neck (for I had hitherto been walking), and cantered up the steep hill before me. When I reached the top, I found myself upon a broad tableland encircled by old and well-grown timber, and at a distance, most tastefully half concealed by ornamental planting, I could catch some glimpse of Callonby. Before, however, I had time to look about me, I heard the tramp of horses' feet behind, and in another moment two ladies dashed up the steep behind, and came towards me at a smart gallop, followed by a groom, who, neither himself nor his horse, seemed to relish the pace of his fair mistresses. I moved off the road into the grass to permit them to pass; but no sooner had they got abreast of me than Sir Roger, anxious for a fair start, flung up both heels at once, pricked up his ears, and with a plunge that very nearly threw me from the saddle, set off at top speed. My first thought was for the ladies beside me, and to my utter horror, I now saw them coming along in full gallop; their horses had got off the road, and were, to my thinking, become quite unmanageable. I endeavored to pull up, but all in vain. Sir Roger had got the bit between his teeth,—a favorite trick of his,—and I was perfectly powerless to hold him. By this time they, being mounted on thoroughbreds, got a full neck before me, and the pace was now tremendous. On we all came, each horse at his utmost stretch. They were evidently gaining, from the better stride of their cattle; and will it be believed, or shall I venture to acknowledge it in these my Confessions, that I, who a moment before would have given my best chance of promotion to be able to pull in my horse, would now have "pledged my dukedom" to be able to give Sir Roger one cut of the whip unobserved? I leave it to the wise to decipher the *rationale,* but such is the fact. It was complete steeple-chasing, and my blood was up.

On we came, and I now perceived that about two hundred yards before me stood an iron gate and piers, without any hedge or wall on either side. Before I could conjecture the meaning of so strange a thing in the midst of a large lawn, I saw the foremost horse, now two or three lengths before the other, still in advance of me, take two or three short strides, and fly about eight feet over a sunk fence; the second followed in the same style, the riders sitting as steadily as in the gallop. It was now my turn, and I confess as I neared the dike I heartily wished myself well over it, for the very possibility of a "mistake" was maddening. Sir Roger came on at a slapping pace, and when within two yards of the brink, rose to it, and cleared it like a deer. By the time I had accomplished this feat, not the less to my satisfaction that both ladies had turned in their saddles to watch me, they were already far in advance. They held on still at the same pace, round a small copse which concealed them an instant from my view, and which when I passed, I perceived that they had just reached the hall door, and were dismounting.

On the steps stood a tall, elderly-looking, gentlemanlike

person, who I rightly conjectured was his lordship. I heard him laughing heartily as I came up. I at last succeeded in getting Sir Roger to a canter; and when a few yards from where the group were standing, sprang off, and hastened up to make my apologies as I best might for my unfortunate runaway. I was luckily spared the awkwardness of an explanation, for his lordship, approaching me with his hand extended, said,—

"Mr. Lorrequer is most welcome at Callonby. I cannot be mistaken, I am sure; I have the pleasure of addressing the nephew of my old friend Sir Guy Lorrequer, of Elton. I am indeed most happy to see you, and not the less so that you are safe and sound, which, five minutes since, I assure you I had my fears for."

Before I could assure his lordship that my fears were all for my competitors in the race,—for such in reality they were,—he introduced me to the two ladies, who were still standing beside him: "Lady Jane Callonby, Mr. Lorrequer; Lady Catherine."

"Which of you young ladies, may I ask, planned this 'escapade;' for I see by your looks it was no accident?"

"I think, papa," said Lady Jane, "you must question Mr. Lorrequer on that head; he certainly started first."

"I confess, indeed," said I, "such was the case."

"Well, you must confess, too, you were distanced," said Lady Jane.

His lordship laughed heartily, and I joined in his mirth, feeling at the same time most terribly provoked to be quizzed on such a matter: that I, a steeple-chase horseman of the first water, should be twitted by a couple of young ladies on the score of a most manly exercise! "But come," said his lordship, "the first bell has rung long since, and I am longing to ask Mr. Lorrequer all about my old college friend of forty years ago. So, ladies, hasten your toilet, I beseech you."

With these words, his lordship, taking my arm, led me into the drawing-room, where we had not been many minutes till we were joined by her ladyship, a tall, stately, handsome woman of a certain age, resolutely bent upon being both young and beautiful, in spite of time and wrinkles. Her reception of me, though not possessing the frankness of his lordship, was still very polite, and intended to be even gracious. I now found, by the reiterated inquiries for my old uncle, Sir Guy, that he it was, and not Hamlet, to whom I owed my present notice; and I must include it among my Confessions that it was about the first advantage I ever derived from the relationship. After half an hour's agreeable chatting, the ladies entered; and then I had time to remark the extreme beauty of their appearance. They were both wonderfully like; and except that Lady Jane was taller and more womanly, it would have been almost impossible to discriminate between them.

Lady Jane Callonby was then about twenty years of age, rather above the middle size, and slightly disposed towards *embonpoint;* her eye was of the deepest and most liquid blue, and rendered apparently darker by long lashes of the blackest jet,—for such was the color of her hair; her nose slightly, but slightly, deviated from the straightness of the Greek, and her upper lip was faultless, as were her mouth and chin. The whole lower part of the face, from the perfect repose and from the carriage of her head, had certainly a great air of hauteur; but the extreme melting softness of her eyes took from this, and when she spoke, there was a quiet earnestness in her mild and musical voice that disarmed you at once of connecting the idea of self with the speaker. The word "fascinating," more than any other I know of, conveys the effect of her appearance; and to produce it, she had, more than any other woman I ever met, that wonderful gift, *l'art de plaire.*

I was roused from my perhaps too earnest, because unconscious, gaze at the lovely figure before me by his lordship saying, "Mr. Lorrequer, her ladyship is waiting for you." I accordingly bowed, and offering my arm, led her into the dinner-room. And here I draw rein for the present, reserving for my next chapter my adventures at Callonby.

CHAPTER III.

LIFE AT CALLONBY.—LOVE-MAKING.—MISS O'DOWD'S ADVENTURE.

MY first evening at Callonby passed off as nearly all first evenings do everywhere. His lordship was most agreeable; talked much of my uncle, Sir Guy, whose fag he had been at Eton half a century before, promised me some capital shooting in his preserves, discussed the state of politics, and as the second decanter of port "waned apace," grew wondrous confidential, and told me of his intention to start his son for the county at the next general election, such being the object which had now conferred the honor of his presence on his Irish estates.

Her ladyship was most condescendingly civil; vouchsafed much tender commiseration for my "exile," as she termed my quarters in Kilrush; wondered how I could possibly exist in a marching regiment (who had never been in the cavalry in my life!); spoke quite feelingly of my *kindness* in joining their stupid family party, for they were living, to use her own phrase, "like hermits;" and wound up all by a playful assurance that as she perceived, from all my answers, that I was bent on preserving a strict incognito, she would tell no tales about me on her return to "town." Now, it may readily be believed that all this and many more of her ladyship's allusions were a "Chaldee manuscript" to me. That she knew certain facts of my family and relations was certain, but that she had interwoven in the humble web of my history a very pretty embroidery of fiction was equally so; and while she thus ran on, with innumerable allusions to Lady Marys and Lord Johns, who she pretended to suppose were dying to hear from me, I could not help muttering to myself, with good Christopher Sly, "An all this be true, then Lord be thanked for my good amends;" for up to that moment I was an ungrateful man for all such high and noble solicitude. One dark doubt shot for an instant across my brain. Mayhap her ladyship had "registered a vow" never to syllable a name unchronicled by Debrett, or was actually only mystifying me for mere amusement. A minute's consideration dispelled this fear; for I found myself treated *en seigneur* by the whole family. As for the daughters of the house, nothing could possibly be more engaging than their manner. The eldest, Lady Jane, was pleased, from my near relationship to her father's oldest friend, to receive me "from the first" on the most friendly footing, while with the younger, Lady Catherine, from her being less reserved than her sister, my progress was even greater; and thus, before we separated for the night, I contrived to "take up my position" in such a fashion as to be already looked upon as one of the family party,—to which object Lord, and indeed Lady Callonby seemed most willing to contribute, and made me promise to spend the entire of the following day at Callonby, and as many of the succeeding ones as my military duties would permit.

As his lordship was wishing me good-night at the door of the drawing-room, he said, in a half-whisper,—

"We were ignorant yesterday, Mr. Lorrequer, how soon we should have the pleasure of seeing you here; and you are therefore condemned to a small room off the library, it being the only one we can insure you as being well aired. I must therefore apprise you that you are not to be shocked at finding yourself surrounded by every member of my family hung up in frames around you. But as the room is usually my own snuggery, I have resigned it without any alteration whatever."

The apartment for which his lordship had so strongly apologized stood in very pleasing contrast to my late one in Kilrush. The soft Persian carpet, on which one's feet sank to the very ankles; the brightly polished dogs, upon which a blazing wood-fire burned; the well-upholstered fauteuils which seemed to invite sleep without the trouble of lying down for it; and, last of all, the ample and luxurious bed, upon whose rich purple hangings the ruddy glare of the fire threw a most mellow light,—were all a pleasing exchange for the *garniture* of the "Hotel Healy."

"Certes, Harry Lorrequer," said I, as I threw myself upon a small ottoman before the fire, in all the slippered ease and *abandon* of a man who has changed a dress-coat for a morning gown,—"certes, thou art destined for great things;

even here, where fate had seemed 'to do its worst' to thee, a little paradise opens, and what to ordinary mortals had proved but a 'flat, stale, and most unprofitable' quarter, presents to thee all the accumulated delight of an hospitable mansion, a kind, almost friendly host, a condescending Madame Mère, and daughters too! ah, ye gods!—But what is this?" And here for the first time lifting up my eyes, I perceived a beautiful water-color drawing in the style of "Chalon," which was placed above the chimney-piece. I rose at once, and taking a candle proceeded to examine it more minutely. It was a portrait of Lady Jane, a full-length too, and wonderfully like; there was more complexion, and perhaps more roundness of the figure than her present appearance would justify; but if anything was gained in brilliancy, it was certainly lost in point of expression, and I infinitely preferred her pale but beautifully fair countenance to the rosy cheek of the picture. The figure was faultless; the same easy grace, the result of perfect symmetry and refinement together, which only one in a thousand of handsome girls possess, was portrayed to the life. The more I looked, the more I felt charmed with it. Never had I seen anything so truly characteristic as this sketch, for it was scarcely more. It was after nearly an hour's quiet contemplation that I began to remember the lateness of the night,—an hour in which my thoughts had rambled from the lovely object before me to wonder at the situation in which I found myself placed; for there was so much of "attention" towards me, in the manner of every member of the family, coupled with certain mistakes as to my habits and acquaintances, as left me perfectly unable to unravel the mystery which so evidently surrounded me. "Perhaps," thought I, "Sir Guy has written in my behalf to his lordship. Oh! he would never do anything half so civil. Well, to be sure, I shall astonish them at headquarters: they'll not believe this. I wonder if Lady Jane saw my Hamlet; for they landed in Cork from Bristol about that time. She is indeed a most beautiful girl. I wish I were a marquis, if it were only for *her* sake. Well, my Lord Callonby, you may be a very wise man in the House of Lords; but I would just ask, is it exactly prudent to introduce into your family, on terms of such perfect intimacy, a young, fas-

cinating, well-looking fellow of four-and-twenty, albeit only
a subaltern, with two such daughters as you have? *Peut-être!*
One thing is certain—*I* have no cause of complaint; and so
good-night, Lady Jane." And with these words I fell asleep,
to dream of the deepest blue eyes and the most melting tones
that ever reduced a poor lieutenant in a marching regiment
to curse his fate that he could not call the Commander of the
Forces his father.

When I descended to the breakfast-room, I found the
whole family assembled in a group around Lord Kilkee, who
had just returned from a distant part of the county, where
he had been canvassing the electors and spouting patriotism
the day before. He was giving an account of his progress
with much spirit and humor as I entered; but on seeing me,
immediately came forward and shook hands with me like an
old acquaintance. By Lord Callonby and the ladies I was
welcomed also with much courtesy and kindness, and some
slight *badinage* passed upon my sleeping in what Lord Kilkee called the "Picture Gallery," which, for all I knew to the
contrary, contained but one fair portrait. I am not a believer
in Mesmer; but certainly there must have been some influence at work very like what we hear of in magnetism, for
before the breakfast was concluded there seemed at once to
spring up a perfect understanding between this family and
myself, which made me feel as much *chez moi* as I had ever
done in my life; and from that hour I may date an intimacy
which every succeeding day but served to increase.

After breakfast Lord Callonby consigned me to the guidance of his son, and we sallied forth to deal destruction
amongst the pheasants, with which the preserves were stocked;
and here I may observe, *en passant,* that with the single exception of fox-hunting, which was ever a passion with me,
I never could understand that inveterate pursuit of game to
which some men devote themselves. Thus, grouse-shooting
and its attendant pleasures of stumping over a boggy mountain from daylight till dark, never had much attraction for
me; and as to the delights of widgeon and wild-duck shooting,
when purchased by sitting up all night in a barrel with your
eye to the bung, I'll none of it. No, no! give me shooting or
angling merely as a *divertimento,* a pleasant interlude be-

tween breakfast and luncheon-time, when, consigning your Manton to a corner and the gamekeeper "to the dogs," you once more humanize your costume to take a canter with the daughters of the house, or, if the day look loweringly, a match of billiards with the men.

I have ever found that the happiest portions of existence are the most difficult to chronicle. We may—nay, we must —impart our miseries and annoyances to our many "dear friends" whose *forte* is sympathy or consolation; and all men are eloquent on the subject of their woes,—not so with their joys. Some have a miser-like pleasure in hoarding them up for their own private gratification; others—and they are prudent—feel that the narrative is scarcely agreeable even to their best friends; and a few—of whom I confess myself one —are content to be happy without knowing why, and to have pleasant souvenirs without being able to explain them.

Such must be my apology for not more minutely entering upon an account of my life at Callonby. A fortnight had now seen me *enfoncé,* the daily companion of two beautiful girls in all their walks and rides through a romantic, unfrequented country, seeing but little of the other members of the family; the gentlemen being entirely occupied with their election tactics, and Lady Callonby, being a late riser, seldom appearing before the dinner hour. There was not a cliff on the bold and rocky coast we did not climb, not a cave upon the pebbly beach unvisited. Sometimes my fair companions would bring a volume of Metastasio down to the little river where I used to angle, and the "gentle craft" was often abandoned for the heart-thrilling verses of that delightful poet. Yes, many years have passed over, and these scenes are still as fresh in my memory as though they had been of yesterday. In *my* memory, I say, "as for thee,—

> "Chi sa se mai
> Ti sovverrai di me?"

At the end of three weeks the house became full of company, from the garret to the cellar. Country gentlemen and their wives and daughters came pouring in on every species of conveyance known since the Flood; family coaches, which but for their yellow panels might have been mistaken for hearses, and high barouches, the ascent to which was accomplished by a step-ladder, followed each other in what appeared a never-ending succession. And here I may note an instance of the anomalous character of the conveyances, from an incident to which I was a witness at the time.

Among the visitors on the second day came a maiden lady from the neighborhood of Ennistimon, Miss Elizabeth O'Dowd, the last of a very old and highly respectable family in the county, and whose extensive property, thickly studded with freeholders, was a strong reason for her being paid every attention in Lord Callonby's power to bestow. Miss Betty O'Dowd—for so she was popularly styled—was the very personification of an old maid; stiff as a ramrod, and so rigid in observance of the proprieties of female conduct that in the estimation of the Clare gentry Diana was a hoyden compared to her.

Miss Betty lived, as I have said, near Ennistimon, and the road from thence to Callonby at the time I speak of—it was before Mr. Nimmo—was as like the bed of a mountain torrent as a respectable highway. There were holes that would have made a grave for any maiden lady within fifty miles, and rocks thickly scattered enough to prove fatal to the strongest wheels that ever issued from "Hutton's." Miss O'Dowd knew this well; she had upon one occasion been upset in travelling it, and a slate-colored silk dress bore the dye of every species of mud and mire to be found there, for many a year after, to remind her of her misfortune and keep open the wound of her sorrow. When, therefore, the invitation to Callonby arrived, a grave council of war was summoned to deliberate upon the mode of transit, for the honor could not be declined, *coûte qu'il coûte.* The chariot was out of the question,—Nicholas declared it would never reach the "Moraan Beg," as the first precipice was called; the inside car was long since pronounced unfit for hazardous enterprise; and the only resource left was what is called in Hibernian parlance a "low-backed car," that is, a car without any back whatever, it being neither more nor less than the common agricultural conveyance of the country, upon which, a feather-bed being laid, the farmers' wives and daughters are gen-

erally conveyed to fairs, wakes, and stations, etc. Putting
her dignity, if not in her pocket, at least wherever it could
be most easily accommodated, Miss O'Dowd placed her fair
self, in all the plenitude of her charms and the grandeur of
a "bran-new green silk," a "little off the grass, and on the
bottle" (I love to be particular), upon this humble conveyance,
and set out on her way, if not "rejoicing," at least consoled
by Nicholas that "It 'id be black dark when they reached the
house, and the devil a one 'id be the wiser than if she came in
a coach and four." Nicholas was right; it was perfectly dark
on their arrival at Callonby, and Miss O'Dowd, having dismounted and shaken her plumage, a little crumpled by her
half-recumbent position for eight miles, appeared in the drawing-room to receive the most courteous attentions from Lady
Callonby, and from his lordship the most flattering speeches
for her kindness in risking herself and bringing "her horses"
on such a dreadful road, and assured her of his getting a pre-
sentment the very next assizes to repair it. "For we intend,
Miss O'Dowd," said he, "to be most troublesome neighbors
to you in future."

The evening passed off most happily. Miss O'Dowd was
delighted with her hosts, whose character she resolved to
uphold in spite of their reputation for pride and haughti-
ness. Lady Jane sang an Irish melody for her, Lady Callonby gave her slips of a rose geranium she got from the
Princess Augusta, and Lord Kilkee won her heart by the
performance of that most graceful step yclept "cover the
buckle," in an Irish jig. But alas! how short-lived is human bliss; for while this estimable lady revelled in the full
enjoyment of the hour, the sword of Damocles hung suspended above her head. In plain English, she had on arriving at Callonby, to prevent any unnecessary scrutiny into
the nature of her conveyance, ordered Nicholas to be at the
door punctually at eleven, and then to take an opportunity of
quietly slipping open the drawing-room door and giving her
an intimation of it, that she might take her leave at once.
Nicholas was up to time; and having disposed the conveyance under the shadow of the porch, made his way to the
door of the drawing-room unseen and unobserved. He
opened it gently and noiselessly, merely sufficient to take a
survey of the apartment, in which, from the glare of the

lights and the busy hum of voices, he was so bewildered that
it was some minutes before he recognized his mistress. At
last he perceived her: she was seated at a card-table, playing
whist with Lord Callonby for her partner. Who the other
players were, he knew not. A proud man was Nicholas as he
saw his mistress thus placed, actually sitting, as he afterwards expressed it, "forenint the lord;" but his thoughts were
bent on other matters, and it was no time to indulge his
vauntings.

He strove for some time patiently to catch her eye,—for
she was so situated as to permit of this,—but without
success. He then made a slight attempt to attract her attention by beckoning with his finger,—all in vain. "Oh,
murther!" said he, "what is this for? I'll have to spake
afther all."

"Four by honors," said his lordship, "and the odd trick.
Another double, I believe, Miss O'Dowd."

Miss O'Dowd nodded a graceful assent, while a sharp-
looking old dowager at the side of the table called out, "A
rubber of four only, my lord;" and now began an explanation from the whole party at once. Nicholas saw this was
his time, and thought that in the *mêlée* his hint might reach
his mistress unobserved by the remainder of the company.
He accordingly protruded his head into the room, and placing his finger on the side of his nose and shutting one eye
knowingly, with an air of great secrecy, whispered out,
"Miss Betty—Miss Betty, alanah!" For some minutes the
hum of the voices drowned his admonitions; but as by degrees
waxing warmer in the cause, he called out more loudly, every
eye was turned to the spot from whence these extraordinary
sounds proceeded; and certainly the appearance of Nicholas at
the moment was well calculated to astonish the company of a
drawing-room. With his one eye fixed eagerly in the direction
of his mistress, his red scratch wig pushed back off his forehead, in the eagerness of his endeavor to be heard, there
he stood, perfectly unmindful of all around, save Miss O'Dowd
herself. It may well be believed that such an apparition could
not be witnessed with gravity, and, accordingly, a general
titter ran through the room, the whist party, still contending
about odd tricks and honors, being the only persons insensible
to the mirth around them. "Miss Betty, arrah, Miss Betty!"

said Nicholas, with a sigh that converted the subdued laughter of the guests into a perfect burst of mirth.

"Eh," said his lordship, turning round, "what is this? We are losing something excellent, I fear."

At this moment he caught a glimpse of Nicholas, and throwing himself back in his chair, laughed immoderately. It was now Miss Betty's turn; she was about to rise from the table, when the well-known accents of Nicholas fell upon her ear. She fell back in her seat,—there he was; the messenger of the foul fiend himself would have been more welcome at that moment. Her blood rushed to her face and temples, her hands tingled, she closed her eyes; and when she opened them, there stood the accursed Nicholas glowering at her still.

"Man—man!" said she at length, "what do you mean? What do you want here?"

Poor Nicholas, little guessing that the question was intended to throw a doubt upon her acquaintance with him, and conceiving that the hour for the announcement had come, hesitated for an instant how he should designate the conveyance. He could not call it a coach; it certainly was not a buggy, neither was it a jaunting car: what should he say? He looked earnestly, and even imploringly, at his mistress, as if to convey some sense of his difficulty, and then, as it were catching a sudden inspiration, winked once more, as he said,—

"Miss Betty—the—the—the—"—and here he looked indescribably droll—"the thing, *you know,* is at the door."

All his lordship's politeness was too little for the occasion, and Miss O'Dowd's tenantry were lost to the Callonby interest forever.

CHAPTER IV.

BOTANICAL STUDIES.—THE NATURAL SYSTEM PREFERABLE TO THE LINNÆAN.

"THE carriage is at the door, my lord," said a servant, entering the luncheon-room where we were all assembled.

"Now then, Mr. Lorrequer," said Lord Callonby, *"allons,* take another glass of wine, and let us away. I expect you to make a most brilliant speech, remember!"

His lordship here alluded to our intention of visiting a remote barony, where a meeting of the freeholders was that day to be held, and at which I was pledged for a "neat and appropriate" oration in abuse of the Corn-laws and the Holy Alliance.

"I beg pardon, my lord," said her ladyship, in a most languishing tone, "but Mr. Lorrequer is pre-engaged. He has for the last week been promising and deferring his visit to the new conservatory with me, where he is to find out four or five of the Swiss shrubs that Collins cannot make out, and which I am dying to know all about."

"Mr. Lorrequer is a false man, then," said Lady Catherine; "for he said at breakfast that we should devote this afternoon to the chalk caves, as the tide will be so far out that we can see them all perfectly."

"And I," said Lord Kilkee, "must put in my plea that the aforesaid Mr. Lorrequer is booked for a coursing-match—'Mouche *versus* Jessie.' Guilty, or not guilty?"

Lady Jane alone of all said not a word.

"Guilty on every count of the indictment," said I; "I throw myself on the mercy of the court."

"Let his sentence then be banishment," said Lady Catherine, with affected anger, "and let him go with papa."

"I rather think," said Lord Kilkee, "the better plan is to let him visit the conservatory; for I'd wager a fifty he finds it more difficult to invent botany than canvass freeholders, eh?"

"I am sure," said Lady Jane, for the first time breaking silence, "that mamma is infinitely flattered by the proposal that Mr. Lorrequer's company is to be conferred upon her for her sins."

"I am not to be affronted nor quizzed out of my chaperon. Here, Mr. Lorrequer," said Lady Callonby, rising, "get Smith's book there, and let me have your arm; and now, young ladies, come along, and learn something, if you can."

"An admirable proviso," said Lord Kilkee, laughing, "if his botany be only as authentic as the autographs he gave

Mrs. MacDermot, and all of which he wrote himself, in my dressing-room, in half an hour. Napoleon was the only difficult one in the number."

Most fortunately this unfair disclosure did not reach her ladyship's ears, as she was busily engaged putting on her bonnet, and I was yet unassailed in reputation to her.

"Good-by, then," said Lord Callonby; "we meet at seven." And in a few moments the little party were scattered to their several destinations.

"How very hot you have this place, Collins," said Lady Callonby, as we entered the conservatory.

"Only seventy-five, my lady, and the magnolias require heat."

I here dropped a little behind, as if to examine a plant, and in a half-whisper said to Lady Jane,—

"How came it that you alone, Lady Jane, should forget that I had made another appointment? I thought you wished to make a sketch of Craigmoran Abbey. Did you forget that we were to ride there to-day?"

Before she could reply, Lady Callonby called out: "Oh! here it is, Mr. Lorrequer. Is this a heath? that is the question."

Here her ladyship pointed to a little scrubby thing that looked very like a birch rod. I proceeded to examine it most minutely, while Collins waited with all the intense anxiety of a man whose character depended on the sentence.

"Collins will have it a jungermania," said she.

"And Collins is right," said I, not trusting myself with the pronunciation of the awful word her ladyship uttered.

Collins looked ridiculously happy.

"Now that is so delightful," said Lady Callonby, as she stopped to look for another puzzle.

"What a wretch it is," said Lady Catherine, covering her face with her handkerchief.

"What a beautiful little flower," said Lady Jane, lifting up the bell of a lobelia splendens.

"You know, of course," said I, "what they call that flower in France,—*L'amour tendre.*"

"Indeed!"

"True, I assure you. May I present you with this sprig

of it?" cutting off a small twig, and presenting it at the same instant unseen by the others.

She hesitated for an instant, and then extending her fair and taper hand, took it. I dared not look at her as she did so, but a proud, swelling triumph at my heart nearly choked me.

"Now, Collins," said Lady Callonby, "I cannot find the Alpen-tree I brought from the Gründenwald."

Collins hurried forward to her ladyship's side.

Lady Catherine was also called to assist in the search.

I was alone with Lady Jane.

"Now or never," thought I. I hesitated—I stammered; my voice faltered. She saw my agitation; she participated in and increased it. At last I summoned up courage to touch her hand; she gently withdrew it, but so gently, it was not a repulse.

"If, Lady Jane," said I at length, "if the devoted—"

"Holloa, there!" said a deep voice without, "is Mr. Lorrequer there?"

It was Lord Kilkee, returning from his coursing-match. None but he who has felt such an interruption can feel for me. I shame to say that his brotherhood to her for whom I would have perilled my life, restrained me not from something very like a hearty commendation of him to the powers that burn.

"Down, dogs! there, down!" continued he; and in a moment after entered the conservatory, flushed and heated with the chase.

"Mouche is the winner,—two to one; and so, Master Shallow, I owe you a thousand pounds."

Would to Heaven that I had lost the wager, had it only taken a little longer to decide it! I of course appeared overjoyed at my dog's success, and listened with great pretence of interest to the narrative of the "run,"—the more so because, that though perhaps more my friend than the older members of the family, Lord Kilkee evidently liked less than they my growing intimacy with his sister; and I was anxious to blind him on the present occasion, when, but for his recent excitement, very little penetration would have enabled him to detect that something unusual had taken place.

It was now so nearly dark that her ladyship's further search for the alpine treasure became impossible, and so we turned our steps towards the garden, where we continued to walk till joined by Lord Callonby. And now began a most active discussion upon agriculture, rents, tithes, and Toryism, in which the ladies took but little part; and I had the mortification to perceive that Lady Jane was excessively bored, and seized the first opportunity to leave the party and return to the house,—while her sister gave me from time to time certain knowing glances, as if intimating that my knowledge of farming and political economy were pretty much on a par with my proficiency in botany.

"One has discovered me, at least," thought I; but the bell had rung to dress for dinner, and I hastened to my room to think over future plans, and once more wonder at the singular position into which fate and the "rules of the service" had thrown me.

CHAPTER V.

PUZZLED.—EXPLANATION MAKES BAD WORSE.—A DUEL.

"ANY letters?" said her ladyship to a servant as she crossed the hall.

"Only one, my lady,—for Mr. Lorrequer, I believe."

"For me!" thought I; "how is this?" My letters had been hitherto always left in Kilrush. Why was this forwarded here? I hurried to the drawing-room, where I found a double letter awaiting me. The writing was Curzon's, and contained the words, "to be forwarded with haste," on the direction. I opened and read as follows:

DEAR LORREQUER,—Have you any recollection, among your numerous "escapades" at Cork, of having grievously insulted a certain Mr. Giles Beamish in thought, word, or deed? If you have, I say, let me know with all convenient despatch whether the offence be one admitting of apology; for if not, the Lord have mercy on your soul! a more wrothy gentleman than the aforesaid it having rarely been my evil for-

tune to foregather with. He called here yesterday to inquire your address, and at my suggestion wrote a note which
I now enclose. I write in great haste, and am ever yours
faithfully,   C. CURZON.

N. B.—I have not seen his note, so explain all and everything.

The enclosed ran thus :—

SIR,—It can scarcely have escaped your memory, though
now nearly two months since, that at the Mayor's *déjeûner* in
Cork, you were pleased to make merry at my expense, and
expose me and my family for your amusement. This is to
demand an immediate apology, or that satisfaction which,
as an officer, you will not refuse your most obedient servant,
                                          GILES BEAMISH.
Swinburne's Hotel.

"Giles Beamish! Giles Beamish!" said I, repeating the name
in every variety of emphasis, hoping to obtain some clew
to the writer. Had I been appointed the umpire between
Dr. Wall and his reviewers, in the late controversy about
"Phonetic signs," I could not have been more completely
puzzled than by the contents of this note. "Make merry
at his expense!" a great offence truly,—I suppose I have
laughed at better men than ever he was; and I can only
say of such innocent amusement, as Falstaff did of sack
and sugar, if such be a sin, "then Heaven help the wicked!"
But I wish I knew who he is, or what he alludes to, provided he is not mad, which I begin to think not improbable.
"By the by, my lord, do you know any such person in
the South as a Mr. Beamish,—Giles Beamish?"
"To be sure," said Lord Callonby, looking up from his
newspaper; "there are several of the name, of the highest
respectability. One is an alderman of Cork,—a very rich
man too; but I don't remember his Christian name."
"An alderman, did you say?"
"Yes, Alderman Beamish is very well known. I have seen
him frequently,—a short, florid little man."

"Oh! it must be he," said I, musingly; "it must have been this worthy alderman from whose worshipful person I tore the robe of office on the night of the fête. But what does he mean by 'my exposing him and his family'? Why, zounds, his wife and children were not with him on the pavement! Oh! I see it; it is the Mansion House school of eloquence: did not Sir William Curtis apologize for not appearing at court from having lost an eye, which he designated as an awful 'domestic calamity'?"

It being now settled to my satisfaction that Mr. Beamish and the great uncloaked were "convertible terms," I set about making the *amende* in the most handsome manner possible. I wrote to the alderman a most pacific epistle, regretting that my departure from Cork deprived me of making reparation before, and expressing a most anxious hope that "he caught no cold," and a fervent wish that "he would live many years to grace and ornament the dignity of which his becoming costume was the emblem." This I enclosed in a note to Curzon, telling him how the matter occurred, and requesting that he would send it by his servant, together with the scarlet vestment, which he would find in my dressing-room. Having folded and sealed this despatch, I turned to give Lord Callonby an account of the business, and showed him Beamish's note, at which he was greatly amused; and, indeed, it furnished food for mirth for the whole party during the evening. The next morning I set out with Lord Callonby on the long-threatened canvassing expedition, with the details of which I need not burden my "Confessions." Suffice it to say that when Lord Kilkee was advocating Toryism in the West, I, his accredited ambassador, was devoting to the infernal gods the prelacy, the peerage, and the pension list,—a mode of canvass well worthy of imitation in these troublesome times; for, not to speak of the great prospect of success from having friends on both sides of the question, the principal can always divest himself of any unpleasant consequences as regards inconsistency by throwing the blame on his friend, "who went too far," as the appropriate phrase is.

Nothing could be more successful than our mission. Lord Callonby was delighted beyond bounds with the prospect, and so completely carried away by high spirits, and so perfectly assured that much of it was owing to my exertions, that on the second morning of our tour—for we proceeded through the country for three days—he came laughing into my dressing-room with a newspaper in his hand.

"Here, Lorrequer," said he, "here's news for you. You certainly must read this." And he handed me a copy of the "Clare Herald," with an account of our meeting the evening before.

After glancing my eye rapidly over the routine usual in such cases,—"Humph, ha—nearly two hundred people— most respectable farmers—room appropriately decorated— 'Callonby Arms'—'after the usual loyal toasts, the chairman rose'— Well, no matter. Ah! here it is: 'Mr. Lorrequer here addressed the meeting with a flow of eloquence it has rarely, if ever, been our privilege to hear equalled. He began by'—humph—"

"Ah!" said his lordship, impatiently, "you will never find it out. Look here: 'Mr. Lorrequer, whom we have mentioned as having made the highly exciting speech, to be found on our first page, is, we understand, the son of Sir Guy Lorrequer, of Elton, in Shropshire, one of the wealthiest baronets in England. If rumor speaks truly, there is a very near prospect of an alliance between this talented and promising young gentleman and the beautiful and accomplished daughter of a certain noble earl with whom he has been for some time domesticated.'"

"Eh, what think you? Son of Sir Guy Lorrequer. I always thought my old friend a bachelor; but you see the 'Clare Herald' knows better. Not to speak of the last piece of intelligence, it is very good, is it not?"

"Capital indeed," said I, trying to laugh, and at the same time blushing confoundedly, and looking as ridiculous as needs be.

It now struck me forcibly that there was something extremely odd in his lordship's mention of this paragraph, particularly when coupled with his and Lady Callonby's manner to me for the last two months. They knew enough of my family, evidently, to be aware of my station and prospects,—or rather my want of both,—and yet in the face of this they not only encouraged me to prolong a most delightful visit, but by a thousand daily and dangerous opportunities absolutely threw me in the way of one of the loveliest of her sex, seemingly without fear on their parts. "Well!" thought I, with my old philosophy, "Time, that 'pregnant old gentleman,' will disclose all, and so let us be patient!"

My reveries on my good and evil fortune were suddenly interrupted by a letter which reached me that evening, having been forwarded from Callonby by a special messenger. "What! another epistle from Curzon," said I, as my eye caught the address; and wondering not a little what pressing emergency had called forth the words on the cover—"To be forwarded with haste,"—I eagerly broke the seal and read the following:—

My dear Harry,—I received yours on the 11th, and immediately despatched your note and the raiment to Mr. Beamish. He was from home at the time, but at eight o'clock I was sent for from the mess to see two gentlemen on most pressing business. I hurried to my quarters, and there found the aforesaid Mr. B., accompanied by a friend, whom he introduced as Dr. de Courcy Finucane, of the North Cork Militia,—as warlike-looking a gentleman, of his inches, some five feet three, as you would wish to see. The moment I appeared, both rose, and commenced a narrative, for such I judge it to be, but so energetically and so completely together that I could only bow politely, and at last request that one or the other would inform me of the object of their visit. Here began the tug of war, the doctor saying, "Arrah, now, Giles;" Mr. Beamish interrupting by "Whisht, I tell ye,—now can't you let *me?* Ye see, Mr. Curzoin,"—for so they both agreed to designate me. At last, completely worn out, I said, "Perhaps you have not received my friend's note?" At this Mr. Beamish reddened to the eyes, and with the greatest volubility poured forth a flood of indignant eloquence that I thought it necessary to check; but in this I failed, for after informing me pretty clearly that he knew nothing of your story of the alderman or his cloak, added that he firmly believed your pretended reparation was only a renewed insult, and that— But, in a word, he used such language that I was compelled to take him short; and the *finale* is, that I agreed you should meet him, though still ignorant of what he calls the "original offence." But Heaven knows, his conduct here last night demands a reprimand, and I hope you may give it; and if you shoot him, we may worm out the secret from his executors. Nothing could exceed the politeness of the parties on my consenting to this arrangement. Dr. Finucane proposed Carrigaholt as the rendezvous,—about twelve miles, I believe, from Kilrush,—and Tuesday evening, at six, as the time, which will be the very earliest moment we can arrive there. So pray be up to time, and believe me yours,

C. CURZON.

Saturday Evening.

It was late on Monday evening when this letter reached me, and there was no time to be lost, as I was then about forty Irish miles from the place mentioned by Curzon; so, after briefly acquainting Lord Callonby that I was called off by duty, I hurried to my room to pack my clothes and again read over this extraordinary epistle.

I confess it did appear something droll, how completely Curzon seemed to imbibe the passion for fighting from these "bloodthirsty Irishmen;" for by his own showing he was utterly ignorant of my ever having offended this Mr. Beamish, of whom I recollected nothing whatever. Yet when that gentleman waxes wrothy, rather than inconvenience him, or perhaps anxious to get back to the mess, he coolly says, "Oh! my friend shall meet you," and then his present jest, "find out the cause of quarrel from his executors"!

"Truly," thought I, "there is no equanimity like his who acts as your second in a duel. The gentlemanlike urbanity with which he waits on the opposite friend; the conciliating tone with which he proffers implacable enmity; the killing kindness with which he refuses all accommodation; the Talleyrand air of his short notes, dated from the Travellers, or Brookes, with the words 'three o'clock' or 'five o'clock' on the cover,—all indicative of the friendly precipitancy of the negotiation. Then, when all is settled, the social style with which he asks you to take a 'cutlet' with him at the Clarendon, 'not to go home,' is only to be equalled by the admirable tact on the ground,—the studiously elegant salute to the adverse party, half *à la Napoléon,* and half Beau Brummell; the politely offered snuff-box, the coquetting raillery about ten paces or twelve, are certainly the *beau idéal* of the stoicism which preludes sending your friend out of the world like a gentleman."

How very often is the face of external nature at variance with the thoughts and actions, "the sayings and doings," we may be most intent upon at the moment! How many a gay and brilliant bridal party has wended its way to St. George's, Hanover Square, amid a downpour of rain one would suppose sufficient to quench the torch of Hymen, though it burned as brightly as Captain Drummond's oxygen light; and, on the other hand, how frequently are the bluest azure of heaven and the most balmy airs shed upon the heart bursting with affliction or the head bowed with grief; and without any desire to impugn, as a much higher authority has done, the moral character of the moon, how many a scene of blood and rapine has its mild radiance illumined! Such reflections as these came thronging to my mind as on the afternoon of Tuesday I neared the little village of our rendezvous. The scene, which in all its peaceful beauty lay before me, was truly a strong contrast to the occasion that led me thither. I stood upon a little peninsula which separates the Shannon from the wide Atlantic. On one side the placid river flowed on its course between fields of waving corn or rich pasturage,—the beautiful island of Scattery, with its picturesque ruins reflected in the unrippled tide; the cheerful voices of the reapers and the merry laugh of the children were mingled with the seaman's cry of the sailors, who were "heaving short" on their anchor, to take the evening tide. The village, which consisted merely of a few small cabins, was still, from its situation, a pleasing object in the picture, and the blue smoke that rose in slender columns from the humble dwellings took from the scene its character of loneliness, and suggested feelings of home and homely enjoyments, which human habitations, however lowly, never fail to do.

"At any other time," thought I, "how I could have enjoyed all this; but now— And, ha! I find it is already past five o'clock, and if I am rightly informed I am still above a mile from 'Carrigaholt,' where we were to meet."

I had dismissed my conveyance when nearing the village,

to avoid observation, and now took a footpath over the hills. Before I had proceeded half a mile the scene changed completely. I found myself traversing a small glen, grown over with a low oak shrub, and not presenting on any side the slightest trace of habitation. I saw that the ground had been selected by an adept. The glen, which grew narrow as I advanced, suddenly disclosed to my view a glimpse of the Atlantic, upon which the declining sun was pouring a flood of purple glory. I had scarcely turned from the contemplation of this beautiful object when a long low whistle attracted my attention. I looked in the direction from whence it proceeded, and discovered at some distance from me three figures standing beside the ruin of an old abbey, which I now for the first time perceived.

If I had entertained any doubt as to who they were, it had been speedily resolved, for I now saw one of the party waving his hat to me, whom I soon recognized to be Curzon. He came forward to meet me; and in the few hundred yards that intervened before our reaching the others, told me as much as he knew of the opposite party, which, after all, was but little. Mr. Beamish, my adversary, he described as a morose, fire-eating Southern, that evidently longed for an "affair" with a military man,—then considered a circumstance of some *éclat* in the South; his second, the doctor, on the contrary, was by far "the best of the cut-throats," a most amusing little personage, full of his own importance, and profuse in his legends of his own doings in love and war, and evidently disposed to take the pleasing side of every occurrence in life. They both agreed in but one point,—a firm and fixed resolve to give no explanation of the quarrel with me. "So then," said I, as Curzon hurried over the preceding account, "you absolutely know nothing whatever of the reason for which I am about to give this man a meeting?"

"No more than you," said Curzon, with imperturbable gravity; "but one thing I am certain of. Had I not at once promised him such, he would have posted you in Limerick the next morning; and as you know our mess-rule in the 4—th, I thought it best—"

"Oh! certainly, quite right; but now are you quite certain I am the man who offended him? For I solemnly assure you I have not the most remote recollection of having ever heard of him."

"That point," said Curzon, "there can be no doubt of; for he not only designated you as Mr. Harry Lorrequer, but the gentleman that made all Cork laugh so heartily by his representation of Othello."

"Stop!" said I; "not a word more. I'm his man."

By this time we had reached the ruins, and turning a corner came in full contact with the enemy. They had been resting themselves on a tombstone, and rose as we approached.

"Allow me," said Curzon, stepping a little in advance of me, "allow me to introduce my friend Mr. Lorrequer, Dr. Finicane: Dr. Finicane, Mr. Lorrequer."

"Finucane, if quite agreeable to you,—Finucane," said the little gentleman, as he lifted his hat straight off his head, and replaced it most accurately, by way of salute. "Mr. Lorrequer, it is with sincere pleasure I make your acquaintance." Here Mr. Beamish bowed stiffly, in return to my salutation; and at the instant a kind of vague sensation crossed my mind that those red whiskers and that fiery face were not seen for the first time,—but the thumb-screws of the Holy Office would have been powerless to refresh my memory as to when.

"Captain," said the doctor, "may I request the favor of your company this way one minute?" They both walked aside; the only words which reached me as I moved off to permit their conference, being an assurance on the part of the doctor "that it was a sweet spot he picked out, for, by having them placed north and south, neither need have a patch of sky behind him." Very few minutes sufficed for preliminaries, and they both advanced, smirking and smiling as if they had just arranged a new plan for the amelioration of the poor or the benefit of the manufacturing classes, instead of making preparations for sending a fellow-creature out of the world.

"Then, if I understand you, Captain," said the doctor, "you step the distance, and I give the word."

"Exactly," said Curzon.

After a joking allusion to my friend's length of limb, at which we all laughed heartily, we were placed, Curzon and the doctor standing and breaking the line between us. The pistols were then put into our hands, the doctor saying, "Now, gentlemen, I'll just retire six paces, and turn round, which will be quite time enough to prepare, and at the word 'Fire!' ye'll blaze away; mind now." With a knowing wink, the doctor delivered this direction, and immediately moved off. The word "Fire!" followed, and both pistols went off together. My hat was struck near the top, and as the smoke cleared away, I perceived that my ball had taken effect upon my adversary; he was wounded a little below the knee, and appeared to steady himself with the greatest difficulty. "Your friend is hit," said Curzon to the doctor, who now came forward with another pistol. "Your friend is hit."

"So I perceive," said he, placing his finger on the spot; "but it is no harm in life; so we proceed, if you please."

"You don't mean to demand another shot?" said Curzon.

"Faith do I," said the doctor, coolly.

"Then," said Curzon, "I must tell you most unequivocally I refuse, and shall now withdraw my friend; and had it not been for a regulation peculiar to our regiment, but never intended to include cases of this nature, we had not been here now, for up to this hour, my principal and myself are in utter ignorance of any cause of offence ever having been offered by him to Mr. Beamish."

"Giles, do you hear this?" said the doctor.

But Giles did not hear it; for the rapid loss of blood from his wound had so weakened him that he had fainted, and lay peaceably on the grass. Etiquette was now at an end, and we all ran forward to assist the wounded man. For some minutes he lay apparently quite senseless, and when he at last rallied and looked wildly about him, it appeared to be with difficulty that he recalled any recollection of the place and the people around him. For a few seconds he fixed his eyes steadily upon the doctor, and with a lip pale and bloodless and a voice quivering from weakness, said:

"Fin! didn't I tell ye that pistol always threw high? Oh!" —and this he said with a sigh that nearly overpowered him —"oh, Fin, if you had only given me the saw-handled one, that *I am used to*— But it is no good talking now."

In my inmost heart I was grateful to the little doctor for

his mistake; for I plainly perceived what "the saw-handled one he was used to" might have done for me, and could not help muttering to myself with good Sir Andrew,—"If I had known he was so cunning of fence, I'd have seen him damned before that I fought with him."

Our first duty was now to remove the wounded man to the high road, about which both he himself and his second seemed disposed to make some difficulty. They spoke together for a few moments in a low tone of voice, and then the doctor addressed us: "We feel, gentlemen, this is not a time for any concealment; but the truth is, we have need of great circumspection here, for I must inform you we are both of us bound over in heavy recognizances to keep the peace."

"Bound over to keep the peace!" said Curzon and myself together.

"Nothing less; and although there is nobody hereabout would tell, yet if the affair got into the papers by any means, why there are some people in Cork would like to press my friend there, for he is a very neat shot when he has the saw-handle." And here the doctor winked.

We had little time permitted us to think upon the oddity of meeting a man in such circumstances, for we were now obliged to contribute our aid in conveying him to the road, where some means might be procured for his transfer to Kilrush or some other town in the neighborhood, for he was by this time totally unable to walk.

After half an hour's toiling we at last did reach the highway, by which time I had ample opportunity, short as the space was, to see something of the character of our two opponents. It appeared that the doctor exercised the most absolute control over his large friend, dictating and commanding in a tone which the other never ventured to resist. For a moment or two Mr. Beamish expressed a great desire to be conveyed by night to Kilrush, where he might find means to cross the Shannon into Kerry. This, however, the doctor opposed strenuously, from the risk of publicity, and finally settled that we should all go in a body to his friend Father Malachi Brennan's house, only two miles off, where the sick man would have the most tender care, and, what the doctor considered equally indispensable, we ourselves a most excellent supper and a hearty welcome.

"You know Father Malachi, of course, Mr. Lorrequer?"

"I am ashamed to say I do not."

"Not know Malachi Brennan, and live in Clare! Well, well, that is strange! Sure he is the priest of this country for twelve miles in every direction of you, and a better man and a pleasanter there does not live in the diocese, though I'm his cousin that says it."

After professing all the possible pleasure it would afford my friend and myself to make the acquaintance of Father Malachi, we proceeded to place Mr. Beamish in a car that was passing at the time, and started for the residence of the good priest. The whole of the way thither I was occupied but by one thought,—a burning anxiety to know the cause of our quarrel; and I longed for the moment when I might get the doctor apart from his friend to make the inquiry.

"There! look down to your left, where you see the lights shining so brightly,—that is Father Malachi's house; as sure as my name is De Courcy Finucane, there's fun going on there this night."

"Why, there certainly does seem a great illumination in the valley there," said I.

"May I never," said the doctor, "if it isn't a station—"

"A station!—pray may I ask—"

"You need not ask a word on the subject; for if I am a true prophet, you'll know what it means before morning."

A little more chatting together brought us to a narrow road, flanked on either side by high hedges of hawthorn, and in a few minutes more we stood before the priest's residence,— a long, whitewashed, thatched house, having great appearance of comfort and convenience. Arrived here, the doctor seemed at once to take on him the arrangement of the whole party; for after raising the latch and entering the house, he returned to us in a few minutes, and said,—

"Wait a while, now; we'll not go in to Father Malachi till we've put Giles to bed."

We accordingly lifted him from the car and assisted him into the house; and following Finucane down a narrow passage, at last reached a most comfortable little chamber, with a neat bed. Here we placed him, while the doctor gave some directions to a bare-headed, red-legged hussy, without shoes or stockings, and himself proceeded to examine the wound, which was a more serious one than it at first appeared.

After half an hour thus occupied, during which time roars of merriment and hearty peals of laughter burst upon us every time the door opened, from a distant part of the house, where his Reverence was entertaining his friends, and which, as often as they were heard by the doctor, seemed to produce in him sensations not unlike those that afflicted the "wedding guest" in the "Ancient Mariner" when he heard the "loud bassoon," and as certainly imparted an equally longing desire to be a partaker in the mirth, we arranged everything satisfactorily for Mr. Beamish's comfort, and with a large basin of vinegar and water to keep his knee cool, and a strong tumbler of hot punch to keep his heart warm,—homœopathic medicine is not half so new as Dr. Hahnemann would make us believe,—we left Mr. Beamish to his own meditations and doubtless regrets that he did not get the "sawhandled one he was used to," while we proceeded to make our bows to Father Malachi Brennan.

But as I have no intention to treat the good priest with ingratitude, I shall not present him to my readers at the tail of a chapter.

CHAPTER VI.

THE PRIEST'S SUPPER.—FATHER MALACHI AND THE
COADJUTOR.—MAJOR JONES AND THE ABBÉ.

AT the conclusion of our last chapter we left our quondam antagonist, Mr. Beamish, stretched at full length upon a bed practising homœopathy, by administering hot punch to his fever, while we followed our chaperon, Dr. Finucane, into the presence of the Reverend Father Brennan.

The company into which we now, without any ceremony on our parts, introduced ourselves consisted of from five and twenty to thirty persons, seated around a large oak table plentifully provided with materials for drinking, and cups, goblets, and glasses of every shape and form. The moment we entered, the doctor stepped forward, and touching Father Malachi on the shoulder,—for so I rightly guessed him to be,—presented himself to his relative, by whom he was welcomed with every demonstration of joy. While their recognitions were exchanged, and while the doctor explained the reasons of our visit, I was enabled, undisturbed and unnoticed, to take a brief survey of the party.

Father Malachi Brennan, P. P. of Carrigaholt, was what I had often pictured to myself as the *beau idéal* of his caste. His figure was short, fleshy, and enormously muscular, and displayed proportions which wanted but height to constitute a perfect Hercules; his legs, so thick in the calf, so taper in the ankle, looked like nothing I know, except, perhaps, the metal balustrades of Carlisle Bridge; his face was large and rosy, and the general expression a mixture of unbounded good-humor and inexhaustible drollery, to which the restless activity of his black and arched eyebrows greatly contributed; and his mouth, were it not for a character of sensuality and voluptuousness about the nether lip, had been actually handsome; his head was bald, except a narrow circle close above the ears, which was marked by a ring of curly dark hair,—sadly insufficient, however, to conceal a development behind that, if there be truth in phrenology, boded but little happiness to the disciples of Miss Martineau.

Add to these external signs a voice rich, fluent, and racy, with the mellow "doric" of his country, and you have some faint resemblance of one "every inch a priest." The very antipodes to the *bonhomie* of this figure confronted him as croupier at the foot of the table. This, as I afterwards learned, was no less a person than Mister Donovan, the coadjutor, or "curate." He was a tall, spare, ungainly looking man of about five and thirty, with a pale; ascetic countenance, the only readable expression of which vibrated between low suspicion and intense vulgarity; over his low, projecting forehead hung down a mass of straight red hair,—indeed (for Nature is not a politician), it almost approached an orange hue. This was cut close to the head all round, and displayed in their full proportions a pair of enormous ears, which stood out in "relief" like turrets from a watch-tower, and with pretty much the same object; his skin was of that peculiar color and texture to which not all "the water in great Neptune's ocean" could impart a look of cleanliness, while his very voice, hard, harsh, and inflexible, was unprepossessing and unpleasant. And yet, strange at it may seem, he, too, was a correct type of his order; the only difference being that Father Malachi was an older coinage, with the impress of Douai or St. Omer, whereas Mister Donovan was the shining metal, fresh stamped from the mint of Maynooth.

While thus occupied in my surveillance of the scene before me, I was roused by the priest saying,—

"Ah, Fin, my darling, you needn't deny it, you're at the old game as sure as my name is Malachi, and ye'll never be easy nor quiet till ye're sent beyond the sea, or maybe have a record of your virtues on half a ton of marble in the churchyard yonder."

"Upon my honor, upon the sacred honor of a De Courcy—"

"Well, well, never mind it now; ye see ye're just keeping your friends cooling themselves there in the corner. Introduce me at once."

"Mr. Lorrequer, I'm sure—"

"My name is Curzon," said the Adjutant, bowing.

"A mighty pretty name, though a little profane. Well, Mr. Curseon," for so he pronounced it, "ye're as welcome as the flowers in May; and it's mighty proud I am to see ye here."

"Mr. Lorrequer, allow me to shake your hand; I've heard of ye before."

There seemed nothing very strange in that; for go where I would through this county, I seemed as generally known as ever was Brummell in Bond Street.

"Fin tells me," continued Father Malachi, "that ye'd rather not be known down here, in regard of a reason;" and here he winked. "Make yourselves quite easy; the king's writ was never but once in these parts, and the 'original and true copy' went back to Limerick in the stomach of the server. They made him eat it, Mr. Lorrequer! But it's as well to be cautious, for there are a good number here. A little dinner, a little quarterly dinner we have among us, Mr. Curseon, to

58

be social together, and raise a 'thrifle' for the Irish college at Rome, where we have a probationer or two ourselves."

"As good as a station, and more drink," whispered Fin into my ear.

"And now," continued the priest, "ye must just permit me to re-christen ye both, and the contribution will not be the less for what I'm going to do; and I'm certain you'll not be the worse for the change, Mr. Curseon,—though 'tis only for a few hours ye'll have a dacent name."

As I could see no possible objection to this proposal, nor did Curzon either, our only desire being to maintain the secrecy necessary for our antagonist's safety, we at once assented; when Father Malachi took me by the hand, but with such a total change in his whole air and deportment that I was completely puzzled by it. He led me forward to the company with a good deal of that ceremonious reverence I have often admired in Sir Charles Vernon when conducting some full-blown dowager through the mazes of a Castle minuet. The desire to laugh outright was almost irresistible as the Rev. Father stood at arm's length from me, still holding my hand, and bowing to the company pretty much in the style of a manager introducing a blushing *débutante* to an audience. A moment more, and I must have inevitably given way to a burst of laughter, when what was my horror to hear the priest present me to the company as their "excellent, worthy, generous, and patriotic young landlord, Lord Kilkee. Cheer, every mother's son of ye; cheer, I say!" and certainly precept was never more strenuously backed by example, for he huzzaed till I thought he would burst a blood-vessel. May I add, I almost wished it, such was the insufferable annoyance, the chagrin, this announcement gave me; and I waited with eager impatience for the din and clamor to subside, to disclaim every syllable of the priest's announcement, and take the consequences of my baptismal epithet, cost what it might. To this I was impelled by many and important reasons. Situated as I was with respect to the Callonby family, my assumption of their name at such a moment might get abroad, and the consequences to me be inevitable ruin; and independent of my natural repugnance to such sailing under false colors, I saw Curzon laughing almost to suffocation at my wretched predicament, and (so strong within me was the dread of ridicule) I thought, "What a pretty narrative he is concocting for the mess this minute!" I rose to reply; and whether Father Malachi, with his intuitive quickness, guessed my purpose or not, I cannot say, but he certainly resolved to out-manœuvre me, and he succeeded. While with one hand he motioned to the party to keep silence, with the other he took hold of Curzon, but with no peculiar or very measured respect, and introduced him as Mr. M'Neesh, the new Scotch steward and improver,—a character at that time whose popularity might compete with a tithe proctor or an exciseman. So completely did this tactic turn the tables upon the poor Adjutant, who the moment before was exulting over me, that I utterly forgot my own woes, and sat down convulsed with mirth at his situation, —an emotion certainly not lessened as I saw Curzon passed from one to the other at table "like a pauper to his parish," till he found an asylum at the very foot, in juxta with the engaging Mr. Donovan,—a propinquity, if I might judge from their countenances, uncoveted by either party.

While this was performing, Dr. Finucane was making his recognitions with several of the company, to whom he had been long known during his visits to the neighborhood. I now resumed my place on the right of "the father," abandoning for the present all intention of disclaiming my rank, and the campaign was opened. The priest now exerted himself to the utmost to recall conversation into the original channels, and if possible to draw off attention from me, which he still feared might perhaps elicit some unlucky announcement on my part. Failing in his endeavors to bring matters to their former footing, he turned the whole brunt of his attentions to the worthy doctor, who sat on his left.

"How goes on the law," said he, "Fin? Any new proofs, as they call them, forthcoming?"

What Fin replied I could not hear; but the allusion to the "suit" was explained by Father Malachi informing us that the only impediment between his cousin and the title of Kinsale lay in the unfortunate fact that his grandmother, "rest her sowl," was not a man.

Dr. Finucane winced a little under the manner in which

this was spoken, but returned the fire by asking if the bishop was down lately in that quarter? The evasive way in which "the father" replied having stimulated my curiosity as to the reason, little entreaty was necessary to persuade the doctor to relate the following anecdote, which was not relished the less by his superior that it told somewhat heavily on Mr. Donovan.

"It was about four years ago," said the doctor, "since the bishop, Dr. Plunkett, took it into his head that he'd make a general inspection, 'a reconnoissance,' as we'd call it, Mr. Lor—that is, my lord!—through the whole diocese, and leave no part, far or near, without poking his nose in it and seeing how matters were doing. He heard very queer stories about his reverence here, and so down he came one morning in the month of July, riding upon an old gray hack, looking just for all the world like any other elderly gentleman in very rusty black. When he got near the village he picked up a little boy to show him the short cut across the fields to the house here; and as his lordship was a 'sharp man and a shrewd,' he kept his eye on everything as he went along, remarking this, and noting down that.

"'Are ye regular in your duties, my son?' said he to the child.

"'I never miss a Sunday,' said the gossoon; 'for it's always walking his reverence's horse I am the whole time av prayers.'

"His lordship said no more for a little while, when he muttered between his teeth, 'Ah! it's just slander; nothing but slander and lying tongues.' This soliloquy was caused by his remarking that on every gate he passed, or from every cabin, two or three urchins would come out half naked, but all with the finest heads of red hair he ever saw in his life.

"'How is it, my son,' said he at length, 'they tell very strange stories about Father Malachi, and I see so many of these children with red hair, eh? Now, Father Malachi's a dark man.'

"'True for ye,' said the boy, 'true for ye, Father Malachi's dark; but the coadjutor,—the coadjutor's as red as a fox.'"

When the laugh this story caused had a little subsided, Father Malachi called out, "Mickey Oulahan! Mickey, I say, hand his lordship over 'the groceries,' "—thus he designated a square decanter containing about two quarts of whiskey and a bowl heaped high with sugar. "A dacent boy is Mickey, my lord, and I'm happy to be the means of making him known to you." I bowed with condescension, while Mr. Oulahan's eyes sparkled like diamonds at the recognition.

"He has only two years of the lease to run, and a 'long charge'" (*anglicè,* a large family), continued the priest.

"I'll not forget him, you may depend upon it," said I.

"Do you hear that?" said Father Malachi, casting a glance of triumph round the table, while a general buzz of commendation on priest and patron went round, with many such phrases as "Och, thin," "it's his riv'rance *can* do it," "na bocklish," "and why not," etc. As for me, I have already "confessed" to my crying sin,—a fatal, irresistible inclination to follow the humor of the moment wherever it led me; and now I found myself as active a partisan in quizzing Mickey Oulahan as though I was not myself a party included in the jest. I was thus fairly launched into my inveterate habit, and nothing could arrest my progress.

One by one the different individuals round the table were presented to me and made known their various wants, with an implicit confidence in my power of relieving them which I with equal readiness ministered to. I lowered the rent of every man at table. I made a general jail-delivery,—an act of grace, I blush to say, which seemed to be peculiarly interesting to the present company. I abolished all arrears, made a new line of road through an impassable bog and over an inaccessible mountain, and conducted water to a mill which (I learned in the morning) was always worked by wind. The decanter had scarcely completed its third circuit of the board when I bid fair to be the most popular specimen of the peerage that ever visited the "Far West." In the midst of my career of universal benevolence, I was interrupted by Father Malachi, whom I found on his legs pronouncing a glowing eulogium on his cousin's late regiment, the famous North Cork.

"That was the corps!" said he. "Bid them do a thing, and they'd never leave off; and so, when they got orders to retire from Wexford, it's little they cared for the comforts of baggage, like many another regiment, for they threw away everything but their canteens, and never stopped till they ran to Ross, fifteen miles farther than the enemy followed them. And when they were all in bed the same night, fatigued and tired with their exertions, as ye may suppose, a drummer-boy called out in his sleep, 'Here they are—they're coming!' they all jumped up and set off in their shirts, and got two miles out of town before they discovered it was a false alarm."

Peal after peal of laughter followed the priest's encomium on the doctor's regiment; and, indeed, he himself joined most heartily in the mirth, as he might well afford to do, seeing that a braver or better corps than the North Cork, Ireland did not possess.

"Well," said Fin, "it's easy to see ye never can forget what they did at Maynooth."

Father Malachi disclaimed all personal feeling on the subject, and I was at last gratified by the following narrative, which I regret deeply I am not enabled to give in the doctor's own words; but writing as I do from memory, in most instances, I can only convey the substance.

It was towards the latter end of the year '98—the year of the troubles—that the North Cork was ordered, "for their sins," I believe, to march from their snug quarters in Fermoy and take up a position in the town of Maynooth,—a very considerable reverse of fortune to a set of gentlemen extremely addicted to dining out and living at large upon a very pleasant neighborhood. Fermoy abounded in gentry; Maynooth, at that time, had few, if any, excepting his Grace of Leinster, and he lived very privately and saw no company. Maynooth was stupid and dull,—there were neither belles nor balls; Fermoy (to use the doctor's well-remembered words) had "great feeding" and "very genteel young ladies, that carried their handkerchiefs in bags, and danced with the officers."

They had not been many weeks in their new quarters when they began to pine over their altered fortunes, and it was with a sense of delight, which a few months before would have been incomprehensible to them, they discovered that one of their officers had a brother, a young priest in the college; he introduced him to some of his confrères, and the natural result followed. A visiting acquaintance began between the regiment and such of the members of the college as had liberty to leave the precincts, who, as time ripened the acquaintance into intimacy, very naturally preferred the mess of the North Cork to the meagre fare of "the refectory." At last, seldom a day went by without one or two of their reverences finding themselves guests at the mess. The North Corkians were of a most hospitable turn, and the fathers were determined the virtue should not rust for want of being exercised; they would just drop in to say a word to "Captain O'Flaherty about leave to shoot in the demesne," as Carton was styled; or they had a "frank from the Duke for the Colonel," or some other equally pressing reason; and they would contrive to be caught in the middle of a very droll story just as the "roast beef" was playing. Very little entreaty then sufficed,—a short apology for the "derangements" of dress, and a few minutes more found them seated at table without further ceremony on either side.

Among the favorite guests from the college, two were peculiarly in estimation,—"the Professor of the Humanities," Father Luke Mooney, and the Abbé d'Array, "the Lecturer on Moral Philosophy and Belles-Lettres;" and certain it is, pleasanter fellows, or more gifted with the "convivial bump," there never existed. He of the Humanities was a droll dog, —a member of the Curran Club, the "monks of the screw," told an excellent story, and sang the "Cruiskeen Lawn" better than did any before or since him; the moral philosopher, though of a different *genre,* was also a most agreeable companion,—an Irishman transplanted in his youth to St. Omer, and who had grafted upon his native humor a considerable share of French smartness and repartee. Such were the two who ruled supreme in all the festive arrangements of this jovial regiment, and were at last as regular at table as the adjutant and the paymaster, and so might they have continued, had not prosperity, that in its blighting influence upon the heart spares neither priests nor laymen, and is equally severe upon mice (see Æsop's fable) and moral philosophers, actually deprived them, for the "nonce," of reason, and tempted them to their ruin. You naturally ask, what did they do? Did they venture upon allusions to the retreat upon Ross? Nothing of the kind. Did they, in that vanity which wine inspires, refer by word, act, or innuendo, to the well-known order of their colonel when reviewing his regiment in "the Phœnix," to "advance two steps backwards, and dress by the gutter"? Far be it from them,—though indeed either of these had been esteemed light in the balance with their real crime. "Then what was their failing? Come, tell it, and burn ye!" They actually—I dread to say it— quizzed the Major *coram* the whole mess! Now, Major John Jones had only lately exchanged into the North Cork from the "Darry Ragement," as he called it. He was a red-hot Orangeman, a deputy-grand something, and vice-chairman of the " 'Prentice Boys" besides. He broke his leg when a schoolboy by a fall incurred in tying an orange handkerchief around King William's august neck in College Green on one 12th of July, and three several times had closed the gates of Derry with his own loyal hands on the famed anniversary, —in a word, he was one that, if his Church had enjoined penance as an expiation for sin, would have looked upon a trip to Jerusalem on his bare knees as a very light punishment for the crime on his conscience that he sat at table with two buck priests from Maynooth, and carved for them, like the rest of the company!

Poor Major Jones, however, had no such solace, and the cankerworm ate daily deeper and deeper into his pining heart. During the three or four weeks of their intimacy with his regiment, his martyrdom was awful. His figure wasted, and his color became a deeper tinge of orange, and all around averred that there would soon be a "move up" in the corps, for the Major had evidently "got his notice to quit" this world and its pomps and vanities. He felt "that he was dying," to use Haynes Bayley's beautiful and apposite words, and meditated an exchange; but that, from circumstances, was out of the question. At last, subdued by grief, and probably his spirit having chafed itself smooth by such constant attrition, he became to all seeming, calmer; but it was only the calm of a broken and weary heart. Such was Major Jones at the time when, *suadente diabolo,* it seemed meet to Fathers Mooney and D'Array to make him the butt of their raillery. At first he could not believe it,—the thing was incredible, impossible; but when he looked around the table,

5

when he heard the roars of laughter, long, loud, and vociferous; when he heard his name bandied from one to the other across the table, with some vile jest tacked to it "like a tin kettle to a dog's tail," he awoke to the full measure of his misery,—the cup was full. Fate had done her worst, and he might have exclaimed with Lear, "Spit, fire—spout, rain," there was nothing in store for him of further misfortune.

A drum-head court martial, a hint "to sell out," ay, a sentence of "dismissed the service," had been mortal calamities, and, like a man, he would have borne them; but that he, Major John Jones, D.G.S.C.P.B., etc., who had drunk the "pious, glorious, and immortal," sitting astride of "the great gun of Athlone," should come to this! Alas and alas! He retired that night to his chamber a "sadder, if not a wiser man;" he dreamed that the "statue" had given place to the unshapely figure of Leo X., and that "Lundy now stood where Walker stood before." He jumped from his bed in a moment of enthusiasm, he vowed his revenge, and he kept his vow.

That day the Major was "acting field-officer." The various patrols, sentries, pickets, and outposts were all under his especial control, and it was remarked that he took peculiar pains in selecting the men for night duty, which, in the prevailing quietness and peace of that time, seemed scarcely warrantable.

Evening drew near, and Major Jones, summoned by the "oft-heard beat," wended his way to the mess. The officers were dropping in, and true as "the needle to the pole," came Father Mooney and the Abbé. They were welcomed with the usual warmth, and, strange to say, by none more than the Major himself, whose hilarity knew no bounds.

How the evening passed, I shall not stop to relate; suffice it to say that a more brilliant feast of wit and jollification not even the North Cork ever enjoyed. Father Luke's drollest stories, his very quaintest humor, shone forth, and the Abbé sang a new *chanson à boire* that Béranger might have envied.

"What are you about, my dear Father d'Array?" said the Colonel. "You are surely not rising yet? Here's a fresh cooper of port just come in; sit down, I entreat."

"I say it with grief, my dear Colonel, we must away; the

half-hour has just chimed, and we must be within 'the gates' before twelve. The truth is, the superior has been making himself very troublesome about our 'carnal amusements,' as he calls our innocent mirth, and we must therefore be upon our guard."

"Well, if it must be so, we shall not risk losing your society altogether for an hour or so now; so, one bumper to our next meeting,—to-morrow, mind; and now, *Monsieur l'Abbé, au revoir.*"

The worthy fathers finished their glasses, and taking a most affectionate leave of their kind entertainers, sallied forth under the guidance of Major Jones, who insisted upon accompanying them part of the way, as, "from information he had received, the sentries were doubled in some places, and the usual precautions against surprise all taken." Much as this polite attention surprised the objects of it, his brother officers wondered still more, and no sooner did they perceive the Major and his companions issue forth than they set out in a body to watch where this most novel and unexpected complaisance would terminate.

When the priests reached the door of the barrack-yard, they again turned to utter their thanks to the Major, and entreat him once more "not to come a step farther. There now, Major, we know the path well, so just give us the pass, and don't stay out in the night air."

"*Ah, oui, Monsieur Jones,*" said the Abbé, "*retournez, je vous prie.* We are, I may say, *chez nous. Ces braves gens, les* North Cork, know us by this time."

The Major smiled, while he still pressed his services to see them past the pickets; but they were resolved, and would not be denied.

"With the word for the night we want nothing more," said Father Luke.

"Well, then," said the Major, in the gravest tone,—and he was naturally grave,—"you shall have your way; but remember to call out loud, for the first sentry is a little deaf, and a very passionate, ill-tempered fellow to boot."

"Never fear," said Father Mooney, laughing; "I'll go bail he'll hear me."

"Well, the word for the night is, 'Bloody end to the Pope,'

—don't forget, now, 'Bloody end to the Pope.'" And with these words he banged the door between him and the unfortunate priests; and as bolt was fastened after bolt, they heard him laughing to himself like a fiend over his vengeance.

"And big bad luck to ye, Major Jones, for the same, every day ye see a paving-stone," was the faint, sub-audible ejaculation of Father Luke, when he was recovered enough to speak.

"*Sacristi! que nous sommes attrapés,*" said the Abbé, scarcely able to avoid laughing at the situation in which they were placed.

"Well, there's the quarter chiming now; we've no time to lose. Major Jones! Major darling; don't now, ah, don't! sure ye know we'll be ruined entirely. There now, just change it, like a dacent fellow! The devil's luck to him, he's gone! Well, we can't stay here in the rain all night, and be expelled in the morning afterwards, so come along."

They jogged along for a few minutes in silence, till they came to that part of the "Duke's" demesne wall where the first sentry was stationed. By this time the officers, headed by the Major, had quietly slipped out of the gate, and were following their steps at a convenient distance.

The fathers had stopped to consult together what they should do in this trying emergency, when, their whisper being overheard, the sentinel called out gruffly, in the genuine dialect of his country, "Who goes *that?*"

"Father Luke Mooney and the Abbé d'Array," said the former, in his most bland and insinuating tone of voice,— a quality he most eminently possessed.

"Stand, and give the countersign."

"We are coming from the mess, and going home to the college," said Father Mooney, evading the question, and gradually advancing as he spoke.

"Stand, or I'll *shot* ye," said the North Corkian.

Father Luke halted, while a muttered "Blessed Virgin!" announced his state of fear and trepidation.

"D'Array, I say, what are we to do?"

"The countersign," said the sentry, whose figure they could perceive in the dim distance of about thirty yards.

"Sure ye'll let us pass, my good lad, and ye'll have a friend in Father Luke the longest day ye live; and ye might have a worse in time of need,—ye understand."

Whether he did understand or not, he certainly did not heed, for his only reply was the short click of a gun-lock, that bespeaks a preparation to fire.

"There's no help now," said Father Luke; "I see he's a haythen; and bad luck to the Major, I say again." And this, in the fulness of his heart, he uttered aloud.

"That's not the countersign," said the inexorable sentry, striking the butt-end of his musket on the ground with a crash that smote terror into the hearts of the priests.

Mumble—mumble—"to the Pope," said Father Luke, pronouncing the last words distinctly, after the approved practice of a Dublin watchman on being awoke from his dreams of row and riot by the last toll of the Post-office, and not knowing whether it has struck "twelve" or "three," sings out the word "o'clock" in a long, sonorous drawl, that wakes every sleeping citizen, and yet tells nothing how "Time speeds on his flight."

"Louder," said the sentry, in a voice of impatience.

"—to the Pope."

"I don't hear the first part."

"Oh, then," said the priest, with a sigh that might have melted the heart of anything but a sentry, "Bloody end to the Pope; and may the saints in heaven forgive me for saying it!"

"Again," called out the soldier, "and no muttering."

"Bloody end to the Pope," cried Father Luke, in bitter desperation.

"Bloody end to the Pope," echoed the Abbé.

"Pass, Bloody end to the Pope, and good-night," said the sentry, resuming his rounds; while a loud and uproarious peal of laughter behind told the unlucky priests they were overheard by others, and that the story would be over the whole town in the morning.

Whether it was that the penance for their heresy took long in accomplishing, or that they never could summon courage sufficient to face their persecutor, certain it is the North Cork saw them no more, nor were they ever observed to pass the precincts of the college while that regiment occupied Maynooth.

Major Jones himself and his confederates could not have more heartily relished this story than did the party to whom the doctor related it. Much, if not all, the amusement it afforded, however, resulted from his inimitable mode of telling, and the power of mimicry with which he conveyed the dialogue with the sentry; and this, alas! must be lost to my readers,—at least to that portion of them not fortunate enough to possess Dr. Finucane's acquaintance.

"Fin! Fin! your long story has nearly famished me," said the *padre,* as the laugh subsided; "and there you sit now with the jug at your elbow this half-hour; I never thought you would forget our old friend Martin Hanegan's aunt."

"Here's to her health," said Fin; "and your reverence will give us the chant."

"Agreed," said Father Malachi, finishing a bumper; and after giving a few preparatory hems, he sang the following "singularly wild and beautiful poem," as some one calls "Christabel :"—

> " Here's a health to Martin Hanegan's aunt
> And I'll tell ye the reason why !
> She eats bekase she is hungry,
> And drinks bekase she is dry.
>
> "And if ever a man
> Stopped the course of a can,
> Martin Hanegan's aunt would cry,—
> 'Arrah, fill up your glass,
> And let the jug pass;
> How d' ye know but your neighbor's dhry ? '

"Come, my lord and gentlemen, *da capo,* if ye please— 'Fill up your glass,' " etc.; and the *chanson* was chorused with a strength and vigor that would have astonished the Philharmonic.

The mirth and fun now grew "fast and furious;" and Father Malachi, rising with the occasion, flung his reckless drollery and fun on every side, sparing none, from his cousin to the coadjutor. It was now that peculiar period in the evening's enjoyment when an expert and practical chairman gives up all interference or management, and leaves everything to take its course; this, then, was the happy moment selected by Father Malachi to propose the little "conthribution." He brought a plate from a side-table, and placing it before him, addressed the company in a very brief but sensible speech, detailing the object of the institution he was advocating, and concluding with the following words: "And now ye'll just give whatever ye like, according to your means in life and what ye can spare."

The admonition, like the "morale" of an income tax, had the immediate effect of pitting each man against his neighbor, and suggested to their already excited spirits all the ardor of gambling, without, however, the prospect of gain. The plate was first handed to me, in honor of my "rank;" and having deposited upon it a handful of small silver, the priest ran his fingers through the coin, and called out,—

"Five pounds at least,—not a farthing less, as I am a sinner. Look, then,—see, now; they tell ye the gentlemen don't care for the like of ye! but see for yourselves. May I trouble y'r lordship to pass the plate to Mr. Mahony,—he's impatient, I see."

Mr. Mahony, about whom I perceived very little of the impatience alluded to, was a grim-looking old Christian in a rabbit-skin waist-coat with long flaps, who fumbled in the recesses of his breeches-pocket for five minutes, and then drew forth three shillings, which he laid upon the plate with what I fancied very much resembled a sigh.

"Six and sixpence, is it, or five shillings? All the same, Mr. Mahony; and I'll not forget the thrifle you were speaking about this morning, any way." And here he leaned over, as interceding with me for him, but in reality to whisper into my ear, "The greatest miser from this to Castlebar."

"Who's that put down the half guinea in goold?" (and this time he spoke truth)—"who's that, I say?"

"Tim Kennedy, your reverence," said Tim, stroking his hair down with one hand, and looking proud and modest at the same moment.

"Tim, ye're a credit to us any day, and I always said so. It's a gauger he'd like' to be, my lord," said he, turning to me in a kind of stage whisper. I nodded, and muttered something, when he thanked me most profoundly, as if his suit had prospered.

"Mickey Oulahan, the Lord's looking at ye, Mickey." This was said *pianissimo* across the table, and had the effect of increasing Mr. Oulahan's donation from five shillings to seven,—the last two being pitched in very much in the style of a gambler making his final *coup,* and crying, *"Va, banque!"* "The Oulahans were always dacent people,—dacent people, my lord."

"Be gorra, the Oulahans was niver dacenter nor the Molowneys, anyhow," said a tall, athletic young fellow, as he threw down three crown pieces with an energy that made every coin leap from the plate.

"They'll do now," said Father Brennan; "I'll leave them to themselves." And truly the eagerness to get the plate and put down the subscription fully equalled the rapacious anxiety I have witnessed in an old maid at loo to get possession of a thirty-shilling pool, be the same more or less, which lingered on its way to her in the hands of many a fair competitor.

"Mr. M'Neesh"—Curzon had hitherto escaped all notice —"Mr. M'Neesh, to your good health," cried Father Brennan. "It's many a secret they'll be getting out o' ye down there about the Scotch husbandry."

Whatever poor Curzon knew of "drills," certainly did not extend to them when occupied by turnips. This allusion of the priest's being caught up by the party at the foot of the table, they commenced a series of inquiries into different Scotch plans of tillage,—his brief and unsatisfactory answers to which, they felt sure, were given in order to evade imparting information. By degrees, as they continued to press him with questions, his replies grew more short, and a general feeling of dislike on both sides was not very long in following.

The father saw this, and determining, with his usual tact, to repress it, called on the Adjutant for a song. Now, whether he had but one in the world, or whether he took this mode of retaliating for the annoyances he had suffered, I know not; but true it is, he finished his tumbler at a draught, and with a voice of no very peculiar sweetness, though abundantly loud, began "The Boyne Water."

He had just reached the word "battle," in the second line, upon which he was bestowing what he meant to be a shake, when, as if the word suggested it, it seemed the signal for a general engagement. Decanters, glasses, jugs, candlesticks, —ay, and the money-dish,—flew right and left, all originally intended, it is true, for the head of the luckless Adjutant, but as they now and then missed their aim, and came in contact with the "wrong man," invariably provoked retaliation, and in a very few minutes the battle became general.

What may have been the doctor's political sentiments on this occasion, I cannot even guess; but he seemed bent upon performing the part of a "convivial Lord Stanley," and maintaining a dignified neutrality. With this apparent object, he mounted upon the table,—to raise himself, I suppose, above the din and commotion of party clamor,—and brandishing a jug of scalding water, bestowed it with perfect impartiality on the combatants on either side. This Whig plan of conciliation, however well intended, seemed not to prosper with either party; and many were the missiles directed at the ill-starred doctor. Meanwhile Father Malachi, whether following the pacific instinct of his order, in seeking an asylum in troublesome times, or equally moved by old habit to gather coin in low places (much of the money having fallen), was industriously endeavoring to insert himself beneath the table. In this, with one vigorous push, he at last succeeded; but in so doing lifted it from its legs, and thus destroying poor "Fin's" gravity, precipitated him, jug and all, into the thickest of the fray, where he met with that kind reception such a benefactor ever receives at the hand of a grateful public. I meanwhile hurried to rescue poor Curzon, who, having fallen to the ground, was getting a cast of his features taken in pewter, for such seemed the operation a stout farmer was performing on the Adjutant's face with a quart. With considerable difficulty, notwithstanding my supposed "lordship," I succeeded in freeing him from his present position; and he concluding, probably, that enough had been done for one "sitting," most willingly permitted me to lead him from the room. I was soon joined by the doctor, who assisted me in getting my poor friend to bed; which being done, he most eagerly entreated me to join the company. This, however, I firmly but mildly declined, very much to his surprise; for, as he remarked, "They'll all be like lambs now, for they don't believe there's a whole bone in his body."

Expressing my deep sense of the Christian-like forbearance of the party, I pleaded fatigue, and bidding him good night, adjourned to my bedroom; and here, although the arrangements fell somewhat short of the luxurious ones appertaining to my late apartment at Callonby, they were most grateful at the moment; and having "addressed myself to slumber," fell fast asleep, and only awoke late on the following morning to wonder where I was; from any doubts as to which I was speedily relieved by the entrance of the priest's bare-footed "colleen," to deposit on my table a bottle of soda-water, and announce breakfast, with his reverence's compliments.

Having made a hasty toilet, I proceeded to the parlor, which, however late events might have impressed upon my memory, I could scarcely recognize. Instead of the long oak table and the wassail-bowl, there stood near the fire a small round table covered with a snow-white cloth, upon which shone in unrivalled brightness a very handsome tea-equipage. The hissing kettle on one hob was balanced by a gridiron with three newly taken trout frying under the reverential care of Father Malachi himself; a heap of eggs, ranged like shot in an ordnance yard, stood in the middle of the table, while a formidable pile of buttered toast browned before the grate; the morning papers were airing upon the hearth,—everything bespoke that attention to comfort and enjoyment one likes to discover in the house where chance may have domesticated him for a day or two.

"Good-morning, Mr. Lorrequer. I trust you have rested well," said Father Malachi, as I entered.

"Never better; but where are our friends?"

"I have been visiting and comforting them in their affliction, and I may with truth assert it is not often my fortune to have three as sickly looking guests. That was a most unlucky affair last night, and I must apologize—"

"Don't say a word, I entreat; I saw how it all occurred, and am quite sure if it had not been for poor Curzon's ill-timed melody—"

"You are quite right," said the father, interrupting me. "Your friend's taste for music—bad luck to it!—was the *teterrima causa belli.*"

"And the subscription," said I,—"how did it succeed?"

"Oh! the money went in the commotion; and although I have got some seven pounds odd shillings of it, the war was a most expensive one to me. I caught old Mahony very busy under the table during the fray— But let us say no more about it now; draw over your chair. Tea or coffee? There's the rum, if you like it in French fashion."

I immediately obeyed the injunction, and commenced a vigorous assault upon the trout,—caught, as he informed me, "within twenty perches of the house."

"Your poor friend's nose is scarcely regimental," said he, "this morning; and as for Fin, he was never remarkable for beauty, so, though they might cut and hack, they could scarcely disfigure him. As Juvenal says—is n't it Juvenal?—

" ' Cantabit vacuus coram latrone viator; '

or, in the vernacular,—

" ' The empty traveller may whistle
Before the robber and his pistil' [pistol].

There's the Chili vinegar,—another morsel of the trout?"

"I thank you. What excellent coffee, Father Malachi!"

A secret I learned at St. Omer's some thirty years since. Any letters, Bridget?"—to a damsel that entered with a packet in her hand.

"A gossoon from Kilrush, y'r reverence, with a bit of a note for the gentleman there."

"For me? Ah, true enough! 'Harry Lorrequer, Esq., Kilrush.—Try Carrigaholt.' " So ran the superscription,—the first part being in a lady's handwriting; the latter very like the "rustic paling" of the worthy Mrs. Healy's style. The seal was a large one, bearing a coronet at top; and the motto, in old Norman-French, told me it came from Callonby.

With what a trembling hand and beating heart I broke it

open, and yet feared to read it,—so much of my destiny might
be in that simple page! For once in my life my sanguine
spirit failed me; my mind could take in but one casualty,
that Lady Jane had divulged to her family the nature of my
attentions, and that in the letter before me lay a cold mandate
of dismissal from her presence forever.

At last I summoned courage to read it; but having scrupled
to present to my readers the Reverend Father Brennan at the
end of a chapter, let me be not less punctilious in the introduction of her ladyship's billet.

CHAPTER VII.

THE LADY'S LETTER.—PETER AND HIS ACQUAINTANCES.—
TOO LATE.

HER ladyship's letter ran thus:—

CALLONBY, Tuesday morning.

MY DEAR MR. LORREQUER,—My lord has deputed me to
convey to you our adieus, and at the same time express our
very great regret that we should not have seen you before
our departure from Ireland. A sudden call of the House,
and some unexpected ministerial changes, require Lord Callonby's immediate presence in town; and probably before this
reaches you we shall be on the road. Lord Kilkee, who left
us yesterday, was much distressed at not having seen you,—
he desired me to say you shall hear from him from Leaming-
ton. Although writing amid all the haste and bustle of departure, I must not forget the principal part of my commission,
nor, ladylike, defer it to a postscript: my lord entreats that
you will, if possible, pass a month or two with us in London
this season; and if any difficulty should occur in obtaining
leave of absence, to make any use of his name you think fit
at the Horse Guards, where he has some influence. Knowing
as I do with what kindness you ever accede to the wishes of
your friends, I need not say how much gratification this will

afford us all; but, *sans réponse,* we expect you. Believe me to remain, yours very sincerely,

CHARLOTTE CALLONBY.

P. S.—We are quite well, except Lady Jane, who has a slight cold and has been feverish for the last day or two.

Words cannot convey any idea of the torrent of contending emotions under which I perused this letter. The suddenness of the departure, without an opportunity of even a moment's leave-taking, completely unmanned me. What would I not have given to be able to see her once more, even for an instant; to say a "good-by;" to watch the feeling with which she parted from me, and augur from it either favorably to my heart's dearest hope or darkest despair. As I continued to read on, the kindly tone of the remainder reassured me; and when I came to the invitation to London, which plainly argued a wish on their part to perpetuate the intimacy, I was obliged to read it again and again before I could convince myself of its reality. There it was, however, most distinctly and legibly impressed in her ladyship's fairest calligraphy; and certainly, great as was its consequence to me at the time, it by no means formed the principal part of the communication. The two lines of postscript contained more, far more, food for hopes and fears than did all the rest of the epistle.

Lady Jane was ill, then; slightly, however,—a mere cold; true, but she was feverish. I could not help asking myself what share had I in causing that flushed cheek and anxious eye, and pictured to myself, perhaps with more vividness than reality, a thousand little traits of manner, all proofs strong as holy writ to my sanguine mind that my affection was returned, and that I loved not in vain. Again and again I read over the entire letter; never, truly, did a *nisi prius* lawyer con over a new Act of Parliament with more searching ingenuity to detect its hidden meaning, than I did to unravel through its plain phraseology the secret intention of the writer towards me.

There is an old and not less true adage that what we wish we readily believe, and so with me. I found myself an easy convert to my own hopes and desires, and actually ended by persuading myself—no very hard task—that my Lord Callonby had not only witnessed but approved of my attachment to his beautiful daughter, and for reasons probably known to him, but concealed from me, opined that I was a suitable *parti*, and gave all due encouragement to my suit. The hint about using his lordship's influence at the Horse Guards I resolved to benefit by,—not, however, in obtaining leave of absence, which I hoped to accomplish more easily, but with his good sanction in pushing my promotion when I should claim him as my right-honorable father-in-law: a point on the propriety of which I had now fully satisfied myself. What visions of rising greatness burst upon my mind as I thought on the prospect that opened before me! But here let me do myself the justice to record that amid all my pleasure and exultation, my proudest thought was in the anticipation of possessing one in every way so much my superior,—the very consciousness of which imparted a thrill of fear to my heart that such good fortune was too much even to hope for.

How long I might have luxuriated in such *châteaux en Espagne,* Heaven knows; thick and thronging fancies came abundantly to my mind, and it was with something of the feeling of the porter in the "Arabian Nights" as he surveyed the fragments of his broken ware hurled down in a moment of glorious dreaminess that I turned to look at the squat and unaristocratic figure of Father Malachi as he sat reading his newspaper before the fire. How came I in such company? Methinks the Dean of Windsor or the Bishop of Durham had been a much more seemly associate for one destined as I was for the flood-tide of the world's favor.

My eye at this instant rested upon the date of the letter, which was that of the preceding morning; and immediately a thought struck me that, as the day was a lowering and gloomy one, perhaps they might have deferred their journey, and I at once determined to hasten to Callonby, and if possible see them before their departure.

"Father Brennan," said I at length, "I have just received a letter which compels me to reach Kilrush as soon as possible. Is there any public conveyance in the village?"

"You don't talk of leaving us, surely," said the priest, "and a haunch of mutton for dinner, and Fin says he'll be down, and your friend too, and we'll have poor Beamish in on a sofa!"

"I am sorry to say my business will not admit of delay; but if possible, I shall return to thank you for all your kindness in a day or two,—perhaps to-morrow."

"Oh! then," said Father Brennan, "if it must be so, why you can have Pether, my own pad, and a better you never laid leg over; only give him his own time, and let him keep the 'canter,' and he'll never draw up from morning till night. And now I'll just go and have him in readiness for you."

After professing my warm acknowledgments to the good father for his kindness, I hastened to take a hurried farewell of Curzon before going. I found him sitting up in bed taking his breakfast. A large strip of black plaster, extending from the corner of one eye across the nose, and terminating near the mouth, denoted the *locale* of a goodly wound; while the blue, purple, and yellow patches into which his face was partitioned out, left you in doubt whether he more resembled the knave of clubs or a new map of the Ordnance Survey. One hand was wrapped up in a bandage; and altogether a more rueful and woe-begone looking figure I have rarely looked upon; and most certainly I am of opinion that the "glorious, pious, and immortal memory" would have brought pleasanter recollections to Daniel O'Connell himself than it did on that morning to the Adjutant of his Majesty's 4—th.

"Ah! Harry," said he, as I entered, "what Pandemonium is this we've got into? Did you ever witness such a business as last night's?"

"Why, truly," said I, "I know of no one to blame but yourself; surely you must have known what a row your infernal song would bring on."

"I don't know now whether I knew it or not; but certainly at the moment I should have preferred anything to the confounded cross-examination I was under, and was glad to end it by any *coup d'état*. One wretch was persecuting me about green crops, and another about the feeding of bullocks,—about either of which I knew as much as a bear does of a ballet."

"Well, truly, you caused a diversion at some expense to your countenance, for I never beheld anything—"

"Stop there," said he; "you surely have not seen the doctor,—he beats me hollow; they have scarcely left so much hair on his head as would do for an Indian's scalplock; and, of a verity, his aspect is awful this morning. He has just been here, and, by the by, has told me all about your affair with Beamish. It appears that somehow you met him at dinner and gave a very flourishing account of a relative of his who, you informed him, was not only selected for some very dashing service, but actually the personal friend of Picton; and after the family having blazed the matter all over Cork, and given a great entertainment in honor of their kinsman, it turns out that on the glorious 18th he ran away to Brussels faster than even the French to Charleroi,—for which act, however, there was no aspersion ever cast upon his courage, that quality being defended at the expense of his honesty; in a word, he was the paymaster of his company, and had what Theodore Hook calls an 'affection of his chest' that required change of air. Looking only to the running away part of the matter, I unluckily expressed some regret that he did not belong to the North Cork, and I remarked the doctor did not seem to relish the allusion, and *as I* only now remember it was *his* regiment, I suppose I'm in for more mischief."

I had no time to enjoy Curzon's dilemma, and had barely informed him of my intended departure, when a voice from without the room proclaimed that "Pether" was ready; and having commissioned the Adjutant to say the "proper" to Mr. Beamish and the doctor, I hurried away, and after a hearty shake of the hand from Father Brennan, and a faithful promise to return soon, I mounted and set off.

Peter's pace was of all others the one least likely to disturb the lucubrations of a castle-builder like myself. Without any admonition from whip or spur, he maintained a steady and constant canter, which, I am free to confess, was more agreeable to sit than it was graceful to behold; for his head being much lower than his tail, he every moment appeared in the attitude of a diver about to plunge into the water, and more than once I had misgivings that I should consult my safety better if I sat with my face to the tail,—however, what will not habit accomplish? Before I had gone a mile or two, I was so lost in my own reveries and reflections that I knew nothing of my mode of progression, and had only thoughts and feelings for the destiny that awaited me. Sometimes I would fancy myself seated in the House of Commons (on the ministerial benches, of course), while some leading oppositionist was pronouncing a glowing panegyric upon the eloquent and statesmanlike speech of the gallant colonel,—myself; then I thought I was making arrangements for setting out for my new appointment,—and Sancho Panza never coveted the government of an island more than I did, though only a West Indian one; and lastly, I saw myself the chosen diplomat on a difficult mission, and was actually engaged in the easy and agreeable occupation of out-manœuvring Talleyrand and Pozzo di Borgo, when Peter suddenly drew up at the door of a small cabin and convinced me that I was still a mortal man and a lieutenant in his Majesty's 4—th. Before I had time afforded me even to guess at the reason of this sudden halt, an old man emerged from the cabin, which I saw now was a road-side ale-house, and presented Peter with a bucket of meal and water,—a species of "refresher" that he evidently was accustomed to at this place, whether bestrode by a priest or an ambassador. Before me lay a long, straggling street of cabins, irregularly thrown, as if riddled over the ground: this I was informed was Kilkee. While my good steed, therefore, was enjoying his potation, I dismounted, to stretch my legs and look about me; and scarcely had I done so when I found half the population of the village assembled round Peter, whose claims to notoriety, I now learned, depended neither upon his owner's fame, nor even my temporary possession of him. Peter, in fact, had been a racer once,—when, the Wandering Jew might perhaps have told, had he ever visited Clare; for not the oldest inhabitant knew the date of his triumphs on the turf, though they were undisputed traditions, and never did any man appear bold enough to call them in question. Whether it was from his patriarchal character, or that he was the only race-horse ever known in his county, I cannot say, but of a truth the Grand Lama could scarcely be a greater object of reverence in Thibet than was Peter in Kilkee.

"Musha, Peter, but it's well y' 'r' looking!" cried one.

"Ah, thin, maybe ye an't fat on the ribs!" cried another.

"An' cockin' his tail like a coult," said a third.

I am very certain, if I might venture to judge from the faces about, that had the favorite for the St. Leger passed through Kilkee at that moment, comparisons very little to his favor had been drawn from the assemblage around me. With some difficulty I was permitted to reach my much-admired steed, and with a cheer which was sustained and caught up by every denizen of the village as I passed through, I rode on my way, not a little amused at my equivocal popularity.

Being desirous to lose no time, I diverged from the straight road which leads to Kilrush, and took a cross bridle-path to Callonby,—this, I afterwards discovered, was a *détour* of a mile or two; and it was already sunset when I reached the entrance to the Park. I entered the avenue; and now my impatience became extreme, for although Peter continued to move at the same uniform pace, I could not persuade myself that he was not foundering at every step, and was quite sure we were scarcely advancing. At last I reached the wooden bridge and ascended the steep slope,—the spot where I had first met her on whom my every thought now rested. I turned the angle of the clump of beech-trees from whence the first view of the house is caught. I perceived, to my inexpressible delight, that gleams of light shot from many of the windows, and could trace their passing from one to the other. I now drew rein, and with a heart relieved from a load of anxiety, pulled up my good steed, and began to think of the position in which a few brief seconds would place me. I reached the small flower-garden, sacred by a thousand endearing recollections. Oh! of how very little account are the many words of passing kindness and moments of light-hearted pleasure, when spoken or felt, compared to the memory of them when hallowed by time or distance!

"The place, the hour, the sunshine and the shade," all reminded me of the happy past, and all brought vividly before me every portion of that dream of happiness in which I was so utterly, so completely steeped,—every thought of the hopelessness of my passion was lost in the intensity of it, and I did not, in the ardor of my loving, stop to think of its possible success.

It was strange enough that the extreme impatience, the hurried anxiety, I had felt and suffered from while riding up the avenue, had now fled entirely, and in its place I felt nothing but a diffident distrust of myself and a vague sense of awkwardness about intruding thus unexpectedly upon the family while engaged in all the cares and preparations for a speedy departure. The hall-door lay, as usual, wide open; the hall itself was strewn and littered with trunks, imperials, and packing-cases, and the hundred *et ceteras* of travelling baggage. I hesitated a moment whether I should not ring, but at last resolved to enter unannounced, and presuming upon my intimacy, see what effect my sudden appearance would have on Lady Jane, whose feelings towards me would be thus most unequivocally tested. I passed along the wide corridor, entered the music-room: it was still. I walked then to the door of the drawing-room: I paused, I drew a full breath; my hand trembled slightly as I turned the lock; I entered. The room was empty, but the blazing fire upon the hearth, the large arm-chairs drawn round, the scattered books upon the small tables, all told that it had been inhabited a very short time before. "Ah!" thought I, looking at my watch, "they are at dinner;" and I began at once to devise a hundred different plans to account for my late absence and present visit. I knew that a few minutes would probably bring them into the drawing-room, and I felt flurried and heated as the time drew near. At last I heard voices without. I started from the examination of a pencil-drawing, partly finished, but the artist of which I could not be deceived in. I listened,—the sounds drew near; I could not distinguish who were the speakers. The door-lock turned, and I rose to make my well-conned but half-forgotten speech, and oh, confounded disappointment! Mrs. Herbert, the housekeeper, entered. She started, not expecting to see me, and immediately said,—

"Oh! Mr. Lorrequer, then you've missed them?"

"Missed them!" said I; "how—when—where?"

"Did you not get a note from my lord?"

"No; when was it written?"

"Oh, dear me, that is so very unfortunate! Why, sir, my

lord sent off a servant this morning to Kilrush in Lord Kilkee's tilbury to request you would meet them all in Ennis
this evening, where they had intended to stop for to-night;
and they waited here till near four o'clock to-day. But when
the servant came back with the intelligence that you were from
home, and not expected to return soon, they were obliged to
set out, and are not going to make any delay now till they
reach London. The last direction, however, my lord gave was
to forward her ladyship's letter to you as soon as possible."

What I thought, said, or felt, might be a good subject of
confession to Father Malachi, for I fear it may be recorded
among my sins, as I doubt not that the agony I suffered vented
itself in no measured form of speech or conduct; but I have
nothing to confess here on the subject, being so totally overwhelmed as not to know what I did or said. My first gleam
of reason elicited itself by asking,—

"Is there, then, no chance of their stopping in Ennis to-
night?" As I put the question, my mind reverted to Peter
and his eternal canter.

"Oh, dear, no, sir! The horses are ordered to take them,
since Tuesday; and they only thought of staying in Ennis
if you came time enough to meet them,—and they will be so
sorry."

"Do you think so, Mrs. Herbert? Do you indeed think
so?" said I, in a most insinuating tone.

"I am perfectly sure of it, sir."

"Oh, Mrs. Herbert, you are too kind to think so! But perhaps—that is—maybe, Mrs. Herbert, she said something—"

"Who, sir?"

"Lady Callonby, I mean. Did her ladyship leave any message for me about her plants? Or did she remember—"

Mrs. Herbert kept looking at me all the time, with her
great wide gray eyes, while I kept stammering and blushing
like a schoolboy.

"No, sir, her ladyship said nothing, sir; but Lady Jane—"

"Yes; well, what of Lady Jane, my dear Mrs. Herbert?"

"Oh, sir! But you look pale,—would not you like to have a
little wine and water, or perhaps—"

"No, thank you, nothing whatever; I am just a little fatigued. But you were mentioning—"

"Yes, sir; I was saying that Lady Jane was mighty particular about a small plant: she ordered it to be left in her dressing-room. Though Collins told her to have some of the handsome ones of the green-house, she would have nothing but this; and if you were only to hear half the directions she gave about keeping it watered, and taking off dead leaves, you'd think her heart was set on it."

Mrs. Herbert would have had no cause to prescribe for my paleness had she only looked at me this time; fortunately, however, she was engaged, housekeeper-like, in bustling among books, papers, etc., which she had come in for the purpose of arranging and packing up,—she being left behind to bring up the rear and the heavy baggage.

Very few moments' consideration were sufficient to show me that pursuit was hopeless. Whatever might have been Peter's performance in the reign of "Queen Anne," he had now become, like the goose so pathetically described by my friend Lover, rather "stiff in his limbs;" and the odds were fearfully against his overtaking four horses starting fresh every ten miles, not to mention their being some hours in advance already. Having declined all Mrs. Herbert's many kind offers anent food and rest, I took a last lingering look at the beautiful picture which still held its place in the room lately mine, and hurried from a place so full of recollections; and notwithstanding the many reasons I had for self-gratulation, every object around and about filled me with sorrow and regret for hours that had passed, never, never, to return.

It was very late when I reached my old quarters at Kilrush. Mrs. Healy, fortunately, was in bed asleep,—fortunately, I say; for had she selected that occasion to vent her indignation for my long absence, I greatly fear that, in my then temper, I should have exhibited but little of that Job-like endurance for which I was once esteemed. I entered my little mean-looking parlor, with its three chairs and lame table; and as I flung myself upon the wretched substitute for a sofa, and thought upon the varied events which a few weeks had brought about, it required the aid of her ladyship's letter, which I had open before me, to assure me I was not dreaming.

The entire of that night I could not sleep; my destiny seemed upon its balance; and whether the scale inclined to this side or that, good or evil fortune seemed to betide me. How many were my plans and resolutions, and how often abandoned,—again to be pondered over, and once more given up! The gray dawn of the morning was already breaking, and found me still doubting and uncertain. At last the die was thrown; I determined at once to apply for leave to my commanding officer (which he could, if he pleased, give me, without any application to the Horse Guards), set out for Elton, tell Sir Guy my whole adventure, and endeavor, by a more moving love-story than ever graced even the Minerva Press, to induce him to make some settlement on me and use his influence with Lord Callonby in my behalf; this done, set out for London, and then—and then—what then? Then for the "Morning Post,"—"orange-flowers;" "happy couple;" "Lord Callonby's seat in Hampshire," etc.

"You wished to be called at five, sir," said Stubbes.

"Yes; is it five o'clock?"

"No, sir; but I heard you call out something about 'four horses,' and I thought you might be hurried, so I came in a little earlier."

"Quite right, Stubbes. Let me have my breakfast as soon as possible, and see that chestnut horse I brought here last night, fed."

"And now for it," said I. After writing a hurried note to Curzon, requesting him to take command of my party at Kilrush till he heard from me, and sending my kind remembrance to my three friends, I despatched the epistle by my servant on Peter, while I hastened to secure a place in the mail for Ennis, on the box-seat of which let my kind reader suppose me seated, as, wrapping my box-coat around me, I lit my cigar and turned my eyes towards Limerick.

CHAPTER VIII.

CONGRATULATIONS.—SICK LEAVE.—HOW TO PASS THE BOARD.

I HAD scarcely seated myself to breakfast at Swinburne's Hotel in Limerick, when the waiter presented me with a letter. As my first glance at the address showed it to be in

Colonel Carden's handwriting, I felt not a little alarmed for the consequences of the rash step I had taken in leaving my detachment; and while quickly thronging fancies of arrest and court-martial flitted before me, I summoned resolution at last to break the seal, and read as follows :—

My dear Lorrequer,—

" 'Dear Lorrequer!' dear me," thought I,—"cool, certainly, from one I have ever regarded as an open enemy."

My dear Lorrequer,—I have just accidentally heard of your arrival here, and hasten to inform you that as it may not be impossible your reasons for so abruptly leaving your detachment are known to me, I shall not visit your breach of discipline very heavily. My old and worthy friend Lord Callonby, who passed through here yesterday, has so warmly interested himself in your behalf that I feel disposed to do all in my power to serve you, independent of my desire to do so on your own account. Come over here, then, as soon as possible, and let us talk over your plans together.

Believe me, most truly yours,
Henry Carden.

Barracks, 10 o'clock.

However mysterious and difficult to unravel have been some of the circumstances narrated in these "Confessions," I do not scruple to avow that the preceding letter was to *me* by far the most inexplicable piece of fortune I had hitherto met with. That Lord Callonby should have converted one whom I believed an implacable foe into a most obliging friend, was intelligible enough, seeing that his lordship had through life been the patron of the Colonel; but why he had so done, and what communications he could possibly have made with regard to me, that Colonel Carden should speak of "my plans" and proffer assistance in them, was a perfect riddle, and the only solution one so ridiculously flattering that I dared not think of it. I read and re-read the note; misplaced the stops; canvassed every expression; did all to detect a meaning different from the obvious one, fearful of a self-deception where so much was at stake. Yet there it stood forth, a plain, straightforward proffer of services for some object evidently known to the writer; and my only conclusion from all was this, that "my Lord Callonby was the gem of his order, and had a most remarkable talent for selecting a son-in-law."

I fell into a deep revery upon my past life and the prospects which I now felt were opening before me. Nothing seemed extravagant to hopes so well founded, to expectations so brilliant; and in my mind's eye I beheld myself one moment leading my young and beautiful bride through the crowded salons of Devonshire House, and at the next I was contemplating the excellence and perfection of my stud arrangements at Melton,—for I resolved not to give up hunting. While in this pleasurable exercise of my fancy I was removing from before me some of the breakfast equipage, or as I then believed it, breaking the trees into better groups upon my lawn, I was once more brought to the world and its dull reality by the following passage, which my eye fell upon in the newspaper before me: "We understand that the 4—th are daily expecting the route for Cork, from whence they are to sail, early in the ensuing month, for Halifax, to relieve the 88th." While it did not take a moment's consideration to show me that though the regiment there mentioned was the one I belonged to, I could have no possible interest in the announcement,—it never coming into my calculation that *I* should submit to such expatriation; yet it gave me a salutary warning that there was no time to be lost in making my application for leave, which once obtained, I should have ample time to manage an exchange into another corps. The wonderful revolution a few days had effected in all my tastes and desires did not escape me at this moment. But a week or two before, and I should have regarded an order for foreign service as anything rather than unpleasant; now, the thought was insupportable. Then, there would have been some charm to me in the very novelty of the *locale* and the indulgence of that vagrant spirit I have ever possessed,—for, like Justice Woodcock, "I certainly should have been a vagabond if Providence had not made me a justice of the peace;" now, I could not even contemplate the thing as possible, and would actually have refused the command of a regiment if the condition of its acceptance were to sail for the colonies.

Besides, I tried—and how ingenious is self-deception—I tried to find arguments in support of my determination totally different from the reasons which governed me. I affected to fear climate and to dread the effect of the tropics upon my health. "It may do very well," thought I, "for men totally destitute of better prospects, with neither talent, influence, nor powerful connection, to roast their cheeks at Sierra Leone, or suck a sugar-cane at St. Lucia. But that you, Harry Lorrequer, should waste your sweetness upon planters' daughters,—that have only to be known to have the world at your feet! The thing is absurd, and not to be thought of! Yes," said I, half aloud, "we read in the army list that Major A. is appointed to the 50th, and Captain B. to the 12th; but how much more near the truth would it be to say, 'That his Majesty, in consideration of the distinguished services of the one, has been graciously pleased to appoint him to ——, a case of blue and collapsed cholera, in India; and also for the bravery and gallant conduct of the other, in his late affair with the "How-dow-dallah Indians," has promoted him to the ——, yellow fever now devastating and desolating Jamaica'?" How far my zeal for the service might have carried me on this point I know not, for I was speedily aroused from my musings by the loud tramp of feet upon the stairs, and the sound of many well-known voices of my brother officers, who were coming to visit me.

"So, Harry, my boy," said the fat Major, as he entered, "is it true we are not to have the pleasure of your company to Jamaica this time?"

"He prefers a pale face, it seems, to a black one; and certainly, with thirty thousand in the same scale, the taste is excusable."

"But, Lorrequer," said a third, "we heard that you had canvassed the county in the Callonby interest. Why, man, where do you mean to pull up?"

"As for me," lisped a large-eyed, white-haired ensign of three months' standing, "I think it devilish hard old Carden didn't send *me* down there too, for I hear there are two girls in the family, eh, Lorrequer?"

Having, with all that peculiar bashfulness such occasions are sure to elicit, disclaimed the happiness my friends so clearly ascribed to me, I yet pretty plainly let it be understood that the more brilliant they supposed my present prospects to be, the more near were they to estimate them justly. One thing certainly gratified me throughout. All seemed rejoiced at my good fortune, and even the old Scotch paymaster made no more caustic remark than that he "wad na wonder if the chiel's black whiskers wad get him made governor of Stirling Castle before he'd dee."

Should any of my most patient listeners to these my humble "Confessions" wonder, either here or elsewhere, upon what very slight foundations I built these my *châteaux en Espagne,* I have only one answer, that from my boyhood I have had a taste for florid architecture, and would rather have put up with any inconvenience of ground than not build at all.

As it was growing late, I hurriedly bade adieu to my friends and hastened to Colonel Carden's quarters, where I found him waiting for me in company with my old friend Fitzgerald, our regimental surgeon. Our first greetings over, the Colonel drew me aside into a window, and said that from certain expressions Lord Callonby had made use of, certain hints he had dropped, he was perfectly aware of the delicate position in which I stood with respect to his lordship's family. "In fact, my dear Lorrequer," he continued, "without wishing in the least to obtrude myself upon your confidence, I must yet be permitted to say you are the luckiest fellow in Europe, and I most sincerely congratulate you on the prospect before you."

"But, my dear Colonel, I assure you—"

"Well, well, there,—not a word more; don't blush now. I know there is always a kind of secrecy thought necessary on these occasions, for the sake of other parties; so let us pass to your plans. From what I have collected, you have not proposed formally. But, of course, you desire a leave. You'll not quit the army, I trust,—no necessity for that; such influence as yours can always appoint you to an unattached commission."

"Once more let me protest, sir, that though for certain reasons most desirous to obtain a leave of absence, I have not the most remote—"

"That's right, quite right; I am sincerely gratified to hear you say so, and so will be Lord Callonby,—for he likes the service."

And thus was my last effort at a disclaimer cut short by the loquacious little Colonel, who regarded my unfinished sentence as a concurrence with his own opinion.

"*Allah il Allah,*" thought I, "it is my Lord Callonby's own plot; and his friend Colonel Carden aids and abets him."

"Now, Lorrequer," resumed the Colonel, "let us proceed. You have, of course, heard that we are ordered abroad,— mere newspaper report for the present; nevertheless, it is extremely difficult, almost impossible, without a sick certificate, to obtain a leave sufficiently long for your purpose." And here he smirked and I blushed, *selon les règles.*

"A sick certificate," said I, in some surprise.

"The only thing for you," said Fitzgerald, taking a long pinch of snuff; "and I grieve to say you have a most villainous look of good health about you."

"I must acknowledge I have seldom felt better."

"So much the worse, so much the worse," said Fitzgerald, despondingly. "Is there no family complaint, no respectable heirloom of infirmity you can lay claim to from your kindred?"

"None that I know of, unless a very active performance on the several occasions of breakfast, dinner, and supper, with a tendency towards port and an inclination to sleep ten in every twenty-four hours, be a sign of sickness. These symptoms I have known many of the family suffer for years without the slightest alleviation, though, strange as it may appear, they occasionally had medical advice."

Fitz took no notice of my sneer at the faculty, but proceeded to strike my chest several times with his finger-tips. "Try a short cough, now," said he. "Ah, that will never do! Do you ever flush,—before dinner, I mean?"

"Occasionally, when I meet with a luncheon."

"I'm fairly puzzled," said poor Fitz, throwing himself into a chair. "Gout is a very good thing; but then, you see, you are only a sub, and it is clearly against the Articles of

War to have it before being a field-officer at least. Apoplexy is the best I can do for you; and, to say the truth, any one who witnesses your performance at mess may put faith in the likelihood of it. Do you think you could get up a fit for the medical board?" said Fitz, gravely.

"Why, if absolutely indispensable," said I, "and with good instruction,—something this way, eh, is it not?"

"Nothing of the kind; you are quite wrong."

"Is there not always a little laughing and crying?" said I.

"Oh, no, no; take the cue from the paymaster any evening after mess, and you'll make no mistake,—very florid about the cheeks; rather a lazy look in one eye, the other closed up entirely; snore a little from time to time, and don't be too much disposed to talk."

"And you think I may pass muster in this way?"

"Indeed you may, if old Camie, the inspector, happen to be (what he is not often) in a good humor. But I confess I'd rather you were really ill, for we've passed a great number of counterfeits latterly, and we may be all pulled up ere long."

"Not the less grateful for your kindness," said I; "but still I'd rather matters stood as they do."

Having at length obtained a very formidable statement of my "case" from the doctor, and a strong letter from the Colonel deploring the temporary loss of so promising a young officer, I committed myself and my portmanteau to the inside of his Majesty's mail, and started for Dublin with as light a heart and high spirits as were consistent with so much delicacy of health and the directions of my doctor.

———

CHAPTER IX.

THE ROAD.—TRAVELLING ACQUAINTANCES.—A PACKET ADVENTURE.

I SHALL not stop now to narrate the particulars of my visit to the worthies of the medical board, the rather as some of my "Confessions" to come have reference to Dublin and many of those that dwell therein. I shall therefore content myself here with stating that without any difficulty I obtained a six months' leave, and having received much advice and more sympathy from many members of that body, took a respectful leave of them and adjourned to Bilton's, where I had ordered dinner and (as I was advised to live low) a bottle of Sneyd's claret. My hours in Dublin were numbered; at eight o'clock on the evening of my arrival I hastened to the Pigeon House pier to take my berth in the packet for Liverpool. And here, gentle reader, let me implore you, if you have bowels of compassion, to commiserate the condition of a sorry mortal like myself. In the days of which I now speak, steam-packets were not,—men knew not then of the pleasure of going to a comfortable bed in Kingstown harbor, and waking on the morning after in the Clarence dock at Liverpool, with only the addition of a little sharper appetite for breakfast before they set out on an excursion of forty miles per hour through the air.

In the time I have now to commemorate, the intercourse between the two countries was maintained by *two* sailing vessels of small tonnage and still scantier accommodation. Of the one now in question I well recollect the name,—she was called the *Alert;* and certainly a more unfortunate misnomer could scarcely be conceived. Well, there was no choice; so I took my place upon the crowded deck of the little craft, and in a drizzling shower of chilly rain, and amid more noise, confusion, and bustle than would prelude the launch of a line-of-battle ship, we "sidled," goose-fashion, from the shore, and began our voyage towards England.

It is not my intention, in the present stage of my "Confessions," to delay on the road towards an event which influenced so powerfully and so permanently my after-life; yet I cannot refrain from chronicling a slight incident which occurred on board the packet, and which, I have no doubt, may be remembered by some of those who throw their eyes on these pages.

One of my fellow-passengers was a gentleman holding a high official appointment in the viceregal court, either comptroller of the household, master of the horse, or something else equally magnificent; however, whatever the nature of the situation, one thing is certain,—one possessed of more courtly manners and more polished address cannot be conceived; to which he added all the attractions of a very handsome person and a most prepossessing countenance. The only thing the most scrupulous critic could possibly detect as faulty in his whole air and bearing was a certain ultra refinement and fastidiousness, which in a man of acknowledged family and connections was somewhat unaccountable, and certainly unnecessary. The fastidiousness I speak of extended to everything round and about him. He never ate of the wrong dish nor spoke to the wrong man in his life; and that very consciousness gave him a kind of horror of chance acquaintances which made him shrink within himself from persons in every respect his equals. Those who knew Sir Stewart Moore will know I do not exaggerate in either my praise or censure; and to those who have not had that pleasure, I have only to say theirs was the loss, and they must take my word for the facts.

The very antithesis to the person just mentioned was another passenger then on board. She—for even in sex they were different—she was a short, squat, red-faced, vulgar-looking woman of about fifty, possessed of a most garrulous tendency, and talking indiscriminately with every one about her, careless what reception her addresses met with, and quite indifferent to the many rebuffs she momentarily encountered. To me, by what impulse driven, Heaven knows, this amorphous piece of womanhood seemed determined to attach herself. Whether in the smoky and almost impenetrable recesses of the cabin, or braving the cold and penetrating rain upon deck, it mattered not, she was ever at my side, and not only martyring me by the insufferable annoyance of her vulgar loquacity, but actually, from the appearance of acquaintanceship such constant association gave rise to, frightening any one else from conversing with me, and rendering me, ere many hours, a perfect pariah among the passengers. By no one were we—for, alas! we had become Siamese—so thoroughly dreaded as by the refined baronet I have mentioned; he appeared to shrink from our very approach, and avoided us as though we had the plagues of Egypt about us. I saw this, I felt it deeply, and as deeply and resolutely I vowed to be revenged; and the time was not long distant in affording me the opportunity.

The interesting Mrs. Mulrooney—for such was my fair companion called—was on the present occasion making her *début* on what she was pleased to call the "says;" she was proceeding to the Liverpool market as proprietor and supercargo over some legion of swine that occupied the hold of the vessel, and whose mellifluous tones were occasionally heard in all parts of the ship. Having informed me on these, together with some circumstances of her birth and parentage, she proceeded to narrate some of the cautions given by her friends as to her safety when making such a long voyage, and also to detail some of the antiseptics to that dread scourge, sea-sickness, in the fear and terror of which she had come on board, and seemed every hour to be increasing in alarm about.

"Do you think then, sir, that pork is no good agin the sickness? Mickey—that's my husband, sir,—says it's the only thing in life for it, av it's toasted."

"Not the least use, I assure you."

"Nor sperits and wather?"

"Worse and worse, ma'am."

"Oh, thin, maybe oaten mail tay would do? It's a beautiful thing for the stomick, anyhow."

"Rank poison on the present occasion, believe me."

"Oh, thin, blessed Mary, what *am* I to do? What is to become of me?"

"Go down at once to your berth, ma'am; lie still and without speaking till we come in sight of land; or"—and here a bright thought seized me—"if you really feel very ill, call for that man there with the fur collar on his coat,—he can give you the only thing I ever knew of any efficacy. He's the steward, ma'am,—Stewart Moore. But you must be on your guard too, as you are a stranger, for he's a conceited fellow, and has saved a trifle, and sets up for a *half* gentleman; so don't be surprised at his manner,—though, after all, you may find him very different; some people, I've heard, think him extremely civil."

"And he has a cure, ye say?"

"The only one I ever heard of,—it is a little cordial of which you take I don't know how much every ten or fifteen minutes."

"And the naygur doesn't let the saycret out, bad manners to him?"

"No, ma'am; he has refused every offer on the subject."

"May I be so bowld as to ax his name again?"

"Stewart Moore, ma'am. Moore is the name, but people always call him Stewart Moore; just say that in a loud, clear voice, and you'll soon have him."

With the most profuse protestations of gratitude and promises of pork *à discrétion* if ever I sojourned at Ballinasloe, my fair friend proceeded to follow my advice and descended to the cabin.

Some hours after, I also betook myself to my rest, from which, however, towards midnight, I was awoke by the heavy working and pitching of the little vessel as she labored in a rough sea. As I looked forth from my narrow crib, a more woe-begone picture can scarcely be imagined than that before me. Here and there through the gloomy cabin lay the victims of the fell malady, in every stage of suffering and in every attitude of misery. Their cries and lamentings mingled with the creaking of the bulkheads and the jarring twang of the dirty lamp, whose irregular swing told plainly how oscillatory was our present motion. I turned from the unpleasant sight, and was about again to address myself to slumber with what success I might, when I started at the sound of a voice in the very berth next to me, whose tones, once heard, there was no forgetting. The words ran, as nearly as I can recollect, thus :—

"Oh, thin, bad luck to ye for pigs that ever brought me into the like of this! Oh, Lord, there it is again!" And here a slight interruption to eloquence took place, during which I was enabled to reflect upon the author of the complaint, who, I need not say, was Mrs. Mulrooney.

"I think a little tay would settle my stomick, if I only could get it; but what's the use of talking in this horrid place? They never mind me no more than if I was a pig. Steward, steward! Oh, thin, it's wishing you well I am for a steward! Steward, I say!" and this she really did say, with an energy of voice and manner that startled more than one sleeper. "Oh, you're coming at last, steward!"

"Ma'am," said a little dapper and dirty personage in a blue

jacket, with a greasy napkin negligently thrown over one arm *ex officio,* "ma'am, did you call?"

"Call!—is it call? No; but I'm roaring for you this half-hour. Come here. Have you any of the cordial dhrops agin the sickness? You know what I mean."

"Is it brandy, ma'am?"

"No, it isn't brandy."

"We have got gin, ma'am, and bottled porter,—cider, ma'am, if you like."

"Agh, no! sure I want the dhrops agin the sickness."

"Don't know, indeed, ma'am."

"Ah, you stupid creature! Maybe you're not the real steward. What's your name?"

"Smith, ma'am."

"Ah, I thought so! Go away, man, go away."

This injunction, given in a *diminuendo* cadence, was quickly obeyed, and all was silence for a moment or two. Once more was I dropping asleep when the same voice as before burst out with,—

"Am I to die here like a haythen, and nobody to come near me? Steward! steward! steward Moore, I say!"

"Who calls *me?*" said a deep, sonorous voice from the opposite side of the cabin, while at the same instant a tall, green-silk nightcap, surmounting a very aristocratic-looking forehead, appeared between the curtains of the opposite berth.

"Steward Moore!" said the lady again, with her eyes straining in the direction of the door by which she expected him to enter.

"This is most strange," muttered the baronet, half aloud. "Why, madam, you are calling *me?*"

"And if I am," said Mrs. Mulrooney, "and if ye heerd me, have ye no manners to answer your name, eh? Are ye Steward Moore?"

"Upon my life, ma'am, I thought so last night when I came on board. But you really have contrived to make me doubt my own identity."

"And is it there ye're lying on the broad of yer back, and me as sick as a dog fornent ye?"

"I concede, ma'am, the fact; the position is a most irksome one on every account."

"Then why don't ye come over to me?" And this Mrs. Mulrooney said with a voice of something like tenderness, —wishing at all hazards to conciliate so important a functionary.

"Why, really, you *are* the most incomprehensible person I ever met."

"I'm what?" said Mrs. Mulrooney, her blood rushing to her face and temples as she spoke,—for the same reason that her fair townswoman is reported to have borne with stoical fortitude every harsh epithet of the language, until it occurred to her opponent to tell her that "the divil a bit better she was nor a pronoun;" so Mrs. Mulrooney, taking *omne ignotum pro horribile,* became perfectly beside herself at the unlucky phrase. "I'm what? Repate it, av ye dare, and I'll tear yer eyes out! Ye dirty bla—guard, to be lying there at yer ease under the blankets, grinning at me. What's your thrade—answer me that—av it isn't to wait on the ladies, eh?"

"Oh! the woman must be mad," said Sir Stewart.

"The divil a taste mad, my dear, I'm only sick. Now just come over to me like a dacent creature, and give me the dhrop of comfort ye have. Come, avick."

"Go over to you?"

"Ay, and why not? Or, if it's so lazy ye are, why then I'll thry and cross over to *your* side."

These words being accompanied by a certain indication of change of residence on the part of Mrs. Mulrooney, Sir Stewart perceived there was no time to lose; and springing from his berth, he rushed half-dressed through the cabin and up the companion-ladder, just as Mrs. Mulrooney had protruded a pair of enormous legs from her couch, and hung for a moment pendulous before she dropped upon the floor and followed him to the deck. A tremendous shout of laughter from the sailors and deck-passengers prevented my hearing the dialogue which ensued; nor do I yet know how Mrs. Mulrooney learned her mistake. Certain it is, she no more appeared amongst the passengers in the cabin, and Sir Stewart's manner the following morning at breakfast amply satisfied me that I had had my revenge.

CHAPTER X.

UPSET,—MIND AND BODY.

NO sooner in Liverpool, than I hastened to take my place in the earliest conveyance for London. At that time the Umpire coach was the perfection of fast travelling; and seated behind the box, enveloped in a sufficiency of broad-cloth, I turned my face towards town with as much anxiety and as ardent expectations as most of those about me. All went on in the regular monotonous routine of such matters until we reached Northampton, passing down the steep street of which town, the near wheel-horse stumbled and fell; the coach, after a tremendous roll to one side, toppled over on the other, and with a tremendous crash and sudden shock, sent all the outsides, myself among the number, flying through the air like sea-gulls. As for me, after describing a very respect-able parabola, my angle of incidence landed me in a bonnet-maker's shop, having passed through a large plate-glass window and destroyed more leghorns and dunstables than a year's pay would recompense. I have but slight recollection of the details of that occasion until I found myself lying in a very spacious bed at the George Inn, having been bled in both arms, and discovering, by the multitude of bandages in which I was enveloped, that at least some of my bones were broken by the fall. That such fate had befallen my collar-bone and three of my ribs, I soon learned; and was horror-struck at hearing from the surgeon who attended me that four or five weeks would be the very earliest period I could bear re-moval with safety. Here then at once there was a large de-duction from my six months' leave, not to think of the misery that awaited me for such a time, confined to my bed in an inn without books, friends, or acquaintances. However, even this could be remedied by patience, and summoning up all I could command, I "bided my time;" but not before I had completed a term of two months' imprisonment, and had be-come, from actual starvation, something very like a living transparency.

No sooner, however, did I feel myself once more on the

road, than my spirits rose, and I felt myself as full of high hope and buoyant expectancy as ever. It was late at night when I arrived in London. I drove to a quiet hotel in the West End, and the following morning proceeded to Portman Square, bursting with impatience to see my friends the Callonbys and recount all my adventures,—for as I was too ill to write from Northampton, and did not wish to intrust to a stranger the office of communicating with them, I judged that they must be exceedingly uneasy on my account, and pictured to myself the thousand emotions my appearance, so indicative of illness, would give rise to, and could scarcely avoid running, in my impatience to be once more among them. How Lady Jane would meet me, I thought of over again and again; whether the same cautious reserve awaited me, or whether her family's approval would have wrought a change in her reception of me, I burned to ascertain. As my thoughts ran on in this way, I found myself at the door, but was much alarmed to perceive that the closed window-shutters and dismantled look of the house proclaimed them from home. I rang the bell, and soon learned from a servant, whose face I had not seen before, that the family had gone to Paris about a month before, with the intention of spending the winter there. I need not say how grievously this piece of intelligence disappointed me, and for a minute or two I could not collect my thoughts. At last the servant said,—

"If you have anything very particular, sir, that my lord's lawyer can do, I can give you his address."

"No, thank you, nothing;" at the same time I muttered to myself, "I'll have some occupation for him, though, ere long. The family were all quite well, didn't you say?"

"Yes, sir, perfectly well. My lord had only a slight cold."

"Ah, yes! And their address is Meurice? Very well."

So saying, I turned from the door, and with slower steps than I had come, returned to my hotel.

My immediate resolve was to set out for Paris; my second was to visit my uncle, Sir Guy Lorrequer, first, and having explained to him the nature of my position and the advantageous prospects before me, endeavor to induce him to make some settlement on Lady Jane, in the event of my obtaining her family's consent to our marriage. This, from his liking great people much, and laying great stress upon the advantages of connection, I looked upon as a matter of no great difficulty; so that although my hopes of happiness were delayed in their fulfilment, I believed they were only to be the more securely realized. The same day I set out for Elton, and by ten o'clock at night reached my uncle's house. I found the old gentleman just as I had left him three years before,—complaining a little of gout in the left foot; praising his old specific, port wine; abusing his servants for robbing him; and drinking the Duke of Wellington's health every night after supper,—which meal I had much pleasure in surprising him at on my arrival, not having eaten since my departure from London.

"Well, Harry," said my uncle, when the servants had left the room and we drew over the spider-table to the fire to discuss our wine with comfort, "what good wind has blown you down to me, my boy? For it's odd enough, five minutes before I heard the wheels on the gravel, I was just wishing some good fellow would join me at the grouse—and you see I have had my wish! The old story, I suppose, 'out of cash.' Would not come down here for nothing, eh? Come, lad, tell truth,—is it not so?"

"Why, not exactly, sir; but I really had rather at present talk about you than about my own matters, which we can chat over to-morrow. How do you get on, sir, with the Scotch steward?"

"He's a rogue, sir,—a cheat, a scoundrel; but it is the same with them all. And your cousin, Harry,—your cousin, that I have reared from his infancy to be my heir [pleasant topic for me!],—he cares no more for me than the rest of them, and would never come near me if it were not that, like yourself, he was hard run for money, and wanted to wheedle me out of a hundred or two."

"But you forget, sir, I told you I have not come with such an object."

"We'll see that, we'll see that in the morning," replied he, with an incredulous shake of the head.

"But Guy, sir, what has Guy done?"

"What has he not done? No sooner did he join that popinjay set of fellows, the —th Hussars, than he turned out what he calls a four-in-hand drag, which dragged nine hundred pounds out of my pocket. Then he has got a yacht at Cowes, a grouse mountain in Scotland, and has actually given Tattersall an unlimited order to purchase the Wreckington pack of harriers, which he intends to keep for the use of the corps. In a word, there is not an amusement of that villainous regiment, not a flask of champagne drunk at their mess, I don't bear my share in the cost of,—all through the kind offices of your worthy cousin, Guy Lorrequer."

This was an exceedingly pleasant *exposé* for me to hear of my cousin indulged in every excess of foolish extravagance by his rich uncle, while I, the son of an elder brother, who unfortunately called me by his own name, Harry, remained the sub in a marching regiment, with not three hundred pounds a year above my pay, and whom any extravagance, if such had been proved against me, would have deprived of even that small allowance. My uncle, however, did not notice the chagrin with which I heard his narrative, but continued to detail various instances of wild and reckless expense the future possessor of his ample property had already launched into.

Anxious to say something, without well knowing what, I hinted that probably my good cousin would reform some of these days, and marry.

"Marry!" said my uncle; "yes, that I believe is the best thing we can do with him; and I hope now the matter is in good train,—so the latest accounts say, at least."

"Ah, indeed!" said I, endeavoring to take an interest where I really felt none, for my cousin and I had never been very intimate friends, and the difference in our fortunes had not, at least to my thinking, been compensated by any advances which he, under the circumstances, might have made to me.

"Why, Harry, did you not hear of it?" said my uncle.

"No, not a word, sir."

"Very strange, indeed,—a great match, Harry; a very great match indeed."

"Some rich banker's daughter," thought I. "What will he say when he hears of *my* fortune?"

"A very fine young woman too, I understand,—quite the *belle* of London,—and a splendid property left by an aunt."

I was bursting to tell him of *my* affair, and that he had another nephew to whom, if common justice were rendered, his fortune was as certainly made for life.

"Guy's business happened this way," continued my uncle, who was quite engrossed by the thought of his favorite's success. "The father of the young lady met him in Ireland, or Scotland, or some such place, where he was with his regiment, was greatly struck with his manner and address, found him out to be my nephew, asked him to his house, and, in fact, almost threw this lovely girl at his head before they were two months acquainted."

"As nearly as possible my own adventure," thought I, laughing to myself.

"But you have not told me who they are, sir," said I, dying to have *his* story finished, and to begin *mine*.

"I'm coming to that, I'm coming to that. Guy came down here, but did not tell me one word of his having ever met the family, but begged of me to give him an introduction to them, as they were in Paris, where he was going on a short leave; and the first thing I heard of the matter was by a letter from the papa demanding from me if Guy was to be my heir, and asking 'how far his attentions in *his* family met with my approval.'"

"Then how did you know, sir, that they were previously known to each other?"

"The family lawyer told me, who heard it all talked over."

"And why, then, did Guy get the letter of introduction from you, when he was already acquainted with them?"

"I am sure I cannot tell, except that you know he always does everything unlike every one else; and, to be sure, the letter seems to have excited some amusement. I must show you his answer to my first note to know how all was going on,—for I felt very anxious about matters,—when I heard from some person who had met them that Guy was everlastingly in the house, and that Lord Callonby could not live without him."

"Lord who, sir?" said I, in a voice that made the old man upset his glass and spring from his chair in horror.

"What the devil is the matter with the boy? What makes you so pale?"

"Whose name did you say at that moment, sir?" said I, with a slowness of speech that cost me agony.

"Lord Callonby, my old schoolfellow and fag at Eton."

"And the lady's name, sir?" said I, in scarcely an audible whisper.

"I'm sure I forget her name; but here's the letter from Guy, and I think he mentions her name in the postscript."

I snatched rudely the half-opened letter from the old man, as he was vainly endeavoring to detect the place he wanted, and read as follows:—

"My adored Jane is all your fondest wishes for my happiness could picture, and longs to see her dear uncle, as she already calls you on every occasion."

I read no more; my eyes swam, the paper, the candles, everything before me was misty and confused; and although I heard my uncle's voice still going on, I knew nothing of what he said.

For some time my mind could not take in the full extent of the base treachery I had met with, and I sat speechless and stupefied. By degrees my faculties became clearer, and with one glance I read the whole business, from my first meeting with them at Kilrush to the present moment. I saw that in their attentions to me they thought they were winning the heir of Elton, the future proprietor of fifteen thousand per annum. From this tangled web of heartless intrigue I turned my thoughts to Lady Jane herself. How had she betrayed me? for certainly she had not only received, but encouraged my addresses,—and so soon too! To think that at the very moment when my own precipitate haste to see her had involved me in a nearly fatal accident, she was actually receiving the attentions of another! Oh, it was too, too bad!

But enough; even now I can scarcely dwell upon the memory of that moment, when the hopes and dreams of many a long day and night were destined to be thus rudely blighted. I seized the first opportunity of bidding my uncle good-night; and having promised him to reveal all my plans on the morrow, hurried to my room.

My plans—alas, I had none! That one fatal paragraph had scattered them to the winds; and I threw myself upon my bed, wretched and almost heart-broken.

I have once before in these "Confessions" claimed to myself the privilege, not inconsistent with a full disclosure of the memorabilia of my life, to pass slightly over those passages, the burden of which was unhappy, and whose memory is still painful. I must now, therefore, claim the "benefit of this act," and beg of the reader to let me pass from this sad portion of my history; and for the full expression of my mingled rage, contempt, disappointment, and sorrow, let me beg of him to receive instead what a learned pope once gave as his apology for not reading a rather polysyllabic word in a Latin letter,—"As for this," said he, looking at the phrase in question, "suppose it said." So say I. And now, *en route.*

CHAPTER XI.

CHELTENHAM.—MATRIMONIAL ADVENTURE, SHOWING HOW
TO MAKE LOVE FOR A FRIEND.

IT was a cold, raw evening in February as I sat in the coffee-room of the Old Plough, in Cheltenham, *Lucullus c. Lucullo,*—no companion save my half-finished decanter of port. I had drawn my chair to the corner of the ample fireplace, and in a half-dreamy state was reviewing the incidents of my early life, like most men who, however young, have still to lament talents misapplied, opportunities neglected, profitless labor, and disastrous idleness. The dreary aspect of the large and ill-lighted room, the close-curtained boxes, the unsocial look of every thing and body about, suited the habit of my soul, and I was on the verge of becoming excessively sentimental; the unbroken silence, where several people were present, had also its effect upon me, and I felt oppressed and dejected. So sat I for an hour; the clock over the mantel ticked sharply on, the old man in the brown surtout had turned in his chair, and now snored louder, the gentleman who read the "Times" had got the "Chronicle," and I

thought I saw him nodding over the advertisements. The
father who, with a raw son of about nineteen, had dined at
six, sat still and motionless opposite his offspring, and only
breaking the silence around by the grating of the decanter
as he posted it across the table. The only thing denoting
active existence was a little shrivelled man, who, with spectacles on his forehead and hotel slippers on his feet, rapidly
walked up and down, occasionally stopping at his table to
sip a little weak-looking negus, which was his moderate potation for two hours. I have been particular in chronicling
these few and apparently trivial circumstances, for by what
mere trifles are our greatest and most important movements
induced! Had the near wheeler of the Umpire been only
safe on his forelegs and— But let me continue. The gloom
and melancholy which beset me, momentarily increased. But
three months before, and my prospects presented everything
that was fairest and brightest,—now all the future was dark
and dismal. Then, my best friends could scarcely avoid envy
at my fortune,—now, my reverses might almost excite compassion even in an enemy. It was singular enough—and I
should not like to acknowledge it, were not these "Confessions" in their very nature intended to disclose the very pene-
tralia of my heart—but singular it certainly was—and so
I have always felt it since, when reflecting on it—that although
much and warmly attached to Lady Jane Callonby, and feeling
most acutely what I must call her abandonment of me, yet
the most constantly recurring idea of my mind on the subject was, What will the mess say? What will they think at
headquarters? The raillery, the jesting, the half-concealed
allusion, the tone of assumed compassion, which all awaited
me, as each of my comrades took up his line of behaving
towards me, was, after all, the most difficult thing to be borne,
and I absolutely dreaded to join my regiment more thoroughly
than did ever schoolboy to return to his labor on the expiration of his holidays. I had framed to myself all manner of
ways of avoiding this dread event. Sometimes I meditated
an exchange into an African corps; sometimes to leave the
army altogether. However I turned the affair over in my
mind, innumerable difficulties presented themselves; and I
was at last reduced to that stand-still point in which, after

continual vacillation, one only waits for the slightest impulse of persuasion from another to adopt any, no matter what, suggestion. In this enviable frame of mind I sat sipping my wine and watching the clock for that hour at which, with a safe conscience, I might retire to my bed, when the waiter roused me by demanding if my name was Mr. Lorrequer, for that a gentleman having seen my card in the bar, had been making inquiry for the owner of it all through the hotel.

"Yes," said I, "such is my name; but I am not acquainted with any one here, that I can remember."

"The gentleman has only arrived an hour since by the London mail, sir, and here he is."

⁎ At this moment a tall, dashing-looking, half-swaggering fellow, in a very sufficient envelope of box-coats, entered the coffee-room, and unwinding a shawl from his throat, showed me the honest and manly countenance of my friend Jack Waller, of the —th Dragoons, with whom I had served in the Peninsula.

Five minutes sufficed for Jack to tell me that he was come down on a bold speculation at this unseasonable time for Cheltenham; that he was quite sure his fortune was about to be made in a few weeks at farthest; and—which seemed nearly as engrossing a topic—that he was perfectly famished, and desired a hot supper *de suite*.

Jack, having despatched this agreeable meal with a traveller's appetite, proceeded to unfold his plans to me as follows:—

There resided *somewhere* near Cheltenham, in what direction he did not absolutely know, an old East India colonel who had returned from a long career of successful staff duties and government contracts with the moderate fortune of two hundred thousand. He possessed, in addition, a son and a daughter: the former, being a rake and a gambler, he had long since consigned to his own devices; and to the latter he had avowed his intention of leaving all his wealth. That she was beautiful as an angel, highly accomplished, gifted, agreeable, and all that, Jack, who had never seen her, was firmly convinced; that she was also bent resolutely on marrying him, or any other gentleman whose claims were principally the want of money, he was quite ready to swear to,—

and, in fact, so assured did he feel that "the whole affair was feasible" (I use his own expression) that he had managed a two months' leave, and was come down express to see, make love to, and carry her off at once.

"But," said I, with difficulty interrupting him, "how long have you known her father?"

"Known him? I never saw him."

"Well, that certainly is cool. And how do you propose making his acquaintance? Do you intend to make him a *particeps criminis* in the elopement of his own daughter, for a consideration to be hereafter paid out of his own money?"

"Now, Harry, you've touched upon the point in which, you must confess, my genius always stood unrivalled. Acknowledge, if you are not dead to gratitude, acknowledge how often should you have gone supperless to bed in our bivouacs in the Peninsula, had it not been for the ingenuity of your humble servant; avow that if mutton was to be had and beef to be purloined within a circuit of twenty miles round, our mess certainly kept no fast-days. I need not remind you of the cold morning on the retreat from Burgos, when the inexorable Lake brought five men to the halberds for stealing turkeys, that at the same moment I was engaged in devising an ox-tail soup from a heifer brought to our tent in jack-boots the evening before, to escape detection by her foot-tracks."

"True, Jack, I never questioned your Spartan talent; but this affair, time considered, does appear rather difficult."

"And if it were not, should I have ever engaged in it? No, no, Harry. I put all proper value upon the pretty girl, with her two hundred thousand pounds pin-money; but I honestly own to you, the intrigue, the scheme, has as great charm for me as any part of the transaction."

"Well, Jack, now for the plan, then!"

"The plan?—oh, the plan! Why, I have several; but since I have seen you, and talked the matter over with you, I have begun to think of a new mode of opening the trenches."

"Why, I don't see how I can possibly have admitted a single new ray of light upon the affair."

"There you are quite wrong. Just hear me out, without interruption, and I'll explain. I'll first discover the *locale* of this worthy Colonel,—'Hydrabad Cottage' he calls it; good, eh? Then I shall proceed to make a tour of the immediate vicinity, and either be taken dangerously ill in his grounds, within ten yards of the hall-door, or be thrown from my gig at the gate of his avenue and fracture my skull,—I don't much care which. Well, then, as I learn the old gentleman is the most kind, hospitable fellow in the world, he'll admit me at once, his daughter will tend my sick couch, nurse, read to me. Glorious fun, Harry! I'll make fierce love to her. And now, the only point to be decided is whether, having partaken of the Colonel's hospitality so freely, I ought to carry her off or marry her with papa's consent. You see there is much to be said for either line of proceeding."

"I certainly agree with you there; but since you seem to see your way so clearly up to that point, why, I should advise you leaving that an 'open question,' as the ministers say when they are hard pressed for an opinion."

"Well, Harry, I consent; it shall remain so. Now for *your* part, for I have now come to that."

"*Mine!*" said I, in amazement; "why, how can I possibly have any character assigned me in the drama?"

"I'll tell you, Harry,—you shall come with me in the gig in the capacity of my valet."

"Your what?" said I, horror-struck at his impudence.

"Come, no nonsense, Harry; you'll have a glorious time of it,—shall choose as becoming a livery as you like; and you'll have the whole female world below stairs dying for you. And all I ask for such an opportunity vouchsafed to you is to puff *me,* your master, in every possible shape and form, and represent me as the finest and most liberal fellow in the world, rolling in wealth, and only striving to get rid of it."

The unparalleled effrontery of Master Jack in assigning to me such an office absolutely left me unable to reply to him; while he continued to expatiate upon the great field for exertion thus open to us both. At last it occurred to me to benefit by an anecdote of a something similar arrangement, of capturing, not a young lady, but a fortified town, by retorting Jack's proposition.

"Come," said I, "I agree, with one only difference,—I'll be the master, and you the man on this occasion."

To my utter confusion, and without a second's consideration, Waller grasped my hand, and cried, "Done!" Of course I laughed heartily at the utter absurdity of the whole scheme, and rallied my friend on his prospects of Botany Bay for such an exploit, never contemplating in the most remote degree the commission of such extravagance.

Upon this, Jack, to use the expressive French phrase, *prit la parole;* touching, with a master-like delicacy, on my late defeat among the Callonbys (which up to this instant I believed him in ignorance of), he expatiated upon the prospect of my repairing that misfortune and obtaining a fortune considerably larger. He cautiously abstained from mentioning the personal charms of the young lady, supposing, from my lachrymose look, that my heart had not yet recovered the shock of Lady Jane's perfidy, and rather preferred to dwell upon the escape such a marriage would open to me from the mockery of the mess-table, the jesting of my brother officers, and the life-long raillery of the service, wherever the story reached.

The fatal facility of my disposition, so often and so frankly chronicled in these "Confessions;" the openness to be led whither any one might take the trouble to conduct me; the easy indifference to assume any character which might be pressed upon me by chance, accident, or design, assisted by my share of three flasks of champagne,—induced me first to listen, then to attend to, soon after to suggest, and finally, absolutely to concur in and agree to a proposal which, at any other moment, I must have regarded as downright insanity. As the clock struck two, I had just affixed my name to an agreement; for Jack Waller had so much of method in his madness that, fearful of my retracting in the morning, he had committed the whole to writing, which, as a specimen of Jack's legal talents, I copy from the original document, now in my possession.

THE PLOUGH, CHELTENHAM,
Tuesday night or morning, two o'clock—be the same more or less.

I, Harry Lorrequer, sub in his Majesty's —th Regiment of Foot, on the one part, and I, John Waller, commonly called Jack Waller, of the —th Light Dragoons, on the other, hereby promise and agree, each for himself, and not one for the other, to the following conditions, which are hereafter subjoined, to wit, I the aforesaid Jack Waller am to serve, obey, and humbly follow the afore-mentioned Harry Lorrequer for the space of one month of four weeks, conducting himself in all respects, modes, ways, manners as his, the aforesaid Lorrequer's own man, skip, valet, or flunkey, duly praising, puffing, and lauding the aforesaid Lorrequer, and in every way facilitating his success to the hand and fortune of—

"Shall we put in her name, Harry, here?" said Jack.
"I think not; we'll fill it up in pencil; that looks very knowing."

At the end of which period, if successful in his suit, the aforesaid Harry Lorrequer is to render to the aforesaid Waller the sum of ten thousand pounds three and a half per cent., with a faithful discharge in writing for his services, as may be. If, on the other hand, and which Heaven forbid! the aforesaid Lorrequer fail in obtaining the hand of ——, that he will evacuate the territory within twelve hours, and repairing to a convenient spot selected by the aforesaid Waller, then and there duly invest himself with a livery chosen by the aforesaid Waller—

"You know, each man uses his choice in this particular," said Jack.

—and for the space of four calendar weeks be unto the aforesaid Waller as his skip, or valet, receiving, in the event of success, the like compensation as aforesaid, each promising strictly to maintain the terms of this agreement, and binding, by a solemn pledge, to divest himself of every right appertaining to his former condition for the space of time there mentioned.

We signed and sealed it formally, and finished another flask to its perfect ratification. This done, and after a hearty shake-hands, we parted and retired for the night.
The first thing I saw on waking the following morning was

Jack Waller standing beside my bed, evidently in excellent spirits with himself and all the world.

"Harry, my boy, I have done it gloriously," said he. "I only remembered on parting with you last night that one of the most marked features in our old Colonel's character is a certain vague idea he has somewhere picked up that he has been at some very remote period of his history a most distinguished officer. This notion, it appears, haunts his mind, and he absolutely believes he has been in every engagement from the Seven Years' War down to the battle of Waterloo. You cannot mention a siege he did not lay down the first parallel for, nor a storming party where he did not lead the forlorn hope; and there is not a regiment in the service, from those that formed the fighting brigade of Picton down to the London train-bands, with which, to use his own phrase, he has not fought and bled. This mania of heroism is droll enough when one considers that the sphere of his action was necessarily so limited; but yet *we* have every reason to be thankful for the peculiarity, as you'll say when I inform you that this morning I despatched a hasty messenger to his villa with a most polite note, setting forth that 'as Mr. Lorrequer'—ay, Harry, all above board; there is nothing like it—'as Mr. Lorrequer, of the —th, was collecting for publication such materials as might serve to commemorate the distinguished achievements of British officers who have at any time been in command, he most respectfully requests an interview with Colonel Kamworth, whose distinguished services on many gallant occasions have called forth the unqualified approval of his Majesty's Government. Mr. Lorrequer's stay is necessarily limited to a few days, as he proceeds from this to visit Lord Anglesey, and therefore would humbly suggest as early a meeting as may suit Colonel K.'s convenience.' What think you now? Is this a master-stroke, or not?"

"Why, certainly we are in for it now," said I, drawing a deep sigh. "But, Jack, what is all this? Why, you're in livery already."

I now for the first time perceived that Waller was arrayed in a very decorous suit of dark gray, with cord shorts and boots, and looked a very knowing style of servant for the side of a tilbury.

"You like it, do you? Well, I should have preferred something a little more showy myself; but as you chose this last night, I of course gave way; and, after all, I believe you're right,—it certainly is neat."

"Did I choose it last night? I have not the slightest recollection of it."

"Yes, you were most particular about the length of the waistcoat and the height of the cockade, and you see I have followed your orders tolerably close; and now adieu to sweet quality for the season, and I am your most obedient servant for four weeks,—see that you make the most of it!"

While we were talking, the waiter entered with a note addressed to me, which I rightly conjectured could only come from Colonel Kamworth. It ran thus:—

Colonel Kamworth feels highly flattered by the polite attention of Mr. Lorrequer, and will esteem it a particular favor if Mr. L. can afford him the few days his stay in this part of the country will permit, by spending them at Hydrabad Cottage. Any information as to Colonel Kamworth's services in the four quarters of the globe, he need not say, is entirely at Mr. L.'s disposal.

Colonel K. dines at six precisely.

When Waller had read the note through, he tossed his hat up in the air, and with something little short of an Indian whoop, shouted out,—

"The game is won already! Harry, my man, give me the check for the ten thousand; she is your own this minute."

Without participating entirely in Waller's exceeding delight, I could not help feeling a growing interest in the part I was advertised to perform, and began my rehearsal with more spirit than I thought I should have been able to command.

The same evening, at the same hour as that in which on the preceding night I sat alone and comfortless by the coffee-room fire, I was seated opposite a very pompous, respectable-looking old man, with a large, stiff queue of white hair, who pressed me repeatedly to fill my glass and pass the decanter. The room was a small library, with handsomely fitted shelves.

There were but four chairs, but each would have made at least three of any modern one; the curtains, of deep crimson cloth, effectually secured the room from draught, and the cheerful wood fire blazing on the hearth, which was the only light in the apartment, gave a most inviting look of comfort and snugness to everything. "This," thought I, "is all excellent, and however the adventure ends, this is certainly pleasant, and I never tasted better madeira."

"And so, Mr. Lorrequer, you heard of my affair at Cantantrabad, when I took the Rajah prisoner?"

"Yes," said I; "the Governor-General mentioned the gallant business the very last time I dined at Government House."

"Ah! did he? Kind of him, though! Well, sir, I received two lacs of rupees on the morning after, and a promise of ten more if I would permit him to escape; but no, I refused flatly."

"Is it possible! And what did you do with the two lacs? Sent them back, of course—"

"No, that I didn't; the wretches know nothing of the use of money. No, no; I have them this moment in good Government security. I believe I never mentioned to you the storming of Java. Fill yourself another glass, and I'll describe it all to you, for it will be of infinite consequence that a true narrative of this meets the public eye,—they really are quite ignorant of it. Here, now, is Fort Cornelius, and there is the moat; the sugar-basin is the citadel, and the tongs is the first trench; the decanter will represent the tall tower towards the southwest angle, and here, the wine-glass, —this is me. Well, it was a little after ten at night that I got the order from the general in command to march upon this plate of figs, which was an open space before Fort Cornelius, and to take up my position in front of the fort, and with four pieces of field artillery—these walnuts here—to be ready to open my fire at a moment's warning upon the sou'west tower— But, my dear sir, you have moved the tower; I thought you were drinking madeira. As I said before,—to open my fire upon the sou'west tower, or, if necessary, to protect the sugar-tongs, which I explained to you was the trench. Just at the same time the besieged were making preparations for a sortie to occupy this dish of almonds and raisins,—the high ground to the left of my position. Put another log on the fire, if you please, sir; for I cannot see myself. I thought I was up near the figs, and I find myself down near the half-moon—"

"It is past nine," said a servant, entering the room; "shall I take the carriage for Miss Kamworth, sir?"

This being the first time the name of the young lady was mentioned since my arrival, I felt somewhat anxious to hear more of her; in which laudable desire I was not, however, to be gratified, for the Colonel, feeling considerably annoyed by the interruption, dismissed the servant by saying,—

"What do you mean, sirrah, by coming in at this moment? Don't you see I am preparing for the attack on the half-moon? Mr. Lorrequer, I beg your pardon for one moment; this fellow has completely put me out,—and besides, I perceive you have eaten the flying artillery; and, in fact, my dear sir, I shall be obliged to lay down the position again."

With this praiseworthy interest the Colonel proceeded to arrange the *matériel* of our dessert in battle array, when the door was suddenly thrown open, and a very handsome girl, in a most becoming *demi-toilette,* sprang into the room, and either not noticing or not caring that a stranger was present, threw herself into the old gentleman's arms with a degree of *empressement* exceedingly vexatious for any third and unoccupied party to witness.

"Mary, my dear," said the Colonel, completely forgetting Java and Fort Cornelius at once, "you don't perceive I have a gentleman to introduce to you,—Mr. Lorrequer, my daughter, Miss Kamworth." Here the young lady curtseyed somewhat stiffly, and I bowed reverently; and we all resumed places. I now found out that Miss Kamworth had been spending the preceding four or five days at a friend's in the neighborhood, and had preferred coming home somewhat unexpectedly to waiting for her own carriage.

My "Confessions," if recorded *verbatim* from the notes of that four weeks' sojourn, would only increase the already too prolix and uninteresting details of this chapter of my life; I need only say that without falling in love with Mary Kamworth, I felt prodigiously disposed thereto. She was extremely pretty, had a foot and ankle to swear by, the most silvery toned voice I almost ever heard, and a certain witchery and archness of manner that by its very tantalizing uncertainty continually provoked attention, and by suggesting a difficulty in the road to success, imparted a more than common zest in the pursuit. She was a little, a very little, blue, —rather a dabbler in the "ologies" than a real disciple. Yet she made collections of minerals and brown beetles and cryptogamias and various other homœopathic doses of the creation, infinitesimally small in their subdivision, in none of which I felt any interest, save in the excuse they gave for accompanying her in her pony-phaeton. This was, however, a rare pleasure, since every morning for at least three or four hours I was obliged to sit opposite the Colonel, engaged in the compilation of that narrative of his deeds which was to eclipse the career of Napoleon, and leave Wellington's laurels but a very faded lustre in comparison. In this agreeable occupation did I pass the greater part of my day, listening to the insufferable prolixity of the most prolix of colonels, and at times, notwithstanding the propinquity of relationship which awaited us, almost regretting that he was not blown up in any of the numerous explosions his memoir abounded with. I may here mention that while my literary labor was thus progressing, the young lady continued her avocations as before,—not, indeed, with me for her companion, but Waller; for Colonel Kamworth, "having remarked the steadiness and propriety of *my* man, felt no scruple in sending him out to drive Miss Kamworth;" particularly as I gave him a most excellent character for every virtue under heaven.

I must hasten on. The last evening of my four weeks was drawing to a close. Colonel Kamworth had pressed me to prolong my visit, and I only waited for Waller's return from Cheltenham, whither I had sent him for my letters, to make arrangements with him to absolve me from my ridiculous bond and accept the invitation. We were sitting round the library fire, the Colonel, as usual, narrating his early deeds and hairbreadth 'scapes. Mary, embroidering an indescribable something, which every evening made its appearance, but seemed never to advance, was rather in better spirits than usual, at the same time her manner was nervous and uncertain; and I could perceive, by her frequent absence of mind, that her thoughts were not as much occupied by the siege of Java as her worthy father believed them. Without laying any stress upon the circumstance, I must yet avow that Waller's not having returned from Cheltenham gave me some uneasiness, and I more than once had recourse to the bell to demand if "my servant had come back yet." At each of these times I well remember the peculiar expression of Mary's look, the half embarrassment, half drollery, with which she listened to the question and heard the answer in the negative. Supper at length made its appearance, and I asked the servant who waited if my man had brought me any letters, varying my inquiry to conceal my anxiety; and again I heard he had not returned. Resolving now to propose in all form for Miss Kamworth the next morning, and by referring the Colonel to my uncle Sir Guy, smooth, as far as I could, all difficulties, I wished them good-night and retired,—not, however, before the Colonel had warned me that they were to have an excursion to some place in the neighborhood the next day, and begging that I might be in the breakfast-room at nine, as they were to assemble there from all parts, and start early on the expedition. I was in a sound sleep the following morning, when a gentle tap at the door awoke me; at the same time I recognized the voice of the Colonel's servant saying, "Mr. Lorrequer, breakfast is waiting, sir."

I sprang up at once, and replying, "Very well, I shall come down," proceeded to dress in all haste; but to my horror I could not discern a vestige of my clothes. Nothing remained of the habiliments I possessed only the day before,—even my portmanteau had disappeared. After a most diligent search, I discovered on a chair in a corner of the room a small bundle tied up in a handkerchief, on opening which, I perceived a new suit of livery of the most gaudy and showy description,—the vest and breeches of yellow plush, with light-blue binding and lace, of which color was also the coat, which had a standing collar and huge cuffs, deeply ornamented with worked button-holes and large buttons. As I turned the things over, without even a guess of what they could mean, for I was scarcely well awake, I perceived a small slip of paper fastened to the coat-sleeve, upon which, in Waller's handwriting, the following few words were written:—

The livery, I hope, will fit you, as I am rather particular about how you'll look. Get quietly down to the stable-yard, and drive the tilbury into Cheltenham, where wait for further orders from your kind master, JOHN WALLER.

The horrible villainy of this wild scamp actually paralyzed me. That I should put on such ridiculous trumpery was out of the question; yet what was to be done? I rang the bell violently. "Where are my clothes, Thomas?"

"Don't know, sir; I was out all the morning, sir, and never seed them."

"There, Thomas, be smart now, and send them up, will you?"

Thomas disappeared, and speedily returned to say that my clothes could not be found anywhere, no one knew anything of them, and begged me to come down, as Miss Kamworth desired him to say that they were still waiting, and she begged Mr. Lorrequer would not make an elaborate toilet, as they were going on a country excursion. An elaborate toilet! I wish to Heaven she saw my costume! No, I'll never do it.

"Thomas, you must tell the ladies, and the Colonel too, that I feel very ill; I am not able to leave my bed; I am subject to attacks,—very violent attacks in my head, and must always be left quiet and alone,—perfectly alone, mind me, Thomas, for a day at least."

Thomas departed; and as I lay distracted in my bed, I heard from the breakfast-room the loud laughter of many persons evidently enjoying some excellent joke. Could it be me they were laughing at? The thought was horrible!

"Colonel Kamworth wishes to know if you'd like the doctor, sir?" said Thomas, evidently suppressing a most inveterate fit of laughing, as he again appeared at the door.

"No, certainly not," said I, in a voice of thunder. "What the devil are you grinning at?"

"You may as well come, my man,—you're found out; they all know it now," said the fellow, with an odious grin.

I jumped out of the bed and hurled the boot-jack at him with all my strength, but had only the satisfaction to hear him go downstairs chuckling at his escape; and as he reached

the parlor, the increase of mirth and the loudness of the
laughter told me that he was not the only one who was merry
at my expense. Anything was preferable to this. Downstairs
I resolved to go at once. But how? A blanket, I thought,
would not be a bad thing, and particularly as I had said I was
ill. I could at least get as far as Colonel Kamworth's dressing-
room and explain to him the whole affair; but then, if I was
detected *en route!* which I was almost sure to be, with so many
people parading about the house. No, that would never do.
There was but one alternative, and dreadful, shocking as it
was, I could not avoid it; and with a heavy heart, and as much
indignation at Waller for what I could not but consider a most
scurvy trick, I donned the yellow inexpressibles; next came
the vest, and last the coat, with its broad flaps and lace ex-
crescences, fifty times more absurd and merry-andrew than
any stage servant who makes off with his table and two chairs
amid the hisses and gibes of an upper gallery.

If my costume leaned towards the ridiculous, I resolved
that my air and bearing should be more than usually austere
and haughty; and with something of the stride of John Kemble in Coriolanus, I was leaving my bedroom, when I accidentally caught a view of myself in the glass,—and so mor-
tified, so shocked was I that I sank into a chair and almost
abandoned my resolution to go on; the very gesture I had
assumed for my vindication only increased the ridicule of
my appearance, and the strange quaintness of the costume
totally obliterated every trace of any characteristic of the
wearer, so infernally cunning was its contrivance. I don't
think that the most saturnine martyr of gout and dyspepsia
could survey me without laughing. With a bold effort I flung
open my door, hurried down the stairs, and reached the hall.
The first person I met was a kind of pantry-boy,—a beast only
lately emancipated from the plough, and destined, after a
dozen years' training as a servant, again to be turned back
to his old employ for incapacity; he grinned horribly for a
minute as I passed, and then, in a half-whisper, said,—

"Maester, I advise ye run for it; they're a-waiting for ye
with the constables in the justice's room."

I gave him a look of contemptuous superiority, at which he
grinned the more, and passed on.

Without stopping to consider where I was going, I opened the door of the breakfast-parlor and found myself at one plunge in a room full of people. My first impulse was to retreat again; but so shocked was I at the very first thing that met my sight that I was perfectly powerless to do anything. Among a considerable number of people who stood in small groups round the breakfast-table, I discerned Jack Waller, habited in a very accurate black frock and dark trousers, supporting upon his arm—shall I confess?—no less a person than Mary Kamworth, who leaned on him with the familiarity of an old acquaintance and chatted gayly with him. The buzz of conversation which filled the apartment when I entered ceased for a second of deep silence; and then followed a peal of laughter so long and so vociferous that in my momentary anger I prayed some one might burst a blood-vessel and frighten the rest. I put on a look of indescribable indignation, and cast a glance of what I intended should be most withering scorn on the assembly; but alas! my infernal harlequin costume ruined the effect, and confound me if they did not laugh the louder! I turned from one to the other with the air of a man who marks out victims for his future wrath, but with no better success; at last, amid the continued mirth of the party, I made my way towards where Waller stood, absolutely suffocated with laughter, and scarcely able to stand without support.

"Waller," said I, in a voice half tremulous with rage and shame together, "Waller, if this rascally trick be yours, rest assured no former term of intimacy between us shall—"

Before I could conclude the sentence, a bustle at the door of the room called every attention in that direction; I turned and beheld Colonel Kamworth, followed by a strong *posse comitatus* of constables, tipstaffs, etc., armed to the teeth, and evidently prepared for vigorous battle. Before I was able to point out my woes to my kind host, he burst out,—

"So you scoundrel, you impostor, you infernal young villain! Pretending to be a gentleman, you get admission into a man's house and dine at his table, when your proper place had been behind his chair! How far he might have gone, Heaven can tell if that excellent young gentleman, his master, had not traced him here this morning; but you'll pay dearly for it, you young rascal, that you shall."

"Colonel Kamworth," said I, drawing myself proudly up (and, I confess, exciting new bursts of laughter), "Colonel Kamworth, for the expressions you have just applied to me a heavy reckoning awaits you,—not, however, before another individual now present shall atone for the insult he has dared to pass upon me."

Colonel Kamworth's passion at this declaration knew no bounds; he cursed and swore absolutely like a madman, and vowed that transportation for life would be a mild sentence for such an iniquity.

Waller at length, wiping the tears of laughter from his eyes, interposed between the Colonel and his victim, and begged that I might be forgiven. "For indeed, my dear sir," said he, "the poor fellow is of rather respectable parentage, and such is his taste for good society that he'd run any risk to be among his betters, although, as in the present case, the exposure brings a rather heavy retribution. However, let me deal with him. Come, Henry," said he, with an air of insufferable superiority, "take my tilbury into town, and wait for me at the George; I shall endeavor to make your peace with my excellent friend Colonel Kamworth, and the best mode you can contribute to that object is to let us have no more of your society."

I cannot attempt to picture my rage at these words; however, escape from this diabolical predicament was my only present object, and I rushed from the room, and springing into the tilbury at the door, drove down the avenue at the rate of fifteen miles per hour, amid the united cheers, groans, and yells of the whole servants' hall, who seemed to enjoy my "detection" more even than their betters. Meditating vengeance, sharp, short, and decisive, on Waller, the Colonel, and every one else in the infernal conspiracy against me,—for I utterly forgot every vestige of our agreement in the surprise by which I was taken,—I reached Cheltenham. Unfortunately, I had no friend there to whose management I could commit the bearing of a message, and was obliged, as soon as I could procure suitable costume, to hasten up to Coventry, where the —th Dragoons were then quartered. I lost no time in selecting an adviser and taking the necessary steps to bring Master Waller to a reckoning; and on the third morning we again reached Cheltenham, I thirsting for vengeance and bursting still with anger. Not so, my friend, however, who never could discuss the affair with common gravity, and even ventured every now and then on a sly allusion to my yellow shorts. As we passed the last toll-bar, a travelling carriage came whirling by, with four horses, at a tremendous pace; and as the morning was frosty, and the sun scarcely risen, the whole team were smoking and steaming so as to be half invisible. We both remarked on the precipitancy of the party; for as our own pace was considerable, the two vehicles passed like lightning. We had scarcely dressed and ordered breakfast, when a more than usual bustle in the yard called us to the window; the waiter, who came in at the same instant, told us that four horses were ordered out to pursue a young lady who had eloped that morning with an officer.

"Ah! our friend in the green travelling-chariot, I'll be bound," said my companion; but as neither of us knew that part of the country, and I was too engrossed by my own thoughts, I never inquired farther. As the chaise in chase drove round to the door, I looked to see what the pursuer was like; and as he issued from the inn, recognized my *ci-devant* host, Colonel Kamworth. I need not say my vengeance was sated at once,—*he* had lost his daughter, and *Waller* was on the road to be married. Apologies and explanations came in due time for all my injuries and sufferings; and I confess the part which pleased me most was that I saw no more of Jack for a considerable period after. He started for the Continent, where he has lived ever since on a small allowance granted by his father-in-law, and never paying me the stipulated sum, as I had clearly broken the compact.

So much for my second attempt at matrimony. One would suppose that such experience should be deemed sufficient to show that my talent did not lie in that way. And here I must rest for the present, with the additional confession that so strong was the memory of that vile adventure that I refused a lucrative appointment under Lord Anglesey's Government when I discovered that his livery included "yellow plush breeches:" to have such *souvenirs* flitting around and about me at dinner and elsewhere, would have left me without a pleasure in existence.

CHAPTER XII.

DUBLIN.—TOM O'FLAHERTY.—A REMINISCENCE OF THE PENINSULA.

DEAR, dirty Dublin, *Io te saluto!* How many excellent things might be said of thee if, unfortunately, it did not happen that the theme is an old one, and has been much better *sung* than it can ever now be *said*. With thus much of apology for no more lengthened panegyric, let me beg of my reader, if he be conversant with that most moving melody, the "Groves of Blarney," to hum the following lines, which I heard shortly after my landing, and which well express my own feelings for the "loved spot:"—

> "Oh! Dublin, sure, there is no doubtin',
> Beats every city upon the *say;*
> 'T is there you 'll see O'Connell spouting,
> And Lady Morgan making *tay.*
> And 't is the capital of the greatest nation,
> With finest peasantry on a fruitful sod,
> Fighting like devils for conciliation,
> And hating each other for the love of God."

Once more, then, I found myself in the "most car-driving-est city," *en route* to join on the expiration of my leave. Since my departure, my regiment had been ordered to Kilkenny, that sweet city so famed in song for its "fire without smoke," but which, were its character in any way to be derived from its past or present representative, might certainly with more propriety reverse the epithet, and read "smoke without fire." My last communication from headquarters was full of nothing but gay doings. Balls, dinners, *déjeûners,* and, more than all, private theatricals, seemed to occupy the entire attention of every man of the gallant —th. I was earnestly entreated to come, without waiting for the end of my leave; that several of my old "parts were kept open for me;" and that, in fact, the "boys of Kilkenny" were on tiptoe in expectation of my arrival, as though his Majesty's mail were to convey a Kean or a Kemble. I shuddered a little as I read this, and recollected "my last appearance on any stage," little anticipating, at the moment, that my next was to be nearly as productive of the ludicrous, as time and my "Confessions" will show. One circumstance, however, gave me considerable pleasure. It was this: I took it for granted that in the varied and agreeable occupations which so pleasurable a career opened, my adventures in love would escape notice, and that I should avoid the merciless raillery my two failures, in six months, might reasonably be supposed to call forth. I therefore wrote a hurried note to Curzon, setting forth the great interest all their proceedings had for me, and assuring him that my stay in town should be as short as possible, for that I longed once more to "strut the monarch of the boards," and concluded with a sly paragraph, artfully intended to act as a *paratonnerre* to the gibes and jests which I dreaded, by endeavoring to make light of my matrimonial speculations. The postscript ran somewhat thus,—

Glorious fun have I had since we met; but were it not that my good angel stood by me, I should write these hurried lines with a wife at my elbow. But luck, that never yet deserted, is still faithful to your old friend   H. LORREQUER.

My reader may suppose—for he is sufficiently behind the scenes with me—with what feelings I penned these words; yet anything was better than the attack I looked forward to: and I should rather have changed into the Cape Rifle Corps, or any other army of martyrs, than meet my mess with all the ridicule my late proceedings exposed me to. Having disburdened my conscience of this dread, I finished my breakfast and set out on a stroll through the town.

I believe it is Coleridge who somewhere says that to transmit the first bright and early impressions of our youth, fresh and uninjured, to a remote period of life, constitutes one of the loftiest prerogatives of genius. If this be true,—and I am not disposed to dispute it,—what a gifted people must be the worthy inhabitants of Dublin; for I scruple not to affirm that of all cities of which we have any record in history, sacred or profane, there is not one so little likely to disturb the tranquil current of such reminiscences. "As it was of old, so it is now," enjoying a delightful permanency in all its habits and customs which no changes elsewhere disturb or affect; and in this respect I defy O'Connell and all the tail to refuse it the epithet of "Conservative."

Had the excellent Rip Van Winkle, instead of seeking his repose upon the cold and barren acclivities of the Kaatskills, —as we are veritably informed by Irving,—but betaken himself to a comfortable bed at Morrisson's or the Bilton, not only would he have enjoyed a more agreeable siesta, but, what the event showed of more consequence, the pleasing satisfaction of not being disconcerted by novelty on his awakening. It is possible that the waiter who brought him the water to shave—for Rip's beard, we are told, had grown uncommonly long—might exhibit a little of that wear and tear to which humanity is liable from time; but had he questioned him as to the ruling topics, the popular amusements of the day, he would have heard, as he might have done twenty years before, that there was a meeting to convert Jews at the Rotunda; another to rob parsons at the Corn Exchange; that the Viceroy was dining with the Corporation and congratulating them on the prosperity of Ireland, while the inhabitants were regaled with a procession of the "broad ribbon weavers," who had not weaved, Heaven knows when! This, with an occasional letter from Mr. O'Connell, and now and then a duel in the "Phaynix," constituted the current pastimes of the city. Such, at least, were they in *my* day; and though far from the dear *locale,* an odd, flitting glance at the newspapers induces me to believe that matters are not much changed since.

I rambled through the streets for some hours, revolving such thoughts as pressed upon me involuntarily by all I saw. The same little gray homunculus that filled my "Prince's mixture" years before, stood behind the counter at Lundy Foot's, weighing out rappee and high toast just as I last saw him. The fat college porter, that I used to mistake in my schoolboy days for the Provost, God forgive me! was there as fat and as ruddy as heretofore and wore his Roman costume of helmet and plush breeches with an air as classic. The state trumpeter at the Castle—another object of my youthful veneration, poor "old God save the King," as we used to call him—walked the streets as of old,—his cheeks, indeed, a little more lanky and tendinous; but then there had been many viceregal changes, and the "one sole melody his heart delighted in" had been more frequently called into requisition as he marched in solemn state with the other antique gentlemen in tabards. As I walked along, each moment some familiar and early association being suggested by the objects around, I felt my arm suddenly seized. I turned hastily round, and beheld a very old companion in many a hard-fought field and merry bivouac, Tom O'Flaherty, of the 8th. Poor Tom was sadly changed since we last met, which was at a ball in Madrid. He was then one of the best-looking fellows of his stamp I ever met, tall and athletic, with the easy bearing of a man of the world, and a certain jauntiness that I have never seen but in Irishmen who have mixed much in society.

There was also a certain peculiar devil-may-care recklessness about the self-satisfied swagger of his gait, and the free-and-easy glance of his sharp black eye, united with a temper that nothing could ruffle, and a courage nothing could daunt. With such qualities as these, he had been the prime favorite of his mess, to which he never came without some droll story to relate, or some choice expedient for future amusement. Such had Tom once been,—now he was much altered; and though the quiet twinkle of his dark eye showed that the spirit of fun within was not "dead, but only sleeping," to myself, who knew something of his history, it seemed almost cruel to awaken him to anything which might bring him back to the memory of bygone days. A momentary glance showed me that he was no longer what he had been, and that the unfortunate change in his condition, the loss of all his earliest and oldest associates, and his blighted prospects, had nearly broken a heart that never deserted a friend nor quailed before an enemy. Poor O'Flaherty was no longer the delight of the circle he once adorned; the wit that "set the table in a roar" was all but departed,—he had been dismissed the service. The story is a brief one.

In the retreat from Burgos, the ——th Light Dragoons, after
a fatiguing day's march, halted at the wretched village of
Cabeñas. It had been deserted by the inhabitants the day
before, who, on leaving, had set it on fire; and the blackened
walls and fallen roof-trees were nearly all that now remained
to show where the little hamlet had once stood.

Amid a downpour of rain that had fallen for several hours,
drenched to the skin, cold, weary, and nearly starving, the
gallant 8th reached this melancholy spot at nightfall, with
little better prospect of protection from the storm than the
barren heath through which their road led might afford them.
Among the many who muttered curses, not loud, but deep,
on the wretched termination to their day's suffering, there
was one who kept up his usual good spirits, and not only
seemed himself nearly regardless of the privations and miseries about him, but actually succeeded in making the others
who rode alongside as perfectly forgetful of their annoyances
and troubles as was possible under such circumstances. Good
stories, joking allusions to the more discontented ones of the
party, ridiculous plans for the night's encampment, followed
each other so rapidly that the weariness of the way was forgotten; and while some were cursing their hard fate that ever
betrayed them into such misfortunes, the little group round
O'Flaherty were almost convulsed with laughter at the wit
and drollery of one over whom, if the circumstances had any
influence, they seemed only to heighten his passion for amusement. In the early part of the morning he had captured a
turkey, which hung gracefully from his holster on one side,
while a small goat-skin of Valencia wine balanced it on the
other. These good things were destined to form a feast that
evening, to which he had invited four others,—that being,
according to his most liberal calculation, the greatest number
to whom he could afford a reasonable supply of wine.

When the halt was made, it took some time to arrange the
dispositions for the night; and it was nearly midnight before
all the regiment had got their billets and were housed, even
with such scanty accommodation as the place afforded. Tom's
guests had not yet arrived, and he himself was busily engaged in roasting the turkey before a large fire, on which
stood a capacious vessel of spiced wine, when the party appeared. A very cursory "reconnoissance" through the house

—one of the only ones untouched in the village—showed that from the late rain it would be impossible to think of sleeping in the lower story, which already showed signs of being flooded; they therefore proceeded in a body upstairs,—and what was their delight to find a most comfortable room, neatly furnished with chairs and a table, but above all, a large old-fashioned bed, an object of such luxury as only an old campaigner can duly appreciate. The curtains were closely tucked in all round, and in their fleeting and hurried glance, they felt no inclination to disturb them, and rather proceeded to draw up the table before the hearth to which they speedily removed the fire from below; and ere many minutes, with that activity which a bivouac life invariably teaches, their supper smoked before them, and five happier fellows did not sit down that night within a large circuit around. Tom was unusually great; stores of drollery, unlocked before, poured from him unceasingly, and what with his high spirits to excite them, and the reaction inevitable after a hard day's severe march, the party soon lost the little reason that usually sufficed to guide them, and became as pleasantly tipsy as can well be conceived. However, all good things must have an end, and so had the wine-skin. Tom had placed it affectionately under his arm like a bagpipe, and failed, with even a most energetic squeeze, to extract a drop. There was now nothing for it but to go to rest,—and, indeed, it seemed the most prudent thing for the party.

The bed became accordingly a subject of grave deliberation; for as it could only hold two, and the party were five, there seemed some difficulty in submitting their chances to lot, which all agreed was the fairest way. While this was under discussion, one of the party had approached the contested prize, and drawing aside the curtains, proceeded to jump in, when what was his astonishment to discover that it was already occupied! The exclamation of surprise he gave forth soon brought the others to his side, and to their horror, drunk as they were, they found that the body before them was that of a dead man arrayed in all the ghastly pomp of a corpse. A little nearer inspection showed that he had been a priest,—probably the *padre* of the village; on his head he had a small velvet skull-cap embroidered with a cross, and his body was swathed in a vestment such as priests usually wear at the mass; in his hand he held a large wax taper, which appeared to have burnt only half down, and probably been extinguished by the current of air on opening the door. After the first brief shock which this sudden apparition had caused, the party recovered as much of their senses as the wine had left them, and proceeded to discuss what was to be done under the circumstances; for not one of them ever contemplated giving up a bed to a dead priest while five living men slept on the ground. After much altercation, O'Flaherty, who had hitherto listened without speaking, interrupted the contending parties, saying, "Stop, lads, I have it!"

"Come," said one of them, "let us hear Tom's proposal."

"Oh!" said he, with difficulty steadying himself while he spoke, "we'll put him to bed with old Ridgeway, the quartermaster!"

The roar of loud laughter that followed Tom's device was renewed again and again, till not a man could speak from absolute fatigue. There was not a dissentient voice. Old Ridgeway was hated in the corps, and a better way of disposing of the priest and paying off the quartermaster could not be thought of.

Very little time sufficed for their preparations; and if they had been brought up under a certain well-known duke, they could not have exhibited a greater taste for a "black job." The door of the room was quickly taken from its hinges, and the priest placed upon it at full length; a moment more sufficed to lift the door upon their shoulders, and, preceded by Tom, who lit a candle in honor of being, as he said, "chief mourner," they took their way through the camp towards Ridgeway's quarters. When they reached the hut where their victim lay, Tom ordered a halt, and proceeded stealthily into the house to "reconnoitre." The old quartermaster he found stretched on his sheepskin before a large fire, the remnants of an ample supper strewed about him, and two empty bottles standing on the hearth; his deep snoring showed that all was safe, and that no fears of his awaking need disturb them. His shako and sword lay near him, but his sabretasche was under his head. Tom carefully withdrew the two former, and hastening to his friends without, proceeded to decorate the priest with them, expressing, at the same time, considerable regret that he feared it might wake Ridgeway if he were to put the velvet skull-cap on him for a night-cap.

Noiselessly and stealthily they now entered, and proceeded to put down their burden, which, after a moment's discussion, they agreed to place between the quartermaster and the fire, of which hitherto he had reaped ample benefit. This done, they quietly retreated, and hurried back to their quarters, unable to speak with laughter at the success of their plot and their anticipation of Ridgeway's rage on awakening in the morning.

It was in the dim twilight of a hazy morning that the bugler of the 8th aroused the sleeping soldiers from their miserable couches, which, wretched as they were, they nevertheless rose from reluctantly, so wearied and fatigued had they been by the preceding day's march. Not one among the number felt so indisposed to stir as the worthy quartermaster; his peculiar avocations had demanded a more than usual exertion on his part, and in the posture he had lain down at night he rested till morning, without stirring a limb. Twice the reveille had rung through the little encampment, and twice the quartermaster had essayed to open his eyes, but in vain; at last he made a tremendous effort, and sat bolt upright on the floor, hoping that the sudden effort might sufficiently arouse him. Slowly his eyes opened, and the first thing they beheld was the figure of the dead priest with a light cavalry helmet on his head, seated before him. Ridgeway, who was a good Catholic, trembled in every joint,—it might be a ghost, it might be a warning; he knew not what to think. He imagined the lips moved; and so overcome with terror was he at last that he absolutely shouted like a maniac, and never ceased till the hut was filled with officers and men, who, hearing the uproar, ran to his aid. The surprise of the poor quartermaster at the apparition was scarcely greater than that of the beholders. No one was able to afford any explanation of the circumstance, though all were assured that it must have been done in jest. The door upon which the priest had been conveyed afforded the clew,—they had forgotten to restore it to its place. Accordingly, the different billets were examined, and at last O'Flaherty was discovered in a most commodious bed, in a large room without a door, still fast asleep, and alone; how and when he had parted from his companions he never could precisely explain, though he has since confessed it was part of his scheme to lead them astray in the village, and then retire to the bed, which he had determined to appropriate to his sole use.

Old Ridgeway's rage knew no bounds; he absolutely foamed with passion, and in proportion as he was laughed at his choler rose higher. Had this been the only result it had been well for poor Tom; but unfortunately the affair got to be rumored through the country. The inhabitants of the village learned the indignity with which the *padre* had been treated; they addressed a memorial to Lord Wellington. Inquiry was immediately instituted; O'Flaherty was tried by court-martial, and found guilty. Nothing short of the heaviest punishment that could be inflicted under the circumstances would satisfy the Spaniards, and at that precise period it was part of our policy to conciliate their esteem by every means in our power. The commander-in-chief resolved to make what he called an "example," and poor O'Flaherty— the life and soul of his regiment, the darling of his mess— was broke, and pronounced incapable of ever serving his Majesty again. Such was the event upon which my poor friend's fortune in life seemed to hinge. He returned to Ireland, if not entirely broken-hearted, so altered that his best friends scarcely knew him. His "occupation was gone;" the mess had been his home; his brother officers were to him in place of relatives; and he had lost all. His after-life was spent in rambling from one watering-place to another,—more with the air of one who seeks to consume than enjoy his time; and with such a change in appearance as the alteration in his fortune had effected, he now stood before me, but altogether so different a man that but for the well-known tones of a voice that had often convulsed me with laughter, I should scarcely have recognized him.

"Lorrequer, my old friend, I never thought of seeing you here. This is indeed a piece of good luck."

"Why, Tom, you surely knew that the 4—th were in Ireland, did n't you?"

"To be sure. I dined with them only a few days ago; but they told me you were off to Paris to marry something super-latively beautiful and most enormously rich,—the daughter of a duke, if I remember right; but *certes,* they said your fortune was made, and I need not tell you there was not a man among them better pleased than I was to hear it."

"Oh! they said so, did they? Droll dogs,—always quizzing; I wonder you did not perceive the hoax, eh? Very good, was it not?" This I poured out in short, broken sentences, blushing like scarlet, and fidgeting like a schoolgirl with downright nervousness.

"A hoax! Devilish well done too," said Tom; "for old Carden believed the whole story, and told me that he had obtained a six months' leave for you to make your *cour,* and, moreover, said that he had got a letter from the nobleman, Lord— Confound his name!"

"Lord Grey, is it?" said I, with a sly look at Tom.

"No, my dear friend," said he, dryly, "it was not Lord Grey. But to continue: he had got a letter from him, dated from Paris, stating his surprise that you had never joined them there, according to promise, and that they knew your cousin Guy, and a great deal of other matter I can't remember. So what does all this mean? Did you hoax the noble lord as well as the Horse Guards, Harry?"

This was indeed a piece of news for me; I stammered out some ridiculous explanation, and promised a fuller detail. Could it be that I had done the Callonbys injustice, and that they never intended to break off my attentions to Lady Jane, —that she was still faithful, and that of all concerned, I alone had been to blame? Oh! how I hoped this might be the case; heavily as my conscience might accuse, I longed ardently to forgive and deal mercifully with myself. Tom continued to talk about indifferent matters, as these thoughts flitted through my mind; perceiving at last that I did not attend, he stopped suddenly, and said,—

"Harry, I see clearly that something has gone wrong, and perhaps I can guess at the mode too. But however, you can do nothing about it now; come and dine with me to-day, and we'll discuss the affair together after dinner; or if you prefer a 'distraction,' as we used to say in Dunkerque, why then I'll arrange something fashionable for your evening's amusement. Come, what say you to hearing Father Keogh preach? or would you like a supper at the Carlingford? or perhaps you prefer a *soirée chez Miladi?* For all of these Dublin affords,—all three good in their way, and very intellectual."

"Well, Tom, I'm yours. But I should prefer your dining with *me,*—I am at Bilton's; we'll have our cutlet quite alone, and—"

"And be heartily sick of each other, you were going to add. No, no, Harry, you must dine with *me;* I have some remarkably *nice* people to present you to. Six is the hour,—sharp six,—number —, Molesworth Street, Mrs. Clanfrizzle's. Easily find it,—large fanlight over the door, huge lamp in the hall, and a strong odor of mutton broth for thirty yards on each side of the premises. And as good luck will have it, I see old Daly, the counsellor, as they call him,—he's the very man to get to meet you; you always liked a character, eh?"

Saying this, O'Flaherty disengaged himself from my arm and hurried across the street towards a portly, middle-aged looking gentleman with the reddest face I ever beheld. After a brief but very animated colloquy, Tom returned and informed me that all was right; he had secured Daly.

"And who is Daly?" said I, inquiringly, for I was rather interested in hearing what peculiar qualification as a diner-out the counsellor might lay claim to, many of Tom's *friends* being as remarkable for being the quizzed as the quizzers.

"Daly," said he, "is the brother of a most distinguished member of the Irish Bar, of which he himself is also a follower,—bearing, however, no other resemblance to the clever man than the name; for as assuredly as the reputation of the one is inseparably linked with success, so unerringly is the other's coupled with failure. And strange to say, the stupid man is fairly convinced that his brother owes all his advancement to him, and that to his disinterested kindness the other is indebted for his present exalted station. Thus it is through life; there seems ever to accompany dulness a sustaining power of vanity that, like a life-buoy, keeps a mass afloat whose weight unassisted would sink into obscurity. Do you know that my friend Denis, there, imagines himself the first man that ever enlightened Sir Robert Peel as to Irish affairs?—and upon my word, his reputation on this head stands incontestably higher than on most others."

"You surely cannot mean that Sir Robert Peel ever consulted with, much less relied upon, the statements of such a person as you describe your friend Denis to be?"

"He did both; and if he was a little puzzled by the information, the only disgrace attaches to a government that sends men to rule over us unacquainted with our habits of thinking, and utterly ignorant of the language—ay, I repeat it. But come, you shall judge for yourself; the story is a short one, and fortunately so, for I must hasten home to give timely notice of your coming to dine with me. When Sir Robert Peel, then Mr. Peel, came over here as secretary to Ireland, a very distinguished political leader of the day invited a party to meet him at dinner, consisting of men of different political leanings, among whom were, as may be supposed, many members of the Irish Bar. The elder Daly was too remarkable a person to be omitted, but as the two brothers resided together, there was a difficulty about getting him; however, he must be had, and the only alternative that presented itself was adopted,—both were invited. When the party descended to the dining-room, by one of those unfortunate accidents which, as the proverb informs us, occasionally take place in the best regulated establishments, the wrong Mr. Daly got placed beside Mr. Peel,—which post of honor had been destined by the host for the more agreeable and talented brother. There was now no help for it; and with a heart somewhat nervous for the consequences of the proximity, the worthy entertainer sat down to do the honors as best he might. He was consoled during dinner by observing that the devotion bestowed by honest Denis on the viands before him effectually absorbed his faculties, and thereby threw the entire of Mr. Peel's conversation towards the gentleman on his other flank. This happiness was, like most others, destined to be a brief one. As the dessert made its appearance, Mr. Peel began to listen with some attention to the conversation of the persons opposite, with one of whom he was struck most forcibly; so happy a power of illustration, so vivid a fancy, such logical precision in argument as he evinced, perfectly charmed and surprised him. Anxious to learn the name of so gifted an individual, he turned towards his hitherto silent neighbor, and demanded who he was.

" 'Who is he, is it?' said Denis, hesitatingly, as if he half doubted such extent of ignorance as not to know the person alluded to.

"Mr. Peel bowed in acquiescence.

" 'That's Bushe!' said Denis, giving at the same time the same sound to the vowel *u* as it obtains when occurring in the word 'rush.'

" 'I beg pardon,' said Mr. Peel, 'I did not hear.'

" 'Bushe!' replied Denis, with considerable energy of tone.

" 'Oh, yes! I know,' said the secretary,—'Mr. Bushe, a very distinguished member of your Bar, I have heard.'

" 'Faith, you may say that!' said Denis, tossing off his wine at what he esteemed a very trite observation.

" 'Pray,' said Mr. Peel, again returning to the charge, though certainly feeling not a little surprised at the singular laconicism of his informant, no less than the mellifluous tones of an accent then perfectly new to him, 'pray, may I ask, what is the peculiar character of Mr. Bushe's eloquence,—I mean, of course, in his professional capacity?'

" 'Eh!' said Denis, 'I don't comprehend you exactly.'

" 'I mean,' said Mr. Peel, 'in one word, what's his forte?'

" 'His forte?'

" 'I mean what his peculiar gift consists in—'

" 'Oh, I perceave; I have ye now,—the juries!'

" 'Ah! addressing a jury.'

" 'Ay, the juries.'

" 'Can you oblige me by giving me an idea of the manner in which he obtains such signal success in this difficult branch of eloquence?'

" 'I'll tell ye,' said Denis, leisurely finishing his glass, and smacking his lips, with the air of a man girding up his loins for a mighty effort, 'I'll tell ye. Well, ye see, the way he has is this,'—here Mr. Peel's expectation rose to the highest degree of interest,—'the way he has is this,—*he first butthers them up, and then slithers them down!* That's all; devil a more of a secret there's in it.' "

How much reason Denis had to boast of imparting early information to the new secretary I leave my English readers to guess; my Irish ones I may trust to do him ample justice.

My friend now left me to my own devices to while away the hours till time to dress for dinner. Heaven help the gentleman so left in Dublin, say I. It is, perhaps, the only city of its size in the world where there is no lounge, no promenade. Very little experience of it will convince you that it abounds in pretty women, and has its fair share of agreeable men; but where are they in the morning? I wish Sir Dick Lauder, instead of speculating where salmon pass the Christmas holidays, would apply his most inquiring mind to such a question as this. True it is, however, they are not to be found. The squares are deserted, the streets are very nearly so, and all that is left to the luckless wanderer in search of the beautiful is to ogle the beauties of Dame Street, who are shopkeepers in Grafton Street, or the beauties of Grafton Street, who are shopkeepers in Dame Street. But, confound it, how cranky I am getting! I must be tremendously hungry. True, it's past six. So now for my suit of sable, and then to dinner.

CHAPTER XIII.

DUBLIN.—THE BOARDING-HOUSE.—SELECT SOCIETY.

PUNCTUAL to my appointment with O'Flaherty, I found myself, a very few minutes after six o'clock, at Mrs. Clanfrizzle's door. My very authoritative summons at the bell was answered by the appearance of a young, pale-faced invalid in a suit of livery, the taste of which bore a very unpleasant resemblance to the one I so lately figured in. It was with considerable difficulty I persuaded this functionary to permit my carrying my hat with me to the drawing-room,—a species of caution on my part, as he esteemed it, savoring much of distrust. This point, however, I carried, and followed him up a very ill-lighted stair to the drawing-room. Here I was announced by some faint resemblance to my real name, but sufficiently near to bring my friend Tom

at once to meet me, who immediately congratulated me on
my fortune in coming off so well, for that the person who
preceded me, Mr. Jones Blennerhasset, had been just announced as Mr. Blatherhashit,—a change the gentleman himself was not disposed to adopt. "But come along, Harry;
while we are waiting for Daly, let me make you known to
some of our party. This, you must know, is a boarding-house,
and always has some capital fun,—queerest people you ever
met. I have only one hint: cut every man, woman, and child
of them, if you meet them hereafter; I do it myself, though
I have lived here these six months." Pleasant people, thought
I, these must be, with whom such a line is advisable, much
less practicable.

"Mrs. Clanfrizzle, my friend Mr. Lorrequer; thinks he'll
stay the summer in town. Mrs. Clan, should like him to be
one of us." The latter was said *sotto voce,* and was a practice he continued to adopt in presenting me to his several
friends through the room.

"Miss Riley,"—a horrid old fright in a bird of paradise
plume and corked eyebrows, gibbeted in gilt chains and pearl
ornaments, and looking, as the grisettes say, *superbe en chry-
solithe,*—"Miss Riley, Captain Lorrequer,—a friend I have
long desired to present to you. Fifteen thousand a year and a
baronetcy, if he has sixpence,"—*sotto* again. "Surgeon
M'Culloch,—he likes the title," said Tom, in a whisper,—
"Surgeon, Captain Lorrequer. By the by, lest I forget it,
he wishes to speak to you in the morning about his health;
he is stopping at Sandymount for the baths,—you could go
out there, eh?" The tall thing in green spectacles bowed, and
acknowledged Tom's kindness by a knowing touch of the
elbow. In this way he made the tour of the room for about
ten minutes, during which brief space I was, according to the
kind arrangements of O'Flaherty, booked as a resident in the
boarding-house, a lover to at least five elderly and three
young ladies, a patient, a client, a second in a duel to a clerk
in the Post-office, and had also volunteered (through him always) to convey, by all of his Majesty's mails, as many parcels, packets, band-boxes, and bird-cages as would have comfortably filled one of Pickford's vans. All this he told me was
requisite to my being well received, though no one thought

much of any breach of compact subsequently, except Mrs. Clan herself. The ladies had, alas! been often treated vilely before; the doctor had never had a patient; and as for the belligerent knight of the dead office, he'd rather have died than fought any day.

The last person to whom my friend deemed it necessary to introduce me was a Mr. Garret Cudmore, from the Reeks of Kerry, lately matriculated to all the honors of freshmanship in the Dublin University. This latter was a low-sized, dark-browed man, with round shoulders and particularly long arms, the disposal of which seemed sadly to distress him. He possessed the most perfect brogue I ever listened to; but it was difficult to get him to speak, for on coming up to town some weeks before, he had been placed by some intelligent friend at Mrs. Clanfrizzle's establishment, with the express direction to mark and thoroughly digest as much as he could of the habits and customs of the circle about him, which he was rightly informed was the very focus of good-breeding and *haut ton,* but on no account, unless driven thereto by the pressure of sickness or the wants of nature, to trust himself with speech, which, in his then unformed state, he was assured would inevitably ruin him among his fastidiously cultivated associates.

To the letter and the spirit of the despatch he had received, the worthy Garret acted rigidly; and his voice was scarcely ever known to transgress the narrow limits prescribed by his friends. In more respects than one was this a good resolve; for so completely had he identified himself with college habits, things, and phrases, that whenever he conversed, he became little short of unintelligible to the vulgar,—a difficulty not lessened by his peculiar pronunciation.

My round of presentation was just completed, when the pale figure in light-blue livery announced Counsellor Daly and dinner; for both came fortunately together. Taking the post of honor, Miss Riley's arm, I followed Tom, who I soon perceived ruled the whole concern, as he led the way with another ancient vestal in black satin and bugles. The long procession wound its snake-like length down the narrow stair and into the dining-room, where at last we all got seated. And here let me briefly vindicate the motives of my friend. Should any unkind person be found to impute to his selection of a residence any base and grovelling passion for "gourmandise," that day's experience should be an eternal vindication of him. The soup—alas! that I should so far prostitute the word, for the black broth of Sparta was mock-turtle in comparison—retired to make way for a mass of beef, whose tenderness I did not question, for it sank beneath the knife of the carver like a feather-bed,—the skill of Saladin himself would have failed to divide it; the fish was a most rebellious pike, and nearly killed every loyal subject at table; and then down the sides were various dishes of chickens with azure bosoms, and hams with hides like a rhinoceros; covered "decoys" of decomposed vegetable matter called spinach and cabbage; potatoes arrayed in small masses and browned, resembling those ingenious architectural structures of mud children raise in the highways and call dirt-pies. Such were the chief constituents of the "feed;" and such, I am bound to confess, waxed beautifully less under the vigorous onslaught of the party.

The conversation soon became both loud and general. That happy familiarity which I had long believed to be the exclusive prerogative of a military mess, where constant daily association sustains the interest of the veriest trifles, I here found in a perfection I had not anticipated,—with this striking difference, that there was no absurd deference to any existing code of etiquette in the conduct of the party generally, each person quizzing his neighbor in the most free-and-easy style imaginable, and all, evidently from long habit and conventional usage, seeming to enjoy the practice exceedingly. Thus, droll allusions, good stories, and smart repartees fell thick as hail and twice as harmless, which, anywhere else that I had ever heard of, would assuredly have called for more explanations, and perhaps gunpowder, in the morning than usually are deemed agreeable. Here, however, they knew better; and though the lawyer quizzed the doctor for never having another patient than the house-dog, all of whose arteries he had tied in the course of the winter for practice, and the doctor retorted as heavily by showing that the lawyer's practice had been other than beneficial to those for whom he was concerned, his *one* client being found guilty mainly through his ingenious defence of him,—yet they never showed any, the slightest irritation; on the contrary, such little playful *badinage* ever led to some friendly passages of taking wine together, or in arrangements for a party to the "Dargle" or "Dunleary." And thus went on the entire party, the young ladies darting an occasional slight at their elders, who certainly returned the fire often with advantage; all uniting now and then, however, in one common cause,—an attack of the whole line upon Mrs. Clanfrizzle herself for the beef or the mutton or the fish or the poultry, each of which was sure to find some sturdy defamer ready and willing to give evidence in dispraise. Yet even these—and I thought them rather dangerous sallies—led to no more violent results than dignified replies from the worthy hostess upon the goodness of her fare and the evident satisfaction it afforded while being eaten, if the appetites of the party were a test. While this was at its height, Tom stooped behind my chair and whispered gently,—

"This is good, isn't it, eh?—life in a boarding-house; quite new to you. But they are civilized now, compared to what you will find them in the drawing-room. When short whist for fivepenny points sets in, then Greek meets Greek, and we'll have it."

During all this *mêlée* tournament, I perceived that the worthy "jib," as he would be called in the parlance of Trinity, Mr. Cudmore, remained perfectly silent and apparently terrified. The noise, the din of voices, and the laughing so completely addled him that he was like one in a very horrid dream. The attention with which I had observed him having been remarked by my friend O'Flaherty, he informed me that the scholar, as he was called there, was then under a kind of cloud,—an adventure which occurred only two nights before being too fresh in his memory to permit him enjoying himself even to the limited extent it had been his wont to do. As illustrative, not only of Mr. Cudmore, but the life I have been speaking of, I may as well relate it.

Soon after Mr. Cudmore's enlistment under the banners of the Clanfrizzle, he had sought and found an asylum in the drawing-room of the establishment, which promised, from its geographical relations, to expose him less to the molestations of conversation than most other parts of the room. This was a small recess beside the fireplace, not uncommon in old-fashioned houses, and which, from its incapacity to hold more than one, secured to the worthy recluse the privacy he longed for; and here, among superannuated hearth-brushes, an old hand-screen, an asthmatic bellows, and a kettle-holder, sat the timid youth, "alone, but in a crowd." Not all the se-ductions of loo, limited to threepence, nor even that most appropriately designated game, beggar-my-neighbor, could withdraw him from his blest retreat. Like his countryman, Saint Kevin,—my friend Petrie has ascertained that the saint was a native of Tralee,—he fled from the temptations of the world and the blandishments of the fair; but alas! like the saint himself, the—

> "poor 'jib' little knew
> All that wily sex can do;"

for while he hugged himself in the security of his fortress, the web of his destiny was weaving. So true is it, as he him-self used, no less pathetically than poetically, to express it, "Misfortune will find you out if ye were hid in a tay-chest."

It happened that in Mrs. Clanfrizzle's establishment the *enfant bleu* already mentioned was the only individual of his sex retained; and without for a moment disparaging the ability or attentions of this gifted person, yet it may reason-ably be credited that in waiting on a party of twenty-five or thirty persons at dinner, all of whom he had admitted as porter and announced as *maître d'hôtel*, with the subsequent detail of his duties in the drawing-room, Peter,—Blue Peter, his boarding-house sobriquet,—not enjoying the bird-like privilege of "being in two places at once," gave one rather the impression of a person of hasty and fidgety habits, for which nervous tendency the treatment he underwent was cer-tainly injudicious,—it being the invariable custom for each guest to put his services in requisition, perfectly irrespective of all other claims upon him, from whatsoever quarter com-ing; and then at the precise moment that the luckless valet was snuffing the candles, he was abused by one for not bring-ing coal; by another for having carried off his teacup, sent on an expedition for sugar; by a third for having left the door open, which he had never been near; and so on to the end of the chapter.

It chanced that a few evenings previous to my appearance at the house, this indefatigable Caleb was ministering as usual to the various and discrepant wants of the large party assembled in the drawing-room. With his wonted alacrity, he had withdrawn from their obscure retreat against the wall sundry little tables, destined for the players at whist, or "spoil five,"—the popular game of the establishment. With a dexterity that savored much of a stage education, he had arranged the candles, the cards, the counters; he had poked the fire, settled the stool for Miss Riley's august feet, and was busily engaged in changing five shillings into small silver for a desperate victim of loo, when Mrs. Clanfrizzle's third, and, as it appeared, last time of asking for the kettle smote upon his ear. His loyalty would have induced him at once to desert everything on such an occasion; but the other party engaged held him fast, saying,—

"Never mind *her,* Peter; you have sixpence more to give me."

Poor Peter rummaged one pocket, then another, discovering at last threepence in copper and some farthings, with which he seemed endeavoring to make a composition with his creditor for twelve shillings in the pound; when, Mrs. Clan's patience finally becoming exhausted, she turned towards Mr. Cudmore, the only unemployed person she could perceive, and with her blandest smile said,—

"Mr. Cudmore, may I take the liberty of requesting you would hand me the kettle beside you?"

Now, though the kettle aforesaid was, as the hostess very properly observed, beside him, yet the fact that in complying with the demand it was necessary for the bashful youth to leave the recess he occupied, and, with the kettle, proceed to walk half across the room, there to perform certain manual operations requiring skill and presence of mind before a large and crowded assembly, was horror to the mind of the poor jib, and he would nearly as soon have acceded to a desire to dance a hornpipe, if such had been suggested as the wish of the company. However, there was nothing for it, and summoning up all his nerve, knitting his brows, clenching his

Mr. Cudmore filling the teapot.

teeth like one prepared to "do or die," he seized the hissing caldron and strode through the room like the personified genius of steam,—very much to the alarm of all the old ladies in the vicinity, whose tasteful drapery benefited but little from his progress. Yet he felt but little of all this; he had brought up his courage to the sticking place, and he was absolutely half unconscious of the whole scene before him. Nor was it till some kind mediator had seized his arm, while another drew him back by the skirts of the coat, that he desisted from the deluge of hot water with which, having filled the tea-pot, he proceeded to swamp everything else upon the tray, in his unfortunate abstraction. Mrs. Clanfrizzle screamed; the old ladies accompanied her; the young ones tittered; the men laughed; and in a word, poor Cudmore, perfectly unconscious of anything extraordinary, felt himself the admired of all admirers,—very little, it is true, to his own satisfaction. After some few minutes' exposure to these signs of mirth, he succeeded in depositing the source of his griefs within the fender, and once more retired to his sanctuary, having registered a vow which, should I speak it, would forfeit his every claim to gallantry forever.

Whether, in the vow aforesaid, Mr. Cudmore had only been engaged in that species of tessellation which furnishes the pavement so celebrated in the lower regions, I know not; but true it is that he retired that night to his chamber very much discomfited at his *début* in the great world, and half disposed to believe that Nature had intended him for neither a Brummell nor a D'Orsay. While he was ruminating on such matters, he was joined by O'Flaherty, with whom he had been always more intimate than any other inmate of the house, Tom's tact having entirely concealed what the manners of the others too plainly evinced,—a perfect appreciation of the student's oddity and singularity. After some few observations on general matters, O'Flaherty began, with a tone of some seriousness, to express towards Cudmore the warm interest he had ever taken in him since his first coming among them, his great anxiety for his welfare, and his firm resolve that no chance or casual inattention to mere ceremonial observances on his part should ever be seized on by the other guests as a ground for detraction or an excuse for ridicule of him.

"Rely upon it, my dear boy," said he, "I have watched over you like a parent; and having partly foreseen that something like this affair of to-night would take place sooner or later—"

"What affair?" said Cudmore, his eyes staring half out of his head.

"The business of the kettle."

"Kett—el. The kettle! What of that?" said Cudmore.

"What of it? Why, if *you* don't feel it, I am sure it is not *my* duty to remind you; only—"

"Feel it, oh, yes! I saw them laughing because I spilled the water over old Mrs. Jones, or something of that sort."

"No, no, my dear young friend, they were not laughing at *that*,—their mirth had another object."

"What the devil was it at, then?"

"You don't know, don't you?"

"No, I really do not."

"Nor can't guess, eh?"

"Confound me if I can."

"Well, I see, Mr. Cudmore, you are really too innocent for these people. But come; it shall never be said that youth and inexperience ever suffered from the unworthy ridicule and cold sarcasm of the base world while Tom O'Flaherty stood by a spectator. Sir," said Tom, striking his hand with energy on the table, and darting a look of fiery indignation from his eye, "sir, you were this night trepanned,—yes, sir, vilely, shamefully trepanned—I repeat the expression—into the performance of a menial office,—an office so degrading, so offensive, so unbecoming the rank, the station, and the habits of gentlemen, my very blood recoils when I only think of the indignity."

The expression of increasing wonder and surprise depicted in Mr. Cudmore's face at these words, my friend Phiz might convey,—I cannot venture to describe it; suffice it to say that even O'Flaherty himself found it difficult to avoid a burst of laughter as he looked at him and resumed,—

"Witnessing, as I did, the entire occurrence, feeling deeply for the inexperience which the heartless worldlings had dared to trample upon, I resolved to stand by you, and here I am come for that purpose."

"Well, but what in the devil's name have I done all this time?"

"What! are you still ignorant? Is it possible? Did you not hand the kettle from the fireplace, and fill the teapot? Answer me that."

"I did," said Cudmore, with a voice already becoming tremulous.

"Is that the duty of a gentleman? Answer me that."

A dead pause stood in place of a reply, while Tom proceeded,—

"Did you ever hear any one ask me, or Counsellor Daly, or Mr. Fogarty, or any other person to do so? Answer me that."

"No, never," muttered Cudmore, with a sinking spirit.

"Well, then, why, may I ask, were *you* selected for that office, that, by your own confession, no one else would stoop to perform? I'll tell you,—because, from your youth and inexperience, your innocence was deemed a fit victim to the heartless sneers of a cold and unfeeling world." And here Tom broke forth into a very beautiful apostrophe, beginning, "Oh, virtue!"—this I am unfortunately unable to present to my readers, and must only assure them that it was a very faithful imitation of the well-known one delivered by Burke in the case of Warren Hastings,—and concluding with an exhortation to Cudmore to wipe out the stain of his wounded honor by repelling with indignation the slightest future attempt at such an insult.

This done, O'Flaherty retired, leaving Cudmore to dig among Greek roots and chew over the cud of his misfortune. Punctual to the time and place, that same evening beheld the injured Cudmore resume his wonted corner, pretty much with the feeling with which a forlorn hope stands, match in hand, to ignite the train destined to explode with ruin to thousands, himself, perhaps, among the number. There he sat, with a brain as burning and a heart as excited as though, instead of sipping his bohea beside a sea-coal fire, he was that instant trembling beneath the frown of Dr. Elrington for the blunders in his Latin theme,—and what terror to the mind of a "jib" can equal that one?

As luck would have it, this was a company night in the

10

boarding-house. Various young ladies, in long blue sashes and very broad ribbon sandals, paraded the rooms, chatting gayly with very distinguished-looking young gentlemen with gold brooches and party-colored inside waistcoats; sundry elderly ladies sat at card-tables, discussing the "lost honor by an odd trick they played," with heads as large as those of Jack or Jill in the pantomime; spruce clerks in public offices (whose vocation the expansive tendency of the right ear, from long pen-carrying, betokened) discussed fashion "and the musical glasses" to some very over-dressed married ladies who preferred flirting to five-and-ten. The tea-table, over which the amiable hostess presided, had also its standing votaries,— mostly grave parliamentary-looking gentlemen, with powdered heads and very long-waisted black coats, among whom the Sir Oracle was a functionary of his Majesty's High Court of Chancery, though, I have reason to believe, not Lord Manners. Meanwhile, in all parts of the room might be seen Blue Peter distributing tea, coffee, and biscuit, and occasionally interchanging a joke with the dwellers in the house. While all these pleasing occupations proceeded, the hour of Cudmore's trial was approaching. The teapot, which had stood the attack of fourteen cups without flinching, at last began to fail, and discovered to the prying eyes of Mrs. Clanfrizzle nothing but an olive-colored deposit of soft matter closely analogous in appearance and chemical property to the residuary precipitate in a drained fish-pond; she put down the lid with a gentle sigh, and turning towards the fire, bestowed one of her very blandest and most captivating looks on Mr. Cudmore, saying as plainly as looks could say, "Cudmore, you're wanting." Whether the youth did, or did not, understand, I am unable to record; I can only say the appeal was made without acknowledgment. Mrs. Clanfrizzle again essayed, and by a little masonic movement of her hand to the teapot, and a sly glance at the hob, intimated her wish,—still hopelessly. At last there was nothing for it but speaking; and she donned her very softest voice and most persuasive tone, saying, "Mr. Cudmore, I am really very troublesome; will you permit me to ask you—"

"Is it for the kettle, ma'am?" said Cudmore, with a voice that startled the whole room, disconcerting three whist-parties,

and so absorbing the attention of the people at loo that the
pool disappeared without any one being able to account for
the circumstance,—"is it for the kettle, ma'am?"

"If you will be so *very* kind," lisped the hostess.

"Well, then, upon my conscience, you *are* impudent," said
Cudmore, with his face crimson to the ears, and his eyes
flashing fire.

"Why, Mr. Cudmore," began the lady, "why, really, this is
so strange! Why, sir, what *can* you mean?"

"Just *that,*" said the imperturbable jib, who, now his courage was up, dared everything.

"But, sir, you must surely have misunderstood me. I only
asked for the kettle, Mr. Cudmore."

"The devil a more," said Cud, with a sneer.

"Well, then, of course—"

"Well, then, I'll tell you, of coorse," said he, repeating her
words, "the sorrow taste of the kettle I'll give you. Call your
own skip,—Blue Pether there; damn me if I'll be your skip
any longer!"

For the uninitiated, I have only to add that "skip" is the
Trinity College appellation for servant, which was therefore
employed by Mr. Cudmore on this occasion as expressing more
contemptuously his sense of the degradation of the office attempted to be put upon him. Having already informed my
reader on some particulars of the company, I leave him to
suppose how Mr. Cudmore's speech was received. Whist
itself was at an end for that evening, and nothing but laughter, long, loud, and reiterated, burst from every corner of
the room for hours after.

As I have so far travelled out of the record of my own
peculiar Confessions as to give a leaf from what might one
day form the matter of Mr. Cudmore's, I must now make
the only *amende* in my power, by honestly narrating that short
as my visit was to the classic precincts of this agreeable establishment, I did not escape without exciting my share of
ridicule, though I certainly had not the worst of the joke, and
may therefore with better grace tell the story, which, happily
for my readers, is a short one. A custom prevailed in Mrs.
Clanfrizzle's household which, from my unhappy ignorance
of boarding-houses, I am unable to predicate if it belong to

the genera at large or this one specimen in particular; however, it is a sufficiently curious fact, even though thereby hang no tale for my stating it here. The decanters on the dinner-table were never labelled with their more appropriate designation of contents, whether claret, sherry, or port, but with the names of their respective owners, it being a matter of much less consequence that any individual at table should mix his wine by pouring "port upon madeira," than commit the truly legal offence of appropriating to his own use and benefit, even by mistake, his neighbor's bottle. However well the system may work among the regular members of the "domestic circle,"—and I am assured that it does succeed extremely,—to the newly arrived guest or uninitiated visitor the affair is perplexing, and leads occasionally to awkward results.

It so chanced, from my friend O'Flaherty's habitual position at the foot of the table, and my post of honor near the head, that on the first day of my appearing there, the distance between us not only precluded close intercourse, but any of those gentle hints as to habits and customs a new arrival looks for at the hands of his better-informed friend. The only mode of recognition, to prove that we belonged to each other, being by that excellent and truly English custom of drinking wine together, Tom seized the first idle moment from his avocation as carver to say,—

"Lorrequer, a glass of wine with you."

Having, of course, acceded, he again asked,—

"What wine do you drink?" intending thereby, as I afterwards learned, to send me from his end of the table what wine I selected. Not conceiving the object of the inquiry, and having hitherto, without hesitation, helped myself from the decanter which bore some faint resemblance to sherry, I immediately turned for correct information to the bottle itself, upon whose slender neck was ticketed the usual slip of paper. My endeavors to decipher the writing occupied time sufficient again to make O'Flaherty ask,—

"Well, Harry, I'm waiting for you. Will you have claret?"

"No, I thank you," I replied, having by this revealed the inscription,—"no, I thank you; I'll just stick to my old friend here, Bob M'Grotty,"—for thus I rendered familiarly the

name of Rt. M'Grotty on the decanter, and which I, in my
ignorance, believed to be the boarding-house sobriquet for bad
sherry. That Mr. M'Grotty himself little relished my familiarity with either his name or property I had a very decisive
proof, for, turning round upon his chair, and surveying
my person from head to foot with a look of fiery wrath, he
thundered out in very broad Scotch,—

"And by my saul, my freend, ye may just as weel finish it
noo, for deil a glass o' his ain wine did Bob M'Grotty, as ye
ca' him, swallow this day."

The convulsion of laughter into which my blunder and the
Scotchman's passion threw the whole board lasted till the
cloth was withdrawn and the ladies had retired to the drawing-room, the only individual at table not relishing the mistake being the injured proprietor of the bottle, who was too
proud to accept reparation from my friend's decanter, and
would scarcely condescend to open his lips during the evening; notwithstanding which display of honest indignation,
we contrived to become exceedingly merry and jocose, most
of the party communicating little episodes of their life, in
which, it is true, they frequently figured in situations that
nothing but their native and natural candor would venture to
avow. One story I was considerably amused at; it was told
by the counsellor, Mr. Daly, in illustration of the difficulty
of rising at the Bar, and which, as showing his own mode
of obviating the delay that young professional men submit
to from hard necessity, as well as in evidence of his strictly
legal turn, I shall certainly recount one of these days for the
edification of the Junior Bar.

CHAPTER XIV.

THE CHASE.

ON the morning after my visit to the boarding-house I
received a few hurried lines from Curzon, informing me
that no time was to be lost in joining the regiment, that a
grand fancy ball was about to be given by the officers of

the *Dwarf* frigate, then stationed off Dunmore, who, when inviting the 4—th, specially put in a demand for my well-known services, to make it go off, and concluding with an extract from the "Kilkenny Moderator," which ran thus: "An intimation has just reached us, from a quarter on which we can place the fullest reliance, that the celebrated amateur performer, Mr. Lorrequer, may shortly be expected among us. From the many accounts we have received of this highly gifted gentleman's powers, we anticipate a great treat to the lovers of the drama," etc. "So you see, my dear Hal," continued Curzon, "thy vocation calls thee; therefore come, and come quickly. Provide thyself with a black satin costume slashed with light-blue, point-lace collar and ruffles, a Spanish hat looped in front, and, if possible, a long rapier with a flat hilt. Carden is not here, so you may show your face under any color with perfect impunity."

This clever epistle "from the side-scenes" sufficed to show that the gallant 4—th had gone clean theatrical mad; and although from my "last appearance on any stage" it might be supposed I should feel no peculiar desire to repeat the experiment, yet the opportunity of joining during Colonel Carden's absence was too tempting to resist, and I at once made up my mind to set out, and without a moment's delay hurried across the street to the coach-office to book myself an inside in the mail of that night. Fortunately, no difficulty existed in my procuring the seat, for the way-bill was a perfect blank, and I found myself the only person who had as yet announced himself a passenger. On returning to my hotel I found O'Flaherty waiting for me. He was greatly distressed on hearing my determination to leave town, explained how he had been catering for my amusement for the week to come, —that a picnic to the Dargle was arranged in a committee of the whole house, and a boating-party, with a dinner at the Pigeon House, was then under consideration. Resisting, however, such extreme temptations, I mentioned the necessity of my at once proceeding to headquarters, and all other reasons for my precipitancy failing, concluded with that really knock-down argument, "I have taken my place." This, I need scarcely add, finished the matter,—at least, *I* have never known it fail in such cases. Tell your friends that your wife is hourly expecting to be confined; your favorite child is in the measles; your best friend waiting your aid in an awkward scrape; your one vote only wanting to turn the scale in an election,—tell them, I say, each or all of these, or a hundred more like them, and from any one you so speak to, the answer is, "Pooh, pooh, my dear fellow! never fear, don't fuss yourself, take it easy,—to-morrow will do just as well." If on the other hand, however, you reject such flimsy excuses, and simply say, "I'm booked in the mail," the opposition at once falls to the ground, and your quondam antagonist, who was ready to quarrel with you, is at once prepared to assist in packing your portmanteau.

Having soon satisfied my friend Tom that resistance was in vain, I promised to eat an early dinner with him at Morrisson's, and spent the better part of the morning in putting down a few notes of my "Confessions" as well as the particulars of Mr. Daly's story, which, I believe, I half or wholly promised my readers at the conclusion of my last chapter, but which I must defer to a more suitable opportunity, when mentioning the next occasion of my meeting him on the southern circuit.

My dispositions were speedily made. I was fortunate in securing the exact dress my friend's letter alluded to among the stray costumes of Fishamble Street; and rich in the possession of the only "properties" it had been my lot to acquire, I despatched my treasure to the coach-office and hastened to Morrisson's, it being by this time nearly five o'clock. There, true to time, I found O'Flaherty deep in the perusal of the bill, along which figured the *novel* expedients for dining I had been in the habit of reading in every Dublin hotel since my boyhood,—"mock-turtle, mutton gravy, roast beef and potatoes; shoulder of mutton and potatoes! ducks and peas, potatoes! ham and chicken, cutlet, steak, and potatoes! apple-tart and cheese." With a slight *cadenza* of a sigh over the distant glories of Véry, or still better the "Frères," we sat down to a very patriarchal repast, and what may be always had *par excellence* in Dublin,—a bottle of Sneyd's claret.

Poor Tom's spirits were rather below their usual pitch; and although he made many efforts to rally and appear gay, he could not accomplish it. However, we chatted away over old times and old friends, and forgetting all else but the topics we talked of, the timepiece over the chimney first apprised me that two whole hours had gone by, and that it was now seven o'clock,—the very hour the coach was to start. I started up at once, and notwithstanding all Tom's representations of the impossibility of my being in time, had despatched waiters in different directions for a jarvey, more than ever determined upon going,—so often is it that when real reasons for our conduct are wanting, any casual or chance opposition confirms us in an intention which before was but wavering. Seeing me so resolved, Tom at length gave way, and advised my pursuing the mail, which must be now gone at least ten minutes, and which, with smart driving, I should probably overtake before getting free of the city, as they have usually many delays in so doing. I at once ordered out the "yellow post-chaise," and before many minutes had elapsed, what with imprecation and bribery, I started in pursuit of his Majesty's Cork and Kilkenny mail-coach, then patiently waiting in the court-yard of the Post-office.

"Which way now, yer honor?" said a shrill voice from the dark,—for such the night had already become, and threatened, with a few heavy drops of straight rain, the fall of a tremendous shower.

"The Naas road," said I; "and hark ye, my fine fellow, if you overtake the coach in half an hour, I'll double your fare."

"Be gorra, I'll do my endayvor," said the youth; at the same instant dashing in both spurs, we rattled down Nassau Street at a very respectable pace for harriers. Street after street we passed, and at last I perceived we had got clear of the city, and were leaving the long line of lamp-lights behind us. The night was now pitch dark; I could not see anything whatever. The quick clattering of the wheels, the sharp crack of the postilion's whip, or the still sharper tone of his "gee-hup," showed me that we were going at a tremendous pace, had I not even had the experience afforded by the frequent visits my head paid to the roof of the chaise, so often as we bounded over a stone or splashed through a hollow. Dark and gloomy as it was, I constantly let down the window, and with half my body protruded, endeavored to catch a glimpse of the "Chase;" but nothing could I see. The rain now fell in actual torrents, and a more miserable night it is impossible to conceive.

After about an hour so spent, we at last came to a check, so sudden and unexpected on my part that I was nearly precipitated, harlequin fashion, through the front window. Perceiving that we no longer moved, and suspecting that some part of our tackle had given way, I let down the sash, and cried out, "Well, now, my lad, anything wrong?" My question was, however, unheard; and although, amid the steam arising from the wet and smoking horses, I could perceive several figures indistinctly moving about, I could not distinguish what they were doing, nor what they said. A laugh I certainly did hear, and heartily cursed the unfeeling wretch, as I supposed him to be, who was enjoying himself at my disappointment. I again endeavored to find out what had happened, and called out still louder than before.

"We are at Ra'coole, your honor," said the boy, approaching the door of the chaise, "and she's only beat us by hafe a mile."

"Who the devil is she?" said I.

"The mail, your honor, is always a female in Ireland."

"Then why do you stop now? You're not going to feed, I suppose?"

"Of coorse not, your honor,—it's little feeding troubles these bastes, anyhow; but they tell me the road is so heavy we'll never take the chaise over the next stage without leaders."

"Without leaders!" said I. "Pooh! my good fellow, no humbugging,—four horses for a light post-chaise and no luggage. Come, get up, and no nonsense."

At this moment a man approached the window with a lantern in his hand, and so strongly represented the dreadful state of the roads from the late rains, the length of the stage, the frequency of accidents latterly from under-horsing, etc., that I yielded a reluctant assent, and ordered out the leaders, comforting myself the while that considering the inside fare of the coach I made such efforts to overtake was under a pound, and that time was no object to me, I was certainly paying somewhat dearly for my character for resolution.

At last we got under way once more and set off, cheered by a tremendous shout from at least a dozen persons, doubtless denizens of that interesting locality, amid which I once again heard the laugh that had so much annoyed me already. The rain was falling if possible more heavily than before, and had evidently set in for the entire night. Throwing myself back into a corner of the "leathern convenience," I gave myself up to the full enjoyment of the Rochefoucauld maxim that there is always a pleasure felt in the misfortunes of even our best friends, and certainly experienced no small comfort in my distress by contrasting my present position with that of my two friends in the saddle as they sweltered on through mud and mire, rain and storm. On we went, splashing, bumping, rocking, and jolting, till I began at last to have serious thoughts of abdicating the seat and betaking myself to the bottom of the chaise, for safety and protection. Mile after mile succeeded; and as after many a short and fitful slumber, which my dreams gave an apparent length to, I awoke only to find myself still in pursuit, the time seemed so enormously protracted that I began to fancy my whole life was to be passed in the dark, in chase of the Kilkenny mail, as we read in the true history of the Flying Dutchman, who for his sins of impatience, like mine, spent centuries vainly endeavoring to double the Cape; or the Indian mariner in Moore's beautiful ballad, of whom we are told, as—

> Many a day to night gave way,
> And many a morn succeeded,
> Yet still his flight, by day and night,
> That restless mariner speeded.

This might have been all very well in the tropics, with a smart craft and doubtless plenty of sea store; but in a chaise, at night, and on the Naas road, I humbly suggest I had all the worst of the parallel.

At last the altered sound of the wheels gave notice of our approach to a town, and after about twenty minutes' rattling over the pavement we entered what I supposed, correctly, to be Naas. Here I had long since determined my pursuit should cease. I had done enough, and more than enough, to vindicate my fame against any charge of irresolution as to leaving Dublin, and was bethinking me of the various modes of prosecuting my journey on the morrow, when we drew up suddenly at the door of the Swan. The arrival of a chaise and four at a small country town inn suggests to the various officials therein anything rather than the traveller in pursuit of the mail, and so the moment I arrived I was assailed with innumerable proffers of horses, supper, bed, and so on. My anxious query was thrice repeated in vain, "When did the coach pass?"

"The mail?" replied the landlord at length. "Is it the down-mail?"

Not understanding the technical, I answered, "Of course not the Down,—the Kilkenny and Cork mail."

"From Dublin, sir?"

"Yes, from Dublin."

"Not arrived yet, sir, nor will it for three-quarters of an hour. They never leave Dublin till a quarter-past seven,—that is, in fact, half-past; and their time here is twenty minutes to eleven."

"Why, you stupid son of a boot-top, we have been posting on all night like the devil, and all this time the coach has been ten miles behind us!"

"Well, we've cotch them, anyhow," said the urchin as he disengaged himself from his wet saddle and stood upon the ground; "and it is not my fault that the coach is not before us."

With a satisfactory anathema upon all innkeepers, waiters, ostlers, and post-boys, with a codicil including coach-proprietors, I followed the smirking landlord into a well-lighted room with a blazing fire, when, having ordered supper, I soon regained my equanimity.

My rasher and poached eggs, all Naas could afford me, were speedily despatched, and as my last glass from my one pint of sherry was poured out, the long-expected coach drew up. A minute after, the coachman entered to take his dram, followed by the guard. A more lamentable spectacle of condensed moisture cannot be conceived: the rain fell from the entire circumference of his broad-brimmed hat, like the ever-flowing drop from the edge of an antique fountain; his drab coat had become of a deep orange hue, while his huge figure loomed still larger as he stood amid a nebula of damp that would have made an atmosphere for the Georgium Sidus.

"Going on to-night, sir?" said he, addressing me. "Severe

weather, and no chance of its clearing,—but of course you're inside."

"Why, there is very little doubt of that," said I. "Are you nearly full inside?"

"Only one, sir, but he seems a real queer chap; made fifty inquiries at the office if he could not have the whole inside to himself, and when he heard that one place had been taken, —yours, I believe, sir,—he seemed like a scalded bear."

"You don't know his name, then?"

"No, sir, he never gave a name at the office, and his only luggage is two brown-paper parcels, without any ticket, and he has them inside,—indeed, he never lets them from him, even for a second."

Here the guard's horn, announcing all ready, interrupted our colloquy and prevented my learning anything further of my fellow-traveller, whom, however, I at once set down in my own mind for some confounded old churl that made himself comfortable everywhere, without ever thinking of any one else's convenience.

As I passed from the inn door to the coach, I once more congratulated myself that I was about to be housed from the terrific storm of wind and rain that railed without.

"Here's the step, sir," said the guard; "get in, sir,—two minutes late already."

"I beg your pardon, sir," said I, as I half fell over the legs of my unseen companion; "may I request leave to pass you?" While he made way for me for this purpose, I perceived that he stooped down towards the guard and said something, who, from his answer, had evidently been questioned as to who I was.

"And how did he get here, if he took his place in Dublin?" asked the unknown.

"Came half an hour since, sir, in a chaise and four," said the guard, as he banged the door behind him and closed the interview.

Whatever might have been the reasons for my fellow-traveller's anxiety about my name and occupation I knew not, yet could not help feeling gratified at thinking that, as I had not given my name at the coach-office, I was as great a puzzle to him as he to me.

"A severe night, sir," said I, endeavoring to break ground in conversation.

"Mighty severe," briefly and half-crustily replied the unknown, with a richness of brogue that might have stood for a certificate of baptism in Cork or its vicinity.

"And a bad road too, sir," said I, remembering my lately accomplished stage.

"That's the reason I always go armed," said the unknown, clinking at the same moment something like the barrel of a pistol.

Wondering somewhat at his readiness to mistake my meaning, I felt disposed to drop any further effort to draw him out, and was about to address myself to sleep as comfortably as I could.

"I'll just trouble ye to lean off that little parcel there, sir," said he, as he displaced from its position beneath my elbow one of the paper packages the guard had already alluded to.

In complying with this rather gruff demand, one of my pocket-pistols, which I carried in my breast pocket, fell out upon his knee; upon which he immediately started, and asked hurriedly, "And are you armed too?"

"Why, yes," said I, laughing; "men of my trade seldom go without something of this kind."

"Be gorra! I was just thinking that same," said the traveller, with a half sigh to himself.

Why he should or should not have thought so, I never troubled myself to canvass, and was once more settling myself in my corner, when I was startled by a very melancholy groan, which seemed to come from the bottom of my companion's heart.

"Are you ill, sir?" said I, in a voice of some anxiety.

"You may say that," replied he, "if you knew who you were talking to, although maybe you've heard enough of me, though you never saw me till now."

"Without having that pleasure even yet," said I, "it would grieve me to think you should be ill in the coach."

"Maybe it might," briefly replied the unknown, with a species of meaning in his words I could not then understand. "Did ye never hear tell of Barney Doyle?" said he.

"Not to my recollection."

"Then I'm Barney," said he, "that's in all newspapers in the metropolis. I'm seventeen weeks in Jervis Street Hospital, and four in the Lunatic, and the devil a better after all. You must be a stranger, I'm thinking, or you'd know me now."

"Why, I do confess I've only been a few hours in Ireland for the last six months."

"Ay, that's the reason; I knew you would not be fond of travelling with me, if you knew who it was."

"Why, really," said I, beginning at the moment to fathom some of the hints of my companion, "I did not anticipate the pleasure of meeting you."

"It's pleasure ye call it; then there's no accountin' for tastes, as Dr. Colles said when he saw me bite Cusack Rooney's thumb off."

"Bite a man's thumb off!" said I in horror.

"Ay," said he, with a kind of fiendish animation, "in one chop. I wish you'd seen how I scattered the consultation; begad! they didn't wait to ax for a fee."

"Upon my soul, a very pleasant vicinity," thought I. "And may I ask, sir," said I, in a very mild and soothing tone of voice, "may I ask the reason for this singular propensity of yours?"

"There it is now, my dear," said he, laying his hand upon my knee familiarly; "that's just the very thing they can't make out. Colles says it's all the ceribellum, ye see, that's inflamed and combusted, and some of the others think it's the spine, and more the muscles; but my real impression is, the devil a bit they know about it at all."

"And have they no name for the malady?" said I.

"Oh! sure enough they have a name for it."

"And, may I ask—"

"Why, I think you'd better not, because, ye see, maybe I might be throublesome to ye in the night,—though I'll not if I can help it; and it might be uncomfortable to you to be here if I was to get one of the fits."

"One of the fits! Why, it's not possible, sir," said I, "you would travel in a public conveyance in the state you mention, —your friends surely would not permit it!"

"Why, if they *knew,* perhaps," slyly responded the interesting invalid,—"if they *knew*, they might not exactly like it; but, ye see, I escaped only last night, and there'll be a fine hubbub in the morning when they find I'm off. Though I'm thinking Rooney's barking away by this time."

"Rooney barking! Why, what does that mean?"

"They always bark for a day or two after they're bit, if the infection comes first from the dog."

"You are surely not speaking of hydrophobia," said I, my hair actually bristling with horror and consternation.

"Ain't I?" replied he. "Maybe you've guessed it, though."

"And have you the malady on you at present?" said I, trembling for the answer.

"This is the ninth day since I took to biting," said he, gravely, perfectly unconscious, as it appeared, of the terror such information was calculated to convey.

"And with such a propensity, sir, do you think yourself warranted in travelling in a public coach, exposing others—"

"You'd better not raise your voice that way," quietly responded he. "If I'm roused, it'll be worse for ye, that's all."

"Well, but," said I, moderating my zeal, "is it exactly prudent, in your present delicate state, to undertake a journey?"

"Ah!" said he, with a sigh, "I've been longing to see the fox-hounds throw off near Kilkenny; these three weeks I've been thinking of nothing else. But I'm not sure how my nerves will stand the cry; I might be troublesome."

"Upon my soul," thought I, "I shall not select that morning for my *début* in the field."

"I hope, sir, there's no river or watercourse on this road, —anything else I can, I hope, control myself against; but water—running water particularly—makes me troublesome."

Well knowing what he meant by the latter phrase, I felt the cold perspiration settling on my forehead as I remembered that we must be within about ten or twelve miles of Leighlin Bridge, where we should have to pass a very wide river. I strictly concealed this fact from him, however, and gave him to understand that there was not a well, brook, or rivulet for forty miles on either side of us. He now sank into a kind of moody silence, broken occasionally by a low muttering noise, as if speaking to himself. What this might portend I knew not, but thought it better, under all circumstances, not to disturb him. How comfortable my present condition was, I need scarcely remark, sitting *vis-à-vis* to a lunatic with a pair of pistols in his possession, who had already avowed his consciousness of his tendency to do mischief and his inability to master it,—all this in the dark, and in the narrow limits of a mail-coach, where there was scarcely room for defence, and no possibility of escape. How heartily I wished myself back in the coffee-room at Morrisson's with my poor friend Tom! The infernal chaise, that I cursed a hundred times, would have been an "exchange" better than into the Life Guards,—ay, even the outside of the coach, if I could only reach it, would, under present circumstances, be a glorious alternative to my existing misfortune. What were rain and storm, thunder and lightning, compared with the chances that awaited me here? Wet through I should inevitably be; but then I had not yet contracted the horror of moisture my friend opposite labored under. "Ha! what is that? Is it possible he can be asleep,— is it really a snore? Heaven grant that little snort be not what the medical people call a premonitory symptom; if so, he'll be in upon me now, in no time. Ah! there it is again,—he must be asleep, surely; now then is my time, or never." With these words muttered to myself, and a heart throbbing almost audibly at the risk of his awakening, I slowly let down the window of the coach, and stretching forth my hand, turned the handle cautiously and slowly; I next disengaged my legs; and by a long continuous effort of creeping—which I had learned perfectly once, when practising to go as a boa-constrictor to a fancy ball—I withdrew myself from the seat and reached the step, when I muttered something very like a thanksgiving to Providence for my rescue. With little difficulty I now climbed up beside the guard, whose astonishment at my appearance was indeed considerable. That any man should prefer the out to the inside of a coach in such a night, was rather remarkable; but that the person so doing should be totally unprovided with a box-coat or other similar protection, argued something so strange that I doubt not, if he were to decide upon the applicability of the statute of lunacy to a traveller in the mail, the palm would certainly have been awarded to me, and not to my late companion. Well, on we rolled, and heavily as the rain poured down, so relieved did I feel at my change of position that I soon fell fast asleep, and never woke till the coach was driving up Patrick Street. Whatever solace to my feelings reaching the outside of the coach might have been attended with at night, the pleasure I experienced on awakening was really not unalloyed. More dead than alive, I sat a mass of wet clothes, like nothing under heaven except it be that morsel of black and spongy wet cotton at the bottom of a schoolboy's ink-bottle, saturated with rain and the black dye of my coat. My hat, too, had contributed its share of coloring matter, and several long black streaks coursed down my "wrinkled front," giving me very much the air of an Indian warrior who had got the first priming of his war-paint. I certainly must have been a rueful object, were I only to judge from the faces of the waiters as they gazed on me when the coach drew up at Rice and Walsh's Hotel. Cold, wet, and weary as I was, my curiosity to learn more of my late agreeable companion was strong as ever within me,—perhaps stronger from the sacrifices his acquaintance had exacted from me. Before, however, I had disengaged myself from the pile of trunks and carpet-bags I had surrounded myself with, he had got out of the coach, and all I could catch a glimpse of was the back of a little short man in a kind of gray upper coat, and long galli-gaskins on his legs. He carried his two bundles under his arm, and stepped nimbly up the steps of the hotel, without ever turning his head to either side.

"Don't fancy you shall escape me *now*, my good friend," I cried out, as I sprang from the roof to the ground with one jump, and hurried after the great unknown into the coffee-room. By the time I reached it he had approached the fire, on the table near which having deposited the mysterious paper parcels, he was now busily engaged in divesting himself of his great-coat; his face was still turned from me, so that I had time to appear employed in divesting myself of my wet drapery before he perceived me. At last the coat was un-buttoned, the gaiters followed, and throwing them carelessly on a chair, he tucked up the skirts of his coat, and spreading himself comfortably, *à l'anglaise*, before the fire, displayed to my wondering and stupefied gaze the pleasant features of Dr. Finucane.

11

"Why, Dr., Dr. Finucane," cried I, "is this possible? Were you then really the inside in the mail last night?"

"Devil a doubt of it, Mr. Lorrequer; and may I make bould to ask were you the outside?"

"Then what, may I beg to know, did you mean by your damned story about Barney Doyle, and the hydrophobia, and Cusack Rooney's thumb, eh?"

"Oh, by the Lord!" said Finucane, "this will be the death of me. And it was *you* that I drove outside in all the rain last night! Oh, it will kill Father Malachi outright with laughing when I tell him." And he burst out into a fit of merriment that nearly induced me to break his head with the poker.

"Am I to understand, then, Mr. Finucane, that this practical joke of yours was contrived for *my* benefit, and for the purpose of holding *me* up to the ridicule of your confounded acquaintances?"

"Nothing of the kind, upon my conscience," said Fin, drying his eyes, and endeavoring to look sorry and sentimental. "If I had only the least suspicion in life that it was you, upon my oath I'd not have had the hydrophobia at all, and to tell you the truth, you were not the only one frightened,— you alarmed me devilishly too."

"I alarmed you! Why, how can that be?"

"Why, the real affair is this. I was bringing these two packages of notes down to my cousin Callaghan's bank in Cork,—fifteen thousand pounds, devil a less; and when you came into the coach at Naas, after driving there with your four horses, I thought it was all up with me. The guard just whispered in my ear that he saw you look at the priming of your pistols before getting in; and faith, I said four Paters and a Hail Mary before you'd count five. Well, when you got seated, the thought came into my mind that maybe, high-wayman as you were, you would not like dying a natural death, more particularly if you were an Irishman; and so I trumped up that long story about the hydrophobia, and the gentleman's thumb, and devil knows what besides; and while I was telling it, the cold perspiration was running down my head and face, for every time you stirred I said to myself, 'Now, he'll do it.' Two or three times, do you know, I was going to offer you ten shillings in the pound, and spare my life; and once, God forgive me, I thought it would not be a bad plan to shoot you 'by mistake,' do you perceive?"

"Why, upon my soul, I'm very much obliged to you for your excessively kind intentions; but really I feel you have done quite enough for me on the present occasion. But come now, Doctor, I must get to bed, and before I go, promise me two things,—to dine with us to-day at the mess, and not to mention a syllable of what occurred last night: it tells, believe me, very badly for both. So keep the secret, for if these confounded fellows of ours ever get hold of it, I may sell out and quit the army; I'll never hear the end of it!"

"Never fear, my boy; trust me. I'll dine with you, and you're as safe as a church-mouse for anything I'll tell them; so now you'd better change your clothes, for I'm thinking it rained last night."

Muttering some very dubious blessings upon the learned Fin, I left the room infinitely more chagrined and chopfallen at the discovery I had made than at all the misery and exposure the trick had consigned me to. "However," thought I, "if the doctor keep his word, all goes well,—the whole affair is between us both solely; but should it not be so, I may shoot half the mess before the other half would give up quizzing me." Revolving such pleasant thoughts, I betook myself to bed, and, what with mulled port and a blazing fire, became once more conscious of being a warm-blooded animal, and fell sound asleep, to dream of doctors, strait-waistcoats, shaved heads, and all the pleasing associations my late companion's narrative so readily suggested.

CHAPTER XV.

MEMS. OF THE NORTH CORK.

AT six o'clock I had the pleasure of presenting the worthy Dr. Finucane to our mess, taking at the same time an opportunity, unobserved by him, to inform three or four of my brother officers that my friend was really a character, abounding in native drollery, and richer in good stories than even the generality of his countrymen.

Nothing could possibly go on better than the early part of the evening. Fin, true to his promise, never once alluded to what I could plainly perceive was ever uppermost in his mind; and what with his fund of humor, quaintness of expression, and quickness at reply, garnished throughout by his most mellifluous brogue, the true "Bocca Corkana," kept us from one roar of laughter to another. It was just as the moment in which his spirits seemed at their highest that I had the misfortune to call upon him for a story which his cousin, Father Malachi, had alluded to on the ever-memorable evening at his house, and which I had a great desire to hear from Fin's own lips. He seemed disposed to escape telling it, and upon my continuing to press my request, dryly remarked,—

"You forget, surely, my dear Mr. Lorrequer, the weak condition I'm in; and these gentlemen here, they don't know what a severe illness I've been laboring under lately, or they would not pass the decanter so freely down this quarter."

I had barely time to throw a mingled look of entreaty and menace across the table when half a dozen others, rightly judging from the doctor's tone and serio-comic expression that his malady had many more symptoms of fun than suffering about it, called out together,—

"Oh, Doctor, by all means tell us the nature of your late attack; pray relate it."

"With Mr. Lorrequer's permission, I'm your slave, gentlemen," said Fin, finishing off his glass.

"Oh! as for me," I cried, "Dr. Finucane has my full permission to detail whatever he pleases to think a fit subject for your amusement."

"Come, then, Doctor, Harry has no objection, you see; so out with it, and we are all prepared to sympathize with your woes and misfortunes, whatever they be."

"Well, I am sure, I never could think of mentioning it without his leave; but now that he sees no objection— Eh, do you, though? If so, then, don't be winking and making faces at me, but say the word, and devil a syllable of it I'll tell to man or mortal."

The latter part of this delectable speech was addressed to
me across the table, in a species of stage whisper, in reply to
some telegraphic signals I had been throwing him, to induce
him to turn the conversation into another channel.

"Then that's enough," continued he, *sotto voce;* "I see you'd
rather I'd not tell it."

"Tell it and be d——d," said I, wearied by the incorrigible pertinacity with which the villain assailed me. My most
unexpected energy threw the whole table into a roar, at the
conclusion of which Fin began his narrative of the mail-coach
adventure.

I need not tell my reader who has followed me throughout in these my "Confessions" that such a story lost nothing
of its absurdity when intrusted to the doctor's powers of
narration. He dwelt with a poet's feeling upon the description
of his own sufferings, and my sincere condolence and commiseration; he touched with the utmost delicacy upon the
distant hints by which he broke the news to me; but when he
came to describe my open and undisguised terror, and my
secret and precipitate retreat to the roof of the coach, there
was not a man at the table that was not convulsed with laughter, and—shall I acknowledge it?—even I myself was unable to withstand the effect, and joined in the general chorus
against myself.

"Well," said the remorseless wretch as he finished his story,
"if ye haven't the hard hearts to laugh at such a melancholy
subject! Maybe, however, you're not so cruel after all; here's
a toast for you: 'A speedy recovery to Cusack Rooney.'"
This was drunk, amid renewed peals, with all the honors, and
I had abundant time before the uproar was over to wish every
man of them hanged. It was to no purpose that I endeavored
to turn the tables by describing Fin's terror at my supposed
resemblance to a highwayman,—his story had the precedence,
and I met nothing during my recital but sly allusions to mad
dogs, muzzles, and doctors; and contemptible puns were let
off on every side at my expense.

"It's little shame I take to myself for the mistake, anyhow,"
said Fin, "for putting the darkness of the night out of the
question, I'm not so sure I would not have ugly suspicions of
you by daylight."

"And besides, Doctor," added I, "it would not be your first blunder in the dark."

"True for you, Mr. Lorrequer," said he, good-humoredly; "and now that I have told them your story, I don't care if they hear mine,—though, maybe, some of ye have heard it already; it's pretty well known in the North Cork."

We all gave our disclaimers on this point, and having ordered in a fresh cooper of port, disposed ourselves in our most easy attitudes while the doctor proceeded as follows:

"It was in the hard winter of the year '99 that we were quartered in Maynooth,—as many said, for our sins; for a more stupid place, the Lord be merciful to it! never were men condemned to. The people at the college were much better off than we; they had whatever was to be got in the country, and never were disturbed by mounting guard or night patrols. Many of the professors were good fellows, that liked grog fully as well as Greek, and understood short whist and five-and-ten quite as intimately as they knew the Vulgate or the Confessions of Saint Augustine. They made no ostentatious display of their pious zeal, but whenever they were not fasting or praying or something of that kind, they were always pleasant and agreeable, and, to do them justice, never refused, by any chance, an invitation to dinner,—no matter at what inconvenience. Well, even this solace to our affliction was soon lost by an unfortunate mistake of that Orange rogue of the world, Major Jones, that gave a wrong pass one night, —Mr. Lorrequer knows the story" (here he alluded to an adventure detailed in an early chapter of my "Confessions"); "and from that day forward we never saw the pleasant faces of the Abbé d'Array or the Professor of the Humanities at the mess. Well, the only thing I could do was just to take an opportunity to drop in at the college in the evening, where we had a quiet rubber of whist and a little social and intellectual conversation, with maybe an oyster and a glass of punch, just to season the thing, before we separated, all done discreetly and quietly; no shouting, or even singing, for the 'superior' had a prejudice about profane songs. Well, one of those nights—it was about the first week in February—I was detained by stress of weather from eleven o'clock, when we usually bade good-night, to past twelve, and then to one o'clock, waiting for a dry moment to get home to the barracks, —a good mile and a half off. Every time old Father Mahony went to look at the weather he came back, saying, 'It's worse it's getting; such a night of rain, glory be to God, never was seen.' So there was no good in going out to be drenched to the skin, and I sat quietly waiting, taking between times a little punch, just not to seem impatient nor distress their rev'rences. At last it struck two, and I thought, 'Well, the decanter is empty now, and I think, if I mean to walk, I've taken enough for the present;' so wishing them all manner of happiness and pleasant dreams, I stumbled my way down-stairs and set out on my journey. I was always in the habit of taking a short cut on my way home across the 'Gurt na brocha,' the priest's meadows, as they call them,—it saved nearly half a mile; although on the present occasion it exposed one wofully to the rain, for there was nothing to shelter under the entire way, not even a tree. Well, out I set in a half trot, for I stayed so late I was pressed for time; besides, I felt it easier to run than to walk,—I'm sure I can't tell why; maybe the drop of drink I took got into my head. Well, I was just jogging on across the common, the rain beating hard in my face, and my clothes pasted to me with the wet; notwith-standing I was singing to myself a verse of an old song to lighten the road, when I heard suddenly a noise near me like a man sneezing. I stopped and listened,—in fact, it was impossible to see your hand, the night was so dark; but I could hear nothing. The thought then came over me, maybe it's something 'not good,' for there were very ugly stories going about what the priests used to do formerly in these meadows; and bones were often found in different parts of them. Just as I was thinking this, another voice came nearer than the last; it might be only a sneeze after all, but in real earnest it was mighty like a groan. 'The Lord be about us!' I said to myself; 'what's this? Have ye the pass?' I cried out. 'Have ye the pass? or what brings ye walking here, *in nomine Patri?*' for I was so confused whether it was a sperit or not, I was going to address him in Latin,—there's nothing equal to the dead languages to lay a ghost, everybody knows. Faith, the moment I said these words, he gave another groan, deeper and more melancholy like than before. 'If it's uneasy ye are,' says I, 'for any neglect of your friends,' for I thought he might be in purgatory longer than he thought convenient, 'tell me what you wish, and go home peaceably out of the rain; for this weather can do no good to living or dead. Go home,' said I; 'and if it's masses ye'd like, I'll give you a day's pay myself, rather than you should fret yourself this way.' The words were not well out of my mouth when he came so near me that the sigh he gave went right through both my ears. 'The Lord be merciful to me!' said I, trembling. 'Amen!' says he, in a husky voice. The moment he said that, my mind was relieved, for I knew it was not a sperit, and I began to laugh heartily at my mistake. 'And who are ye at all,' said I, 'that's roving about at this hour of the night? Ye can't be Father Luke, for I left him asleep on the carpet before I quitted the college; and faith, my friend, if you hadn't the taste for diversion, ye would not be out now.' He coughed then so hard that I could not make out well what he said, but just perceived that he had lost his way on the common, and was a little disguised in liquor. 'It's a good man's case,' said I, 'to take a little too much, though it's what I don't ever do myself; so take a hold of my hand, and I'll see you safe.' I stretched out my hand, and got him, not by the arm, as I hoped, but by the hair of the head, for he was all dripping with wet, and had lost his hat. 'Well, you'll not be better of this night's excursion,' thought I, 'if ye are liable to the rheumatism. And now, whereabouts do you live, my friend? for I'll see you safe before I leave you.' What he said then I never could clearly make out, for the wind and rain were both beating so hard against my face that I could not hear a word; however, I was able just to perceive that he was very much disguised in drink, and spoke rather thick. 'Well, never mind,' said I, 'it's not a time of day for much conversation; so come along, and I'll see you safe to the guard-house, if you can't remember your own place of abode in the meanwhile.' It was just at the moment I said this that I first discovered he was not a gentleman. Well, now, you'd never guess how I did it; and, faith, I always thought it a very 'cute thing of me, and both of us in the dark."

"Well, I really confess it must have been a very difficult

thing, under the circumstances; pray how did you contrive?"
said the Major.

"Just guess how."

"By the tone of his voice, perhaps, and his accent," said
Curzon.

"Devil a bit; for he spoke remarkably well, considering how
far gone he was in liquor."

"Well, probably by the touch of his hand,—no bad test."

"No, you're wrong again, for it was by the hair I had a
hold of him for fear of falling; for he was always stooping
down. Well, you'd never guess it,—it was just by the touch
of his foot."

"His foot! Why, how did that give you any information?"

"There it is now,—that's just what only an Irishman would
ever have made anything out of; for while he was stumbling
about, he happened to tread upon my toes, and never since
I was born did I feel anything like the weight of him. 'Well,'
said I, 'the loss of your hat may give you a cold, my friend,
but upon my conscience you are in no danger of wet feet
with such a pair of strong brogues as you have on you.' Well,
he laughed at that till I thought he'd split his sides, and in
good truth I could not help joining in the fun, although my
foot was smarting like mad; and so we jogged along through
the rain, enjoying the joke just as if we were sitting by a good
fire, with a jorum of punch between us. I am sure I can't
tell you how often we fell that night; but my clothes the next
morning were absolutely covered with mud, and my hat
crushed in two,—for he was so confoundedly drunk it was
impossible to keep him up, and he always kept boring along
with his head down, so that my heart was almost broke in
keeping him upon his legs. I'm sure I never had a more fatiguing march in the whole Peninsula than that blessed mile
and a half; but every misfortune has an end at last, and it was
four o'clock striking by the college clock as we reached the
barracks. After knocking a couple of times and giving the
countersign, the sentry opened the small wicket, and my
heart actually leaped with joy that I had done with my friend;
so I just called out the sergeant of the guard and said, 'Will
you put that poor fellow on the guard-bed till morning? for

I found him on the common, and he could neither find his way home nor tell me where he lived.' 'And where is he?' said the sergeant. 'He's outside the gate there,' said I, 'wet to the skin, and shaking as if he had the ague.' 'And is this him?' said the sergeant, as we went outside. 'It is,' said I; 'maybe you know him.' 'Maybe I've a guess,' said he, bursting into a fit of laughing that I thought he'd choke with. 'Well, Sergeant,' said I, 'I always took you for a humane man; but if that's the way you treat a fellow-creature in distress—' 'A fellow-creature!' said he, laughing louder than before. 'Ay, a fellow-creature,' said I,—for the sergeant was an Orangeman,—'and if he differs from you in matters of religion, sure he's your fellow-creature still.' 'Troth, Doctor, I think there's another trifling difference betune us,' said he. 'Damn your politics,' said I; 'never let them interfere with true humanity.' Wasn't I right, Major? 'Take good care of him, and here's half-a-crown for ye.' So, saying these words, I steered along by the barrack wall, and after a little groping about, got upstairs to my quarters, when, thanks to a naturally good constitution and regular habits of life, I soon fell fast asleep."

When the doctor had said thus much, he pushed his chair slightly from the table, and taking off his wine, looked about him with the composure of a man who has brought his tale to a termination.

"Well, but, Doctor," said the Major, "you are surely not done. You have not yet told us who your interesting friend turned out to be."

"That's the very thing, then, I'm not able to do."

"But of course," said another, "your story does not end there."

"And where the devil would you have it end?" replied he. "Didn't I bring my hero home, and go asleep afterwards myself; and then, with virtue rewarded, how could I finish it better?"

"Oh! of course; but still you have not accounted for a principal character in the narrative," said I.

"Exactly so," said Curzon. "We were all expecting some splendid catastrophe in the morning,—that your companion turned out to be the Duke of Leinster at least, or perhaps a rebel general with an immense price upon his head."

"Neither the one nor the other," said Fin, dryly.

"And do you mean to say there never was any clew to the discovery of him?"

"The entire affair is wrapped in mystery to this hour," said he. "There was a joke about it, to be sure, among the officers, but the North Cork never wanted something to laugh at."

"And what was the joke?" said several voices together.

"Just a complaint from ould Mickey Oulahan, the postmaster, to the Colonel in the morning that some of the officers took away his blind mare off the common, and that the letters were late in consequence."

"And so, Doctor," called out seven or eight, "your friend turned out to be—"

"Upon my conscience they said so, and that rascal the sergeant would take his oath of it; but my own impression I'll never disclose to the hour of my death."

CHAPTER XVI.

THEATRICALS.

OUR *séance* at the mess that night was a late one, for after we had discussed some coopers of claret, there was a very general public feeling in favor of a broiled bone and some devilled kidneys, followed by a very ample bowl of bishop, over which simple condiments we talked "green-room" till near the break of day.

From having been so long away from the corps I had much to learn of their doings and intentions to do, and heard with much pleasure that they possessed an exceedingly handsome theatre, well stocked with scenery, dresses, and decorations, that they were at the pinnacle of public estimation from what they had already accomplished, and calculated on the result of my appearance to crown them with honor. I had, indeed, very little choice left me in the matter; for not only had they booked me for a particular part, but bills were already in circulation, and sundry little three-cornered notes enveloping them were sent to the *élite* of the surrounding country, setting forth that "on Friday evening the committee of the garrison theatricals, intending to perform a dress rehearsal of 'The Family Party,' request the pleasure of Mr. —— and Mrs. ——'s company on the occasion. Mr. Lorrequer will undertake the part of Captain Beaugarde. Supper at twelve. An answer will oblige."

The sight of one of these pleasant little epistles, of which the foregoing is a true copy, was presented to me as a great favor that evening, it having been agreed upon that I was to know nothing of their high and mighty resolves till the following morning. It was to little purpose that I assured them all, collectively and individually, that of Captain Beaugarde I absolutely knew nothing; had never read the piece, nor even seen it performed. I felt, too, that my last appearance in character in a "Family Party" was anything but successful; and I trembled lest, in the discussion of the subject, some confounded allusion to my adventure at Cheltenham might come out. Happily they seemed all ignorant of this; and fearing to bring conversation in any way to the matter of my late travels, I fell in with their humor, and agreed that if it were possible in the limited time allowed me to manage it,—I had but four days,—I should undertake the character. My concurrence failed to give the full satisfaction I expected, and they so habitually did what they pleased with me that, like all men so disposed, I never got the credit for concession which a man more niggardly of his services may always command.

"To be sure you will do it, Harry," said the Major; "why not? I could learn the thing myself in a couple of hours, as for that."

Now, be it known that the aforesaid Major was so incorrigibly slow of study and dull of comprehension that he had been successively degraded at our theatrical board from the delivering of a stage message to the office of check-taker.

"He's so devilish good in the love-scene," said the junior ensign, with the white eyebrows. "I say, Curzon, you'll be confoundedly jealous though, for he is to play with Fanny."

"I rather think not," said Curzon, who was a little tipsy.

"Oh, yes," said Frazer, "Hepton is right. Lorrequer has Fanny for his *première;* and, upon my soul, I should feel tempted to take the part myself upon the same terms,—though

I verily believe I should forget I was acting, and make fierce love to her on the stage."

"And who may *la charmante* Fanny be?" said I, with something of the air of the Dey of Algiers in my tone.

"Let Curzon tell him," said several voices together; "he is the only man to do justice to such perfection."

"Quiz away, my merry men," said Curzon. "All I know is that you are a confoundedly envious set of fellows; and if so lovely a girl had thrown her eyes on one amongst you—"

"Hip! hip! hurrah!" said old Fitzgerald, "Curzon is a gone man. He'll be off to the palace for a license some fine morning, or I know nothing of such matters."

"Well, but," said I, "if matters are really as you all say, why does not Curzon take the part you destine for me?"

"We dare not trust him," said the Major; "Lord bless you, when the call-boy would sing out for Captain Beaugarde in the second act, we'd find that he had levanted with our best slashed trousers and a bird-of-paradise feather in his cap."

"Well," thought I, "this is better at least than I anticipated; for if nothing else offers, I shall have rare fun teasing my friend Charley,"—for it was evident that he had been caught by the lady in question.

"And so you'll stay with us? Give me your hand,—you are a real trump." These words, which proceeded from a voice at the lower end of the table, were addressed to my friend Finucane.

"I'll stay with ye, upon my conscience," said Fin; "ye have a most seductive way about ye, and a very superior taste in milk punch."

"But, Doctor," said I, "you must not be a drone in the hive; what will you do for us? You should be a capital Sir Lucius O'Trigger, if we could get up 'The Rivals.' "

"My forte is the drum,—the big drum; put me among what the Greeks call the *mousikoi,* and I'll astonish ye."

It was at once agreed that Fin should follow the bent of his genius; and after some other arrangements for the rest of the party, we separated for the night, having previously toasted the "Fanny," to which Curzon attempted to reply, but sank, overpowered by punch and feelings, and looked unutterable things, without the power to frame a sentence.

During the time which intervened between the dinner and the night appointed for our rehearsal I had more business upon my hands than a Chancellor of the Exchequer the week of the budget being produced. The whole management of every department fell, as usual, to my share, and all those who, previously to my arrival, had contributed their quota of labor, did nothing whatever now but lounge about the stage, or sit half the day in the orchestra, listening to some confounded story of Finucane's, who contrived to have an everlasting mob of actors, scene-painters, fiddlers, and call-boys always about him, who from their uproarious mirth and repeated shouts of merriment nearly drove me distracted, as I stood almost alone and unassisted in the whole management. Of *la belle* Fanny, all I learned was that she was a professional actress of very considerable talent and extremely pretty; that Curzon had fallen desperately in love with her the only night she had appeared on the boards there; and that, to avoid his absurd persecution of her, she had determined not to come into town until the morning of the rehearsal, she being at that time on a visit to the house of a country gentleman in the neighborhood. Here was a new difficulty I had to contend with,—to go through my part alone was out of the question to making it effective; and I felt so worried and harassed that I often fairly resolved on taking the wings of the mail and flying away to the uttermost parts of the South of Ireland till all was still and tranquil again. By degrees, however, I got matters into better train; and by getting over our rehearsal early before Fin appeared, as he usually slept somewhat later after his night at mess, I managed to have things in something like order,—he and his confounded drum, which, whenever he was not story-telling, he was sure to be practising on, being, in fact, the greatest difficulties opposed to my managerial functions. One property he possessed, so totally at variance with all habits of order that it completely baffled me. So numerous were his narratives that no occasion could possibly arise, no chance expression be let fall on the stage, but Fin had something he deemed *à propos,* and which, *sans façon,* he at once related for the benefit of all whom it might concern,—that was usually the entire *corps dramatique,* who eagerly turned from stage directions and groupings to laugh at his ridiculous jests. I shall give an instance of this habit of interruption, and let the unhappy wight who has filled such an office as mine pity my woes.

I was standing one morning on the stage, drilling my corps as usual. One most refractory spirit, to whom but a few words were intrusted, and who bungled even those, I was endeavoring to train into something like his part.

"Come, now, Elsmore, try it again,—just so. Yes, come forward in this manner,—take her hand tenderly; press it to your lips; retreat towards the flat; and then, bowing deferentially,—thus,—say 'Good night, good night!' That's very simple, eh? Well, now, that's all you have to do, and that brings you over here; so you make your exit at once."

"Exactly so, Mr. Elsmore; always contrive to be near the door under such circumstances. That was the way with my poor friend Curran. Poor Philpot, when he dined with the Guild of Merchant Tailors they gave him a gold box with their arms upon it,—a goose proper with needles saltier-wise, or something of that kind,—and they made him free of their 'ancient and loyal corporation' and gave him a very grand dinner. Well, Curran was mighty pleasant and agreeable, and kept them laughing all night, till the moment he rose to go away, and then he told them that he never spent so happy an evening and all that. 'But, gentlemen,' said he, 'business has its calls; I must tear myself away. So wishing you now' —there were just eighteen of them—'wishing you now every happiness and prosperity, permit me to take my leave'— and here he stole near the door—'to take my leave, and bid you *both* good night.' "

With a running fire of such stories, it may be supposed how difficult was my task in getting anything done upon the stage.

Well, at last the long-expected Friday arrived, and I rose in the morning with all that peculiar *tourbillon* of spirits that a man feels when he is half pleased and whole frightened with the labor before him. I had scarcely accomplished dressing when a servant tapped at my door and begged to know if I could spare a few moments to speak to Miss Ersler, who was in the drawing-room. I replied, of course, in the affirmative, and rightly conjecturing that my fair friend must be the lovely Fanny already alluded to, followed the servant downstairs.

"Mr. Lorrequer," said the servant; and closing the door behind me, left me in sole possession of the lady.

"Will you do me the favor to sit here, Mr. Lorrequer?" said one of the sweetest voices in the world as she made room for me on the sofa beside her. "I am particularly short-sighted; so pray sit near me, as I really cannot talk to any one I don't see."

I blundered out some platitude of a compliment to her eyes,—the fullest and most lovely blue that ever man gazed into,—at which she smiled as if pleased, and continued: "Now, Mr. Lorrequer, I have really been longing for your coming, for your friends of the 4—th are doubtless very dashing, spirited young gentlemen, perfectly versed in war's alarms; but pardon me if I say that a more wretched company of strolling wretches never graced a barn. Now, come, don't be angry, but let me proceed. Like all amateur people, they have the happy knack, in distributing the characters, to put every man in his most unsuitable position; and then that poor dear thing, Curzon,—I hope he's not a friend of yours,— by some dire fatality always plays the lovers' parts, ha! ha! ha! True, I assure you, so that if you had not been announced as coming this week, I should have left them and gone off to Bath."

Here she rose and adjusted her brown ringlets at the glass, giving me ample time to admire one of the most perfect figures I ever beheld. She was most becomingly dressed, and betrayed a foot and ankle which for symmetry and "small-ness" might have challenged the Rue Rivoli itself to match it.

My first thought was poor Curzon; my second, happy and thrice fortunate Harry Lorrequer! There was no time, how-ever, for indulgence in such very pardonable gratulations; so I at once proceeded, *pour faire l'aimable,* to profess my utter inability to do justice to her undoubted talents, but slyly added that in the love-making part of the matter she should never be able to discover that I was not in earnest. We chatted then gayly for upwards of an hour, until the arrival of her friend's carriage was announced, when tender-ing me most graciously her hand, she smiled benignly, and saying, *"Au revoir, donc,"* drove off.

As I stood upon the steps of the hotel, viewing her "out of the visible horizon," I was joined by Curzon, who evidently, from his self-satisfied air and jaunty gait, little knew how he stood in the fair Fanny's estimation.

"Very pretty, very pretty indeed; deeper and deeper still," cried he, alluding to my most courteous salutation as the carriage rounded the corner and its lovely occupant kissed her hand once more. "I say, Harry, my friend, you don't think that was meant for you, I should hope?"

"What! the kiss of the hand? Yes, faith, but I do."

"Well, certainly, that is good! Why, man, she just saw me coming up that instant. She and I,—we understand each other; never mind, don't be cross,—no fault of yours, you know."

"Ah! so she is taken with you," said I, "eh, Charley?"

"Why, I believe that. I may confess to *you* the real state of matters. She was devilishly struck with me the first time we rehearsed together. We soon got up a little flirtation; but the other night, when I played Mirabel to her, it finished the affair. She was quite nervous, and could scarcely go through with her part. I saw it, and upon my soul I am sorry for it; she's a prodigiously fine girl,—such lips and such teeth. Egad! I was delighted when you came; for, you see, I was in a manner obliged to take one line of character, and I saw pretty plainly where it must end. And you know with you it's quite different; she'll laugh and chat and all that sort of thing, but she'll not be carried away by her feelings. You understand me."

"Oh, perfectly; it's quite different, as you observed."

If I had not been supported internally during this short dialogue by the recently expressed opinion of the dear Fanny herself upon my *friend* Curzon's merits, I think I should have been tempted to take the liberty of wringing his neck off. However, the affair was much better as it stood, as I had only to wait a little with proper patience, and I had no fears but that my friend Charley would become the hero of a very pretty episode for the mess.

"So I suppose you must feel considerably bored by this kind of thing," I said, endeavoring to draw him out.

"Why, I do," replied he, "and I do not. The girl is very pretty. The place is dull in the morning, and altogether it helps to fill up time."

"Well," said I, "you are always fortunate, Curzon. You have ever your share of what floating luck the world affords."

"It is not exactly all luck, my dear friend; for, as I shall explain to you—"

"Not now," replied I, "for I have not yet breakfasted." So saying, I turned into the coffee-room, leaving the worthy Adjutant to revel in his fancied conquest and pity such unfortunates as myself.

After an early dinner at the club-house I hastened down to the theatre, where numerous preparations for the night were going forward. The green-room was devoted to the office of a supper-room, to which the audience had been invited. The dressing-rooms were many of them filled with the viands destined for the entertainment, where, among the wooden fowls and "impracticable" flagons, were to be seen very imposing pasties and flasks of champagne littered together in most admirable disorder. The confusion naturally incidental to all private theatricals was tenfold increased by the circumstances of our projected supper. Cooks and scene-shifters, fiddlers and waiters, were most inextricably mingled; and as in all similar cases, the least important functionaries took the greatest airs upon them, and appropriated without hesitation whatever came to their hands. Thus, the cook would not have scrupled to light a fire with the violoncello of the orchestra; and I actually caught one of the "marmitons" making a "soufflé" in a brass helmet I had once worn when astonishing the world as Coriolanus!

Six o'clock struck. "In another short hour and we begin," thought I, with a sinking heart, as I looked upon the littered stage crowded with hosts of fellows that had nothing to do there. Figaro himself never wished for ubiquity more than I did as I hastened from place to place, entreating, cursing, begging, scolding, execrating, and imploring by turns. To mend the matter, the devils in the orchestra had begun to tune their instruments, and I had to bawl like a boatswain of a man-of-war to be heard by the person beside me.

As seven o'clock struck I peeped through the small aperture

in the curtain, and saw, to my satisfaction,—mingled, I confess, with fear,—that the house was nearly filled, the lower tier of boxes entirely so. There were a great many ladies, handsomely dressed, chatting gayly with their chaperons, and I recognized some of my acquaintances on every side; in fact, there was scarcely a family of rank in the county that had not at least some member of it present. As the orchestra struck up the overture to "Don Giovanni," I retired from my place to inspect the arrangements behind.

Before the performance of "The Family Party" we were to have a little one-act piece called "A Day in Madrid," written by myself; the principal characters being expressly composed for "Miss Ersler and Mr. Lorrequer."

The story of this trifle it is not necessary to allude to,—indeed, if it were, I should scarcely have patience to do so, so connected is my recollection of it with the distressing incident which followed.

In the first scene of the piece, the curtain, rising, displays *la belle* Fanny sitting at her embroidery in the midst of a beautiful garden surrounded with statues, fountains, etc.; at the back is seen a pavilion, in the ancient Moorish style of architecture, over which hang the branches of some large and shady trees. She comes forward expressing her impatience at the delay of her lover, whose absence she tortures herself to account for by a hundred different suppositions; and after a very sufficient *exposé* of her feelings, and some little explanatory details of her private history, conveying a very clear intimation of her own amiability and her guardian's cruelty, she proceeds, after the fashion of other young ladies similarly situated, to give utterance to her feelings by a song. After, therefore, a suitable prelude from the orchestra, for which, considering the impassioned state of her mind, she waits patiently, she comes forward and begins a melody,—

" Oh! why is he far from the heart that adores him? "

in which, for two verses, she proceeds with sundry *sol feggi* to account for the circumstances and show her own disbelief of the explanation in a very satisfactory manner. Meanwhile, for I must not expose my reader to an anxiety on my account similar to what the dear Fanny here labored under, I was making the necessary preparations for flying to her presence and clasping her to my heart,—that is to say, I had already gummed on a pair of mustachios, had corked and arched a ferocious pair of eyebrows, which, with my rouged cheeks, gave me a look half Whiskerando, half Grimaldi; these operations were performed, from the stress of circumstances, sufficiently near the object of my affections to afford me the pleasing satisfaction of hearing from her own sweet lips her solicitude about me,—in a word, all the dressing-rooms but two being filled with hampers of provisions, glass, china, and crockery, from absolute necessity I had no other spot where I could attire myself unseen, except in the identical pavilion already alluded to. Here, however, I was quite secure, and had abundant time also; for I was not to appear till scene the second, when I was to come forward in full Spanish costume, "every inch a hidalgo." Meantime, Fanny had been singing, "Oh! why is he far," etc. At the conclusion of the last verse, just as she repeats the words "Why, why, why," in a very distracted and melting cadence, a voice behind startles her; she turns and beholds her guardian,—so, at least, runs the course of events in the real drama; that it should follow thus now, however, *Diis aliter visum,* for just as she came to the very moving apostrophe alluded to, and called out, "Why comes he not?" a gruff voice from behind answered in a strong Cork brogue, "Ah! would ye have him come in a state of nature?" At the instant a loud whistle ran through the house, and the pavilion scene slowly drew up, discovering me, Harry Lorrequer, seated on a small stool before a cracked looking-glass, my only habiliments, as I am an honest man, being a pair of long white-silk stockings and a very richly embroidered shirt with point-lace collar. The shouts of laughter are yet in my ears; the loud roar of inextinguishable mirth which, after the first brief pause of astonishment gave way, shook the entire building. My recollection may well have been confused at such a moment of unutterable shame and misery; yet I clearly remember seeing Fanny, the sweet Fanny herself, fall into an arm-chair nearly suffocated with convulsions of laughter. I cannot go on; what I did I know not. I suppose my exit was additionally ludicrous, for a new *éclat de rire* followed me out. I rushed out of the theatre, and wrapping only my cloak round me, ran without stopping to the barracks. But I must cease; these are woes too sacred for even "Confessions" like mine, so let me close the curtain of my room and my chapter together, and say adieu for a season.

CHAPTER XVII.

THE WAGER.

IT might have been about six weeks after the events detailed in my last chapter had occurred that Curzon broke suddenly into my room one morning before I had risen, and throwing a precautionary glance around, as if to assure himself that we were alone, seized my hand with a most unusual earnestness, and steadfastly looking at me, said:

"Harry Lorrequer, will you stand by me?"

So sudden and unexpected was his appearance at the moment that I really felt but half awake, and kept puzzling myself for an explanation of the scene, rather than thinking of a reply to his question; perceiving which, and auguring but badly from my silence, he continued,—

"Am I, then, really deceived in what I believed to be an old and tried friend?"

"Why, what the devil's the matter?" I cried out. "If you are in a scrape, why of course you know I'm your man; but still, it's only fair to let one know something of the matter in the meanwhile."

"In a scrape!" said he, with a long-drawn sigh intended to beat the whole Minerva Press in its romantic cadence.

"Well, but get on a bit," said I, rather impatiently; "who is the fellow you've got the row with? Not one of ours, I trust?"

"Ah, my dear Hal," said he, in the same melting tone as before, "how your imagination does run upon rows and broils and duelling *rencontres!*" (he, the speaker, be it known to the reader, was the fire-eater of the regiment). "As if life had nothing better to offer than the excitement of a challenge or the mock heroism of a meeting."

As he made a dead pause here, after which he showed no disposition to continue, I merely added,—

"Well, at this rate of proceeding we shall get at the matter in hand on our way out to Corfu, for I hear we are the next regiment for the Mediterranean."

The observation seemed to have some effect in rousing him from his lethargy, and he added,—

"If you only knew the nature of the attachment, and how completely all my future hopes are concerned upon the issue—"

"Ho!" said I; "so it's a money affair, is it? And is it old Watson has issued the writ? I'll bet a hundred on it."

"Well, upon my soul, Lorrequer," said he, jumping from his chair, and speaking with more energy than he had before evinced, "you are, without exception, the most worldly-minded, cold-blooded fellow I ever met. What have I said that could have led you to suppose I had either a duel or a law-suit upon my hands this morning? Learn once and for all, man, that I am in love,—desperately and over head and ears in love."

"*E poi?*" said I, coolly.

"And intend to marry immediately."

"Oh! very well," said I; "the fighting and debt will come later, that's all. But to return,—now for the lady."

"Come, you must make a guess."

"Why, then, I really must confess my utter inability; for your attentions have been so generally and impartially distributed since our arrival here that it may be any fair one, from your venerable partner at whist last evening to Mrs. Henderson, the pastry-cook, inclusive, for whose macaroni and cherry-brandy your feelings have been as warm as they are constant."

"Come, no more quizzing, Hal. You surely must have remarked that lovely girl I waltzed with at Power's ball on Tuesday last."

"Lovely girl! Why, in all seriousness, you don't mean the small woman with the tow wig?"

"No, I do *not* mean any such thing, but a beautiful creature, with the brightest locks in Christendom,—the very light brown waving ringlets Domenichino loved to paint, and a foot— Did you see her foot?"

"No; that was rather difficult, for she kept continually bobbing up and down, like a boy's cork-float in a fishpond."

"Stop there. I shall not permit this any longer; I came not here to listen to—"

"But, Curzon, my boy, you're not angry?"

"Yes, sir, I am angry."

"Why, surely, you have not been serious all this time?"

"And why not, pray?"

"Oh! I don't exactly know,—that is, faith, I scarcely thought you were in earnest, for if I did, of course I should honestly have confessed to you that the lady in question struck me as one of the handsomest persons I ever met."

"You think so really, Hal?"

"Certainly I do; and the opinion is not mine alone,—she is, in fact, universally admired."

"Come, Harry, excuse my bad temper; I ought to have known you better. Give me your hand, old boy, and wish me joy; for, with your aiding and abetting, she is mine to-morrow morning."

I wrung his hand heartily, congratulating myself, meanwhile, how happily I had got out of my scrape; as I now, for the first time, perceived that Curzon was actually in earnest.

"So you will stand by me, Hal?" said he.

"Of course. Only show me how, and I'm perfectly at your service. Anything, from riding postilion on the leaders to officiating as bridesmaid, and I am your man. And if you are in want of such a functionary, I shall stand *in loco parentis* to the lady, and give her away with as much *onction* and tenderness as though I had as many marriageable daughters as King Priam himself. It is with me in marriage as in duelling, —I'll be anything rather than a principal; and I have long since disapproved of either method as a means of 'obtaining satisfaction.'"

"Ah! Harry, I shall not be discouraged by your sneers; you've been rather unlucky, I'm aware. But now to return. Your office on this occasion is an exceedingly simple one; and yet that which I could only confide to one as much my friend as yourself. You must carry my dearest Louisa off."

"Carry her off! Where? when? how?"

"All that I have already arranged, as you shall hear."

"Yes. But first of all please to explain why, if going to run away with the lady, you don't accompany her yourself."

"Ah! I knew you would say that,—I could have laid a wager you'd ask that question; for it is just that very explanation will show all the native delicacy and feminine propriety of my darling Loo. And first I must tell you that old Sir Alfred Jonson, her father, has some confounded prejudice against the army, and never would consent to her marriage with a red-coat; so that, his consent being out of the question, our only resource is an elopement. Louisa consents to this, but only upon one condition, and this she insists upon so firmly—I had almost said obstinately—that, notwithstanding all my arguments and representations, and even entreaties against it, she remains inflexible; so that I have at length yielded, and she is to have her own way."

"Well, and what is the condition she lays such stress upon?"

"Simply this, that we are never to travel a mile together until I obtain my right to do so by making her my wife. She has got some trumpery notions in her head that any slight transgression over the bounds of delicacy made by women before marriage is ever after remembered by the husband to their disadvantage, and she is therefore resolved not to sacrifice her principle even at such a crisis as the present."

"All very proper, I have no doubt; but still, pray explain what I confess appears somewhat strange to me at present. How does so very delicately minded a person reconcile herself to travelling with a perfect stranger under such circumstances?"

"That I can explain perfectly to you. You must know that when my darling Loo consented to take this step, which I induced her to do with the greatest difficulty, she made the proviso I have just mentioned; I at once showed her that I had no maiden aunt or married sister to confide her to at such a moment, and what was to be done? She immediately replied, 'Have you no elderly brother officer, whose years and discretion will put the transaction in such a light as to silence the slanderous tongues of the world? For with such a man I am quite ready and willing to trust myself.' You see I was hard pushed there. What could I do? Whom could I select? Old Hayes, the paymaster, is always tipsy; Jones is five and forty,—but still, if he found out there was thirty thousand pounds in the case, egad! I'm not so sure I'd have found my betrothed at the end of the stage. You were my only hope; I knew I could rely upon you,—you would carry on the whole affair with tact and discretion. And as to age, your stage experience would enable you, with a little assistance from costume, to pass muster,—besides that, I have always represented you as the very Methuselah of the corps; and in the gray dawn of an autumnal morning—with maiden bashfulness assisting—the scrutiny is not likely to be a close one. So now, your consent is alone wanting to complete the arrangements which, before this time to-morrow, shall have made me the happiest of mortals."

Having expressed in fitting terms my full sense of obligation for the delicate flattery with which he pictured me as "Old Lorrequer" to the lady, I begged a more detailed account of his plan, which I shall shorten for my reader's sake, by the following brief *exposé*.

A post-chaise and four was to be in waiting at five o'clock in the morning to convey me to Sir Alfred Jonson's residence, about twelve miles distant. There I was to be met by a lady at the gate-lodge, who was subsequently to accompany me to a small village on the Nore, where an old college friend of Curzon's happened to reside as parson, and by whom the treaty was to be concluded.

This was all simple and clear enough, the only condition necessary to insure success being punctuality, particularly on the lady's part. As to mine, I readily promised my best aid and warmest efforts in my friend's behalf.

"There is only one thing more," said Curzon. "Louisa's younger brother is a devilish hot-headed, wild sort of a fellow, and it would be as well, just for precaution's sake, to have your pistols along with you, if, by any chance, he should make out what was going forward,—not but that you know, if anything serious was to take place, I should be the person to take all that upon my hands."

"Oh! of course, I understand," said I. Meanwhile I could not help running over in my mind the pleasant possibilities such an adventure presented, heartily wishing that Curzon had been content to marry by banns, or any other of the legitimate modes in use, without risking his friend's bones. The other *pros* and *cons* of the matter, with full and accurate directions as to the road to be taken on obtaining possession of the lady, being all arranged, we parted, I to settle my costume and appearance for my first performance in an old man's part, and Curzon to obtain a short leave for a few days from the commanding officer of the regiment.

When we again met, which was at the mess-table, it was not without evidence on either side of that peculiar consciousness which persons feel who have, or think they have, some secret in common which the world wots not of. Curzon's unusually quick and excited manner would at once have struck any close observer as indicating the eve of some important step, no less than continual allusions to whatever was going on, by sly and equivocal jokes and ambiguous jests. Happily, however, on the present occasion, the party were otherwise occupied than watching him, being most profoundly and learnedly engaged in discussing medicine and matters medical with all the acute and accurate knowledge which characterizes such discussions among the non-medical public.

The present conversation originated from some mention our senior surgeon, Fitzgerald, had just made of a consultation which he was invited to attend on the next morning at the distance of twenty miles, and which necessitated him to start at a most uncomfortably early hour. While he continued to deplore the hard fate of such men as himself, so eagerly sought after by the world that their own hours were eternally broken in upon by external claims, the juniors were not sparing of their mirth on the occasion at the expense of the worthy doctor, who, in plain truth, had never been disturbed by a request like the present within any one's memory. Some asserted that the whole thing was a puff got up by Fitz himself, who was only going to have a day's partridge-shooting; others hinting that it was a blind to escape the vigilance of Mrs. Fitzgerald—a well-known virago in the regiment—while Fitz enjoyed himself; and a third party, pretending to sympathize with the doctor, suggested that a hundred pounds would be the least he could possibly be offered for such services as his on so grave an occasion.

"No, no, only fifty," said Fitz, gravely.

"Fifty! Why, you tremendous old humbug, you don't mean to say you'll make fifty pounds before we are out of our beds in the morning?" cried one.

"I'll take your bet on it," said the doctor, who had in this instance reason to suppose his fee would be a large one.

During this discussion the claret had been pushed round rather freely; and fully bent as I was upon the adventure before me, I had taken my share of it as a preparation. I thought of the amazing prize I was about to be instrumental in securing for my friend,—for the lady had really thirty thousand pounds,—and I could not conceal my triumph at such a prospect of success in comparison with the meaner object of ambition. They all seemed to envy poor Fitzgerald. I struggled with my secret for some time; but my pride and the claret together got the better of me, and I called out, "Fifty pounds on it, then, that before ten to-morrow morning I'll make a better hit of it than you, and the mess shall decide between us afterwards as to the winner. And if you will," said I, seeing some reluctance on Fitz's part to take the wager, and getting emboldened in consequence, "let the judgment be pronounced over a couple of dozen of champagne, paid by the loser."

This was a *coup d'état* on *my* part, for I knew at once there were so many parties to benefit by the bet, terminate which way it might, there could be no possibility of evading it. My device succeeded, and poor Fitzgerald, fairly badgered into a wager, the terms of which he could not in the least comprehend, was obliged to sign the conditions inserted in the Adjutant's note-book, his greatest hope in so doing being in the quantity of wine he had seen me drink during the evening. As for myself, the bet was no sooner made than I began to think upon the very little chance I had of winning it; for even supposing my success perfect in the department allotted to me, it might with great reason be doubted what peculiar benefit I myself derived as a counterbalance to the fee of the doctor. For this, my only trust lay in the justice of a de-

cision which I conjectured would lean more towards the goodness of a practical joke than the equity of the transaction.
The party at mess soon after separated, and I wished my
friend good-night for the last time before meeting him as a
bridegroom.

I arranged everything in order for my start. My pistol-
case I placed conspicuously before me, to avoid being forgotten in the haste of departure; and having ordered my servant to sit up all night in the guard-room until he heard
the carriage at the barrack-gate, threw myself on my bed, but
not to sleep. The adventure I was about to engage in suggested to my mind a thousand associations, into which many
of the scenes I have already narrated entered. I thought
how frequently I had myself been on the verge of that state
which Curzon was about to try, and how it always happened
that when nearest to success failure had intervened. From
my very schoolboy days, my love adventures had the same unfortunate abruptness in their issue; and there seemed to be
something very like a fatality in the invariable unsuccess of my
efforts at marriage. I feared, too, that my friend Curzon
had placed himself in very unfortunate hands, if augury were
to be relied upon. "Something will surely happen," thought
I, "from my confounded ill luck, and all will be blown up."
Wearied at last with thinking, I fell into a sound sleep for
about three quarters of an hour, at the end of which I was
awoke by my servant informing me that a chaise and four
was drawn up at the end of the barrack lane.

"Why, surely they are too early, Stubbes? It's only four
o'clock."

"Yes, sir; but they say that the road for eight miles is very
bad, and they must go it almost at a walk."

"That is certainly pleasant," thought I; "but I'm in for it
now, so can't help it."

In a few minutes I was up and dressed, and so perfectly
transformed by the addition of a brown scratch-wig and large
green spectacles and a deep-flapped waistcoat that my servant,
on re-entering my room, could not recognize me. I followed
him now across the barrack-yard, as with my pistol-case under
one arm, and a lantern in his hand, he proceeded to the barrack-gate.

As I passed beneath the Adjutant's window I saw a light; the sash was quickly thrown open, and Curzon appeared.

"Is that you, Harry?"

"Yes; when do you start?"

"In about two hours. I've only eight miles to go; you have upwards of twelve, and no time to lose. Success attend you, my boy! We'll meet soon."

"Here's the carriage, sir; this way."

"Well, my lads, you know the road, I suppose?"

"Every inch of it, your honor's glory,—we're always coming in for doctors and 'pothecaries; they're never a week without them."

I was soon seated, the door clapped to, the words "all right" given, and away we went.

Little as I had slept during the night, my mind was too much occupied with the adventure I was engaged in to permit any thoughts of sleep now, so that I had abundant opportunity afforded me of pondering over all the bearings of the case with much more of deliberation and caution than I had yet bestowed upon it. One thing was certain, whether success did or did not attend our undertaking, the risk was mine and mine only; and if by any accident the affair should be already known to the family, I stood a very fair chance of being shot by one of the sons, or stoned to death by the tenantry, while my excellent friend Curzon should be eating his breakfast with his reverend friend and only interrupting himself in his fourth muffin to wonder "what could keep them." And besides, for minor miseries will, like the blue devils in "Don Giovanni," thrust up their heads among their better-grown brethren, my fifty-pound bet looked rather blue; for even under the most favorable light considered, however Curzon might be esteemed a gainer, it might well be doubted how far I had succeeded better than the doctor when producing his fee in evidence. Well, well, I'm in for it now; but it certainly is strange all these very awkward circumstances never struck me so forcibly before. And, after all, it was not quite fair of Curzon to put any man forward in such a transaction,—the more so as such a representation might be made of it at the Horse Guards as to stop a man's promotion, or seriously affect his prospects for life; and I at last began to convince myself that many a man so placed would carry the lady off himself, and leave the Adjutant to settle the affair with the family. For two mortal hours did I conjure up every possible disagreeable contingency that might arise. My being mulcted of my fifty, and laughed at by the mess, seemed inevitable, even were I fortunate enough to escape a duel with the fire-eating brother. Meanwhile a thick, misty rain continued to fall, adding so much to the darkness of the early hour that I could see little of the country about me, and knew nothing of where I was.

Troubles are like laudanum, a small dose only excites, a strong one sets you to sleep,—not a very comfortable sleep, mayhap, but still it is sleep, and often very sound sleep; so it now happened with me. I had pondered over, weighed, and considered all the *pros, cons,* turnings, and windings of this awkward predicament, till I had fairly convinced myself that I was on the high road to a confounded scrape; and then, having established that fact to my entire satisfaction, I fell comfortably back in the chaise and sank into a most profound slumber.

If to any of my readers I may appear here to have taken a very despondent view of this whole affair, let him only call to mind my invariable ill luck in such matters, and how always it had been my lot to see myself on the fair road to success only up to that point at which it is certain; besides— But why explain? These are my "Confessions." I may not alter what are matters of fact, and my reader must only take me with all the imperfections of wrong motives and headlong impulses upon my head, or abandon me at once.

Meanwhile the chaise rolled along, and the road being better and the pace faster, my sleep became more easy; thus about an hour and a half after I had fallen asleep passed rapidly over, when the sharp turning of an angle disturbed me from my leaning position, and I awoke. I started up and rubbed my eyes; several seconds elapsed before I could think where I was or whither going. Consciousness at last came, and I perceived that we were driving up a thickly-planted avenue. Why, confound it, they can't have mistaken it, thought I, or are we really going up to the house instead of waiting at the lodge? I at once lowered the sash, and stretching out my head, cried out, "Do you know what ye are about, lads,—is this all right?" but unfortunately, amid the rattling of the gravel and the clatter of the horses, my words were unheard; and thinking I was addressing a request to go faster, the villains cracked their whips, and breaking into a full gallop, before five minutes flew over, they drew up with a jerk at the foot of a long portico to a large and spacious cut-stone mansion. When I rallied from the sudden check, which had nearly thrown me through the window, I gave myself up for lost; here I was, *vis-à-vis* the very hall-door of the man whose daughter I was about to elope with,—whether so placed by the awkwardness and blundering of the wretches who drove me, or delivered up by their treachery, it mattered not, my fate seemed certain; before I had time to determine upon any line of acting in this confounded dilemma, the door was jerked open by a servant in sombre livery, who, protruding his head and shoulders into the chaise, looked at me steadily for a moment and said, "Ah! then, Doctor, darlin', but ye're welcome." With the speed with which sometimes the bar of an air long since heard, or the passing glance of an old familiar face can call up the memory of our very earliest childhood bright and vivid before us, did that one single phrase explain the entire mystery of my present position, and I saw in one rapid glance that I had got into the chaise intended for Dr. Fitzgerald, and was absolutely, at that moment, before the hall-door of the patient. My first impulse was an honest one to avow the mistake and retrace my steps, taking my chance to settle with Curzon, whose matrimonial scheme I foresaw was doomed to the untimely fate of all those I had ever been concerned in. My next thought—how seldom is the adage true which says that "second thoughts are best!" —was upon my luckless wager; for even supposing that Fitzgerald should follow me in the other chaise, yet as I had the start of him, if I could only pass muster for half an hour, I might secure the fee and evacuate the territory. Besides that, there was a great chance of Fitz's having gone on *my* errand, while I was journeying on *his,* in which case I should be safe from interruption. Meanwhile, Heaven only could tell what his interference in poor Curzon's business might not involve. These serious reflections took about ten seconds to pass through my mind as the grave-looking old servant proceeded to encumber himself with my cloak and my pistol-case, remarking as he lifted the latter, "And may the Lord grant ye won't want the instruments this time, Doctor, for they say he is better this morning." Heartily wishing amen to the benevolent prayer of the honest domestic for more reasons than one, I descended leisurely, as I conjectured a doctor ought to do, from the chaise, and with a solemn pace and grave demeanor followed him into the house.

In the small parlor to which I was ushered sat two gentlemen somewhat advanced in years, who I rightly supposed were my medical *confrères*. One of these was a tall, pale, ascetic-looking man, with gray hair and retreating forehead, slow in speech and lugubrious in demeanor. The other, his antithesis, was a short, rosy-cheeked, apoplectic-looking subject, with a laugh like a suffocating wheeze, and a paunch like an alderman, his quick, restless eye and full nether lip denoting more of the *bon vivant* than the abstemious disciple of Æsculapius. A moment's glance satisfied me that if I had only these to deal with, I was safe, for I saw that they were of the stamp of country practitioner,—half-physician, half-apothecary,—who rarely come in contact with the higher orders of their art, and then only to be dictated to, obey, and grumble.

"Doctor, may I beg to intrude myself, Mr. Phipps, on your notice? Dr. Phipps, or Mr., it's all one; but I have only a license in pharmacy, though they call me doctor. Surgeon Riley, sir, a very respectable practitioner," said he, waving his hand towards his rubicund *confrère*.

I at once expressed the great happiness it afforded me to meet such highly informed and justly celebrated gentlemen; and fearing every moment the arrival of the real Simon Pure should cover me with shame and disgrace, begged they would afford me, as soon as possible, some history of the case we were convened for. They accordingly proceeded to expound, in a species of duet, some curious particulars of an old gentleman who had the evil fortune to have them for his doctors, and who labored under some swelling of the neck which they differed as to the treatment of, and in consequence of which the aid of a third party (myself, Heaven bless the mark!) was requested.

As I could by no means divest myself of the fear of Fitz's arrival, I pleaded the multiplicity of my professional engagements as a reason for at once seeing the patient; upon which I was conducted upstairs by my two brethren, and introduced to a half-lighted chamber. In a large easy-chair sat a florid-looking old man, with a face in which pain and habitual ill-temper had combined to absorb every expression.

"This is the doctor of the regiment, sir, that you desired to see," said my tall coadjutor.

"Oh! then, very well; good-morning, sir. I suppose you will find out something new the matter, for them two there have been doing so every day this two months."

"I trust, sir," I replied stiffly, "that with the assistance of my learned friends much may be done for you. Ha! hem! so this is the malady. Turn your head a little to that side." Here an awful groan escaped the sick man, for I, it appears, had made considerable impression upon rather a delicate part, —not unintentionally, I must confess; for as I remembered Hoyle's maxim at whist, "when in doubt play a trump," so I thought it might be true in physic, when posed by a difficulty, to do a bold thing also. "Does that hurt you, sir?" said I, in a soothing and affectionate tone of voice.

"Like the devil," growled the patient.

"And here?" said I.

"Oh! oh! I can't bear it any longer."

"Oh! I perceive," said I, "the thing is just as I expected." Here I raised my eyebrows, and looked indescribably wise at my *confrères*.

"No aneurism, Doctor," said the tall one.

"Certainly not."

"Maybe," said the short man, "maybe it's a stay-at-home-with-us tumor after all,"—so at least he appeared to pronounce a confounded technical, which I afterwards learned was "steatomatous." Conceiving that my rosy friend was disposed to jeer at me, I gave him a terrific frown and resumed, "This must not be touched."

"So you won't operate upon it," said the patient.

"I would not take a thousand pounds to do so," I replied.

"Now, if you please, gentlemen," said I, making a step towards the door, as if to withdraw for consultation; upon which they accompanied me downstairs to the breakfast-room. As it was the only time in my life I had performed in this character, I had some doubts as to the propriety of indulging a very hearty breakfast appetite, not knowing if it were unprofessional to eat; but from this doubt my learned friends speedily relieved me, by the entire devotion which they bestowed for about twenty minutes upon ham, rolls, eggs, and cutlets, barely interrupting these important occupations by sly allusions to the old gentleman's malady and his chance of recovery.

"Well, Doctor," said the pale one, as at length he rested from his labors, "what are we to do?"

"Ay," said the other, "there's the question."

"Go on," said I, "go on as before; I can't advise you better." Now, this was a deep stroke of mine, for up to the present moment I did not know what treatment they were practising; but it looked a shrewd thing to guess it, and it certainly was civil to approve of it.

"So you think that will be best?"

"I am certain that I know nothing better," I answered.

"Well, I'm sure, sir, we have every reason to be gratified for the very candid manner in which you have treated us. Sir, I'm your most obedient servant," said the fat one.

"Gentlemen, both your good healths and professional success also." Here I swallowed a glass of brandy, thinking all the while there were worse things than the practice of physic.

"I hope you are not going?" said one, as my chaise drew up at the door.

"Business calls me," said I, "and I can't help it."

"Could not you manage to see our friend here again in a day or two?" said the rosy one.

"I fear it will be impossible," replied I; "besides, I have a notion he may not desire it."

"I have been commissioned to hand you this," said the tall doctor, with a half sigh, as he put a check into my hand.

I bowed slightly, and stuffed the crumpled paper with a half-careless air into my waistcoat pocket; and wishing them both every species of happiness and success, shook hands four times with each, and drove off, never believing myself safe till I saw the gate-lodge behind me, and felt myself flying on the road to Kilkenny at about twelve miles Irish an hour.

CHAPTER XVIII.

.THE ELOPEMENT.

IT was past two o'clock when I reached the town. On entering the barrack-yard I perceived a large group of officers chatting together, and every moment breaking into immoderate fits of laughter. I went over and immediately learned the source of their mirth, which was this. No sooner had it been known that Fitzgerald was about to go to a distance on a professional call than a couple of young officers laid their heads together and wrote an anonymous note to Mrs. Fitz, who was the very dragon of jealousy, informing her that her husband had feigned the whole history of the patient and consultation as an excuse for absenting himself on an excursion of gallantry, and that if she wished to satisfy herself of the truth of the statement she had only to follow him in the morning and detect his entire scheme; the object of these amiable friends being to give poor Mrs. Fitz a twenty miles' jaunt, and confront her with her injured husband at the end of it.

Having a mind actively alive to suspicions of this nature, the worthy woman made all her arrangements for a start; and scarcely was the chaise-and-four, with her husband, out of the town than she was on the track of it, with a heart bursting with jealousy, and vowing vengeance to the knife against all concerned in this scheme to wrong her.

So far the plan of her persecutors had perfectly succeeded; they saw her depart on a trip of, as they supposed, twenty miles, and their whole notions of the practical joke were limited to the *éclaircissement* that must ensue at the end. Little, however, were they aware how much more near the suspected crime was the position of the poor doctor to turn out; for as, by one blunder, I had taken his chaise, so he, without any inquiry whatever, had got into the one intended for me, and never awoke from a most refreshing slumber till shaken by the shoulder by the postilion, who whispered in his ear, "Here we are, sir; this is the gate."

"But why stop at the gate? Drive up the avenue, my boy."

"His honor told me, sir, not for the world to go farther than the lodge, nor to make as much noise as a mouse."

"Ah! very true. He may be very irritable, poor man! Well, stop here, and I'll get out."

Just as the doctor had reached the ground, a very smart-looking soubrette tripped up and said to him,—

"Beg pardon, sir, but you are the gentleman from the barrack, sir?"

"Yes, my dear," said Fitz, with a knowing look at the pretty face of the damsel; "what can I do for you?"

"Why, sir, my mistress is here in the shrubbery; but she is so nervous and so frightened, I don't know she'll go through it."

"Ah! she's frightened, poor thing, is she? Oh! she must keep up her spirits; while there's life there's hope."

"Sir?"

"I say, my darling, she must not give way. I'll speak to her a little. Is not *he* rather advanced in life?"

"Oh, Lord, no, sir! Only two and thirty, my mistress tells me."

"Two and thirty! Why, I thought he was above sixty."

"Above sixty! Law, sir, you have a bright fancy! This is the gentleman, ma'am. Now, sir, I'll just slip aside for a moment and let you talk to her."

"I am grieved, ma'am, that I have not the happiness to make your acquaintance under happier circumstances."

"I must confess, sir, though I am ashamed—"

"Never be ashamed, ma'am; your grief, although I trust causeless, does you infinite honor.—Upon my soul, she is rather pretty," said the doctor to himself here.

"Well, sir, as I have the most perfect confidence in you, from all I have heard of you, I trust you will not think me abrupt in saying that any longer delay here is dangerous."

"Dangerous! Is he in so critical a state as that, then?"

"Critical a state, sir,—why, what do you mean?"

"I mean, ma'am, do you think, then, it must be done to-day?"

"Of course I do, sir; and I shall never leave the spot without your assuring me of it."

"Oh! in that case make your mind easy; I have the instruments in the chaise."

"The instruments in the chaise! Really, sir, if you are not jesting,—I trust you don't think this is a fitting time for such, —I entreat of you to speak more plainly and intelligibly."

"Jesting, ma'am! I'm incapable of jesting at such a moment."

"Ma'am, ma'am! I see one of the rangers, ma'am, at a distance; so don't lose a moment, but get into the chaise at once."

"Well, sir, let us away; for I have now gone too far to retract."

"Help my mistress into the chaise, sir. Lord! what a man it is."

A moment more saw the poor doctor seated beside the young lady, while the postilions plied whip and spur with their best energy, and the road flew beneath them. Meanwhile the delay caused by the short dialogue enabled Mrs. Fitz's slower conveyance to come up with the pursuit, and her chaise had just turned the angle of the road as she caught a glimpse of a muslin dress stepping into the carriage with her husband.

There are no words capable of conveying the faintest idea of the feelings that agitated Mrs. Fitz at this moment. The fullest confirmation to her worst fears was before her eyes,— just at the very instant when a doubt was beginning to cross over her mind that it might have been merely a hoax that was practised on her, and that the worthy doctor was innocent and blameless. As for the poor doctor himself, there seemed little chance of his being enlightened as to the real state of matters; for from the moment the young lady had taken her place in the chaise, she had buried her face in her hands and sobbed continually. Meanwhile he concluded that they were approaching the house by some back entrance to avoid noise and confusion, and waited with due patience for the journey's end.

As, however, her grief continued unabated, Fitz at length

began to think of the many little consolatory acts he had successfully practised in his professional career, and was just insinuating some very tender speech on the score of resignation, with his head inclined towards the weeping lady beside him, when the chaise of Mrs. Fitz came up alongside, and the postilions having yielded to the call to halt, drew suddenly up, displaying to the enraged wife the *tableau* we have mentioned.

"So, wretch!" she screamed rather than spoke, "I have detected you at last."

"Lord bless me! Why, it is my wife."

"Yes, villain! your injured, much-wronged wife! And you, madam, may I ask what have you to say for thus eloping with a married man?"

"Shame! My dear Jemima," said Fitz, "how can you possibly permit your foolish jealousy so far to blind your reason? Don't you see I am going upon a professional call?"

"Oh, you are, are you? Quite professional, I'll be bound!"

"Oh, sir, oh, madam, I beseech you, save me from the anger of my relatives and the disgrace of exposure! Pray take me back at once."

"Why, Heavens! ma'am, what do *you* mean? You are not gone mad, as well as my wife!"

"Really, Mr. Fitz," said Mrs. F., "this is carrying the joke too far. Take your unfortunate victim—as I suppose she is such—home to her parents, and prepare to accompany me to the barrack; and if there be law and justice in—"

"Well! may the Lord in his mercy preserve my senses, or you will both drive me clean mad."

"Oh, dear! oh, dear!" sobbed the young lady, while Mrs. Fitzgerald continued to upbraid at the top of her voice, heedless of the disclaimers and protestations of innocence poured out with the eloquence of despair by the poor doctor. Matters were in this state when a man dressed in a fustian jacket, like a groom, drove up to the side of the road in a tax-cart; he immediately got down, and tearing open the door of the doctor's chaise, lifted out the young lady and deposited her safely in his own conveyance, merely adding,—

"I say, master, you're in luck this morning that Mr. William took the lower road; for if *he* had come up with you instead of me, he'd blow the roof off your skull, that's all."

While these highly satisfactory words were being addressed to poor Fitz, Mrs. Fitzgerald had removed from her carriage to that of her husband,—perhaps preferring four horses to two; or perhaps she had still more unexplained views of the transaction, which might as well be told on the road homeward.

Whatever might have been the nature of Mrs. F.'s dissertation, nothing is known. The chaise containing these turtle-doves arrived late at night at Kilkenny, and Fitz was installed safely in his quarters before any one knew of his having come back. The following morning he was reported ill, and for three weeks he was but once seen, and at that time only at his window, with a flannel nightcap on his head, looking particularly pale, and rather dark under one eye.

As for Curzon, the last thing known of him that luckless morning was his hiring a post-chaise for the Royal Oak, from whence he posted to Dublin, and hastened on to England. In a few days we learned that the Adjutant had exchanged into a regiment in Canada; and to this hour there are not three men in the 4—th who know the real secret of that morning's misadventures.

CHAPTER XIX.

DETACHMENT DUTY.—AN ASSIZE TOWN.

AS there appeared to be but little prospect of poor Fitzgerald ever requiring any explanation from me as to the events of that morning, for he feared to venture from his room lest he might be recognized and prosecuted for abduction, I thought it better to keep my own secret also; and it was therefore with a feeling of anything but regret that I received an order, which under other circumstances would have rendered me miserable, to march on detachment duty. To any one at all conversant with the life we lead in the army, I need not say how unpleasant such a change usually is. To surrender your capital mess with all its well-appointed equipments, your jovial brother officers, your West India Madeira, your cool Lafitte, your daily, hourly, and half-hourly flirta-

tions with the whole female population,—never a deficient
one in a garrison town,—not to speak of your matches at trotting, coursing, and pigeon-shooting, and a hundred other delectable modes of getting over the ground through life till
it please your ungrateful country and the Horse Guards to
make you a major-general,—to surrender all these, I say, for
the noise, dust, and damp disagreeables of a country inn, with
bacon to eat, whiskey to drink, and the priest or the constabu-
lary chief to get drunk with (I speak of Ireland here), and
your only affair *par amours* being the occasional ogling of
the apothecary's daughter opposite as often as she visits the
shop in the exciting occupation of measuring out garden seeds
and senna. These are, indeed, the exchanges, with a difference, for which there is no compensation; and for my own
part, I never went upon such duty that I did not exclaim
with the honest Irishman when the mail went over him, "O
Lord! what is this for?" firmly believing that in the earthly
purgatory of such duties I was reaping the heavy retribution
attendant on past offences.

Besides, from being rather a crack man in my corps, I
thought it somewhat hard that my turn for such duty should
come round about twice as often as that of my brother officers. But so it is; I never knew a fellow a little smarter
than his neighbors that was not pounced upon by his colonel
for a victim. Now, however, I looked at these matters in a
very different light. To leave headquarters was to escape
being questioned; while there was scarcely any post to which
I could be sent where something strange or adventurous
might not turn up and serve me to erase the memory of the
past and turn the attention of my companions in any quarter
rather than towards myself.

My orders on the present occasion were to march to Clon-
mel, from whence I was to proceed a short distance to the
house of a magistrate upon whose information, transmitted
to the Chief Secretary, the present assistance of a military
party had been obtained; and not without every appearance
of reason. The assizes of the town were about to be held,
and many capital offences stood for trial in the calendar; and
as it was strongly rumored that in the event of certain convictions being obtained, a rescue would be attempted, a gen-

eral attack upon the town seemed a too natural consequence; and if so, the house of so obnoxious a person as him I have alluded to would be equally certain of being assailed. Such, at least, is too frequently the history of such scenes. Beginning with no one definite object,—sometimes a slight one,—more ample views and wider conceptions of mischief follow, and what has begun in a drunken riot, a casual *rencontre,* may terminate in the slaughter of a family or the burning of a village. The finest peasantry—God bless them!—are a quick people, and readier at taking a hint than most others, and have, withal, a natural taste for fighting that no acquired habits of other nations can pretend to vie with.

As the worthy person to whose house I was now about to proceed was, and, if I am rightly informed, is, rather a remarkable character in the local history of Irish politics, I may as well say a few words concerning him. Mr. Joseph Larkins, Esq.,—for so he signed himself,—had only been lately elevated to the bench of magistrates. He was originally one of that large but intelligent class called in Ireland "small farmers," remarkable chiefly for a considerable tact in driving hard bargains, a great skill in wethers, a rather national dislike to pay all species of imposts, whether partaking of the nature of tax, tithe, grand jury cess, or anything of that nature whatsoever. So very accountable—I had almost said (for I have been long quartered in Ireland) so very laudable—a propensity excited but little of surprise or astonishment in his neighbors, the majority of whom entertained very similar views,—none, however, possessing anything like the able and lawyer-like ability of the worthy Larkins for the successful evasion of these inroads upon the liberty of the subject. Such, in fact, was his talent, and so great his success in this respect, that he had established what, if it did not actually amount to a statute of exemption in law, served equally well in reality; and for several years he enjoyed a perfect immunity on the subject of money-paying in general. His "little houldin'," as he unostentatiously called some five hundred acres of bog, mountain, and sheep-walk, lay in a remote part of the county; the roads were nearly impassable for several miles in that direction; land was of little value; the agent was a timid man with a large family; of three tithe-proctors who had penetrated into the forbidden territory, two labored under a dyspepsia for life, not being able to digest parchment and sealing-wax, for they usually dined on their own writs, and the third gave five pounds out of his pocket to a large, fresh-looking man, with brown whiskers and beard, that concealed him two nights in a hayloft to escape the vengeance of the people,—which act of philanthropy should never be forgotten, if some ill-natured people were not bold enough to say that the kind individual in question was no other man than Larkins himself.

However this may be, true it is that this was the last attempt made to bring within the responsibilities of the law so refractory a subject; and so powerful is habit that although he was to be met with at every market and cattle-fair in the county, an arrest of his person was no more contemplated than if he enjoyed the privilege of parliament to go at large without danger.

When the country became disturbed, and nightly meetings of the peasantry were constantly held, followed by outrages against life and property to the most frightful extent, the usual resources of the law were employed unavailingly. It was in vain to offer high rewards; approvers could not be found; and so perfectly organized were the secret associations that few beyond the very ringleaders knew anything of consequence to communicate. Special commissions were sent down from Dublin, additional police force, detachments of military; long correspondences took place between the magistracy and the government. But all in vain, the disturbances continued, and at last to such a height had they risen that the country was put under martial law; and even this was ultimately found perfectly insufficient to repel what now daily threatened to become an open rebellion rather than mere agrarian disturbance. It was at this precise moment, when all resources seemed to be fast exhausting themselves, that certain information reached the Castle of the most important nature. The individual who obtained and transmitted it had perilled his life in so doing; but the result was a great one,—no less than the capital conviction and execution of seven of the most influential amongst the disaffected peasantry. Confidence was at once shaken in the secrecy of their associates; distrust and suspicion followed. Many of the boldest sank beneath the fear of betrayal, and themselves became evidence for the Crown; and in five months a county abounding in midnight meetings and blazing with insurrectionary fires became almost the most tranquil in its province. It may well be believed that he who rendered this important service on this trying emergency could not be passed over, and the name of J. Larkins soon after appeared in the "Gazette" as one of his Majesty's justices of the peace for the county,—pretty much in the same spirit in which a country gentleman converts the greatest poacher in his neighborhood by making him his gamekeeper.

In person he was a large and powerfully built man, considerably above six feet in height, and possessing great activity, combined with powers of enduring fatigue almost incredible. With an eye like a hawk and a heart that never knew fear, he was the person of all others calculated to strike terror into the minds of the country people. The reckless daring with which he threw himself into danger, the almost impetuous quickness with which he followed up a scent whenever information reached him of an important character, had their full effect upon a people who, long accustomed to the slowness and the uncertainty of the law, were almost paralyzed at beholding detection and punishment follow on crime as certainly as the thunder-crash follows the lightning.

His great instrument for this purpose was the obtaining information from sworn members of the secret societies, and whose names never appeared in the course of a trial or a prosecution until the measure of their iniquity was completed, when they usually received a couple of hundred pounds blood-money, as it was called, with which they took themselves away to America or Australia,—their lives being only secured while they remained by the shelter afforded them in the magistrate's own house. And so it happened that constantly there numbered from ten to twelve of these wretches, inmates of his family, each of whom had the burden of participation in one murder at least, waiting for an opportunity to leave the country unmolested and unwatched.

Such a frightful and unnatural state of things can hardly be conceived; and yet, shocking as it was, it was a relief to that which led to it. I have dwelt, perhaps, too long upon this painful subject; but let my reader now accompany me a little farther, and the scene shall be changed. Does he see that long, low white house, with a tall, steep roof, perforated with innumerable narrow windows? There are a few straggling beech-trees upon a low, bleak-looking field before the house, which is called by courtesy the lawn; a pig or two, some geese, and a tethered goat are here and there musing over the state of Ireland; while some rosy, curly-headed, noisy, and bare-legged urchins are gambolling before the door. This is the dwelling of the worshipful justice, to which myself and my party were now approaching with that degree of activity which attends on most marches of twenty miles under the oppressive closeness of a day in autumn. Fatigued and tired as I was, yet I could not enter the little enclosure before the house without stopping for a moment to admire the view before me. It was a large tract of rich country, undulating on every side, and teeming with corn-fields in all the yellow gold of ripeness; here and there, almost hid by small clumps of ash and alder, were scattered some cottages, from which the blue smoke rose in a curling column into the calm evening sky. All was graceful and beautifully tranquil, and you might have selected the picture as emblematic of that happiness and repose we so constantly associate with our ideas of the country; and yet before that sun had even set which now gilded the landscape, its glories would be replaced by the lurid glare of nightly incendiarism and— But here, fortunately for my reader, and perhaps myself, I am interrupted in my meditations by a rich, mellifluous accent, saying, in the true Doric of the South,—

"Mr. Lorrequer, you're welcome to Curryglass, sir! You've had a hot day for your march. Maybe you'd take a taste of sherry before dinner? Well, then, we'll not wait for Molowny, but order it up at once."

So saying, I was ushered into a long, low drawing-room, in which were collected together about a dozen men, to whom I was specially and severally presented, and among whom I was happy to find my boarding-house acquaintance, Mr. Daly, who, with the others, had arrived that same day for the assizes, and who were all members of the legal profession, either barristers, attorneys, or clerks of the peace.

The hungry aspect of the guests, no less than the speed
with which dinner made its appearance after my arrival,
showed me that my coming was only waited for to complete
the party, the Mr. Molowny before alluded to being unani-
mously voted present. The meal itself had but slight pretensions to elegance,—there were no delicacies of Parisian
taste, no triumphs of French cookery; but in their place stood
a lordly fish of some five and twenty pounds weight, a massive sirloin, with all the usual armament of fowls, ham,
pigeon-pie, beefsteak, etc., lying in rather a promiscuous order
along either side of the table. The party were evidently disposed to be satisfied, and I acknowledge I did not prove an
exception to the learned individuals about me, either in my
relish for the good things, or my appetite to enjoy them.
Dulce est desipere in loco, says some one,—by which I suppose is meant that a rather slang company is occasionally
good fun. Whether from my taste for the "humanities" or
not, I am unable to say, but certainly in my then humor I
should not have exchanged my position for one of much
greater pretensions to elegance and *ton*. There was first a
general onslaught upon the viands, crashing of plates, jingling of knives, mingling with requests for "more beef," "the
hard side of the salmon," or "another slice of ham." Then
came a dropping fire of drinking wine, which quickly increased, the decanters of sherry for about ten minutes resting
upon the table about as long as Taglioni touches this mortal
earth in one of her flying movements. Acquaintances were
quickly formed between the members of the Bar and myself,
and I found that my momentary popularity was likely to
terminate in my downfall; for as each introduction was followed by a bumper of strong sherry, I did not expect to last
till the end of the feast. The cloth at length disappeared, and
I was just thanking Providence for the respite from hob-
nobbing which I imagined was to follow, when a huge square
decanter of whiskey appeared, flanked by an enormous jug
of boiling water, and renewed preparations for drinking upon
a large scale seriously commenced. It was just at this moment that I for the first time perceived the rather remarkable
figure who had waited upon us at dinner, and who, while I
chronicle so many things of little import, deserves a slight

mention. He was a little old man of about fifty-five or sixty years, wearing upon his head a barrister's wig, and habited in clothes which originally had been the costume of a very large and bulky person, and which, consequently, added much to the drollery of his appearance. He had been for forty years the servant of Judge Vandeleur, and had entered his present service rather in the light of a preceptor than a menial, invariably dictating to the worthy justice upon every occasion of etiquette or propriety by a reference to what "the judge himself" did, which always sufficed to carry the day in Nicholas's favor, opposition to so correct a standard never being thought of by the justice.

"That's Billy Crow's own whiskey, the *'small still,'*" said Nicholas, placing the decanter upon the table; "make much of it, for there isn't such dew in the county."

With this commendation upon the liquor, Nicholas departed, and we proceeded to fill our glasses.

I cannot venture—perhaps it is so much the better that I cannot—to give any idea of the conversation which at once broke out, as if the barriers that restrained it had at length given way. But law-talk in all its plenitude followed; and for two hours I heard of nothing but writs, detainers, declarations, traverses in prox, and alibis, with sundry hints for *qui tam processes,* interspersed, occasionally, with sly jokes about packing juries and confounding witnesses, among which figured the usual number of good things attributed to the Chief-Baron O'Grady and the other sayers of smart sayings at the Bar.

"Ah!" said Mr. Daly, drawing a deep sigh at the same instant, "the Bar is sadly fallen off since I was called in the year '76. There was not a leader in one of the circuits at that time that couldn't puzzle any jury that ever sat in a box; and as for driving through an Act of Parliament, it was, as Sancho Panza says, cakes and gingerbread to them. And then there is one special talent lost forever to the present generation,—just like stained glass, and illuminated manuscripts, and slow poisons, and the like, that were all known years ago, —I mean the beautiful art of addressing the judge before the jury, and not letting them know you were quizzing them, if ye like to do that same. Poor Peter Purcell for that—rest

his ashes!—he could cheat the devil himself if he had need,
—and maybe he has had before now. Peter is sixteen years
dead last November."

"And what was Peter's peculiar tact in that respect, Mr.
Daly?" said I.

"Oh! then, I might try for hours to explain it to you in vain!
but I'll just give you an instance that'll show you better than
all my dissertations on the subject, and I was present myself
when it happened, more by token it was the first time I ever
met him on circuit.

"I suppose there is scarcely any one here now, except myself, that remembers the great cause of Mills *versus* Mulcahy,
a Widow and Others, that was tried in Ennis in the year '82.
It's no matter if there is not. Perhaps it may be more agreeable for me, for I can tell my story in my own way, and not
be interrupted. Well, that was called 'the old record,' for
they tried it seventeen times. I believe, on my conscience,
it killed old Jones, who was in the Common Pleas; he used
to say, if he put it for trial on the day of judgment, one of
the parties would be sure to lodge an appeal. Be that as it
may, the Millses engaged Peter special, and brought him down
with a great retainer, in a chaise-and-four, flags flying, and
favors in the postilion's hats, and a fiddler on the roof, playing the 'Hare in the Corn.' The inn was illuminated the same
evening, and Peter made a speech from the windows upon
the liberty of the Press and religious freedom all over the
globe, and there wasn't a man in the mob didn't cheer him,—
which was the more civil because few of them knew a word
of English, and the others thought he was a play-actor. But it
all went off well, nevertheless, for Peter was a clever fellow;
and although he liked money well, he liked popularity more,
and he never went anywhere 'special' that he hadn't a public
meeting of some kind or other, either to abolish rents, or
suppress parsons, or some such popular and beneficial scheme,
which always made him a great favorite with the people and
got him plenty of clients. But I am wandering from the
record. Purcell came down, as I said before, special for Mills;
and when he looked over his brief, and thought of the
case, he determined to have it tried by a gentleman jury,
for although he was a great man with the mob, he liked the

country gentlemen better in the jury-box, for he was always coming out with quotations from the classics, which, whether the grand jury understood or not, they always applauded very much. Well, when he came into court that morning you may guess his surprise and mortification to find that the same jury that had tried a common ejectment case were still in the box, and waiting, by the chief-justice's direction, to try Mills *versus* Mulcahy, the great case of the assizes.

"I hear they were a set of common clod-hopping wretches, with frieze coats and brogues, that no man could get round at all, for they were as cunning as foxes, and could tell blarney from good sense rather better than people with better coats on them.

"Now, the moment that Mr. Purcell came into the court, after bowing politely to the judge, he looked up to the box; and when he saw the dirty faces of the dealers in pork and potatoes, and the unshaven chins of the small farmers, his heart fell within him, and he knew in a minute how little they'd care for the classics if he quoted Cæsar's Commentaries itself for them, ignorant creatures as they were.

"Well, the cause was called, and up gets Peter, and he began to 'express,' as he always called it himself, 'the great distress his client and himself would labor under if the patient and most intelligent jury then on the panel should come to the consideration of so very tedious a case as this promised to be, after their already most fatiguing exertions;' he commented upon their absence from their wives and families, their farms neglected, their crops hazarded, and in about fifteen minutes he showed them they were, if not speedily released and sent home, worse treated and harder used than many of the prisoners condemned to three months' imprisonment; and actually so far worked upon the feelings of the chief himself that he turned to the foreman of the jury and said that although it was a great deviation from his habitual practice, if at this pressing season their prospects were involved to the extent the learned counsel had pictured, why then he would so far bend his practice on this occasion, and they should be dismissed. Now, Peter, I must confess, here showed the most culpable ignorance in not knowing that a set of country fellows, put up in a jury box, would rather let every blade of corn rot in the ground than give up what they always supposed so very respectable an appointment; for they invariably imagine in these cases that they are something very like my lord the judge, 'barrin' the ermine;' besides that on the present occasion Peter's argument in their favor decided them upon staying, for they now felt like martyrs, and firmly believed that they were putting the chief-justice under an obligation to them for life.

"When, therefore, they heard the question of the court, it did not take a moment's time for the whole body to rise *en masse,* and bowing to the judge, call out, 'We'll stay, my lord, and try every mother's son of them for you,—ay, if it lasted till Christmas.'

"'I am sure, my lord,' said Peter, collecting himself for an effort, 'I cannot sufficiently express my gratitude for the great sacrifice these gifted and highly intelligent gentlemen are making in my client's behalf; for being persons who have great interests in the country at stake, their conduct on the present occasion is the more praiseworthy; and I am certain they fully appreciate, as does your lordship, the difficulty of the case before us, when documents will be submitted requiring a certain degree of acquaintance with such testimonials sufficiently to comprehend. Many of the title-deeds, as your lordship is aware, being obtained under old abbey charters, are in the learned languages; and we all know how home to our hearts and bosoms comes the beautiful line of the Greek poet, "Vacuus viator cantabit ante latronem."' The sound of the quotation roused the chief-justice, who had been in some measure inattentive to the preceding part of the learned counsel's address, and he called out rather sharply, 'Greek! Mr. Purcell,—why, I must have mistaken. Will you repeat the passage?'

"'With pleasure, my lord. I was just observing to your lordship and the jury, with the eloquent poet Hergesius, "Vacuus viator cantabit ante latronem."'

"'Greek, did you call it?'

"'Yes, my lord, of *course* I did.'

"'Why, Mr. Purcell, you are quoting Latin to me. And what do you mean by talking of the learned Hergesius and Greek all this time? The line is Juvenal's.'

" 'My lord, with much submission to your lordship, and every deference to your great attainments and very superior talents, let me still assure you that I am quoting Greek, and that your lordship is in error.'

" 'Mr. Purcell, I have only to remark that if you are desirous to make a jest of the court, you had better be cautious, I say, sir;' and here the judge waxed exceeding wroth. 'I say the line is Latin,—Latin, sir; Juvenal's Latin, sir,—every schoolboy knows it.'

" 'Of course, my lord,' said Peter, with great humility, 'I bow myself to the decision of your lordship; the line is, therefore, Latin. Yet I may be permitted to hint that were your lordship disposed to submit this question, as you are shortly about to do another and a similar one, to those clear-sighted and intelligent gentlemen there, I am satisfied, my lord, it would be Greek to every man of them.'

"The look, the voice, and the peculiar emphasis with which Peter gave these words were perfectly successful. The acute judge anticipated the wish of the counsel, the jury were dismissed, and Peter proceeded to his case before those he knew better how to deal with, and with whom the result was more certain to be as he wished it."

To this anecdote of the counsellor succeeded many others, of which, as the whiskey was potent and the hour late, my memory is not over retentive; the party did not break up till near four o'clock, and even then our *séance* only concluded because some one gravely remarked that as we should be all actively engaged on the morrow, early hours were advisable.

CHAPTER XX.

THE ASSIZE TOWN.

I HAD not been above a week in my new quarters when my servant presented me, among my letters one morning, with a packet which, with considerable pains, I at length recognized to be directed to me. The entire envelope was covered with writing in various hands, among which I detected something which bore a faint resemblance to my name; but the address which followed was perfectly unreadable, not only to me, as it appeared, but also to the "experts" of the different post-offices, for it had been followed by sundry directions to try various places beginning with T, which seemed to be the letter commencing the "great unknown locality,"—thus I read, "Try Tralee," "Try Tyrone," "Try Tanderagee," etc. I wonder that they didn't add, "Try Teheran;" and I suppose they would at last, rather than abandon the pursuit.

"But, Stubbes," said I, as I conned over the various addresses on this incomprehensible cover, "are you sure this is for me?"

"The postmaster, sir, desired me to ask if you'd have it, for he has offered it to every one down in these parts lately; the waterguard officers will take it at 8*d*., sir, if you won't, but I begged you might have the refusal."

"Oh! very well; I am happy to find matters are managed so impartially in the post-office here. Nothing like a public auction for making matters find their true level. Tell the postmaster, then, I'll keep the letter, and the rather, as it happens, by good luck, to be intended for me."

"And now for the interior," said I, as I broke the seal and read:—

PARIS, RUE CASTIGLIONE.

MY DEAR MR. LORREQUER,—As her ladyship and my son have in vain essayed to get anything from you in the shape of a reply to their letters, it has devolved upon me to try my fortune, which, were I to augur from the legibility of my writing, may not, I should fear, prove more successful than the [what can the word be?—"the—the"—why, it can't be "damnable," surely?—no, it is "amiable," I see]—than the amiable epistle of my lady. I cannot, however, permit myself to leave this without apprising you that we are about to start for Baden, where we purpose remaining a month or two. Your cousin Guy, who has been staying for some time with us, has been obliged to set out for Geneva, but hopes to join in some weeks hence. He is a great favorite with us all, but has not effaced the memory of our older friend, yourself. Could you not find means to come over and see us, if only a flying visit? Rotterdam is the route, and a few days would bring you to our quarters. Hoping that you may feel so disposed, I have enclosed herewith a letter to the Horse Guards, which I trust may facilitate your obtaining leave of absence. I know of no other mode of making your peace with the ladies, who are too highly incensed at your desertion to send one civil postscript to this letter, and Kilkee and myself are absolutely exhausted in our defence of you.

Believe me, yours truly,

CALLONBY.

Had I received an official notification of my being appointed paymaster to the forces or chaplain to Chelsea Hospital, I believe I should have received the information with less surprise than I perused this letter. That after the long interval which had elapsed, during which I had considered myself totally forgotten by this family, I should now receive a letter, —and such a letter too, quite in the vein of our former intimacy and good feeling, inviting me to their house, and again professing their willingness that I should be on the terms of our old familiarity,—was little short of wonderful to me. I read, too,—with what pleasure!—that slight mention of my cousin whom I had so long regarded as my successful rival, but who I began now to hope had not been preferred to me. Perhaps it was not yet too late to think that all was not hopeless. It appeared, too, that several letters had been written which had never reached me; so, while I accused them of neglect and forgetfulness, I was really more amenable to the charge myself; for from the moment I had heard of my cousin Guy's having been domesticated amongst them, and the rumors of his marriage had reached me, I suffered my absurd jealousy to blind my reason, and never wrote another line after. I ought to have known how *bavard* Guy always was; that he never met with the most commonplace attentions anywhere that he did not immediately write home about settlements and pin-money, and portions for younger children, and all that sort of nonsense. Now I saw it all plainly; and ten thousand times quicker than my hopes were extinguished they were again kindled, and I could not refrain from regarding Lady Jane as a mirror of constancy, and myself the most fortunate man

in Europe. My old castle-building propensities came back
upon me in an instant, and I pictured myself with Lady Jane
as my companion wandering among the beautiful scenery of
the Neckar beneath the lofty ruins of Heidelberg, or skimming the placid surface of the Rhine, while "mellowed by distance" came the rich chorus of a student's melody filling the
air with its flood of song. How delightful I thought to be
reading the lyrics of Uhland or Bürger with one so capable of
appreciating them, with all the hallowed associations of the
"Vaterland" about us! "Yes," said I aloud, repeating the
well-known line of a German *Lied:*—

"Bekränzt mit Laub, den lieben vollen Becher."

"Upon my conscience," said Mr. Daly, who had for some
time past been in silent admiration of my stage-struck appearance,—"upon my conscience, Mr. Lorrequer, I had no
conception you knew Irish."

The mighty talisman of the counsellor's voice brought me
back in a moment to a consciousness of where I was then
standing, and the still more unfortunate fact that I was only
a subaltern in his Majesty's 4—th.

"Why, my dear counsellor, that was German I was quoting,
not Irish."

"With all my heart," said Mr. Daly, breaking the top off
his third egg,—"with all my heart; I'd rather you'd talk it
than me. Much conversation in that tongue, I'm thinking,
would be mighty apt to loosen one's teeth."

"Not at all; it is the most beautiful language in Europe,
and the most musical too. Why, even for your own peculiar
taste in such matters, where can you find any language so rich
in Bacchanalian songs as German?"

"I'd rather hear the 'Cruiskeen Lawn,' or the 'Jug of
Punch,' as my old friend Pat Samson could sing them, than
a score of your High-Dutch jawbreakers."

"Shame upon ye, Mr. Daly! And for pathos, for true
feeling, where is there anything equal to Schiller's ballads?"

"I don't think I've ever heard any of his; but if you will
talk of ballads," said the counsellor, "give me old Mosey

M'Garry's. What's finer than"—and here he began, with a most nasal twang and dolorous emphasis, to sing,—

> " 'And I stepped up unto her,
> An' I made a congee,
> And I axed her her pardon
> For the making so free.'

"And then the next verse she says,—

> " 'Are you goin' to undo me,
> In this desert alone?'—

There's a shake there."

"For Heaven's sake," I cried, "stop! When I spoke of ballads, I never meant such infernal stuff as that."

"I'll not give up my knowledge of ballads to any man breathing," said Mr. Daly; "and with God's blessing, I'll sing you one this evening, after dinner, that will give you a cramp in the stomach."

An animated discussion upon lyrical poetry was here interrupted by a summons from our host to set out for the town. My party were, by the desire of the magistracy, to be in readiness near the court-house in the event of any serious disturbance, which there existed but too much reason to apprehend, from the highly excited state of feeling on the subject of the approaching trials. The soldiers were, under the guidance of Mr. Larkins, safely ensconced in a tan-yard; and I myself having consigned them for the present to a non-commissioned officer, was left at perfect liberty to dispose of my time and person as it might please me.

While these arrangements were taking place, I had entirely lost sight of Mr. Daly, under whose guidance and protection I trusted to obtain a place within the bar to hear the trials; so that I was now perfectly alone, for my host's numerous avocations entirely precluded any thought of my putting myself under his care.

My first object was to reach the court-house, and there could be little difficulty in finding it, for the throng of persons in the street were all eagerly bending their way thither. I accordingly followed with the stream, and soon found myself among an enormous multitude of frieze-coated and red-cloaked people of both sexes in a large open square which formed the market-place, one side of which was flanked by the court-house,—for as such I immediately recognized a massive-looking gray stone building,—in which the numerous windows, all open and filled with people, exhaled a continued steam from the crowded atmosphere within. To approach it was perfectly impossible; for the square was packed so closely that as the people approached by the various streets they were obliged to stand in the avenues leading to it, and regard what was going on from a distance. Of this large multitude I soon became one, hoping that at length some fortunate opportunity might enable me to obtain admission through some of my legal acquaintances.

That the fate of those who were then upon their trial for their lives absorbed the entire feelings of those without, a momentary glance at the hundreds of anxious and careworn faces in the crowd would completely satisfy. Motionless and silent they stood; they felt no fatigue, no want of food or refreshment; their interest was one and undivided,—all their hopes and fears were centred in the events then passing at a short distance from them, but to which their ignorance imparted an additional and more painful excitement; the only information of how matters were going on being by an occasional word, sometimes a mere gesture, from some one stationed in the windows to a friend in the crowd.

When the contemplation of this singularly impressive scene was beginning to weary from the irksomeness of my position, I thought of retiring, but soon discovered how impossible was such a step. The crowd had blocked up so completely all the avenues of approach that even had I succeeded in getting from the market-place, it would be only to remain firmly impacted among the mob in the street.

It now also occurred to me that although I had been assured by Larkins no call could possibly be made upon my services or those of my party till after the trial, yet were that to conclude at any moment, I should be perfectly unable to gain the place where I had stationed them, and the most serious consequences might ensue from the absence of their officer if the men were required to act.

From the time this thought took possession of me, I became excessively uncomfortable. Every expression of the people that denoted the progress of the trial only alarmed me for the conclusion, which I supposed might not be distant, and I began, with all my ingenuity, to attempt my retreat, which, after half an hour's severe struggle, I completely abandoned, finding myself scarcely ten yards from where I started.

At length the counsel for the Crown, who had been speaking to evidence, ceased; and an indistinct murmur was heard through the court-house, which was soon repressed by the voice of the crier calling "Silence!" All now seemed still and silent as the grave; yet, on listening attentively for some time, you could catch the low tones of a voice speaking, as it appeared, with great deliberation and slowness. This was the judge addressing the jury. In a short time this also ceased; and for about half an hour the silence was perfectly unbroken, and both within and without there reigned one intense and aching sense of anxiety that absorbed every feeling, and imparted to every face an expression of almost agonizing uncertainty. It was, indeed, a moment well calculated to excite such emotions. The jury had retired to deliberate upon their verdict. At length a door was heard to open, and the footsteps of the jury, as they resumed their places, sounded through the court, and were heard by those without. How heavily upon many a stout heart those footsteps fell! They had taken their seats; then came another pause, after which the monotonous tones of the clerk of the court were heard, addressing the jury for their verdict. As the foreman rises, every ear is bent, every eye strained, every heart-string vibrates. His lips move, but he is not heard; he is desired by the judge to speak louder; there is another pause; he appears to labor for a few seconds with a mighty effort, and at last pronounces the words, "Guilty, my lord; all guilty!"

I have heard the wild war-whoop of the Red Indian as in his own pine-forest he has unexpectedly come upon the track of his foe, and the almost extinguished hope of vengeance has been kindled again in his cruel heart; I have listened to the scarcely less savage hurrah of a storming party as they have surmounted the crumbling ruins of a breach and devoted to fire and sword, with that one yell, all who await them; and once in my life it has been my fortune to hear the last yell of defiance from a pirate crew as they sank beneath the raking fire of a frigate rather than surrender, and went down with a cheer of defiance that rose even above the red artillery that destroyed but could not subdue them,—but never, in any or all of these awful moments, did my heart vibrate to such sounds as rent the air when the fatal "Guilty" was heard by those within, and repeated to those 'without. It was not grief, it was not despair, neither was it the cry of sharp and irrepressible anguish from a suddenly blighted hope; but it was the long pent-up and carefully concealed burst of feeling which called aloud for vengeance,—red and reeking revenge upon all who had been instrumental in the sentence then delivered. It ceased, and I looked towards the court-house, expecting that an immediate and desperate attack upon the building and those whom it contained would at once take place. But nothing of the kind ensued; the mob were already beginning to disperse, and before I recovered perfectly from the excitement of these few and terrible moments, the square was nearly empty, and I almost felt as if the wild and frantic denunciation that still rang through my ears had been conjured up by a heated and fevered imagination.

When I again met our party at the dinner-table, I could not help feeling surprised on perceiving how little they sympathized in my feeling for the events of the day, which indeed they only alluded to in a professional point of view,—criticising the speeches of the counsel on both sides, and the character of the different witnesses who were examined.

"Well," said Mr. Daly, addressing our host, "you never could have had a conviction to-day if it wasn't for Mike. He's the best evidence I ever heard. I'd like to know very much how you ever got so clever a fellow completely in your clutches."

"By a mere accident, and very simply," replied the justice. "It was upon one of our most crowded fair-days, half the county was in town, when the information arrived that the Walshes were murdered the night before at the cross-roads above Telenamuck Mills. The news reached me as I was signing some tithe-warrants, one of which was against Mickey. I sent for him into the office, knowing that as he was in the se-

cret of all the evil doings, I might as well pretend to do him a
service and offer to stop the warrant out of kindness, as it
were. Well, one way or another, he was kept waiting several
hours while I was engaged in writing, and all the country
people, as they passed the window, could look in and see
Mickey Sheehan standing before me while I was employed
busily writing letters. It was just at this time that a mounted
policeman rode in with the account of the murder, upon which
I immediately issued a warrant to arrest the two MacNeills
and Owen Shirley upon suspicion. I thought I saw Mike
turn pale as I said the names over to the sergeant of police,
and I at once determined to turn it to account; so I immediately began talking to Mickey about his own affairs, breaking off, every now and then, to give some directions about
the men to be captured. The crowd outside was increasing
every instant, and you need not have looked at their faces
twice to perceive that they had regarded Mickey as an ap-
prover; and the same night that saw the MacNeills in custody,
witnessed the burning of Sheehan's house and haggart, and
he only escaped by a miracle over to Curryglass, where, once
under my protection, with the imputation upon his character
of having turned king's evidence, I had little trouble in persuading him that he might as well benefit by the report as
enjoy the name without the gain. He soon complied, and the
convictions of this day are partly the result."

When the applause which greeted this clever stroke of our
host had subsided, I inquired what results might, in all likelihood, follow the proceedings of which I had that day been
a witness.

"Nothing will be done immediately," replied the justice,
"because we have a large force of police and military about
us; but let either, or unhappily both, be withdrawn, and the
cry you heard given in the market-place to-day will be the
death-wail for more than one of those who are well and hearty
at this moment."

The train of thought inevitably forced upon me by all I had
been a spectator of during the day but little disposed me to be
a partaker in the mirth and conviviality which, as usual,
formed the staple of the assize dinners of Mr. Larkins; and I
accordingly took an early opportunity to quit the company and
retire for the night.

CHAPTER XXI.

A DAY IN DUBLIN.

ON the third day of my residence at Curryglass arrived
my friend Mortimer to replace me, bringing my leave
from the colonel and a most handsome letter, in which he
again glanced at the prospect before me in the Callonby family, and hinted at my destination, which I had not alluded to,
adding that if I made the pretence of study in Germany the
reason for my application at the Horse Guards, I should be
almost certain to obtain a six months' leave. With what
spirits I ordered Stubbes to pack up my portmanteau and secure our places in the Dublin mail for that night, while I myself hurried to take leave of my kind entertainer and his guests,
as well as to recommend to their favor and attention my excellent friend Mortimer! He, being a jovial fellow, not at
all in love, was a happy exchange for me, since despite Daly's
capital stories, I had spent the last two days in watching the
highroad for my successor's arrival.

Once more, then, I bade adieu to Curryglass and its hospitable owner, whose labors for "justice to Ireland" I shall
long remember, and depositing myself in the bowels of his
Majesty's mail, gave way to the full current of my hopes and
imaginings, which at last ended in a sound and refreshing
sleep, from which I only awoke as we drew up at the door of
the Hibernian, in Dawson Street.

Even at that early hour there was considerable bustle and
activity of preparation, which I was at some loss to account
for till informed by the waiter that there were upwards of
three hundred strangers in the house, it being the day of his
Majesty's expected arrival on his visit to Ireland, and a very
considerable section of the county of Galway being at that
moment, with their wives and families, installed for the occasion in this their favorite hotel.

Although I had been reading of this approaching event
every day for the last three months, I could not help feeling
surprised at the intense appearance of excitement it occasioned, and in the few minutes' conversation I held with the
waiter, learned the total impossibility of procuring a lodging

anywhere, and that I could not have a bed, even were I to offer five guineas for it. Having, therefore, no inclination for sleep, even upon easier terms, I ordered my breakfast to be ready at ten, and set out upon a stroll through the town. I could not help, in my short ramble through the streets, perceiving how admirably adapted were the worthy Dublinites for all the honors that awaited them. Garlands of flowers, transparencies, flags, and the other insignia of rejoicing were everywhere in preparation, and at the end of Sackville Street a considerable erection, very much resembling an impromptu gallows, was being built, for the purpose, as I afterwards learned, of giving the worshipful the lord mayor the opportunity of opening the city gates to royalty,—creating the obstacle where none existed being a very ingenious conceit, and considerably Irish into the bargain. I could not help feeling some desire to witness how all should go off, to use the theatrical phrase; but in my anxiety to get on to the Continent, I at once abandoned every thought of delay. When I returned to the coffee-room of my hotel, I found it crowded to excess; every little table, originally destined for the accommodation of one, having at least two, and sometimes three occupants. In my hurried glance round the room to decide where I should place myself, I was considerably struck with the appearance of a stout elderly gentleman with red whiskers and a high, bald forehead; he had, although the day was an oppressively hot one, three waistcoats on, and by the brown York tan of his long-topped boots evinced a very considerable contempt either for weather or fashion; in the quick glance of his sharp gray eye I read that he listened half doubtingly to the narrative of his companion, whose back was turned towards me, but who appeared, from the occasional words which reached me, to be giving a rather marvellous and melodramatic version of the expected pleasures of the capital. There was something in the tone of the speaker's voice that I thought I recognized; I accordingly drew near, and what was my surprise to discover my friend Tom O'Flaherty. After our first salutation was over, Tom presented me to his friend Mr. Burke, of somewhere, who, he continued to inform me, in a stage whisper, was a "regular quiz," and never in Dublin in his life before.

"And so you say, sir, that his Majesty cannot enter without the permission of the lord mayor?"

"And the aldermen too," replied Tom. "It is an old feudal ceremony. When his Majesty comes up to the gate, he demands admission, and the lord mayor refuses, because he would be thus surrendering his great prerogative of head of the city; then the aldermen get about him and cajole him, and by degrees he's won over by the promise of being knighted, and the king gains the day and enters."

"Upon my conscience, a mighty ridiculous ceremony it is, after all," said Mr. Burke, "and very like a bargain for sheep in Ballinasloe fair, when the buyer and seller appear to be going to fight, till a mutual friend settles the bargain between them."

At this moment Mr. Burke suddenly sprang from his chair, which was nearest the window, to look out; I accordingly followed his example, and beheld a rather ludicrous procession, if such it could be called, consisting of so few persons. The principal individual in the group was a florid, fat, happy-looking gentleman of about fifty, with a profusion of nearly white whiskers which met at his chin mounted upon a sleek charger, whose half-ambling, half-prancing pace had evidently been acquired by long habit of going in procession; this august figure was habited in a scarlet coat and cocked-hat having "tags" and all the other appanage of a general officer; he also wore tight buckskin breeches and high jack-boots, like those of the Horse Guards. As he looked from side to side, with a self-satisfied, contented air, he appeared quite insensible of the *cortège* which followed and preceded him,—the latter consisting of some score of half-ragged boys, yelling and shouting with all their might, and the former being a kind of instalment in hand of the Dublin Militia Band, and who, in numbers and equipment, closely resembled the "army" which accompanies the first appearance of Bombastes, the only difference, that these I speak of did not play the "Rogue's March," which might have perhaps appeared personal.

As this goodly procession advanced, Mr. Burke's eyes became riveted upon it; it was the first wonder he had yet beheld, and he devoured it.

"May I ask, sir," said he, at length, "who that is?"

"Who that is?" said Tom, surveying him leisurely as he spoke, "why surely, sir, you must be jesting, or you would not ask such a question! I trust, indeed, every one knows who he is,—eh, Harry?" said he, looking at me for a confirmation of what he said, and to which, of course, I assented by a look.

"Well, but, my dear Mr. O'Flaherty, you forget how ignorant I am of everything here—"

"Ah, true!" said Tom, interrupting; "I forget you never saw him before."

"And who is he, sir?"

"Why, that's the Duke of Wellington, sir!"

"Lord have mercy upon me; is it?" said Mr. Burke, as he upset the table and all its breakfast equipage, and rushed through the coffee-room like one possessed. Before I could half recover from the fit of laughing this event threw me into, I heard him, as he ran full speed down Dawson Street, waving his hat, and shouting at the top of his lungs, "God bless your Grace! Long life to your Grace! Hurrah for the hero of Waterloo! the great captain of the age!" etc., which I grieve to say, for the ingratitude of the individual lauded, seemed not to afford him half the pleasure and none of the amusement it did the mob, who re-echoed the shouts and cheering till he was hid within the precincts of the Mansion House.

"And now," said Tom to me, "finish your breakfast as fast as possible; for when Burke comes back, he will be boring me to dine with him, or some such thing, as a kind of acknowledgment of his gratitude for showing him the duke. Do you know, he has seen more wonders through my poor instrumentality within the last three days in Dublin than a six months' trip to the Continent would show most men. I have made him believe that Burke Bethel is Lord Brougham, and I am about to bring him to a *soirée* at *Miladi's*, whom he supposes to be the Marchioness of Conyngham. *À propos* to the dear 'Blew,' let me tell you of a 'good hit' I was witness to a few nights since. You know, perhaps, old Sir Charles Giesecke, eh?"

"I have seen him once, I think,—the professor of mineralogy."

"Well, poor old Sir Charles, one of the most modest and

retiring men in existence, was standing the other night among the mob, in one of the drawing-rooms, while a waltzing-party were figuring away, at which, with that fondness for *la danse* that characterizes every German of any age, he was looking with much interest, when my lady came tripping up, and the following short dialogue ensued within my earshot:—

"'Ah! *mon cher Sir Charles, ravie de vous voir.* But why are you not dancing?'

"'*Ah! Miladi, je ne puis pas,—c'est-à-dire, ich kann es nicht;* I am too old; *ich bin*—'

"'Oh, you horrid man! I understand you perfectly. You hate ladies; that is the real reason. You do,—you know you do.'

"'*Ah, Miladi, gnädige Frau, glauben Sie mich;* I do loave de ladies; I do adore de sex. Do you know, *Miladi,* when I was in Greenland I did keep four womans.'

"'Oh, shocking, horrid, vile Sir Charles! How could you tell *me* such a story? I shall die of it!'

"'*Ah, mein Gott, Miladi, Sie irren sich; vous vous trompez.* You are quite in mistake; it was only to *row my boat!*'

"I leave you to guess how my lady's taste for the broadside of the story, and poor Sir Charles's vindication of himself, in regard to his estimation of *le beau sexe,* amused all who heard it; as for me, I had to leave the room, half-choked with suppressed laughter. And now let us bolt, for I see Burke coming; and, upon my soul, I am tired of telling him lies, and must rest on my oars for a few hours at least."

"But where is the necessity for so doing?" said I. "Surely where there is so much of novelty as a large city presents to a visitor for the first time there is little occasion to draw upon imagination for your facts."

"Ah, my dear Harry, how little do you know of life! There is a kind of man whose appetite for the marvellous is such that he must be crammed with miracles, or he dies of inanition; and you might as well attempt to feed a tiger upon *pâté de foie gras* as satisfy him by mere naked, unvarnished truth. I'll just give you an easy illustration: you saw his delight this morning when the 'duke' rode past; well, I'll tell you the converse of that proposition now. The night before last, having nothing better to do, we went to the theatre; the piece was 'La Pérouse,' which they have been playing here for the last two months to crowded houses, to exhibit some North American Indians whom some theatrical speculator brought over 'special,' in all the horrors of fur, wampum, and yellow ochre. Finding the 'spectacle' rather uninteresting, I leaned back in my box and fell into a doze. Meanwhile, my inquiring friend Mr. Burke, who felt naturally anxious, as he always does, to get *au fond* of matters, left his place to obtain information about the piece, the audience, and, above all, the authenticity of the Indians, who certainly astonished him considerably.

"Now it so happened that about a fortnight previously some violent passion to return home to their own country had seized these interesting individuals, and they felt the most irresistible longing to abandon the savage and unnatural condiments of roast beef and Guinness's porter and resume their ancient and more civilized habits of life. In fact, like the old African lady mentioned by the missionary at the Cape, they felt they could die happy if they 'could only once more have a roast child for supper;' and as such luxuries are dear in this country, stay another week they would not, whatever the consequences might be. The manager reasoned, begged, implored, and threatened by turns, all would not do, go they were determined; and all that the unfortunate proprietor could accomplish was to make a purchase of their properties in fur, belts, bows, arrows, and feathers, and get them away quietly without the public being the wiser. The piece was too profitable a one to abandon, so he looked about anxiously to supply the deficiency in his *corps dramatique*. For several days nothing presented itself to his thoughts, and the public were becoming more clamorous for the repetition of a drama which had greatly delighted them. What was to be done? In a mood of doubt and uncertainty the wretched manager was taking his accustomed walk upon the lighthouse pier while a number of unfortunate country fellows, bare-legged and lanky, with hay ropes fastening their old gray coats around them, were standing beside a packet, about to take their departure for England for the harvest. Their uncouth appearance, their wild looks, their violent gestures, and, above all, their strange and guttural language,—for they were all speaking Irish,—attracted the attention of the manager; the effect, to his professional eye, was good. The thought struck him at once: here were the very fellows he wanted. It was scarcely necessary to alter anything about them; they were ready made to his hand, and in many respects better savages than their prototypes. Through the mediation of some whiskey, the appropriate liquor in all treaties of this nature, a bargain was readily struck, and in two hours more these 'forty thieves' were rehearsing upon the classic boards of our theatre, and once more 'La Pérouse,' in all the glory of red capital letters, shone forth in the morning advertisements. The run of the piece continued unabated; the Indians were the rage; nothing else was thought or spoken of in Dublin, and already the benefit of Ashewaballagh Ho was announced,—who, by the by, was a little fellow from Martin's estate in Connemara, and one of the drollest dogs I ever heard of. Well, it so happened that it was upon one of their nights of performing that I found myself, with Mr. Burke, a spectator of their proceedings; I had fallen into an easy slumber, when a dreadful row in the box lobby roused me from my dream, and the loud cry of 'Turn him out!' 'Pitch him over!' 'Beat his brains out!' and other humane proposals of the like nature, effectually restored me to consciousness. I rushed out of the box into the lobby, and there, to my astonishment, in the midst of a considerable crowd, beheld my friend Mr. Burke belaboring the box-keeper with all his might with a cotton umbrella of rather unpleasant proportions, accompanying each blow with an exclamation of 'Well, are they Connaught-men now, you rascal, eh? Are they all west of Athlone, tell me that, now? I wonder what's preventing me beating the soul out of ye.' After obtaining a short cessation of hostilities, and restoring poor Sharkey to his legs, much more dead than alive from pure fright, I learned at last the *teterrima causa belli*. Mr. Burke, it seems, had entered into conversation with Sharkey, the box-keeper, as to all the particulars of the theatre and the present piece, but especially as to the real and authentic history of the Indians, whose language he remarked in many respects to resemble Irish. Poor Sharkey, whose benefit night was approaching, thought he might secure a friend for life by im-

parting to him an important state secret; and when, therefore, pressed rather closely as to the 'savages' whereabout,'
resolved to try a bold stroke and trust his unknown interrogator. 'And so you don't really know where they come from,
nor can't guess?' 'Maybe, Peru,' said Mr. Burke, innocently.
'Try again, sir,' said Sharkey, with a knowing grin. 'Is it
Behring's Straits?' said Mr. Burke. 'What do you think of
Galway, sir?' said Sharkey, with a leer intended to cement
a friendship for life. The words were no sooner out of his
lips than Burke, who immediately took them as a piece of
direct insolence to himself and his country, felled him to the
earth, and was in the act of continuing the discipline when I
arrived on the field of battle."

CHAPTER XXII.

A NIGHT AT HOWTH.

"AND you must really leave us so soon!" said Tom, as
we issued forth into the street. "Why, I was just plan-
ning a whole week's adventure for you. Town is so full of
all kinds of idle people, I think I could manage to make your
time pass pleasantly enough."

"Of that," I replied, "I have little doubt; but, for the reasons I have just mentioned, it is absolutely necessary that I
should not lose a moment; and after arranging a few things
here, I shall start to-morrow by the earliest packet, and hasten
up to London at once."

"By Jupiter," said Tom, "how lucky! I just remember
something which comes admirably à propos. You are going
to Paris,—is it not so?"

"Yes, direct to Paris."

"Nothing could be better. There is a particularly nice
person, a great friend of mine, Mrs. Bingham, waiting for
several days in hopes of a chaperon to take care of herself and
daughter—a lovely girl, only nineteen, you wretch—to London, *en route* to the Continent; the mamma a delightful
woman and a widow, with a very satisfactory jointure,—you

understand,—but the daughter a regular, downright beauty
and a ward in Chancery, with how many thousand pounds
I am afraid to trust myself to say. You must know, then,
they are the Binghams of— Upon my soul, I forget where,
but highly respectable."

"I regret I have not the pleasure of their acquaintance, and
the more because I shall not be able to make it now."

"As why?" said Tom, gravely.

"Because, in the first place, I am so confoundedly pressed
for time that I could not possibly delay under any contingency that might arise; and your fair friends are, doubtless,
not so eagerly determined upon travelling night and day till
they reach Paris. Secondly, to speak candidly, with my
present hopes and fears weighing upon my mind, I should not
be the most agreeable travelling companion to two ladies with
such pretensions as you speak of; and thirdly—" •

"Confound your thirdly! I suppose we shall have six-
teenthly, like a Presbyterian minister's sermon, if I let you
go on. Why, they'll not delay you one hour. Mrs. Bingham,
man, cares as little for the road as yourself; and as for your
petits soins, I suppose if you get the fair ladies through the
Custom House and see them safe in a London hotel, it is all
that will be required at your hands."

"Notwithstanding all you say, I see the downright impossibility of my taking such a charge at this moment, when
my own affairs require all the little attention I can bestow, and
when, were I once involved with your fair friends, it might
be completely out of my power to prosecute my own plans."

As I said this, we reached the door of a handsome-looking
house in Kildare Street, upon which Tom left my arm, and
informing me that he desired to drop a card, knocked loudly.

"Is Mrs. Bingham at home?" said he, as the servant opened
the door.

"No, sir, she's out in the carriage."

"Well, you see, Harry, your ill-luck befriends you; for I
was resolved on presenting you to my friends and leaving the
rest to its merits."

"I can safely assure you that I should not have gone upstairs," said I. "Little as I know of myself, there is one
point of my character I have never been deceived in,—the

fatal facility by which every new incident or adventure can turn me from following up my best-matured and longest-digested plans; and as I feel this weakness and cannot correct it, the next best thing I can do is to fly the causes."

"Upon my soul," said Tom, "you have become quite a philosopher since we met. There is an old adage which says, 'No king is ever thoroughly gracious if he has not passed a year or two in dethronement;' so I believe your regular lady-killer—yourself, for instance—becomes a very quiet animal for being occasionally jilted. But now, as you have some commissions to do, pray get done with them as fast as possible, and let us meet at dinner. Where do you dine to-day?"

"Why, upon that point I am at your service completely."

"Well, then, I have got a plan which I think will suit you. You said you wished to go by Holyhead, for fear of delay; so we'll drive down at six o'clock to Skinner's, and dine with him on board the packet at Howth. Bring your luggage with you, and it will save you a vast deal of fuss and trouble in the morning."

Nothing could be better management for me than this, so I accordingly promised accquiescence; and having appointed a rendezvous for six o'clock, bade O'Flaherty good-by, inwardly rejoicing that my plans were so far forwarded, and that I was not to be embarrassed with either Mrs. Bingham or her daughter, for whose acquaintance or society I had no peculiar ambition.

My commissions, though not very numerous, occupied the few hours which remained, and it was already a few minutes past six o'clock when I took my stand under the piazza of the Post-office to wait for O'Flaherty. I had not long to do so, for immediately after I had reached the spot he arrived in an open barouche and four posters, with three other young men to whom he severally introduced me, but whose names I have totally forgotten; I only remember that two of the party were military men then quartered in town.

When I had taken my seat, I could not help whispering to Tom that although his friend Skinner might be *bon* for a visitation for two at his dinner, yet as we were now so strong a party, it might be as well to dine at the hotel.

"Oh!" said he, "I have arranged all that; I have sent him a special messenger two hours since, and so make your mind easy,—we shall not be disappointed, nor he short-taken."

Our drive, although a long one, passed quickly over, and before we had reached our destination I had become tolerably intimate with all the party, who were evidently picked men, selected by O'Flaherty for a pleasant evening.

We drove along the pier to the wharf where the steamer lay, and were received at once by Tom's friend with all the warm welcome and hospitality of a sailor, united with the address and polish of a very finished gentleman. As we descended the companion-ladder to the cabin, my mind became speedily divested of any fears I might have indulged in as to the want of preparation of our entertainer. The table was covered with handsome plate and cut glass, while the side-tables glittered with a magnificent dessert, and two large wine-coolers presented an array of champagne necks shining with their leaden cravats that would have tempted an anchorite.

I remember very little else of that evening than the *coup d'œil* I have mentioned. Besides, were my memory more retentive, I might scruple to trespass farther on my reader's patience by the detail of those pleasures, which, like love-letters, however agreeable to the parties immediately concerned, are very unedifying to all others. I do remember, certainly, that good stories and capital songs succeeded each other with a rapidity only to be equalled by the popping of corks, and have also a very vague and indistinct recollection of a dance round the table,—evidently to finish a chorus, but which, it appears, finished me too, for I saw no more that night.

How many have commemorated the waking sensations of their fellow-men after a night's debauch! Yet at the same time, I am not aware of any one having perfectly conveyed even a passing likeness to the mingled throng of sensations which crowd one's brain on such an occasion. The doubt of what has passed, by degrees yielding to the half-consciousness of the truth; the feeling of shame inseparable, except to the habitually hard-goer, from the events thus dimly pictured; the racking headache and intense thirst, with the horror of the potation recently indulged in; the recurring sense of the fun or drollery of a story or an incident which provokes us again to laugh, despite the jarring of our brain from the shaking,—all this, and more, most men have felt; and happy are they when their waking thoughts are limited to such, at times like these. The matter becomes considerably worse when the following morning calls for some considerable exertion for which, even in your best and calmest moments, you barely find yourself equal.

It is truly unpleasant, on rubbing your eyes and opening your ears, to discover that the great bell is ringing the half-hour before your quarterly examination at college, while Locke, Lloyd, and Lucian are dancing a reel through your brain little short of madness; scarcely less agreeable is it to learn that your friend Captain Wildfire is at the door in his cab, to accompany you to the Phœnix, to stand within twelve paces of a cool gentleman who has been sitting with his arm in cold water for the last half-hour, that he may pick you out "artist-like." There are, besides these, innumerable situations in which our preparations of the night would appear as none of the wisest; but I prefer going at once to my own, which, although considerably inferior in difficulty, was not without its own *désagréments.*

When I awoke, therefore, on board the *Firefly* the morning after our dinner-party, I was perfectly unable, by any mental process within my reach, to discover where I was. On shipboard I felt I must be,—the narrow berth, the gilded and panelled cabin which met my eye through my half-open curtains, and that peculiar swelling motion inseparable from a vessel in the water, all satisfied me of this fact. I looked about me, but could see no one to give me the least idea of my position. Could it be that we were on our way out to Corfu, and that I had been ill for some time past?

But this cabin had little resemblance to a transport. Perhaps it might be a frigate,—I knew not. Then, again, were we sailing, or at anchor? for the ship was nearly motionless. At this instant a tremendous noise like thunder crashed through my head, and for a moment I expected we had exploded and would all be blown up; but an instant after, I discovered it must be the escape of the steam, and that I was on board a packet-ship. Here, then, was some clew to my situation, and one which would probably have elicited all in due season; but just at this moment a voice on deck saved me from any further calculations. Two persons were conversing, whose voices were not altogether unknown to me, but why, I knew not.

"Then, Captain, I suppose you consider this as an excellent passage?"

"Yes, of course I do," replied the captain; "it's only five hours since we left Howth, and now, you see, we are nearly in. If we have this run of the tide, we shall reach the Head before twelve o'clock."

"Ha, ha,!" said I to myself; "now I begin to learn something. So we have crossed the Channel while I was sleeping,—not the least agreeable thing for a man to hear who suffers martyrdom from sea-sickness. But let me listen again."

"And that large mountain there, is that Snowdon?"

"No, you cannot see Snowdon, there is too much mist about it; that mountain is Capel Curig! And there, that bold bluff to the eastward, that is Penmaenmawr."

"Come, there is no time to be lost," thought I; so springing out of my berth, accoutred as I was, in merely trousers and slippers, with a red handkerchief fastened, nightcap fashion, round my head, I took my way through the cabin.

My first thought on getting upon my legs was, how tremendously the vessel pitched, which I had not remarked while in my berth, but now I could scarce keep myself from falling at every step. I was just about to call the steward when I again heard the voices on deck.

"You have but few passengers this trip?"

"I think only yourself and a Captain Lorrequer," replied the captain,—"who, by the by, is losing all this fine coast, which is certainly a great pity."

"He shall not do so much longer," thought I; "for as I find that there are no other passengers, I'll make my toilet on deck, and enjoy the view besides." With this determination I ascended slowly and cautiously the companion-ladder, and stepped out upon the deck; but scarcely had I done so when a roar of the loudest laughter made me turn my head towards the poop, and there, to my horror of horrors, I beheld Tom

O'Flaherty seated between two ladies, whose most vociferous mirth I soon perceived was elicited at my expense.

All the party of the preceding night were also there, and as I turned from their grinning faces to the land, I saw, to my shame and confusion, that we were still lying beside the pier at Howth; while the bandboxes, trunks, and imperials of new arrivals were incessantly pouring in, as travelling carriages kept driving up to the place of embarkation. I stood perfectly astounded and bewildered. Shame for my ridiculous costume would have made me fly at any other time; but there I remained to be laughed at patiently, while that villain O'Flaherty, leading me passively forward, introduced me to his friends: "Mrs. Bingham, Mr. Lorrequer; Mr. Lorrequer, Miss Bingham. Don't be prepossessed against him, ladies, for when not in love and properly dressed, he is a marvellously well-looking young gentleman; and as—"

What the remainder of the sentence might be, I knew not; for I rushed down into the cabin, and locking the door, never opened it till I could perceive from the stern windows that we were really off on our way to England, and recognized once more the laughing face of O'Flaherty, who, as he waved his hat to his friends from the pier, reminded them that "they were under the care and protection of his friend Lorrequer, who, he trusted, would condescend to increase his wearing apparel under the circumstances."

CHAPTER XXIII.

THE JOURNEY.

WHEN I did at last venture upon deck, it was with a costume studiously accurate, and as much of manner as I could possibly muster to endeavor at once to erase the unfortunate impression of my first appearance; this, however, was not destined to be a perfectly successful manœuvre, and I was obliged, after a few minutes, to join the laugh, which I found could not be repressed, at my expense. One good result certainly followed from all this,—I became almost immediately on intimate terms with Mrs. Bingham and her daughter, and much of the awkwardness in my position as their chaperon, which, *bon gré, mal gré,* I was destined to be, was at once got over. Mrs. Bingham herself was of that style of widow which comes under the "fat, fair, and forty" category, with a never-ceasing flow of high, almost boisterous spirits, an excellent temper, good health, and a well-stocked purse. Life to her was like a game of her favorite "speculation." When she *believed* the "company honest," and *knew* her cards trumps, she was tolerably easy for the result. She liked Kingstown; she liked whist; she liked the military; she liked "the Junior Bar," of which she knew a good number; she had a well-furnished house in Kildare Street and a well-cushioned pew in St. Anne's; she was a favorite at the Castle, and Dr. Labatt "knew her constitution." Why, with all these advantages, she should ever have thought of leaving the "happy valley" of her native city, it was somewhat hard to guess. Was it that thoughts of matrimony, which the Continent held out more prospect for, had invaded the fair widow's heart? Was it that the altered condition to which politics had greatly reduced Dublin had effected this change of opinion? Or was it like that indescribable longing for the unknown something which we read of in the pathetic history of the fair lady celebrated, I believe, by Petrarch? But I quote from memory,—

> " Mrs. Gill is very ill;
>   Nothing can improve her
> But to see the Tuileries
> And waddle through the Louvre."

None of these, I believe, however good and valid reasons in themselves, were the moving powers upon the present occasion; the all-sufficient one being that Mrs. Bingham had a daughter. Now, Miss Bingham was Dublin too,—but Dublin of a later edition, and a finer, more hot-pressed copy than her mamma. She had been educated at Mrs. Somebody's seminary in Mountjoy Square, had been taught to dance by Montague, and had learned French from a Swiss governess, with a number of similar advantages,—a very pretty figure, dark eyes, long eyelashes and a dimple, and last, but of course least, the deserved reputation of a large fortune. She had made a most successful *début* in the Dublin world, where she was much admired and flattered, and which soon suggested to her quick mind, as it has often done in similar cases to a young provincial *débutante,* not to waste her attractions upon the minor theatres, but at once to appear upon the "great boards," —so far evidencing a higher flight of imagination and enterprise than is usually found among the class of her early associates, who may be characterized as that school of young ladies who admire "The Corsair" and Kingstown, and say, "Ah, don't!"

She possessed much more common sense than her mamma, and promised, under proper advantages, to become speedily quite sufficiently acquainted with the world and its habitudes. In the mean while, I perceived that she ran a very considerable risk of being carried off by some mustachioed Pole, with a name like a sneeze, who might pretend to enjoy access to the fashionable circles of the Continent.

Very little study of my two friends enabled me to see thus much, and very little "usage" sufficed to render me speedily intimate with both; the easy good-nature of the mamma, who had a very methodistical appreciation of what the "connection" call "creature comforts," amused me much, and opened one ready path to her good graces by the opportunity afforded of getting up a luncheon of veal cutlets and London porter, of which I partook,—not a little to the evident loss of the fair daughter's esteem.

While, therefore, I made the tour of the steward's cell in search of Harvey's sauce, I brushed up my memory of "The Corsair" and "Childe Harold," and alternately discussed Stilton and Southey, Shelley and lobsters, Haynes Bayley and ham.

The day happened to be particularly calm and delightful, so that we never left the deck, and the six hours which brought us from land to land quickly passed over in this manner; and ere we reached "the Head," I had become the warm friend and legal adviser of the mother; and with the daughter I was installed as chief confidant of all her griefs and sorrows, both of which appointments cost me a solemn promise to take care of them till their arrival in Paris, where they had many friends and acquaintances awaiting them. Here, then, as usual, was the fatal facility with which I gave myself up to any one who took the trouble to influence me! One thing, nevertheless, I was determined on,—to let no circumstance defer my arrival at Paris a day later than was possible; therefore, though my office as chaperon might engage me on the road, it should not interfere with the object before me. Had my mind not been so completely engaged with my own immediate prospects, when hope, suddenly and unexpectedly revived, had become so tinged with fears and doubts as to be almost torture, I must have been much amused with my present position, as I found myself seated with my two fair friends, rolling along through Wales in their comfortable travelling carriage, giving all the orders at the different hotels, seeing after the luggage, and acting *en maître* in every respect.

The good widow enjoyed particularly the difficulty which my precise position with regard to her and her daughter threw the different innkeepers on the road into, sometimes supposing me to be her husband, sometimes her son, and once her son-in-law,—which very alarming conjecture brought a crimson tinge to the fair daughter's cheek; an expression, which, in my ignorance, I thought looked very like an inclination to faint in my arms.

At length we reached London; and having been there safely installed at Mivart's, I sallied forth to present my letter to the Horse Guards and obtain our passport for the Continent.

"Number 9, Poland Street, sir," said the waiter, as I inquired the address of the French consul. Having discovered that my interview with the commander-in-chief was appointed for four o'clock, I determined to lose no time, but make every possible arrangement for leaving London in the morning.

A cab quietly conveyed me to the door of the consul, around which stood several other vehicles of every shape and fashion, while in the doorway were to be seen numbers of people, thronging and pressing, like the opera-pit on a full night. Into the midst of this assemblage I soon thrust myself, and borne upon the current, at length reached a small back parlor filled also with people. A door opening into another small room in the front showed a similar mob there, with the addition of a small elderly man in a bag-wig and spectacles, very much begrimed with snuff, and speaking in a very choleric tone to the various applicants for passports, who, totally ignorant of French, insisted upon interlarding their demands with an occasional stray phrase, making a kind of tessellated pavement of tongues which would have shamed Babel. Nearest to the table at which the functionary sat stood a mustachioed gentleman in a blue frock and white trousers, a white hat jauntily set upon one side of his head, and primrose gloves. He cast a momentary glance of a very undervaluing import upon the crowd around him, and then, turning to the consul, said in a very soprano tone,—

"*Passe-port, monsieur!*"

"*Que voulez-vous que je fasse?*" replied the old Frenchman, gruffly.

"*Je suis—j'ai*—that is, *donnez-moi passe-port.*"

"Where do you go?" replied the consul.

"*Calai.*"

"*Comment, diable!* Speak Inglis, an' I understan' you as besser. Your name?"

"Lorraine Snaggs, *gentilhomme.*"

"What age have you,—how old?"

"Twenty-two."

"*C'est ça,*" said the old consul, flinging the passport across the table with the air of a man who thoroughly comprehended the applicant's pretension to the designation of *gentilhomme anglais.*

As I followed the worthy representative of Seven Dials with my eye, another person had neared the table. She was a rather pretty young woman, with blue eyes and brown hair braided quietly on her forehead, and wearing a plain close bonnet of a very coquettish appearance.

"Will you be seated, mamselle?" said the polite old Frenchman, who had hitherto been more like a bear than a human being. "*Où allez-vous donc?* where to, *ma chère?*"

"To Paris, sir."

"By Calais?"

"No, sir; by Boulogne."

"*C'est bon; quel âge avez-vous?* What old, *ma belle?*"

"Nineteen, sir, in June."

"And are you alone quite, eh?"

"No, sir, my little girl."

"Ah! your leetel girl—*c'est fort bien; je m'aperçois.* And your name?"

"Fanny Linwood, sir."

"*C'est fini, ma chère,*—Mademoiselle Fanny Linwood," said the old man, as he wrote down the name.

"Oh, sir, I beg your pardon, but you have put me down 'mademoiselle,' and—and—you see, sir, I have my little girl."

"*Ah! c'est égal, mamselle;* they don't mind these things in France. *Au plaisir de vous voir, adieu!*"

" 'They don't mind these things in France!' " said I to myself, repeating the old consul's phrase, which I could not help feeling as a whole chapter on his nation.

My business was soon settled, for I spoke nothing but English, very little knowledge of the world teaching me that when we have any favor, however slight, to ask, it is always good policy to make the demand by propitiating the self-esteem of the granter,—if, happily, there be an opportunity for so doing.

When I returned to Mivart's, I found a written answer to my letter of the morning, stating that his lordship of the Horse Guards was leaving town that afternoon, but would not delay my departure for the Continent, to visit which a four months' leave was granted me, with a recommendation to study at Weimar.

The next day brought us to Dover, in time to stroll about the cliffs during the evening, when I again talked sentiment with the daughter till very late. The mamma herself was too tired to come out, so that we had our walk quite alone. It is strange enough how quickly this travelling together has shaken us into intimacy. Isabella says she feels as if I were her brother, and I begin to think myself she is *not* exactly like a sister. She has a marvellously pretty foot and ankle.

The climbing of cliffs is a very dangerous pastime. How true the French adage,—*C'est plus facile de glisser sur le gazon que sur la glace.* But still nothing can come of it; for if Lady Jane be not false, I must consider myself an engaged man.

"Well, but I hope," said I, rousing myself from a revery of some minutes, and inadvertently pressing the arm which leaned upon me, "your mamma will not be alarmed at our long absence?"

"Oh! not in the least; for she knows I'm with *you*."

And here I felt a return of the pressure,—perhaps also inadvertently given, but which, whether or not, effectually set all my reasonings and calculations astray; and we returned to the hotel silent on both sides.

The appearance of "mamma" beside the hissing tea-urn brought us both back to ourselves; and after an hour's chatting we said "Good-night," to start on the morrow for the Continent.

CHAPTER XXIV.

CALAIS.

IT was upon a lovely evening in autumn as the Dover steamboat rounded the wooden pier at Calais, amid a fleet of small boats filled with eager and anxious faces, soliciting, in every species of bad English and *patois* French, the attention and patronage of the passengers.

"*Hôtel des Bains, milor.*"

"*Hôtel d'Angleterre,*" said another, in a voice of the most imposing superiority. "*C'est superbe,*—pretty well."

"*Hôtel du Nord, votre Excellence; remise de poste* and delays [query, relays] at all hours."

"*Commissionnaire, miladi,*" sang out a small shrill treble from the midst of a crowded cock-boat, nearly swamped beneath our paddle-wheel.

What a scene of bustle, confusion, and excitement does the deck of a steamer present upon such an occasion. Every one is running hither or thither. *Sauve qui peut* is now the watchword; and friendships that promised a lifelong endurance only half an hour ago, find here a speedy dissolution. The lady who slept all night upon deck enveloped in the folds of your Astrakhan cloak scarcely deigns an acknowledgment of you as she adjusts her ringlets before the looking-glass over the stove in the cabin; the polite gentleman that would have flown for a reticule or a smelling-bottle upon the high seas, won't leave his luggage in the harbor; and the gallantry and devotion that stood the test of half a gale of wind and a wet jacket is not proof when the safety of a carpet-bag or the security of a "Mackintosh" is concerned.

And thus here, as elsewhere is prosperity the touchstone of good feeling. All the various disguises which have been assumed *per viaggio* are here immediately abandoned, and stripped of the travelling costume of urbanity and courtesy, which they put on for the voyage, they stand forth in all the unblushing front of selfishness and self-interest.

Some tender scenes yet find their place amid the ruins of this chaotic state. Here may be seen a careful mother adjusting innumerable shawls and handkerchiefs round the throat of a sea-green young lady with a cough,—her maid, at the same instant, taking a tender farewell of the steward in the after-cabin.

Here is a very red-faced and hot individual, with punch-colored breeches and gaiters, disputing "one brandy too much" in his bill, and vowing that the company shall hear of it when he returns to England. There, a tall, elderly woman, with a Scotch-gray eye and a sharp cheek-bone, is depositing within her muff various seizable articles, that, until now, had been lying quietly in her trunk. Yonder, that raw-looking young gentleman, with the crumpled frock-coat and loose cravat and sea-sick visage, is asking every one if they think he may land without a passport. You scarcely recognize him for the cigar-smoking dandy of yesterday, that talked as if he had lived half his life on the Continent. While there, a rather pretty girl is looking intently at some object in the blue water beside the rudder post. You are surprised you cannot make it out; but then, she has the advantage of you, for the tall, well-looking man, with the knowing whiskers, is evidently whispering something in her ear.

"Steward, this is not my trunk; mine was a leather—"

"All the 'leathers' are gone in the first boat, sir."

"Most scandalous way of doing business."

"Trouble you for two-and-sixpence, sir."

"There's Matilda coughing again," says a thin, shrewish woman, with a kind of triumphant scowl at her better half; "but you *would* have her wear that thin shawl!"

"Whatever may be the fault of the shawl, I fancy no one will reproach her ankles for thinness," murmurs a young guardsman as he peeps up the companion-ladder.

Amid all the Babel of tongues and uproar of voices, the thorough bass of the escape steam keeps up its infernal thunders till the very brain reels; and sick as you have been of the voyage, you half wish yourself once more at sea, if only to have a moment of peace and tranquillity.

Numbers now throng the deck who have never made their appearance before. Pale, jaundiced, and crumpled, they have all the sea-sick look and haggard cheek of the real martyr,— all except one, a stout, swarthy, brown-visaged man, of about forty, with a frame of iron and a voice like the fourth string of a violoncello. You wonder why he should have taken to his bed. Learn, then, that he is his Majesty's courier from the Foreign Office, with despatches to Constantinople, and that as he is not destined to lie down in a bed for the next fourteen days, he is glad even of the narrow resemblance to one he finds in the berth of a steamboat. At length you are on shore, and marched off in a long string, like a gang of convicts, to the Bureau de l'Octroi; and here is begun an examination of the luggage which promises, from its minuteness, to last for the three months you destined to spend in Switzerland. At the end of an hour you discover that the *soi-disant commissionnaire* will transact all this affair for a few francs; and after a tiresome wait in a filthy room, jostled, elbowed, and trampled upon by boors with sabots, you adjourn to your inn and begin to feel that you are not in England.

Our little party had but few of the miseries here recounted to contend with. My *savoir faire,* with all modesty be it spoken, had been long schooled in the art and practice of travelling; and while our less-experienced fellow-travellers were deep in the novel mysteries of cotton stockings and petticoats, most ostentatiously displayed upon every table of the Bureau, we were comfortably seated in the handsome salon of the Hôtel du Nord, looking out upon a pretty grass-plot surrounded with orange-trees, and displaying in the middle a fountain about the size of a walking-stick.

"Now, Mr. Lorrequer," said Mrs. Bingham, as she seated herself by the open window, "never forget how totally dependent we are upon your kind offices. Isabella has discovered already that the French of Mountjoy Square, however intelligible in that neighborhood, and even as far as Mount Street, is Coptic and Sanscrit here; and as for myself, I intend to affect deaf-and-dumbness till I reach Paris, where I hear every one can speak English a little."

"Now, then, to begin my functions," said I, as I rang for the waiter and ran over in my mind rapidly how many invaluable hints for my new position my present trip might afford me, "always provided," as the lawyers say, that Lady Jane Callonby might feel herself tempted to become my travelling companion, in which case— But, confound it, how I am castle-building again! Meanwhile, Mrs. Bingham is looking as hungry and famished as though she would eat the waiter. "Ha! this is the *carte.*"

"Now, then, to order supper."

"*Cotelettes d'agneau.*"

"*Mayonnaise de homard.*"

"*Perdreaux rouges aux truffes,*—mark that, *aux truffes.*"

"*Gelée au maraschino.*"

"And the wine, sir," said the waiter, with a look of approval at my selection. "Champagne,—no other wine, sir?"

"No," said I, "champagne only. *Frappé,* of course," I added. And the waiter departed with a bow that would have graced St. James's.

As long as our immaterial and better part shall be doomed to keep company with its fleshly tabernacle, with all its attendant miseries of gout and indigestion, how much of our enjoyment in this world is dependent upon the mere accessory circumstances by which the business of life is carried on and maintained, and to despise which is neither good policy nor sound philosophy. In this conclusion, a somewhat long experience of the life of a traveller has fully established me. And nowhere does it press more forcibly upon the mind than when first arrived in a Continental inn, after leaving the best hotels of England still fresh in your memory. I do not for a moment dispute the very great superiority in comfort of the latter, by which I would be understood to mean all those resemblances to one's own home which an English hotel so eminently possesses, and every other one so markedly wants;

but I mean that in contrivances to elevate the spirit, cheer the jaded and tired wayfarer by objects which, however they may appeal to the mere senses, seem, at least, but little sensual, give me a foreign inn. Let me have a large, spacious salon, with its lofty walls and its airy, large-paned windows (I shall not object if the cornices and mouldings be gilded, because such is usually the case) ; let the sun and heat of a summer's day come tempered through the deep lattices of a well-fitting *jalousie* bearing upon them the rich incense of a fragrant orange-tree in blossom, and the sparkling drops of a neighboring fountain, the gentle plash of which is faintly audible amid the hum of the drone-bee; let such be the *agréments* without; while within, let the more substantial joys of the table await, in such guise as only a French *cuisine* can present them,—give me these, I say, and I shall never sigh for the far-famed and long-deplored comforts of a box in a coffee-room like a pew in a parish church, though certainly not so well cushioned, and fully as dull, with a hot waiter and a cold beefsteak; the only thing higher than your game being your bill, and the only thing less drinkable than your port being the porter.

With such exotic notions, imagine, my dear reader, whether or not I felt happy as I found myself seated between my two fair friends doing the honors of a little supper, and assisting the exhilaration of our champagne by such efforts of wit as, under favorable circumstances like these, are ever successful, and which, being like the foaming liquid which washes them down, to be swallowed without waiting, are ever esteemed good from the excitement that results, and never seriously canvassed for any more sterling merit. Nothing ever makes a man so agreeable as the belief that he is so; and certainly my fair companions appeared to have the most excellent idea of my powers in that respect; and I fancy that I made more *bons mots,* hit off more epigrams, and invented more choice incidents on that happy evening than, if now remembered, would suffice to pay my tailor's bill when collated for "Bentley's Miscellany," and illustrated by Cruikshank. Alas! that, like the good liquor that seasoned them, both are gone by, and I am left but to chronicle the memory of the fun in dulness, and counterfeit the effervescence of the grape-juice by soda-water. One thing, however, is certain,—we formed a most agreeable party; and if the feeling of gloom ever momentarily shot through my mind, it was that evenings like these came so rarely in this work-a-day world that each such should be looked on as our last.

If I had not already shown myself up to my reader as a weathercock of the first water, perhaps I should now hesitate about confessing that I half regretted the short space during which it should be my privilege to act as the guide and mentor of my two friends. The impetuous haste which I before felt necessary to exercise in reaching Paris immediately was now tempered by prudent thoughts about travelling at night, and reflections about sun-stroke by day; and even moments most devoted to the object of my heart's aspirations were fettered by the very philosophic idea that it could never detract from the pleasure of the happiness that awaited me if I travelled on the primrose path to its attainment. I argued thus: if Lady Jane be true, if—if, in a word, I am destined to have any success in the Callonby family, then will a day or two more not risk it. My present friends I shall, of course, take leave of at Paris, where their own acquaintances await them; and, on the other hand, should I be doomed once more to disappointment, I am equally certain I should feel no disposition to form a new attachment. Thus did I reason, and thus I believed; and though I was a kind of "consultation opinion" among my friends in "suits of love," I was really then unaware that at no time is a man so prone to fall in love as immediately after his being jilted. If common-sense will teach us not to dance a bolero upon a sprained ankle, so might it also convey the equally important lesson not to expose our more vital and inflammatory organ to the fire the day after its being singed.

Reflections like these did not occur to me at this moment; besides that, I was "going the pace" with a forty-horse power of agreeability that left me little time for thought,—least of all, for serious thought. So stood matters. I had just filled our tall, slender glasses with the creaming and "sparkling" source of wit and inspiration when the loud crack, crack,

crack of a postilion's whip, accompanied by the shaking trot of a heavy team and the roll of wheels, announced a new arrival.

"Here they come!" said I. "Only look at them,—four horses and one postilion, all apparently straggling and straying after their own fancy, but yet going surprisingly straight, notwithstanding. See how they come through that narrow archway,—it might puzzle the best four-in-hand in England to do it better."

"What a handsome young man, if he had not those odious mustachios! Why, Mr. Lorrequer, he knows *you,*—see, he is bowing to you."

"*Me!* Oh! no. Why, surely, it must be! The devil,— it is Kilkee, Lady Jane's brother! I know his temper well. One five minutes' observation of my present intimacy with my fair friends, and adieu to all hopes for me of calling Lord Callonby my father-in-law. There is not, therefore, a moment to lose."

As these thoughts revolved through my mind, the confusion I felt had covered my face with scarlet, and with a species of blundering apology for abruptly leaving them for a moment, I ran downstairs only in time sufficient to anticipate Kilkee's questions as to the number of my apartment, to which he was desirous of proceeding at once. Our first greetings over, Kilkee questioned me as to my route, adding that his now was necessarily an undecided one, for if his family happened not to be at Paris, he should be obliged to seek after them among the German watering-places. "In any case, Lorrequer," said he, "we shall hunt them in couples. I must insist upon your coming along with me."

"Oh! that," said I, "you must not think of. Your carriage is a *coupé,* and I cannot think of crowding you."

"Why, you don't seriously wish to affront me, I hope; for I flatter myself that a more perfect carriage for two people cannot be built. Hobson made it on a plan of my own, and I am exceedingly proud of it, I assure you. Come,—that matter is decided; now for supper. Are there many English here just now? By the by, the ladies I think I saw you standing with on the balcony, who are they?"

"Oh! the ladies; oh! yes, people I came over with—"

"One was pretty, I fancied. Have you supped? Just order something, will you; meanwhile, I shall write a few lines before the post leaves." Saying which, he dashed upstairs after the waiter, and left me to my meditations.

"This begins to be pleasant," thought I, as the door closed, leaving me alone in the salon. In circumstances of such moment I had never felt so nonplussed as now. How to decline Kilkee's invitation, without discovering my intimacy with the Binghams,—and yet I could not, by any possibility, desert them thus abruptly. Such was the dilemma. "I see but one thing for it," said I gloomily, as I strode through the coffee-room with my head sunk and my hands behind my back; "I see but one thing left,—I must be taken ill to-night, and not be able to leave my bed in the morning: a fever, a contagious fever; blue and red spots all over me; and be raving wildly before breakfast-time; and if ever any discovery takes place of my intimacy above stairs, I must only establish it as a premonitory symptom of insanity, which seized me in the packet. And now for a doctor that will understand my case and listen to reason, as they would call it in Ireland." With this idea uppermost, I walked out into the court-yard to look for a *commissionnaire* to guide me in my search. Around on every side of me stood the various carriages and vehicles of the hotel and its inmates, to the full as distinctive and peculiar in character as their owners. "Ah! there is Kilkee's," said I, as my eye lighted upon the well-balanced and elegant little carriage which he had been only with justice encomiumizing. "It is certainly perfect; and yet I'd give a handful of louis d'or if it was like that venerable cabriolet yonder, with the one wheel and no shafts. But, alas! those springs give little hope of a break-down, and that confounded axle will outlive the patentee. But still, can nothing be done, eh? Come, the thought is a good one. I say, *garçon,* who greases the wheels of the carriages here?"

"*C'est moi, monsieur,*" said a great oaf in wooden shoes and a blouse.

"Well, then, do you understand these?" said I, touching the patent axle-boxes with my cane.

He shook his head.

"Then who does here?"

"Ah! Michel understands them perfectly."

"Then bring him here," said I.

In a few minutes a little, shrewd old fellow, with a smith's apron, made his appearance and introduced himself as M. Michel. I had not much difficulty in making him master of my plan, which was to detach one of the wheels, as if for the purpose of oiling the axle, and afterwards render it incapable of being replaced,—at least for twenty-four hours.

"This is my idea," said I; "nevertheless, do not be influenced by me. All I ask is, disable the carriage from proceeding to-morrow, and here are three louis d'or at your service."

"*Soyez bien tranquille, monsieur;* milor shall spend to-morrow in Calais if I know anything of my art." Saying which, he set out in search of his tools, while I returned to the salon with my mind relieved, and fully prepared to press the urgency of my reaching Paris without any delay.

"Well, Lorrequer," said Kilkee, as I entered, "here is supper waiting, and I am as hungry as a wolf."

"Oh! I beg pardon, I've been getting everything in readiness for our start to-morrow morning; for I have not told you how anxious I am to get to Paris before the 8th,—some family business which requires my looking after, compelling me to do so."

"As to that, let your mind be at rest, for I shall travel to-morrow night if you prefer it. Now, for the *Volnay*. Why, you are not drinking your wine. What do you say to our paying our respects to the fair ladies above stairs? I am sure the attentions you have practised coming over would permit the liberty."

"Oh, hang it, no! There's neither of them pretty, and I should rather avoid the risk of making a regular acquaintance with them," said I.

"As you like, then; only as you'll not take any wine, let us have a stroll through the town."

After a short ramble through the town, in which Kilkee talked the entire time, but of what I know not, my thoughts being upon my own immediate concerns, we returned to the hotel. As we entered the *porte-cochère* my friend Michel passed me, and as he took off his hat in salutation, gave me one rapid glance of his knowing eye that completely satisfied me that Hobson's pride in my friend's carriage had by that time received quite sufficient provocation to throw him into an apoplexy.

"By the by," said I, "let us see your carriage. I am curious to look at it," and so I was.

"Well, then, come along this way; they have placed it under some of these sheds, which they think coach-houses."

I followed my friend through the court till we arrived near the fatal spot; but before reaching it he caught a glimpse of the mischief, and shouted out a most awful imprecation upon the author of the deed which met his eye. The fore-wheel of the *coupé* had been taken from the axle, and in the difficulty of so doing, from the excellence of the workman-ship, two of the spokes were broken, the patent box was a mass of rent metal, and the end of the axle turned downwards like a hoe.

I cannot convey any idea of poor Kilkee's distraction,—and, in reality, my own was little short of it; for the wretch had so far outstripped my orders that I became horrified at the cruel destruction before me. We both, therefore, stormed in the most imposing English and French, first separately, and then together. We offered a reward for the apprehension of the culprit, whom no one appeared to know,—although, as it hap-pened, every one in a large household was aware of the trans-action but the proprietor himself. We abused all, innkeeper, waiters, ostlers, and chambermaids, collectively and individ-ually, condemned Calais as a den of iniquity, and branded all Frenchmen as rogues and vagabonds. This seemed to allevi-ate considerably my friend's grief and excite my thirst,—for-tunately, perhaps, for us; for if our eloquence had held out much longer, I am afraid our auditory might have lost their patience,—and, indeed, I am quite certain, if our French had not been in nearly as disjointed a condition as the spokes of the *calèche,* such must have been the case.

"Well, Lorrequer, I suppose, then, we are not destined to be fellow-travellers; for if you must go to-morrow—"

"Alas! it is imperative," said I.

"Then, in any case, let us arrange where we shall meet, for I hope to be in Paris the day after you."

"I'll stop at Meurice's."

"Meurice's be it," said he; "so now good-night till we meet in Paris."

CHAPTER XXV.

THE GENDARME.

I HAD fortunately sufficient influence upon my fair friends to persuade them to leave Calais early on the morning following; and two hours before Kilkee had opened his eyes upon this mortal life we were far upon the road to Paris.

Having thus far perfectly succeeded in my plot, my spirits rose rapidly, and I made every exertion to make the road appear short to my fellow-travellers. This part of France is unfortunately deficient in any interest from scenery; large undivided tracts of waving corn-fields, with a background of apparently interminable forests, and occasionally, but rarely, the glimpse of some old time-worn château, with its pointed gable and terraced walk, are nearly all that the eye can detect in the intervals between the small towns and villages. Nothing, however, is "flat or unprofitable" to those who desire to make it otherwise; good health, good spirits, and fine weather are wonderful travelling companions, and render one tolerably independent of the charms of scenery. Every mile that separated me from Calais, and took away the chance of being overtaken, added to my gayety, and I flatter myself that a happier party have rarely travelled that well-frequented road.

We reached Abbeville to dinner, and adjourned to the beautiful little garden of the inn for our coffee; the evening was so delightful that I proposed to walk on the Paris road until the coming up of the carriage, which required a screw, or a washer, or some such trifle, as always occurs in French posting. To this "mamma" objected, she being tired; but added that Isabella and I might go on, and that she would take us up in half an hour. This was an arrangement so very agreeable and unlooked-for by me that I pressed Miss Bingham as far as I well could, and at last succeeded in overcoming her scruples and permitting me to shawl her. One has always a tremendous power of persuasion with the uninitiated abroad, by a reference to a standard of manners and habits totally different from our own. Thus the talismanic words, "Oh! don't be shocked; remember you are in France," did more to satisfy my young friend's mind than all I could have said for an hour. Little did she know that in England only has an unmarried young lady any liberty, and that the standard of foreign propriety on this head is far, very far, more rigid than our own.

"*La première rue à gauche,*" said an old man of whom I inquired the road. "*Et puis?*" added I.

"And then quite straight; it is a *chaussée* all the way, and you cannot mistake it."

"Now for it, mademoiselle," said I. "Let us try if we cannot see a good deal of the country before the carriage comes up."

We had soon left the town behind, and reached a beautifully shaded high-road, with blossoming fruit-trees and honeysuckle-covered cottages; there had been several light showers during the day, and the air had all the fresh, fragrant feeling of an autumn evening, so tranquillizing and calming that few there are who have not felt, at some time or other of their lives, its influence upon their minds. I fancied my fair companion did so, for as she walked beside me, her silence and the gentle pressure of her arm were far more eloquent than words.

If that extraordinary flutter and flurry of sensations which will now and then seize you when walking upon a lonely country road with a pretty girl for your companion, whose arm is linked in yours, and whose thoughts, as far as you can guess, at least, are travelling the same path with your own,—if this be animal magnetism, or one of its phenomena, then do I swear by Mesmer. Whatever it be, delusion or otherwise, it has given me the brightest moments of my life; these are the real "winged dreams" of pleasures which outlive others of more absorbing and actual interest at the time. After all, for how many of our happiest feelings are we indebted to the weakness of our nature? The man that is wise at nineteen, *je lui en fais mes compliments,* but I assuredly do not envy him; and now, even now, when I number more years than I should like to "confess," rather than suffer the suspicious watchfulness of age to creep on me, I prefer to "go on believing," even though every hour of the day should show me duped and deceived. While I plead guilty to this impeachment, let me show, in mitigation, that it has its enjoyments. First, although I am the most constant and devoted man breathing, as a very cursory glance at these "Confessions" may prove, yet I have never been able to restrain myself from a propensity to make love merely as a pastime. The gambler that sits down to play cards or dice against himself may perhaps be the only person that can comprehend this tendency of mine. We both of us are playing for nothing (or love, which I suppose is synonymous), we neither of us put forth our strength; for that very reason—and in fact, like the waiter at Vauxhall, who was complimented upon the dexterity with which he poured out the lemonade, and confessed that he spent his mornings "practysing with vater,"—we pass a considerable portion of our lives in a mimic warfare which, if it seem unprofitable, is nevertheless pleasant.

After all this long tirade, need I say how our walk proceeded? We had fallen into a kind of discussion upon the singular intimacy which had so rapidly grown up between us, and which years long might have failed to engender. We attempted also to analyze the reasons for and the nature of the friendship thus so suddenly established,—a rather dangerous and difficult topic when the parties were both young, one eminently handsome, and the other disposed to be most agreeable. Oh! my dear young friends of either sex, whatever your feelings be for one another, keep them to yourselves; I know of nothing half so hazardous as that "comparing of notes" which sometimes happens. Analysis is a beautiful thing in mathematics or chemistry, but it makes sad havoc when applied to the "functions of the heart."

"Mamma appears to have forgotten us," said Isabella, as she spoke, after walking for some time in silence beside me.

"Oh! depend upon it the carriage has taken all this time to repair; but are you tired?"

"Oh! by no means; the evening is delightful, but—"

"Then perhaps you are *ennuyée*," said I, half pettishly, to provoke a disclaimer, if possible. To this insidiously put query

I received, as I deserved, no answer, and again we sauntered on without speaking.

"To whom does that château belong, my old friend?" said I, addressing a man on the roadside.

"To Monsieur le Marquis, sir," replied he.

"But what's his name, though?"

"Ah! that I can't tell you," replied the man again.

There you may perceive how, even yet, in provincial France the old respect for the aristocracy still survives. It is sufficient that the possessor of that fine place is "Monsieur le Marquis;" but any other knowledge of who he is, and what, is superfluous. "How far are we from the next village, do you know?"

"About a league."

"Indeed! Why, I thought La Scarpe was quite near us."

"Ah! you are thinking of the Amiens road."

"Yes, of course; and is not this the Amiens road?"

"Oh, no! The Amiens road lies beyond those low hills to the right. You pass the turn at the first *barrière*."

"Is it possible we could have come wrong?"

"Oh! Mr. Lorrequer, don't say so, I entreat of you."

"And what road is this, then, my friend?"

"This is the road to Albert and Péronne."

"Unfortunately, I believe he is quite right. Is there any cross-road from the village before us now to the Amiens road?"

"Yes; you can reach it about two leagues hence."

"And we can get a carriage at the inn, probably?"

"Ah! that I am not sure of. Perhaps at the Lion d'Or you may."

"But why not go back to Abbeville?"

"Oh! Mrs. Bingham must have left long since, and besides, you forget the distance; we have been walking two hours."

"Now for the village," said I as I drew my friend's arm closer within mine, and we set out in a fast walk.

Isabella seemed terribly frightened at the whole affair; what her mamma might think, and what might be her fears at not finding us on the road, and a hundred other encouraging reflections of this nature, she poured forth unceasingly. As for myself, I did not know well what to think of it, my old fondness ever for adventure being sufficiently strong in me to give a relish to anything which bore the least resemblance to one. This I now concealed, and sympathized with my fair friend upon our mishap, assuring her at the same time that there could be no doubt of our overtaking Mrs. Bingham before her arrival at Amiens.

"Ah! there is the village in the valley; how beautifully situated!"

"Oh! I can't admire anything now, Mr. Lorrequer; I am so frightened."

"But surely without cause," said I, looking tenderly beneath her bonnet.

"Is this," she answered, "nothing?" And we walked on in silence again.

On reaching the Lion d'Or we discovered that the only conveyance to be had was a species of open market-cart drawn by two horses, and in which it was necessary that my fair friend and myself should seat ourselves side by side upon straw. There was no choice; and as for Miss Bingham, I believe if an ass with panniers had presented itself, she would have preferred it to remaining where she was. We therefore took our places, and she could not refrain from laughing as we set out upon our journey in this absurd equipage, every jolt of which threw us from side to side, and rendered every attention on my part requisite to prevent her being upset.

After about two hours' travelling we arrived at the Amiens road and stopped at the *barrière*. I immediately inquired if a carriage had passed resembling Mrs. Bingham's, and learned that it had, about an hour before, and that the lady in it had been informed that two persons, like those she asked after, had been seen in a *calèche* driving rapidly to Amiens, upon which she set out as fast as possible in pursuit.

"Certainly," said I, "the plot is thickening; but for that unlucky mistake, she might in all probability have waited here for us. Amiens is only two leagues now, so our drive will not be long, and before six o'clock we shall all be laughing over the matter as a very good joke."

On we rattled, and as the road became less frequented, and the shadows lengthened, I could not but wonder at the strange situations which the adventurous character of my life had so often involved me in. Meanwhile, my fair friend's spirits became more and more depressed, and it was not without the greatest difficulty I was enabled to support her courage. I assured her, and not altogether without reason, that though so often in my eventful career accidents were occurring which rendered it dubious and difficult to reach the goal I aimed at, yet the results had so often been more pleasant than I could have anticipated, that I always felt a kind of involuntary satisfaction at some apparent obstacle to my path, setting it down as some especial means of fortune, to heighten the pleasure awaiting me; "And now," added I, "even here, perhaps, in this very mistake of our road, the sentiments I have heard, the feelings I have given utterance to—" What I was about to say, Heaven knows,—perhaps nothing less than a downright proposal was coming; but at that critical moment a *gendarme* rode up to the side of our wagon and surveyed us with the peculiarly significant scowl his order is gifted with. After trotting alongside for a few seconds he ordered the driver to halt, and, turning abruptly to us, demanded our passports. Now, our passports were at that precise moment peaceably reposing in the side-pocket of Mrs. Bingham's carriage; I, therefore, explained to the *gendarme* how we were circumstanced, and added that on arriving at Amiens the passports should be produced. To this he replied that all might be perfectly true, but he did not believe a word of it; that he had received an order for the apprehension of two English persons travelling that road; and that he should accordingly request our company back to Chantraine, the *commissaire* of which place was his officer.

"But why not take us to Amiens?" said I; "particularly when I tell you that we can there show our passports."

"I belong to the Chantraine district," was the laconic answer; and like the gentleman who could not weep at the sermon because he belonged to another parish, this specimen of a French Dogberry would not hear reason except in his own district.

No arguments which I could think of had any effect upon him, and amid a volley of entreaty and imprecation, both equally vain, we saw ourselves turn back upon the road to

Amiens, and set out at a round trot to Chantraine, on the road to Calais.

Poor Isabella, I really pitied her! Hitherto her courage had been principally sustained by the prospect of soon reaching Amiens; now there was no seeing where our adventure was to end. Besides that, actual fatigue from the wretched conveyance began to distress her, and she was scarcely able to support herself, though assisted by my arm. What a perilous position mine,—whispering consolation and comfort to a pretty girl on a lonely road, the only person near being one who comprehended nothing of the language we spoke in! Ah, how little do we know of fate, and how often do we despise circumstances that determine all our fortunes in the world! To think that a *gendarme* should have anything to do with my future lot in life, and that the real want of a passport to travel should involve the probable want of a license to marry. "Yes, it is quite in keeping," thought I, "with every step I have taken through life. I may be brought before the *maire* as a culprit, and leave him as a Benedict."

On reaching the town, we were not permitted to drive to the inn, but at once conveyed to the house of the *commissaire,* who was also the *maire* of the district. The worthy functionary was long since in bed, and it was only after ringing violently for half an hour that a head, surmounted with a dirty cotton nightcap, peeped from an upper window, and seemed to survey the assemblage beneath with patient attention. By this time a considerable crowd had collected from the neighboring ale-houses and *cabarets,* who deemed it a most fitting occasion to honor us with the most infernal yells and shouts, as indicating their love of justice and delight in detecting knavery; and that we were both involved in such suspicion we had not long to learn. Meanwhile, the poor old *maire,* who had been an *employé* in the stormy days of the Revolution and also under Napoleon, and who fully concurred with Swift that "a crowd is a mob, if composed even of bishops," firmly believing that the uproar beneath in the street was the announcement of a new change of affairs at Paris, determined to be early in the field, and shouted, therefore, with all his lungs: *"Vive la nation! Vive la charte! A bas les autres!"* A tremendous shout of laughter saluted this exhibition of unexpected republicanism, and the poor *maire* retired from the window, having learned his mistake, covered with shame and confusion.

Before the mirth caused by this blunder had subsided, the door had opened, and we were ushered into the bureau, accompanied by the anxious crowd, all curious to know the particulars of our crime.

The *maire* soon appeared, his nightcap being replaced by a small black-velvet skull-cap, and his lanky figure enveloped in a tarnished silk dressing-gown; he permitted us to be seated while the *gendarme* recounted the suspicious circumstances of our travelling, and produced the order to arrest an Englishman and his wife who had arrived in one of the late Boulogne packets, and who had carried off from some banking-house money and bills to a large amount.

"I have no doubt these are the people," said the *gendarme;* "and here is the *carte descriptive.* Let us compare it: 'Forty-two or forty-three years of age.'"

"I trust, Monsieur le Maire," said I, overhearing this, "that ladies do not recognize me as so much."

"'Of a pale and cadaverous aspect,'" continued the *gendarme.*

"Civil and complimentary, certainly," added I.

"'Squints much with the left eye.' Look at Monsieur le Maire, if you please, sir," said the *gendarme.*

Upon this the old functionary, wiping his spectacles with a snuffy handkerchief, as if preparing them to examine an eclipse of the sun, regarded me fixedly for several minutes, and said, "Oh, yes, I perceive it plainly; continue the description."

"'Five feet three inches,'" said the *gendarme.*

"Six feet one in England, whatever this climate may have done since."

"'Speaks broken and bad French.'"

"Like a native," said I,—"at least, so said my friends in the Chaussée d'Antin in the year fifteen."

Here the catalogue ended, and a short conference between the *maire* and the *gendarme* ensued, which ended in our being committed for examination on the morrow; meanwhile, we were to remain at the inn under the surveillance of the *gendarme*.

On reaching the inn my poor friend was so completely exhausted that she at once retired to her room, and I proceeded to fulfil a promise I had made her to despatch a note to Mrs. Bingham at Amiens by a special messenger, acquainting her with all our mishaps and requesting her to come or send to our assistance. This done, and a good supper smoking before me, of which, with difficulty, I persuaded Isabella to partake in her own room, I again regained my equanimity, and felt once more at ease.

The *gendarme* in whose guardianship I had been left was a fine specimen of his caste,—a large and powerfully built man of about fifty, with an enormous beard of grizzly brown and gray hair, meeting above and beneath his nether lip; his eyebrows were heavy and beetling, and nearly concealed his sharp gray eyes, while a deep sabre-wound had left upon his cheek a long white scar, giving a most warlike and ferocious look to his features.

As he sat apart from me for some time, silent and motionless, I could not help imagining in how many a hard-fought day he had borne a part, for he evidently, from his age and bearing, had been one of the soldiers of the Empire. I invited him to partake of my bottle of Médoc, by which he seemed flattered. When the flask became low, and was replaced by another, he appeared to have lost much of his constrained air, and seemed forgetting rapidly the suspicious circumstances which he supposed attached to me, waxed wondrous confidential and communicative, condescending to impart some traits of a life which was not without its vicissitudes, for he had been, as I suspected, one of the "Garde,"—the old Garde, —was wounded at Marengo, and received his decoration on the field of Wagram from the hands of the Emperor himself. The headlong enthusiasm of attachment to Napoleon which his brief and stormy career elicited, even from those who suffered long and deeply in his behalf, is not one of the least singular circumstances which this portion of history displays. While the rigors of the conscription had invaded every family in France, from Normandy to La Vendée; while the untilled fields, the ruined granaries, the half-deserted villages, all attested the depopulation of the land,—those talismanic words, *l'Empereur et la Gloire,* by some magic mechanism seemed all-sufficient, not only to repress regret and suffering, but even stimulate pride and nourish valor; and even yet, when it might be supposed that, like the brilliant spectacle of a magic lantern, the gaudy pageant had passed away, leaving only the darkness and desolation behind it, the memory of those days under the Empire survives untarnished and unimpaired, and every sacrifice of friends or fortune is accounted but little in the balance when the honor of *la belle France* and the triumphs of the *grande armée* are weighed against them. The infatuated and enthusiastic followers of this great man would seem, in some respects, to resemble the drunkard in the *vaudeville,* who alleged as his excuse for drinking, that whenever he was sober, his poverty disgusted him. "My cabin," said he, "is a cell, my wife a mass of old rags, my child a wretched object of misery and malady. But give me brandy, let me only have that, and then my hut is a palace, my wife is a princess, and my child the very picture of health and happiness." So with these people,—intoxicated with the triumphs of their nation, *tête montée* with victory, they cannot exist in the horror of sobriety which peace necessarily enforces; and whenever the subject turns in conversation upon the distresses of the time or the evil prospects of the country, they call out, not, like the drunkard, for brandy, but in the same spirit they say, "Ah, if you would again see France flourishing and happy, let us once more have our *croix d'honneur,* our epaulets, our voluntary contributions, our Murillos, our Velasquez, our spoils from Venice, and our increased territories to rule over." This is the language of the Bonapartist everywhere and at all seasons; and the mass of the nation is wonderfully disposed to participate in the sentiment. The Empire was the "Æneid" of the nation, and Napoleon the only hero they could believe in. You may satisfy yourself of this easily. Every *café* will give evidence of it, every society bears testimony to it, and even the most wretched *vaudeville,* however trivial the interest, however meagre the story and poor the diction, let the Emperor but have his *rôle,* let him be as laconic as possible, carry his hands behind his back, wear the well-known low cocked hat and the *redingote grise,* the success is certain, every sentence he utters is applauded, and not a single allusion to the Pyramids, the sun of Austerlitz, *la gloire, et la Vieille Garde,* but is sure to bring down thunders of acclamation. But I am forgetting myself, and perhaps my reader too; the conversation of the old *gendarme* accidentally led me into reflections like these, and he was well calculated in many ways to call them forth. His devoted attachment, his personal love of the Emperor, of which he gave me some touching instances, was admirably illustrated by an incident which I am inclined to tell, and hope it may amuse the reader as much as it did myself on hearing it.

When Napoleon had taken possession of the papal dominions, as he virtually did, and carried off the pope, Pius VI., to Paris, this old soldier, then a musketeer in the Garde, formed part of the company that mounted guard over the holy father. During the earlier months of the holy father's confinement he was at liberty to leave his apartments at any hour he pleased, and cross the courtyard of the palace to the chapel where he performed mass. At such moments the portion of the Imperial Guard then on duty stood under arms, and received from the august hand of the pope his benediction as he passed. But one morning a hasty express arrived from the Tuileries, and the officer on duty communicated his instructions to his party that the apostolic vicar was not to be permitted to pass, as heretofore, to the chapel, and that a most rigid superintendence was to be exercised over his movements. My poor companion had his turn for duty on that ill-starred day; he had not been long at his post when the sound of footsteps was heard approaching, and he soon saw the procession, which always attended the holy father to his devotions, advancing towards him. He immediately placed himself across the passage, and with his musket in rest, barred the exit, declaring at the same time that such were his orders. In vain the priests who formed the *cortège* addressed themselves to his heart and spoke to his feelings, and at last, finding little success by these methods, explained to him the mortal sin and crime, for which eternal damnation itself might not be a too heavy retribution, if he persisted in preventing his Holiness to pass, and thus be the means of opposing an obstacle to the head of the whole Catholic Church from celebrating the mass. The soldier remained firm and unmoved, the only answer he returned being that he had his orders, and dared not disobey them. The pope, however, persisted in his resolution. and endeavored to get by, when the hardy veteran retreated a step, and placing his musket and bayonet at the charge, called out, *"Au nom de l'Empereur,"* when the pious party at last yielded, and slowly retired within the palace.

Not many days after, this severe restriction was recalled, and once more the father was permitted to go to and from the chapel of the palace at such times as he pleased, and again, as before, in passing the corridor, the guards presented arms and received the holy benediction,—all except one; upon him the head of the Church frowned severely and turned his back, while extending his pious hands towards the others. "And yet," said the poor fellow, in concluding his story,— "and yet I could not have done otherwise. I had my orders, and must have followed them; and had the Emperor commanded it, I should have run my bayonet through the body of the holy father himself.

"Thus you see, my dear sir, how I have loved the Emperor, for I have many a day stood under fire for him in this world, *et il faut que j'aime encore au feu pour lui après ma mort."*

He received in good part the consolations I offered him on this head; but I plainly saw they did not, could not, relieve his mind from the horrible conviction he lay under,—that his soul's safety forever had been bartered for his attachment to the Emperor.

This story had brought us to the end of the third bottle of Médoc; and as I was neither the pope, nor had any very decided intentions of saying mass, he offered no obstacle to my retiring for the night and betaking myself to my bed.

CHAPTER XXVI.

THE INN AT CHANTRAINE.

WHEN contrasted with the comforts of an English bed-room in a good hotel, how miserably short does the appearance of a French one fall in the estimation of the tired traveller! In exchange for the carpeted floor, the well-curtained windows, the richly-tapestried bed, the well-cushioned arm-chair, and the innumerable other luxuries which await him, he has nought but a narrow, uncurtained bed, a bare floor (occasionally a flagged one), three hard cane-bottomed chairs, and a looking-glass which may convey an idea of how you would look under the combined influence of the cholera and a stroke of apoplexy, one half of your face being twice the length of the other, and the entire of it of a bluish-green tint,—pretty enough in one of Turner's landscapes, but not at all becoming when applied to the "human face divine." Let no late arrival from the Continent contradict me here by his late experiences, which a stray twenty pounds and the railroads (confound them for the same!) have enabled him to acquire. I speak of matters before it occurred to all Charing Cross and Cheapside to "take the water" between Dover and Calais, and inundate the world with the wit of the Cider Cellars and the Hole in the Wall. No! In the days I write of, the travelled were of another genus, and you might dine at Véry's, or have your box at *Les Italiens,* without being dunned by your tailor at the one, or confronted with your washerwoman at the other. Perhaps I have written all this in the spite and malice of a man who feels that his sovereign only goes half as far now as heretofore, and attributes all his diminished enjoyments and restricted luxuries to the unceasing current of his countrymen, whom fate and the law of imprisonment for debt impel hither. Whether I am so far guilty or not, is not now the question; suffice it to say that Harry Lorrequer, for reasons best known to himself, lives abroad, where he will be most happy to see any of his old and former friends who take his quarters *en route;* and in the words of a bellicose brother of the pen, but in a far different spirit, he would add "that any person who feels himself here alluded to may learn the author's address at his publisher's." "Now let us go back to our muttons," as Barney Coyle used to say in the Dublin Library formerly,—for Barney was fond of French allusions, which occasionally, too, he gave in their own tongue; as once describing an interview with Lord Cloncurry, in which he broke off suddenly the conference, adding, "I told him I never could consent to such a proposition, and putting my *château* (*chapeau*) on my head, I left the house at once."

It was nearly three o'clock in the morning as, accompanied by the waiter, who, like others of his tribe, had become a kind of somnambulist *ex officio,* I wended my way up one flight of stairs, and down another, along a narrow corridor, down two steps, through an ante-chamber, and into another corridor to No. 82, my habitation for the night. Why I should have been so far conducted from the habitable portion of the house I had spent my evening in, I leave the learned in such matters to explain; as for me, I have ever remarked it, while asking for a chamber in a large, roomy hotel, the singular pride with which you are ushered up grand staircases, down passages, through corridors, and up narrow back flights till the blue sky is seen through the skylight, to No. 199, "the only spare bedroom in the house," while the silence and desolation of the whole establishment would seem to imply far otherwise, —the only evidence of occupation being a pair of dirty Wellingtons at the door of No. 7.

"Well, we have arrived at last," said I, drawing a deep sigh as I threw myself upon a rickety chair and surveyed rapidly my meagre-looking apartment.

"Yes, this is Monsieur's chamber," said the waiter, with a very peculiar look, half servile, half droll. *"Madame couche No.* 28."

"Very well, good night!" said I, closing the door hastily, and not liking the further scrutiny of the fellow's eye as he fastened it on me, as if to search what precise degree of relationship existed between myself and my fair friend, whom he had called "madame" purposely to elicit an observation from me. "Ten to one, though," said I, as I undressed myself, "but they think she is my wife. How good! But again— Ay, it is very possible, considering we are in France. *Numéro vingt-huit,*—quite far enough 'from this part of the house, I should suppose, from my number. That old *gendarme* was a fine fellow. What strong attachment to Napoleon! and the story of the pope,—I hope I may remember *that*. Isabella, poor girl, this adventure must really distress her,—hope she is not crying over it. What a devil of a hard bed!—and it is not five feet long, too. And bless my soul, is this all by way of covering? Why, I shall be perished here! Oh! I must certainly put all my clothes over me in addition; unfortunately there is no hearth-rug. Well, there is no help for it now, so let me try to sleep,—*numéro vingt-huit.*"

How long I remained in a kind of uneasy, fitful slumber, I cannot tell; but I awoke shivering with cold, puzzled to tell where I was, and my brain addled with the broken fragments of half-a-dozen dreams, all mingling and mixing themselves with the unpleasant realities of my situation. "What an infernal contrivance for a bed," thought I, as my head came thump against the top, while my legs projected far beyond the foot-rail, the miserable portion of clothing over me at the same time being only sufficient to temper the night air, which in autumn is occasionally severe and cutting. "This will never do. I must ring the bell and rouse the house, if only to get a fire, if they don't possess such a thing as blankets." I immediately rose, and groping my way along the wall, endeavored to discover the bell, but in vain; and for the same satisfactory reason that Von Troil did not devote one chapter of his work on Iceland to "snakes,"—because there were none such there. What was now to be done? About the geography of my present abode I knew, perhaps, as much as the public at large know about the Coppermine River and Behring's Straits. The world, it was true, was before me, "where to choose,"—admirable things for an epic, but decidedly an unfortunate circumstance for a very cold gentleman in search of a blanket. Thus thinking, I opened the door of my chamber, and not in any way resolved how I should proceed, I stepped forth into the long corridor, which was dark as midnight itself.

Tracing my path along the wall, I soon reached a door, which I in vain attempted to open; in another moment I found another and another, each of which was locked. Thus along the entire corridor I felt my way, making every effort to discover where any of the people of the house might have concealed themselves, but without success. What was to be done now? It was of no use to go back to my late abode, and find it comfortless as I left it, so I resolved to proceed in my search; by this time I had arrived at the top of a small flight of stairs which I remembered having come up, and which led to another long passage similar to the one I had explored, but running in a transverse direction; down this I now crept and reached the landing, along the wall of which I was guided by my hand, as well for safety as to discover the architrave of some friendly door where the inhabitant might be sufficiently Samaritan to lend some portion of his bed-clothes. Door after door followed in succession along this confounded passage, which I began to think as long as the gallery of the lower one; at last, however, just as my heart was sinking within me from disappointment, the handle of a lock turned, and I found myself inside a chamber. How was I now to proceed? For if this apartment did not contain any of the people of the hotel, I had but a sorry excuse for disturbing the repose of any traveller who might have been more fortunate than myself in the article of blankets. To go back, however, would be absurd, having already taken so much trouble to find out a room that was inhabited,—for that such was the case, a short, thick snore assured me,—so that my resolve was at once made to waken the sleeper and endeavor to interest him in my destitute situation. I accordingly approached the place where the nasal sounds seemed to issue from, and soon reached the post of a bed. I waited for an instant, and then began,—

"Monsieur, voulez-vous bien me permettre—"

."As to short whist, I never could make it out, so there is an end of it," said my unknown friend, in a low, husky voice, which, strangely enough, was not totally unfamiliar to me; but when or how I had heard it before I could not then think.

"Well," thought I, "he is an Englishman, at all events, so I hope his patriotism may forgive my intrusion; so here goes once more to rouse him, though he seems a confoundedly heavy sleeper.—I beg your pardon, sir, but unfortunately, in a point like the present, perhaps—"

"Well, do you mark the points, and I'll score the rubber," said he.

"The devil take the gambling fellow's dreaming!" thought I, raising my voice at the same time. "Perhaps a cold night, sir, may suffice as my apology."

"Cold? Oh, ay! put a hot poker in it," muttered he; "a hot poker, a little sugar, and a spice of nutmeg,—nothing else, —then it's delicious."

"Upon my soul, this is too bad," said I to myself. "Let us see what shaking will do.—Sir, sir, I shall feel obliged by—"

"Well, then, don't shake me, and I'll tell you where I hid the cigars,—they are under my straw hat in the window."

"Well, really," thought I, "if this gentleman's confessions were of an interesting nature, this might be good fun; but as the night is cold, I must shorten the *séance,* so here goes for one effort more.—If, sir, you could kindly spare me even a small portion of your bed-clothes—"

"No, thank you, no more wine, but I'll sing with pleasure;" and here the wretch, in something like the voice of a frog with the quinsy, began; " 'I mourn the hopes that leave me.' "

"You shall mourn something else for the same reason," said I, as, losing all patience, I seized quilt and blankets by the corner, and with one vigorous pull wrenched them from the bed and darted from the room. In a second I was in the corridor, trailing my spoil behind, which in my haste I had not time to collect in a bundle. I flew rather than ran along the passage, reached the stairs, and in another minute had gained the second gallery, but not before I heard the slam of a door behind me, and the same instant the footsteps of a person running along the corridor, who could be no other than my pursuer, effectually aroused by my last appeal to his charity. I darted along the dark and narrow passage, but soon to my horror discovered that I must have passed the door of my chamber; for I had reached the foot of the narrow back stair which led to the *grenier* and the servants' rooms, beneath the roof. To turn now would only have led me plump in the face of my injured countryman, of whose thew and sinew I was perfectly ignorant, and did not much like to venture upon. There was little time for reflection, for he had just reached the top of the stair, and was evidently listening for some clew to guide him on; stealthily and silently, and scarcely drawing breath, I mounted the narrow stairs step by step, but before I had arrived at the landing, he heard the rustle of the bed-clothes and again gave chase. There was something in the unrelenting ardor of his pursuit which suggested to my mind the idea of a most uncompromising foe; and as fear added speed to my steps, I dashed along beneath the low-roofed passage, wondering what chance of escape might yet present itself. Just at this instant the hand by which I had guided myself along the wall touched the handle of a door, I turned it, it opened, I drew in my precious bundle, and closing the door noiselessly, sat down, breathless and still, upon the floor.

Scarcely was this, the work of a second, accomplished, when the heavy tread of my pursuer resounded on the floor.

"Upon my conscience it's strange if I haven't you now, my friend," said he; "you're in a *cul-de-sac* here, as they say, if I know anything of the house; and faith, I'll make a salad of you when I get you, that's all. Devil a dirtier trick ever I heard tell of."

Need I say these words had the true smack of an Irish accent?—which circumstance, from whatever cause, did not by any means tend to assuage my fears in the event of discovery.

However, from such a misfortune my good genius now delivered me; for after traversing the passage to the end, he at last discovered another, which led by a long flight to the second story, down which he proceeded, venting at every step his determination for vengeance, and his resolution not to desist from the pursuit if it took the entire night for it.

"Well, now," thought I, "as he will scarcely venture up here again, and as I may, by leaving this, be only incurring the risk of encountering him, my best plan is to stay where I am, if it be possible." With this intent, I proceeded to explore the apartment, which from its perfect stillness I concluded to be unoccupied. After some few minutes' groping I reached a low bed, fortunately empty; and although the touch of the bedclothes led to no very favorable augury of its neatness or elegance, there was little choice at this moment, so I rolled myself up in my recent booty and resolved to wait patiently for daybreak to regain my apartment.

As always happens in such circumstances, sleep came on unawares,—so, at least, every one's experience, I am sure, can testify, that if you are forced to wake early to start by some morning coach, and that unfortunately you have not got to bed till late at night, the chances are ten to one that you get no sleep whatever, simply because you are desirous of it; but make up your mind ever so resolutely that you'll not slumber, and whether your determination be built on motives of propriety, duty, convenience, or health, the chances are just as strong that you are sound and snoring before ten minutes.

How many a man has found it impossible, with every effort of his heart and brain aiding his good wishes, to sit with unclosed eyes and ears through a dull sermon in the dog-days! How many an expectant, longing heir has yielded to the drowsy influence when endeavoring to look contrite under the severe correction of a lecture on extravagance from his uncle! Who has not felt the irresistible tendency to "drop off" in the half-hour before dinner at a stupid country-house? I need not catalogue the thousand other situations in life infinitely more "sleep-compelling" than morphine; for myself, my pleasantest and soundest moments of perfect forgetfulness of this dreary world and all its cares have been taken on an oaken bench, seated bolt upright, and *vis-à-vis* a lecturer on botany, whose calming accents, united with the softened light of an autumnal day, piercing its difficult rays through the narrow and cobwebbed windows, the odor of the recent plants and flowers aiding and abetting, all combined to steep the soul in sleep, and you sank by imperceptible and gradual steps into that state of easy slumber in which "come no dreams," and the last sounds of the lecturer's "hypogenous and perigenous" died away, becoming beautifully less, till your senses sank into rest, the syllable "rigging us—rigging us," seeming to melt away in the distance and fade from your memory. Peace be with you, Dr. A.! If I owe gratitude anywhere, I have my debt with you. The very memory I bear of you has saved me no inconsiderable sum in hop and henbane. Without any assistance from the sciences on the present occasion, I was soon asleep, and woke not till the cracking of whips and trampling of horses' feet on the pavement of the coach-yard apprised me that the world had risen to its daily labor, and that so ought I. From the short survey of my present chamber which I took on waking, I conjectured it must have been the den of some of the servants of the house upon occasion. Two low truckle-beds of the meanest description lay along the wall opposite to mine; one of them appeared to have been slept in during the past night, but by what species of animal the Fates alone can tell. An old demi-peak saddle capped and tipped with brass, some rusty bits and stray stirrup-irons, lay here and there upon the floor; while upon a species of clothes-rack, attached to a rafter, hung a tarnished suit of postilion's livery, cap, jacket, leathers, and jack-boots, all ready for use, and evidently, from their arrangement, supposed by the owner to be a rather creditable "turn-out."

I turned over these singular habiliments with much of the curiosity with which an antiquary would survey a suit of chain-armor; the long epaulets of yellow cotton cord, the heavy belt with its brass buckle, the cumbrous boots, plaited and bound with iron-like churns, were in rather a ludicrous contrast to the equipment of our light and jockey-like boys, in nankeen jackets and neat tops, that spin along over our level "Macadam."

"But," thought I, "it is full time I should get back to No. 82 and make my appearance below stairs;" though in what part of the building my room lay, and how I was to reach it without my clothes, I had not the slightest idea. A blanket is an exceedingly comfortable article of wearing apparel when in bed, but as a walking costume is by no means convenient or appropriate; while as to making a *sortie en sauvage,* however appropriate during the night, there were many serious objections if done in broad day, and with the whole establishment awake and active. The noise of mopping, scrubbing, and polishing, which is eternally going forward in a foreign inn, amply testified there was nothing which I could adopt in my present naked and forlorn condition save the uncouth and ridiculous dress of the postilion; and I need not say the thought of so doing presented nothing agreeable. I looked from the narrow window out upon the tiled roof, but without any prospect of being heard if I called ever so loudly.

The infernal noise of floor-cleansing, assisted by a Norman peasant's *chanson du pays,* the "time" being well marked by her heavy sabots, gave even less chance to me within; so that after more than half an hour passed in weighing difficulties and canvassing plans, I determined upon donning "the blue and yellow" and setting out for my own room without delay, hoping sincerely that, with proper precaution, I should be able to reach it unseen and unobserved.

As I laid but little stress upon the figure I should make in my new habiliments, it did not cause me much mortification to find that the clothes were considerably too small, the jacket scarcely coming beneath my arms, and the sleeves being so short that my hands and wrists projected beyond the cuffs like two enormous claws; the leathers were also limited in their length, and when drawn up to a proper height, permitted my knees to be seen beneath, like the short costume of a Spanish *toreador,* but scarcely as graceful. Not wishing to encumber myself in the heavy and noisy masses of wood, iron, and leather they call *les bottes fortes,* I slipped my feet into my slippers and stole gently from the room. How I must have looked at the moment, I leave my reader to guess, as with anxious and stealthy pace I crept along the low gallery that led to the narrow staircase, down which I proceeded step by step; but just as I reached the bottom, perceived, a little distance from me, with her back turned towards me, a short, squat peasant on her knees belaboring with a brush the well-waxed floor. To pass, therefore, unobserved was impossible, so that I did not hesitate to address her, and endeavor to interest her in my behalf and enlist her as my guide.

"*Bon jour, ma chère,*" said I, in a soft, insinuating tone. She did not hear me, so I repeated, "*Bon jour, ma chère, bon jour.*"

Upon this she turned round, and looking fixedly at me for a second, called out in a thick patois, "*Ah, bon Dieu, qu'il est drôle comme ça, François! Mais ce n'est pas François!*" Saying which, she sprang from her kneeling position to her feet, and with a speed that her shape and sabots seemed little to promise, rushed down the stairs as if she had seen the devil himself.

"Why, what is the matter with the woman?" said I. "Surely, if I am not François,—which, God be thanked, is true,—yet I cannot look so frightful as all this would imply." I had not much time given me for consideration now, for before I had well deciphered the number over a door before me, the loud noise of several voices on the floor beneath attracted my attention, and the moment after, the heavy tramp of feet followed, and in an instant the gallery was thronged by the men and women of the house,—waiters, ostlers, cooks, scullions, *filles de chambre,* mingled with *gendarmes,* peasants, and townspeople,—all eagerly forcing their way upstairs; yet all, on arriving at the landing-place, seemed disposed to keep at a respectful distance, and bundled themselves at one end of the corridor, while I, feelingly alive to the ridiculous appearance I made, occupied the other. The gravity with which they seemed at first disposed to regard me soon gave way, and peal after peal of laughter broke out, and young and old, men and women, even to the most severe *gendarmes,* all appeared incapable of controlling the desire for merriment my most singular figure inspired. And unfortunately this emotion seemed to promise no very speedy conclusion; for the jokes and witticisms made upon my appearance threatened to renew the festivities *ad libitum.*

"*Regardez donc ses épaules,*" said one.

"*Ah, mon Dieu! Il me fait l'idée d'une grenouille avec ses jambes jaunes,*" cried another.

"*Il vaut son pesant de fromage pour un vaudeville,*" said the director of the strolling theatre of the place. "I'll give seventy francs a week *d'appointements,* and Scribe shall write a piece expressly for himself, if he'll take it."

"May the devil fly away with your grinning baboon faces!" said I, as I rushed up the stairs again, pursued by the mob at full cry. Scarcely, however, had I reached the top step when the rough hand of the *gendarme* seized me by the shoulder, while he said in a low, husky voice, "*C'est inutile, monsieur,* you cannot escape. The thing was well contrived, it is true; but the *gendarmes* of France are not easily outwitted, and you could not have long avoided detection, even in that dress."

It was my turn to laugh now, which, to their very great amazement, I did, loud and long. That I should have thought my present costume could ever have been the means of screening me from observation, however it might have been calculated to attract it, was rather too absurd a supposition even for the mayor of a village to entertain; besides, it only now occurred to me that I was figuring in the character of a prisoner. The continued peals of laughing which this mistake on their part elicited from me seemed to afford but slight pleasure to my captor, who gruffly said,—

"When you have done amusing yourself, *mon ami,* perhaps you will do us the favor to come before the mayor."

"Certainly," I replied; "but you will first permit me to resume my own clothes. I am quite sick of masquerading *en postillon.*"

"Not so fast, my friend," said the suspicious old follower of Fouché,—"not so fast; it is but right the *maire* should see you in the disguise you attempted your escape in. It must be especially mentioned in the *procès-verbal.*"

"Well, this is becoming too ludicrous," said I. "It need not take five minutes to satisfy you why, how, and where I put on these confounded rags—"

"Then tell it to the *maire,* at the bureau."

"But for that purpose it is not necessary I should be conducted through the streets in broad day, to be laughed at. No, positively, I'll not go. In my own dress I'll accompany you with pleasure."

"Victor, Henri, Guillaume!" said the *gendarme,* addressing his companions, who immediately closed round me. "You see," added he, "there is no use in resisting."

Need I recount my own shame and ineffable disgrace? Alas! it is too, too true. Harry Lorrequer—whom Stultz entreated to wear his coats, the ornament of Hyde Park, the last appeal in dress, fashion, and equipage—was obliged to parade through the mob of a market-town in France, with four *gendarmes* for his companions, and he himself habited in a mongrel character, half postilion, half Delaware Indian. The incessant yells of laughter, the screams of the children, and the outpouring of every species of sarcasm and ridicule at my expense were not all; for as I emerged from the

Lorrequer as Postillion.

inn-door I saw Isabella in the window. Her eyes were red with weeping, but no sooner had she beheld me than she broke out into a fit of laughter that was audible even in the street.

Rage had now taken such a hold upon me that I forgot my ridiculous appearance in my thirst for vengeance. I marched on through the grinning crowd with the step of a martyr. I suppose my heroic bearing and warlike deportment must have heightened the drollery of the scene, for the devils only laughed the more. The bureau of the *maire* could not contain one tenth of the anxious and curious individuals who thronged the entrance, and for about twenty minutes the whole efforts of the *gendarmes* were little enough to keep order and maintain silence. At length the *maire* made his appearance; and accustomed as he had been for a long life to scenes of an absurd and extraordinary nature, yet the ridicule of my look and costume was too much, and he laughed outright. This was of course the signal for renewed mirth from the crowd, while those without doors, infected by the example, took up the jest, and I had the pleasure of a short calculation, *à la Babbage,* of how many maxillary jaws were at that same moment wagging at my expense.

However, the examination commenced; and I at length obtained an opportunity of explaining under what circumstances I had left my room, and how and why I had been induced to don this confounded cause of all my misery.

"This may be very true," said the mayor, "as it is very plausible, if you have evidence to prove what you have stated—"

"If it's evidence only is wanting, Mr. Maire, I'll confirm one part of the story," said a voice in the crowd, in an accent and tone that assured me the speaker was the injured proprietor of the stolen blankets. I turned round hastily to look at my victim, and what was my surprise to recognize a very old Dublin acquaintance, Mr. Arthur O'Leary.

"Good morning, Mr. Lorrequer," said he. "This is mighty like our old practices in College Green; but upon my conscience the *maire* has the advantage of Gabbet. It's lucky for you I know his worship, as we'd call him at home, or this might be a serious business. Nothing would persuade them that you were not Lucien Bonaparte, or the Iron Mask, or something of that sort, if they took it into their heads."

Mr. O'Leary was as good as his word. In a species of French that I'd venture to say would be perfectly intelligible in Mullingar, he contrived to explain to the *maire* that I was neither a runaway nor a swindler, but a very old friend of his, and consequently most respectable. The official was now as profuse of his civilities as he had before been of his suspicions, and most hospitably pressed us to stay for breakfast. This, for many reasons, I was obliged to decline,—not the least of which was my impatience to get out of my present costume. We accordingly procured a carriage and I returned to the hotel, screened from the gaze but still accompanied by the shouts of the mob, who evidently took a most lively interest in the entire proceeding.

I lost no time in changing my costume, and was about to descend to the salon, when the master of the house came to inform me that Mrs. Bingham's courier had arrived with the carriage, and that she expected us at Amiens as soon as possible.

"That is all right. Now, Mr. O'Leary, I must pray you to forgive the liberty I have taken with you, and also permit me to defer the explanation of many circumstances which seem at present strange, till—"

"Till *sine die,* if the story be a long one, my dear sir. There's nothing I hate so much, except cold punch."

"You are going to Paris," said I, "is it not so?"

"Yes, I'm thinking of it. I was up at Trolhatten, in Norway, three weeks ago, and I was obliged to leave it hastily, for I've an appointment with a friend in Geneva."

"Then how do you travel?"

"On foot, just as you see, except that I have a tobacco-bag upstairs and an umbrella."

"Light equipment, certainly; but you must allow me to give you a set down as far as Amiens, and also to present you to my friends there."

To this Mr. O'Leary made no objection; and as Miss Bingham could not bear any delay, in her anxiety to join her mother, we set out at once,—the only thing to mar my full enjoyment at the moment being the sight of the identical vest-ments I had so lately figured in, bobbing up and down before my eyes for the whole length of the stage, and leading to innumerable mischievous allusions from my friend Mr. O'Leary, which were far too much relished by my fair companion.

At twelve we arrived at Amiens, when I presented my friend Mr. O'Leary to Mrs. Bingham.

CHAPTER XXVII.

MR. O'LEARY.

AT the conclusion of my last chapter I was about to introduce to my reader's acquaintance my friend Mr. O'Leary; and as he is destined to occupy some place in the history of these "Confessions," I may perhaps be permitted to do so at more length than his intrinsic merit at first sight might appear to warrant.

Mr. O'Leary was, and I am induced to believe is, a particularly short, fat, greasy-looking gentleman, with a head as free from phrenological development as a billiard-ball, and a countenance which, in feature and color, nearly resembled the face of a cherub carved in oak as we see them in old pulpits.

Short as is his stature, his limbs compose the least part of it. His hands and feet, forming some compensation by their ample proportions, give to his entire air and appearance somewhat the look of a small fish, with short, thick fins, vulgarly called a cobbler's thumb. His voice, varying in cadence from a deep baritone to a high falsetto, maintains throughout the distinctive characteristics of a Dublin accent and pronunciation, and he talks of the "Veel of Ovoca," and a "beef-*steek*," with some pride of intonation. What part of *the* Island he came originally from, or what may be his age, are questions I have the most profound ignorance of; I have heard many anecdotes which would imply his being what the French call *d'un âge mûr,* but his own observations are generally limited to events occurring since the peace of "fifteen." To his personal attractions, such as they are, he has never been solicitous of contributing by the meretricious aids of dress. His coat, calculating from its length of waist and ample skirt, would fit Bumbo Green, while his trousers, being made of some cheap and shrinking material, have gradually contracted their limits, and look now exactly like knee-breeches, without the usual buttons at the bottom.

These, with the addition of a pair of green spectacles, the glass of one being absent, and permitting the look-out of a sharp gray eye, twinkling with drollery and good-humor, form the most palpable of his externals. In point of character, they who best knew him represented him as the best-tempered, best-hearted fellow breathing, ever ready to assist a friend, and always postponing his own plans and his own views, when he had any, to the wishes and intentions of others. Among the many odd things about him was a constant preference to travelling on foot, and a great passion for living abroad, both of which tastes he gratified, although his size might seem to offer obstacles to the one, and his total ignorance of every Continental language would appear to preclude the other. With a great liking for tobacco, which he smoked all day, a fondness for whist and malt liquors, his antipathies were few; so that except when called upon to shave more than once in the week, or wash his hands twice on the same day, it was difficult to disconcert him. His fortune was very ample; but although his mode of living was neither very ostentatious nor costly, he contrived always to spend his income. Such was the gentleman I now presented to my friends, who, I must confess, appeared strangely puzzled by his manner and appearance. This feeling, however, soon wore off; and before he had spent the morning in their company, he had made more way in their good graces, and gone farther to establish intimacy, than many a more accomplished person, with an unexceptionable coat and accurate whisker, might have effected in a fortnight. What were his gifts in this way, I am, alas! most deplorably ignorant of; it was not, Heaven knows, that he possessed any conversational talent,—of successful flattery he knew as much as a negro does of the national debt,—and yet the *bonhomie* of his character seemed to tell at once; and I never knew him fail in any one instance to establish an interest for himself before he had completed the ordinary period of a visit.

I think it is Washington Irving who has so admirably depicted the mortification of a dandy angler who, with his
beaver garnished with brown hackles, his well-poised rod, polished gaff, and handsome landing-net, with everything befitting, spends his long summer day whipping a trout stream
without a rise or even a ripple to reward him, while a ragged
urchin, with a willow wand and a bent pin, not ten yards distant, is covering the greensward with myriads of speckled and
scaly backs, from one pound weight to four. So it is in everything,—"the race is not to the swift;" the elements of success
in life, whatever be the object of pursuit, are very, very different from what we think of them at first sight. And so it
was with Mr. O'Leary; and I have more than once witnessed
the triumph of his homely manner and blunt humor over the
more polished and well-bred taste of his competitors for favor;
and what might have been the limit to such success, Heaven
can only tell, if it were not that he labored under a counter-
balancing infirmity sufficient to have swamped a line-of-
battle ship itself. It was simply this,—a most unfortunate
propensity to talk of the wrong place, person, or time in any
society he found himself; and this taste for the *mal à propos*
extended so far that no one ever ventured into company with
him as his friend without trembling for the result. But even
this, I believe his only fault, resulted from the natural goodness of his character and intentions; for believing, as he did,
in his honest simplicity, that the arbitrary distinctions of class
and rank were held as cheaply by others as himself, he felt
small scruple at recounting to a duchess a scene in a *cabaret,*
and with as little hesitation would he, if asked, have sung
the "Cruiskeen Lawn" or the "Jug of Punch," after Lablache
had finished the "Al Idea" from "Figaro." *Mauvaise honte*
he had none; indeed, I am not sure that he had any kind of
shame whatever,—except, possibly, when detected with a
coat that bore any appearance of newness, or if over-per-
suaded to wear gloves, which he ever considered as a special
effeminacy.

Such was he; and how far he insinuated himself into their
good graces, let the fact tell that on my return to the breakfast-room, after about an hour's absence, I heard him detailing the particulars of a route they were to take by his advice,

and also learned that he had been offered, and had accepted, a seat in their carriage to Paris.

"Then I'll do myself the pleasure of joining your party, Mrs. Bingham," said he. "Bingham, I think, madam, is your name?"

"Yes, sir."

"Any relation, may I ask, of a most dear friend of mine, of the same name, from Currynaslattery, in the county of Wexford?"

"I am really not aware," said Mrs. Bingham. "My husband's family are, I believe, many of them from that county."

"Ah, what a pleasant fellow was Tom!" said Mr. O'Leary, musingly, and with that peculiar tone which made me tremble, for I knew well that a reminiscence was coming. "A pleasant fellow indeed."

"Is he alive, sir, now?"

"I believe so, ma'am; but I hear the climate does not agree with him."

"Ah, then, he's abroad,—in Italy, probably?"

"No, ma'am, in Botany Bay. His brother, they say, might have saved him, but he left poor Tom to his fate, for he was just then paying his court to a Miss Crow, I think, with a large fortune. O Lord! what have I said! It's always the luck of me!" The latter exclamation was the result of a heavy plump upon the floor, Mrs. Bingham having fallen in a faint, she being the identical lady alluded to, and her husband the brother of pleasant Tom Bingham.

To hurl Mr. O'Leary out of the room by one hand, and ring the bell with the other, was the work of a moment; and with proper care and in due time, Mrs. Bingham was brought to herself, when, most fortunately, she entirely forgot the cause of her sudden indisposition, and of course neither her daughter nor myself suffered any clew to escape us which might lead to its discovery.

When we were once more upon the road, to efface, if it might be necessary, any unpleasant recurrence to the late scene, I proceeded to give Mrs. Bingham an account of my adventure at Chantraine, in which, of course, I endeavored to render my friend O'Leary all the honors of being laughed at in preference to myself, laying little stress upon my masquerading in the jack-boots.

"You are quite right," said O'Leary, joining in the hearty laugh against him, "quite right; I was always a very heavy sleeper,—indeed, if I wasn't, I wouldn't be here now, travelling about *en garçon,* free as air;" and here he heaved a sigh, which, from its incongruity with his jovial look and happy expression, threw us all into renewed laughter.

"But why, Mr. O'Leary, what can your sleepiness have to do with such tender recollections,—for such, I am sure, that sigh bespeaks them?"

"Ah! ma'am, it may seem strange, but it is, nevertheless, true, if it were not for that unfortunate tendency, I should now be the happy possessor of a most accomplished and amiable lady and eight hundred per annum three-and-a-half per cent. stock."

"You overslept yourself on the wedding-day, I suppose?"

"You shall hear, ma'am; the story is but a short one. It is now about eight years ago, I was rambling through the South of France and had just reached Lyons, where the confounded pavement, that sticks up like pears with the points upwards, had compelled me to rest some days and recruit. For this purpose I installed myself in the *pension* of Madame Gourgeaud, Rue des Petits-Carmes,—a quiet house, where we dined at twelve, ten in number, upon about two pounds of stewed beef, with garlic and carrots, a light soup (being the water which accompanied the same, to render it tender in stewing), some preserved cherries and an omelette, with a pint bottle of Beaune (*sixième qualité,* I believe), a species of pyroligneous wine, made from the vine-stalks, but pleasant in summer with your salad. Then we played dominos in the evening, or whist for sou-points, leading altogether a very quiet and virtuous existence, or, as Madame herself expressed it, '*une vie tout à fait patriarchale,*'—of this I cannot myself affirm how far she was right in supposing the patriarchs did exactly like us. But to proceed: in the same establishment there lived a widow, an Englishwoman, whose late husband had been a wine merchant at Dijon; he had also, I suppose, from residing in that country, been imitating the patriarchs, for he died one day. Well, the lady was delayed at Lyons for some law business, and thus it came about that her husband's testament and the sharp paving-stones in the streets determined that we should be acquainted. I cannot express to you the delight of my fair countrywoman at finding that a person who spoke English had arrived at the *pension,*—a feeling I myself somewhat participated in; for, to say truth, I was not at that time a very great proficient in French. We soon became intimate,—in less time, probably, than it could otherwise have happened; for, from the ignorance of all the others of one word of English, I was enabled, during dinner, to say many soft and tender things which one does not usually venture on in company.

"I recounted my travels and told various adventures of my wanderings, till at last, from being merely amused, I found that my fair friend began to be interested in my narratives; and frequently, when passing the *bouillon* to her, I have seen a tear in the corner of her eye. In a word, 'she loved me for the dangers I had passed,' as Othello says. Well, laugh away if you like, but it's truth I am telling you." At this part of Mr. O'Leary's story we all found it impossible to withstand the ludicrous mock-heroic of his face and tone, and laughed loud and long. When we at length became silent he resumed: "Before three weeks had passed over, I had proposed and was accepted,—just your own way, Mr. Lorrequer, taking the ball at the hop; the very same way you did at Cheltenham, the time the lady jilted you and ran off with your friend Mr. Waller. I read it all in the news, though I was then in Norway, fishing." Here there was another interruption by a laugh,—not, however, at Mr. O'Leary's expense. I gave him a most menacing look, while he continued: "The settlements were soon drawn up, and consisted, like all great diplomatic documents, of a series of 'gains and compensations:' thus, she was not to taste anything stronger than *kirschwasser* or Nantz brandy; and I limited myself to a pound of short-cut weekly; and so on. But to proceed: the lady, being a good Catholic, insisted upon being married by a priest of her own persuasion, before the performance of the ceremony at the British embassy in Paris; to this I could offer no objection, and we were accordingly united in the holy bonds the same morning, after signing the law papers."

"Then, Mr. O'Leary, you are really a married man."

"That's the very point I'm coming to, ma'am; for I've consulted all the jurists upon the subject, and they never can agree. But you shall hear. I despatched a polite note to Bishop Luscombe, and made every arrangement for the approaching ceremony, took a quarter in the Rue du Helder, near the Estaminet, and looked forward with anxiety for the day which was to make me happy, for our marriage in Lyons was only a kind of betrothal. Now, my fair friend had but one difficulty remaining, poor dear soul,—I refrain from mentioning her name for delicacy's sake,—but poor dear Mrs. Ram could not bear the notion of our going up to Paris in the same conveyance, for long as she had lived abroad, she had avoided everything French, even the language; so she proposed that I should go in the early diligence, which starts at four o'clock in the morning, while she took her departure at nine. Thus I should be some hours sooner in Paris, and ready to receive her on her arriving, besides sparing her bashfulness all reproach of our travelling together. It was no use my telling her that I always travelled on foot and hated a diligence; she coolly replied that at our time of life we could not spare the time necessary for a pilgrimage to Jerusalem, for so she supposed the journey from Lyons to Paris to be; so fearing lest any doubt might be thrown upon the ardor of my attachment, I yielded at once, remembering at the moment what my poor friend Tom Bing— O Lord, I'm at it again!"

"Sir, I did not hear."

"Nothing, ma'am; I was just going to observe that ladies of a certain time of life, and widows especially, like a lover that seems a little ardent or so, all the better." Here Mrs. Bingham blushed, her daughter bridled, and I nearly suffocated with shame and suppressed laughter.

"After a most tender farewell of my bride, or wife, I don't know which, I retired for the night with a mind vacillating between my hopes of happiness and my fears for the result of a journey so foreign to all my habits of travelling, and in which I could not but tremble at the many casualties my habitual laziness and dislike to any hours but my own choosing might involve me in.

"I had scarcely lain down in bed ere these thoughts took such possession of me that sleep, for once in my life, was out of the question; and then the misery of getting up at four in the morning, putting on your clothes by the flickering light of the porter's candle, getting your boots on the wrong feet, and all that kind of annoyance,—I am sure I fretted myself into the feeling of a downright martyr before an hour was over. 'Well, at least,' thought I, 'one thing is well done,— I have been quite right in coming to sleep at the Messageries Hôtel, where the diligence starts from, or the chances are ten to one that I never should wake till the time was past. Now, however, they are sure to call me, so I may sleep tranquilly till then.' Meanwhile I had forgotten to pack my trunk, and my papers, etc., lay all about the room in a state of considerable confusion. I rose at once with all the despatch I could muster; this took a long time to effect, and it was nearly two o'clock ere I finished and sat down to smoke a solitary pipe,— the last, as I supposed, it might be my lot to enjoy for Heaven knows how long, Mrs. R. having expressed rather late in our intimacy, I confess, strong opinions against tobacco within doors.

"When I had finished my little sac of the 'weed,' the clock struck three, and I started to think how little time I was destined to have in bed. In bed! 'Why,' said I, 'there is no use thinking of it now, for I shall scarcely have lain down ere I shall be obliged to get up again.' So thinking, I set about dressing myself for the road; and as the season was winter and the weather dreadfully severe, took care to array myself in all the covering I could lay hands upon, and by the time I had enveloped myself in a pair of long Hungarian gaiters, and a *kurtcha* of sheep's wool, with a brown bearskin outside, with a Welsh wig and a pair of large dark glass goggles to defend the eyes from the snow, I was not only perfectly impervious to all effects of the weather, but so thoroughly defended from any influence of sight or sound that a volcano might be hissing and thundering within ten yards of me without attracting my slightest attention. Now, I thought, instead of remaining here, I'll just step down to the coach and get snugly into the diligence, and having secured the corner of the *coupé,* resign myself to sleep with the certainty of not being left behind, and probably, too, be some miles on my journey before awaking.

"I accordingly went downstairs, and to my surprise found even at that early hour that many of the *garçons* of the house were stirring and bustling about, getting all the luggage up in the huge wooden leviathan that was to convey us on our road. There they stood, like bees around a hive, clustering and buzzing, and all so engaged that with difficulty could I get an answer to my question of what diligence it was.

"'*La diligence pour Paris, monsieur.*'

"'Ah! all right, then,' said I; so, watching an opportunity to do so unobserved, for I supposed they might have laughed at me, I stepped quietly into the *coupé,* and amid the creaking of cordage and the thumping of feet on the roof fell as sound asleep as ever I did in my life, these sounds coming to my muffled ears soft as the echoes on the Rhine. When it was that I awoke, I cannot say; but as I rubbed my eyes and yawned after a most refreshing sleep, I perceived that it was still quite dark all around, and that the diligence was standing before the door of some inn and not moving. 'Ah!' thought I, 'this is the first stage; how naturally one always wakes at the change of horses,—a kind of instinct implanted by Providence, I suppose, to direct us to a little refreshment on the road.' With these pious feelings I let down the glass and called out to the *garçon* for a glass of brandy and a cigar. While he was bringing them, I had time to look about, and perceived, to my very great delight, that I had the whole *coupé* to myself. 'Are there any passengers coming in here?' said I, as the waiter came forward with my liquor. 'I should think not, sir,' said the fellow, with a leer. 'Then I shall have the whole *coupé* to myself?' said I. 'Monsieur need have no fear of being disturbed; I can safely assure him that he will have no one there for the next twenty-four hours.' This was really pleasant intelligence; so I chucked him a ten-sou piece, and closing up the window, as the morning was cold, once more lay back to sleep with a success that has never failed me. It was to a bright blue cloudless sky, and the sharp clear air of a fine day in winter, that I at length opened my eyes. I pulled out my watch, and discovered it was exactly two o'clock; I next lowered the glass and looked about me, and very much to my surprise discovered that the diligence was not moving, but standing very peaceably in a very crowded congregation of other similar and dissimilar conveyances, all of which seemed, I thought, to labor under some physical ailment, some wanting a box, others a body, etc., and, in fact, suggesting the idea of an infirmary for old and disabled carriages of either sex, mails and others. 'Oh! I have it,' cried I; 'we are arrived at Mont-Géran, and they are all at dinner, and from my being alone in the *coupé,* they have forgotten to call me.' I immediately opened the door and stepped out into the inn-yard, crowded with *conducteurs,* grooms, and ostlers, who, I thought, looked rather surprised at seeing me emerge from the diligence.

" 'You did not know I was there?' said I, with a knowing wink at one of them as I passed.

" '*Assurément non,*' said the fellow, with a laugh, that was the signal for all the others to join in it.

" 'Is the *table d'hôte* over?' said I, regardless of the mirth around me.

" 'Monsieur is just in time,' said the waiter, who happened to pass with a soup-tureen in his hand; 'have the goodness to step this way.'

"I had barely time to remark the close resemblance of the waiter to the fellow who presented me with my brandy and cigar in the morning, when he ushered me into a large room, with about forty persons sitting at a long table, evidently waiting with impatience for the *potage* to begin their dinner. Whether it was they enjoyed the joke of having neglected to call me, or that they were laughing at my travelling costume, I cannot say; but the moment I came in, I could perceive a general titter run through the assembly.

" 'Not too late, after all, gentlemen,' said I, marching gravely up to the table.

" 'Monsieur is in excellent time,' said the host, making room for me beside his chair.

"Notwithstanding the incumbrance of my weighty habiliments, I proceeded to do ample justice to the viands before me, apologizing laughingly to the host by pleading a traveller's appetite.

" 'Then you have, perhaps, come far this morning,' said a gentleman opposite.

" 'Yes,' said I, 'I have been on the road since four o'clock.'

" 'And how are the roads?' said another.

" 'Very bad,' said I, 'the first few stages from Lyons; afterwards much better.' This was said at a venture, as I began to be ashamed of being always asleep before my fellow-travellers. They did not seem, however, to understand me perfectly; and one old fellow, putting down his spectacles from his forehead, leaned over and said,—

" 'And where, may I ask, has Monsieur come from this morning?'

" 'From Lyons,' said I, with the proud air of a man who has done a stout feat, and is not ashamed of the exploit.

" 'From Lyons!' said one. 'From Lyons!' cried another. 'From Lyons!' repeated a third.

" 'Yes,' said I. 'What the devil is so strange in it? Travelling is so quick nowadays, one thinks nothing of twenty leagues before dinner.'

"The infernal shout of laughing that followed my explanation is still in my ears. From one end of the table to the other there was one continued ha, ha, ha! From the greasy host to the little hunchbacked waiter, they were all grinning away.

" 'And how did Monsieur travel?' said the old gentleman, who seemed to carry on the prosecution against me.

" 'In the *coupé* of the *Aigle noir,*' said I, giving the name with some pride that I was not altogether ignorant of the conveyance.

" 'Then you should certainly not complain of the roads,' said the host, chuckling; 'for the only journey that diligence has made this day has been from the street-door to the inn. For as they found, when the luggage was nearly packed, that the axle was almost broken through, they wheeled it round to the *cour,* and prepared another for the travellers.'

" 'And where am I now?' said I.

" 'In Lyons,' said twenty voices, half choked with laughter at my question.

"I was thunderstruck at the news at first; but as I proceeded with my dinner I joined in the mirth of the party, which certainly was not diminished on my telling them the object of my intended journey.

" 'I think, young man,' said the old fellow with the spectacles, 'that you should take the occurrence as a warning of Providence that marriage will not suit you.'

"I began to be of the same opinion; but then, there was the jointure. To be sure, I was to give up tobacco, and perhaps I should not be as free to ramble about as when a *garçon*. So, taking all things into consideration, I ordered in another bottle of Burgundy to drink Mrs. Ram's health, got my passport *viséd* for Barèges, and set out for the Pyrenees the same evening."

"And have you never heard anything more of the lady?" said Mrs. Bingham.

"Oh, yes! She was faithful to the last; for I found out when at Rome last winter that she had offered a reward for me in the newspapers, and indeed had commenced a regular pursuit of me through the whole Continent. And to tell the real fact, I should not now fancy turning my steps towards Paris if I had not very tolerable information that she is in full cry after me through the Wengern Alp, I having contrived a paragraph in 'Galignani' to seduce her thither, and where, with the blessing of Providence, if the snow sets in early, she must pass the winter."

CHAPTER XXVIII.

PARIS.

NOTHING more worthy of recording occurred before our arrival at Meurice's on the third day of our journey. My friend O'Leary had, with his usual good fortune, become indispensable to his new acquaintance, and it was not altogether without some little lurking discontent that I perceived how much less often my services were called in requests since his having joined our party; his information, notwithstanding its very scanty extent, was continually relied upon, and his very imperfect French everlastingly called into requisition to interpret a question for the ladies. "Yes,"

thought I, " 'Othello's occupation's gone.' One of two
things has certainly happened,—either Mrs. Bingham and her
daughter have noticed my continued abstraction of mind, and
have attributed it to the real cause, the preoccupation of my
affections, or thinking, on the other hand, that I am desperately in love with one or other of them, have thought that
a little show of preference to Mr. O'Leary may stimulate me
to a proposal at once." In either case I resolved to lose no
time in taking my leave, which there could be no difficulty in
doing now, as the ladies had reached their intended destination, and had numerous friends in Paris to advise and assist
them; besides that, I had too long neglected the real object
of my trip, and should lose no time in finding out the Callonbys, and at once learn what prospect of success awaited me
in that quarter. Leaving my fair friends, then, to refresh
themselves after the journey, and consigning Mr. O'Leary
to the enjoyment of his meerschaum, through the aid of
which he had rendered his apartment like a Dutch swamp
in autumn, the only portion of his own figure visible through
the mist being his short legs and heavy shoes, I set forth at
last.

On reaching the house in the Rue de la Paix, where the
Callonbys had resided, I learned that they were still at Baden,
and were not expected in Paris for some weeks; that Lord
Kilkee had arrived that morning, and was then dining at
the Embassy, having left an invitation for me to dine with
him on the following day, if I happened to call. As I turned
from the door, uncertain whither to direct my steps, I walked
on unconsciously towards the Boulevard, and, occupied as I
was, thinking over all the chances before me, did not perceive
where I stood till the bright glare of a large gas-lamp over
my head apprised me that I was at the door of the well-
known Salon des Etrangers, at the corner of the Rue Riche-
lieu; carriages, *citadines,* and *vigilantes* were crowding,
crashing, and clattering on all sides, as the host of fashion
and the gaming-table were hastening to their *champ de ba-
taille.* Not being a member of the Salon, and having little
disposition to enter if I had been, I stood for some minutes
looking at the crowd as it continued to press on towards the
splendid and brilliantly lighted stairs which led from the very

street to the rooms of this palace, for such, in the magnificence and luxury of its decorations, it really was. As I was on the very eve of turning away, a large and very handsome cab-horse turned the corner from the Boulevard, with the most perfect appointment of harness and carriage I had seen for a long time.

While I continued to admire the taste and propriety of the equipage, a young man in deep mourning sprang from the inside and stood upon the pavement before me. *"A deux heures,* Charles," said he to his servant, as the cab turned slowly round. The voice struck me as well known. I waited till he approached the lamp, to catch a glimpse of the face, and what was my surprise to recognize my cousin, Guy Lorrequer, of the 10th, whom I had not met with for six years before. My first impulse was not to make myself known to him. Our mutual position with regard to Lady Jane was so much a mystery, as regarded myself, that I feared the result of any meeting until I was sufficiently aware of how matters stood, and whether we were to meet as friends and relations, or rivals, and consequently enemies.

Before I had time to take my resolution, Guy had recognized me, and seizing me by the hand with both his, called, "Harry, my old friend, how are you? How long have you been here? And never to call on me! Why, man, what is the meaning of this?" Before I had time to say that I was only a few hours in Paris, he again interrupted me by saying, "And how comes it that you are not in mourning? You must surely have heard it!"

"Heard what?" I cried, nearly hoarse from agitation.

"Our poor old friend Sir Guy—didn't you know?—is dead."

Only those who have felt how strong the ties of kindred are, as they decrease in number, can tell how this news fell upon my heart. All my poor uncle's kindnesses came full upon my memory; his affectionate letters of advice, his well-meant chidings too, even dearer to me than his praise and approval, completely unmanned me; and I stood speechless and powerless before my cousin as he continued to detail to me the rapid progress of Sir Guy's malady,—an attack of gout in the head,—which carried him off in three days. Letters had been sent to me in different places, but none reached; and at the very moment the clerk of my uncle's lawyer was in pursuit of me through the Highlands, where some mistaken information had induced him to follow me.

"You are, therefore," continued Guy, "unaware that our uncle has dealt so fairly by you, and, indeed, by both of us. I have got the Somersetshire estates, which go with the baronetcy, but the Cumberland property is all yours; and I heartily wish you joy of having nearly eight thousand per annum, and one of the sweetest villas that ever man fancied on Derwentwater. But come along here," continued he, and he led me through the crowded corridor and up the wide stair. "I have much to tell you, and we can be perfectly alone here; no one will trouble themselves with us."

Unconscious of all around me, I followed Guy along the gilded and glittering lobby which led to the Salon, and it was only as the servant in rich livery came forward to take my hat and cane that I remembered where I was. Then the full sense of all I had been listening to rushed upon me, and the unfitness, and indeed the indecency, of the place for such communications as we were engaged in came most forcibly before me. Sir Guy, it is true, had always preferred my cousin to me; he it was who was always destined to succeed both to his title and his estates, and his wildness and extravagance had ever met with a milder rebuke and weaker chastisement than my follies and my misfortunes. Yet still he was my last remaining relative,—the only one I possessed in all the world to whom in any difficulty or trial I had to look up; and I felt in the very midst of my newly acquired wealth and riches, poorer and more alone than ever I had done in my lifetime. I followed Guy to a small and dimly-lighted cabinet off the great Salon, where, having seated ourselves, he proceeded to detail to me the various events which a few short weeks had accomplished. Of himself he spoke but little, and never once alluded to the Callonbys at all,—indeed, all I could learn was that he had left the army, and purposed remaining for the winter at Paris, where he appeared to have entered into all its gayety and dissipation at once.

"Of course," said he, "you will give up 'sodgering' now, —at the best it is but poor sport after five and twenty, and is perfectly unendurable when a man has the means of pushing himself in the gay world. And now, Harry, let us mix a little among the mob here; for *Messieurs les Banquiers* don't hold people in estimation who come here only for the *chapons au riz* and the *champagne frappé,* as we should seem to do were we to stay here much longer."

Such was the whirl of my thoughts, and so great the confusion in my ideas from all I had just heard, that I felt myself implicitly following every direction of my cousin with a child-like obedience, of the full extent of which I became only conscious when I found myself seated at the table of the Salon, between my cousin Guy and an old, hard-visaged, pale-countenanced man, who, he told me in a whisper, was Polignac the minister.

What a study for the man who would watch the passions and emotions of his fellow-men would the table of a *rouge-et-noir* gambling-house present; the skill and dexterity which games of other kinds require being here wanting, leave the player free to the full abandonment of the passion. The interest is not a gradually increasing or vacillating one, as fortune and knowledge of the game favor; the result is uninfluenced by anything of his doing: with the last turned card of the croupier is he rich or ruined; and thus in the very abstraction of the anxiety is this the most painfully exciting of all gambling whatever. The very rattle of the dice-box to the hazard-player is a relief; and the thought that he is in some way instrumental to his good or bad fortune gives a turn to his thoughts. There is something so like the inevitable character of fate associated with the result of a chance, which you can in no way affect or avert, that I have, notwithstanding a strong bias for play, ever dreaded and avoided the *rouge-et-noir* table. Hitherto prudential motives had their share in the resolve; a small loss at play becomes a matter of importance to a sub in a marching regiment; and therefore I was firm in my determination to avoid the gambling-table. Now, my fortunes were altered; and as I looked at the heap of shining louis d'or which Guy pushed before me in exchange for a *billet de banque* of large amount, I felt the full importance of my altered position, mingling with the old and long-practised prejudices which years had been accumulating to fix. There is, besides, some wonderful fascination to most men in the very aspect of high play. To pit your fortune against that of another; to see whether or not your luck shall not exceed some other's,—are feelings that have a place in most bosoms, and are certainly, if not naturally existing, most easily generated in the bustle and excitement of the gambling-house. The splendor of the decorations, the rich profusion of gilded ornaments, the large and gorgeously framed mirrors, the sparkling lustres, mingled their effect with the perfumed air of the apartment, filled with orange-trees and other aromatic shrubs, the dress of the company, among whom were many ladies in costumes not inferior to those of a court, the glitter of diamonds, the sparkle of stars and decorations, rendered more magical by knowing that the wearers were names in history. There, with his round but ample shoulder and large, massive head, covered with long, snow-white hair, stands one, the maker and unmaker of kings, watching with a look of ill-concealed anxiety the progress of his game. Here is Soult, with his dogged look and beetle brow; there stands Balzac, the author,—his gains here are less derived from the betting than the bettors; he is evidently "making his own" of some of them, while in the seeming *bonhomie* of his careless manner and easy *abandon* they scruple not to trust him with anecdotes and traits that from the crucible of his fiery imagination come forth like the purified gold from the furnace. And there,—look at that old and weather-beaten man, with gray eyebrows and mustachios, who throws from the breast pocket of his frock, ever and anon, a handful of gold pieces upon the table; he evidently neither knows nor cares for the amount, for the banker himself is obliged to count over the stake for him. That is Blücher, the never-wanting attendant at the Salon; he has been an immense loser, but plays on, and with the same stern perseverance with which he would pour his bold cavalry through a ravine torn by artillery, he stands by the still waning chance with a courage that never falters.

One strong feature of the levelling character of a taste for play has never ceased to impress me most forcibly; not only do the individual peculiarities of the man give way before the all-absorbing passion, but, stranger still, the very boldest traits of nationality even fade and disappear before it, and man seems, under the high-pressure power of this greatest of all stimulants, resolved into a most abstract state.

Among all the traits which distinguish Frenchmen from natives of every country, none is more prominent than a kind of never-failing elasticity of temperament which seems almost to defy all the power of misfortune to depress. Let what will happen, the Frenchman seems to possess some strong resource within himself, in his ardent temperament, upon which he can draw at will; and whether on the day after a defeat, the moment of being deceived in his strongest hopes of returned affection, the overthrow of some long-cherished wish, it matters not, he never gives way entirely. But see him at the gaming-table; watch the intense, the aching anxiety with which his eye follows every card as it falls from the hand of the croupier; behold the look of cold despair that tracks his stake as the banker rakes it in among his gains,—and you will at once perceive that here, at least, his wonted powers fail him. No jest escapes the lips of one that would joke upon the steps of the guillotine. The mocker who would jeer at the torments of revolution stands like a coward quailing before the impassive eye and pale cheek of a croupier. While I continued to occupy myself by observing the different groups about me, I had been almost mechanically following the game, placing at each deal some gold upon the table; the result, however, had interested me so slightly that it was only by remarking the attention my game had excited in others that my own was drawn towards it. I then perceived that I had permitted my winnings to accumulate upon the board, and that in the very deal then commencing, I had a stake of nearly five hundred pounds.

"*Faites votre jeu! Le jeu est fait,*" said the croupier; "*trente-deux.*"

"You have lost, by Jove!" said Guy, in a low whisper, in which I could detect some trait of agitation.

"*Trente-et-un,*" added the croupier. "*Rouge perd, et couleur.*"

There was a regular buzz of wonder through the room at my extraordinary luck, for thus, with every chance against me, I had won again.

As the croupier placed the *billets de banque* upon the table I overheard the muttered commendations of an old veteran behind me upon the coolness and judgment of my play. "So much for fortune," thought I. "My judgment consists in a perfect ignorance of the chances, and my coolness is merely a thorough indifference to success." Whether it was now that flattery had its effect upon me, or that the passion for play, so long dormant, had suddenly seized hold upon me, I know not, but my attention became from that moment riveted upon the game, and I played every deal. Guy, who had been from the first betting with the indifferent success which I have so often observed to attend upon the calculations of old and experienced gamblers, now gave up, and employed himself merely in watching my game.

"Harry," said he, at last, "I am completely puzzled as to whether you are merely throwing down your louis at hazard, or are not the deepest player I have ever met with."

"You shall see," said I, as I stooped over towards the banker and whispered, "How far is the betting permitted?"

"Fifteen thousand francs," said the croupier, with a look of surprise.

"Here goes, then!" said I; *"quinze mille francs,—rouge."*

In a moment the *rouge* won, and the second deal I repeated the bet, and so continuing on with the like success. When I was preparing my rouleau for the fifth, the banker rose, and saying, *"Messieurs, le banque est fermée pour ce soir,"* proceeded to lock his *cassette* and close the table.

"You are satisfied now," said Guy, rising; "you see you have broken the bank. And a very pretty incident to commence with, on your first introduction to a campaign in Paris."

Having changed my gold for notes, I stuffed them, with an air of well-affected carelessness, into my pocket, and strolled through the Salon, where I had now become an object of considerably more interest than all the marshals and ministers about me.

"Now, Hal," said Guy, "I'll just order our supper in the cabinet, and join you in a moment."

As I remained for some minutes awaiting Guy's return, my attention was drawn towards a crowd, in a smaller salon, among whom the usual silent decorum of the play-table seemed held in but small respect, for every instant some burst of hearty laughter, or some open expression of joy or anger burst forth, by which I immediately perceived that they were the votaries of the roulette-table,—a game at which the strict propriety and etiquette ever maintained at *rouge-et-noir* are never exacted. As I pressed nearer, to discover the cause of the mirth, which every moment seemed to augment, guess my surprise to perceive among the foremost rank of the players my acquaintance Mr. O'Leary, whom I at that moment believed to be solacing himself with his meerschaum at Meurice's. My astonishment at how he obtained admission to the Salon was even less than my fear of his recognizing me. At no time is it agreeable to find that the man who is regarded as the *buffo* of a party turns out to be your friend; but still less is this so when the individual claiming acquaintance with you presents any striking absurdity in his dress or manner, strongly at contrast with the persons and things about him. And thus it now happened. Mr. O'Leary's external man as we met him on the Calais road, with its various accompaniments of blouse, cap, spectacles, and tobacco-pipe, were nothing very remarkable; but when the same figure presented itself among the *élégants* of the Parisian world, redolent of *eau de Portugal,* and superb in the glories of brocade waistcoats and velvet-coats, the thing was too absurd, and I longed to steal away before any chance should present itself of a recognition. This, however, was impossible, as the crowd from the other table were all gathered round us, and I was obliged to stand fast, and trust that the excitement of the game, in which he appeared to be thoroughly occupied, might keep his eye fixed on another quarter. I now observed that the same scene in which I had so lately been occupied at the *rouge-et-noir* table was enacting here, under rather different circumstances. Mr. O'Leary was the only player, as I had just been,—not, however, because his success absorbed all the interest of the bystanders, but that, unfortunately, his constant want of it elicited some strong expression of discontent and mistrust from him, which excited the loud laughter of the others, but of which, from his great anxiety in the game, he seemed totally unconscious.

"Faites votre jeu, messieurs," said the croupier.

"Wait a bit till I change this," said Mr. O'Leary, producing an English sovereign; the action interpreted his wishes, and the money was converted into *coupons de jeu.*

I now discovered one great cause of the mirth of the bystanders,—at least the English portion of them. Mr. O'Leary, when placing his money upon the table, observed the singular practice of announcing aloud the amount of his bet, which, for his own information, he reduced to Irish currency; thus the stillness of the room was every instant broken by a strong Irish accent pronouncing something of this sort,—"five francs, four and a penny;" "ten francs, eight and three ha'pence." The amusement thus caused was increased by the excitement his losses threw him into. He now ceased to play for several times, when at last he made an offering of his usual stake.

"Perd," said the croupier, raking in the piece with a contemptuous air at the smallness of the bet, and in no way pleased that the interest Mr. O'Leary excited should prevent the other players from betting.

"Perd," said O'Leary, again. "Devil another song you sing than *perd;* and I'm not quite clear you're not cheating all the while,—only, God help you if you are!"

As he so said, the head of a huge blackthorn stick was half protruded across the table, causing renewed mirth; for among other regulations, every cane, however trifling, is always demanded at the door, and thus a new subject of astonishment arose as to how he had succeeded in carrying it with him into the Salon.

"Here's at you again," said O'Leary, regardless of the laughter, and covering three or four numbers with his *jetons.*

Round went the ball once more, and once more he lost.

"Look, now, devil a lie in it; he makes them go wherever he pleases. I'll take a turn now at the tables,—fair play's a jewel; and we'll see how you'll get on."

So saying, he proceeded to insinuate himself into the chair of the croupier, whom he proposed to supersede, by no very gentle means. This was of course resisted, and as the loud mirth of the bystanders grew more and more boisterous, the cries of *"A la porte! A la porte!"* from the friends of the bank rang through the crowd.

"Go it, Pat, go it, Pat!" said Guy, over my shoulder, who seemed to take a prodigious interest in the proceedings.

At this unexpected recognition of his nativity,—for Mr. O'Leary never suspected he could be discovered by his accent, —he looked across the table and caught my eye at once.

"Oh, I'm safe now! Stand by me, Mr. Lorrequer, and we'll clear the room."

So saying, and without any further provocation, he upset the croupier, chair and all, with one sudden jerk upon the floor, and giving a tremendous kick to the *cassette,* sent all the five-francs pieces flying over him; he then jumped upon the table, and brandishing his blackthorn through the ormolu lustre, scattered the wax-lights on all sides, accompanying the exploit by a yell that would have called up all Connemara at midnight, if it had only been heard there. In an instant the *gendarmes,* always sufficiently near to be called in if required, came pouring into the room, and supposing the whole affair had been a preconcerted thing to obtain possession of the money in the bank, commenced capturing different members of the company who appeared, by enjoying the confusion, to be favoring and assisting it. My cousin Guy was one of the first so treated,—a proceeding to which he responded by an appeal rather in favor with most Englishmen, and at once knocked down the *gendarme.* This was the signal for a general engagement; and accordingly, before an explanation could possibly be attempted, a most terrific combat ensued, the Frenchmen in the room siding with the *gendarmerie* and making common cause against the English, who, although greatly inferior in number, possessed considerable advantage, from long habit in street-rows and boxing encounters. As for myself, I had the good fortune to be pitted against a very pursy and unwieldy Frenchman, who *sacré'd* to admiration, but never put in a single blow at me. While, therefore, I amused myself practising what old Cribb called "the one, two," upon his fat carcase I had abundant time and opportunity to watch all that was doing about me; and truly a more ludicrous affair I never beheld. Imagine about fifteen or sixteen young Englishmen, most of them powerful, athletic fellows, driving an indiscriminate mob of about five times their number before them, who, with courage enough to resist, were yet so totally ignorant of the boxing art that they retreated pell-mell before the battering phalanx of their sturdy opponents,—the most ludicrous figure of all being Mr. O'Leary himself, who, standing upon the table, laid about him with a brass lustre that he had unstrung, and did considerable mischief with this novel instrument of warfare, crying out the entire time, "Murder every mother's son of them!" "Give them another taste of Waterloo!" Just as he had uttered the last patriotic sentiment, he received a slight admonition from behind by the point of a *gendarme's* sword, which made him leap from the table with the alacrity of a harlequin, and come plump down among the thickest of the fray. My attention was now directed elsewhere, for above all the din and *tapage* of the encounter I could plainly hear the row-dow-dow of the drums and the measured tread of troops approaching, and at once guessed that a reinforcement of the *gendarmerie* were coming up. Behind me there was a large window with a heavy scarlet curtain before it; my resolution was at once taken; I floored my antagonist, whom I had till now treated with the most merciful forbearance, and immediately sprang behind the curtain. A second's consideration showed that in the search that must ensue this would afford no refuge, so I at once opened the sash and endeavored to ascertain at what height I was above the ground beneath me. The night was so dark that I could see nothing; but judging from the leaves and twigs that reached to the window that it was a garden beneath, and auguring from the perfumed smell of the shrubs that they could not be tall trees, I resolved to leap,—a resolve I had little time to come to, for the step of the soldiers was already heard upon the stair. Fixing my hat, then, down upon my brows, and buttoning my coat tightly, I let myself down from the window-stool by my hands, and fell upon my legs in the soft earth of the garden, safe and unhurt. From the increased clamor and din overhead, I could learn the affray was at its height, and had little difficulty in detecting the sonorous accent and wild threats of my friend Mr. O'Leary high above all the other sounds around him. I did not wait long, however, to enjoy them, but at once set about securing my escape from my present bondage. In this I had little difficulty, for I was directed by a light to a small door, which, as I approached, I found led into the den of the *concierge,* and also communicated by another door with the street. I opened it therefore at once, and was in the act of opening the second, when I felt myself seized by the collar by a strong hand, and on turning round saw the sturdy figure of the *concierge* himself, with a drawn bayonet within a few inches of my throat. *"Tenez, mon ami,"* said I, quietly; and placing half a dozen louis, some of my recent spoils, in his hand, at once satisfied him that, even if I were a robber, I was at least one that understood and respected the conveniences of society. He at once relinquished his hold and dropped his weapon, and pulling off his cap with one hand, to draw the cord which opened the *porte-cochère* with the other, bowed me politely to the street. I had scarcely had time to insinuate myself into the dense mass of the people whom the noise and confusion within had assembled around the house, when the double door of the building opened, and a file of *gendarmerie* came forth, leading between them my friend Mr. O'Leary and some others of the rioters,—among whom I rejoiced to find my cousin did not figure. If I were to judge from his disordered habiliments and scarred visage, Mr. O'Leary's resistance to the constituted authorities must have been a vigorous one; and the drollery of his appearance was certainly not decreased by his having lost the entire brim of his hat,— the covering of his head bearing, under these distressing circumstances, a strong resemblance to a saucepan.

As I could not at that moment contribute in any way to his rescue, I determined on the following day to be present at his examination and render him all the assistance in my power. Meanwhile, I returned to Meurice's, thinking of every adventure of the evening much more than of my own changed condition and altered fortunes.

CHAPTER XXIX.

PARIS.

THE first thing which met my eye when waking in the morning, after the affair at the Salon, was the *rouleau* of *billets de banque* which I had won at play; and it took several minutes before I could persuade myself that the entire recollection of the evening had any more solid foundation than a heated brain and fevered imagination. The sudden spring from being a subaltern in the 4—th, with a few hundreds per annum, *pour tout potage,* to becoming the veritable proprietor of several thousands, with a handsome house in Cumberland, was a consideration which I could scarcely admit into my mind, so fearful was I that the very first occurrence of the day should dispel the illusion and throw me back into the dull reality which I was hoping to escape from.

There is no adage more true than the old Roman one, that what we wish, we readily believe; so I had little difficulty in convincing myself that all was as I desired,— although, certainly, my confused memory of the past evening contributed little to that conviction. It was, then, amid a very whirl of anticipated pleasures and new schemes for enjoying life that I sat down to a breakfast, at which, that I might lose no time in commencing my race, I had ordered the most exquisite viands which even French cookery could accomplish for the occasion.

My plans were soon decided upon. I resolved to remain only long enough in Paris to provide myself with a comfortable travelling carriage, secure a good courier, and start for Baden, when I trusted that my pretensions, whatever favor they might have been once received with, would certainly now, at least, be listened to with more prospect of being successful.

I opened the "Galignani's" paper of the day to direct me in my search, and had scarcely read a few lines before a paragraph caught my eye which not a little amused me; it was headed: "Serious Riot at the Salon des Etrangers, and Attempt to rob the Bank."

"Last evening, among the persons who presented themselves at the table of this fashionable resort, were certain individuals who, by their manners and dress, bespoke anything
rather than the rank and condition of those who usually
resort there, and whose admission is still unexplained, notwithstanding the efforts of the police to unravel the mystery.
The proprietors of the bank did not fail to remark these
persons, but scrupled, from fear of disturbing the propriety of
the Salon, to take the necessary steps for their exclusion,
reserving their intention to the adoption of precautions
against such intrusions in future,—unfortunately, as it turned
out eventually; for towards eleven o'clock one of these individuals, having lost a considerable sum at play, proceeded in
a very violent and outrageous manner to denounce the bank,
and went so far as to accuse the croupier of cheating. This
language, having failed to excite the disturbance it was evidently intended to promote, was soon followed up by a most
dreadful personal attack upon the banker, in which he was
thrown from his seat, and the *cassette,* containing several
thousand francs in gold and notes, immediately laid hold of.
The confusion now became considerable, and it was apparent
that the whole had been a preconcerted scheme. Several persons, leaping upon the table, attempted to extinguish the great
lustre of the Salon, in which bold attempt they were most
spiritedly resisted by some of the other players and the *gendarmes,* who had by this time arrived in force. The riot was
quelled after a prolonged and desperate resistance, and the
rioters, with the exception of two, were captured and conveyed to prison, where they await the result of a judicial in-
vestigation, of which we shall not fail to lay the particulars
before our readers.

"Since our going to press we have learned that one of the
ringleaders in this vile scheme is a noted English *escroc,*—a
swindler, who was already arrested at C—— for travelling
with a false passport, but who contrives, by some collusion
with another of the gang, to evade the local authorities. If
this be the case, we trust he will speedily be detected and
brought to punishment."

Whatever amusement I had found in reading the commencing portion of this ridiculous misstatement, the allu-

sion in the latter part by no means afforded me equal pleasure; and I saw in one rapid glance how much annoyance,
and how many delays and impediments, a charge even of this
ridiculous nature might give rise to in my present circumstances. "My passport, however, will settle all," thought I,
as I thrust my hand towards my pocket, in which I had
placed it along with some letters.

Guess my misery to discover that the whole of the pocket
had been cut away,—probably in the hope of obtaining the
billets de banque I had won at play, but which I had changed
from that pocket to a breast one on leaving the table. This
at once led me to suspect that there might be some truth in
the suspicion of the newspaper writer of a preconcerted
scheme, and at once explained to me what had much puzzled me before,—the extreme rapidity with which the elements of discord were propagated; for the whole affair was
the work of a few seconds. While I continued to meditate
on these matters, the waiter entered with a small note in an
envelope, which a *commissionnaire* had just left at the hotel
for me, and went away, saying there was no answer. I
opened it hastily, and read :—

DEAR H.,—The confounded affair of last night has induced
me to leave this for a few days; besides that, I have obtained
a most excellent reason for absenting myself in the presence
of a black eye which will prevent my appearance in public
for a week to come. As you are a stranger here, you need
not fear being detected. With all its *désagréments,* I can't
help laughing at the adventure, and I am heartily glad to have
had the opportunity of displaying old Jackson's science upon
those wretched *gendarmes.*

Yours truly,

G. L.

"This certainly," thought I, "improves my position. Here
is my cousin Guy—the only one to whom, in any doubt
or difficulty here, I could refer—here he is, flown, without letting me know where to address him or find him
out." I rang my bell hastily, and having written a line on
my card requesting Lord Kilkee to come to me as soon as
he could, despatched it to the Rue de la Paix. The mes-

senger soon returned with an answer that Lord Kilkee had been obliged to leave Paris late the evening before, having received some important letters from Baden. My anxiety now became greater. I did not know but that the moment I ventured to leave the hotel I should be recognized by some of the witnesses of the evening's fray; and all thoughts of succoring poor O'Leary were completely forgotten in my fear for the annoyances the whole of this ridiculous affair might involve me in. Without any decision as to my future steps, I dressed myself and proceeded to pay my respects to Mrs. Bingham and her daughter, who were in the same hotel, and whom I had not seen since our arrival.

As I entered the drawing-room I was surprised to find Miss Bingham alone. She appeared to have been weeping,— at least the efforts she made to appear easy and in good spirits contrasted a good deal with the expression of her features as I came in. To my inquiries for Mrs. Bingham, I received for answer that the friends Mrs. Bingham had expected having left a few days before for Baden, she had resolved on following them, and had now merely driven out to make a few purchases before her departure, which was to take place in the morning.

There is something so sad in the thought of being deserted and left by one's friends under any circumstances that I cannot express how much this intelligence affected me. It seemed, too, like the last drop of bad news filling up the measure, that I was to be suddenly deprived of the society of the very few friends about me just as I stood most in need of them.

Whether or not Miss Bingham noticed my embarrassment, I cannot say; but certainly she seemed not displeased, and there was in the half-encouraging tone of her manner something which led me to suspect that she was not dissatisfied with the impression her news seemed to produce upon me.

Without at all alluding to my own improved fortune, or to the events of the preceding night, I began to talk over the coming journey, and expressed my sincere regret that, having lost my passport under circumstances which might create some delay, I could not join their party as I should otherwise have done.

Miss Bingham heard this speech with rather more emotion than so simple a declaration was calculated to produce; and while she threw down her eyes beneath their long dark lashes and colored slightly, asked,—

"And did you really wish to come with us?"

"Undoubtedly," said I.

"And is there no other objection than the passport?"

"None whatever," said I, warming as I spoke; for the interest she appeared to take in me completely upset all my calculations. Besides that, I had never seen her looking so handsome; and *that,* as the French wisely remark, *vaut toujours quelque chose.*

"Oh! then, pray come with us, which you can do, for mamma has just got a passport for her nephew along with her own; and as we really don't want *him,* nor *he us,* we shall both be better pleased to be free of each other, and you can easily afterwards have your own forwarded to Baden by post."

"Ah! but," said I, "how shall I be certain, if I take so flattering an offer, that you will forgive me for filling up the place of the dear cousin? For, if I conjecture aright, it is *le cher Edouard* that purposes to be your companion."

"Yes, you have guessed quite correctly. But you must not tax me with inconsistency, but really I have grown quite tired of my poor cousin since I saw him last night."

"And you used to admire him most prodigiously."

"Well, well, that is all true; but I do so no longer."

"Eh! *perche?*" said I, looking cunningly in her eye.

"For reasons that Mr. Lorrequer shall never know if he has to ask them," said the poor girl, covering her eyes with her hands and sobbing bitterly.

What I thought, said, or did upon this occasion, with all my most sincere desire to make a clean breast of it in these "Confessions," I know not; but this I do know,—that two hours after, I found myself still sitting upon the sofa beside Miss Bingham, whom I had been calling Emily all the while, and talking more of personal matters and my own circumstances than is ever safe or prudent for a young man to do with any lady under the age of his mother.

All that I can now remember of this interview is the fact

of having arranged my departure in the manner proposed by Miss Bingham,—a proposition to which I acceded with an affectation of satisfaction that I fear went very far to deceive my fair friend. Not that the pleasure I felt in the prospect was altogether feigned; but certainly the habit of being led away by the whim and temper of the moment had so much become part of my nature that I had long since despaired of ever guarding myself against the propensity I had acquired of following every lead which any one might throw out for me. And thus, as poor Harry Lorrequer was ever the first man to get into a row at the suggestion of a friend, so he only waited the least possible pressing on any occasion to involve himself in any scrape or misfortune that presented itself, provided there was only some one good enough to advise him to do so.

As I entered my own room to make preparations for my departure, I could not help thinking over all the events thus crowded into the space of a few hours. My sudden possession of wealth; my prospects at Callonby still undecided; my scrape at the Salon; my late interview with Miss Bingham, in which I had only stopped short of a proposal to marry,—were almost sufficient to occupy any reasonable mind; and so I was beginning to suspect, when the waiter informed me that the *commissaire* of police was in waiting below and wished to speak to me. Affecting some surprise at the request, which I at once perceived the object of, I desired him to be introduced. I was quite correct in my guess. The information of my being concerned in the affair at the Salon had been communicated to the authorities, and the *commissaire* had orders to obtain bail for my appearance at the Tribunal de Justice on that day week, or commit me at once to prison. The *commissaire* politely gave me till evening to procure the required bail, satisfying himself that he could adopt measures to prevent my escape, and took his leave. He had scarcely gone when Mr. Edward Bingham was announced,—the reason for this visit I could not so easily divine; but I had little time allowed for my conjectures, as the same instant a very smart, dapper little gentleman presented himself, dressed in all the extravagance of French mode. His hair, which was permitted to curl upon his shoulders, was divided along the middle of the head; his mustachios were slightly upturned and carefully waxed; and his small chin-tuft, or Henri-Quatre, most gracefully pointed; he wore three most happily contrasting colored waistcoats, and spurs of glittering brass. His visit was of scarcely five minutes' duration, but was evidently the opening of a breaching battery by the Bingham family in all form,—the object of which I could at least guess at.

My embarrassments were not destined to end here; for scarcely had I returned Mr. Bingham's eighth salutation at the end of the staircase when another individual presented himself before me. This figure was in every respect the opposite of my last visitor. Although framed perfectly upon the late Parisian school of dandyism, his, however, was the *Ecole militaire*. Le Capitaine Eugène de Joncourt, for so he introduced himself, was a portly personage of about five and thirty or forty years of age, with that mixture of *bonhomie* and ferocity in his features which the soldiers of Napoleon's army either affected or possessed naturally. His features, which were handsome, and the expression of which was pleasing, were, as it seemed, perverted, by the warlike turn of a most terrific pair of whiskers and mustachios, from their naturally good-humored bent; and the practised frown and quick turn of his dark eye were evidently only the acquired advantages of his military career. A handsome mouth, with singularly regular and good teeth, took much away from the stern look of the upper part of his face, and contributed, with the aid of a most pleasing voice, to impress you in his favor. His dress was a blue braided frock decorated with the *cordon* of the Legion; but neither these, nor the clink of his long cavalry spurs, were necessary to convince you that the man was a soldier. Besides that, there was that mixture of urbanity and *aplomb* in his manner which showed him to be perfectly accustomed to the usages of the best society.

"May I beg to know," said he, as he seated himself slowly, "if this card contains your name and address?" handing me at the same moment one of my visiting-cards. I immediately replied in the affirmative.

"You are in the English service?"

"Yes."

"Then may I entreat your pardon for the trouble of these questions and explain the reason of my visit? I am the friend of Le Baron d'Haultpenne, with whom you had the altercation last night at the Salon, and in whose name I have come to request the address of a friend on your part."

"Ho, ho!" thought I, "the baron is then the stout gentleman that I pummelled so unmercifully near the window. But how came he by my card? And besides, in a row of that kind, I am not aware how far the matter can be conceived to go farther than what happens at the moment." These were the thoughts of a second of time, and before I could reply, the captain resumed,—

"You seem to have forgotten the circumstance, and so, indeed, should I like to do; but, unfortunately, D'Haultpenne says that you struck him with your walking-cane, so you know, under such a state of things, there is but one course."

"But gently," added I; "I had no cane whatever last evening."

"Oh! I beg pardon," interrupted he. "But my friend is most positive in his account, and describes the altercation as having continued from the Salon to the street, when you struck him, and at the same time threw him your card. Two of your officers were also present; and although, as it appears from your present forgetfulness, the thing took place in the heat and excitement of the moment, still—"

"But still," said I, catching up his last words, "I never did strike the gentleman as you describe, never had any altercation in the street, and—"

"Is that your address?" said the Frenchman, with a slight bow.

"Yes, certainly it is."

"Why, then," said he, with a mild curl of his upper lip, half smile, half derision,—

"Why, then, make yourself perfectly easy," I replied. "If any one has by an accident made use of my name, it shall not suffer by such a mistake. I shall be quite at your service the moment I can find out a friend to refer you to."

I had much difficulty to utter these few words with a suitable degree of temper, so stung was I by the insolent demeanor of the Frenchman, whose coolness and urbanity seemed only to increase every moment.

"Then I have the honor to salute you," said he, rising, with great mildness in his voice, "and shall take the liberty to leave my card for the information of your friend."

So saying, he placed his card upon the table: "Le Capitaine Eugène de Joncourt, Cuirassiers de la Garde."

"I need not press upon Monsieur the value of despatch."

"I shall not lose a moment," said I, as he clattered down the stairs of the hotel with that perfect swaggering *nonchalance* which your foreigner is always an adept in; and I returned to my room to meditate upon my numerous embarrassments and think over the difficulties which every moment was contributing to increase the number of.

"The indictment has certainly many counts," thought I.

Imprimis, a half-implied but fully comprehended promise to marry a young lady, with whom, I confess, I only intend to journey this life—as far as Baden.

Secondly, a charge of swindling—for such the imputation amounts to—at the Salon.

Thirdly, another unaccountable delay in joining the Callonbys, with whom I am every hour in the risk of being *compromis.*

And lastly, a duel in perspective with some confounded Frenchman who is at this very moment practising at a pistol-gallery.

Such were the heads of my reflections, and such the agreeable impressions my visit to Paris was destined to open with; how they were to be followed up remains to be told.

CHAPTER XXX.

CAPTURE TREVANION'S ADVENTURE.

AS the day was now waning apace, and I was still unprovided with any one who could act as my second, I set out upon a search through the various large hotels in the neighborhood, trusting that amid my numerous acquaintance I should be fortunate enough to find some of them at Paris. With a most anxious eye I scanned the lists of arrivals at the usual haunts of my countrymen in the Rue Rivoli and the Place Vendôme, but without success; there were long catalogues of "milors," with their "couriers," etc., but not one name known to me in the number.

I repaired to Galignani's Library, which, though crowded as ever with English, did not present to me one familiar face. From thence I turned into the Palais Royal, and at last, completely jaded by walking and sick from disappointment, I sat down upon a bench in the Tuileries Gardens.

I had scarcely been there many minutes when a gentleman accosted me in English, saying, "May I ask if this be your property?" showing at the same time a pocket-book which I had inadvertently dropped in pulling out my handkerchief. As I thanked him for his attention, and was about to turn away, I perceived that he continued to look very steadily at me. At length he said,—

"I think I am not mistaken; I have the pleasure to see Mr. Lorrequer, who may, perhaps, recollect my name, Trevanion, of the 43d. The last time we met was at Malta."

"Oh! I remember perfectly. Indeed, I should be very ungrateful if I did not; for to your kind offices there I am indebted for my life. You must surely recollect the street row near the battery?"

"Yes, that was rather a brisk affair while it lasted; but, pray, how long have you been here?"

"Merely a few days; and most anxious am I to leave as soon as possible,—for independently of pressing reasons to wish myself elsewhere, I have had nothing but trouble and worry since my arrival, and at this instant am involved in a duel without the slightest cause that I can discover, and, what is still worse, without the aid of a single friend to undertake the requisite negotiation for me."

"If my services can in any way assist—"

"Oh, my dear Captain, this is really so great a favor that I cannot say how much I thank you."

"Say nothing whatever, but rest quite assured that I am completely at your disposal; for although we are not very old friends, yet I have heard so much of you from some of ours that I feel as if we had been long acquainted."

This was an immense piece of good fortune to me; for of all the persons I knew, he was the most suited to aid me at this moment. In addition to a thorough knowledge of the Continent and its habits, he spoke French fluently, and had been the most distinguished authority in the duello to a large military acquaintance; joining to a consummate tact and cleverness in his diplomacy a temper that never permitted itself to be ruffled, and a most unexceptionable reputation for courage. In a word, to have had Trevanion for your second was not only to have secured odds in your favor, but, still better, to have obtained the certainty that, let the affair take what turn it might, you were sure of coming out of it with credit.

He was the only man I have ever met who had much mixed himself in transactions of this nature, and yet never, by any chance, had degenerated into the fire-eater; more quiet, unassuming manners it was impossible to meet with, and in the various anecdotes I had heard of him, I had always traced a degree of forbearance that men of less known bravery might not have ventured to practise. At the same time, when once roused by anything like premeditated insult or predetermined affront, he became almost ungovernable, and it would be safer to beard the lion in his den than cross his path. Among the many stories, and there were a great many current in his regiment, concerning him, there was one so singularly characteristic of the man that as I have passingly mentioned his name here, I may as well relate it; at the same time premising that as it is well known, I may only be repeating an often-heard tale to many of my readers.

When the regiment to which Trevanion belonged became part of the army of occupation in Paris, he was left at Versailles seriously ill from the effects of a sabre-wound he received at Waterloo, and from which his recovery at first was exceedingly doubtful. At the end of several weeks, however, he became out of danger, and was able to receive the visits of his brother officers whenever they were fortunate enough to obtain a day's leave of absence to run down and see him. From them he learned that one of his oldest friends in the regiment had fallen in a duel during the time of his illness, and that two other officers were dangerously wounded,—one of whom was not expected to survive. When he inquired as to the reasons of these many disasters, he was informed that since the entrance of the allies into Paris the French officers, boiling with rage and indignation at their recent defeat, and smarting under the hourly disgrace which the presence of their conquerors suggested, sought out, by every means in their power, opportunities of insult; but always so artfully contrived as to render the opposite party the challenger, thus reserving to themselves the choice of the weapons. When, therefore, it is borne in mind that the French are the most expert swordsmen in Europe, little doubt can exist as to the issue of these combats; and, in fact, scarcely a morning passed without three or four English or Prussian officers being carried through the Barrière de l'Etoile, if not dead, at least seriously wounded, and condemned to carry with them through life the inflictions of a sanguinary and savage spirit of vengeance.

While Trevanion listened to this sad recital,—and scarcely did a day come without adding to the long catalogue of disasters,—he at once perceived that the quiet deportment and unassuming demeanor which so strongly characterize the English officer were construed by their French opponents into evidences of want of courage, and saw that to so systematic a plan for slaughter no common remedy could be applied, and that some *coup d'état* was absolutely necessary to put it down once and forever.

In the history of these sanguinary *rencontres* one name was continually recurring, generally as the principal, sometimes the instigator, of the quarrel. This was an officer of a chasseur regiment who had the reputation of being the best swordsman in the whole French army, and was no less distinguished for his "skill at fence" than his uncompromising hatred of the British, with whom alone, of all the allied forces, he was ever known to come in contact. So celebrated was the Capitaine Auguste Gendemar for his pursuits that it was well known at that time in Paris that he was the president of a duelling club associated for the express and avowed object of provoking to insult, and as certainly dooming to death every English officer upon whom they could fasten a quarrel.

The Café Phillidor, at that period in the Rue Vivienne, was the rendezvous of this reputable faction; and here *le capitaine* reigned supreme, receiving accounts of the various "affairs" which were transacting, counselling and plotting for the future. His ascendency among his countrymen was perfectly undisputed; and being possessed of great muscular strength, with that peculiar *farouche* exterior without which courage is nothing in France, he was in every way calculated for the infamous leadership he assumed.

It was, unfortunately, to this same café, being situated in what was called the English quarter, that the officers of the 43d regiment were in the habit of resorting, totally unaware of the plots by which they were surrounded, and quite unsuspecting the tangled web of deliberate and cold-blooded assassination in which they were involved; and here took place the quarrel, the result of which was the death of Trevanion's friend, a young officer of great promise, and universally beloved in his regiment.

As Trevanion listened to these accounts, his impatience became daily greater that his weak state should prevent his being among his brother officers when his advice and assistance were so imperatively required, and where, amid all the solicitude for his perfect recovery, he could not but perceive they ardently wished for his presence.

The day at last arrived; and restored to something like his former self, Trevanion once more appeared in the messroom of his regiment. Amid the many sincere and hearty congratulations on his recovered looks were not a few half-expressed hints that he should not go much out into the world for some little time to come. To these friendly admonitions Trevanion replied by a good-humoured laugh and a ready assurance that he understood the intended kindness, and felt in no wise disposed to be invalided again. "In fact," said he, "I have come up here to enjoy life a little,—not to risk it; but among the sights of your gay capital, I must certainly have a peep at your famed captain, of whom I have heard too much not to feel an interest in him."

Notwithstanding the many objections to this, made with a view to delay his visit to the Phillidor to a later period, it was at length agreed that they should all repair to the *café* that evening, but upon the express understanding that every cause of quarrel should be strictly avoided, and that their stay should be merely sufficient to satisfy Trevanion's curiosity as to the appearance of the renowned captain.

It was rather before the usual hour of the *café's* filling that a number of English officers, among whom was Trevanion, entered the salon of the Phillidor; having determined not to attract any unusual attention, they broke into little knots and parties of threes and fours, and dispersed through the·room, where they either sipped their coffee or played at dominoes, then, as now, the staple resource of a French *café*.

The clock over the *comptoir* struck eight, and at the same instant a waiter made his appearance, carrying a small table, which he placed beside the fire; and having trimmed a lamp and placed a large armchair before it, was about to withdraw, when Trevanion, whose curiosity was roused by the singularity of these arrangements, determined upon asking for whose comfort they were intended. The waiter stared for a moment at the question with an air as if doubting the seriousness of him who put it, and at last replied, *"Pour Monsieur le Capitaine, je crois,"* with a certain tone of significance upon the latter words.

"Le capitaine! but what captain?" said he, carelessly; "for I am a captain, and that gentleman there,—and there, too, is another," at the same instant throwing himself listlessly into the well-cushioned chair, and stretching out his legs at full length upon the hearth.

The look of horror which this quiet proceeding on his part elicited from the poor waiter so astonished Trevanion that he could not help saying, "Is there anything the matter with you, my friend? Are you ill?"

"No, monsieur, not ill,—nothing the matter with *me;* but *you,* sir, oh, you, sir, pray come away!"

"Me!" said Trevanion,—"me! Why, my good man, I was never better in my life; so now just bring me my coffee and the 'Moniteur,' if you have it. There, don't stare that way, but do as I bid you."

There was something in the assured tone of these few

words that either overawed or repressed every rising feeling of the waiter for his interrogator, for, silently handing his coffee and the newspaper, he left the room; not, however, without bestowing a parting glance so full of terror and dismay that our friend was obliged to smile at it. All this was the work of a few minutes, and not until the noise of new arrivals had attracted the attention of his brother officers did they perceive where he had installed himself, and to what danger he was thus, as they supposed, unwittingly exposed.

In perfect misery at what they conceived their own fault in not apprising him of the sacred character of that place, they stood silently looking at him as he continued to sip his coffee, apparently unconscious of every thing and person about him.

It was now, however, too late for remonstrance; for already several French officers had noticed the circumstance, and by their interchange of looks and signs openly evinced their satisfaction at it, and their delight at the catastrophe which seemed inevitable to the luckless Englishman.

There was now a more than ordinary silence in the *café,* which at all times was remarkable for the quiet and noiseless demeanor of its frequenters, when the door was flung open by the ready waiter, and the Capitaine Auguste Gendemar entered. He was a large, squarely-built man, with a most savage expression of countenance, which a bushy beard and shaggy, overhanging mustache served successfully to assist; his eyes were shaded by deep, projecting brows and long eyebrows slanting over them and increasing their look of piercing sharpness; there was in his whole air and demeanor that certain French air of swaggering bullyism which ever remained in those who, having risen from the ranks, maintained the look of ruffianly defiance which gave their early character for courage its peculiar merit.

To the friendly salutations of his countrymen he returned the slightest and coldest acknowledgments, throwing a glance of disdain around him as he wended his way to his accustomed place beside the fire; this he did with as much of noise and swagger as he could well contrive, his sabre and sabretasche clanking behind, his spurs jangling, and his heavy step made purposely heavier to draw upon him the notice and attention he sought for. Trevanion alone testified no consciousness of his entrance, and appeared totally engrossed by the columns of his newspaper, from which he never lifted his eyes for an instant. *Le capitaine* at length reached the fire-place, when, no sooner did he behold his accustomed seat in the possession of another than he absolutely started back with surprise and anger.

What might have been his first impulse it is hard to say, for as the blood rushed to his face and forehead, he clenched his hands firmly, and seemed for an instant, as he eyed the stranger, like a tiger about to spring upon its victim; this was but for a second, for turning rapidly round towards his friends, he gave them a look of peculiar meaning, showing two rows of white teeth, with a grin which seemed to say, "I have taken my line;" and he had done so. He now ordered the waiter, in a voice of thunder, to bring him a chair. This he took roughly from him and placed, with a crash, upon the floor, exactly opposite that of Trevanion, and still so near as scarcely to permit of his sitting down upon it. The noisy vehemence of this action at last appeared to have roused Trevanion's attention, for he now, for the first time, looked up from his paper and quietly regarded his *vis-à-vis*. There could not in the world be a stronger contrast to the bland look and courteous expression of Trevanion's handsome features than the savage scowl of the enraged Frenchman, in whose face the strong and ill-repressed workings of passion were twitching and distorting every lineament and line; indeed, no words could ever convey half so forcibly as did that look, insult,—open, palpable, deep, determined insult!

Trevanion's eyes, which had been merely for a moment lifted from his paper, again fell, and he appeared to take no notice whatever of the extraordinary proximity of the Frenchman, still less of the savage and insulting character of his looks.

Le capitaine, having thus failed to bring on the explanation he sought for, proceeded to accomplish it by other means; for taking the lamp, by the light of which Trevan-

ion was still reading, he placed it at his side of the table,
and at the same instant stretching across his arm, he
plucked the newspaper from his hand, giving at the same
moment a glance of triumph towards the bystanders, as
though he would say, "You see what he must submit to."
Words cannot describe the astonishment of the British officers as they beheld Trevanion, under this gross and open
insult, content himself by a slight smile and half bow, as
if returning a courtesy, and then throw his eyes downwards,
as if engaged in deep thought, while the triumphant sneer
of the French at this unaccountable conduct was absolutely
maddening to them to endure.

But their patience was destined to submit to stronger proof;
for at this instant *le capitaine* stretched forth one enormous
leg, cased in his massive jack-boot, and with a crash deposited
the heel upon the foot of their friend Trevanion. At length
he is roused, thought they, for a slight flush of crimson flitted
across his cheek, and his upper lip trembled with a quick,
spasmodic twitching; but both these signs were over in a
second, and his features were as calm and unmoved as before,
and his only appearance of consciousness of the affront was
given by his drawing back his chair and placing his legs beneath it, as if for protection.

This last insult, and the tame forbearance with which it
was submitted to, produced all their opposite effects upon
the bystanders, and looks of ungovernable rage and derisive
contempt were every moment interchanging; indeed, were it
not for the all-absorbing interest which the two great actors
in the scene had concentrated upon themselves, the two parties
must have come at once into open conflict.

The clock of the *café* struck nine,—the hour at which
Gendemar always retired; so calling to the waiter for his
glass of brandy, he placed his newspaper upon the table, and
putting both his elbows upon it, and his chin upon his hands,
he stared full in Trevanion's face with a look of the most
derisive triumph, meant to crown the achievement of the
evening. To this, as to all his former insults, Trevanion appeared still insensible, and merely regarded him with his
never-changing half-smile. The brandy arrived; *le capitaine*
took it in his hand, and with a nod of most insulting famili-

arity saluted Trevanion, adding with a loud voice, so as to be heard on every side,—"*À votre courage, Anglais.*" He had scarcely swallowed the liquor when Trevanion rose slowly from his chair, displaying to the astonished gaze of the Frenchman the immense proportions and gigantic frame of a man well known as the largest officer in the British army; with one stride he was beside the chair of the Frenchman, and with the speed of lightning he seized his nose by one hand, while with the other he grasped his lower jaw, and wrenching open his mouth with the strength of an ogre, he spat down his throat.

So sudden was the movement that before ten seconds had elapsed all was over, and the Frenchman rushed from the room, holding the fragments of his jaw-bone (for it was fractured!), and followed by his countrymen, who from that hour deserted the Café Phillidor; nor was there ever any mention of the famous captain during the stay of the regiment in Paris.

CHAPTER XXXI.

DIFFICULTIES.

WHILE we walked together towards Meurice's I explained to Trevanion the position in which I stood; and having detailed at full length the row at the Salon and the imprisonment of O'Leary, entreated his assistance in behalf of him, as well as to free me from some of my many embarrassments.

It was strange enough—though at first so preoccupied was I with other thoughts that I paid but little attention to it—that no part of my eventful evening seemed to make so strong an impression on him as my mention of having seen my cousin Guy and heard from him of the death of my uncle. At this portion of my story he smiled with so much significance of meaning that I could not help asking his reason.

"It is always an unpleasant task, Mr. Lorrequer, to speak in any way, however delicately, in a tone of disparagement of a man's relative; and therefore, as we are not long enough acquainted—"

"But pray," said I, "waive that consideration, and only remember the position in which I now am. If you know anything of this business, I entreat you to tell me; I promise to take whatever you may be disposed to communicate, in the same good part it is intended."

"Well, then, I believe you are right. But first, let me ask you how do you know of your uncle's death? For I have reason to doubt it."

"From Guy; he told me himself."

"When did you see him, and where?"

"Why, I have just told you; I saw him last night at the Salon."

"And you could not be mistaken?"

"Impossible! Besides, he wrote to me a note which I received this morning,—here it is."

"Hem, ha! Well, are you satisfied that it is his handwriting?" said Trevanion, as he perused the note slowly twice over.

"Why, of course— But stop— You are right; it is not his hand, nor do I know the writing, now that you direct my attention to it. But what can that mean? You surely do not suppose that I have mistaken any one for him? For, independent of all else, his knowledge of my family and my uncle's affairs would quite disprove that."

"This is really a complex affair," said Trevanion, musingly. "How long may it be since you saw your cousin,—before last night, I mean?"

"Several years,—above six, certainly."

"Oh! it is quite possible, then," said Trevanion, musingly. "Do you know, Mr. Lorrequer, this affair seems more puzzling to me than to you, and for this plain reason,—I am disposed to think you never saw your cousin last night."

"Why, confound it, there is one circumstance that I think may satisfy you on that head. You will not deny that I saw some one who very much resembled him; and, certainly, as he lent me above three thousand francs to play with at the table, it looks rather more like his act than that of a perfect stranger."

"Have you got the money?" asked Trevanion, dryly.

"Yes," said I; "but certainly you are the most unbeliev-ing of mortals, and I am quite happy that I have yet in my possession two of the *billets de banque;* for, I suppose, with-out them, you would scarcely credit me." I here opened my pocket-book and produced the notes.

He took them, examined them attentively for an instant, held them between him and the light, refolded them, and, having placed them in my pocket-book, said: "I thought as much,—they are forgeries."

"Hold!" said I; "my cousin Guy, whatever wildness he may have committed, is yet totally incapable of—"

"I never said the contrary," replied Trevanion, in the same dry tone as before.

"Then what can you mean? For I see no alternative be-tween that and totally discrediting the evidence of my senses."

"Perhaps I can suggest a middle course," said Trevanion; "lend me, therefore, a patient hearing for a few moments, and I may be able to throw some light upon this difficult matter. You may never have heard that there is, in this same city of Paris, a person so extremely like your cousin Guy that his most intimate friends have daily mistaken one for the other; and this mistake has the more often been made from the circumstances of their both being in the habit of frequenting the same class in society, where, knowing and walking with the same people, the difficulty of discriminating has been greatly increased. This individual, who has too many aliases for one to know which to particularize him by, is one of that numerous order of beings which a high state of civilization is always engendering and throwing up on the surface of society; he is a man of low birth and mean con-nections, but gifted with most taking manners and an un-exceptional address and appearance. These advantages, and the possession of apparently independent means, have opened to him the access to a certain set of people who are well known and well received in society, and obtained for him, what he prizes much more, the admission into several clubs where high play is carried on. In this mixed assemblage, which sporting habits and gambling (that grand leveller of all distinctions) have brought together, this man and your cousin Guy met frequently; and from the constant allusion to the wonderful resemblance between them, your eccentric cousin, who, I must say, was never too select in his acquaintances, frequently amused himself by practical jokes upon his friends which served still more to nurture the intimacy between them; and from this habit, Mr. Dudley Morewood— for such is his latest patronymic—must have enjoyed frequent opportunities of hearing much of your family and relations,— a species of information he never neglected, though at the moment it might appear not so immediately applicable to his purposes. Now, this man, who knows of every new English arrival in Paris with as much certainty as the police itself, would at once be aware of your being here; and having learned from Guy how little intercourse there had been of late years between you, would not let slip an opportunity of availing himself of the likeness if anything could thereby turn to his profit."

"Stop!" cried I. "You have opened my eyes completely; for now I remember that as I continued to win last night, this man, who was playing hazard at another table, constantly borrowed from me, but always in gold, invariably refusing the bank-notes as too high for his game."

"There his object was clear enough; for besides obtaining *your* gold, he made you the means of disseminating his false *billets de banque.*"

"So that I have been actually playing and winning upon this fellow's forgeries," said I, "and am perhaps at this very instant inscribed in the *Livre noir* of the police as a most accomplished swindler! But what could be the intention of his note this morning?"

"As to that," said Trevanion, "it is hard to say. One thing you may assuredly rely upon,—it is not an unnecessary epistle, whatever be its object; he never wastes his powder when the game flies too high. So we must only wait patiently for the unravelment of his plans, satisfied that we, at least, know something. What most surprises me is his venturing at present to appear in public; for it is not above two months since an escapade of his attracted so much attention in the play world here that he was obliged to leave and it was supposed that he would never return to Paris."

"One piece of good fortune there is at least," said I, "which, I can safely say, repays me for any and all the annoyance this unhappy affair may cause me,—it is, that my poor old uncle is still alive and well. Not all my anticipated pleasures in newly acquired wealth could have afforded me the same gratification that this fact does; for although never so much his favorite as my cousin, yet the sense of protection, the feeling of confidence which is inseparable from the degree of relationship between us, standing, as he has ever done, in the light of a father to me, is infinitely more pleasurable than the possession of riches, which must ever suggest to me the recollection of a kind friend lost to me forever. But so many thoughts press on me, so many effects of this affair are staring me in the face, I really know not which way to turn, nor can I even collect my ideas sufficiently to determine what is first to be done."

"Leave all that to me," said Trevanion; "it is a tangled web, but I think I can unravel it. Meanwhile, where does the captain reside? For among all your pressing engagements, this affair with the Frenchman must come off first; and for this reason, although you are not really obliged to give him satisfaction, by his merely producing your card and insisting that you are to be responsible for the misdeeds of any one who might show it as his own address, yet I look upon it as a most fortunate thing, while charges so heavy may be at this moment hanging over your head as the proceedings of last night involve, that you have a public opportunity of meeting an antagonist in the field,—thereby evincing no fear of publicity nor any intention of absconding; for be assured that the police are at this moment in possession of what has occurred, and from the *fracas* which followed, are well disposed to regard the whole as a concerted scheme to seize upon the property of the *banque,*—a not uncommon wind-up here when luck fails. My advice is, therefore, meet the man at once; I shall take care that the prefect is informed that you have been imposed upon by a person passing himself off as your relative, and enter bail for your appearance whenever you are called upon. That being done, we shall have time for a moment's respite to look around us and consider the other bearings of this difficult business."

"Here, then, is the card of address," said I: "Eugène de Joncourt, Capitaine de Cavalerie, No. 8, Chaussée d'Antin."

"De Joncourt! why, confound it, this is not so pleasant; he is about the best shot in Paris, and a very steady swordsman besides. I don't like this."

"But you forget, he is the friend, not the principal, here."

"The more good fortune yours," said Trevanion, dryly; "for I acknowledge I should not give much for your chance at twenty paces opposite his pistol. Then who is the other?"

"Le Baron d'Haultpenne," said I, "and his name is all that I know of him; his very appearance is unknown to me."

"I believe I am acquainted with him," said Trevanion; "but here we are at Meurice's. Now I shall just write a few lines to a legal friend who will manage to liberate Mr. O'Leary, whose services we shall need,—two persons are usual on each side in this country,—and then 'to business.'"

The note written and despatched, Trevanion jumped into a cab and set out for the Chaussée d'Antin, leaving me to think over, as well as I could, the mass of trouble and confusion in which twenty-four hours of life in Paris had involved me.

CHAPTER XXXII.

EXPLANATION.

IT was past seven o'clock when Trevanion made his appearance, accompanied by O'Leary; and having in a few words informed me that a meeting was fixed for the following morning near St. Cloud, proposed that we should at once go to dinner at Véry's, after which we should have plenty of time to discuss the various steps to be taken. As we were leaving the hotel for this purpose, a waiter requested of me to permit M. Meurice to speak a few words to me; which having agreed to, I entered the little bureau where this Czar of Hotels sits enthroned,—and what was my surprise to learn the request he had to prefer was nothing less than that I would so far oblige him as to vacate the apartment I possessed in the hotel, adding that my compliance would confer upon him the power to accommodate a "Milord" who had written for apartments and was coming with a large suite of servants. Suspecting that some rumor of the late affair at Frascati's might have influenced my friend Meurice in this unusual demand, I abruptly refused, and was about to turn away, when he, perhaps guessing that I had not believed his statements, handed me an open letter, saying, "You see, sir, this is the letter; and as I am so pressed for spare room, I must now refuse the ·writer."

As my eye glanced at the writing, I started back with amazement to perceive it was in my cousin Guy's hand requesting that apartments might be retained for Sir Guy Lorrequer, my uncle, who was to arrive in Paris by the end of the week. If any doubt had remained on my mind as to the deception I had been duped by, this would completely have dispelled it; but I had long before been convinced of the trick, and only wondered how the false Guy—Mr. Dudley Morewood—had contrived to present himself to me so opportunely, and by what means, in so short a space of time, he had become acquainted with my personal appearance.

As I mentioned this circumstance of the letter to Trevanion, he could not conceal his satisfaction at his sagacity in unravelling the mystery, while this new intelligence confirmed the justness and accuracy of all his explanations.

As we walked along towards the Palais Royal, Trevanion endeavored, not very successfully, to explain to my friend O'Leary the nature of the trick which had been practised, promising at another time some revelations concerning the accomplished individual who had planned it, which in boldness and daring eclipsed even this.

Any one who in waking has had the confused memory of a dream in which events have been so mingled and mixed as to present no uniform narrative, but only a mass of strange and incongruous occurrences, without object or connection, may form some notion of the state of restless excitement my brain suffered from as the many and conflicting ideas my late adventures suggested, presented themselves to my mind in rapid succession.

The glare, the noise, and the clatter of a French *café* are

certainly not the agents most in request for restoring a man
to the enjoyment of his erring faculties; and if I felt addled
and confused before, I had scarcely passed the threshold of
Véry's when I became absolutely like one in a trance. The
large salon was more than usually crowded, and it was with
difficulty that we obtained a place at a table where some other
English were seated, among whom I recognized my lately
made acquaintance, Mr. Edward Bingham.

Excepting a cup of coffee, I had taken nothing the entire
day; and so completely did my anxieties of different kinds
subdue all appetite that the most exquisite viands of this
well-known restaurant did not in the least tempt me. The
champagne alone had any attraction for me; and seduced by
the icy coldness of the wine, I drank copiously. This was
all that was wanting to complete the maddening confusion
of my brain, and the effect was instantaneous: the lights
danced before my eyes; the lustres whirled round; and as
the scattered fragments of conversation on either side met
my ear, I was able to form some not very inaccurate conception of what insanity might be. Politics and literature,
Mexican bonds and Noblet's legs, *pâtés de perdreaux* and
the quarantine laws, the *extrême gauche* and *roulette*, Victor
Hugo and *rouge-et-noir*, had formed a species of grand *ballet
d'action* in my fevered brain, and I was perfectly beside myself. Occasionally, too, I would revert to my own concerns,
although I was scarcely able to follow up any train of thought
for more than a few seconds together, and totally inadequate
to distinguish the false from the true. I continued to confound the counterfeit with my cousin, and wonder how my
poor uncle, for whom I was about to put on the deepest
mourning, could possibly think of driving me out of my lodgings. Of my duel for the morning I had the most shadowy
recollection, and could not perfectly comprehend whether it
was O'Leary or myself was the principal, and, indeed, cared
but little. In this happy state of independent existence I
must have passed a considerable time; and as my total silence
when spoken to, or my irrelevant answers, appeared to have
tired out my companions, they left me to the uninterrupted
enjoyment of my own pleasant imaginings.

"Do you hear, Lorrequer," at last said Trevanion,—"are

you asleep, my dear friend? This gentleman has been good enough to invite us to breakfast to-morrow at St. Cloud."

I looked up, and was just able to recognize the well-trimmed mustachio of Mr. Edward Bingham as he stood mumbling something before me.

"St. Cloud,—what of St. Cloud?" said I.

"We have something in that quarter to-morrow."

"What is it, O'Leary? Can we go?"

"Oh! certainly. Our engagement is an early one."

"We shall accept your polite invitation with pleasure—" Here he stooped over and whispered something in my ear, —what, I cannot say; but I know that my reply, now equally lost to me, produced a hearty fit of laughing to my two friends.

My next recollection is finding myself in a crowded box at the theatre. It seems that O'Leary had acceded to a proposal from some of the other party to accompany them to the Porte St. Martin, where Mrs. Bingham and her daughter had engaged a box. Amid all the confusion which troubled thoughts and wine produced in me, I could not help perceiving a studied politeness and attention on the part of Mr. Edward Bingham towards me; and my first sobering reflection came on finding that a place was reserved for me beside Miss Bingham, into which, by some contrivance I can in no wise explain, I found myself almost immediately installed. To all the excitement of champagne and punch, let the attractions of a French ballet be added, and with a singularly pretty companion at your side, to whom you have already made sufficient advances to be aware that you are no longer indifferent to her, and I venture to predict that it is much more likely your conversation will incline to flirting than political economy, and, moreover, that you make more progress during the performance of one single *pas de deux* upon the stage than you have hitherto done in ten morning calls, with an unexceptionable whisker and the best-fitting gloves in Paris. Alas! alas! it is only the rich man that ever wins at *rouge-et-noir*. The well-insured Indiaman, with her cargo of millions, comes safe into port; while the whole venture of some hardy veteran of the wave founders within sight of his native shore. So

is it ever. Where success would be all and everything, it
never comes; but only be indifferent or regardless, and fortune is at your feet, suing and imploring your acceptance
of her favors. What would I not have given for one half
of that solicitude now so kindly expressed in my favor by
Miss Bingham if syllabled by the lips of Lady Jane Callonby! How would my heart have throbbed for one light
smile from one, while I ungratefully basked in the openly
avowed preference of the other! These were my first
thoughts,—what were the succeeding ones?

"Elle est très bien!" said a Frenchwoman, turning round
in the box next to us, and directing at the same moment the
eyes of a mustachioed hero upon my fair companion.

What a turn to my thoughts did this unexpected ejaculation give rise to! I now began to consider her more
attentively, and certainly concurred fully in the Frenchwoman's verdict. I had never seen her look half so well
before. The great fault in her features, which were most
classically regular, lay in the monotony and uniform character of their expression. Now this was quite changed. Her
cheek was slightly flushed, and her eyes more brilliant than
ever; while her slightly parted lips gave a degree of speaking
earnestness to her expression that made her perfectly beautiful.

Whether it was from this cause, I cannot say, but I certainly never felt so suddenly decided in my life from one
course to its very opposite, as I now did to pay attention to
my lovely companion. And here, I fear, I must acknowledge, in the honesty of these confessional details, that
vanity had also its share in the decision. To be the admitted and preferred suitor of the prettiest woman in company, is generally a strong inducement to fall desperately
in love with her, independently of other temptations for so
doing.

How far my successes tallied with my good intentions in
this respect, I cannot now say. I only remember that more
than once O'Leary whispered to me something like a caution
of some sort or other; but Emily's encouraging smiles and
still more encouraging speeches had far more effect upon me
than all the eloquence of the united service, had it been en-

gaged in my behalf, would have effected. Mrs. Bingham, too,—who, to do her justice, seemed but little cognizant of our proceedings,—from time to time evinced that species of motherly satisfaction which *very* young men rejoice much in, and older ones are considerably alarmed at.

The play over, O'Leary charged himself with the protection of madam, while I enveloped Emily in her shawl and drew her arm within my own. What my hand had to do with hers, I knew not; it remains one of the unexplained difficulties of that eventful evening. I have, it is true, a hazy recollection of pressing some very taper and delicately formed fingers; and remember, too, the pain I felt next morning on awaking, by the pressure of a too tight ring, which had, by some strange accident, found its way to my finger, for which its size was but ill adapted.

"You will join us at supper, I hope," said Mrs. Bingham, as Trevanion handed her to her carriage. "Mr. Lorrequer, Mr. O'Leary, we shall expect you."

I was about to promise to do so, when Trevanion suddenly interrupted me, saying that he had already accepted an invitation which would, unfortunately, prevent us; and having hastily wished the ladies good-night, hurried me away so abruptly that I had not a moment given for even one parting look at the fair Emily.

"Why, Trevanion," said I, "what invitation are you dreaming of? I, for one, should have been delighted to have gone home with the Binghams."

"So I perceived," said Trevanion, gravely; "and it was for that precise reason I so firmly refused what, individually, I might have been most happy to accept."

"Then pray have the goodness to explain—"

"It is easily done. You have already, in recounting your manifold embarrassments, told me enough of these people to let me see that they intend you should marry among them; and, indeed, you have gone quite far enough to encourage such an expectation. Your present excited state has led you sufficiently far this evening, and I could not answer for your not proposing in all form before the supper was over; therefore I had no other course open to me than positively to refuse Mrs. Bingham's invitation. But

here we are now at the *Cadran Rouge;* we shall have our
lobster and a glass of Moselle, and then to bed, for we must
not forget that we are to be at St. Cloud by seven."

"Ah! that is a good thought of yours about the lobster,"
said O'Leary; "and now, as you understand these matters,
just order supper, and let us enjoy ourselves."

With all the accustomed despatch of a restaurant, a
most appetizing little supper made its speedy appearance;
and although now perfectly divested of the high excitement
which had hitherto possessed me, my spirits were excellent, and I never more relished our good fare and good
fellowship.

After a full bumper to the health of the fair Emily had
been proposed and drained by all three, Trevanion again
explained how much more serious difficulty would result
from any false step in that quarter than from all other
scrapes collectively.

This he represented so strongly that for the first time I
began to perceive the train of ill consequences that must inevitably result, and promised most faithfully to be guided by
any counsel he might feel disposed to give me.

"Ah! what a pity," said O'Leary, "it is not my case. It's
very little trouble it would cost any one to break off a match
for *me*. I had always a most peculiar talent for those things."

"Indeed!" said Trevanion. "Pray, may we know your
secret? For, perhaps, ere long we may have occasion for its
employment."

"Tell it by all means," said I.

"If I do," said O'Leary, "it will cost you a patient hearing; for my experiences are connected with two episodes in
my early life which, although not very amusing, are certainly
instructive."

"Oh! by all means let us hear them," said Trevanion; "for
we have yet two bottles of Chambertin left, and must finish
them ere we part."

"Well, agreed," said O'Leary; "only once for all, as what
I am about to confide is strictly confidential, you must promise
never even to allude to it hereafter in even the most remote
manner, much less indulge in any unseemly mirth at what I
shall relate."

Having pledged ourselves to secrecy and a becoming seriousness, O'Leary began his story as follows.

CHAPTER XXXIII.

MR. O'LEARY'S FIRST LOVE.

"IT was during the viceroyalty of the Duke of Richmond that the incidents I am about to mention took place. That was a few years since, and I was rather younger and a little more particular about my dress than at present." Here the little man threw a calm glance of satisfaction upon his uncouth habiliments that nearly made us forget our compact and laugh outright. "Well, in those wild and headstrong days of youthful ardor I fell in love,—desperately in love; and as always is, I believe, the case with our early experiments in that unfortunate passion, the object of my affection was in every way unsuited to me. She was a tall, dark-haired, dark-eyed maiden, with a romantic imagination and a kind of half-crazed poetic fervor that often made me fear for her intellect. I'm a short, rather fat,—I was always given this way,"—here he patted a waistcoat that would fit Daniel Lambert,—"happy-minded little fellow, that liked my supper of oysters at the Pigeon-house, and my other creature comforts, and hated everything that excited or put me out of my way, just as I would have hated a blister. Then, the devil would have it—for as certainly as marriages are made in heaven, flirtations have something to say to the other place— that I should fall most irretrievably in love with Lady Agnes Moreton. Bless my soul, it absolutely puts me in a perspiration, this hot day, just to think over all I went through on her account! For, strange to say, the more I appeared to prosper in her good graces, the more did she exact on my part; the pursuit was like Jacob's ladder,—if it did lead to heaven, it was certainly an awfully long journey, and very hard on one's legs. There was not an amusement she could think of, no matter how unsuited to my tastes or my abilities, that she did not immediately take a violent fancy to; and

then there was no escaping, and I was at once obliged to go
with the tide, and Heaven knows if it would not have carried
me to my grave if it were not for the fortunate (I now call
it) accident that broke off the affair forever. One time she
took a fancy for yachting; and all the danglers about her—
and she had always had a *cordon* of them, young *aides-de-
camp* of her father the general, and idle hussars in clanking
sabretasches and most absurd mustaches—approved of the
taste, and so kept filling her mind with anecdotes of corsairs
and smugglers that at last nothing would satisfy her till I—
I, who always would rather have waited for low water and
waded the Liffey in all its black mud than cross over in the
ferry-boat, for fear of sickness—*I* was obliged to put an ad-
vertisement in the newspaper for a pleasure-boat, and before
three weeks saw myself owner of a clinker-built schooner of
forty-eight tons that by some mockery of fortune was called
The Delight. I wish you saw me, as you might have done
every morning for about a month, as I stood on the Custom-
house quay giving orders for the outfit of the little craft. At
first, as she bobbed and pitched with the flood-tide, I used
to be a little giddy and rather qualmish, but at last I learned
to look on without my head reeling. I began to fancy myself
very much of a sailor,—a delusion considerably encouraged
by a huge blue jacket and a sou'wester, both of which, though
it was in the dog-days, Agnes insisted upon my wearing, saying I looked more like Dirk Hatteraick, who, I understood,
was one of her favorite heroes in Walter Scott. In fact, after
she suggested this, she and all her friends called me nothing
but 'Dirk.'

"Well, at last, after Heaven knows how many excuses on
my part and entreaties for delay, a day was appointed for our
first excursion. I shall never forget that day,—the entire
night before it I did not close my eyes; the skipper had told
me, in his confounded sea-jargon, that if the wind was in
one quarter we should have a short, tossing sea; and if in
another, a long, rolling swell; and if in a third, a happy
union of both: in fact, he made it out that it could not possibly blow right,—an opinion I most heartily coincided in;
and most devoutly did I pray for a calm that would not
permit of our stirring from our moorings, and thus mar our

projected party of pleasure. My prayer was unheard; but my hopes rose, on the other hand, for it blew tremendously during the entire night, and although there was a lull towards morning, the sea, even in the river, was considerable.

"I had just come to the conclusion that I was safe for this time, when the mate poked his head into the room and said,—

" 'Mr. Brail wishes to know, sir, if he'll bend the new main-sail to-day, as it's blowing rather fresh, and he thinks the spars light.'

" 'Why, the devil take him, he would not have us go out in a hurricane! Surely, Pipes, we could not take out ladies to-day?'

" 'Oh! bless your heart, yes, sir; it blows a bit, to be sure, but she's a good sea-boat, and we can run for Arklow or the Hook if it comes fresher.'

" 'Oh, nonsense! there's no pleasure in that; besides, I'm sure they won't like it,—the ladies won't venture, you'll see.'

" 'Ay, sir, but they're all on board a'ready; there's eight ladies in the cabin and six on deck, and as many hampers of victuals and as much crockery as if we were goin' to Madeira. Captain Grantham, sir, the soldier officer with the big beard, is a-mixing punch in the grog-tub.'

" 'From the consequences of this day I proclaim myself innocent,' said I, with a solemn voice, as I drew on my duck trousers and prepared to set out.

" 'And the mainsail, sir?' said the mate, not understanding what I said.

" 'I care not which,' said I, doggedly; 'act or part in this wilful proceeding I'll not take.'

" 'Ay, ay, sir,' said the stupid wretch; 'then I'll say you're a coming, and he may stretch the large canvas; for the skipper says he likes a wet jacket when he has gentlemen out.'

"Never did a victim put on a flame-colored garment, the emblem of fate, and set out on the march of death with a heavier heart than did I put on my pilot-coat that morning to join my friends.

"My last hope deserted me as I saw the little vessel lying beside the quay; for I continued to trust that in getting out from the dock some accident or mischance might occur to spoil our sport. But no; there she lay, rolling and pitching in such a way that, even at anchor, they could not stand on the deck without holding. Amid the torrent of compliments for the perfection of all my arrangements, and innumerable sweet things on my taste in the decoration and fitting up of my cabin, I scarcely felt myself afloat for some minutes, and we got under way amid a noise and uproar that absolutely prevented the possibility of reflection.

"Hitherto our destination had not been mentioned, and as all the party appealed to Lady Agnes, I could not be less gallant, and joined them in their request.

" 'Well, then, what do you think of Lambay?' said she, looking at the same moment towards the skipper.

" 'We can make it, my lady,' said the man, 'but we'll have a roughish sea of it, for there's a strong point of westward in the wind.'

" 'Then don't think of it,' said I. 'We have come out for pleasure, not to make our friends sick or terrify them. It does very well for us men.'

" 'There you are, Dirk, with your insolent sneers about women's nerves and female cowardice. Now, nothing but Lambay will content me,—what say you, ladies?'

"A general reply of approval met this speech, and it was carried by acclamation.

" 'Lambay then be it,' said I, with the voice of a man who, entreating to be shot, is informed that he cannot be afforded that pleasure, as his sentence is to be hanged.

"But I must hasten over these painful recollections. We dropped down the river, and soon left the lighthouse and its long pier behind us, the mast bending like a whip, and the sea boiling like barm over the lee gunwale. Still, the spirit of our party only rose the lighter, and nothing but eulogies upon the trim and sailing of the craft resounded on all sides. The din and buzz of the conversation went on only more loudly and less restrictedly than if the party had been on shore, and all, even myself, seemed happy, for up to this moment I had not been sea-sick; yet certain treacherous sensations, that alternately evinced themselves in my stomach and my head, warned me of what was in store for me. The word was now given to tack; I was in the act of essaying a soft speech to Lady Agnes, when the confounded cry was heard of 'Ready about! Starboard there; let go sheets and tacks! Stand by, haul!' The vessel plunged head-foremost into the boiling sea, which hissed on either bow; the heavy boom swung over, carrying my hat along with it—and almost my head too. The rest of the party, possibly better informed than myself, speedily changed their places to the opposite side of the boat, while I remained holding on fast by the gunwale, till the sea, rushing over what was now become the lee side, carried me head over heels into the shingle ballast in the waist. Lord, how they did laugh! Agnes, too, who never before could get beyond a very faint smile, grew almost hysterical at my performance. As for me, I only wanted this to complete my long-threatened misfortune; sea-sickness, in all its most miserable forms, set in upon me, and ere half an hour I lay upon that heap of small stones as indifferent to all around and about me as though I were dead. Oh, the long, dreary hours of that melancholy day! it seemed like a year. They tacked and tacked, they wore, beat, and tacked again, the sea washing over me, and the ruffianly sailors trampling upon me without the slightest remorse, whenever they had any occasion to pass back or forward. From my long trance of suffering I was partly roused by the steward shaking my shoulder, saying,—

" 'The gentlemen wish to know, sir, if you'd like sum'at to eat, as they're a goin' to have a morsel; we are getting into slack water now.'

" 'Where are we?' I replied, in a sepulchral voice.

" 'Off the Hook, sir. We have had a most splendid run, but I fear we'll catch it soon; there's some dirty weather to the westward.'

" 'God grant it!' said I, piously and in a low tone.

" 'Did you say you'd have a bit to eat, sir?'

" 'No! Eat! Am I a cannibal? Eat—go away. Mark me, my good fellow, I'll pay you your wages, if ever we get ashore; you'll never set another foot aboard with me.'

"The man looked perfectly astounded as he moved away, and my thoughts were soon engrossed by the proceedings near me. The rattle of knives and the jingling of plates and glasses went on very briskly for some time, accompanied by various pleasant observations of my guests, for such I judged them, from the mirth which ever followed them. At last I thought I heard my name, or at least what they pleased to use as its substitute, mentioned; I strained my ears to listen, and learned that they were pretending to plan a run over to Cowes and see the regatta. This they discussed then for about twenty minutes in a very loud voice, purposely to see its effects upon me; but as I was now aware of the trick, I gave no signs of any intelligence.

" 'Poor Dirk,' said Grantham, 'I believe by this time he cares very little which way her head lies; but here comes something better than all our discussions. Lady Agnes, sit here; Miss Pelham, here's a dry cushion for you. Did you say a wing, Lady Mary?'

"Now began the crash and clatter of dinner,—champagne corks popping, glasses ringing, and all that peculiar admixture of *fracas* and fun which accompanies a scrambled meal. How they did laugh and eat, ay, and drink too! Grantham's punch seemed to have its success, for, sick as I was, I could perceive the voices of the men grow gradually louder, and discovered that two gentlemen who had been remarkably timid in the morning, and scarcely opened their lips, were now rather uproariously given, and one even proposed to sing.

" 'If any man,' thought I, 'were to look for an instant at the little scene now enacted here, what a moral would he reap from it! Talk of the base ingratitude of the world, you cannot say too much of it. Who would suppose that it was *my* boat these people were assembled in; that it was *my* champagne these people were drinking; that *my* venison and *my* pheasants were feeding those lips which rarely spoke except to raise a joke at my expense?' My chagrin increased my sickness, and my sickness redoubled my chagrin.

" 'Mr. Brail,' said I, in a low whisper, 'Mr. Brail.'

" 'Did you speak, sir?' said he, with about as much surprise in his manner as though he had been addressed by a corpse.

" 'Mr. Brail,' said I, 'is there any danger here?'

" 'Lord love you, no, sir; she's walking Spanish, and the sea going down. We shall have lovely weather, and they're all enjoying it, sir,—the ladies.'

" 'So I perceive,' said I, with a groan,—'so I perceive; but, Mr. Brail, could you do nothing—just to—to—startle them

a little, I mean for fun only? Just ship a heavy sea or two,—
I don't care for a little damage, Mr. Brail; and if it were
to wash over the dinner service and all the wine, I should
not like it worse.'

" 'Why, sir, you are getting quite funny; the sickness is
going.'

" 'No, Mr. Brail, worse than ever; my head is in two pieces,
and my stomach in the back of my mouth. But I should
like you to do this,—so just manage it, will you? And there's
twenty pounds in my pocket-book, you can have it,—there
now, won't you oblige me? And hark ye, Mr. Brail, if
Captain Grantham were to be washed over by mere accident,
it cannot be helped; accidents are always occurring in boating
parties. Go now; you know what I mean.'

" 'But, sir—' began he.

" 'Well, then, Mr. Brail, you won't,—very well. Now all
I have to say is this, that the moment I can find strength to do
it, I'll stave out a plank; I'll scuttle the vessel,—that's all;
I have made up my mind, and look to yourselves now.'

"Saying these words, I again threw myself upon the ballast,
and as the gay chorus of a drinking-song was wafted across
me, prayed devoutly that we might all go down to the bottom. The song over, I heard a harsh, gruff voice mixing with
the more civilized tones of the party, and soon perceived
that Mr. Brail was recounting my proposal, amid the most uproarious shouts of laughter I ever listened to. Then followed
a number of pleasant suggestions for my future management,
one proposing to have me tried for mutiny and sentenced to a
good ducking over the side; another, that I should be tarred
on my back,—to which latter most humane notion the fair
Agnes subscribed, averring that she was resolved upon my
deserving my sobriquet of Dirk Hatteraick. My wrath was
now the master even of deadly sickness. I got upon my knees,
and having in vain tried to reach my legs, I struggled aft.
In this posture did I reach the quarter-deck. What my
intention precisely was in this excursion, I have no notion of
now, but I have some very vague idea that I meant to react
the curse of Kehama upon the whole party. At last I mustered strength to rise; but alas! I had scarcely reached the
standing position when a tremendous heel of the boat to

one side threw me in the gunwale, and before I was able to recover my balance, a second lurch pitched me headlong into the sea. I have, thank God, no further recollection of my misfortunes. When I again became conscious, I found myself wrapped up in a pilot-coat while my clothes were drying. The vessel was at anchor in Wexford, my attached friends had started for town with post-horses, leaving me no less cured of love than aquatics.

"The Delight passed over in a few days to some more favored son of Neptune, and I hid my shame and my misfortunes by a year's tour on the Continent."

"Although I acknowledge," said Trevanion, "that hitherto I have reaped no aid from Mr. O'Leary's narrative, yet I think it is not without a moral."

"Well, but," said I, "he has got another adventure to tell us; we have quite time for it, so pray pass the wine and let us have it."

"I have just finished the Burgundy," said O'Leary; "and if you will ring for another flask, I have no objection to let you hear the story of my second love."

CHAPTER XXXIV.

MR. O'LEARY'S SECOND LOVE.

"YOU may easily suppose," began Mr. O'Leary, "that the unhappy termination of my first passion served as a shield to me for a long time against my unfortunate tendencies towards the fair; and such was really the case. I never spoke to a young lady for three years after without a reeling in my head, so associated in my mind was love and sea-sickness. However, at last, what will not time do? It was about four years from the date of this adventure when I became so oblivious of my former failure as again to tempt my fortune! My present choice, in every way unlike the last, was a gay, lively girl of great animal spirits and a considerable turn for raillery that spared no one; the members of her own family were not even sacred in her eyes, and her father, a reverend dean, as frequently figured among the ludicrous as his neighbors.

"The Evershams had been very old friends of a rich aunt of mine,—who never, by the by, had condescended to notice me till I made their acquaintance; but no sooner had I done so than she sent for me and gave me to understand that in the event of my succeeding to the hand of Fanny Eversham, I should be her heir and the possessor of about sixty thousand pounds. She did not stop here, but by canvassing the dean in my favor, speedily put the matter on a most favorable footing, and in less than two months I was received as the accepted suitor of the fair Fanny, then one of the reigning *belles* of Dublin.

"They lived at this time about three miles from town, in a very pretty country, where I used to pass all my mornings, and many of my evenings too, in a state of happiness that I should have considered perfect if it were not for two unhappy blots,—one, the taste of my betrothed for laughing at her friends; another, the diabolical propensity to talk politics of my intended father-in-law. To the former I could submit; but with the latter, submission only made bad worse; for he invariably drew up as I receded, dryly observing that with men who had no avowed opinions, it was ill agreeing, or that with persons who kept their politics as a schoolboy does his pocket-money, never to spend, and always ready to change, it was unpleasant to dispute. Such taunts as these I submitted to as well as I might, secretly resolving that as I never knew the meaning of Whig and Tory, I'd contrive to spend my life, after marriage, out of the worthy dean's diocese.

"Time wore on, and at length to my most pressing solicitations it was conceded that a day for our marriage should be appointed. Not even the unlucky termination of this my second love affair can deprive me of the happy *souvenir* of the few weeks which were to intervene before our destined union.

"The mornings were passed in ransacking all the shops where wedding finery could be procured; laces, blondes, velvets, and satins littered every corner of the deanery; and there was scarcely a carriage in a coachmaker's yard in the city that I had not sat and jumped in, to try the springs, by the special directions of Mrs. Eversham, who never ceased to impress me with the awful responsibility I was about to take upon me in marrying so great a prize as her daughter,—a feeling I found very general among many of my friends at the Kildare Street Club.

"Among the many indispensable purchases which I was to make, and about which Fanny expressed herself more than commonly anxious, was a saddle-horse for me. She was a great horsewoman, and hated riding with only a servant, and had given me to understand as much about half a dozen times each day for the last five weeks. How shall I acknowledge it? Equestrianism was never my forte. I had all my life considerable respect for the horse as an animal,—pretty much as I regarded a lion or a tiger; but as to any intention of mounting upon the back of one and taking a ride, I should as soon have dreamed of taking an airing upon a giraffe; and as to the thought of buying, feeding, and maintaining such a beast at my own proper cost, I should just as soon have determined to purchase a pillory or a ducking-stool by way of amusing my leisure hours.

"However, Fanny was obstinate. Whether she suspected anything or not, I cannot say; but nothing seemed to turn her from her purpose. And although I pleaded a thousand things in delay, yet she each day grew more impatient, and at last I saw that there was nothing for it but to submit.

"When I arrived at this last and bold resolve, I could not help feeling that to possess a horse and not be able to mount him, was only deferring the ridicule; and as I had so often expressed the difficulty I felt in suiting myself as a cause of my delay, I could not possibly come forward with anything very objectionable, or I should be only the more laughed at. There was then but one course to take; a fortnight still intervened before the day which was to make me happy, and I resolved to take lessons in riding during the interval, and by every endeavor in my power become, if possible, able to pass muster in the saddle before my bride.

"Poor old Lalouette understood but little of the urgency of the case when I requested his leave to take my lessons each morning at six o'clock, for I dared not absent myself during the day without exciting suspicion. And never, I will venture to assert, did knight-errant of old strive harder for the hand of his lady love than did I during that weary fortnight. If a hippogriff had been the animal I bestrode, instead of being, as it was, an old wall-eyed gray, I could not have felt more misgivings at my temerity, or more proud of my achievement. In the first three days the unaccustomed exercise proved so severe that when I reached the deanery I could hardly move, and crossed the floor pretty much as a pair of compasses might be supposed to do if performing that exploit. Nothing, however, could equal the kindness of my poor dear mother-in-law in embryo, and even the dean too. Fanny, indeed, said nothing, but I rather think she was disposed to giggle a little. But my rheumatism, as it was called, was daily inquired after, and I was compelled to take some infernal stuff in my port wine at dinner that nearly made me sick at table.

" 'I am sure you walk too much,' said Fanny, with one of her knowing looks. 'Papa, don't you think he ought to ride? It would be much better for him.'

" 'I do, my dear,' said the dean. 'But then, you see, he is so hard to be pleased in a horse. Your old hunting days have spoiled you; but you must forget Melton and Grantham, and condescend to keep a hack.'

"I must have looked confoundedly foolish here, for Fanny never took her eyes off me, and continued to laugh in her own wicked way.

"It was now about the ninth or tenth day of my purgatorial performances; and certainly if there be any merit in fleshly mortifications, these religious exercises of mine should stand my part hereafter. A review had been announced in the Phœnix Park which Fanny had expressed herself most desirous to witness; and as the dean would not permit her to go without a chaperon, I had no means of escape, and promised to escort her. No sooner had I made this rash pledge than I hastened to my confidential friend Lalouette, and having imparted to him my entire secret, asked him, in a solemn and imposing manner, 'Can I do it?'

"The old man shook his head dubiously, looked grave, and muttered at length, 'Mosch depend on de horse.'

" 'I know it, I know it, I feel it,' said I, eagerly; 'then where are we to find an animal that will carry me peaceably through this awful day,—I care not for its price?'

" '*Votre affaire ne sera pas trop chère,*' said he.

" 'Why, how do you mean?' said I.

"He then proceeded to inform me that by a singularly fortunate chance there took place that day an auction of 'cast horses,' as they are termed, which had been used in the horse police force, and that from long riding, and training to stand fire, nothing could be more suitable than one of these, being both easy to ride and not given to start at noise.

"I could have almost hugged the old fellow for his happy suggestion, and waited with impatience for three o'clock to come, when we repaired together to Essex Bridge, at that time the place selected for these sales.

"I was at first a little shocked at the look of the animals drawn up; they were mostly miserably thin, most of them swelled in the legs, few without sore backs, and not one eye, on an average, in every three; but still they were all high-steppers, and carried a great tail.

" 'There's your *affaire,*' said the old Frenchman, as a long-legged, fiddle-headed beast was led out, turning out his fore-legs so as to endanger the man who walked beside him.

" 'Yes, there's blood for you,' said Charley Dycer, seeing my eye fixed on the wretched beast; 'equal to fifteen stone with any fox-hounds. Safe in all his paces, and warranted sound,—except,' added he, in a whisper, 'a slight spavin in both hind legs, ring bone, and a little touched in the wind.' Here the animal gave an approving cough. 'Will any gentleman say fifty pounds to begin?'

"But no gentleman did. A hackney coachman, however, said five, and the sale was opened; the beast trotting up and down nearly over the bidders at every moment, and plunging on so that it was impossible to know what was doing.

" 'Five ten—fifteen—six pounds; thank you, sir,—guineas.'

" ' Seven pounds,' said I, bidding against myself, not perceiving that I had spoken last.

" 'Thank you, Mr. Moriarty,' said Dycer, turning towards an invisible purchaser supposed to be in the crowd; 'thank you, sir,—you'll not let a good one go in that way.'

22

"Every one here turned to find out the very knowing gentleman, but he could nowhere be seen.

"Dycer resumed: 'Seven ten for Mr. Moriarty. Going for seven ten, —a cruel sacrifice. There's action for you,—playful beast.'

"Here the devil had stumbled, and nearly killed a basket-woman with two children.

" 'Eight,' said I, with a loud voice.

" 'Eight pounds,—quite absurd,' said Dycer, almost rudely; 'a charger like that for eight pounds—going for eight pounds —going—nothing above eight pounds—no reserve, gentlemen, you are aware of that! They are all, as it were, his Majesty's stud—no reserve whatever—last time—eight pounds—gone!'

"Amid a very hearty cheer from the mob,—God knows why, but a Dublin mob always cheer,—I returned, accompanied by a ragged fellow, leading my new purchase after me with a hay halter. 'What is the meaning of those letters?' said I, pointing to a very conspicuous 'G. R.,' with sundry other enigmatical signs, burned upon the animal's hind-quarter.

" 'That's to show he was a po-lis,' said the fellow, with a grin; 'and whin ye ride with ladies, ye must turn the decoy side.'

"The auspicious morning at last arrived; and strange to say, the first waking thought was of the unlucky day that ushered in my yachting excursion four years before. Why this was so, I cannot pretend to guess; there was but little analogy in the circumstances,—at least so far as anything had then gone. 'How is Marius?' said I to my servant as he opened my shutters. Here let me mention that a friend of the Kildare Street Club had suggested this name from the remarkably classic character of my steed's countenance; his nose, he assured me, was perfectly Roman.

" 'Marius is doing finely, sir, barring his cough and the thrifle that ails his hind legs.'

" 'He'll carry me quietly, Simon, eh?'

" 'Quietly. I'll warrant he'll carry you quietly, if that's all.'

"Here was comfort; for Simon had lived forty years as pantry boy with my mother, and knew a great deal about horses. I dressed myself, therefore, in high spirits; and if my pilot jacket and oil-skin cap in former days had half persuaded me that I was born for marine achievements, certainly my cords and tops that morning went far to convince me that I must have once been a very keen sportsman somewhere without knowing it.

"It was a delightful July day that I set out to join my friends, who, having recruited a large party, were to rendezvous at the corner of Stephen's Green; thither I proceeded in a certain ambling trot which I have often observed is a very favorite pace with timid horsemen and gentlemen of the medical profession. I was hailed with a most hearty welcome by a large party as I turned out of Grafton Street, among whom I perceived several friends of Miss Eversham, and some young dragoon officers, not of my acquaintance, but who appeared to know Fanny intimately, and were laughing heartily with her as I rode up.

"I don't know if other men have experienced what I am about to mention or not; but certainly to me there is no more painful sensation than to find yourself among a number of well-mounted, well-equipped people, while the animal you yourself bestride seems only fit for the kennel. Every look that is cast at your unlucky steed and every whispered observation about you are so many thorns in your flesh, till at last you begin to feel that your appearance is for very little else than the amusement and mirth of the assembly, and every time you rise in your stirrups you excite a laugh.

" 'Where, for mercy's sake, did you find that creature?' said Fanny, surveying Marius through a glass.

" 'Oh, him, eh? Why, he is a handsome horse, if in condition,—a charger, you know; that's his style.'

" 'Indeed,' lisped a young lancer, 'I should be devilish sorry to charge or be charged with him.' And here they all chuckled at this puppy's silly joke, and I drew up to repress further liberties.

" 'Is he anything of a fencer?' said a young country gentleman.

" 'To judge from his near eye, I should say much more of a boxer,' said another.

"Here commenced a running fire of pleasantry at the expense of my poor steed, which, not content with attacking his physical, extended to his moral qualities; an old gentleman near me observing that I ought not to have mounted him at all, seeing that he was so deuced groggy! To which I replied by insinuating that if others present were as free from the influence of ardent spirits, society would not be a sufferer,—an observation that I flatter myself turned the mirth against the old fellow, for they all laughed for a quarter of an hour after.

"Well, at last we set out in a brisk trot, and, placed near Fanny, I speedily forgot all my annoyances in the prospect of figuring to advantage before her. When we reached College Green the leaders of the party suddenly drew up, and we soon found that the entire street opposite the Bank was filled with a dense mob of people, who appeared to be swayed hither and thither like some mighty beast as the individuals composing it were engaged in close conflict. It was nothing more nor less than one of those almost weekly rows which then took place between the students of the University and the townspeople, and which rarely ended without serious consequences. The numbers of people pressing on to the scene of action soon blocked up our retreat, and we found ourselves most unwilling spectators of the conflict. Political watchwords were loudly shouted by each party; and at last the students, who appeared to be yielding to superior numbers, called out for the intervention of the police. The aid was nearer than they expected; for at the same instant a body of mounted policemen, whose high helmets rendered them sufficiently conspicuous, were seen trotting at a sharp pace down Dame Street. On they came, with drawn sabres, led by a well-looking gentleman-like personage in plain clothes, who dashed at once into the midst of the fray, issuing his orders and pointing out to his followers to secure the ringleaders. Up to this moment I had been a most patient and rather amused spectator of what was doing. Now, however, my part was to commence, for at the word 'charge,' given in a harsh, deep voice by the sergeant of the party, Marius, remembering his ancient instinct, pricked up his ears, cocked his tail, flung up both his hind legs till they nearly broke the provost's windows, and plunged into the thickest of the fray like a devil incarnate.

"Self-preservation must be a strong instinct, for I well remember how little pain it cost me to see the people tumbling

Mr. O'Leary charges a mob.

and rolling before and beneath me, while I continued to keep my seat. It was only the moment before, and that immense mass were in man-to-man encounter; now, all the indignation of both parties seemed turned upon me. Brick-bats were loudly implored, and paving-stones begged to throw at my devoted head; the wild huntsman of the German romance never created half the terror nor one tenth of the mischief that I did in less than fifteen minutes, for the ill-starred beast continued twining and twisting like a serpent, plunging and kicking the entire time, and occasionally biting too,—all which accomplishments, I afterwards learned, however little in request in civil life, are highly prized in the horse police.

"Every new order of the sergeant was followed in his own fashion by Marius, who very soon contrived to concentrate in my unhappy person all the interest of about fifteen hundred people.

" 'Secure that scoundrel!' said the magistrate, pointing with his finger towards me as I rode over a respectable-looking old lady with a gray muff. 'Secure him! Cut him down!'

" 'Ah, devil's luck to him if he do!' said a newsmonger with a broken shin.

"On I went, however; and now, as the Fates would have it, instead of bearing me out of further danger, the confounded brute dashed onwards to where the magistrate was standing, surrounded by policemen. I thought I saw him change color as I came on. I suppose my own looks were none of the pleasantest, for the worthy man evidently liked them not. Into the midst of them we plunged, upsetting a corporal, horse and all, and appearing as if bent upon reaching the alderman.

" 'Cut him down, for Heaven's sake! Will nobody shoot him?' said he, with a voice trembling with fear and anger.

"At these words a wretch lifted up his sabre and made a cut at my head. I stooped suddenly, and throwing myself from the saddle, seized the poor alderman around the neck, and we both came rolling to the ground together. So completely was he possessed with the notion that I meant to assassinate him that while I was endeavoring to extricate myself from his grasp, he continued to beg his life in the most heartrending manner.

"My story is now soon told. So effectually did they rescue

the alderman from his danger that they left me insensible; and I only came to myself some days after by finding myself in the dock in Green Street, charged with an indictment of nineteen counts, the only word of truth of which lay in the preamble, for the 'devil inciting' me only, would ever have made me the owner of that infernal beast, the cause of all my misfortunes. I was so stupefied with my beating that I know little of the course of the proceedings. My friends told me afterwards that I had a narrow escape from transportation; but for the greatest influence exerted in my behalf I should certainly have passed the autumn in the agreeable recreation of pounding oyster-shells or carding wool; and it certainly must have gone hard with me, for, stupefied as I was, I remember the sensation in court when the alderman made his appearance with a patch over his eye. The affecting admonition of the little judge—who, when passing sentence upon me, adverted to the former respectability of my life and the rank of my relatives—actually made the galleries weep.

"Four months to Newgate and a fine to the king then rewarded my taste for horse-exercise; and it's no wonder if I prefer going on foot.

"As to Miss Eversham, the following short note from the dean concluded my hopes in that quarter:—

"DEANERY, Wednesday morning.

"SIR,—After the very distressing publicity to which your late conduct has exposed you, the so open avowal of political opinions at variance with those (I will say) of every gentleman, and the recorded sentence of a judge on the verdict of twelve of your countrymen, I should hope that you will not feel my present admonition necessary to inform you that your visits at my house shall cease.

"The presents you made my daughter when under our unfortunate ignorance of your real character, have been addressed to your hotel, and I am your most obedient, humble servant,   "OLIVER EVERSHAM."

"Here ended my second affair *par amours;* and I freely confess to you that if I can only obtain a wife in a sea-voyage or a steeplechase, I am likely to fulfil one great condition in modern advertising, 'as having no incumbrance, nor any objection to travel.' "

CHAPTER XXXV.

THE DUEL.

MR. O'LEARY had scarcely concluded the narrative of his second adventure when the gray light of the breaking day was seen faintly struggling through the half-closed curtains, and apprising us of the lateness of the hour.

"I think we shall just have time for one finishing flask of Chambertin," said O'Leary, as he emptied the bottle into his glass.

"I forbid the banns, for one," cried Trevanion. "We have all had wine enough, considering what we have before us this morning; and besides, you are not aware it is now past four o'clock. So, *garçon, garçon,* there!—how soundly the poor fellow sleeps!—let us have some coffee, and then inquire if a carriage is in waiting at the corner of the Rue Vivienne."

The coffee made its appearance,—very much, as it seemed, to Mr. O'Leary's chagrin, who, however, solaced himself by sundry "small glasses" to correct the coldness of the wine he had drunk, and at length recovered his good-humor.

"Do you know, now," said he, after a short pause, in which we had all kept silence, "I think what we are about to do is the very ugliest way of finishing a pleasant evening. For my own part, I like the wind-up we used to have in 'Old Trinity' formerly, when, after wringing off half a dozen knockers, breaking the lamps at the post-office, and getting out the fire-engines of Werburgh's parish, we beat a few watchmen and went peaceably to bed."

"Well, not being an Irishman," said Trevanion, "I'm half disposed to think that even our present purpose is nearly as favorable to life and limb; but here comes my servant. Well, John, is all arranged and the carriage ready?"

Having ascertained that the carriage was in waiting, and that the small box—brass-bound and Bramah-locked—reposed within, we paid our bill and departed. A cold, raw, misty-looking morning, with masses of dark, lowering clouds overhead, and channels of dark and murky water beneath, were the pleasant prospects which met us as we issued forth from the *café*. The lamps which hung suspended midway across the street—we speak of some years since—creaked, with a low and plaintive sound, as they swung backwards and forwards in the wind. Not a footstep was heard in the street, nothing but the heavy patter of the rain as it fell ceaselessly upon the broad pavement. It was, indeed, a most depressing and dispiriting accompaniment to our intended excursion; and even O'Leary, who seemed to have but slight sympathy with external influences, felt it, for he spoke but little, and was scarcely ten minutes in the carriage till he was sound asleep. This was, I confess, a great relief to me; for however impressed I was, and to this hour am, with the many sterling qualities of my poor friend, yet I acknowledge that this was not precisely the time I should have cared for their exercise, and would have much preferred the companionship of a different order of person, even though less long acquainted with him. Trevanion was, of all others, the most suitable for this purpose; and I felt no embarrassment in opening my mind freely to him upon subjects which, but twenty-four hours previous, I could not have imparted to a brother.

There is no such unlocker of the secrets of the heart as the possibly near approach of death. Indeed, I question if a great deal of the bitterness the thought of it inspires does not depend upon that very circumstance. The reflection that the long-treasured mystery of our lives (and who is there without some such?) is about to become known, and the secret of our inmost heart laid bare, is in itself depressing. Not one kind word nor one embracing adieu to those we are to leave forever can be spoken or written without calling up its own story of half-forgotten griefs, or, still worse, at such a moment, of happiness never again to be partaken of.

"I cannot explain why," said I to Trevanion, "but although it has unfortunately been pretty often my lot to have gone out on occasions like this, both as principal and friend, yet never before did I feel so completely depressed and low-spirited; and never, in fact, did so many thoughts of regret arise before me for much of the past, and sorrow for the chance of abandoning the future—"

"I can understand," said Trevanion, interrupting. "I have heard of your prospects in the Callonby family, and certainly, with such hopes, I can well conceive how little one would be disposed to brook the slightest incident which could interfere with their accomplishment; but now that your cousin Guy's pretensions in that quarter are at an end, I suppose, from all I have heard, that there can be no great obstacle to yours."

"Guy's pretensions at an end! For Heaven's sake tell me all you know of this affair; for up to this moment I am in utter ignorance of everything regarding his position in the Callonby family."

"Unfortunately," replied Trevanion, "I know but little; but still that little is authentic, Guy himself having imparted the secret to a very intimate friend of mine. It appears, then, that your cousin had heard that the Callonbys had been very civil to you in Ireland and made all manner of advances to you,— having done so under the impression that you were the *other* nephew of Sir Guy, and consequently the heir of a large fortune, that is, Guy himself,—and that they had never discovered the mistake during the time they resided in Ireland, when they not only permitted, but even encouraged the closest intimacy between you and Lady Jane. Is so far true?"

"I have long suspected it. Indeed, in no other way can I account for the reception I met with from the Callonbys. But is it possible that Lady Jane could have lent herself to anything so unworthy—"

"Pray hear me out," said Trevanion, who was evidently struck by the despondency of my voice and manner. "Guy, having heard of their mistake, and arguing well to himself from this evidence of their disposition, no sooner heard of their arrival in Paris than he came over here and got introduced to them. From that time he scarcely ever left their house, except to accompany them into society or to the theatres. It is said that with Lady Jane he made no progress. Her manner, at the beginning cold and formal, became daily more so, until at last he was half disposed to abandon the pursuit,—in which, by the by, he has since confessed, am-

bitious views entered more than any affection for the lady,
—when the thought struck him to benefit by what he supposed at first to be the great bar to his success. He suddenly
pretended to be only desirous of intimacy with Lady Jane from
having heard so much of her from you; affected to be greatly
in your confidence; and, in fact, assumed the character of
a friend cognizant of all your feelings and hopes, and ardently
desiring, by every means in his power, to advance your interests—"

"And was it thus he succeeded?" I broke in.

" 'Twas thus he endeavored to succeed," said Trevanion.

"Ah! with what success I but too well know," said I. "My
uncle himself showed me a letter from Guy in which he absolutely speaks of the affair as settled, and talks of Lady Jane
as about to be his wife."

"That may be all quite true; but a little consideration of
Guy's tactics will show what he intended, for I find that he
induced your uncle, by some representations of his, to make
the most handsome proposals, with regard to the marriage,
to the Callonbys, and that, to make the story short, nothing
but the decided refusal of Lady Jane—who at length saw
through his entire game,—prevented the match."

"And then she did refuse him?" said I, with ill-repressed
exultation.

"Of that there can be no doubt; for independently of all
the gossip and quizzing upon the subject to which Guy was
exposed in the coteries, he made little secret of it himself,
openly avowing that he did not consider a repulse a defeat,
and that he resolved to sustain the siege as vigorously as ever."

However interested I felt in all Trevanion was telling me,
I could not help falling into a train of thinking over my first
acquaintance with the Callonbys. There are, perhaps, but
few things more humiliating than the knowledge that any
attention or consideration we have met with has been paid us
in mistake for another; and in the very proportion that they
were prized before, are they detested when the truth is known
to us.

To all the depressing influences these thoughts suggested,
came the healing balm that Lady Jane was true to me; that
she at least, however others might be biassed by worldly con-

siderations,—that she cared for me, for myself alone. My reader (alas! for my character for judgment) knows upon how little I founded the conviction; but I have often, in these "Confessions," avowed my especial failing to be a great taste for self-deception, and here was a capital occasion for its indulgence.

"We shall have abundant time to discuss this later on," said Trevanion, laying his hand upon my shoulder to rouse my wandering attention, "for now, I perceive, we have only eight minutes to spare."

As he spoke, a dragoon officer, in an undress, rode up to the window of the carriage, and looking steadily at our party for a few seconds, asked if we were *"Messieurs les Anglais;"* and almost without waiting for reply, added, "You had better not go any farther in your carriage, for the next turn of the road will bring you in sight of the village."

We accordingly stopped the driver, and having with some difficulty aroused O'Leary, got out upon the road. The stranger here gave his horse to a groom and proceeded to guide us through a corn-field by a narrow path, with whose windings and crossings he appeared quite conversant. We at length reached the brow of a little hill, from which an extended view of the country lay before us, showing the Seine winding its tranquil course between the richly tilled fields, dotted with many a pretty cottage. Turning abruptly from this point, our guide led us, by a narrow and steep path, into a little glen planted with poplars and willows. A small stream ran through this, and by the noise we soon detected that a mill was not far distant, which another turning brought us at once in front of.

And here I cannot help dwelling upon the scene which met our view. In the porch of the little rural mill sat two gentlemen, one of whom I immediately recognized as the person who had waited upon me, and the other I rightly conjectured to be my adversary. Before them stood a small table covered with a spotless napkin, upon which a breakfast equipage was spread,—a most inviting melon and a long, slender-necked bottle, reposing in a little ice-pail, forming part of the picture. My opponent was coolly enjoying his cigar, a half-finished cup of coffee beside him; his friend was occupied in examining the caps of the duelling-pistols, which were placed upon a chair. No sooner had we turned the angle which brought us in view than they both rose, and taking off their hats with much courtesy, bade us good-morning.

"May I offer you a cup of coffee?" said Monsieur de Joncourt to me as I came up, at the same time filling it out, and pushing over a little flask of cognac towards me.

A look from Trevanion decided my acceptance of the proffered civility, and I seated myself in the chair beside the baron. Trevanion meanwhile had engaged my adversary in conversation along with the stranger who had been our guide, leaving O'Leary alone unoccupied, which, however, he did not long remain; for although uninvited by the others, he seized a knife and fork and commenced a vigorous attack upon a partridge-pie near him, and with equal absence of ceremony uncorked the champagne and filled out a foaming goblet, nearly one third of the whole bottle, adding,—

"I think, Mr. Lorrequer, there's nothing like showing them that we are just as cool and unconcerned as themselves."

If I might judge from the looks of the party, a happier mode of convincing them of our "free and easy" feelings could not possibly have been discovered. From any mortification this proceeding might have caused me, I was speedily relieved by Trevanion calling O'Leary to one side while he explained to him that he must nominally act as second on the ground, as Trevanion, being a resident in Paris, might become liable to a prosecution should anything serious arise, while O'Leary, as a mere passer through, could cross the country into Germany and avoid all trouble.

O'Leary at once acceded,—perhaps the more readily because he expected to be allowed to return to his breakfast; but in this he soon found himself mistaken, for the whole party now rose, and, preceded by the baron, followed the course of the little stream.

After about five minutes walking we found ourselves at the outlet of the glen, which was formed by a large stone quarry, making a species of amphitheatre, with lofty walls of rugged granite rising thirty or forty feet on either side of us. The ground was smooth and level as a boarded floor, and certainly, to amateurs in this sort of matters, presented a most perfect spot for a "meeting."

The stranger who had just joined us could not help remarking our looks of satisfaction at the choice of the ground, and observed to me,—

"This is not the first affair that this little spot has witnessed, and the 'Mill of St. Cloud' is, I think, the very best 'meet' about Paris."

Trevanion, who during these few minutes had been engaged with De Joncourt, now drew me aside.

"Well, Lorrequer, have you any recollection now of having seen your opponent before, or can you make a guess at the source of all this?"

"Never till this instant," said I, "have I beheld him," as I looked towards the tall, stoutly built figure of my adversary, who was very leisurely detaching a cordon from his tightly fitting frock,—doubtless to prevent its attracting my aim.

"Well, never mind, I shall manage everything properly. What can you do with the small-sword, for they have rapiers at the mill?"

"Nothing whatever; I have not fenced since I was a boy."

"No matter, then, we'll fight at a *barrière*,—I know they're not prepared for that from Englishmen; so just step on one side now, and leave me to talk it over."

As the limited nature of the ground did not permit me to retire to a distance, I became involuntarily aware of a dialogue which even the seriousness of the moment could scarcely keep me from laughing at, outright.

It was necessary, for the sake of avoiding any possible legal difficulty in the result, that O'Leary should give his assent to every step of the arrangement; and being almost totally ignorant of French, Trevanion had not only to translate for him, but also to render in reply O'Leary's own comments or objections to the propositions of the others.

"Then it is agreed,—we fight at a *barrière*," said Captain de Joncourt.

"What's that, Trevanion?"

"We have agreed to place them at a *barrière*," replied Trevanion.

"That's strange," muttered O'Leary to himself, who, knowing that the word meant a "turnpike," never supposed it had any other signification.

"*Vingt-quatre pas, n'est-ce-pas?*" said De Joncourt.

"Too far," interposed Trevanion.

"What does he say now?" asked O'Leary.

"Twenty-four paces for the distance."

"Twenty-four of my teeth, he means," said O'Leary, snapping his fingers. "What does he think of the length of Sackville Street? Ask him that, will ye?"

"What says Monsieur?" said the Frenchman.

"He thinks the distance much too great."

"He may be mistaken," said the Captain, half sneeringly. "My friend is *de la première force.*"

"That must be something impudent, from your looks, Mr. Trevanion. Isn't it a thousand pities I can't speak French?"

"What say you, then, to twelve paces? Fire together, and two shots each, if the first fire be inconclusive," said Trevanion.

"And if necessary," added the Frenchman, carelessly, "conclude with these," touching the swords with his foot as he spoke.

"The choice of the weapon lies with us, I opine," replied Trevanion. "We have already named pistols, and by them we shall decide this matter."

It was at length, after innumerable objections, agreed upon that we should be placed back to back, and, at a word given, each walk forward to a certain distance marked out by a stone, where we were to halt, and at the signal *"Un," "Deux,"* turn round and fire.

This, which is essentially a French invention in duelling, was perfectly new to me, but by no means so to Trevanion, who was fully aware of the immense consequence of not giving even a momentary opportunity for aim to my antagonist; and in this mode of firing the most practised and deadly shot is liable to err, particularly if the signal be given quickly.

While Trevanion and the Captain were measuring out the ground, a little circumstance which was enacted near me was certainly not over-calculated to strengthen my nerve. The stranger who had led us to the ground had begun to examine the pistols, and finding that one of them was loaded, turned towards my adversary, saying, "D'Haultpenne, you have forgotten to draw the charge. Come, let us see what vein you are in." At the same time, drawing off his large cavalry glove, he handed the pistol to his friend. "A double-napoleon you don't hit the thumb."

"Done!" said the other, adjusting the weapon in his hand. The action was scarcely performed, when the bettor flung the glove into the air with all his force. My opponent raised his pistol, waited for an instant till the glove, having attained its greatest height, turned to fall again; then click went the trigger, the glove turned round and round half a dozen times, and fell about twenty yards off, and the thumb was found cut clearly off at the juncture with the hand.

This—which did not occupy half as long as I have spent in recounting it—was certainly a pleasant introduction to standing at fifteen yards from the principal actor; and I should doubtless have felt it in all its force, had not my attention been drawn off by the ludicrous expression of grief in O'Leary's countenance, who evidently regarded me as already defunct.

"Now, Lorrequer, we are ready," said Trevanion, coming forward; and then, lowering his voice, added "All is in your favor; I have won the 'word,' which I shall give the moment you halt. So turn and fire at once. Be sure not to go too far round in the turn,—that is the invariable error in this mode of firing; only, no hurry!—Be calm."

"Now, messieurs," said De Joncourt as he approached with his friend leaning upon his arm, and placed him in the spot allotted to him. Trevanion then took my arm, and placed me back to back to my antagonist. As I took up my ground, it so chanced that my adversary's spur slightly grazed me, upon which he immediately turned round, and with the most engaging smile, begged a "thousand pardons," and hoped I was not hurt.

O'Leary, who saw the incident and guessed the action aright, called out,—

"Oh, the cold-blooded villain! the devil a chance for you, Mr. Lorrequer."

"Messieurs, your pistols," said De Joncourt, who, as he

handed the weapons and repeated once more the conditions of the combat, gave the word to march.

I now walked slowly forward to the place marked out by the stone; but it seemed that I must have been in advance of my opponent, for I remember some seconds elapsed before Trevanion coughed slightly, and then with a clear, full voice called out, *"Un," "Deux!"* I had scarcely turned myself half round, when my right arm was suddenly lifted up, as if by a galvanic shock. My pistol jerked upwards and exploded the same moment, and then dropped powerlessly from my hand, which I now felt was covered with warm blood from a wound near the elbow. From the acute but momentary pang this gave me, my attention was soon called off; for scarcely had my arm been struck, when a loud clattering noise to the left induced me to turn, and then, to my astonishment, I saw my friend O'Leary about twelve feet from the ground, hanging on by some ash twigs that grew from the clefts of the granite. Fragments of broken rock were falling around him, and his own position momentarily threatened a downfall. He was screaming with all his might; but what he said was entirely lost in the shouts of laughter of Trevanion and the Frenchmen, who could scarcely stand with the immoderate exuberance of their mirth.

I had no time to run to his aid,—which, although wounded, I should have done,—when the branch he clung to slowly yielded with his weight, and the round, plump figure of my poor friend rolled over the little cleft of rock, and after a few faint struggles came tumbling heavily down, and at last lay peaceably in the deep heather at the bottom, his cries the whole time being loud enough to rise even above the vociferous laughter of the others.

I now ran forward, as did Trevanion, when O'Leary, turning his eyes towards me, said, in the most piteous manner,—

"Mr. Lorrequer, I forgive you; here is my hand. Bad luck to their French way of fighting, that's all; it's only good for killing one's friend. I thought I was safe up there, come what might."

"My dear O'Leary," said I, in an agony which prevented my minding the laughing faces around me, "surely you don't mean to say that I have wounded *you?*"

"No, dear, not wounded, only killed me outright,—through the brain it must be, from the torture I'm suffering."

The shout with which this speech was received sufficiently aroused me; while Trevanion, with a voice nearly choked with laughter, said,—

"Why, Lorrequer, did you not see that your pistol, on being struck, threw your ball high up on the quarry? Fortunately, however, about a foot and a half above Mr. O'Leary's head, whose most serious wounds are his scratched hands and bruised bones from his tumble."

This explanation, which was perfectly satisfactory to me, was by no means so consoling to poor O'Leary, who lay quite unconscious to all around, moaning in the most melancholy manner. Some of the blood, which continued to flow fast from my wound, having dropped upon his face, roused him a little, but only to increase his lamentation for his own destiny, which he believed was fast accomplishing.

"Through the skull, clean through the skull, and preserving my senses to the last! Mr. Lorrequer, stoop down,—it is a dying man asks you: don't refuse me a last request. There's neither luck nor grace, honor nor glory, in such a way of fighting; so just promise me you'll shoot that grinning baboon there when he's going off the ground, since it's the fashion to fire at a man with his back to you. Bring him down, and I'll die easy."

And with these words he closed his eyes and straightened out his legs, stretched his arms on either side, and arranged himself as much corpse fashion as the circumstances of the ground would permit, while I now freely participated in the mirth of the others, which, loud and boisterous as it was, never reached the ears of O'Leary.

My arm had now become so painful that I was obliged to ask Trevanion to assist me in getting off my coat. The surprise of the Frenchmen on learning that I was wounded was very considerable, O'Leary's catastrophe having exclusively engaged all attention. My arm was now examined, when it was discovered that the ball had passed through from one side to the other, without apparently touching the bone; the bullet and the portion of my coat carried in by it both lay in my sleeve. The only serious consequence to be apprehended was the wound of the blood-vessel, which continued to pour forth blood unceasingly, and I was just surgeon enough to guess that an artery had been cut.

Trevanion bound his handkerchief tightly across the wound and assisted me to the high road, which, so sudden was the loss of blood, I reached with difficulty. During all these proceedings nothing possibly could be more kind and considerate than the conduct of our opponents. All the bold and swaggering air which they had deemed the *essentiel* before, at once fled, and in its place we found the most gentlemanlike attention and true politeness.

As soon as I was enabled to speak upon the matter, I begged Trevanion to look to poor O'Leary, who still lay upon the ground in a state of perfect unconsciousness. Captain de Joncourt, on hearing my wish, at once returned to the quarry, and with the greatest difficulty persuaded my friend to rise and endeavor to walk, which at last he did attempt, calling him to bear witness that it perhaps was the only case on record where a man with a bullet in his brain had made such an exertion.

With a view to my comfort and quiet, they got him into D'Haultpenne's cab; and having undertaken to send Dupuytren to me immediately on my reaching Paris, took their leave, and Trevanion and I set out homeward.

Not all my exhaustion and debility, nor even the acute pain I was suffering, could prevent my laughing at O'Leary's adventure; and it required all Trevanion's prudence to prevent my indulging too far in my recollection of it.

When we reached Meurice's I found Dupuytren in waiting, who immediately pronounced the main artery of the limb as wounded, and almost as instantaneously proceeded to pass a ligature round it. This painful business being concluded, I was placed upon a sofa; and being plentifully supplied with lemonade and enjoined to keep quiet, left to my own meditations, such as they were, till evening,—Trevanion having taken upon him to apologize for our absence at Mrs. Bingham's *déjeuner,* and O'Leary being fast asleep in his own apartment.

CHAPTER XXXVI.

EARLY RECOLLECTIONS.—A FIRST LOVE.

I KNOW of no sensations so very nearly alike as those felt on awaking after very sudden and profuse loss of blood, and those resulting from a large dose of opium. The dizziness, the confusion, and the abstraction at first, gradually yielding, as the senses become clearer, to a vague and indistinct consciousness; then the strange mistiness in which fact and fiction are wrapped up,—the confounding of persons and places and times, not so as to embarrass and annoy, for the very debility you feel subdues all irritation, but rather to present a panoramic picture of odd and incongruous events more pleasing than otherwise.

Of the circumstances by which I was thus brought to a sick couch I had not even the most vague recollection; the faces and the dress of all those I had lately seen were vividly before me, but how, and for what purpose, I knew not. Something in their kindness and attention had left an agreeable impression upon my mind, and without being able, or even attempting to trace it, I felt happy in the thought. While thus the "hour before" was dim and indistinct, the events of years past were vividly and brightly pictured before me; and strange, too, the more remote the period, the more did it seem palpable and present to my imagination. For so it is, there is in memory a species of mental long-sightedness which, though blind to the object close beside you, can reach the blue mountains and the starry skies which lie full many a league away. Is this a malady? or is it rather a providential gift to alleviate the tedious hours of the sick-bed and cheer the lonely sufferer, whose thoughts are his only realm?

My school-boy days in all their holiday excitement; the bank where I had culled the earliest cowslips of the year; the clear but rapid stream where days long I have watched the speckled trout as they swam peacefully beneath, or shook their bright fins in the gay sunshine; the gorgeous dragon-fly that played above the water and dipped his bright wings in its ripple,—they were all before me. And then came the thought of school itself, with its little world of boyish cares and emulations,—the early imbibed passion for success; the ardent longing for superiority; the high and swelling feeling of the heart, as home drew near, to think that I had gained the wished-for prize, the object of many an hour's toil, the thought of many a long night's dream; my father's smile; my mother's kiss! Oh! what a very world of tender memory that one thought suggests; for what are all our later successes in life—how bright soever our fortune be—compared with the early triumphs of our infancy! Where, among the jealous rivalry of some, the cold and half-wrung praise of others, the selfish and unsympathizing regard of all, shall we find anything to repay us for the swelling ecstasy of our young hearts as those who have cradled and loved us grow proud in our successes? For myself, a life that has failed in every presage of those that prophesied favorably, years that have followed on each other only to blight the promise that kind and well-wishing friends foretold, leave but little to dwell upon that can be reckoned as success. And yet, some moments I have had which half seemed to realize my early dream of ambition and rouse my spirit within me; but what were they all, compared to my boyish glories? What the passing excitement one's own heart inspires in its lonely and selfish solitude when compared with that little world of sympathy and love our early home teemed with, as, proud in some trifling distinction, we fell into a mother's arms and heard our father's "God bless you, boy"? No, no; the world has no requital for this. It is like the bright day-spring, which, as its glories gild the east, displays before us a whole world of beauty and promise. Blighted hopes have not withered, false friendships have not scathed, cold, selfish interest has not yet hardened our hearts or dried up our affections, and we are indeed happy; but equally like the burst of morning is it fleeting and short-lived, and equally so, too, does it pass away, never, never to return.

From thoughts like these my mind wandered on to more advanced years, when, emerging from very boyhood, I half believed myself a man, and was fully convinced I was in love.

Perhaps, after all, for the time it lasted—ten days, I

think—it was the most sincere passion I ever felt. I had been spending some weeks at a small watering-place in Wales with some relatives of my mother. There were, as might be supposed, but few "distractions" in such a place, save the scenery and an occasional day's fishing in the little river of Dolgelly, which ran near. In all these little rambles which the younger portion of the family made together, frequent mention was ever being made of a visit from a very dear cousin, and to which all looked forward with the greatest eagerness,—the elder ones of the party with a certain air of quiet pleasure, as though they knew more than they said, and the younger with all the childish exuberance of youthful delight. Clara Mourtray seemed to be, from all I was hourly hearing, the very paragon and pattern of everything. If any one was praised for beauty, Clara was immediately pronounced much prettier; did any one sing, Clara's voice and taste were far superior. In our homeward walk, should the shadows of the dark hills fall with a picturesque effect upon the blue lake, some one was sure to say, "Oh, how Clara would like to sketch that!" In short, there was no charm nor accomplishment ever the gift of woman that Clara did not possess, or, what amounted pretty much to the same thing, that my relatives did not implicitly give her credit for. The constantly recurring praises of the same person affect us always differently as we go on in life. In youth the prevailing sentiment is an ardent desire to see the prodigy of whom we have heard so much; in after years, heartily to detest what hourly hurts our self-love by comparisons,—we would take any steps to avoid meeting what we have inwardly decreed to be a "bore." The former was my course; and though my curiosity was certainly very great, I had made up my mind to as great a disappointment, and half wished for the long arrival as a means of criticising what they could see no fault in.

The wished-for evening at length came, and we all set out upon a walk to meet the carriage which was to bring the long-wished-for Clara among us. We had not walked above a mile when the eager eye of the foremost detected a cloud of dust upon the road at some distance, and after a few minutes more, four posters were seen coming along at a tremendous rate. The next moment *she* was making the tour of about a dozen uncles, aunts, cousins, and *cousines,* none of whom, it appeared to me, felt any peculiar desire to surrender the hearty embrace to the next of kin in succession. At last she came to me, when, perhaps, in the confusion of the moment, not exactly remembering whether or not she had seen me before, she stood for a moment silent, a deep blush mantling her lovely cheek, masses of waving brown hair disordered and floating upon her shoulders, her large and liquid blue eyes beaming upon me. One look was enough; I was deeply, irretrievably in love.

"Our cousin Harry, Harry Lorrequer,—wild Harry, as we used to call him, Clara," said one of the girls, introducing me.

She held out her hand and said something with a smile,—what, I know not, nor can I tell how I replied; but something absurd it must have been, for they all laughed heartily, and the worthy papa himself tapped my shoulder jestingly, adding,—

"Never mind, Harry; you will do better one day, or I am much mistaken in you."

Whether I was conscious that I had behaved foolishly or not, I cannot well say; but the whole of that night I thought over plans innumerable how I should succeed in putting myself forward before "Cousin Clara," and vindicating myself against any imputation of schoolboy mannerism that my first appearance might have caused.

The next day we remained at home. Clara was too much fatigued to walk out, and none of us would leave her. What a day of happiness that was! I knew something of music, and could sing a second. Clara was delighted at this, for the others had not cultivated singing much. We therefore spent part of the morning in this way. Then she produced her sketch-book, and I brought out mine, and we had a mutual interchange of prisoners. What cutting out of leaves and detaching of rice-paper landscapes! Then she came out upon the lawn to see my pony leap, and promised to ride him the following day. She patted the greyhounds, and said Gypsy, which was mine, was the prettiest. In a word, before night fell, Clara had won my heart in its every fibre, and I went to my room the very happiest of mortals.

I need not chronicle my next three days,—to me the most glorious *trois jours* of my life. Clara had evidently singled me out and preferred me to all the rest. It was beside *me* she rode, upon *my* arm she leaned in walking, and, to fill me with delight unutterable, I overheard her say to my uncle: "Oh, I doat upon dear Harry! And it is so pleasant, for I'm sure Mortimer will be so jealous."

"And who is Mortimer?" thought I; "he is a new character in the piece, of whom we have seen nothing."

I was not long in doubt upon this head, for that very day, at dinner, the identical Mortimer presented himself. He was a fine, dashing-looking, soldier-like fellow, of about thirty-five, with a heavy mustache, and a bronzed cheek,— rather grave in his manner, but still perfectly good-natured, and when he smiled showing a most handsome set of regular teeth. Clara seemed less pleased (I thought) at his coming than the others, and took pleasure in tormenting him by a thousand pettish and frivolous ways, which I was sorry for, as I thought he did not like it, and used to look half chidingly at her from time to time, but without any effect, for she just went on as before, and generally ended by taking my arm and saying: "Come away, Harry. *You* always are kind, and never look sulky; I can agree with *you*." These were delightful words for me to listen to; but I could not hear them without feeling for him, who evidently was pained by Clara's avowed preference for me, and whose years —for I thought thirty-five at that time a little verging upon the patriarchal—entitled him to more respect.

"Well," thought I, one evening, as this game had been carried rather farther than usual, "I hope she is content now, for certainly Mortimer is jealous;" and the result proved it, for the whole of the following day he absented himself, and never came back till late in the evening. He had been, I found, from a chance observation I overheard, at the bishop's palace, and the bishop himself, I learned, was to breakfast with us in the morning.

"Harry, I have a commission for you," said Clara. "You must get up very early to-morrow, and climb the Cader mountain, and bring me a grand bouquet of the blue and purple heath that I liked so much the last time I was there. Mind, very early, for I intend to surprise the bishop to-morrow with my taste in a nosegay."

The sun had scarcely risen as I sprang from my bed and started upon my errand. Oh, the glorious beauty of that morning's walk! As I climbed the mountain, the deep mists lay upon all around, and except the path I was treading, nothing was visible; but before I reached the top, the heavy masses of vapor were yielding to the influence of the sun, and as they rolled from the valleys up the mountain sides, were every instant opening new glens and ravines beneath me, bright in all their verdure, and speckled with sheep, whose tinkling bells reached me even where I stood.

I counted above twenty lakes, at different levels below me,—some brilliant and shining like polished mirrors; others, not less beautiful, dark and solemn with some mighty mountain shadow. As I looked landward, the mountains reared their huge crests, one above the other, to the farthest any eye could reach. Towards the opposite side, the calm and tranquil sea lay beneath me, bathed in the yellow gold of a rising sun; a few ships were peaceably lying at anchor in the bay; and the only thing in motion was a row-boat, the heavy, monotonous stroke of whose oars rose in the stillness of the morning air. Not a single habitation of man could I descry, nor any vestige of a human being, except that mass of something upon a rock far down beneath were one, and I think it must have been, for I saw a sheep-dog ever returning again and again to the same spot.

My bouquet was gathered, the gentian of the Alps, which is found here, also contributing its evidence to show where I had been to seek it, and I turned home.

The family were at breakfast as I entered,—at least so the servants said, for I only remembered then that the bishop was our guest, and that I could not present myself without some slight attention to my dress. I hastened to my room, and scarcely had I finished, when one of my cousins, a little girl of eight years, came to the door and said,—

"Harry, come down; Clara wants you."

I rushed downstairs, and as I entered the breakfast-parlor, stood still with surprise. The ladies were all dressed in white, and even my little cousin wore a gala costume that almost amazed me.

"My bouquet, Harry! I hope you have not forgotten it," said Clara, as I approached.

I presented it at once, when she gayly and coquettishly held out her hand for me to kiss. This I did, my blood rushing to my face and temples the while, and almost depriving me of consciousness.

"Well, Clara, I *am* surprised at you," said Mortimer. "How can you treat the poor boy so?"

I grew deadly pale at these words, and turning round, looked at the speaker full in the face. "Poor fellow!" thought I, "he is jealous, and I am really grieved for him;" and turned again to Clara.

"Here it is—oh, how handsome, papa!" said one of the younger children, running eagerly to the window as a very pretty open carriage with four horses drew up before the house.

"The bishop has taste," I murmured to myself, scarcely deigning to give a second look at the equipage.

Clara now left the room, but speedily returned, her dress changed, and shawled as if for a walk. What could all this mean? And the whispering, too, what is all that? And why are they all so sad? Clara has been weeping.

"God bless you, my child! Good by!" said my aunt, as she folded her in her arms for the third time.

"Good by, good by!" I heard on every side. At length, approaching me, Clara took my hand and said,—

"My poor Harry, so we are going to part! I am going to Italy."

"To Italy, Clara? Oh, no, say no! Italy! I shall never see you again!"

"Won't you wear this ring for me, Harry? It is an old favorite of yours; and when we meet again—"

"Oh, dearest Clara!" I said, "do not speak thus."

"Good by, my poor boy, good by!" said Clara, hurriedly, and rushing out of the room, she was lifted by Mortimer into the carriage, who immediately jumped in after her. The whip cracked, the horses clattered, and all was out of sight in a second.

"Why is she gone with him?" said I, reproachfully, turning towards my aunt.

"Why, my dear, a very sufficient reason. She was married this morning."

This was my first love!

CHAPTER XXXVII.

WISE RESOLVES.

MUSING over this boyish adventure, I fell into a deep slumber, and on awakening it took me some minutes before I could recall my senses sufficiently to know where I was. The whole face of things in my room was completely changed. Flowers had been put in the china vases upon the tables; two handsome lamps, shaded with gauzes, stood upon the consoles; illustrated books, prints, and caricatures were scattered about. A pianoforte had, also, by some witchcraft, insinuated itself into a recess near the sofa; a handsome little tea-service, of old Dresden china, graced a small marqueterie table; and a little piquet table stood most invitingly beside the fire. I had scarcely time to turn my eyes from one to the other of these new occupants when I heard the handle of my door gently turn, as if by some cautious hand, and immediately closed my eyes and feigned sleep. Through my half-shut lids I perceived the door opened. After a pause of about a second, the skirt of a white muslin dress appeared; then a pretty foot stole a little farther; and at last the slight and graceful figure of Emily Bingham advanced noiselessly into the room. Fear had rendered her deadly pale; but the effect of her rich brown hair, braided plainly on either side of her cheek, suited so well the character of her features, I thought her far handsomer than ever. She came forward towards the table, and I now could perceive that she had something in her hand resembling a letter. This she placed near my hand,—so near as almost to touch it. She leaned over me; I felt her breath upon my brow, but never moved. At this instant a tress of her hair, becoming unfastened, fell over upon my face. She started; the motion threw me off my guard, and I looked up. She gave a faint, scarcely audible shriek, and shrank into the chair beside me. Recovering, however, upon the instant, she grasped the letter she had just laid down, and having crushed it between her fingers, threw it into the fire. This done,—as if the effort had been too much for her strength,—she again fell back upon her seat, and looked so pale I almost thought she had fainted.

Before I had time to speak she rose once more; and now her face was bathed in blushes, her eyes swam with rising tears, and her lips trembled with emotion as she spoke.

"Oh, Mr. Lorrequer, what will you—what can you think of this? If you but knew—" And here she faltered and again grew pale, while I, with difficulty rising from the sofa, took her hand and led her to the chair beside it.

"And may I not know," said I, "may I not know, my dear" —I am not sure I did not say "dearest"—"Miss Bingham, when perhaps the knowledge might make me the happiest of mortals?"

This was a pretty plunge as a sequel to my late resolutions. She hid her face between her hands and sobbed for some seconds.

"At least," said I, "as that letter was destined for me but a few moments since, I trust that you will let me hear its contents."

"Oh, no, not now!" said she, entreatingly; and rising at the same time, she turned to leave the room.

I still held her hand, and pressed it within mine. I thought she returned the pressure. I leaned forward to catch her eye, when the door was opened hastily, and a most extraordinary figure presented itself.

It was a short, fat man, with a pair of enormous mustachios of a fiery red, huge bushy whiskers of the same color, a blue frock covered with braiding and decorated with several crosses and ribbons, tight pantaloons, and Hessian boots with long brass spurs. He held a large gold-headed cane in his hand, and looked about with an expression of very equivocal drollery, mingled with fear.

"May I ask, sir," said I, as this individual closed the door behind him, "may I ask the reason for this intrusion?"

"Oh, upon my conscience, I'll do, I'm sure to pass muster now," said the well-known voice of Mr. O'Leary, whose pleasant features began to dilate amid the forest of red hair he was disguised in. "But I see you are engaged," said he, with a sly look at Miss Bingham, whom he had not yet recognized; "so I must contrive to hide myself elsewhere, I suppose."

"It is Miss Bingham," said I, "who has been kind enough to come here with her maid to bring me some flowers. Pray present my compliments to Mrs. Bingham, and say how deeply I feel her kind attention."

Emily rose at the instant, and recovering her self-possession at once, said,—

"You forget, Mr. Lorrequer, it is a secret from whom the flowers came,—at least, mamma hoped to place them in your vases without your knowing. So pray don't speak of it, and I'm sure Mr. O'Leary will not tell."

If Mr. O'Leary heard one word of this artful speech, I know not, but he certainly paid no attention to it nor the speaker, who left the room without his appearing aware of it.

"Now that she is gone,—for which Heaven be praised!" said I to myself,—"let me see what this fellow can mean."

As I turned from the door I could scarcely avoid laughing aloud at the figure before me. He stood opposite a large mirror, his hat on one side of his head, one arm in his breast, and the other extended, leaning upon his stick; a look of as much ferocity as such features could accomplish had been assumed, and his whole attitude was a kind of caricature of a melodramatic hero in a German drama.

"Why, O'Leary, what is all this?"

"Hush, hush!" said he, in a terrified whisper; "never mention that name again till we are over the frontier."

"But, man, explain,—what do you mean?"

"Can't you guess?" said he, dryly.

"Impossible; unless the affair at the Salon has induced you to take this disguise, I cannot conceive the reason."

"Nothing further from it, my dear friend,—much worse than that."

"Out with it, then, at once."

"She's come; she's here,—in this very house, No. 29, above the *entresol.*"

"Who is here in No. 29, above the *entresol?*"

"Who but Mrs. O'Leary herself! I was near saying, 'Bad luck to her.' "

"And does she know you are here?"

"That is what I can't exactly say," said he; "but she has had the *Livre des Voyageurs* brought up to her room, and has been making rather unpleasant inquiries for the proprietor of certain hieroglyphics beginning with O which have given me great alarm,—the more so as all the waiters have been sent for in turn and subjected to long examination by her. So I have lost no time, but under the auspices of your friend Trevanion, have become the fascinating figure you find me, and am now Count O'Linski, a Pole of noble family, banished by the Russian Government, with a father in Siberia and all that; and I hope, by the end of the week, to be able to cheat at *écarté* and deceive the very police itself."

The idea of O'Leary's assuming such a metamorphosis was too absurd not to throw me into a hearty fit of laughing, in which the worthy *émigré* indulged also.

"But why not leave this at once," said I, "if you are so much in dread of recognition?"

"You forget the trial," added O'Leary. "I must be here on the 18th, or all my bail is forfeited."

"True, I had forgotten that. Well, now, your plans."

"Simply to keep very quiet here till the affair of the tribunal is over, and then quit France at once. Meanwhile, Trevanion thinks that we may, by a bold stratagem, send Mrs. O'Leary off on a wrong scent, and has requested Mrs. Bingham to contrive to make her acquaintance and ask her to tea in her room, when she will see me, *en Polonais,* at a distance, you know,—hear something of my melancholy destiny from Trevanion,—and leave the hotel quite sure she has no claim on me. Meanwhile, some others of the party are to mention incidentally having met Mr. O'Leary somewhere, or heard of his decease, or any pleasant little incident that may occur to them."

"The plan is excellent," said I; "for in all probability she

may never come in your way again, if sent off on a good
errand this time."

"That's what I'm thinking," said O'Leary, "and I am
greatly disposed to let her hear that I'm with Belzoni in
Egypt, with an engagement to spend the Christmas with the
Dey of Algiers. That would give her a very pretty tour for
the remainder of the year, and show her the Pyramids. But,
tell me fairly, am I a good Pole?"

"Rather short," said I, "and a little too fat, perhaps."

"That comes from the dash of the Tartar blood,—nothing
more. And my mother was a Fin," said he,—"she'll never
ask whether from the Blackwater or the Baltic. How I revel
in the thought that I may smoke in company without a
breach of the unities! But I must go; there is a gentleman
with a quinsy in No. 8, that gives me a lesson in Polish this
morning. So good by, and don't forget to be well enough
to-night, for you must be present at my *début*."

O'Leary had scarcely gone when my thoughts reverted to
Emily Bingham. I was not such a coxcomb as to fancy her
in love with me, yet certainly there was something in the
affair which looked not unlike it; and though, by such a circumstance, every embarrassment which pressed upon me had
become infinitely greater, I could not dissemble from myself
a sense of pleasure at the thought. She was really a very
pretty girl, and improved vastly upon acquaintance. *Les ab-
sents ont toujours tort* is the truest proverb in any language,
and I felt it, in its fullest force, when Trevanion entered my
room.

"Well, Lorrequer," said he, "your time is not likely to hang
heavily on your hands in Paris if occupation will prevent it,
for I find you are just now booked for a new scrape."

"What can you mean?" said I, starting up.

"Why, O'Leary, who has been, since your illness, a constant visitor at the Binghams,—dining there every day and
spending his evenings,—has just told me that the mamma is
only waiting for the arrival of Sir Guy Lorrequer in Paris
to open the trenches in all form; and from what she has
heard of Sir Guy, she deems it most likely he will give her
every aid and support to making you the husband of the fair
Emily."

"And with good reason too," said I; "for if my uncle were only given to understand that I had once gone far in my attentions, nothing would induce him to break off the match. He was crossed in love himself when young, and has made a score of people miserable since, in the benevolent idea of marrying them against every obstacle."

"How very smart you have become!" said Trevanion, taking a look round my room, and surveying in turn each of the new occupants. "You must certainly reckon upon seeing your fair friend here, or all this elegance is sadly wasted."

This was the time to explain all about Miss Bingham's visit; and I did so,—of course omitting any details which might seem to me needless, or involving myself in inconsistency.

Trevanion listened patiently to the end; was silent for some moments; then added,—

"And you never saw the letter?"

"Of course not. It was burned before my eyes."

"I think the affair looks very serious, Lorrequer. You may have won this girl's affections. It matters little whether the mamma be a hackneyed matchmaker, or the cousin a bullying duellist. If the girl have a heart, and you have gained it—"

"Then I must marry, you would say."

"Exactly so,—without the prompting of your worthy uncle; I see no other course open to you without dishonor. My advice, therefore, is ascertain—and that speedily—how far your attentions have been attended with the success you dread, and then decide at once. Are you able to get as far as Mrs. Bingham's room this morning? If so, come along. I will take all the *frais* of *la chère maman* off your hands while you talk to the daughter, and half an hour's courage and resolution will do it all."

Having made the most effective toilet my means would permit, my right arm in a sling and my step trembling from weakness, I sallied forth with Trevanion to make love with as many fears for the result as the most bashful admirer ever experienced when pressing his suit upon some haughty belle, —but for a far different reason.

CHAPTER XXXVIII.

THE PROPOSAL.

ON reaching Mrs. Bingham's apartment we found that she had just left home to wait upon Mrs. O'Leary, and consequently that Miss Bingham was alone. Trevanion, therefore, having wished me a safe deliverance through my trying mission, shook my hand warmly and departed.

I stood for some moments irresolutely, with my hand upon the lock of the door. To think that the next few minutes may decide the fortune of one's after-life is a sufficiently anxious thought; but that your fate may be so decided, by compelling you to finish in sorrow what you have begun in folly, is still more insupportable. Such, then, was my condition. I had resolved within myself, if the result of this meeting should prove that I had won Miss Bingham's affections, to propose for her at once in all form and make her my wife. If, on the other hand, I only found that she too had amused herself with a little passing flirtation, why then, I was a free man once more; but on catechising myself a little closer, I discovered that I was not indisposed to make love *de novo.*

With the speed of lightning my mind ran over every passage of our acquaintance,—our first meeting; our solitary walks; our daily, hourly associations; our travelling intimacy; the adventure at Chantraine. There was, it is true, nothing in all this which could establish the fact of wooing, but everything which should convince an old offender like myself that the young lady was *en prise,* and that I myself—despite my really strong attachment elsewhere—was not entirely scathless.

"Yes," said I, half aloud, as I once more reviewed the past, "it is but another chapter in my history in keeping with all the rest,—one step has ever led me to a second, and so on to a third; what with other men have passed for mere trifles, have ever with me become serious difficulties, and the false enthusiasm with which I ever follow any object in life blinds me for the time, and mistaking zeal for inclination, I never feel how little my heart is interested in success till the fever of pursuit is over."

These were pleasant thoughts for one about to throw himself at a pretty girl's feet and pour out his "soul of love before her;" but that with me was the least part of it. Curran, they say, usually picked up his facts in a case from the opposite counsel's statements. I always relied for my conduct in carrying on anything to the chance circumstances of the moment, and trusted to my animal spirits to give me an interest in whatever, for the time being, engaged me.

I opened the door. Miss Bingham was sitting at a table, her head leaning upon her hands, some open letters which lay before her evidently so occupying her attention that my approach was unheard. On my addressing her, she turned round suddenly, and became at first deep scarlet, then pale as death; while, turning to the table, she hurriedly threw her letters into a drawer, and motioned me to a place beside her.

After the first brief and commonplace inquiry for my health, and hopes for my speedy recovery, she became silent; and I, too, primed with topics innumerable to discuss, knowing how short my time might prove before Mrs. Bingham's return, could not say a word.

"I hope, Mr. Lorrequer," said she at length, "that you have incurred no risk by leaving your room so early."

"I have not," I replied; "but even were there a certainty of it, the anxiety I labored under to see and speak with you alone, would have overcome all fears on that account. Since this unfortunate business has confined me to my chamber, I have done nothing but think over circumstances which have at length so entirely taken possession of me that I must, at any sacrifice, have sought an opportunity to explain to you—" Here Emily looked down, and I continued: "I need scarcely say, what my feelings must long since have betrayed, that to have enjoyed the daily happiness of living in your society, of estimating your worth, of feeling your fascinations, were not the means most in request for him who knew, too well, how little he deserved, either by fortune or desert, to hope to make you his; and yet, how little has prudence or caution to do with situations like this." She did not

24

guess the animus of this speech. "I felt all I have described; and yet, and yet I lingered on, prizing too dearly the happiness of the present hour to risk it by any avowal of sentiments which might have banished me from your presence forever. If the alternation of these hopes and fears has proved too strong for my reason at last, I cannot help it; and this it is which now leads me to make this avowal to you."

Emily turned her head away from me, but her agitated manner showed how deeply my words had affected her; and I too, now that I had finished, felt that I had been "coming it rather strong," though perhaps not very intelligibly.

"I had hoped, Mr. Lorrequer," said she, at length,—"I had hoped, I confess, to have had an opportunity of speaking with you." Then, thought I, the game is over, and Bishop Luscombe is richer by ten pounds than I wish him. "Something, I know not what, in your manner led me to suspect that your affections might lean towards me; hints you have dropped, and, now and then, your chance allusions, strengthened the belief, and I determined at length that no feeling of maidenly shame on my part should endanger the happiness of either of us, and I resolved to see you. This was so difficult that I wrote a letter, and that letter, which might have saved me all distressing explanation, I burned before you this morning."

"But why, dearest girl,"—here was a plunge—"why, if the letter could remove any misconstruction, or could be the means of dispelling any doubt, why not have let me see it?"

"Hear me out," cried she eagerly, and evidently not heeding my interruption; "I determined, if your affections were indeed—" A flood of tears here broke forth and drowned her words; her head sank between her hands, and she sobbed bitterly.

"*Corpo di Baccho!*" said I to myself, "it is all over with me; the poor girl is evidently jealous, and her heart will break."

"Dearest, dearest Emily," said I, passing my arm round her, and approaching my head close to hers, "if you think that any other love than yours could ever beat within this heart; that I could see you hourly before me, live beneath your smile, and gaze upon your beauty, and, still more than all,—pardon the boldness of the thought,—feel that I was not indifferent to you—"

"Oh! spare me this at least," said she, turning round her tearful eyes upon me, and looking most bewitchingly beautiful. "Have I then shown you this plainly?"

"Yes, dearest girl! That instinct which tells us we are loved has spoken within me. And here in this beating heart—"

"Oh! say no more," said she; "if I have *indeed* gained your affections—"

"*If—if* you have," said I, clasping her to my heart, while she continued to sob still violently, and I felt half disposed to blow my brains out for my success. However, there is something in love-making, as in fox-hunting, which carries you along in spite of yourself; and I continued to pour forth whole rhapsodies of love that the Pastor Fido could not equal.

"Enough," said she; "it is enough that you love me and that I have encouraged your your so doing. But, oh! tell me once more, and think how much of future happiness may rest upon your answer,—tell me, may not this be some passing attachment, which circumstances have created and others may dispel? Say, might not absence, time, or another more worthy—"

This was certainly a very rigid cross-examination when I thought the trial was over; and not being exactly prepared for it, I felt no other mode of reply than pressing her taper fingers alternately to my lips, and muttering something that might pass for a declaration of love unalterable, but, to my own ears, resembled a lament on my folly.

"She is mine now," thought I, "so we must e'en make the best of it; and truly she is a very handsome girl, though not a Lady Jane Callonby. The next step is the mamma; but I do not anticipate much difficulty in that quarter."

"Leave me now," said she, in a low and broken voice, "but promise not to speak of this meeting to any one before we meet again. I have my reasons,—believe me, they are sufficient ones; so promise me this before we part."

Having readily given the pledge required, I again kissed her hand and bade farewell, not a little puzzled the whole time at perceiving that ever since my declaration and accep-

tance Emily seemed anything but happy, and evidently struggling against some secret feeling, of which I knew nothing.
"Yes," thought I, as I wended my way along the corridor,
"the poor little girl is tremendously jealous, and I must have
said many a thing during our intimacy to hurt her. However, that is all past and gone; and now comes a new character for me: my next appearance will be in the part of the
'happy husband.' "

CHAPTER XXXIX.

THOUGHTS UPON MATRIMONY IN GENERAL, AND IN THE
ARMY IN PARTICULAR.—THE KNIGHT OF KERRY AND BILLY
M'CABE.

"SO," thought I, as I closed the door of my room behind
me, "I am accepted; the die is cast which makes me a
Benedict. Yet Heaven knows that never was a man less disposed to be over-joyous at his good fortune!" What a happy
invention it were if, when adopting any road in life, we could
only manage to forget that we had ever contemplated any
other! It is the eternal looking back in this world that forms
the staple of all our misery; and we are but ill-requited for
such unhappiness by the brightest anticipations we can conjure up for the future. How much of all that "past" was now
to become a source of painful recollection, and to how little
of the future could I look forward with even hope!

Our weaknesses are much more constantly the spring of
all our annoyances and troubles than even our vices. The
one we hold in some sort of subjection; we are perfectly
slaves to the others. This thought came home most forcibly to my bosom as I reflected upon the step which led me
on imperceptibly to my present embarrassment. "Well, *c'est
fini,* now," said I, drawing upon that bountiful source of consolation ever open to the man who mars his fortune,—that
"what is past can't be amended;" which piece of philosophy,
as well as its twin brother, that "all will be the same a hundred years hence," have been golden rules to me from my
childhood.

The transition from one mode of life to another perfectly different has ever seemed to me a great trial of a man's moral courage, besides that the fact of quitting forever anything, no matter how insignificant or valueless, is always attended with painful misgivings. My bachelor life had its share of annoyances and disappointments, it is true, but upon the whole it was a most happy one; and now I was about to surrender it forever, not yielding to the impulse of affection and love for one without whom life were valueless to me, but merely a recompense for the indulgence of that fatal habit I had contracted of pursuing with eagerness every shadow that crossed my path. All my early friends, all my vagrant fancies, all my day-dreams of the future, I was now to surrender; for what becomes of any man's bachelor friends when he is once married? Where are his rambles in high and by ways when he has a wife? And what is left for anticipation after his wedding, except, perhaps, to speculate upon the arrangement of his funeral? To a military man more than to any other these are serious thoughts. All the fascinations of an army life, in war or peace, lie in the daily, hourly associations with your brother officers,—the morning cigar, the barrack-square lounge, the afternoon ride, the game of billiards before dinner, the mess (that perfection of dinner society), the plans for the evening, the devilled kidney at twelve,—forming so many points of departure whence you sail out upon your daily voyage through life. *Versus* these you have that awful perversion of all that is natural,—an officer's wife. She has been a beauty when young, had black eyes and high complexion, a good figure, rather inclined to *embonpoint,* and a certain springiness in her walk and a jauntiness in her air that are ever sure attractions to a sub in a marching regiment. She can play backgammon and sing *"Di tanti palpiti,"* and, if an Irishwoman, is certain to be able to ride a steeple-chase, and has an uncle a lord, who (*en parenthèse*) always turns out to be a creation made by King James after his abdication. In conclusion, she breakfasts *en papillotes,* wears her shoes down at heel, calls every officer of the regiment by his name, has a great taste for increasing his Majesty's lieges, and delights in London porter. To this genus of "vrow" I have never ceased to entertain the most thrilling abhorrence,—and yet how often have I seen what appeared to be pretty and interesting girls fall into something of this sort; and how often have I vowed any fate to myself rather than become the husband of a baggage-wagon wife!

Had all my most sanguine hopes promised realizing, had my suit with Lady Jane been favorable, I could scarcely have bade adieu to my bachelor life without a sigh. No prospect of future happiness can ever perfectly exclude all regret at quitting our present state forever. I am sure if I had been a caterpillar, it would have been with a heavy heart that I should have donned my wings as a butterfly; now the metamorphosis was reversed. Need it be wondered if I were sad?

So completely was I absorbed in my thoughts upon this matter that I had not perceived the entrance of O'Leary and Trevanion, who, unaware of my being in the apartment, as I was stretched upon a sofa in a dark corner, drew their chairs towards the fire and began chatting.

"Do you know, Mr. Trevanion," said O'Leary, "I am half afraid of this disguise of mine. I sometimes think I am not like a Pole; and if she should discover me—"

"No fear of that in the world; your costume is perfect, your beard unexceptionable. I could, perhaps, have desired a little less paunch; but then—"

"That comes of fretting, as Falstaff says; and you must not forget that I am banished from my country."

"Now as to your conversation, I should advise you saying very little,—not one word of English. You may, if you like, call in the assistance of Irish when hard pressed."

"I have my fears on that score. There is no knowing where that might lead to,—perhaps discovery. You know the story of the Knight of Kerry and Billy M'Cabe?"

"I fear I must confess my ignorance; I have never heard of it."

"Then maybe you never knew Giles Dackson?"

"I have not that pleasure either."

"Lord bless me, how strange that is! I thought he was better known than the Duke of Wellington or the travelling piper. Well, I must tell you the story, for it has a moral too, —indeed, several morals; but you'll find that out for yourself.

Well, it seems that one day the Knight of Kerry was walking along the Strand in London, killing an hour's time till the House was done prayers and Hume tired of hearing himself speaking; his eye was caught by an enormous picture displayed upon the wall of a house, representing a human figure covered with long, dark hair, with huge nails upon his hands, and a most fearful expression of face. At first the Knight thought it was Dr. Bowring; but on coming nearer he heard a man with a scarlet livery and a cocked hat call out, 'Walk in, ladies and gentlemen! The most vonderful curiosity ever exhibited—only one shilling—the vild man from Chippoo-wango, in Africay—eats raw wittles without being cooked, and many other surprising and pleasing performances.'

"The Knight paid his money and was admitted. At first the crowd prevented his seeing anything, for the place was full to suffocation, and the noise awful; for, besides the exclamations and applause of the audience, there were three barrel-organs playing 'Home, sweet Home!' and 'Cherry Ripe!' and the wild man himself contributed his share to the uproar. At last the Knight obtained, by dint of squeezing and some pushing, a place in the front, when, to his very great horror, he beheld a figure that far eclipsed the portrait without doors.

"It was a man nearly naked, covered with long, shaggy hair that grew even over his nose and cheek-bones. He sprang about, sometimes on his feet, sometimes all-fours, but always uttering the most fearful yells, and glaring upon the crowd in a manner that was really dangerous. The Knight did not feel exactly happy at the whole proceeding, and began heartily to wish himself back in the House, even upon a committee of privileges, when suddenly the savage gave a more frantic scream than before, and seized upon a morsel of raw beef which a keeper extended to him upon a long fork like a tandem whip,—he was not safe, it appears, at close quarters. This he tore to pieces eagerly, and devoured in the most voracious manner, amid great clapping of hands and other evidences of satisfaction from the audience. 'I'll go now,' thought the Knight, 'for God knows whether, in his hungry moods, he might not fancy to conclude his dinner by a member of Parliament.' Just at this instant some sounds struck upon his ear that surprised him not a little. He listened more attentively, and conceive, if you can, his amazement to find that amid his most fearful cries and wild yells the savage was talking Irish. Laugh if you like, but it's truth I am telling you,—nothing less than Irish. There he was, jumping four feet high in the air, eating his raw meat, pulling out his hair by handfuls, and, amid all this, cursing the whole company to his heart's content in as good Irish as ever was heard in Tralee. Now, though the Knight had heard of red Jews and white negroes, he had never happened to read any account of an African Irishman; so he listened very closely, and by degrees not only the words were known to him, but the very voice was familiar. At length something he heard left no further doubt upon his mind, and turning to the savage, he addressed him in Irish, at the same time fixing a look of most scrutinizing import upon him.

" 'Who are you, you scoundrel?' said the Knight.

" 'Billy M'Cabe, your honor.'

" 'And what do you mean by playing off these tricks here, instead of earning your bread like an honest man?'

" 'Whisht!' said Billy, 'and keep the secret. I'm earning the rent for your honor. One must do many a queer thing that pays two pound ten an acre for bad land.'

"This was enough; the Knight wished Billy every success, and left him amid the vociferous applause of a well-satisfied audience. This adventure, it seems, has made the worthy Knight a great friend to the introduction of poor-laws; for he remarks, very truly, more of Billy's countrymen might take a fancy to a savage life if the secret was found out."

It was impossible for me to preserve my *incognito* as Mr. O'Leary concluded his story, and I was obliged to join in the mirth of Trevanion, who laughed loud and long as he finished it.

CHAPTER XL.

A REMINISCENCE.

O'LEARY and Trevanion had scarcely left the room when the waiter entered with two letters,—the one bore a German post-mark and was in the well-known hand of Lady Callonby; the other in a writing with which I was no less familiar, that of Emily Bingham.

Let any one who has been patient enough to follow me through these "Confessions," conceive my agitation at this moment. There lay my fate before me, coupled, in all likelihood, with a view of what it might have been under happier auspices,—at least so in anticipation did I read the two unopened epistles. My late interview with Miss Bingham left no doubt upon my mind that I had secured her affections; and acting in accordance with the counsel of Trevanion, no less than my own sense of right, I resolved upon marrying her,—with what prospect of happiness I dared not to think.

Alas and alas! there is no infatuation like the taste for flirtation,—mere empty, valueless, heartless flirtation. You hide the dice-box and the billiard-cue, lest your son become a gambler; you put aside the Racing Calendar, lest he imbibe a jockey predilection,—but you never tremble at his fondness for white muslin and a satin slipper, far more dangerous tastes though they be, and infinitely more perilous to a man's peace and prosperity than all the "queens of trumps" that ever figured, whether on pasteboard or the Doncaster! "Woman's my wakeness, yer honor," said an honest Patlander on being charged before the lord mayor with having four wives living; and without having any such "Algerine act" upon my conscience, I must, I fear, enter a somewhat similar plea for my downfallings, and avow in humble gratitude that I have scarcely had a misfortune through life unattributable to them in one way or another. And this I say without any reference to country, class, or complexion, "black, brown, or fair;" from my first step forth into life, a raw sub in the gallant 4—th, to this same hour, I have no other avowal, no other confession to make. "Be always ready with the pistol," was the dying advice of an Irish statesman to his sons; mine, in a similar circumstance, would rather be *"Gardez-vous des femmes,"* and more especially if they be Irish.

There is something almost treacherous in the facility with which an Irish girl receives your early attentions, and appears to like them, that invariably turns a young fellow's head very long before he has any prospect of touching *her* heart. She thinks it so natural to be made love to that there is neither any affected coyness nor any agitated surprise. She listens to your declaration of love as quietly as the chief justice would to one of law, and refers the decision to a packed jury of her relatives, who rarely recommend you to mercy. Love and fighting, too, are so intimately united in Ireland that a courtship rarely progresses without at least one exchange of shots between some of the parties concerned. My first twenty-four hours in Dublin is so pleasantly characteristic of this that I may as well relate it here while the subject is before us; besides, as these "Confessions" are intended as warnings and guides to youth, I may convey a useful lesson, showing why a man should not "make love in the dark."

It was upon a raw, cold, drizzling morning in February, 18—, that our regiment landed on the North-wall from Liverpool, whence we had been hurriedly ordered to repress some riots and disturbances then agitating Dublin.

We marched to the Royal Barracks, our band playing "Patrick's Day," to the very considerable admiration of as naked a population as ever loved music. The —th Dragoons were at the same time quartered there,—right pleasant, jovial fellows, who soon gave us to understand that the troubles were over before we arrived, and that the great city authorities were now returning thanks for their preservation from fire and sword by a series of entertainments of the most costly, but somewhat incongruous, kind; the company being scarce less mixed than the dishes. Peers and play-actors, judges and jailers, archbishops, tailors, attorneys, rope-makers, and apothecaries, all uniting in the festive delight of good feeding and drinking the "glorious memory,"—but of whom, half the company knew not, only surmising "it was something agin the Papists." You may smile, but these were pleasant times, and I scarcely care to go back there since they were changed.

But to return. The —th had just received an invitation to a ball to be given by the high sheriff, and to which they most considerately said we should also be invited. This negotiation was so well managed that before noon we all received our cards from a green-liveried youth mounted upon a very emaciated pony,—the whole turn-out not auguring flatteringly of the high sheriff's taste in equipage.

We dined with the —th, and, as customary before going to an evening party, took the "other bottle" of claret that lies beyond the frontier of prudence. In fact, from the lieutenant-colonel down to the newly-joined ensign, there was not a face in the party that did not betray "signs of the times" that promised most favorably for the mirth of the sheriff's ball. We were so perfectly up to the mark that our major, a Connemara man, said, as we left the mess-room, "a liqueur glass would spoil us."

In this acme of our intellectual wealth we started about eleven o'clock upon every species of conveyance that chance could press into the service. Of hackney coaches there were few; but in jingles, noddies, and jaunting-cars, with three on a side and "one in the well," we mustered strong. Down Barrack Street we galloped, the mob cheering us, we laughing, and I'm afraid shouting a little too, the watchmen springing their rattles, as if instinctively at any noise, and the whole population up and awake, evidently entertaining a high opinion of our convivial qualities. Our voices became gradually more decorous, however, as we approached the more civilized quarter of the town; and with only the slight stoppage of the procession to pick up an occasional dropper-off as he lapsed from the seat of a jaunting-car, we arrived at length at our host's residence, somewhere in Sackville Street.

Had our advent conferred the order of knighthood upon the host, he could not have received us with more delight. He shook us all in turn by the hand, to the number of eight and thirty, and then presented us *seriatim* to his spouse, a very bejewelled lady of some forty years, who, what between bugles, feathers, and her turban, looked exceedingly like a Chinese pagoda upon a saucer. The rooms were crowded to suffocation, the noise awful, and the company crushing and elbowing rather a little more than you expect where the moiety are of the softer sex. However, we all so perfectly fell in with the habits of the place that ere half an hour we squeezed, ogled, leered, and drank champagne like the rest of the corporation.

"Devilish hot work, this!" said the Colonel, as he passed me with a rosy-cheeked, smiling lady on each arm. "The mayor —that little fellow in the punch-colored shorts—has very nearly put me *hors de combat* with strong negus; take care of him, I advise you."

Tipsy as I felt myself, I was yet sufficiently clear to be fully alive to the drollery of the scene before me. Flirtations that under other circumstances would demand the secrecy and solitude of a country green lane or some garden bower, were here conducted in all the open effrontery of wax-lights and lustres; looks were interchanged, hands were squeezed, soft things whispered, and smiles returned, till the intoxication of "punch negus" and spiced port gave way to the far greater one of bright looks and tender glances. Quadrilles and country dances (waltzing there was none, perhaps all for the best), whist, backgammon, loo unlimited for uproar, sandwiches and warm liquors, employed us pretty briskly till supper was announced, when a grand squeeze took place on the stairs, the population tending thitherward with an eagerness that a previous starvation of twenty-four hours could alone justify. Among this dense mass of moving muslin, velvet, and broadcloth I found myself chaperoning an extremely tempting little damsel, with a pair of laughing blue eyes and dark eyelashes, who had been committed to my care and guidance for the passage.

"Miss Moriarty, Mr. Lorrequer," said an old lady in green and spangles, who I afterwards found was the lady mayoress.

"The nicest girl in the room," said a gentleman with a Tipperary accent, "and has a mighty sweet place near Athlone."

The hint was not lost upon me, and I speedily began to "make up" to my charge; and before we reached the supper-room, learned certain particulars of her history which I have not yet forgotten. She was, it seems, sister to a lady then in the room, the wife of an attorney who rejoiced in the pleasing and classical appellation of Mr. Mark Anthony Fitzpatrick; the aforesaid Mark Anthony being a tall, raw-boned,

black-whiskered, ill-looking dog, that from time to time contrived to throw very uncomfortable-looking glances at me
and Mary Anne—for she was so named—the whole time of
supper. After a few minutes, however, I totally forgot him,
and indeed everything else, in the fascination of my fair
companion. She shared her chair with me, upon which I
supported her by my arm passed round the back; we ate
our pickled salmon, jelly, blanc-mange, cold chicken, ham,
and custard off the same plate, with an occasional squeeze
of the finger, as our hands met, her eyes making sad havoc
with me all the while, as I poured my tale of love—love,
lasting, burning, all-consuming—into her not unwilling
ear.

"Ah! now, ye're not in earnest?"

"Yes, Mary Anne, by all that's—"

"Well, there, now, don't swear, and take care; sure Mark
Anthony is looking."

"Mark Anthony be—"

"Oh! how passionate you are! I'm sure I never could live
easy with you. There, now give me some sponge-cake, and
don't be squeezing me, or they'll see you."

"Yes, to my heart, dearest girl."

"Och! it's cheese you're giving me," said she, with a gri-
mace that nearly cured my passion.

"A cottage, a hut, with you—with *you!*" said I, in a cadence
that I defy Macready to rival. "What is worldly splendor
or the empty glitter of rank?"

I here glanced at my epaulets, upon which I saw her eyes
riveted.

"Isn't the ginger-beer beautiful!" said she, emptying a glass
of champagne.

Still, I was not to be roused from my trance, and continued
my courtship as warmly as ever.

"I suppose you will come home *now,*" said a gruff voice
behind Mary Anne.

I turned, and perceived Mark Anthony with a grim look
of peculiar import.

"Oh! Mark, dear, I'm engaged to dance another set with
this gentleman."

"Ye are, are ye?" replied Mark, eying me askance. "Troth,

and I think the gentleman would be better if he went off to his flea-bag himself."

In my then mystified intellect this west-country synonym for a bed a little puzzled me.

"Yes, sir, the lady is engaged to *me,*—have you anything to say to that?"

"Nothing, at present, at all," said Mark, almost timidly.

"Oh dear, oh dear!" sobbed Mary Anne; "they're going to fight, and he'll be killed, I know he will."

For which of us this fate was destined, I stopped not to consider; but taking the lady under my arm, elbowed my way to the drawing-room amid a very sufficient patting upon the back and thumping between the shoulders, bestowed by members of the company who approved of my proceedings. The three fiddles, the flute and bassoon, that formed our band, being by this time sufficiently drunk, played after a fashion of their own, which, by one of those strange sympathies of our nature, imparted its influence to our legs, and a country dance was performed in a style of free and easy gesticulation that defies description. At the end of eighteen couple, tired of my exertions,—and they were not slight,—I leaned my back against the wall of the room, which I now, for the first time, perceived was covered with a very peculiar and novel species of hanging,—no less than a kind of rough, green-baize cloth, that moved and floated at every motion of the air. I paid little attention to this, till suddenly turning my head, something gave way behind it. I felt myself struck upon the back of the neck, and fell forward into the room, covered by a perfect avalanche of fenders, fire-irons, frying-pans, and copper kettles, mingled with the lesser artillery of small nails, door-keys, and holdfasts. There I lay amid the most vociferous mirth I ever listened to, under the confounded torrent of iron-mongery that half stunned me. The laughter over, I was assisted to rise; and having drunk about a pint of vinegar, and had my face and temples washed in strong whiskey punch, —the allocation of the fluids being mistaken,—I learned that our host, the high sheriff, was a celebrated tin and iron man, that his ball-room was no other than his magazine of metals, and that to conceal the well-filled shelves from the gaze of his aristocratic guests, they were clothed in the manner related,—which my unhappy head, by some misfortune, displaced, and thus brought on a calamity scarcely less afflicting to him than to myself. I should scarcely have stopped to mention this here, were it not that Mary Anne's gentle nursing of me in my misery went far to complete what her fascination had begun; and although she could not help laughing at the occurrence, I forgave her readily for her kindness.

"Remember," said I, trying to ogle through a black eye, painted by the angle of a register grate,—"remember, Mary Anne, I am to see you home."

"Oh, dear, sir! sure I don't know how you can manage it—"

Here Mark Anthony's entrance cut short her speech, for he came to declare that some of the officers had taken his coach, and was, as might be supposed, in a towering passion.

"If, sir," said I, with an air of the most balmy courtesy, —"if I can be of any use in assisting you to see your friends home—"

"Ah! then, ye're a nice-looking article to see ladies home. I wish you seen yourself this minute," said he.

As I felt it would be no breach of the unities—time, place, and everything considered—to smash his skull, I should certainly have proceeded to do so, had not a look of the most imploring kind from Mary Anne restrained me. By this time he had taken her under the arm and was leading her away. I stood irresolute, till a glance from my charmer caught me; when I rallied at once, and followed them downstairs. Here the scene was to the full as the above; the cloaking, shawling, shoeing, etc., of the ladies being certainly as mirth-moving a process as I should wish to see. Here were mothers trying to collect their daughters, as a hen her chickens, and, as in that case, the pursuit of one usually lost all the others; testy papas swearing; lovers leering as they twisted the boas round the fair throats of their sweethearts; vows of love mingling with lamentations for a lost slipper or a stray mantle. Sometimes the candles were extinguished, and the *mêlée* became greater, till the order and light were restored together. Meanwhile, each of our fellows had secured his fair one, save myself, and I was exposed to no small ridicule for my want of tact. Nettled by this, I made a plunge to the corner of the room, where Mary Anne was shawling; I recognized her pink sash, threw her cloak over her shoulders, and at the very moment that Mark Anthony drew his wife's arm within his, I performed the same by *my* friend, and followed them to the door. Here the grim brother-in-law turned round to take Mary Anne's arm, and seeing her with me, merely gave a kind of hoarse chuckle, and muttered: "Very well, sir; upon my conscience, you *will* have it, I see." During this brief interval, so occupied was I in watching him that I never once looked in my fair friend's face; but the gentle squeeze of her arm, as she leaned upon me, assured me that I had her approval of what I was doing.

What was the precise train of my thoughts, and what the subjects of conversation between us, I am unfortunately now unable to recollect. It is sufficient to remember that I could not believe five minutes had elapsed, when we arrived at York Street.

"Then you confess you love me," said I, as I squeezed her arm to my side. "Then, by this kiss I swear never to relinquish—"

What I was about to add, I am sure I know not; but true it is that a certain smacking noise here attracted Mr. Mark Anthony's attention, who started round, looked us full in the face, and then gravely added: "Enough is as good as a feast. I wish you pleasant drames, Mr. Larry Kar, if that's your name; and you'll hear from me in the morning."

"I intend it," said I. "Good night, dearest; think of—" The slam of the street-door in my face spoiled the peroration, and I turned towards home.

By the time I reached the barracks, the united effects of champagne, sherry, and Sheffield iron had in a good measure subsided, and my head had become sufficiently clear to permit a slight retrospect of the evening's amusement.

From two illusions I was at last awakened: first, the high-sheriff's ball was *not* the most accurate representation of high society; secondly, I was *not* deeply enamoured of Mary Anne Moriarty. Strange as it may seem, and how little soever the apparent connection between those two facts, the truth of one had a considerable influence in deciding the other. *"N'importe,"* said I, "the thing is over; it was rather good fun, too, upon the whole,—saving the *chute des casseroles;* and as to the lady, she must have seen it was a joke as well as myself. At least, so I am decided it shall be; and as there was no witness to our conversation, the thing is easily got out of."

The following day, as I was dressing to ride out, my servant announced no less a person than Mr. Mark Anthony Fitzpatrick, who said that he came upon a little business and must see me immediately.

Mr. Fitzpatrick, upon being announced, speedily opened his negotiation by asking, in very terse and unequivocal phrase, my intentions regarding his sister-in-law. After professing the most perfect astonishment at the question and its possible import, I replied that she was a most charming person, with whom I intended to have nothing whatever to do.

"And maybe you never proposed for her at the ball last night?"

"Propose for a lady at a ball the first time I ever met her!"

"Just so. Can you carry your memory so far back? Or perhaps I had better refresh it;" and he here repeated the whole substance of my conversation on my way homeward, sometimes in the very words I used.

"But, my dear sir, the young lady could never have supposed I used such language as this you have repeated?"

"So, then, you intend to break off? Well, then, it's right to tell you that you're in a very ugly scrape, for it was my wife you took home last night,—not Miss Moriarty; and I leave you to choose at your leisure whether you'd rather be defendant in a suit for breach of promise or seduction. And, upon my conscience, I think it's civil in me to give you a choice."

What a pretty disclosure was here! So that while I was imagining myself squeezing the hand and winning the heart of the fair Mary Anne, I was merely making a case of strong evidence for a jury, that might expose me to the world and half ruin me in damages. There was but one course open,— to make a fight for it; and from what I saw of my friend Mark Anthony, this did not seem difficult.

I accordingly assumed a high tone,—laughed at the entire affair; said it was a "way that we had in the army;" that "we never meant anything by it," etc.

In a few minutes I perceived the bait was taking. Mr. Fitzpatrick's west-country blood was up; all thought of the legal resource was abandoned; and he flung out of the room to find a friend, I having given him the name of "one of ours" as mine upon the occasion.

Very little time was lost, for before three o'clock that afternoon a meeting was fixed for the following morning at the North Bull; and I had the satisfaction of hearing that I only escaped the malignant eloquence of Holmes in the King's Bench, to be "blazed" at by the best shot on the western circuit. The thought was not agreeable, and I indemnified myself for the scrape by a very satisfactory anathema upon the high-sheriff and his ball and his confounded saucepans; for to the lady's sympathy for my sufferings I attributed much of my folly.

At eight the next morning I found myself standing, with Curzon and the doctor, upon the bleak portion of her Majesty's dominions they term the North Bull, waiting, in a chilly rain and a raw fog, till it pleased Mark Anthony Fitzpatrick to come and shoot me,—such being the precise terms of our combat, in the opinion of all parties.

The time, however, passed on, and half-past eight, three-quarters, and at last nine o'clock, without his appearing; when just as Curzon had resolved upon our leaving the ground, a hack jaunting-car was seen driving at full speed along the road near us. It came nearer, and at length drew up; two men leaped off and came towards us, one of whom, as he came forward, took off his hat politely and introduced himself as Mr. O'Gorman, the fighting friend of Mark Anthony.

"It's a mighty unpleasant business I'm come upon, gentlemen," said he. "Mr. Fitzpatrick has been unavoidably prevented from having the happiness to meet you this morning—"

"Then you can't expect us, sir, to dance attendance upon him here to-morrow," said Curzon, interrupting.

"By no manner of means," replied the other, placidly, "for it would be equally inconvenient for him to be here then. But I have only to say that as I'm here for my friend, and know all the particulars of the case, maybe you'd have the kindness to waive all etiquette and let me stand in his place."

"Certainly and most decidedly not," said Curzon. "Waive

etiquette! Why, sir, we have no quarrel with you, never saw you before."

"Well, now, isn't this hard?" said Mr. O'Gorman, addressing his friend, who stood by with a pistol-case under his arm; "but I told Mark that I was sure they'd be standing upon punctilio, for they were English. Well, sir," said he, turning towards Curzon, "there's but one way to arrange it now, that I see. Mr. Fitzpatrick, you must know, was arrested this morning for a trifle of £140. If you or your friend there will join us in the bail, we can get him out, and he'll fight you in the morning to your satisfaction."

When the astonishment this proposal had created, subsided, we assured Mr. O'Gorman that we were noways disposed to pay such a price for our amusement,—a fact that seemed considerably to surprise both him and his friend; and adding that to Mr. Fitzpatrick personally we should feel bound to hold ourselves pledged at a future period, we left the ground, Curzon laughing heartily at the original expedient thus suggested, while I inwardly pronounced a most glowing eulogy on the law of imprisonment for debt.

Before Mr. Fitzpatrick obtained the benefit of the Act, we were ordered abroad, and I have never since heard of him.

CHAPTER XLI.

THE TWO LETTERS.

FROM the digression of the last chapter I was recalled by the sight of the two letters which lay during my revery unopened before me. I first broke the seal of Lady Callonby's epistle, which ran thus :—

MUNICH, La Croix Blanche.

MY DEAR MR. LORREQUER,—I have just heard from Kilkee that you are at length about to pay us your long-promised visit, and write these few lines to beg that before leaving Paris you will kindly execute for me the commissions of which I enclose a formidable list, or at least as many of them as you can conveniently accomplish. Our stay here now will be so short that it will require all your despatch to overtake us before reaching Milan, Lady Jane's health requiring an immediate change of climate. Our present plans are to winter in Italy, although such will interfere considerably with Lord Callonby, who is pressed much by his friends to accept office. However, all this and other gossip I reserve for our meeting. Meanwhile, adieu! and if any of my commissions bore you, omit them at once, except the white roses and the Brussels veil, which Lady Jane is most anxious for.

Sincerely yours,
CHARLOTTE CALLONBY.

How much did these few and apparently commonplace lines convey to *me?* First, my visit was not only expected, but actually looked forward to, canvassed, perhaps I might almost whisper to myself the .flattery,—wished for. Again, Lady Jane's health was spoken of as precarious,—less actual illness, I said to myself, than mere delicacy requiring the bluer sky and warmer air of Italy. Perhaps her spirits were affected,—some mental malady; some ill-placed passion: *que sais-je?* In fact, my brain ran on so fast in its devisings that by a quick process, less logical than pleasing, I satisfied myself that the lovely Lady Jane Callonby was actually in love— with whom, let the reader guess. And Lord Callonby, too, about to join the Ministry,—well, all the better to have one's father-in-law in power; promotion *is* so cursed slow nowadays. And lastly the sly allusion to the commissions,—the malice of introducing *her* name to interest me. With such materials as these to build upon, frail as they may seem to others, I found no difficulty in regarding myself as the dear friend of the family and the acknowledged suitor of Lady Jane.

In the midst, however, of all my self-gratulation, my eye fell upon the letter of Emily Bingham, and I suddenly remembered how fatal to all such happy anticipations it might prove. I tore it open in passionate haste and read:

MY DEAR MR. LORREQUER,—As from the interview we have had this morning I am inclined to believe that I have gained your affections, I think that I should ill requite such a state of your feeling for me were I to conceal that I cannot return you mine,—in fact, that they are not mine to bestow. This frank avowal, whatever pain it may have cost me, I think I owe to you to make. You will perhaps say the confession should have been earlier. To which I reply, it should have been so, had I known, or even guessed at, the nature of your feelings for me; for—and I write it in all truth and perfect respect for you—I only saw in your attentions the flirting habits of a man of the world with a very unformed and igno- rant girl of eighteen, with whom, as it was his amusement to travel, he deemed it worth his while to talk. I now see, and bitterly regret, my error, yet deem it better to make this pain- ful confession than suffer you to remain in a delusion which may involve your happiness in the wreck of mine. I am most faithfully your friend,   EMILY BINGHAM.

"What a charming girl she is!" I cried, as I finished the letter; "how full of true feeling, how honorable, how straight- forward! And yet it is devilish strange how cunningly she played her part, and it seems now that I never did touch her affections. Master Harry, I begin to fear you are not al- together the awful lady-killer you have been thinking." Thus did I meditate upon this singular note; my delight at being once more "free" mingling with some chagrin that I was jock- eyed, and by a young miss of eighteen too. "Confoundedly disagreeable if the mess knew it," thought I. *"Per Bacco!"* how they would quiz upon my difficulty to break off a match, when the lady was only anxious to get rid of *me*.

"This affair must never come to their ears, or I am ruined; and now, the sooner all negotiations are concluded, the better. I must obtain a meeting with Emily, acknowledge the truth and justice of all her views, express my deep regret at the issue of the affair, slyly hint that I have been merely playing her own game back upon her,—for it would be the devil to let her go off with the idea that she had singed me, yet never caught fire herself,—so that we both shall draw stakes and part friends."

This valiant resolution taken, I wrote a very short note, begging an interview, and proceeded to make as formidable a toilet as I could for the forthcoming meeting; before I had concluded which, a verbal answer by her maid informed me that "Miss Bingham was alone, and ready to receive me."

As I took my way along the corridor I could not help feeling that among all my singular scrapes and embarrassing situations through life my present mission was certainly not the least, the difficulty, such as it was, being considerably increased by my own confounded *amour-propre,* that would not leave me satisfied with obtaining my liberty if I could not insist upon coming off scathless also. In fact, I was not content to evacuate the fortress if I were not to march out with all the honors of war. This feeling I neither attempt to palliate nor defend; I merely chronicle it as are too many of these "Confessions,"—a matter of truth, yet not the less a subject for sorrow.

My hand was upon the lock of the door. I stopped, hesitated, and listened. I certainly heard something. Yes, it is too true,—she is sobbing. What a total overthrow of all my selfish resolves, all my egotistical plans, did that slight cadence give! She was crying,—her tears for the bitter pain she concluded I was suffering mingling doubtless with sorrow for her own sources of grief; for it was clear to me that whoever may have been my favored rival, the attachment was either unknown to or unsanctioned by the mother. I wished I had not listened; all my determinations were completely routed, and as I opened the door I felt my heart beating almost audibly against my side.

In a subdued half-light, tempered through the rose-colored curtains with a small china cup of newly plucked moss-roses upon the table, sat, or rather leaned, Emily Bingham, her face buried in her hands as I entered. She did not hear my approach, so that I had above a minute to admire the graceful character of her head and the fine, undulating curve of her neck and shoulders, before I spoke.

"Miss Bingham," said I.

She started, looked up; her dark-blue eyes, brilliant though tearful, were fixed upon me for a second, as if searching my very inmost thoughts. She held out her hand, and turning her head aside, made room for me on the sofa beside her. "Strange girl," thought I, "that in the very moment of breaking with a man forever, puts on her most fascinating toilet, arrays herself in her most bewitching manner, and gives him a reception only calculated to turn his head and render him ten times more in love than ever." Her hand, which remained still in mine, was burning as if in fever, and the heaving movement of her neck and shoulders showed me how much this meeting cost her. We were both silent, till at length, feeling that any chance interruption might leave us as far as ever from understanding each other, I resolved to begin.

"My dear, dear Emily," I said, "do not, I entreat of you, add to the misery I am this moment enduring by letting me see you thus. Whatever your wrongs towards me, this is far too heavy a retribution. My object was never to make you wretched; if I am not to obtain the bliss to strive and make you happy—"

"Oh, Harry!"—this was the first time she had ever so called me—"how like you to think of me,—of *me,* at such a time, as if I was not the cause of all our present unhappiness. But not wilfully, not intentionally. Oh, no, no! your attentions, the flattery of your notice, took me at once, and in the gratification of my self-esteem I forgot all else. I heard, too, that you were engaged to another; and believing, as I did, that you were trifling with my affections, I spared no effort to win yours. I confess it, I wished this with all my soul."

"And now," said I, "that you have gained them,"—here was a pretty sequel to my well-matured plans!—"and now, Emily—"

"But have I really done so?" said she, hurriedly turning round and fixing her large, full eyes upon me, while one of her hands played carelessly through my hair—"have I your heart,—your whole heart?"

"Can you doubt it, dearest?" said I, passionately pressing her to my bosom, and at the same time muttering, "What the devil's in the wind now? We are surely not going to patch up our separation and make love in earnest?"

There she lay, her head upon my shoulder, her long brown, waving ringlets falling loosely across my face and on my bosom, her hand in mine. What were her thoughts I cannot guess; mine—God forgive me!—were a fervent wish either for her mother's appearance, or that the hotel would suddenly take fire, or some other extensive calamity arise to put the finishing stroke to this embarrassing situation.

None of these, however, were destined to occur; and Emily lay still and motionless as she was, scarce seeming to breathe, and pale as death. "What can this mean?" said I. "Surely this is not the usual way to part with a rejected suitor? If it be, why then, by Jupiter, the successful one must have rather the worst of it; and I fervently hope that Lady Jane be not at this moment giving her *congé* to some disappointed swain." She slowly raised her large, black-fringed eyelids, and looked into my face with an expression at once so tender and so plaintive that I felt a struggle within myself whether to press her to my heart or— What the deuce was the alternative? I hope my reader knows, for I really do not. "And after all," thought I, "if we are to marry, I am only anticipating a little; and if not, why then a *'chaste salute,'* as Winifred Jenkins calls it, she'll be none the worse for." Acting at once upon this resolve, I leaned downwards, and was passing back her ringlets from her now flushed cheek, when I was startled by my name, which I heard called several times in the corridor. The door at the same instant was burst suddenly open, and Trevanion appeared.

"Harry, Harry Lorrequer!" cried he, as he entered; then, suddenly checking himself, added: "A thousand, ten thousand pardons, but—"

"But what," cried I, passionately, forgetting all save the situation of poor Emily at the moment,—"what can justify—"

"Nothing certainly can justify such an intrusion," said Trevanion, finishing my sentence for me, "except the very near danger you run this moment in being arrested. O'Leary's imprudence has compromised your safety, and you must leave Paris within an hour."

"Oh, Mr. Trevanion," said Emily, who by this time had regained a more befitting attitude, "pray speak out! What is it? Is Harry—is Mr. Lorrequer, I mean—in any danger?"

"Nothing of consequence, Miss Bingham, if he only act with prudence and be guided by his friends. Lorrequer, you will find me in your apartments in half an hour; till then adieu."

While Emily poured forth question after question as to the nature and extent of my present difficulty, I could not help thinking of the tact by which Trevanion escaped, leaving me to make my adieus to Emily as best I might; for I saw in a glance that I must leave Paris at once. I therefore briefly gave her to understand the affair at the Salon, which I suspected to be the cause of the threatened arrest, and was about to profess my unaltered and unalterable attachment, when she suddenly stopped me.

"No, Mr. Lorrequer, no. All is over between us. We must never meet again, never. We have been both playing a part. Good by—good by! Do not altogether forget me—and once more, Harry, good by!"

What I might have said, thought, or done, I know not; but the arrival of Mrs. Bingham's carriage at the door left no time for anything but escape. So once more pressing her hand firmly to my lips, I said, *"Au revoir,* Emily, *au revoir,* —not good by;"* and rushing from the room, regained my room just as Mrs. Bingham reached the corridor.

CHAPTER XLII.

MR. O'LEARY'S CAPTURE.

"DOES she really care for me?" was my first question to myself as I left the room. "Is this story about pre-engaged affections merely a got-up thing to try the force of my attachment for her? For if not, her conduct is most inexplicable; and great as my experience has been in such affairs, I avow myself out-manœuvred." While I thought over this difficulty, Trevanion came up, and in a few words informed me more fully upon what he had hinted at before. It appeared that O'Leary, much more alive to the imperative necessity of avoiding detection by his wife than of involving himself with the police, had thrown out most dark and mysterious hints in the hotel as to the reason of his residence at Paris, fully impressed with the idea that to be a good Pole he need only talk "revolutionary," devote to the powers below all kings, czars, and kaisers, weep over the wrongs of his nation, wear rather seedy habiliments, and smoke profusely. The latter were with him easy conditions; and he so completely acted the former to the life that he had been that morning arrested in the Tuileries gardens under several treasonable charges,—among others, the conspiracy, with some of his compatriots, to murder the minister of war.

However laughable such an accusation against poor O'Leary, one circumstance rendered the matter anything but ludicrous. Although he must come off free of this grave offence, yet, as the Salon transaction would necessarily now become known, I should be immediately involved, and my departure from Paris prevented.

"So," said Trevanion, as he briefly laid before me the difficulty of my position, "you may perceive that however strongly your affections may be engaged in a certain quarter, it is quite as well to think of leaving Paris without delay. O'Leary's arrest will be followed by yours, depend upon it, and once under the surveillance of the police, escape is impossible."

"But, seriously, Trevanion," said I, nettled at the tone of raillery he spoke in, "you must see that there is nothing whatever in that business. I was merely taking my farewell of the fair Emily. Her affections have been long since engaged, and I—"

"Only endeavoring to support her in her attachment to the more favored rival. Is it not so?"

"Come, no quizzing! Faith! I began to feel very uncomfortable about parting with her the moment that I discovered that I must do so."

"So I guessed," said Trevanion, with a dry look, "from the interesting scene I so abruptly trespassed upon. But you are right; a little bit of tenderness is never misplaced, so long as the object is young, pretty, and, still more than all, disposed for it."

"Quite out; perfectly mistaken, believe me. Emily not only never cared for me, but she has gone far enough to tell me so."

"Then, from all I know of such matters," replied he, "you were both in a very fair way to repair that mistake on her part. But hark! what is this?"

A tremendous noise in the street here interrupted our colloquy, and on opening the window, a strange scene presented itself to our eyes. In the middle of a dense mass of moving rabble, shouting, yelling, and screaming with all their might, were two *gendarmes* with a prisoner between them. The unhappy man was followed by a rather over-dressed, middle-aged looking woman, who appeared to be desirous of bestowing the most *coram publico* endearments upon the culprit, whom a second glance showed us was O'Leary.

"I tell you, my dear madam, you are mistaken," said O'Leary, addressing her with great sternness of manner and voice.

"Mistaken? Never, never! How could I ever be mistaken in that dear voice, those lovely eyes, that sweet little nose?"

"Take her away, she's deranged," said O'Leary to the *gendarmes*. "Sure, if I'm a Pole, that's enough of misfortune."

"I'll follow him to the end of the earth, I will."

"I'm going to the galleys, God be praised!" said O'Leary.

"To the galleys, to the guillotine,—anywhere," responded she, throwing herself upon his neck,—much less, as it seemed, to his gratification than that of the mob, who laughed and shouted most uproariously.

"Mrs. Ram, ain't you ashamed?"

"He calls me by my name," said she, "and he attempts to disown me. Ha! ha! ha! ha!" and immediately fell off into a strong paroxysm of kicking and pinching and punching the bystanders,—a malady well known under the name of hysterics, but being little more than a privileged mode, among certain ladies, of paying off some scores which it is not thought decent to do in their more sober moments.

"Lead me away,—anywhere; convict me of what you like," said he, "but don't let her follow me."

The *gendarmes,* who little comprehended the nature of the scene before them, were not sorry to anticipate a renewal of it on Mrs. Ram's recovery, and accordingly seized the opportunity to march on with O'Leary, who turned the corner of the Rue Rivoli under a shower of execrations from the mob that fell fortunately most unconsciously upon his ears.

The possibility of figuring in such a procession contributed much to the force of Trevanion's reasonings, and I resolved to leave Paris at once.

"Promise me, then, to involve yourself in no more scrapes

for half an hour. Pack everything you may want with you, and by seven o'clock I will be here with your passport and all ready for a start."

With a beating brain and in a whirlwind of conflicting thoughts, I threw my clothes hither and thither into my trunk. Lady Jane and Emily both flitting every instant before my imagination, and frequently an irresolution to proceed stopping all my preparations for departure, I sat down musing upon a chair, and half determined to stay where I was, come what might of it. Finally, the possibility of exposure in a trial had its weight. I continued my occupation till the last coat was folded and the lock turned, when I seated myself opposite my luggage and waited impatiently for my friend's return.

CHAPTER XLIII.

THE JOURNEY.

TREVANION came at last. He had obtained my passport and engaged a carriage to convey me about eight miles, where I should overtake the diligence,—such a mode of travelling being judged more likely to favor my escape, by attracting less attention than posting. It was past ten when I left the Rue St. Honoré, having shaken hands with Trevanion for the last time, and charged him with ten thousand soft messages for the "friends" I left behind me.

When I arrived at the village of St. Jacques, the diligence had not come up. To pass away the time, I ordered a little supper and a bottle of St. Julien. Scarcely had I seated myself to my cutlet when the rapid whirl of wheels was heard without, and a cab drew up suddenly at the door. So naturally does the fugitive suspect pursuit that my immediate impression was that I was followed. In this notion I was strengthened by the tones of a cracked, discordant voice, asking in very peculiar French if the "diligence had passed." Being answered in the negative, he walked into the room where I was, and speedily, by his appearance, removed any apprehensions I had felt as to my safety. Nothing could less resemble

the tall port and sturdy bearing of a *gendarme* than the di-
minutive and dwarfish individual before me. His height
could scarcely have reached five feet, of which the head
formed fully a fourth part; and even this was rendered in appearance still greater by a mass of loosely floating black hair
that fell upon his neck and shoulders, and gave him much
the air of a "black lion" on a signboard. His black frock fur-
collared and braided, his ill-made boots, his meerschaum projecting from his breast-pocket, above all, his unwashed
hands and a heavy gold ring upon his thumb,—all made an
ensemble of evidences that showed he could be nothing but
a German. His manner was bustling, impatient, and had it
not been ludicrous, would certainly be considered as insolent
to every one about him, for he stared each person abruptly in
the face, and mumbled some broken expressions of his opinion of them half-aloud in German. His comments ran on:
"Bon soir, Monsieur," to the host; *"ein Bösewicht, ganz
sicher,"*—"a scoundrel, without doubt;" and then added, still
lower, "Rob you here as soon as look at you." *"Ah, postillon! comment va?"*—"Much more like a brigand after all,—
I know which I'd take you for." *"Verfluchte Frau,"*—"How
ugly the woman is!" This compliment was intended for the
hostess, who curtseyed down to the ground in her ignorance.
At last, approaching me, he stopped, and having steadily surveyed me, muttered, *"Ein echter Engländer,"*—"A thorough
Englishman; always eating." I could not resist the temptation to assure him that I was perfectly aware of his flattering
impression in my behalf; though I had speedily to regret my
precipitancy, for, less mindful of the rebuke than pleased at
finding some one who understood German, he drew his chair
beside me and entered into conversation.

Every one has surely felt, some time or other in life, the
insufferable annoyance of having his thoughts and reflections
interfered with and broken in upon by the vulgar imperti-
nence and egotism of some "bore" who, mistaking your abstraction for attention, and your despair for delight, inflicts
upon you his whole life and adventures, when your own immediate destinies are perhaps vacillating in the scale.

Such a doom was now mine! Occupied as I was by the
hope of the future, and my fears lest any impediment to my

escape should blast my prospects forever, I preferred appearing to pay attention to this confounded fellow's "personal narrative," lest his questions, turning on my own affairs, might excite suspicions as to the reasons of my journey.

I longed most ardently for the arrival of the diligence, trusting that, with true German thrift, my friend might prefer the cheapness of the *intérieur* to the magnificence of the *coupé,* and that thus I should see no more of him. But in this pleasing hope I was destined to be disappointed, for I was scarcely seated in my place when I found him beside me. The third occupant of this "privileged den," as well as my lamp-light survey of him permitted, afforded nothing to build on as a compensation for the German. He was a tall, lanky, lantern-jawed man, with a hook nose and projecting chin; his hair, which had only been permitted to grow very lately, formed that curve upon his forehead we see in certain old-fashioned horse-shoe wigs; his compressed lip and hard features gave the expression of one who had seen a good deal of the world, and didn't think the better of it in consequence. I observed that he listened to the few words we spoke while getting in with some attention, and then, like a person who did not comprehend the language, turned his shoulder towards us and soon fell asleep. I was now left to the "tender mercies" of my talkative companion, who certainly spared me not. Notwithstanding my vigorous resolves to turn a deaf ear to his narratives, I could not avoid learning that he was the director of music to some German prince; that he had been to Paris to bring out an opera, which, having, as he said, an "immense success," he was about to repeat in Strasburg. He further informed me that a *député* from Alsace had obtained for him a government permission to travel with the courier; but that he, being "social" withal, and noways proud, preferred the democracy of the diligence to the solitary grandeur of the *calèche* (for which Heaven confound him!), and thus became my present companion.

Music in all its shapes and forms made up the staple of the little man's talk. There was scarcely an opera or an overture, from Mozart to Donizetti, that he did not insist upon singing a scene from; and wound up all by a very pathetic lamentation over English insensibility to music, which he in great part attributed to our having only one opera, which he kindly informed me was "Bob et Joan." However indisposed to check the current of his loquacity by any effort of mine, I could not avoid the temptation to translate for him a story which Sir Walter Scott once related to me, and which was so far *à propos* as conveying my own sense of the merits of our national music, such as we have it, by its associations with scenes and persons and places we are all familiar with, however unintelligible to the ear of a stranger.

A young French vicomte was fortunate enough to obtain in marriage the hand of a singularly pretty Scotch heiress of an ancient family and good fortune, who, amongst her other endowments, possessed a large old-fashioned house in a remote district of the Highlands, where her ancestors had resided for centuries. Thither the young couple repaired to pass the honeymoon; the enamoured bridegroom gladly availing himself of the opportunity to ingratiate himself with his new connection by adopting the reclusion he saw practised by the English on such occasions. However consonant to our notions of happiness, and however conducive to our enjoyment this custom be,—and I have strong doubts upon the subject,—it certainly prospered ill with the volatile Frenchman, who pined for Paris, its *cafés,* its boulevards, its *maisons de jeu,* and its *soirées.* His days were passed in looking from the deep and narrow windows of some oak-framed room upon the bare and heath-clad moors, or watching the cloud shadows as they passed across the dark pine-trees that closed the distance.

Bored to death, and convinced that he had sacrificed enough, and more than enough, to the barbarism which demanded such a *séjour,* he was sitting one evening listlessly upon the terrace in front of the house, plotting a speedy escape from his gloomy abode, and meditating upon the life of pleasure that awaited him, when the discordant twang of some savage music broke upon his ear and roused him from his revery. The wild scream and fitful burst of a Highland pibroch is certainly not the most likely thing in nature to allay the irritable and ruffled feelings of an irascible person,—unless, perhaps, the hearer eschew breeches. So thought the vicomte. He started hurriedly up, and straight before him, up the gravel walk, beheld the stalwart figure and bony frame of an old Highlander, blowing, with all his lungs, the "Gathering of the Clans." With all the speed he could muster he rushed into the house, and calling his servants, ordered them to expel the intruder and drive him at once outside the demesne. When the mandate was made known to the old piper, it was with the greatest difficulty he could be brought to comprehend it; for, time out of mind, his approach had been hailed with every demonstration of rejoicing, and now— But no, the thing was impossible; there must be a mistake somewhere. He was accordingly about to recommence, when a second and stronger hint suggested to him that it were safer to depart. "Maybe the carl didna like the pipes," said the Highlander, musingly, as he packed them up for his march; "maybe he didna like *me;* perhaps, too, he was na in the humor for music." He paused for an instant, as if reflecting,—not satisfied, probably, that he had hit upon the true solution,—when suddenly his eye brightened, his lips curled, and fixing a look upon the angry Frenchman, he said: "Maybe ye are right enow,—ye heard them ower muckle in Waterloo to like the skirl o' them ever since;" with which satisfactory explanation, made in no spirit of bitterness or raillery, but in the simple belief that he had hit the mark of the vicomte's antipathy, the old man gathered up his plaid and departed.

However disposed I might have felt towards sleep, the little German resolved I should not obtain any; for when, half an hour together, I would preserve a rigid silence, he, nowise daunted, had recourse to some German *Lied,* which he gave forth with an energy of voice and manner that must have aroused every sleeper in the diligence; so that, fain to avoid this, I did my best to keep him on the subject of his adventures, which, as a man of successful gallantry, were manifold indeed. Wearying, at last, even of this subordinate part, I fell into a kind of half-doze, the words of a student-song he continued to sing without ceasing for above an hour being the last waking thought on my memory.

Less as a *souvenir* of the singer than a specimen of its class, I give here a rough translation of the well-known *Burschen* melody called—

THE POPE.

I.

The Pope he leads a happy life,—
He fears not married care nor strife;
He drinks the best of Rhenish wine:
I would the Pope's gay lot were mine!

CHORUS.

He drinks the best of Rhenish wine:
I would the Pope's gay lot were mine.

II.

But then all happy's not his life,—
He has not maid, nor blooming wife,
Nor child has he to raise his hope:
I would not wish to be the Pope.

III.

The Sultan better pleases me,—
His is a life of jollity;
His wives are many as he will:
I would the Sultan's throne then fill.

IV.

But even he's a wretched man,—
He must obey his Alcoran,
And dares not drink one drop of wine:
I would not change his lot for mine.

V.

So then I'll hold my lowly stand,
And live in German Vaterland;
I'll kiss my maiden fair and fine,
And drink the best of Rhenish wine.

VI.

Whene'er my maiden kisses me,
I'll think that I the Sultan be;
And when my cheery glass I tope,
I'll fancy then I am the Pope.

CHAPTER XLIV.

THE JOURNEY.

IT was with a feeling of pleasure I cannot explain that I awoke in the morning and found myself upon the road. The turmoil, the bustle, the never-ending difficulties of my late life in Paris had so over-excited and worried me that I could neither think nor reflect. Now, all these cares and troubles were behind me, and I felt like a liberated prisoner as I looked upon the gray dawn of the coming day as it gradually melted from its dull and leaden tint to the pink and yellow hue of the rising sun. The broad and richly colored plains of *la belle France* were before me,—and it is *la belle France,* however inferior to parts of England in rural beauty,—the large tracts of waving yellow corn, undulating like a sea in the morning breeze, the interminable reaches of forest, upon which the shadows played and flitted, deepening the effect and mellowing the mass as we see them in Ruysdael's pictures, while now and then some tall-gabled, antiquated château, with its mutilated terrace and dowager-like air of bygone grandeur, would peep forth at the end of some long avenue of lime-trees, all having their own features of beauty, and a beauty with which every object around harmonizes well. The sluggish peasant, in his blouse and striped nightcap; the heavily caparisoned horse, shaking his head amidst a Babel-tower of gaudy worsted tassels and brass bells; the deeply laden wagon creeping slowly along,—are all in keeping with a scene where the very mist that rises from the valley seems indolent and lazy, and unwilling to impart the rich perfume of verdure with which it is loaded. Every land has its own peculiar character of beauty. The glaciered mountain, the Alpine peak, the dashing cataracts of Switzerland and the Tyrol, are not finer in their way than the long, flat moorlands of a Flemish landscape, with its clump of stunted willows clustering over some limpid brook, in which the oxen are standing for shelter from the noon-day heat, while, lower down, some rude water-wheel is mingling its sounds with the summer bees and the merry voices of the miller and his companions.

So strayed my thoughts as the German shook me by the arm, and asked if I were not ready for my breakfast? Luckily, to this question there is rarely but the one answer. Who is not ready for his breakfast when on the road? How delightful, if on the Continent, to escape from the narrow limits of the dungeon-like diligence, where you sit with your knees next your collar-bone, fainting with heat and suffocated by dust, and to find yourself suddenly beside the tempting *plats* of a little French *déjeuner,* with its cutlets, its fried fish, its *poulet,* its salads, and its little *entrée* of fruit, tempered with a not despicable bottle of Beaune. If in England, the exchange is nearly as grateful; for though our travelling be better, and our position less irksome, still it is no small alteration from the stage-coach to the inn parlor, redolent of aromatic black tea, eggs, and hot toast, with a hospitable sideboard of lordly sirloins and York hams that would make a Jew's mouth water. While in America the change is greatest of all, as any one can vouch for who has been suddenly emancipated from the stove-heat of a "nine-inside" leathern "conveniency," bumping ten miles an hour over a corduroy road, the company smoking, if not worse, to the ample display of luxurious viands displayed upon the breakfast-table, where, what with buffalo steaks, pumpkin pie, "chicken fixings," and other aristocratically called temptations, he must be indeed fastidious who cannot employ his half-hour. Pity it is, when there is so much good to eat, that people will not partake of it like civilized beings and with that air of cheerful thankfulness that all other nations more or less express when enjoying the earth's bounties. But true it is that there is a spirit of discontent in the Yankee that seems to accept of benefits with a tone of dissatisfaction, if not distrust. I once made this remark to an excellent friend of mine, now no more, who, however, would not permit of my attributing this feature to the Americans exclusively, adding, "Where have you more of this than in Ireland? And surely you would not call the Irish ungrateful?" He illustrated his first remark by the following short anecdote:—

The rector of the parish my friend lived in was a man who added to the income he derived from his living a very handsome private fortune, which he devoted entirely to the benefit of the poor around him. Among the objects of his bounty one old woman—a childless widow—was remarkably distinguished. Whether commiserating her utter helplessness or her complete isolation, he went farther to relieve her than to many, if not all, the other poor. She frequently was in the habit of pleading her poverty as a reason for not appearing in church among her neighbors; and he gladly seized an opportunity of so improving her condition that on this score, at least, no impediment existed. When all his little plans for her comfort had been carried into execution, he took·the opportunity one day of dropping in, as if accidentally, to speak to her. By degrees he led the subject to her changed condition in life,—the alteration from a cold, damp, smoky hovel to a warm, clean, slated house; the cheerful garden before the door that replaced the mud-heap and the duck-pool; and all the other happy changes which a few weeks had effected. And he then asked, did she not feel grateful to a bountiful Providence that had showered down so many blessings upon her head?

"Ah, troth! it's thrue for yer honor, I am grateful," she replied, in a whining, discordant tone, which astonished the worthy parson.

"Of course you are, my good woman, of course you are; but I mean to say, don't you feel that every moment you live is too short to express your thankfulness to this kind Providence for what he has done?"

"Ah, darlin'! it's all thrue; he's very good, he's mighty kind, so he is."

"Why, then, not acknowledge it in a different manner?" said the parson, with some heat. "Has he not housed you and fed you and clothed you?"

"Yes, alanah, he done it all."

"Well, where is your gratitude for all those mercies?"

"Ah! sure, if he did," said the old crone, roused at length by the importunity of the questioner,—"sure, if he did, *doesn't he take it out o' me in the corns?*"

CHAPTER XLV.

A REMINISCENCE OF THE EAST.

THE breakfast-table assembled around it the three generations of men who issued from the three subdivisions of the diligence, and presented that motley and mixed assemblage of ranks, ages, and countries which forms so very amusing a part of a traveller's experience.

First came the *haute aristocratie* of the *coupé,* then the middle class of the *intérieur,* and lastly, the *tiers état* of the *rotonde,* with its *mélange* of Jew money-lenders, under-officers and their wives, a Norman nurse with a high cap and a red jupe; while, to close the procession, a German student descended from the roof, with a beard, a blouse, and a meerschaum. Of such materials was our party made up; and yet, differing in all our objects and interests, we speedily amalgamated into a very social state of intimacy, and chatted away over our breakfast with much good humor and gayety, each person of the number seeming pleased at the momentary opportunity of finding a new listener, save my tall companion of the *coupé.* He preserved a dogged silence, unbroken by even a chance expression to the waiter, who observed his wants and supplied them by a species of quick instinct evidently acquired by practice. As I could not help feeling somewhat interested about the hermit-like attachment he evinced for solitude, I watched him narrowly for some time, and at length, as the *rôti* made its appearance before him, after he had helped himself and tasted it, he caught my eye fixed upon him, and looking at me intently for a few seconds, he seemed to be satisfied in some passing doubt he labored under, as he said, with a most peculiar shake of the head: *"No mangez, no mangez cela."*

"Ah!" said I, detecting in my friend's French his English origin, "you are an Englishman, I find."

"The devil a doubt of it, darling," said he half testily.

"An Irishman too,—still better," said I.

"Why, then, isn't it strange that my French always shows me to be English, and my English proves me Irish? It's lucky for me there's no going farther, anyhow."

Delighted to have thus fallen upon a "character," as the Irishman evidently appeared, I moved my chair towards his; finding, however, he was not half pleased at the manner in which my acquaintance had been made with him, and knowing his country's susceptibility of being taken by a story, I resolved to make my advances by narrating a circumstance which had once befallen me in my early life.

Our countrymen, English and Irish, travel so much nowadays that one ought never to feel surprised at finding them anywhere. The instance I am about to relate will verify to a certain extent the fact, by showing that no situation is too odd or too unlikely to be within the verge of calculation.

When the 10th Foot, to which I then belonged, were at Corfu, I obtained, with three other officers, a short leave of absence to make a hurried tour of the Morea and take a passing glance at Constantinople,—in those days much less frequently visited by travellers than at present.

After rambling pleasantly about for some weeks, we were about to return, when we determined that before sailing we would accept an invitation some officers of the "Blazer" frigate, then stationed here, had given us to pass a day at Pera and picnic on the mountain.

One fine bright morning was therefore selected, a most appetizing little dinner being carefully packed up, and we set out, a party of fourteen, upon our excursion.

The weather was glorious, and the scene far finer than any of us had anticipated,—the view from the mountain extending over the entire city, gorgeous in the rich coloring of its domes and minarets; while at one side the Golden Horn was visible, crowded with ships of every nation, and at the other a glimpse might be had of the Sea of Marmora, blue and tranquil as it lay beneath. The broad bosom of the Bosporus was sheeted out like a map before us,—peace-

ful, yet bustling with life and animation. Here lay the
Union-Jack of Old England, floating beside the lilies of
France (we speak of times when lilies were, and barricades
were not), the tall and taper spars of a Yankee frigate towering above the low timbers and heavy hull of a Dutch
schooner, the gilded poop and carved galleries of a Turkish
three-decker anchored beside the raking mast and curved
deck of a suspicious-looking craft, whose red-capped, dark-
visaged crew needed not the naked creese at their sides to
bespeak them Malays. The whole was redolent of life, and
teeming with food for one's fancy to conjure from.

While we were debating upon the choice of a spot for
our luncheon which should command the chief points of view
within our reach, one of the party came to inform us
that he had just discovered the very thing we were in
search of. It was a small kiosk, built upon a projecting rock
that looked down upon the Bosporus and the city, and had
evidently, from the extended views it presented, been selected
as the spot to build upon. The building itself was a small
octagon, open on every side, and presenting a series of prospects, land and seaward, of the most varied and magnificent
kind.

Seeing no one near, nor any trace of habitation, we resolved to avail ourselves of the good taste of the founder;
and spreading out the contents of our hampers, proceeded
to discuss a most excellent cold dinner. When the good
things had disappeared, and the wine begun to circulate, one
of the party observed that we should not think of enjoying
ourselves before we had filled a bumper to the brim to the
health of our good king, whose birthday it chanced to be.
Our homeward thoughts and loyalty uniting, we filled our
glasses and gave so hearty a "hip, hip, hurrah" to our toast
that I doubt if the echoes of those old rocks ever heard the
equal of it.

Scarcely was the last cheer dying away in the distance,
when the door of the kiosk opened, and a negro, dressed in
white muslin, appeared, his arms and ankles bearing those
huge rings of massive gold which only persons of rank distinguish their servants by.

After a most profound obeisance to the party, he explained, in very tolerable French, that his master, the Effendi Ben Mustapha Al Halak, at whose charge (in house-rent) we were then feasting, sent us greeting, and begged that if not considered as contrary to our usage, etc., we should permit him and his suite to approach the kiosk and observe us at our meal.

Independent of his politeness in the mode of conveying the request, as *he* would prove fully as entertaining a sight to us as *we* could possibly be to him, we immediately expressed our great willingness to receive his visit, coupled with a half-hint that perhaps he might honor us by joining the party.

After a half-hour's delay the door was once more thrown open, and a venerable old Turk entered. He salaamed three times most reverently, and motioned to us to be seated, declining at the same time, by a gentle gesture of his hand, our invitation. He was followed by a train of six persons, all splendidly attired, and attesting, by their costume and manner, the rank and importance of their chief. Conceiving that his visit had but one object,—to observe our convivial customs,—we immediately re-seated ourselves and filled our glasses.

As one after another the officers of the Effendi's household passed round the apartments, we offered them a goblet of champagne, which they severally declined with a polite but solemn smile,—all except one, a large, savage-looking Turk, with a most ferocious scowl and the largest black beard I ever beheld. He did not content himself with a mute refusal of our offer, but stopping suddenly, he raised up his hands above his head and muttered some words in Turkish, which one of the party informed us was a very satisfactory recommendation of the whole company to Satan for their heretic abomination.

The procession moved slowly round the room, and when it reached the door again, retired, each member of it salaaming three times as he had done on entering. Scarcely had they gone, when we burst into a loud fit of laughter at the savage-looking fellow who thought proper to excommunicate us, and were about to discuss his more than common appearance of disgust at our proceedings, when again the door opened, and a turbaned head peeped in; but so altered were the features that although seen but the moment before, we could hardly believe them the same. The dark complexion, the long and bushy beard were there; but instead of the sleepy and solemn character of the Oriental, with heavy eye and closed lip, there was a droll half-devilry in the look and partly open mouth that made a most laughable contrast with the head-dress. He looked stealthily around him for an instant, as if to see that all was right, and then, with an accent and expression I shall never forget, said, *"I'll taste your wine, gentlemen, av it be pleasing to ye."*

CHAPTER XLVI.

A DAY IN THE PHŒNIX.

WHEN we were once more in the *coupé* of the diligence, I directed my entire attention towards my Irish acquaintance, as well because of his apparent singularity, as to avoid the little German in the opposite corner.

"You have not been long in France, then, sir," said I, as we resumed our conversation.

"Three weeks; and it seems like three years to me,— nothing to eat, nothing to drink, and nobody to speak to. But I'll go back soon; I only came abroad for a month."

"You'll scarcely see much of the Continent in so short a time."

"Devil a much *that* will grieve me; I didn't come to see it."

"Indeed!"

"Nothing of the kind; I only came—to be away from home."

"Oh! I perceive."

"You're quite out there," said my companion, misinterpreting my meaning. "It wasn't anything of that kind. I don't owe sixpence. I was laughed out of Ireland,—that's all; though that same is bad enough."

"Laughed out of it?"

"Just so; and little you know of Ireland if that surprises you."

After acknowledging that such an event was perfectly possible, from what I myself had seen of that country, I obtained the following very brief account of my companion's reasons for foreign travel.

"Well, sir," began he, "it is about four months since I brought up to Dublin from Galway a little chestnut mare, with cropped ears and a short tail, square-jointed, and rather low,—just what you'd call a smart hack for going to cover with; a lively thing on the road with a light weight. Nobody ever suspected that she was a clean-bred thing,— own sister to Jenny, that won the Corinthians, and ran second to Giles for the Riddlesworth; but so she was, and a better-bred mare never leaped the pound in Ballinasloe. Well, I brought her to Dublin, and used to ride her out two or three times a week, making little matches sometimes to trot,—and for a thoroughbred she was a clipper at trotting,— to trot a mile or so on the grass; another day to gallop the length of the Nine Acres opposite the Lodge; and then sometimes back her for a ten-pound note to jump the biggest furze-bush that could be found,—all of which she could do with ease, nobody thinking, all the while, that the cock-tailed pony was by Scroggins, out of a 'Lamp-lighter mare.' As every fellow that was beat to-day was sure to come back to-morrow with something better, either of his own or a friend's, I had matches booked for every day in the week; for I always made my little boy, that rode, win by half a neck or a nostril, and so we kept on day after day pocketing from ten to thirty pounds or thereabouts. It was mighty pleasant while it lasted, for besides winning the money, I had my own fun laughing at the spoonies that never could book my bets fast enough,—young infantry officers and the Junior Bar; they were for the most part mighty nice to look at, but very raw about racing. How long I might have gone on in this way, I cannot say; but one morning I fell in with a fat, elderly gentleman in shorts and gaiters, mounted on a dun cob pony that was very fidgety and hot-tempered, and appeared to give the rider a great deal of uneasiness.

" 'He's a spicy hack you're on, sir,' said I, 'and has a go in him, I'll be bound.'

" 'I rayther think he has,' said the old gentleman, half testily.

" 'And can trot a bit too?'

" 'Twelve Irish miles in fifty minutes, with my weight.' Here he looked down at a paunch like a sugar hogshead.

" 'Maybe he's not bad across a country,' said I, rather to humor the old fellow, who, I saw, was proud of his pony.

" 'I'd like to see his match, that's all.' Here he gave a rather contemptuous glance at my hack.

"Well, one word led to another, and it ended at last in our booking a match, with which one party was no less pleased than the other. It was this: each was to ride his own horse, starting from the school in the Park, round the Fifteen Acres, outside the Monument, and back to the start,—just one heat, about a mile and a half; the ground good, and only soft enough. In consideration, however, of his greater weight, I was to give odds, in the start; and as we could not well agree on how much, it was at length decided that he was to get away first, and I to follow as fast as I could, after drinking a pewter quart full of Guinness's double stout,—droll odds, you'll say; but it was the old fellow's own thought, and as the match was a *soft* one, I let him have his way.

"The next morning the Phœnix was crowded as if for a review. There were all the Dublin notorieties swarming in barouches and tilburies and outside jaunting-cars; smart clerks in the Post-office, mounted upon kicking devils from Dycer's and Lalouette's stables; attorneys' wives and daughters from York Street; and a stray doctor or so on a hack that looked as if it had been lectured on for the six winter months at the College of Surgeons. My antagonist was half an hour late, which time I occupied in booking bets on every side of me,—offering odds of ten, fifteen, and at last, to tempt the people, twenty-five to one against the dun. At last the fat gentleman came up on a jaunting-car, followed by a groom leading the cob. I wish you had heard the cheer that greeted him on his arrival, for it appeared he was a well-known character in town, and much in favor with the mob. When he got off the car he bundled into a tent, followed by a few of his friends, where they remained for about five minutes, at the end of which he came out in full racing costume,—blue and yellow-striped jacket, blue cap, and leathers,—looking as funny a figure as ever you set eyes upon. I now thought it time to throw off my white surtout and show out in pink-and-orange,—the colors I had been winning in for two months past. While some of the party were sent on to station themselves at different places round the Fifteen Acres, to mark out the course, my fat friend was assisted into his saddle, and gave a short preliminary gallop of a hundred yards or so that set us all a laughing. The odds were now fifty to one in my favor, and I gave them wherever I could find takers. 'With you, sir, if you please, in pounds, and the gentleman in the red whiskers too, if he likes,—very well, in half-sovereigns, if you prefer it.' So I went on, betting on every side, till the bell rang to mount. As I knew I had plenty of time to spare, I took little notice, and merely giving a look to my girths, I continued leisurely booking my bets. At last the time came, and at the word 'Away!' off went the fat gentleman on the dun at a spluttering gallop that flung the mud on every side of us, and once more threw us all a laughing. I waited patiently till he got near the upper end of the park, taking bets every minute; now that he was away, every one offered to wager. At last, when I had let him get nearly half round, and found no more money could be had, I called out to his friends for the porter, and throwing myself into the saddle, gathered up the reins in my hand. The crowd fell back on each side, while from the tent I have already mentioned, out came a thin fellow with one eye, with a pewter quart in his hand. He lifted it up towards me, and I took it; but what was my fright to find that the porter was boiling, and the vessel so hot I could barely hold it. I endeavored to drink, however; the first mouthful took all the skin off my lips and tongue, the second half choked, and the third nearly threw me into an apoplectic fit, the mob cheering all the time like devils. Meantime the old fellow had reached the furze, and was going along like fun. Again I tried the porter, and a fit of coughing came on which lasted five minutes. The pewter was so hot that the edge of the quart took away a piece

of my mouth at every effort. I ventured once more, and with
the desperation of a madman I threw down the hot liquid to
its last drop. My head reeled, my eyes glared, and my brain
was on fire. I thought I beheld fifty fat gentlemen riding on
every side of me, and all the sky raining jackets in blue
and yellow. Half mechanically I took the reins and put spurs
to my horse; but before I got well away, a loud cheer from
the crowd assailed me. I turned, and saw the dun coming
in at a floundering gallop, covered with foam, and so dead
blown that neither himself nor the rider could have got twenty
yards farther. The race was, however, won. My odds were
lost to every man on the field, and, worse than all, I was so
laughed at that I could not venture out in the streets without
hearing allusions to my misfortune; for a certain friend of
mine, one Tom O'Flaherty—"

"Tom, of the 11th Light Dragoons?"

"The same; you know Tom, then? Maybe you have heard
him mention me,—Maurice Malone?"

"Not Mr. Malone, of Fort Peak?"

"Bad luck to him! I am as well known in connection with
Fort Peak as the Duke is with Waterloo. There is not a part
of the globe where he has not told that confounded story!"

As my readers may not possibly be all numbered in Mr.
O'Flaherty's acquaintance, I shall venture to give the anecdote which Mr. Malone accounted to be so widely circulated.

CHAPTER XLVII.

AN ADVENTURE IN CANADA.

TOWARDS the close of the last war with America a
small detachment of military occupied the little block-
house of Fort Peak, which, about eight miles from the Falls
of Niagara, formed the last outpost on the frontier. The fort,
in itself inconsiderable, was only of importance as commanding a part of the river where it was practicable to ford, and
where the easy ascent of the bank offered a safe situation for

the enemy to cross over whenever they felt disposed to carry the war into our territory.

There having been, however, no threat of invasion in this quarter, and the natural strength of the position being considerable, a mere handful of men, with two subaltern officers, were allotted for this duty,—such being conceived ample to maintain it till the arrival of succor from headquarters, then at Little York, on the opposite side of the lake. The officers of this party were our old acquaintance Tom O'Flaherty and our newly made one, Maurice Malone.

Whatever may be the merits of commanding officers, one virtue they certainly can lay small claim to; namely, any insight into character, or at least any regard for the knowledge. Seldom are two men sent off on detachment duty to some remote quarter, to associate daily and hourly for months together, that they are not, by some happy chance, the very people who never, as the phrase is, "took to each other" in their lives. The gray-headed, weather-beaten, disappointed "Peninsular" is coupled with the essenced and dandified Adonis of the corps; the man of literary tastes and cultivated pursuits with the empty-headed, ill-formed youth fresh from Harrow or Westminster. This case offered no exception to the rule; for though there were few men possessed of more assimilating powers than O'Flaherty, yet certainly his companion did put the faculty to the test, for anything more unlike him there never existed. Tom, all good-humor and high spirits, making the best of everything, never nonplussed, never taken aback, perfectly at home, whether flirting with a Lady Charlotte in her drawing-room, or crossing a grouse-mountain in the Highlands, sufficiently well read to talk on any ordinary topic, and always ready-witted enough to seem more so; a thorough sportsman, whether showing forth in his "pink" at Melton, whipping a trout-stream in Wales, or filling a country-house with black-cock and moor-fowl; an unexceptionable judge of all the good things in life, from a pretty ankle to a well-hung tilbury,—from the odds at hazard to the "Comet vintage." Such, in brief, was Tom. Now, his *confrère* was none of these; he had been drafted from the Galway militia to the line for some election services rendered by his family to the

Government candidate; was of a saturnine and discontented habit, always miserable about some trifle or other, and never at rest till he had drowned his sorrows in Jamaica rum, which, since the regiment was abroad, he had copiously used as a substitute for whiskey. To such an extent had this passion gained upon him that a corporal's guard was always in attendance whenever he dined out, to convey him home to the barracks.

The wearisome monotony of a close garrison, with so un-genial a companion, would have damped any man's spirits but O'Flaherty's. He, however, upon this, as other occasions in life, rallied himself to make the best of it; and by short excursions within certain prescribed limits along the river side, contrived to shoot and fish enough to get through the day and improve the meagre fare of his mess-table. Malone never appeared before dinner,—his late sittings at night re-quiring all the following day to recruit him from a new attack upon the rum-bottle.

Now, although his seeing so little of his brother officer was anything but unpleasant to O'Flaherty, yet the *ennui* of such a life was gradually wearing him, and all his wits were put in requisition to furnish occupation for his time. Never a day passed without his praying ardently for an attack from the enemy; any alternative, any reverse, had been a blessing compared with his present life. No such spirit, however, seemed to animate the Yankee troops; not a soldier was to be seen for miles around, and every straggler that passed the Fort concurred in saying that the Americans were not within four days' march of the frontier.

Weeks passed over, and the same state of things remain-ing unchanged, O'Flaherty gradually relaxed some of his strictness as to duty; small foraging parties of three and four being daily permitted to leave the Fort for a few hours, to which they usually returned laden with wild turkeys and fish, both being found in great abundance near them.

Such was the life of the little garrison for two or three long summer months, each day so resembling its fellow that no difference could be found.

As to how the war was faring, or what the aspect of af-fairs might be, they absolutely knew nothing. Newspapers never reached them; and whether from having so much occupation at headquarters, or that the difficulty of sending letters prevented, their friends never wrote a line; and thus they jogged on a very vegetable existence, till thought at last was stagnating in their brains, and O'Flaherty half envied his companion's resource in the spirit-flask.

Such was the state of affairs at the Fort, when one evening O'Flaherty appeared to pace the little rampart that looked towards Lake Ontario, with an appearance of anxiety and impatience strangely at variance with his daily phlegmatic look. It seemed that the corporal's party he had despatched that morning to forage near the Falls had not returned, and already were four hours later than their time away.

Every imaginable mode of accounting for their absence suggested itself to his mind. Sometimes he feared that they had been attacked by the Indian hunters, who were far from favorably disposed towards their poaching neighbors. Then, again, it might be merely that they had missed their track in the forest; or could it be that they had ventured to reach Goat Island in a canoe, and had been carried down the rapids? Such were the torturing doubts that passed, as some shrill squirrel or hoarse night-owl pierced the air with a cry, and then all was silent again. While thus the hours went slowly by, his attention was attracted by a bright light in the sky. It appeared as if part of the heavens were reflecting some strong glare from beneath, for as he looked, the light, at first pale and colorless, gradually deepened into a rich mellow hue, and at length, through the murky blackness of the night, a strong, clear current of flame rose steadily upwards from the earth and pointed towards the sky. From the direction, it must have been either at the Falls or immediately near them; and now the horrible conviction flashed upon his mind that the party had been waylaid by the Indians, who were, as is their custom, making a war-feast over their victims. ·

Not an instant was to be lost. The little garrison beat to arms; and as the men fell in, O'Flaherty cast his eyes around, while he selected a few brave fellows to accompany him. Scarcely had the men fallen out from the ranks, when the sentinel at the gate was challenged by a well-known voice, and in a moment more the corporal of the foraging party was among them. Fatigue and exhaustion had so overcome him that for some minutes he was speechless. At length he recovered sufficiently to give the following brief account:—

The little party, having obtained their supply of venison above Queenston, were returning to the Fort, when they suddenly came upon a track of feet, and little experience in forest life soon proved that some new arrivals had reached the hunting-grounds; for on examining them closely, they proved neither to be Indian tracks, nor yet those made by the shoes of the Fort party. Proceeding with caution to track them backwards for three or four miles, they reached the bank of the Niagara River above the whirlpools, where the crossing is most easily effected from the American side. The mystery was at once explained,—it was a surprise party of the Yankees, sent to attack Fort Peak; and now the only thing to be done was to hasten back immediately to their friends and prepare for their reception.

With this intent they took the river path, as the shortest, but had not proceeded far when their fears were confirmed; for in a little embayment of the bank they perceived a party of twenty blue coats, who, with their arms piled, were lying around as if waiting for the hour of attack. The sight of this party added greatly to their alarm, for they now perceived that the Americans had divided their force, —the foot-tracks first seen being evidently those of another division. As the corporal and his few men continued, from the low and thick brushwood, to make their reconnoissance of the enemy, they observed with delight that they were not regulars, but a militia force. With this one animating thought they again, with noiseless step, regained the forest and proceeded upon their way. Scarcely, however, had they marched a mile, when the sound of voices and loud laughter apprised them that another party was near, which, as well as they could observe in the increasing gloom, was still larger than the former. They were now obliged to make a considerable circuit and advance still deeper into the forest, their anxiety hourly increasing lest the enemy should reach the Fort before themselves. In this dilemma it was resolved that the party should separate, the corporal determining to proceed alone by the river bank, while the others, by a *détour* of some miles, should endeavor to learn the force of the Yankees, and as far as they could, their mode of attack. From that instant the corporal knew no more; for after two hours' weary exertion he reached the Fort, which, had it been but another mile distant, his strength had not held out for him to attain.

However gladly poor O'Flaherty might have hailed such information under other circumstances, now it came like a thunderbolt upon him. Six of his small force were away, —perhaps ere this made prisoners by the enemy,—the Yankees, as well as he could judge, were a numerous party, and he himself totally without a single adviser; for Malone had dined, and was, therefore, by this time in that pleasing state of indifference in which he could only recognize an enemy in the man that did not send round the decanter.

In the half-indulged hope that his state might permit some faint exercise of the reasoning faculty, O'Flaherty walked towards the small den they had designated as the mess-room, in search of his brother-officer.

As he entered the apartment, little disposed as he felt to mirth at such moment, the tableau before him was too ridiculous not to laugh at. At one side of the fireplace sat Malone, his face florid with drinking, and his eyeballs projecting. Upon his head was a small Indian skull-cap with two peacock's feathers, 'and a piece of scarlet cloth which hung down behind. In one hand he held a smoking goblet of rum-punch, and in the other a long Indian Chibook pipe. Opposite to him, but squatted upon the floor, reposed a Red Indian that lived in the Fort as a guide, equally drunk, but preserving, even in his liquor, an impassive, grave aspect, strangely contrasting with the high excitement of Malone's face. The red man wore Malone's uniform coat, which he had put on back foremost,—his head-dress having, in all probability, been exchanged for it, as an amicable courtesy between the parties. There they sat, looking fixedly at each other; neither spoke, nor even smiled,—the rum-bottle, which at brief intervals passed from one to the other, maintained a friendly intercourse that each was content with.

To the hearty fit of laughing of O'Flaherty, Malone replied by a look of drunken defiance, and then nodded to his red friend, who returned the courtesy. As poor Tom left the room he saw that nothing was to be hoped for in this quarter, and determined to beat the garrison to arms without any further delay. Scarcely had he closed the door behind him, when a sudden thought flashed through his brain. He hesitated, walked forward a few paces, stopped again, and calling out to the corporal, said,—

"You are certain they were militia?"

"Yes, sir; quite sure."

"Then, by Jove, I have it," cried O'Flaherty. "If they should turn out to be the Buffalo Fencibles, we may get through this scrape better than I hoped for."

"I believe you are right, sir; for I heard one of the men as I passed observe, 'What will they say in Buffalo when it's over?'"

"Send Mathers here, corporal; and do you order four rank and file, with side-arms, to be in readiness immediately."

"Mathers, you have heard the news," said O'Flaherty, as the sergeant entered. "Can the Fort hold out against such a force as Jackson reports? You doubt,—well, so do I; so let's see what's to be done. Can you remember, was it not the Buffalo militia that were so tremendously thrashed by the Delawares last autumn?"

"Yes, sir; they chased them for two days and nights, and had they not reached the town of Buffalo, the Delawares would not have left a scalp in the regiment."

"Can you recollect the chief's name,—it was Carran—something, eh?"

"Caudan-dacwagae."

"Exactly. Where is he supposed to be now?"

"Up in Detroit, sir, they say, but no one knows; those fellows are here to-day, and there to-morrow."

"Well then, sergeant, here's my plan." Saying these words, O'Flaherty proceeded to walk towards his quarters, accompanied by the sergeant, with whom he conversed for some time eagerly; occasionally replying, as it appeared, to objections, and offering explanations as the other seemed to require them. The colloquy lasted half an hour; and although the veteran sergeant seemed difficult of conviction, it ended by his saying, as he left the room,—

419

"Well, sir, as you say, it can only come to hard knocks at worst. Here goes. I'll send off the scout party to make the fires and choose the men for the out-pickets, for no time is to be lost."

In about an hour's time from the scene I have mentioned, a number of militia officers, of different grades, were seated round a bivouac fire upon the bank of the Niagara River. The conversation seemed of an angry nature, for the voices of the speakers were loud and irascible, and their gestures evidenced a state of high excitement.

"I see," said one, who seemed the superior of the party,— "I see well where this will end. We shall have another Queenston affair, as we had last fall with the Delawares."

"I only say," replied another, "that if you wish our men to stand fire to-morrow morning, the less you remind them of the Delawares the better. What is that noise? Is not that a drum beating?"

The party at these words sprang to their legs, and stood in an attitude of listening for some seconds.

"Who goes there?" sang out a sentinel from his post; and then, after a moment's delay, added: "Pass flag of truce to Major Brown's quarters."

Scarcely were the words spoken, when three officers in scarlet, preceded by a drummer with a white flag, stood before the American party.

"To whom may I address myself?" said one of the British, —who, I may inform my reader, *en passant,* was no other than O'Flaherty,—"to whom may I address myself as the officer in command?"

"I am Major Brown," said a short, plethoric little man in a blue uniform and round hat. "And who are you?"

"Major O'Flaherty, of his Majesty's Fifth Foot," said Tom, with a very sonorous emphasis on each word, "the bearer of a flag of truce and an amicable proposition from Major-General Allen, commanding the garrison of Fort Peak."

The Americans, who were evidently taken by surprise at their intentions of attack being known, were silent, while he continued:—

"Gentlemen, it may appear somewhat strange that a garrison possessing the natural strength of a powerful position, supplied with abundant ammunition and every muniment of war, should despatch a flag of truce on the eve of an attack in preference to waiting for the moment when a sharp and well-prepared reception might best attest its vigilance and discipline. But the reasons for this step are soon explained. In the first place, you intend a surprise. We have been long aware of your projected attack. Our spies have tracked you from your crossing the river above the whirlpool to your present position. Every man of your party is numbered by us, and, what is still more, numbered by our allies; yes, gentlemen, I must repeat it, 'allies,' though as a Briton I blush at the word. Shame and disgrace forever be that man's portion who first associated the honorable usages of war with the atrocious and bloody cruelties of the savage. Yet so it is; the Delawares of the hills"—here the Yankees exchanged very peculiar looks—"have this morning arrived at Fort Peak with orders to ravage the whole of your frontier, from Fort George to Lake Erie. They brought us the information of your approach, and their chief is, while I speak, making an infamous proposition, by which a price is to be paid for every scalp he produces in the morning. Now, as the General cannot refuse to co-operate with the savages without compromising himself with the commander-in-chief, neither can he accept of such assistance without some pangs of conscience, he has taken the only course open to him; he has despatched myself and my brother officers here"—O'Flaherty glanced at two privates dressed up in his regimentals—"to offer you terms—"

O'Flaherty paused when he arrived thus far, expecting that the opposite party would make some reply; but they continued silent,—when suddenly, from the dense forest, there rang forth a wild and savage yell that rose and fell several times, like the pibroch of the Highlander, and ended at last in a loud whoop that was echoed and re-echoed again and again for several seconds after.

"Hark!" said O'Flaherty, with an accent of horror. "Hark! the war-cry of the Delawares! The savages are eager for their prey. May it yet be time enough to rescue you from such a fate! Time presses. Our terms are these,—as they do not admit of discussion, and must be at once accepted or rejected, to your own ear alone can I impart them."

Saying which, he took Major Brown aside, and walking apart from the others, led him, by slow steps, into the forest. While O'Flaherty continued to dilate upon the atrocities of Indian war and the revengeful character of the savages, he contrived to be always advancing towards the river side, till at length the glare of a fire was perceptible through the gloom. Major Brown stopped suddenly, and pointed in the direction of the flame.

"It is the Indian picket," said O'Flaherty, calmly; "and as the facts I have been detailing may be more palpable to your mind, you shall see them with your own eyes. Yes, I repeat it, you shall, through the cover of this brushwood, see Caudandacwagae himself; for he is with them in person."

As O'Flaherty said this, he led Major Brown, now speechless with terror, behind a massive cork-tree, from which spot they could look down upon the river side, where in a small creek sat five or six persons in blankets and scarlet headdresses, their faces streaked with patches of yellow and red paint, to which the glare of the fire lent fresh horror. In the midst sat one whose violent gestures and savage cries gave him the very appearance of a demon as he resisted with all his might the efforts of the others to restrain him, shouting like a maniac all the while, and struggling to rise.

"It is the chief," said O'Flaherty; "he will wait no longer. We have bribed the others to keep him quiet, if possible, a little time; but I see they cannot succeed."

A loud yell of triumph from below interrupted Tom's speech, the infuriated savage—who was no other than Mr. Malone—having obtained the rum-bottle, for which he was fighting with all his might; his temper not being improved in the struggle by occasional admonitions from the red end of a cigar applied to his naked skin by the other Indians, who were his own solidiers acting under O'Flaherty's orders.

"Now," said Tom, "that you have convinced yourself, and can satisfy your brother officers, will you take your chance, or will you accept the honorable terms of the General,—pile your arms, and retreat beyond the river before daybreak? Your muskets and ammunition will offer a bribe to the cupidity of the savage and delay his pursuit till you can reach some place of safety."

Major Brown heard the proposal in silence, and at last determined upon consulting his brother officers.

"I have outstayed my time," said O'Flaherty. "But stop: the lives of so many are at stake, I consent." Saying which, they walked on without speaking, till they arrived where the others were standing around the watch-fire.

As Brown retired to consult with the officers, Tom heard with pleasure how much *his* two companions had worked upon the Yankees' fears during his absence, by details of the vindictive feelings of the Delawares, and their vows to annihilate the Buffalo militia.

Before five minutes they had decided. Upon a solemn pledge from O'Flaherty that the terms of the compact were to be observed as he stated them, they agreed to march with their arms to the ford, where, having piled them, they were to cross over and make the best of their way home.

By sunrise the next morning all that remained of the threatened attack on Fort Peak were the smouldering ashes of some wood fires, eighty muskets piled in the fort, and the yellow ochre and red stripes that still adorned the countenance of the late Indian chief, but now snoring Lieutenant—Maurice Malone.

CHAPTER XLVIII.

THE COURIER'S PASSPORT.

A SECOND night succeeded to the long, dreary day of the diligence, and the only agreeable reflection arose in the feeling that every mile travelled was diminishing the chance of pursuit and removing me still farther from that scene of trouble and annoyance that was soon to furnish gossip for Paris under the title of the *"Affaire O'Leary."*

How *he* was ever to extricate himself from the numerous and embarrassing difficulties gave me, I confess, less uneasiness than the uncertainty of my own fortunes. Luck seemed ever to befriend *him,*—*me* it had always accompanied far enough through life to make its subsequent desertion more painful. How far I should blame myself for this, I stopped not to consider, but brooded over the fact in a melancholy and discontented mood. The one thought uppermost in my mind was: How will Lady Jane receive me? Am I forgotten, or am I only remembered as the subject of that unlucky mistake when, under the guise of an elder son, I was fêted and made much of? What pretensions I had, without fortune, rank, influence, or even expectations of any kind, to seek the hand of the most beautiful girl of the day, with the largest fortune as her dowry, I dared not ask myself; the reply would have dashed all my hopes, and my pursuit would have at once been abandoned. "Tell the people you are an excellent preacher," was the advice of an old and learned divine to a younger and less-experienced one,—"tell them so every morning and every noon and every evening, and at last they will begin to believe it." "So," thought I, "I shall impress upon the Callonbys that I am a most unexceptionable *parti*. Upon every occasion they shall hear it, as they open their newspapers at breakfast, as they sip their soup at luncheon, as they adjust their napkin at dinner, as they chat over their wine at night. My influence in the house shall be unbounded, my pleasures consulted, my dislikes remembered. The people in favor with me shall dine there three times a week; those less fortunate shall be put into schedule B. My opinions on all subjects shall be a law, whether I pronounce upon politics or discuss a dinner; and all this I shall accomplish by a successful flattery of my lady, a little bullying of my lord, a devoted attention to the youngest sister, a special cultivation of Kilkee, and a very *prononcé* neglect of Lady Jane." These were my half-waking thoughts as the heavy diligence rumbled over the *pavé* into Nancy; and I was aroused by the door being suddenly jerked open and a bronzed face, with a black beard and mustache, being thrust in amongst us.

"Your passports, Messieurs," as the lantern was held up in succession across our faces, and we handed forth our crumpled and worn papers to the official.

The night was stormy and dark; gusts of wind sweeping along, bearing with them the tail of some thunder-cloud, mingled their sounds with a falling tile from the roofs or a broken chimney-pot. The officer in vain endeavored to hold open the passports while he inscribed his name; and just as the last scrawl was completed, the lantern went out. Muttering a heavy curse upon the weather, he thrust them in upon us *en masse,* and banging the door to, called out to the conductor, *"En route."*

Again we rumbled on, and ere we cleared the last lamps of the town, the whole party were once more sunk in sleep, save myself. Hour after hour rolled by, the rain pattering upon the roof, and the heavy plash of the horses' feet contributing their mournful sounds to the melancholy that was stealing over me. At length we drew up at the door of a little inn, and by the noise and bustle without I perceived there was a change of horses. Anxious to stretch my legs, and relieve, if even for a moment, the wearisome monotony of the night, I got out and strode into the little parlor of the inn. There was a cheerful fire in an open stove, beside which stood a portly figure in a sheepskin *bunta* and a cloth travelling-cap with a gold band, his legs cased in high Russia-leather boots, —all evident signs of the profession of the wearer, had even his haste at supper not bespoke the fact that he was a government courier.

"You had better make haste with the horses, Antoine, if you don't wish the postmaster to hear of it," said he as I entered, his mouth filled with pie-crust and *vin de Beaune* as he spoke.

A lumbering peasant, with a blouse, sabots, and a striped night-cap, replied in some unknown patois, when the courier again said,—

"Well, then, take the diligence-horses; I must get on at all events,—they are not so hurried, I'll be bound. Besides, it will save the *gendarmes* some miles of a ride if they overtake them here."

"Have we another *visé* of our passports here, then?" said I, addressing the courier; "for we have already been examined at Nancy."

"Not exactly a *visé,*" said the courier, eying me most suspiciously as he spoke, and then continuing to eat with his former voracity.

"Then what, may I ask, have we to do with the *gendarmes?"*

"It is a search," said the courier, gruffly, and with the air of one who desired no further questioning.

I immediately ordered a bottle of Burgundy, and filling a large goblet before him, said, with much respect,—

"*A votre bon voyage, Monsieur le Courier.*"

To this he at once replied by taking off his cap and bowing politely as he drank off the wine.

"Have we any runaway felon or stray galley slave among us," said I, laughingly, "that they are going to search us?"

"No, Monsieur," said the courier; "but there has been a government order to arrest a person on this road connected with the dreadful Polish plot that has just *éclaté* at Paris. I passed a vidette of cavalry at Nancy, and they will be up here in half an hour."

"A Polish plot! Why, I left Paris only two days ago and never heard of it."

"*C'est bien possible, Monsieur.* Perhaps, after all, it may only be an affair of the police; but they have certainly arrested one prisoner at Meurice's, charged with this, as well as the attempt to rob Frascati and murder the croupier."

"Alas!" said I, with a half-suppressed groan, "it is too true; that infernal fellow O'Leary has ruined me, and I shall be brought back to Paris, and only taken from prison to meet the open shame and disgrace of a public trial."

What was to be done? Every moment was precious. I walked to the door to conceal my agitation. All was dark and gloomy. The thought of escape was my only one; but how to accomplish it? Every stir without suggested to my anxious mind the approaching tread of horses; every rattle of the harness seemed like the clink of accoutrements.

While I yet hesitated, I felt that my fate was in the balance. Concealment where I was, was impossible; there were no means of obtaining horses to proceed. My last only hope then rested in the courier,—he perhaps might be bribed to assist me at this juncture. Still, his impression as to the enormity of the crime imputed, might deter him; and there was no time for explanation, if even he would listen to it. I returned to the room; he had finished his meal, and was now engaged in all the preparations for encountering a wet and dreary night. I hesitated; my fears that if he should refuse

my offers, all chance of my escape was gone, deterred me for
a moment. At length, as he wound a large woollen shawl
around his throat and seemed to have completed his costume,
I summoned nerve for the effort, and with as much boldness
in my manner as I could muster, said,—

"Monsieur le Courier, one word with you." I here closed
the door, and continued: "My fortunes, my whole prospects
in life depend upon my reaching Strasburg by to-morrow
night. You alone can be the means of my doing so. Is there
any price you can mention for which you will render me this
service? If so, name it."

"So, then, Monsieur," said the courier, slowly, "so, then,
you are the—"

"You have guessed it," said I, interrupting. "Do you accept my proposal?"

"It is impossible," said he, "utterly impossible; for even
should I be disposed to run the risk on my own account, it
would avail you nothing. The first town we entered, your
passport would be demanded, and not being *viséd* by the minister to travel *en courier,* you would at once be detained and
arrested."

"Then am I lost," said I, throwing myself upon a chair;
at the same instant my passport, which I carried in my breast-
pocket, fell out at the feet of the courier. He lifted it and
opened it leisurely. So engrossed was I by my misfortunes
that for some minutes I did not perceive that, as he continued
to read the passport, he smiled from time to time, till at length
a hearty fit of laughing awoke me from my abstraction. My
first impulse was to seize him by the throat; controlling my
temper, however, with an effort, I said,—

"And pray, Monsieur, may I ask in what manner the position I stand in at this moment affords you so much amusement? Is there anything so particularly droll, anything so
excessively ludicrous, in my situation; or what particular gift
do you possess that shall prevent me from throwing you out
of the window?"

"*Mais, Monsieur,*" said he, half stifled with laughter, "do
you know the blunder I fell into? It is really too good. Could
you only guess whom I took you for, you would laugh too."

Here he became so overcome with merriment that he was

obliged to sit down, which he did opposite to me, and actually shook with laughter.

"When this comedy is over," thought I, "we may begin to understand each other." Seeing no prospect of this, I became at length impatient, and jumping on my legs, said,—

"Enough, sir, quite enough of this foolery. Believe me, you have every reason to be thankful that my present embarrassment should so far engross me that I cannot afford time to give you a thrashing."

"*Pardon, mille pardons,*" said he humbly; "but you will, I am sure, forgive me when I tell you that I was stupid enough to mistake you for the fugitive Englishman whom the *gendarmes* are in pursuit of. How good, eh?"

"Oh! devilish good; but what do you mean?"

"Why, the fellow that caused the attack at Frascati and all that, and—"

"Yes—well, eh? Did you think I was he?"

"To be sure I did, till I saw your passport."

"Till you saw my passport! Why, what on earth can he mean?" thought I. "No, but," said I, half jestingly, "how could you make such a blunder?"

"Why, your confused manner, your impatience to get on, your hurried questions, all convinced me. In fact, I'd have wagered anything you were the Englishman."

"And what, in Heaven's name, does he think me now?" thought I, as I endeavored to join in the laugh so ludicrous a mistake occasioned.

"But we are delaying sadly," said the courier. "Are you ready?"

"Ready? Ready for what?"

"To go on with me, of course. Don't you wish to get early to Strasburg?"

"To be sure I do."

"Well, then, come along. But pray don't mind your luggage, for my *calèche* is loaded. Your instruments can come in the diligence."

"My instruments in the diligence! He's mad, that's flat."

"How they will laugh at Strasburg at my mistake!"

"That they will," thought I. "The only doubt is, will *you* join in the merriment?"

So saying, I followed the courier to the door, jumped into his *calèche,* and in another moment was hurrying over the *pavé* at a pace that defied pursuit and promised soon to make up for all our late delay. Scarcely was the fur-lined apron of the *calèche* buttoned around me, and the German blinds let down, when I set to work to think over the circumstance that had just befallen me. As I had never examined my passport from the moment Trevanion handed it to me at Paris, I knew nothing of its contents; therefore, as to what impression it might convey of me, I was totally ignorant. To ask the courier for it now might excite suspicion; so that I was totally at sea how to account for his sudden change in my favor, or in what precise capacity I was travelling beside him. Once, and once only, the thought of treachery occurred to me. "Is he about to hand me over to the *gendarmes?* and are we now only retracing our steps towards Nancy? If so, Monsieur le Courier, whatever be *my* fate, *yours* is certainly an unenviable one." My reflections on this head were soon broken in upon, for my companion again returned to the subject of his "singular error," and assured me that he was as near as possible leaving me behind, under the mistaken impression of my being "myself," and informed me that all Strasburg would be delighted to see me,—which latter piece of news was only the more flattering that I knew no one there, nor had ever been in that city in my life; and after about an hour's mystification as to my tastes, habits, and pursuits, he fell fast asleep, leaving me to solve the difficult problem as to whether I was not somebody else, or the only alternative, whether travelling *en courier* might not be prescribed by physicians as a mode of treating insane patients.

CHAPTER XLIX.

A NIGHT IN STRASBURG.

WITH the dawn of day my miseries recommenced; for after letting down the sash and venting some very fervent imprecations upon the postilion for not going faster than his horses were able, the courier once more recurred to his last night's blunder, and proceeded very leisurely to catechize me as to my probable stay at Strasburg, whither I should go from thence, and so on. As I was still in doubt what or whom he took me for, I answered with the greatest circumspection,—watching, the while, for any clew that might lead me to a discovery of myself. Thus occasionally evading all pushing and home queries, and sometimes, when hard pressed, feigning drowsiness, I passed the long and anxious day, the fear of being overtaken ever mingling with the thoughts that some unlucky admission of mine might discover my real character to the courier, who at any post-station might hand me over to the authorities. "Could I only guess at the part I am performing," thought I, "I might manage to keep up the illusion;" but my attention was so entirely engrossed by fencing off all his thrusts that I could find out nothing. At last, as night drew near, the thought that we were approaching Strasburg rallied my spirits, suggesting an escape from all pursuit, as well as the welcome prospect of getting rid of my present torturer, who, whenever I awoke from a doze, reverted to our singular meeting with a pertinacity that absolutely seemed like malice.

"As I am aware that this is your first visit to Strasburg," said the courier, "perhaps I can be of service to you in recommending a hotel. Put up, I advise you, at the 'Bear,'—a capital hotel, and not ten minutes' distance from the theatre."

I thanked him for the counsel; and rejoicing in the fact that my prototype, whoever he might be, was unknown in the city, began to feel some little hope of getting through this scrape as I had done so many others.

"They have been keeping the 'Huguenots' for your arrival, and all Strasburg is impatient for your coming."

"Indeed!" said I, mumbling something meant to be modest. "Who the devil am I, then, to cause all this *fracas?* Heaven grant, not the new 'prefect,' or the commander of the forces."

"I am told the 'Zauberflöte' is your favorite opera?"

"I can't say that I ever heard it,—that is, I mean that I could say—well got up."

Here I floundered on, having so far forgot myself as to endanger everything.

"How very unfortunate! Well, I hope you will not long have as much to say. Meanwhile, here we are,—this is the 'Bear.' "

We rattled into the ample *porte-cochère* of a vast hotel, the postilion cracking his enormous whip, and bells ringing on every side, as if the Crown Prince of Russia had been the arrival, and not a poor sub in the 4—th.

The courier jumped out, and running up to the landlord, whispered a few words in his ear, to which the other answered by a deep *"Ah, vraiment!"* and then saluted me with an obsequiousness that made my flesh quake.

"I shall make *mes hommages* in the morning," said the courier, as he drove off at full speed to deliver his despatches, and left me to my own devices to perform a character without even being able to guess what it might be. My passport, too, the only thing that could throw any light upon the affair, he had taken along with him, promising to have it *viséd,* and save me any trouble.

Of all my difficulties and puzzling situations in life, this was certainly the worst; for however often my lot had been to personate another, yet hitherto I had had the good fortune to be aware of what and whom I was performing. Now I might be anybody; from Marshal Soult to Monsieur Scribe; one thing only was certain,—I must be a "celebrity." The confounded pains and trouble they were taking to receive me attested that fact, and left me to the pleasing reflection that my detection, should it take place, would be sure of attracting a very general publicity. Having ordered my supper from the landlord with a certain air of reserve sufficient to prevent even an Alsace host from obtruding any questions upon me, I took my opportunity to stroll from the inn down to the river-side. There lay the broad, rapid Rhine, separating me, by how narrow a limit, from that land where, if I once arrived, my safety was certain. Never did that great boundary of nations strike me so forcibly as now when my own petty interests and fortunes were at stake. Night was fast settling upon the low, flat banks of the stream, and nothing stirred save the ceaseless ripple of the river. One fishing bark alone was on the water. I hailed the solitary tenant of it, and after some little parley induced him to ferry me over. This, however, could only be done when the night was farther advanced,—it being against the law to cross the river except at certain hours and between two established points, where officers of the revenue were stationed. The fisherman was easily bribed, however, to evade the regulation, and only bargained that I should meet him on the bank before day-break. Having settled this point to my satisfaction, I returned to my hotel in better spirits; and with a Strasburg *pâté* and a flask of Niersteiner, drank to my speedy deliverance.

How to consume the long, dreary hours between this time and that of my departure I knew not, for though greatly fatigued, I felt that sleep was impossible; the usual resource of a gossip with the host was equally out of the question; and all that remained was the theatre, which I happily remembered was not far from the hotel.

It was an opera-night, and the house was crowded to excess; but with some little management, I obtained a place in a box near the stage. The piece was "Les Francs Maçons," which was certainly admirably supported, and drew down from the audience—no mean one as judges of music—the loudest thunders of applause. As for me, the house was as great a curiosity as the opera. The novel spectacle of some hundred people relishing and appreciating the highest order of musical genius, was something totally new and surprising to me. The curtain at length fell upon the fifth act; and now the deafening roar of acclamation was tremendous; and amid a perfect shout of enthusiasm, the manager announced the opera for the ensuing evening. Scarcely had this subsided when a buzz ran through the house, at first subdued, but gradually getting louder, extending from the boxes to the balcony, from the balcony to the parterre, and finally even to the galleries. Groups of people stood upon the benches and looked fixedly in one part of the house, then changed and regarded as eagerly the other.

"What can this mean?" thought I. "Is the theatre on fire? Something surely has gone wrong!"

In this conviction, with the contagious spirit of curiosity, I mounted upon a seat and looked about me on every side; but unable still to catch the object which seemed to attract the rest, as I was about to resume my place my eyes fell upon a well-known face, which in an instant I remembered was that of my late fellow-traveller, the courier. Anxious to avoid his recognition, I attempted to get down at once; but before I could accomplish it, the wretch had perceived and recognized me, and I saw him even, with a gesture of delight, point me out to some friends beside him.

"Confound the fellow!" muttered I; "I must leave this at once, or I shall be involved in some trouble."

Scarcely was my resolve taken, when a new burst of voices arose from the pit, the words *"L'Auteur!"* mingling with loud cries for "Meyerbeer!" "Meyerbeer!" to appear. "So," thought I, "it seems the great composer is here. Oh, by Jove! I must have a peep at him before I go." So, leaning over the front rail of the box, I looked anxiously about to catch one hasty glimpse of one of the great men of his day and country. What was my surprise, however, to perceive that about two thousand eyes were firmly riveted upon the box I was seated in, while about half the number of tongues called out unceasingly, *"M. Meyerbeer! vive Meyerbeer! vive l'Auteur des Francs Maçons! vive les Francs Maçons!"* etc. Before I could turn to look for the hero of the scene, my legs were taken from under me, and I felt myself lifted by several strong men and held out in front of the box, while the whole audience, rising *en masse,* saluted me—yes, me, Harry Lorrequer—with a cheer that shook the building. Fearful of precipitating myself into the pit beneath if I made the least effort, and half wild with terror and amazement, I stared about like a maniac, while a beautiful young woman tripped along the edge of the box, supported by her companion's hand, and placed lightly upon my brow a chaplet of roses and laurel. Here the applause was like an earthquake.

"May the devil fly away with half of you!" was my grateful response to as full a cheer of applause as ever the walls of the house re-echoed to.

"On the stage, on the stage!" shouted that portion of the audience who, occupying the same side of the house as myself, preferred having a better view of me; and to the stage I was accordingly hurried, down a narrow stair, through a side scene, and over half the *corps de ballet,* who were waiting for their *entrée.* Kicking, plunging, buffeting like a madman, they

carried me to the "flats," when the manager led me forward
to the footlights, my wreath of flowers contrasting rather rue-
fully with my bruised cheeks and torn habiliments. Human
beings, God be praised! are only capable of certain efforts;
so that one half the audience were coughing their sides out,
while the other were hoarse as bull-frogs from their enthusiasm in less than five minutes.

"You'll have what my friend Rooney calls a *chronic bron-
chitis* for these three weeks," said I,—"that's one comfort,"
as I bowed my way back to the "practicable" door, through
which I made my exit, with the thousand faces of the parterre
shouting my name, or, as fancy dictated, that of one of *my*
operas. I retreated behind the scenes to encounter very nearly
as much, and at closer quarters too, as that lately sustained
before the audience. After an embrace of two minutes' duration from the manager, I ran the gauntlet from the prima
donna to the last triangle of the orchestra, who cut away
a back button of my coat as a souvenir. During all this, I
must confess, very little acting was needed on my part. They
were so perfectly contented with their self-deception that if
I had made an affidavit before the mayor,—if there be such
a functionary in such an insane town,—they would not have
believed me. Wearied and exhausted at length by all I had
gone through, I sat down upon a bench, and affecting to be
overcome by my feelings, concealed my face in my handkerchief. This was the first moment of relief I experienced since
my arrival; but it was not to last long, for the manager,
putting down his head close to my ear, whispered,—

"Monsieur Meyerbeer, I have a surprise for you such as
you have not had for some time, I venture to say."

"I defy you on this head," thought I. "If they make me
out King Solomon now, it will not amaze me."

"And when I tell you my secret," continued he, "you will
acknowledge I cannot be of a very jealous disposition. Madame Baptiste has just told me she knew you formerly, and
that she—that is, you—were, in fact—you understand—there
had been—so to say—a little something between you."

I groaned in spirit as I thought, "Now am I lost without
a chance of escape; the devil take her reminiscences!"

Lorrequer's début at Strasburg.

"I see," continued *le bon mari,* "you cannot guess of whom I speak; but when I tell you of Amélie Grandet, your memory will perhaps be better."

"Amélie Grandet!" said I, with a stage start; I need not say that I had never heard the name before,—"Amélie Grandet here?"

"Yes, that she is," said the manager, rubbing his hands; "and *my* wife too."

"Married! Amélie Grandet married! No, no, it is impossible; I cannot believe it. But were it true,—true, mark me,—for worlds would I not meet her."

"Comme il est drôle," said the manager, soliloquizing aloud; "for my wife takes it much easier, seeing they never met each other since they were fifteen."

"Ho, ho!" thought I, "the affair is not so bad either; time makes great changes in that space. And does she still remember me?" said I, in a very Romeo-in-the-garden voice.

"Why, so far as remembering the little boy that used to play with her in the orchard at her mother's cottage near Pirna, and with whom she used to go boating upon the Elbe, I believe the recollection is perfect. But come along; she insists upon seeing you, and is at this very moment waiting supper in our room for you."

"A thorough German she must be," thought I, "with her sympathies and her supper, her reminiscences and her Rhine wine, hunting in couples through her brain."

Summoning courage from the fact of our long absence from each other, I followed the manager through a wilderness of pavilions, forests, clouds, and cataracts, and at length arrived at a little door, at which he knocked gently.

"Come in," said a soft voice inside. We opened, and beheld a very beautiful young woman in Tyrolese costume,—she was to perform in the afterpiece,—her low bodice and short scarlet petticoat displaying the most perfect symmetry of form and roundness of proportion. She was dressing her hair before a low glass as we came in, and scarcely turned at our approach; but in an instant, as if some sudden thought struck her, she sprang fully round, and looking at me fixedly for above a minute,—a very trying one for me,—she glanced

435

at her husband, whose countenance plainly indicated that she was right, and calling out, *"C'est lui,—c'est bien lui!"* threw herself into my arms and sobbed convulsively.

"If this were to be the only fruits of my impersonation," thought I, "it is not so bad; but I am greatly afraid these good people will find out a wife and seven babies for me before morning."

Whether the manager thought that enough had been done for stage effect, I know not; but he gently disengaged the lovely Amélie and deposited her upon a sofa, to a place upon which she speedily motioned me by a look from a pair of very seducing blue eyes.

"François, mon cher, you must put off 'La Chaumière.' I can't play to-night."

"Put it off! But only think of the audience, *ma mie,*— they will pull down the house."

"C'est possible," said she carelessly. "If that give them any pleasure, I suppose they must be indulged; but I, too, must have a little of my own way. I shall not play!"

The tone this was said in—the look, the easy gesture of command, no less than the afflicted helplessness of the luckless husband—showed me that Amélie, however docile as a sweetheart, had certainly her own way as wife.

While *le cher François* then retired to make his proposition to the audience of substituting something for the "Chaumière," —"the sudden illness of Madame Baptiste having prevented her appearance,"—we began to renew our old acquaintance by a thousand inquiries into that long-past time when we were sweethearts and lovers.

"You remember me then so well?" said I.

"As of yesterday. You are much taller, and your eyes darker; but still there is something— You know, however, I have been expecting to see you these two days; and tell me frankly, how do you find me looking?"

"More beautiful, a thousand times more beautiful, than ever, —all save in one thing, Amélie—"

"And that is—"

"You are married."

"How you jest! But let us look back. Do you ever think of any of our old compacts?" Here she pulled a leaf from a rosebud in her bouquet and kissed it. "I wager you have forgotten *that*."

How I should have replied to this masonic sign, Heaven knows! But the manager fortunately entered, to assure us that the audience had kindly consented not to pull down the house, but to listen to a five-act tragedy instead, in which he had to perform the principal character. "So, then, don't wait supper, Amélie, but take care of Monsieur Meyerbeer till my return."

Thus once more were we left to our souvenirs, in which, whenever hard pushed myself, I regularly carried the war into the enemy's camp, by allusions to incidents which, I need not observe, had never occurred. After a thousand stories of our early loves, mingled with an occasional sigh over their fleeting character,—now indulging a soft retrospect of the once happy past, now moralizing on the future,—Amélie and I chatted away the hours till the conclusion of the tragedy.

By this time the hour was approaching for my departure; so, after a very tender leave-taking with my new friend and my old love, I left the theatre and walked slowly along to the river.

"So much for early associations," thought I; "and how much better pleased are we ever to paint the past according to our own fancy, than to remember it as it really was. Hence all the insufferable cant about happy infancy and 'the glorious schoolboy days,' which have generally no more foundation in fact than have the *châteaux en Espagne* we build up for the future. I wager that the real *amant d'enfance,* when he arrives, is not half so great a friend with the fair Amélie as his unworthy shadow. At the same time, I had just as soon that Lady Jane should have no 'early loves' to look back upon, except such as I have performed a character in."

The plash of oars near me broke my reflections, and the next moment found me skimming the rapid Rhine as I thought for the last time, "What will they say in Strasburg to-morrow? How will they account for the mysterious disappearance of M. Meyerbeer? Poor Amélie Grandet!" for so completely had the late incidents engrossed my attention that I had for the moment lost sight of the most singular event of all,— how I came to be mistaken for the illustrious composer.

CHAPTER L.

A SURPRISE.

IT was late upon the following day ere I awoke from the long, deep sleep that closed my labors in Strasburg. In the confusion of my waking thoughts I imagined myself still before a crowded and enthusiastic audience; the glare of the footlights, the crash of the orchestra, the shouts of *"L'Auteur!" "L'Auteur!"* were all before me, and so completely possessed me that as the waiter entered with hot water, I could not resist the impulse to pull off my nightcap with one hand, and press the other to my heart in the usual theatrical style of acknowledgments for a most flattering reception. The startled look of the poor fellow as he neared the door to escape, roused me from my hallucination and awakened me to the conviction that the suspicion of lunacy might be a still heavier infliction than the personation of M. Meyerbeer.

With thoughts of this nature I assumed my steadiest demeanor, ordered my breakfast in the most orthodox fashion, ate it like a man in his senses, and when I threw myself back in the wicker conveniency they call a *calèche,* and bid adieu to Kehl, the whole fraternity of the inn would have given me a certificate of sanity before any court in Europe.

"Now for Munich," said I, as we rattled along down the steep street of the little town,—"now for Munich, with all the speed that first of postmasters and slowest of men, the Prince of Tour and Taxis, will afford us."

The future engrossed all my thoughts; and puzzling as my late adventures had been to account for, I never for a moment reverted to the past. "Is she to be mine?" was the ever-rising question in my mind. The thousand difficulties that had crossed my path might long since have terminated a pursuit where there was so little of promise, did I not cherish the idea in my heart that I was fated to succeed. Sheridan answered the ribald sneers of his first auditory by saying, "Laugh on; but I have it in me, and by —— it shall come out." So I whispered to myself: "Go on, Harry. Luck has been hitherto against you, it is true; but you have yet one throw of the dice, and something seems to say a fortunate one, in store; and if so—" But I cannot trust myself with such anticipations. I am well aware how little the world sympathizes with the man whose fortunes are the sport of his temperament; that April-day frame of mind is ever the jest and scoff of those hardier and sterner natures who, if never overjoyed by success, are never much depressed by failure. That I have been cast in the former mould, these "Confessions" have, alas! plainly proved; but that I regret it, I fear also, for my character for sound judgment, I must answer "No."

> " Better far to be
> In utter darkness lying
> Than be blest with light and see
> That light forever flying "—

is doubtless very pretty poetry, but very poor philosophy. For myself—and some glimpses of sunshine this fair world has afforded me, fleeting and passing enough, in all conscience; and yet I am not so ungrateful as to repine at my happiness because it was not permanent, while I am thankful for those bright hours of "Love's Young Dream" which, if nothing more, are at least delightful souvenirs. They form the golden thread in the tangled web of our existence, ever appearing amid the darker surface around, and throwing a fair halo of brilliancy on what, without it, were cold, bleak, and barren. No, no,—

> "The light that lies
> In woman's eyes"

were it twice as fleeting as—as it is ten times more brilliant than—the forked lightning, irradiates the dark gloom within us for many a long day after it has ceased to shine upon us. As in boyhood it is the humanizing influence that tempers the fierce and unruly passions of our nature, so in manhood it forms the goal to which all our better and higher aspirations tend, telling us there is something more worthy than gold, and a more lofty pinnacle of ambition than the praise and envy of our fellow-men; and we may rest assured that when this feeling dies within us, all the ideal of life dies with it, and nothing remains save the dull reality of our daily cares and occupations. "I have lived and have loved," saith Schiller; and if it were not that there seems some tautology in the phrase, I should say such is my own motto. "If Lady Jane but prove true; if I have really succeeded; if, in a word— But why speculate upon such chances? What pretensions have I, what reasons, to look for such a prize? Alas and alas! were I to catechize myself too closely, I fear that my horses' heads would face towards Calais, and that I should turn my back upon the only prospect of happiness I can picture to myself in this world."

In reflections such as these the hours rolled over, and it was already late at night when we reached the little village of Merchem. While fresh horses were being got ready, I seized the occasion to partake of the *table d'hôte* supper of the inn, at the door of which the diligence was drawn up. Around the long and not over-scrupulously clean table sat the usual assemblage of a German "Eilwagen," smoking, dressing salad, knitting, and occasionally picking their teeth with their forks, until the soup should make its appearance. Taking my place amid this motley assemblage of mustachioed shopkeepers and voluminously petticoated Fraus, I sat calculating how long human patience could endure such companionship, when my attention was aroused by hearing a person near me narrate to his friend the circumstances of my *début* at Strasburg, with certain marginal notes of his own that not a little surprised me.

"And so it turned out not to be Meyerbeer after all," said the listener.

"Of course not," replied the other. "Meyerbeer's passport was stolen from him in the diligence by this English *escroc,* and the consequence was that our poor countryman was arrested, the other passport being found upon him; while the Englishman, proceeding to Strasburg, took his benefit at the opera and walked away with above twelve thousand florins."

"*Sappermint!*" said the other, tossing off his beer. "He must have been a clever fellow, though, to lead the orchestra in the *Francs Maçons.*"

"That is the most astonishing part of all; for they say in Strasburg that his performance upon the violin was far finer than Paganini's. But there seems some secret in it, after all;

for Madame Baptiste swears that he is Meyerbeer,—and, in fact, the matter is far from being cleared up, nor can it be till he is apprehended."

"Which shall not be for some time to come," said I to myself, as, slipping noiselessly from the room, I regained my *calèche,* and in ten minutes more was proceeding on my journey. "So much for correct information," thought I. "One thing, however, is certain,—to the chance interchange of passports I owe my safety, with the additional satisfaction that my little German acquaintance is reaping a pleasant retribution for all his worry and annoyance of me in the *coupé."*

Only he who has toiled over the weary miles of a long journey exclusively occupied with one thought, one overpowering feeling, can adequately commiserate my impatient anxiety as the days rolled slowly over on the long, tiresome road that leads from the Rhine to the South of Germany.

The morning was breaking on the fourth day of my journey as the tall spires of Munich rose to my view, amid the dull and arid desert of sand that city is placed in. "At last!" was my exclamation as the postilion tapped at the window with his whip, and then pointed towards the city,—"at last! Oh! what would be the ecstasy of my feelings now, could I exchange the torturing anxieties of suspense for the glorious certainty my heart throbs for; now my journey is nearing its end, to see me claim as my own what I only barely aspire to in the sanguine hope of a heart that *will* not despair. But cheer up, Harry! It is a noble stake you play for, and it is ever the bold gambler that wins." Scarcely was this reflection made half aloud, when a sudden shock threw me from my seat. I fell towards the door, which, bursting open, launched me out upon the road, at the same moment that the broken axle-tree of the *calèche* had upset it on the opposite side, carrying one horse along with it, and leaving the other, with the postilion on his back, kicking and plunging with all his might. After assisting the frightened fellow to dismount, and having cut the traces of the restive animal, I then perceived that in the *mêlée* I had not escaped scathless. I could barely stand, and on passing my hand along my instep, perceived I had sprained my ankle in the fall. The day was only breaking, and no one was in sight; so that after a few minutes' consideration, the best thing to do appeared to be to get the other horse upon his legs, and despatching the postilion to Munich, then about three leagues distant, for a carriage, wait patiently on the road-side for his return. No sooner was the resolve made than carried into execution; and in less than a quarter of an hour from the moment of the accident, I was seated upon the bank, watching the retiring figure of the postilion as he disappeared down a hill on his way to Munich. When the momentary burst of impatience was over, I could not help congratulating myself that I was so far fortunate in reaching the end of my journey ere the mischance befell me. Had it occurred at Stuttgart, I really think that it would have half driven me distracted.

I was not long in my present situation when a number of peasants, with broad-brimmed hats and many-buttoned coats, passed on their way to work. They all saluted me respectfully; but although they saw the broken carriage, and might well guess at the nature of my accident, yet not one ever thought of proffering his services or even indulging curiosity by way of inquiry. "How thoroughly German!" I thought. "These people are the Turks of Europe,—stupefied with tobacco and strong beer. They have no thought for anything but themselves and their own immediate occupations." Perceiving at length one whose better dress and more intelligent look bespoke a rank above the common, I made the effort, with such *Platt-Deutsch* as I could muster, to ask if there were any house near, where I could remain till the postilion's return; and learned, greatly to my gratification, that by taking the path which led through a grove of pine-trees near me, I should find a château. But who was the proprietor he knew not,— indeed, the people were only newly come, and he believed were foreigners; English, he thought. Oh! how my heart jumped as I said, "Can they be the Callonbys?—Are they many in family? Are there ladies,—young ladies among them?" He knew not. Having hastily arranged with my new friend to watch the carriage till my return, I took the path he showed me, and, smarting with pain at every step, hurried along as best I could towards the château. I had not walked many minutes when a break in the wood gave me a view of the old mansion, and at once dispelled the illusion that was momentarily gaining upon me. "They could not be the Callonbys." The house was old, and though it had once been a fine and handsome structure, exhibited now abundant traces of decay: the rich cornices which supported the roof had fallen in many places, and lay in fragments upon the terrace beneath; the portico of the door was half tumbling, and the architraves of the windows were broken and dismantled; the tall and once richly ornamented chimneys were bereft of all their tracery, and stood bolt upright in all their nakedness above the high-pitched roof. A straggling *jet d'eau* was vigorously fighting its way amid a mass of creeping shrubs and luxuriant lichens that had grown around and above a richly carved fountain, and fell in a shower of sparkling dew upon the rank grass and tall weeds around. The gentle murmur was the only sound that broke the stillness of the morning.

A few deities in lead and stone, mutilated and broken, stood like the *Genii loci,* guarding the desolation about them, while an old superannuated peacock, with drooping, ragged tail, was the only living thing to be seen. All bespoke the wreck of what once was great and noble, and all plainly told me that such could not be the abode of the Callonbys.

Half doubting that the house were inhabited, and half scrupling, if so, to disturb its inmates from their rest, I sat down upon the terrace steps and fell into a fit of musing on the objects about. That strange propensity of my countrymen to settle down in remote and unfrequented spots upon the Continent had never struck me so forcibly; for although unquestionably there were evident traces of the former grandeur of the place, yet it was a long-past greatness, and in the dilapidated walls, weed-grown walks, the dark and gloomy pine-groves, there were more hints for sadness than I should willingly surround myself by, in a residence. The harsh grating of a heavy door behind roused me; I turned and beheld an old man in a species of tarnished and worm-eaten livery, who, holding the door, again gazed at me with a mingled expression of fear and curiosity. Having briefly explained the circumstances which had befallen me, and appealed to the broken *calèche* upon the road to corroborate my testimony, which I perceived needed such aid, the old man invited me to enter, saying that his master and mistress had not yet risen, but that he would himself give me some breakfast, of which by this time I stood much in want. The room into which I was ushered corresponded well with the exterior of the house. It was large, bleak, and ill-furnished; the ample, uncurtained windows, the cold, white-panelled walls, the uncarpeted floor, all giving it an air of uninhabitable misery. A few chairs of the Louis-Quatorze taste, with blue velvet linings, faded and worn, a cracked marble table upon legs that once had been gilt, two scarcely detectable portraits of a mail-clad hero and a scarcely less formidable fair with a dove upon her wrist, formed the principal articles of furniture in this dismal abode, where so sad and depressing did everything appear that I half regretted the curiosity that had tempted me from the balmy air and cheerful morning without, to the gloom and solitude around me.

The old man soon reappeared with a not-despicable cup of *café noir* and a piece of bread as large as a teaspoon, and used by the Germans pretty much in the same way. As the adage of the "gift horse" is of tolerably general acceptance, I ate and was thankful, mingling my acknowledgments from time to time with some questions about the owners of the mansion, concerning whom I could not help feeling curious. The ancient servitor, however, knew little or nothing of those he served; his master was the honorable baron, but of his name he was ignorant; his mistress was young; they had not been many months there; they knew no one, had no visitors; he had heard they were English, but did not know it himself; they were *gute Leute,* "good people," and that was enough for him. How strange did all this seem, that two persons, young, too, should separate themselves from all the attractions and pleasures of the world and settle down in this dark and dreary solitude, where every association was of melancholy, every object a text for sad reflections. Lost in these thoughts, I sat down beside the window, and heeded not the old man as he noiselessly left the room. My thoughts ran on over the strange phases in which life presents itself, and how little, after all, external influences have to do with that peace of mind whose origin is within. "The Indian, whose wigwam is beside the cataract, heeds not its thunders nor feels its sprays as they fall in everlasting dews upon him; the Arab of the desert sees no bleakness in those never-ending plains upon whose horizon his eye has rested from childhood to age. Who knows but he who inhabits this lonely dwelling may have once shone in the gay world, mixing in its follies, tasting of its fascination? And to think that now—" The low murmurs of the pine-tops, the gentle rustle of the water through the rank grass, and my own thoughts combining, overcame me at length, and I slept,—how long I know not; but when I awoke, certain changes about showed me that some length of time had elapsed: a gay wood-fire was burning on the hearth, an ample breakfast covered the table, and the broad sheet of the "Times" newspaper was negligently reposing in the deep hollow of an arm-chair. Before I had well thought how to apologize for the cool *insouciance* of my intrusion, the door opened, and a tall, well-built man entered; his shooting-jacket and gaiters were evidence of his English origin, while a bushy mustache and most ample "Henri Quatre" nearly concealed features that still were not quite unknown to me. He stopped, looked steadily at me, placed a hand on either shoulder, and calling out, "Harry—Harry Lorrequer, by all that's glorious!" rushed from the room in a transport of laughter.

If my escape from the gallows depended upon my guessing my friend, I should have submitted to the last penalty of the law; never was I so completely nonplussed. "Confound him, what does he mean by running away in that fashion! It would serve him right were I to decamp by one of the windows before he comes back. But hark! some one is approaching."

"I tell you I cannot be mistaken," said the man's voice from without.

"Oh, impossible!" said a ladylike accent that seemed not heard by me for the first time.

"Judge for yourself,—though certainly the last time you saw him may confuse your memory a little."

"What the devil does he mean by that?" said I, as the door opened and a very beautiful young woman came forward, who, after a moment's hesitation, called out,—

"True, indeed, it is Mr. Lorrequer; but he seems to have forgotten me."

The eyes, the lips, the tone of the voice, were all familiar. "What! can it be possible?" Her companion, who had now entered, stood behind her holding his sides with ill-suppressed mirth, and at length called out,—

"Harry, my boy, you scarcely were more discomposed the last morning we parted, when the yellow plush—"

"By Jove, it is!" said I, as I sprang forward, and seizing my fair friend in my arms, saluted upon both cheeks my quondam flame Miss Kamworth, now the wife of my old friend, Jack Waller, of whom I have made due mention in an early chapter of these "Confessions."

Were I given a muster-roll of my acquaintance to say which of them might inhabit this deserted mansion, Jack Waller would certainly have been the last I should have selected,— the gay, lively, dashing, high-spirited Jack, fond of society, dress, equipage, living entirely in the world, known to and liked by everybody, of universal reputation. Did you want a cavalier to see your wife through a crush at the Opera, a friend in a duel, a rider for your kicking horse in a stiff steeplechase, a bow-oar for your boat at a rowing-match, Jack was your man. Such, then, was my surprise at finding him here that although there were many things I longed to inquire about, my first question was,—

"And how came you here?"

"Life has its vicissitudes," replied Jack, laughing; "many stranger things have come to pass than *my* reformation. But first of all let us think of breakfast; you shall have ample satisfaction for all your curiosity afterwards."

"Not now, I fear; I am hurrying on to Munich."

"Oh, I perceive! But you are aware that—your friends are not there."

"The Callonbys not at Munich!" said I, with a start.

"No, they have been at Salzburg, in the Tyrol, for some weeks. But don't fret yourself; they are expected to-morrow in time for the court masquerade, so that until then at least you are my guest."

Overjoyed at this information, I turned my attention towards Madame, whom I found much improved; the *embonpoint* of womanhood had still further increased the charms of one who had always been handsome, and I could not help acknowledging that my friend was warrantable in any scheme for securing such a prize.

CHAPTER LI.

JACK WALLER'S STORY.

THE day passed quickly over with my newly found friends, whose curiosity to learn my adventures since we parted anticipated me in my wish to learn theirs. After an early dinner, however, with a fresh log upon the hearth, a crusty flask of red hermitage before us, Jack and I found ourselves alone and at liberty to speak freely together.

"I scarcely could have expected such would be our meeting, Jack," said I, "from the way we last parted."

"Yes, by Jove, Harry, I believe I behaved but shabbily ·to you in that affair; but 'Love and War,' you know,—and, besides, we had a distinct agreement drawn up between us."

"All true; and, after all, you are perhaps less to blame than my own miserable fortune that lies in wait to entrap and disappoint me at every turn in life. Tell me, what do you know of the Callonbys?"

"Nothing personally. We have met them at dinner, a visit passed subsequently between us, *et voilà tout;* they have been scenery hunting, picture hunting, and all that sort of thing since their arrival, and rarely much in Munich. But how do you stand there? 'To be, or not to be,' eh?"

"That is the very question of all others I would fain solve, and yet am in most complete ignorance of all about it; but the time approaches which must decide all. I have neither temper nor patience for further contemplation of it. So here goes: 'Success to the Enterprise.'"

"Or," said Jack, tossing off his glass at the moment, "or, as they would say in Ireland, 'Your health and inclinations, if they be virtuous.'"

"And now, Jack, tell me something of your own fortunes since the day you passed me in the post-chaise and four."

"The story is soon told. You remember that when I carried off Mary, I had no intention of leaving England whatever; my object was, after making her my wife, to open negotiations with the old Colonel, and after the approved routine of penitential letters, imploring forgiveness and setting

447

forth happiness only wanting his sanction to make it heaven itself, to have thrown ourselves at his feet *selon les règles,* sobbed, blubbered, blew our noses, and dressed for dinner, very comfortable inmates of that particularly snug residence, 'Hydrabad Cottage.' Now, Mary, who behaved with great courage for a couple of days after that, got low-spirited and depressed; the desertion of her father, as she called it, weighed upon her mind, and all my endeavors to rally and comfort her were fruitless and unavailing. Each day, however, I expected to hear something of or from the Colonel that would put an end to this feeling of suspense,—but no, three weeks rolled on; although I took care that he knew of our address, we never received any communication. You are aware that when I married I knew Mary had, or was to have had, a large fortune, and that I myself had not then enough in the world to pay the common expenses of our wedding-tour. My calculation was this: the reconciliation will possibly, what with delays of post, distance, and deliberation, take a month,—say five weeks; now, at forty pounds per week, that makes exactly two hundred pounds,—such being the precise limit of my exchequer when, blessed with a wife, a man, and a maid, three imperials, a cap-case, and a poodle, I arrived at the Royal Hotel in Edinburgh. Had I been Lord Francis Somebody, with his hundred thousand a year, looking for a new 'distraction' at any price, or still more, were I a London shopkeeper spending a Sunday in Boulogne-sur-Mer, and trying to find out something 'expensive, as he had only one day to stay,' I could not have more industriously sought out opportunities for extravagance; and each day contrived to find out some two or three acquaintances to bring home to dinner. And as I affected to have been married for a long time, Mary felt less awkward among strangers, and we got on famously; still, the silence of the Colonel weighed upon her mind, and although she partook of none of my anxieties from that source, being perfectly ignorant of the state of my finances, she dwelt so constantly upon this subject that I at length yielded to her repeated solicitations and permitted her to write to her father. Her letter was a most proper one, combining a dutiful regret for leaving her home, with the hope that her choice had been such as to excuse her rashness, or at least pal-

liate her fault. It went on to say that her father's acknowledgment of her was all she needed or cared for to complete her
happiness, and asked for his permission to seek it in person.
This was the substance of the letter, which, upon the whole,
satisfied me, and I waited anxiously for the reply. At the end
of five days the answer arrived. It was thus :—

DEAR MARY,—You have chosen your own path in life, and
having done so, I have neither the right nor inclination to interfere with your decision; I shall neither receive you nor the
person you have made your husband; and to prevent any further disappointment, inform you that as I leave this to-morrow, any future letters you might think proper to address will
not reach,

Yours very faithfully,
C. KAMWORTH.

Hydrabad Cottage.

"This was a tremendous *coup,* and not in the least anticipated by either of us. Upon me the effect was stunning,
knowing, as I did, that our fast-diminishing finances were
nearly expended. Mary, on the other hand, who neither knew
nor thought of the exchequer, rallied at once from her de-
pression, and after a hearty fit of crying, dried her eyes, and
putting her arm round my neck, said,—

" 'Well, Jack, I must only love you the more, since papa
will not share any of my affection.'

" 'I wish he would his purse, though,' muttered I, as I
pressed her in my arms and strove to seem perfectly happy.

"I shall not prolong my story by dwelling upon the agitation this letter cost me; however, I had yet a hundred pounds
left and an aunt in Harley Street, with whom I had always
been a favorite. This thought—the only rallying one I possessed—saved me for the time; and as fretting was never my
forte, I never let Mary perceive that anything had gone wrong,
and managed so well in this respect that my good spirits raised
hers, and we set out for London one fine sunshiny morning
as happy a looking couple as ever travelled the north road.

"When we arrived at the Clarendon, my first care was to
get into a cab and drive to Harley Street. I rang the bell;

and not waiting to ask if my aunt was at home, I dashed up-stairs to the drawing-room. In I bolted; and instead of the precise old Lady Lilford, sitting at her embroidery, with her fat poodle beside her, beheld a strapping-looking fellow, with a black mustache, making fierce love to a young lady on the sofa beside him.

" 'Why, how is this? I really—there must be some mistake here.' In my heart I knew that such doings in my good aunt's dwelling were impossible.

" 'I should suspect there is, sir,' drawled out he of the mustache, as he took a very cool survey of me through his glass.

" 'Is Lady Lilford at home, may I ask?' said I, in a very apologetic tone of voice.

" 'I haven't the honor of her ladyship's acquaintance,' replied he, in a lisp, evidently enjoying my perplexity, which was every moment becoming more evident.

" 'But this is her house,' said I; 'at least—'

" 'Lady Lilford is at Paris, sir,' said the young lady, who now spoke for the first time. 'Papa has taken the house for the season, and that may perhaps account for your mistake.'

"What I muttered by way of apology for my intrusion, I know not; but I stammered, the young lady blushed, the beau chuckled and turned to the window, and when I found myself in the street, I scarcely knew whether to laugh at my blunder or curse my disappointment.

"The next morning I called upon my aunt's lawyer, and having obtained her address in Paris, sauntered to the 'Junior Club' to write her a letter before post-hour. As I scanned over the morning papers, I could not help smiling at the flaming paragraph which announced my marriage to the only daughter and heiress of the millionnaire Colonel Kamworth. Not well knowing how to open the correspondence with my worthy relative, I folded the paper containing the news, and addressed it to 'Lady Lilford, Hôtel de Bristol, Paris.'

"When I arrived at the Clarendon, I found my wife and her maid surrounded by cases and bandboxes; laces, satins, and velvets were displayed on all sides, while an emissary from Storr and Mortimer was arranging a grand review of jewelry on a side-table, one half of which would have ruined the Rajah of Mysore to purchase. My advice was immediately called into requisition; and pressed into service, I had nothing left for it but to canvass, criticise, and praise, between times, which I did with a good grace, considering that I anticipated the 'Fleet' for every flounce of Valenciennes lace, and could not help associating a rich diamond aigrette with hard labor for life and the climate of New South Wales. The utter abstraction I was in led to some awkward *contretemps,* and as my wife's enthusiasm for her purchases increased, so did my revery gain ground.

" 'Is it not beautiful, Jack? How delicately worked! It must have taken a long time to do it.'

" 'Seven years,' I muttered, as my thoughts ran upon a very different topic.

" 'Oh, no, not so much!' said she, laughing; 'and it must be such a hard thing to do.'

" 'Not half so hard as carding wool or pounding oyster-shells.'

" 'How absurd you are! Well, I'll take this; it will look so well in—'

" 'Botany Bay,' said I, with a sigh that set all the party laughing, which at last roused me and enabled me to join in the joke.

"As at length one half of the room became filled with millinery and the other glittered with jewels and *bijouterie,* my wife grew weary with her exertions, and we found ourselves alone.

"When I told her that my aunt had taken up her residence in Paris, it immediately occurred to her how pleasant it would be to go there too; and although I concurred in the opinion for very different reasons, it was at length decided that we should do so; and the only difficulty now existed as to the means, as though the daily papers teemed with 'four ways to go from London to Paris,' they all resolved themselves into one, and that one, unfortunately, to me the most difficult and impracticable,—by money.

"There was, however, one last resource open,—the sale of my commission. I will not dwell upon what it cost me to resolve upon this; the determination was a painful one, but it was soon come to, and before five o'clock that day, Cox and

Greenwood had got their instructions to sell out for me, and had advanced a thousand pounds of the purchase. Our bill settled, the waiters bowing to the ground (it is your ruined man that is always the most liberal), the post-horses harnessed, and impatient for the road, I took my place beside my wife, while my valet held a parasol over the soubrette in the rumble,—all in the approved fashion of those who have an unlimited credit with Coutts or Drummond,—the whips cracked, the leaders capered, and with a patronizing bow to the proprietor of the Clarendon, away we rattled to Dover.

"After the usual routine of sea-sickness, fatigue, and poisonous cookery, we reached Paris on the fifth day, and put up at the Hôtel de Londres, Place Vendôme.

"To have an adequate idea of the state of my feelings as I trod the splendid apartments of this princely hotel, surrounded by every luxury that wealth can procure or taste suggest, you must imagine the condition of a man who is regaled with a sumptuous banquet on the eve of his execution. The inevitable termination to all my present splendor was never for a moment absent from my thoughts, and the secrecy with which I was obliged to conceal my feelings formed one of the greatest sources of my misery. 'The *coup,* when it does come, will be sad enough, and poor Mary may as well have the comfort of the deception as long as it lasts, without suffering as I do.' Such was the reasoning by which I met every resolve to break to her the real state of our finances, and such the frame of mind in which I spent my days at Paris,—the only really unhappy ones I can ever charge my memory with.

"We had scarcely got settled in the hotel when my aunt, who inhabited the opposite side of the Place, came over to see us and wish us joy. She had seen the paragraph in the 'Post,' and, like all other people with plenty of money, fully approved a match like mine.

"She was delighted with Mary, and despite the natural reserve of the old maiden lady, became actually cordial, and invited us to dine with her that day, and every succeeding one we might feel disposed to do so. 'So far so well,' thought I, as I offered her my arm to see her home; 'but if she knew of what value even this small attention is to us, am I quite so sure she would offer it? However, no time is to be lost; I cannot live in this state of hourly agitation; I must make some one the confidant of my sorrows; and none so fit as she who can relieve as well as advise upon them.' Although such was my determination, yet somehow I could not pluck up courage for the effort. My aunt's congratulations upon my good luck made me shrink from the avowal; and while she ran on upon the beauty and grace of my wife,—topics I fully concurred in,—I almost chimed in with her satisfaction at the prudential and proper motives which led to the match. Twenty times I was on the eve of interrupting her and saying, 'But, madam, I am a beggar; my wife has not a shilling; I have absolutely nothing; her father disowns us; my commission is sold; and in three weeks the Hôtel de Londres and the Palais Royal will be some hundred pounds the richer, and I without the fare of a cab to drive me down to the Seine to drown myself.'

"Such were my thoughts; but whenever I endeavored to speak them, some confounded fulness in my throat nearly choked me, my temples throbbed, my hands trembled; and whether it was shame or the sickness of despair, I cannot say, but the words would not come, and all that I could get out was some flattery of my wife's beauty, or some vapid eulogy upon my own cleverness in securing such a prize. To give you in one brief sentence an idea of my state, Harry, know, then, that though loving Mary with all my heart and soul, as I felt she deserved to be loved, fifty times a day I would have given my life itself that you had been the successful man on the morning that I carried her off, and that Jack Waller was once more a bachelor, to see the only woman he ever loved the wife of another.

"But this is growing tedious, Harry; I must get over the ground faster. Two months passed over at Paris, during which we continued to live at the Londres, giving dinners, *soirées, déjeuners*. With the prettiest equipage in the Champs Elysées, we were quite the mode; for my wife—which is rare enough for an Englishwoman—knew how to dress herself. Our evening-parties were the most distinguished things going, and if I were capable of partaking of any pleasure in the *éclat,* I had my share, having won all the pigeon-matches in the Bois de Boulogne, and beat Lord Henry Seymour himself in a steeplechase. The continual round of occupation in which pleasure involves a man is certainly its greatest attraction,—reflection is impossible; the present is too full to admit any of the past, and very little of the future; and even I, with all my terrors awaiting me, began to feel a half indifference to the result in the manifold cares of my then existence. To this state of fatalism—for such it was becoming—had I arrived, when the vision was dispelled in a moment by a visit from my aunt, who came to say that, some business requiring her immediate presence in London, she was to set out that evening, but hoped to find us in Paris on her return. I was thunderstruck at the news. Although as yet I had obtained no manner of assistance from the old lady, yet I felt that her very presence was a kind of security to us, and that in every sudden emergency she was there to apply to. My money was nearly expended, the second and last instalment of my commission was all that remained, and much of even that I owed to tradespeople. I now resolved to speak out. 'The worst must be known,' thought I, 'in a few days, and now or never be it.' So saying, I drew my aunt's arm within my own, and telling her that I wished a few minutes' conversation alone, led her to one of the less frequented walks in the Tuileries gardens. When we had got sufficiently far to be removed from all listeners, I began thus: 'My dearest aunt, what I have suffered in concealing from you so long the subject of my present confession, will plead as my excuse in not making you sooner my confidant.' When I had got thus far, the agitation of my aunt was such that I could not venture to say more for a minute or two. At length she said, in a kind of hurried whisper, 'Go on;' and although then I would have given all I possessed in the world to have continued, I could not speak a word.

" 'Dear John, what is it? Anything about Mary? For Heaven's sake, speak!'

" 'Yes, dearest aunt, it is about Mary, and entirely about Mary.'

" 'Ah, dear me! I feared it long since; but then, John, consider, she is very handsome, very much admired, and—'

" 'That makes it all the heavier, my dear aunt; the prouder

her present position, the more severely will she feel the reverse.'

" 'Oh! but surely, John, your fears must exaggerate the danger.'

" 'Nothing of the kind,—I have not words to tell you.'

" 'Oh, dear, oh, dear! don't say so,' said the old lady, blushing; 'for though I have often remarked a kind of gay flirting manner she has with men, I am sure she means nothing by it; she is so young and so—'

"I stopped, stepped forward, and looking straight into my aunt's face, broke out into a fit of laughter, so that she, mistaking it for hysterical from its violence, nearly fainted upon the spot.

"As soon as I could sufficiently recover gravity to explain to my aunt her mistake, I endeavored to do so; but so ludicrous was the *contretemps*, and so ashamed the old lady for her gratuitous suspicions, that she would not listen to a word, and begged me to return to her hotel. Such an unexpected turn to my communication routed all my plans; and after a very awkward silence of some minutes on both sides, I mumbled something about her expensive habits of life, costly equipage, number of horses, etc., and hinted at the propriety of retrenchment.

" 'Mary rides beautifully,' said my aunt drily.

" 'Yes; but, my dear aunt, it was not exactly of that I was going to speak, for, in fact—'

" 'Oh! John,' said she, interrupting, 'I know your delicacy too well to suspect; but, in fact, I have myself perceived what you allude to, and wished very much to have some conversation with you on the subject.'

" 'Thank God!' said I to myself; 'at length we understand each other, and the ice is broken at last.'

" 'Indeed, I think I have anticipated your wish in the matter; but as time presses, and I must look after all my packing, I shall say good-by for a few weeks; and in the evening, Jepson, who stays here, will bring you *what I mean* over to your hotel. Once more, then, good by!'

" 'Good by, my dearest, kindest friend!' said I, taking a most tender adieu of the old lady. 'What an excellent creature she is!' said I, half aloud, as I turned towards home;

'how considerate, how truly kind, to spare me, too, all the pain of explanation. Now I begin to breathe once more. If there be a flask of Johannisberg in the Londres, I'll drink your health this day, and so shall Mary.' So saying, I entered the hotel with a lighter heart and a firmer step than ever it had been my fortune to do hitherto.

" 'We shall miss the old lady, I'm sure, Mary, she is so kind.'

" 'Oh! indeed she is; but then, John, she is *such* a prude.'

"Now, I could not help recurring in my mind to some of the conversation in the Tuileries gardens, and did not feel exactly at ease.

" 'Such a prude, and so very old-fashioned in her notions.'

" 'Yes, Mary,' said I, with more gravity than she was prepared for, 'she is a prude; but I am not certain that in foreign society, where less liberties are tolerated than in our country, such a bearing be not wiser.' What I was going to plunge into, Heaven knows; for the waiter entered at the moment, and presenting me with a large and carefully sealed package, said, *'De la part de Miladi Lilfore.'* 'But stay, here comes, if I am not mistaken, a better eulogy upon my dear aunt than any I can pronounce.'

" 'How heavy it is,' said I to myself, balancing the parcel in my hand. 'There is no answer,' said I aloud to the waiter, who stood as if expecting one.

" 'The servant wishes to have some acknowledgment in writing, sir, that it has been delivered into your own hands.'

" 'Send him here, then,' said I.

"Jepson entered. 'Well, George, your parcel is all right, and here is a napoleon to drink my health.'

"Scarcely had the servants left the room when Mary, whose curiosity was fully roused, rushed over and tried to get the packet from me. After a short struggle I yielded, and she flew to the end of the room, and tearing open the seals, several papers fell to the ground. Before I could have time to snatch them up, she had read some lines written on the envelope, and turning towards me, threw her arms round my neck and said, 'Yes, Jack, she is indeed all you have said. Look here!' I turned and read, with what feeling I leave to you to guess, the following—

Dear Nephew and Niece,—The enclosed will convey to
you, with my warmest wishes for your happiness, a ticket on
the Frankfort Lottery, of which I enclose the scheme. I also
take the opportunity of saying that I have purchased the Hungarian pony for Mary, which we spoke of this morning. It
it at Johnston's stable, and will be delivered on sending for it.

" 'Think of that, Jack,—the Borghese pony, with the silky
tail, mine! Oh, what a dear, good old soul! It was the very
thing of all others I longed for, for they told me the princess
had refused every offer for it.'

"While Mary ran on in this strain, I sat mute and stupefied; the sudden reverse my hopes had sustained deprived
me for a moment of all thought, and it was several minutes
before I could rightly take in the full extent of my misfortunes.

"How that crazy old maid—for such, alas! I called her to
myself now—could have so blundered all my meaning, how
she could so palpably have mistaken, I could not conceive.
What a remedy for a man overwhelmed with debt,—a ticket
in a German lottery and a cream-colored pony! As if my
whole life had not been one continued lottery, with every day
a blank; and as to horses, I had eleven in my stables already.
Perhaps she thought twelve would read better in my schedule,
when I, next week, surrendered as insolvent.

"Unable to bear the delight, the childish delight, of Mary
on her new acquisition, I rushed out of the house and wandered for several hours on the Boulevards. At last I summoned up courage to tell my wife. I once more turned
towards home and entered her dressing-room, where she was
having her hair dressed for a ball at the Embassy. My
resolution failed me. 'Not now,' thought I; 'to-morrow will
do as well. One night more of happiness for her, and
then—' I looked on with pleasure and pride as ornament after
ornament, brilliant with diamonds and emeralds, shone in her
hair and upon her arms, still heightening her beauty and
lighting up with a dazzling brilliancy her lovely figure. 'But
then it must come, and whenever the hour arrives, the reverse
will be fully as bitter; besides, I am able now, and when I may
again be so, who can tell? Now then be it,' said I as I told

the waiting-maid to retire; and taking a chair beside my wife, put my arm round her.

" 'There, John, dearest, take care; don't you see you'll crush all that great affair of Malines lace which Rosetta has been breaking her heart to manage this half hour?'

" '*Et puis?*' said I.

" '*Et puis* I could not go to the ball, naughty boy. I am bent on great conquest to-night; so pray don't mar such good intentions.'

" 'And would be greatly disappointed were you not to go?'

" 'Of course I should. But what do you mean,—is there any reason why I should not? You are silent, John; speak, oh, speak! Has anything occurred to my—'

" 'No, no, dearest; nothing that I know has occurred to the Colonel.'

" 'Well, then, who is it? Oh, tell me at once!'

" 'Oh! my dear, there is no one in the case but ourselves.' So saying, despite the injunction about the lace, I drew her towards me, and in as few words, but as clearly as I was able, explained all our circumstances,—my endeavor to better them, my hopes, my fears, and now my bitter disappointment, if not despair.

"The first shock over, Mary showed not only more courage, but more sound sense than I could have believed. All the frivolity of her former character vanished at the first touch of adversity,—just as of old, Harry, we left the tinsel of our gay jackets behind when active service called upon us for something more sterling. She advised, counselled, and encouraged me by turns; and in half an hour the most poignant regret I had was in not having sooner made her my confidant, and checked the progress of our enormous expenditure somewhat earlier.

"I shall not detain you much longer. In three weeks we had sold our carriages and horses, our pictures (we had begun this among our extravagances), and soon after our china followed; and under the plea of ill-health we set out for Baden, not one among our Paris acquaintances ever suspecting the real reason of our departure, and never attributing any pecuniary difficulties to us,—for we paid our debts.

"The same day we left Paris I despatched a letter to my

aunt, explaining fully all about us, and suggesting that as I had now left the army forever, perhaps she would interest some of her friends—and she had powerful ones—to do something for me.

"After some little loitering on the Rhine, we fixed upon Hesse-Cassel for our residence. It was very quiet, very cheap; the country around picturesque, and last, but not least, there was not an Englishman in the neighborhood. The second week after our arrival brought us letters from my aunt. She had settled four hundred a year upon us for the present, and sent the first year in advance; and pledging herself not to forget when an opportunity of serving me should offer, promised us a visit as soon as we were ready to receive her.

"From that moment to this," said Jack, "all has gone well with us. We have, it is true, not many luxuries, but we have no wants, and, better still, no debts. The dear old aunt is always making us some little present or other, and somehow I have a kind of feeling that better luck is still in store. But faith, Harry, as long as I have a happy home and a warm fireside for a friend when he drops in upon me I scarcely can say that better luck need be wished for."

"There is only one point, Jack, you have not enlightened me upon,—how came you here? You are some hundred miles from Hesse in your present château."

"Oh! by Jove, that was a great omission in my narrative; but come, this will explain it. See here." So saying, he drew from a little drawer a large lithographic print of a magnificent castellated building, with towers and bastions, keep, moat, and even drawbridge, the walls bristling with cannon, and an eagled banner floating proudly above them.

"What, in the name of the sphinxes, is this?"

"There," said Jack, "is the Schloss von Eberhausen, or, if you like it in English, Eberhausen Castle, as it was in the year of the deluge; since the present mansion that we are now sipping our wine in bears no close resemblance to it. But to make the mystery clear, this was the great prize in the Frankfort lottery, the ticket of which my aunt's first note contained, and which we were fortunate enough to win. We have only been here a few weeks; and though the affair looks somewhat meagre, we have hopes that in a little time, and with some pains, much may be done to make it habitable. There is a capital *chasse* of some hundred acres, plenty of wood and innumerable rights, seignorial, manorial, etc., which, fortunately for my neighbors, I neither understand nor care for; and we are therefore the best friends in the world. Among others, I am styled the Graf, or Count—"

"Well, then, Monsieur le Comte," said his wife, coming in, "do you intend favoring me with your company at coffee this evening? For already it is ten o'clock; and considering my former claim upon Mr. Lorrequer, you have let me enjoy very little of his society."

We now adjourned to the drawing-room, where we gossiped away till past midnight; and I retired to my room, meditating over Jack's adventures, and praying in my heart that, despite all his mischances, my own might end as happily.

CHAPTER LII.

MUNICH.

THE rest and quietness of the preceding day had so far recovered me from the effects of my accident that I resolved, as soon as breakfast was over, to take leave of my kind friends and set out for Munich.

"We shall meet to-night, Harry," said Waller, as we parted,—"we shall meet at the Casino; and don't forget that the Croix Blanche is your hotel, and Schnetz, the tailor in the Grande Place, will provide you with everything you need in the way of dress."

This latter piece of information was satisfactory, inasmuch as the greater part of my luggage, containing my uniform, etc., had been left in the French diligence; and as the ball was patronized by the court, I was greatly puzzled how to make my appearance.

Bad roads and worse horses made me feel the few leagues before me the most tiresome part of my journey. But of course in this feeling impatience had its share. A few hours

more, and my fate would be decided; and yet I thought the
time would never come. "If the Callonbys should not arrive;
if, again, my evil star be in the ascendant, and any new impediment to our meeting arise— But I cannot, will not, think
this; Fortune must surely be tired of persecuting me by this
time, and, even to sustain her old character for fickleness,
must befriend me now. Ah! here we are in Munich, and this
is the Croix Blanche. What a dingy old mansion!"

Beneath a massive porch, supported by heavy stone pil-
lars, stood the stout figure of Andreas Behr, the host. A
white napkin, fastened in one button-hole and hanging
gracefully down beside him, a soup-ladle held sceptre-wise
in his right hand, and the grinding motion of his nether
jaw, all showed that he had risen from his *table d'hôte* to
welcome the new arrival; and certainly, if noise and uproar
might explain the phenomenon, the clatter of my equipage
over the pavement might have roused the dead.

While my postilion was endeavoring by mighty efforts,
with a heavy stone, to turn the handle of the door, and thus
liberate me from my cage, I perceived that the host came
forward and said something to him; on replying to which,
he ceased his endeavors to open the door, and looked vacantly
about him. Upon this I threw down the sash and called
out,—

"I say, is not this the Croix Blanche?"

"Ja," said the man-mountain with the napkin.

"Well, then, open the door, pray; I'm going to stop here."

"Nein."

"No! What do you mean by that? Has not Lord Callonby
engaged rooms here?"

"Ja."

"Well, then, I am a particular friend of his, and will stay
here too."

"Nein."

"What the devil are you at, with your *Ja* and *Nein!"* said
I. "Has your confounded tongue nothing better than a mono-
syllable to reply with?"

Whether disliking the tone the controversy was assuming,
or remembering that his dinner waited, I know not; but at
these words my fat friend turned leisurely round and wad-

dled back into the house, where, in a moment after, I had the pleasure of beholding him, at the head of a long table, distributing viands with a very different degree of activity from what he displayed in dialogue.

With one vigorous jerk I dashed open the door, upsetting at the same time the poor postilion, who had recommenced his operations on the lock, and, foaming with passion, strode into the *salle à manger*. Nothing is such an immediate damper to any sudden explosion of temper as the placid and unconcerned faces of a number of people who, ignorant of yourself and your peculiar miseries at the moment, seem only to regard you as a madman. This I felt strongly as, flushed in face and tingling in my fingers, I entered the room.

"Take my luggage," said I to a gaping waiter, "and place a chair there, do you hear?"

There seemed, I suppose, something in my looks that did not admit of much parley; for the man made room for me at once at the table, and left the room, as if to discharge the other part of my injunction, without saying a word. As I arranged my napkin before me, I was collecting my energies and my German, as well as I was able, for the attack of the host, which, I anticipated from his recent conduct, must now ensue; but, greatly to my surprise, he sent me my soup without a word, and the dinner went on without any interruption. When the dessert had made its appearance, I beckoned the waiter towards me, and asked what the landlord meant by his singular reception of me. The man shrugged his shoulders and raised his eyebrows without speaking, as if to imply, "It's his way."

"Well, then, no matter," said I. "Have you sent my luggage upstairs?"

"No, sir, there is no room,—the house is full."

"The house full? Confound it, this is too provoking! I have most urgent reasons for wishing to stay here. Cannot you make some arrangement? See about it, waiter." I here slipped a napoleon into the fellow's hand, and hinted that as much more awaited the *finale* of the negotiation.

In about a minute after, I perceived him behind the host's chair pleading my cause with considerable energy; but to my complete chagrin I heard the other answer all his eloquence by a loud *"Nein,"* that he grunted out in such a manner as closed the conference.

"I cannot succeed, sir," said the man as he passed behind me; "but don't leave the house till I speak with you again."

"What confounded mystery is there in all this?" thought I. "Is there anything so suspicious in my look or appearance that the old bear in the fur-cap will not even admit me? What can it all mean? One thing I'm resolved upon, nothing less than force shall remove me."

So saying, I lit my cigar, and in order to give the waiter an opportunity of conferring with me unobserved by his master, walked out into the porch and sat down.

In a few minutes he joined me, and after a stealthy look on each side, said,—

"The Herr Andreas is a hard man to deal with, and when he says a thing, never goes back of it. Now, he has been expecting the new English Chargé d'Affaires here these last ten days, and has kept the hotel half empty in consequence; and as Milor Callonby has engaged the other half, why, we have nothing to do; so that when he asked the postilion if you were milor, and found that you were not, he determined not to admit you."

"But why not have the civility to explain that?"

"He seldom speaks, and when he does, only a word or two at a time. He is quite tired with what he has gone through to-day, and will retire very early to bed; and for this reason I have requested you to remain, for as he never ventures upstairs, I will then manage to give you one of the ambassador's rooms, which, even if he come, he'll never miss. So that if you keep quiet, and do not attract any particular attention towards you, all will go well."

This advice seemed so reasonable that I determined to follow it, any inconvenience being preferable, provided I could be under the same roof with my beloved Jane; and from the waiter's account, there seemed no doubt whatever of their arrival that evening. In order, therefore, to follow his injunctions to the letter, I strolled out towards the Place in search of the tailor, and also to deliver a letter from Waller to the chamberlain to provide me with a card for the ball. Monsieur Schnetz, who was the very pinnacle of politeness, was nevertheless, in fact, nearly as untractable as my host of the Cross. All his people were engaged in preparing a suit for the English Chargé d'Affaires, whose trunks had been sent in a wrong direction, and who had despatched a courier from Frankfort to order a uniform. This second thwarting, and from the same source, so nettled me that I greatly fear all my respect for the Foreign Office, and those who live thereby, would not have saved them from something most unlike a blessing, had not Monsieur Schnetz saved diplomacy from such desecration by saying that if I could content myself with a plain suit, such as civilians wore, he would do his endeavor to accommodate me.

"Anything, Monsieur Schnetz; dress me like the Pope's Nuncio or the Lord Mayor of London, if you like, but only enable me to go."

Although my reply did not seem to convey a very exalted idea of my taste in costume to the worthy artist, it at least evinced my anxiety for the ball; and running his measure over me, he assured me that the dress he would provide was both well-looking and becoming; adding, "At nine o'clock, sir, you'll have it,—exactly the same size as his Excellency the Chargé d'Affaires."

"Confound the Chargé d'Affaires!" I added, and left the house.

CHAPTER LIII.

INN AT MUNICH.

AS I had never been in Munich before, I strolled about the town till dusk. At that time the taste of the King had not enriched the capital with the innumerable objects of art which render it now second to none in Europe. There were, indeed, then but few attractions,—narrow streets, tall, unarchitectural-looking houses, and gloomy, unimpressive churches. Tired of this, I turned towards my inn, wondering in my mind if Antoine had succeeded in procuring me the room, or whether I should be obliged to seek my lodging elsewhere. Scarcely had I entered the porch when I found him awaiting my arrival, candle in hand. He conducted me at once up the wide oaken stair, then along the gallery, into a large wainscoted room with a most capacious bed. A cheerful wood fire burned and crackled away in the grate, the cloth was already spread for supper (remember, it was in Germany), the newspapers of the day were placed before me, and in a word, every attention showed that I had found the true avenue to Antoine's good graces, who now stood bowing before me, in apparent ecstasy at his own cleverness.

"All very well done, Antoine; and now for supper. Order it yourself for me,—I never can find my way in a German *Speisekarte;* and be sure to have a *fiacre* here at nine,—nine precisely."

Antoine withdrew, leaving me to my own reflections, which now, if not gloomy, were still of the most anxious kind.

Scarcely was the supper placed upon the table, when a tremendous tramping of horses along the street, and loud cracking of whips, announced a new arrival.

"Here they are!" said I, as, springing up, I upset the soup and nearly threw the *rôti* into Antoine's face as he was putting it before me.

Downstairs I rushed through the hall, pushing aside waiters and overturning chambermaids in my course. The carriage was already at the door. "Now for a surprise," thought I, as I worked through the crowd in the porch, and reached the door just as the steps were clattered down, and a gentleman began to descend, whom twenty expectant voices, now informed of his identity, welcomed as the new Chargé d'Affaires.

"May all the—"

What I wished for his Excellency it would not be polite to repeat, nor most discreet even to remember; but, certes, I mounted the stairs with as little good-will towards the envoy extraordinary as was consistent with due loyalty.

When once more in my room, I congratulated myself that now at least no more "false starts" could occur; "The eternal Chargé d'Affaires, of whom I have been hearing since my arrival, cannot come twice. He is here now, and I hope I've done with him."

The supper—some greasiness apart—was good, the wine excellent. My spirits were gradually rising, and I paced my room in that mingled state of hope and fear that, amid all its anxieties, has such moments of ecstasy. A new noise without,—some rabble in the street; hark! it comes nearer,— I hear the sound of wheels; yes, there go the horses,—nearer and nearer. Ah! it is dying away again—stay—yes, yes, here it is, here they are! The noise and tumult without now increased every instant, the heavy trot of six or eight horses shook the very street, and I heard the round, dull, rumbling sound of a heavy carriage as it drew up at last at the door of the inn. Why it was, I know not, but this time I could not stir; my heart beat almost loud enough for me to hear, my temples throbbed, and then a cold and clammy perspiration came over me, and I sank into a chair. Fearing that I was about to faint, sick as I was, I felt angry with myself, and tried to rally, but could not, and only at length was roused by hearing that the steps were let down, and shortly after, the tread of feet coming along the gallery towards my room.

"They are coming,—she is coming," thought I. "Now then for my doom!"

There was some noise of voices outside. I listened, for I still felt unable to rise. The talking grew louder; doors were opened and shut; then came a lull; then more slamming of doors and more talking; then all was still again; and at last I heard the steps of people as if retiring, and in a few minutes after, the carriage-door was jammed to, and again the heavy tramp of the horses rattled over the *pavé*. At this instant Antoine entered.

"Well, Antoine," said I, in a voice trembling with weakness and agitation,—"well, who has arrived?"

"It was his Grace the Grand Maréchal," said Antoine, scarcely heeding my question, in the importance of the illustrious visitor who had come.

"Ah! the Grand Maréchal," said I, carelessly; "does he live here?"

"*Sappermint, nein, mein Herr;* but he has just been to pay his respects to his Excellency the new Chargé d'Affaires."

In the name of all patience, I ask, who could endure this?

Arrival of the " Chargé d'Affaires."

From the hour of my arrival I am haunted by this one image,—the Chargé d'Affaires. For him I have been almost condemned to go houseless and naked; and now the most sacred feelings of my heart are subject to his influence. I walked up and down in an agony. "Another such disappointment, and my brain will turn," thought I, "and they may write my epitaph,—'Died of love and a Chargé d'Affaires.'"

"It is time to dress," said the waiter.

"I could strangle him with my own hands," muttered I, worked up into a real heat by the excitement of my passion.

"The Chargé—"

"Say that name again, villain, and I'll blow your brains out," cried I, seizing Antoine by the throat and pinning him against the wall; "only dare to mutter it, and you'll never breathe another syllable."

The poor fellow grew green with terror, and fell upon his knees before me.

"Get my dressing things ready," said I, in a more subdued tone. "I did not mean to terrify you,—but beware of what I told you."

While Antoine occupied himself with the preparations for my toilet, I sat broodingly over the wood embers, thinking of my fate.

A knock came to the door. It was the tailor's servant with my clothes. He laid down the parcel and retired, while Antoine proceeded to open it and exhibit before me a blue uniform with embroidered collar and cuffs,—the whole, without being gaudy, being sufficiently handsome, and quite as showy as I could wish.

The poor waiter expressed his unqualified approval of the costume, and talked away about the approaching ball as something pre-eminently magnificent.

"You had better look after the *fiacre,* Antoine," said I; "it is past nine."

He walked towards the door, opened it, and then turning round, said, in a kind of low, confidential whisper, pointing, with the thumb of his left hand, towards the wall of the room as he spoke,—

"He wont go; very strange that."

"Whom do you mean?" said I, quite unconscious of the allusion.

"The Chargé d'Aff—"

I made one spring at him; but he slammed the door to, and before I could reach the lobby, I heard him rolling from top to bottom of the oak staircase, making noise enough in his fall to account for the fracture of every bone in his body.

CHAPTER LIV.

THE BALL.

AS I was informed that the King would himself be present at the ball, I knew that court etiquette required that the company should arrive before his Majesty; and although at every minute I expected the arrival of the Callonbys, I dared not defer my departure any longer.

"They are certain to be at the ball," said Waller; and that sentence never left my mind.

So saying, I jumped into the *fiacre,* and in a few minutes found myself in the long line of carriages that led to the *Hof-saal.* Any one who has been in Munich will testify for me that the ball-room is one of the most beautiful in Europe; and to me, who for some time had not been living much in the world, its splendor was positively dazzling. The glare of the chandeliers, the clang of the music, the magnificence of the dresses, the beauty of the Bavarian women, too, all surprised and amazed me. There were several hundred people present, but the King not having yet arrived, dancing had not commenced. Feeling as I did then, it was rather a relief to me than otherwise that I knew no one. There was quite amusement enough in walking through the saloons, observing the strange costumes, and remarking the various groups as they congregated around the trays of ices and the *champagne frappé.* The buzz of talking and the sounds of laughter and merriment prevailed over even the orchestra; and as the gay crowds paraded the rooms, all seemed pleasure and excitement. Suddenly a tremendous noise was heard without; then came a loud roll of the drums, which lasted for several seconds, and the clank of musketry; then a cheer,—it is the King.

"The King!" resounded on all sides; and in another moment the folding-doors at the end of the *Saal* were thrown open, and the music struck up the national anthem of Bavaria.

His Majesty entered, accompanied by the Queen, his brother, two or three archduchesses, and a long suite of officers.

I could not help remarking upon the singular good taste with which the assembly—all anxious and eager to catch a glimpse of his Majesty—behaved on this occasion. There was no pressing forward to the *estrade* where he stood, no vulgar curiosity evinced by any one, but the groups continued, as before, to gather and scatter; the only difference being that the velvet chair and cushion, which had attracted some observers before, were, now that they were tenanted by royalty, passed with a deep and respectful salutation. "How proper this," thought I, "and what an inducement for a monarch to come among his people, who remember to receive him with such true politeness!" While these thoughts were passing through my mind, and I was leaning against a pillar that supported the gallery of the orchestra, a gentleman whose dress, covered with gold and embroidery, bespoke him as belonging to the court, eyed me with his lorgnette, and then passed rapidly on. A quadrille was now forming near me, and I was watching, with some interest, the proceeding, when the same figure that I remarked before, approached me, bowing deeply at every step, and shaking a halo of powder from his hair at each reverence.

"May I take the liberty of introducing myself to you?" said he. "Le Comte Benningsen." Here he bowed again, and I returned the obeisance still deeper. "Regret much that I was not fortunate enough to make your acquaintance this evening when I called upon you," said he, with another salutation.

"Never heard of that," said I to myself.

"Your Excellency arrived this evening?"

"Yes," said I; "only a few hours since."

"How fond these Germans are of titles!" thought I. Remembering that in Vienna every one is "his Grace," I thought it might be Bavarian politeness to call every one "his Excellency."

"You have not been presented, I believe?"

"No," said I; "but I hope to take an early opportunity of paying *mes hommages* to his Majesty."

"I have just received his orders to present you now," replied he, with another bow.

"The devil you have!" thought I. "How very civil that!" And although I had heard innumerable anecdotes of the free-and-easy habits of the Bavarian court, this certainly surprised me, so that I actually, to prevent a blunder, said: "Am I to understand you, Monsieur le Comte, that his Majesty was graciously pleased—"

"If you will follow me," replied the courtier, motioning with his chapeau; and in another moment I was elbowing my way through the mob of marquises and duchesses on my way to the raised platform where the King was standing.

"Heaven grant I have not misunderstood all he has been saying!" was my last thought as the crowd of courtiers fell back on either side, and I found myself before his Majesty. How the Grand Maréchal entitled me, I heard not; but when the King addressed me immediately in English, saying, "I hope your Excellency has had a good journey?" I said to myself, "Come, there is no mistake here, Harry; and it is only another freak of fortune, who is now in good-humor with you."

The King, who was a fine, tall, well-built man, with a large, bushy mustache, possessed, though not handsome, a most pleasing expression; his utterance was very rapid, and his English none of the best, so that it was with the greatest difficulty I contrived to follow his questions, which came thick as hail upon me. After some commonplaces about the roads, the weather, and the seasons, his Majesty said,—

"My Lord Callonby has been residing some time here. You know him?" And then, not waiting for a reply, added: "Pleasant person; well informed; like him much, and his daughters too,—how handsome they are!" Here I blushed, and felt most awkward, while the King continued,—

"Hope they will remain some time,—quite an ornament to our court. Monsieur le Comte, his Excellency will dance."

I here muttered an apology about my sprained ankle, and the King turned to converse with some of the ladies of the court. His Majesty's notice brought several persons now around me, who introduced themselves; and in a quarter of an hour I felt myself surrounded by acquaintances, each vying with the other in showing me attention.

"Worse places than Munich, Master Harry!" thought I, as I chaperoned a fat duchess, with fourteen quarterings, towards the refreshment-room, and had just accepted invitations enough to occupy me three weeks in advance.

"I have been looking everywhere for your Excellency," said the Grand Maréchal, bustling his way to me, breathless and panting. "His Majesty desires you will make one of his party at whist; so pray come at once."

"Figaro quà, Figaro là," muttered I; "never was man in such request. Heaven grant the whole royal family of Bavaria be not mad, for this looks very like it! Lady Jane had better look sharp, for I have only to throw my eyes on an archduchess, to be king of the Bavarian Tyrol some fine morning."

"You play whist, of course,—every Englishman does," said the King. "You shall be my partner."

Our adversaries were the Prince Maximilian, brother to his Majesty, and the Prussian ambassador. As I sat down at the table, I could not help saying in my heart, "Now is your time, Harry; if my Lord Callonby should see you, your fortune is made." Waller passed at this moment, and as he saluted the King I saw him actually start with amazement as he beheld me. "Better fun this than figuring in the yellow plush, Master Jack," I muttered, as he passed on, actually thunderstruck with amazement. But the game was begun, and I was obliged to be attentive. We won the first game, and the King was in immense good-humor as he took some franc-pieces from the Prussian minister, who, small as the stake was, seemed not to relish losing. His Majesty now complimented me upon my play, and was about to add something, when he perceived some one in the crowd, and sent an aide-de-camp for him.

"Ah, my lord, we expected you earlier!" and then said some words in too low a tone for me to hear, motioning towards me as he spoke.

If Waller was surprised at seeing me where I was, it was nothing to the effect produced upon the present party, whom I now recognized as Lord Callonby. Respect for the presence we were in restrained any expression on either side, and a more ludicrous tableau than we presented can scarcely be conceived. What I would have given that the whist party was over, I need not say; and certainly his Majesty's eulogy upon my play came too soon, for I was now so discomposed, my eyes wandering from the table to see if Lady Jane was near, that I lost every trick, and finished by revoking. The King rose half pettishly, observing that "His Excellency seems fatigued;" and I rushed forward to shake hands with Lord Callonby, totally forgetting the royal censure in my delight at discovering my friend.

"Lorrequer, I am indeed rejoiced to see you. And when did you arrive?"

"This evening."

"This evening! and how the deuce have you contrived already, eh? Why, you seem quite at home here!"

"You shall hear all," said I, hastily; "but is Lady Callonby here?"

"No. Kilkee only is with me,—there he is, figuranting away in a galop. The ladies were too tired to come, particularly as they dine at court to-morrow; the fatigue would be too great."

"I have his Majesty's order to invite your Excellency to dinner to-morrow," said the Grand Maréchal, coming up at this instant.

I bowed my acknowledgments, and turned again to Lord Callonby, whose surprise now seemed to have reached the climax.

"Why, Lorrequer, I never heard of this! When did you adopt this new career?"

Not understanding the gist of the question, and conceiving that it applied to my success at court, I answered at random something about "falling upon my legs, good luck," etc., and once more returned to the charge, inquiring most anxiously for Lady Callonby's health.

"Ah! she is tolerably well. Jane is the only invalid; but then we hope Italy will restore her."

Just at this instant Kilkee caught my eye, and rushing over from his place beside his partner, shook me by both hands, saying,—

"Delighted to see you here, Lorrequer; but as I can't stay now, promise to sup with me to-night at the Cross."

I accepted, of course, and the next instant he was whirling along in his waltz with one of the most lovely German girls I ever saw. Lord Callonby saw my admiration of her, and as it were replying to my gaze, remarked,—

"Yes, very handsome indeed; but really Kilkee is going too far with it. I rely very much upon you to reason him out of his folly; and we have all agreed that you have most influence over him, and are most likely to be listened to patiently."

Here was a new character assigned me,—the confidential friend and adviser of the family, trusted with a most delicate and important secret, likely to bring me into most intimate terms of intercourse with them all; for the "we" of Lord Callonby bespoke a family consultation, in which I was deputed as the negotiator. I at once promised my assistance, saying at the same time that if Kilkee really was strongly attached, and had also reason to suppose that the lady liked him, it was not exactly fair,—that, in short, if the matter had gone beyond flirtation, any interference of mine would be imprudent, if not impertinent. Lord Callonby smiled slightly as he replied,—

"Quite right, Lorrequer. I am just as much against constraint as yourself, if only no great barriers exist; but here, with a difference of religion, country, language, habits, in fact everything that can create disparity, the thing is not to be thought of."

I suspected that his Lordship read in my partial defence of Kilkee a slight attempt to prop up my own case, and I felt confused and embarrassed beyond measure at the detection.

"Well, we shall have time enough for all this. Now let us

hear something of my old friend Sir Guy. How is he looking?"

"I am unfortunately unable to give you any account of him. I left Paris the very day before he was expected to arrive there."

"Oh! then I have all the news myself in that case; for in his letter, which I received yesterday, he mentions that we are not to expect him before Tuesday."

"Expect him! Is he coming here then?"

"Yes. Why, I thought you were aware of that. He has been long promising to pay us a visit; and at last, by great persuasion, we have succeeded in getting him across the sea, —and, indeed, were it not that he was coming, we should have been in Florence before this."

A gleam of hope shot through my heart as I said to myself, "What can this visit mean?" and the moment after, I felt sick, almost fainting, as I asked if my Cousin Guy was also expected.

"Oh, yes! We shall want him, I should think," said Lord Callonby, with a very peculiar smile.

I thought I should have fallen at these few words. "Come, Harry," thought I, "it is better to learn your fate at once. Now or never; death itself were preferable to this continued suspense. If the blow is to fall, it can scarcely sink me lower than I now feel." So reasoning, I laid my hand upon Lord Callonby's arm, and with a face pale as death, and a voice all but inarticulate, said,—

"My lord, you will pardon, I am sure—"

"My dear Lorrequer," said his Lordship, interrupting me, "for Heaven's sake sit down. How ill you are looking! We must nurse you, my poor fellow."

I sank upon a bench, the light danced before my eyes, the clang of the music sounded like the roar of a waterfall, and I felt a cold perspiration burst over my face and forehead. At the instant I recognized Kilkee's voice, and without well knowing why or how, discovered myself in the open air.

"Come, you are better now," said Kilkee, "and will be quite well when you get some supper and a little of the tokay his Majesty has been good enough to send us."

"His Majesty desires to know if his Excellency is better," said an aide-de-camp.

I muttered my most grateful acknowledgments.

"One of the court carriages is in waiting for your Excellency," said a venerable old gentleman in a tie-wig, whom I recognized as the Minister for Foreign Affairs, as he added, in a lower tone, to Lord Callonby, "I fear he has been greatly overworked lately. His exertions on the subject of the Greek Loan are well known to his Majesty."

"Indeed!" said Lord Callonby, with a start of surprise; "I never heard of that before."

If it had not been for that start of amazement, I should have died of terror. It was the only thing that showed me I was not out of my senses, which I now concluded the old gentleman must be; for I had never heard of the Greek Loan in my life before.

"Farewell! *mon cher collègue,*" said the venerable minister as I got into the carriage, wondering, as well I might, what singular band of brotherhood united one of his Majesty's 4—th with the Minister for Foreign Affairs of the Court of Bavaria.

When I arrived at the White Cross I found my nerves, usually proof to anything, so shaken and shattered that, fearing, with the difficult game before me, any mistake, however trivial, might mar all my fortunes forever, I said a "goodnight" to my friends and went to bed.

CHAPTER LV.

A DISCOVERY.

" A NOTE for Monsieur," said the waiter, awaking me at the same time from the soundest sleep and the most delightful dream. The billet was thus:—

If your "Excellency" does not intend to slumber during the next twenty-four hours, it might be as well to remember that we are waiting breakfast. Ever yours,

KILKEE.

"It is true, then," said I, following up the delusion of my dream,—"it is true I am really domesticated once more with the Callonbys; my suit is prospering, and at length the long-sought, long-hoped-for moment is come—"

"Well, Harry," said Kilkee, as he dashed open the door,—"well, Harry, how are you? Better than last night, I hope?"

"Oh, yes, considerably! In fact, I can't think what could have been the matter with me; but I felt confoundedly uncomfortable."

"You did! Why, man, what can you mean? Was it not a joke?"

"A joke!" said I, with a start.

"Yes, to be sure. I thought it was only the sequel of the other humbug."

"'The sequel of the other humbug!' Gracious mercy!" thought I, getting pale with horror, "is it thus he ventures to designate my attachment to his sister?"

"Come, come, it's all over now. What the devil could have persuaded you to push the thing so far?"

"Really, I am so completely in the dark as to your meaning that I only get deeper in the mystery by my chance replies. What do you mean?"

"What do I mean? Why, the affair of last night, of course. All Munich is full of it; and most fortunately for you, the King has taken it all in the most good-humored way, and laughs more than any one else about it."

"Oh! then," thought I, "I must have done or said something last night, during my illness, that I can't remember now.—Come, Kilkee, out with it. What happened last night that has served to amuse the good people of Munich? For as I am a true man, I forget all you are alluding to."

"And don't remember the Greek Loan, eh?"

"The Greek Loan?"

"And your Excellency's marked reception by his Majesty? By Jove! though, it was the rarest piece of impudence I ever heard of; hoaxing a crowned head, quizzing one of the Lord's anointed, is *un peu trop fort.*"

"If you really do not wish to render me insane at once,

for the love of mercy say, in plain terms, what all this means."

"Come, come, I see you are incorrigible: but as breakfast is waiting all this time, you shall have your explanations below stairs."

Before I had time for another question, Kilkee passed his arm within mine and led me along the corridor, pouring out, the entire time, a whole rhapsody about the practical joke of my late illness, which he was pleased to say would ring from one end of Europe to the other.

Lord Callonby was alone in the breakfast-room when we entered, and the moment he perceived me, called out,—

"Eh, Lorrequer, you here still? Why, man, I thought you'd have been over the frontier early this morning."

"Indeed, my lord! I am not exactly aware of any urgent reason for so rapid a flight."

"You are not? The devil you are not! Why, you must surely have known his Majesty to be the best-tempered man in his dominions, then, or you would never have played off such a *ruse,*—though, I must say, there never was anything better done. Old Heldersteen, the Minister for Foreign Affairs, is nearly deranged this morning about it. It seems that he was the first that fell into the trap. But, seriously speaking, I think it would be better if you got away from this. The King, it is true, has behaved with the best possible good feeling, but—"

"My lord, I have a favor to ask, perhaps—indeed, in all likelihood—the last I shall ever ask of your Lordship; it is this: What are you alluding to all this while? and for what especial reason do you suggest my immediate departure from Munich?"

"Bless my heart and soul! you surely cannot mean to carry the thing on any farther? You never can intend to assume your ministerial functions by daylight?"

"My what?—my ministerial functions?"

"Oh, no! that were too much, even though his Majesty did say that you were the most agreeable diplomatist he had met for a long time."

"I a diplomatist!"

"You, certainly! Surely you cannot be acting now! Why,

gracious mercy, Lorrequer! can it be possible that you were not doing it by design? Do you really not know in what character you appeared last night?"

"If in any other than that of Harry Lorrequer, my lord, I pledge my honor I am ignorant."

"Nor the uniform you wore,—don't you know what it meant?"

"The tailor sent it to my room."

"Why, by Jove! this will kill me!" said Lord Callonby, bursting into a fit of laughter, in which Kilkee, a hitherto silent spectator of our colloquy, joined to such an extent that I thought he might burst a blood-vessel. "Why, man, you went as the Chargé d'Affaires."

"I the Chargé d'Affaires!"

"That you did, and a most successful *début* you made of it."

While shame and confusion covered me from head to foot at the absurd and ludicrous blunder I had been guilty of, the sense of the ridiculous was so strong in me that I fell upon a sofa and laughed on with the others for full ten minutes.

"Your Excellency is, I am rejoiced to find, in good spirits," said Lady Callonby, entering, and presenting her hand.

"He is so glad to have arranged the Greek Loan," said Lady Catherine, smiling, with a half-malicious twinkle of the eye.

Just at this instant another door opened, and Lady Jane appeared. Luckily for me, the increased mirth of the party, as Lord Callonby informed them of *my* blunder, prevented their paying any attention to me; for as I half sprang forward towards her, my agitation would have revealed to any observer the whole state of my feelings. I took her hand, which she extended to me without speaking, and bowing deeply over it, raised my head and looked into her eyes, as if to read at one glance my fate; and when I let fall her hand, I would not have exchanged my fortune for a kingdom.

"You have heard, Jane, how our friend opened his campaign in Munich last night?"

"Oh! I hope, Mr. Lorrequer, they are only quizzing. You surely could not—"

"Could not! What he could not, what he would not do, is beyond my calculation to make out," said Kilkee, laughing, —"anything in life, from breaking an axletree to hoaxing a king." I turned, as may be imagined, a deaf ear to this allusion, which really frightened me, not knowing how far Kilkee's information might lead, nor how he might feel disposed to use it. Lady Jane turned a half-reproachful glance at me, as if rebuking my folly; but the interest she thus took in me I would not have bartered for the smile of the proudest queen in Christendom.

Breakfast over, Lord Callonby undertook to explain to the court the blunder by which I had unwittingly been betrayed into personating the newly arrived minister; and as the mistake was more of their causing than my own, my excuses were accepted, and when his Lordship returned to the hotel, he brought with him an invitation for me to dine at court in my own unaccredited character. By this time I had been carrying on the siege as briskly as circumstances permitted; Lady Callonby, being deeply interested in her newly arrived purchases, and Lady Catherine, being good-natured enough to pretend to be so also, left me, at intervals, many opportunities of speaking to Lady Jane.

As I feared that such occasions would not often present themselves, I determined on making the best use of my time, and at once led the conversation towards the goal I aimed at, by asking if Lady Jane had completely forgotten the wild cliffs and rocky coast of Clare, amid the tall mountains and glaciered peaks of the Tyrol?

"Far from it," she replied. "I have a most clear remembrance of bold Moher and the rolling swell of the blue Atlantic, and long to feel its spray once more upon my cheek. But then, I knew it in childhood,—your acquaintance with it was of a later date, and connected with fewer happy associations."

"Fewer happy associations,—how can you say so? Was it not there the brightest hours of my whole life were passed; was it not there I first met—"

"Kilkee tells me," said Lady Jane, interrupting me shortly, "that Miss Bingham is extremely pretty."

This was turning my flank with a vengeance; so I muttered something about difference of tastes, etc., and continued: "I understand my worthy cousin Guy had the good fortune to make your acquaintance in Paris."

It was now her turn to blush, which she did deeply, and said nothing.

"He is expected, I believe, in a few days at Munich," said I, fixing my eyes upon her, and endeavoring to read her thoughts. She blushed more deeply, and the blood at my own heart ran cold as I thought over all I had heard, and I muttered to myself, "She loves him."

"Mr. Lorrequer, the carriage is waiting; and as we are going to the Gallery this morning and have much to see, pray let us have your escort."

"Oh! I'm sure," said Catherine, "his assistance will be considerable,—particularly if his knowledge of art only equals his tact in botany. Don't you think so, Jane?" But Jane was gone.

They left the room to dress, and I was alone,—alone with my anxious, now half-despairing thoughts, crowding and rushing upon my beating brain. "She loves him, and I have only come to witness her becoming the wife of another. I see it all too plainly,—my uncle's arrival; Lord Callonby's familiar manner; Jane's own confession. All, all convince me that my fate is decided. Now, then, for one last brief explanation, and I leave Munich, never to see her more."

Just as I had so spoken, she entered. Her gloves had been forgotten in the room, and she came in, not knowing that I was there. What would I not have given at that moment for the ready-witted assurance, the easy self-possession, with which I should have made my advances had my heart not been as deeply engaged as I now felt it! Alas! my courage was gone; there was too much at stake, and I preferred, now that the time was come, any suspense, any vacillation, to the dreadful certainty of refusal.

These were my first thoughts as she entered; how they were followed, I cannot say. The same wild confusion of my brain, which I once felt when mounting the breach in a storm-party, now completely beset me; and as then, when death and destruction raged on every side, I held on my way, regardless of every obstacle, and forgetting all save the goal before me, so did I now, in the intensity of my excitement, disregard everything save the story of my love, which I poured forth with that fervor which truth only can give. But she spoke not; her averted head, her cold and tremulous hand and half-drawn sigh, were all that replied to me as I waited for that one word upon which hung all my fortune. At length her hand, which I scarcely held within my own, was gently withdrawn. She lifted it to her eyes, but still was silent.

"Enough," said I; "I seek not to pain you more. The daring ambition that prompted me to love you has met its heaviest retribution. Farewell. *You,* Lady Jane, have nothing to reproach yourself with,—*you* never encouraged, you never deceived me. I, and I alone, have been to blame, and mine must be the suffering. Adieu, then, once more, and forever."

She turned slowly round, and as the handkerchief fell from her hand,—her features were pale as marble,—I saw that she was endeavoring to speak, but could not; and at length, as the color came slowly back to her cheek, her lips moved, and just as I leaned forward, with beating heart, to hear, her sister came running forward, and suddenly checked herself in her career as she said, laughingly,—

"Mille pardons, Jane, but his Excellency must take another occasion to explain the quadruple alliance; for mamma has been waiting in the carriage these ten minutes."

I followed them to the door, placed them in the carriage, and was turning again towards the house, when Lady Callonby said,—

"Oh, Mr. Lorrequer, we count upon you! You must not desert us."

I muttered something about not feeling well.

"And then, perhaps, the Greek Loan is engaging your attention," said Catherine,—"or, mayhap, some reciprocity treaty is not prospering."

The malice of this last sally told; for Jane blushed deeply, and I felt overwhelmed with confusion.

"But pray come; the drive will do you good."

"Your Ladyship will, I am certain, excuse—"

Just as I had got so far, I caught Lady Jane's eye, for the

first time since we had left the drawing-room. What I read there I could not, for the life of me, say; but instead of finishing my sentence, I got into the carriage and drove off, very much to the surprise of Lady Callonby, who, never having studied magnetism, knew very little the cause of my sudden recovery.

The thrill of hope that shot through my heart, succeeding so rapidly the dark gloom of my despairing thoughts, buoyed me up; and while I whispered to myself, "All may not yet be lost," I summoned my best energies to my aid. Luckily for me, I was better qualified to act as cicerone in a gallery than as a guide in a green-house; and with the confidence that knowledge of a subject ever inspires, I rattled away about art and artists,—greatly to the edification of Lady Callonby, much to the surprise of Lady Catherine, and, better than all, evidently to the satisfaction of her to win whose praise I would gladly have risked my life.

"There," said I, as I placed my fair friend before a delicious little Madonna of Carlo Dolce,—"there is, perhaps, the triumph of coloring. From the downy softness of that cheek, the luscious depth of that blue eye, the waving richness of those sunny locks, all is perfect. Fortunately so beautiful a head is not a monopoly, for he painted many copies of this picture."

"Quite true," said a voice behind; "and mine at Elton is, I think, if anything, better than this."

I turned, and beheld my good old uncle, Sir Guy, who was standing beside Lady Callonby. While I welcomed my worthy relative, I could not help casting a glance around to see if Guy were also there; and not perceiving him, my heart beat freely again.

My uncle, it appeared, had just arrived, and lost no time in joining us at the gallery. His manner to me was cordial to a degree; and I perceived that, immediately upon being introduced to Lady Jane, he took considerable pains to observe her, and paid her the most marked attention.

The first moment I could steal unnoticed, I took the opportunity of asking if Guy were come. That one fact was to me all, and upon the answer to my question I hung with deep anxiety.

"Guy here? No, not yet. The fact is, Harry, my boy, Guy has not got on here as well as I could have wished. Everything had been arranged among us; Callonby behaved most handsomely, and as far as regarded myself I threw no impediment in the way. But still, I don't know how it was, but Guy did not advance, and the matter now—"

"Pray, how does it stand? Have you any hopes to put all to rights again?"

"Yes, Harry, I think, with your assistance, much may be done."

"Oh! count upon me, by all means," said I, with a sneering bitterness that my uncle could not have escaped remarking, had his attention not been drawn off by Lady Callonby.

"What have I done, what sin did I meditate before I was born, that I should come into the world branded with failure in all I attempt? Is it not enough that my cousin, my elder by some months, should be rich while I am poor, honored and titled while I am unknown and unnoticed, but is he also to be preferred to me in every station in life? Is there no feeling of the heart so sacred that it must not succumb to primogeniture?"

"What a dear old man Sir Guy is!" said Catherine, interrupting my sad reflections, "and how gallant! He is absolutely flirting with Lady Jane."

And quite true it was. The old gentleman was paying his devoirs with a studied anxiety to please that went to my very heart as I witnessed it. The remainder of that day to me was a painful and suffering one. My intention of suddenly leaving Munich had been abandoned,—why, I knew not. I felt that I was hoping against hope, and that my stay was only to confirm, by the most "damning proof," how surely I was fated to disappointment. My reasonings all ended in one point. "If she really love Guy, then my present attentions can only be a source of unhappiness to her; if she do not, is there any prospect that, from the bare fact of my attachment, so proud a family as the Callonbys will suffer their daughter to make a mere love-match?"

There was but one answer to this question, and I had at last the courage to make it; and yet the Callonbys had marked me out for their attentions, and had gone unusually

out of their way to inflict injury upon me, if all were meant
to end in nothing. "If I only could bring myself to think
that this was a systematic game adopted by them to lead to
the subsequent arrangement with my cousin; if I could but
satisfy my doubts on this head—" What threats of vengeance I muttered, I cannot remember, for I was summoned
at that critical moment to attend the party to the palace.

The state of excitement I was in was an ill preparative
for the rigid etiquette of a court dinner. All passed off, however, happily, and the King, by a most good-natured allusion
to the blunder of the night before, set me perfectly at ease on
that head.

I was placed next to Lady Jane at dinner; and half from
wounded pride, half from the momentarily increasing conviction that all was lost, chatted away gayly, without any evidence of a stronger feeling than that which the mere vicinity
of a pretty person is sure to inspire. What success this game
was attended with, I know not; but the suffering it cost me,
I shall never cease to remember. One satisfaction I certainly
did experience,—she was manifestly piqued, and several times
turned towards the person on the other side of her, to avoid
the tone of indifference in which I discussed matters that
were actually wringing my own heart at the moment. Yet
such was the bitterness of my spirit that I set down this conduct on her part as coquetry, and quite convinced myself that
any slight encouragement she might ever have given my attentions was only meant to indulge a spirit of vanity, by
adding another to the list of her conquests.

As the feeling grew upon me, I suppose my manner to her
became more palpably cutting, for it ended at last in our dis-
continuing to speak; and when we retired from the palace, I
accompanied her to the carriage in silence, and wished her a
cold and distant good-night, without any advance to touch her
hand at parting,—and yet that parting I had destined for our
last.

The greater part of that night I spent in writing letters.
One was to Jane herself, owning my affections, confessing
that even the rudeness of my late conduct was the fruit of
it, and finally assuring her that failing to win from her any
return of my passion, I had resolved never to meet her more.

I also wrote a short note to my uncle, thanking him for all he had formerly done in my behalf, but coldly declining for the future any assistance upon his part, resolving that upon my own efforts alone should I now rest my fortunes. To Lord Callonby I wrote at greater length, recapitulating the history of our early intimacy, and accusing him of encouraging me in expectations which, as he never intended to confirm them, were fated to prove my ruin. More, much more, I said, which to avow I should gladly shrink from, were it not that I have pledged myself to honesty in these "Confessions;" and as they depict the bitterness and misery of my spirit, I must plead guilty to them here. In a word, I felt myself injured. I saw no outlet for redress, and the only consolation open to my wounded pride and crushed affection was to show that if I felt myself a victim, at least I was not a dupe. I set about packing up for the journey,—whither, I knew not. My leave was nearly expired, yet I could not bear the thought of rejoining the regiment. My only desire was to leave Munich, and that speedily. When all my arrangements were completed, I went down noiselessly to the inn-yard to order posthorses by daybreak; there, to my surprise, I found all activity and bustle. Though so late at night, a courier had arrived from England for Lord Callonby, with some important despatches from the government. This would, at any other time, have interested me deeply; now I heard the news without a particle of feeling, and I made all the necessary dispositions for my journey, without paying the slightest attention to what was going on about me. I had just finished, when Lord Callonby's valet came to say that his Lordship wished to see me immediately in his dressing-room. Though I would gladly have declined any further interview, I saw no means of escape, and followed the servant to his Lordship's room.

There I found Lord Callonby in his dressing-gown and nightcap, surrounded by papers, letters, despatch-boxes, and red-tape-tied parcels, that all bespoke business.

"Lorrequer, sit down, my boy. I have much to say to you; and as we have no time to lose, you must forego a little sleep. Is the door closed? I have just received most important news from England; and to begin." Here his Lordship opened a letter and read as follows:—

My dear Lord,—They are out at last,—the majority on Friday increased to forty yesterday evening, when they resigned; the Duke has meanwhile assumed the reins till further arrangements can be perfected, and despatches are now preparing to bring all our friends about us. The only rumors as yet are, L—— for the Colonies, H—— to the Foreign Office, W—— President of the Council, and, we anxiously hope, yourself Viceroy in Ireland. In any case, lose no time in coming back to England. The struggle will be a sharp one, as the outs are distracted, and we shall want you much. Ever yours, my dear lord,   Henry ——.

"This is much sooner than I looked for, Lorrequer,—perhaps almost than I wished; but as it has taken place, we must not decline the battle. Now, what I wanted with you is this: if I go to Ireland, I should like your acceptance of the Private Secretary's office. Come, come, no objections; you know that you need not leave the army,—you can become unattached; I'll arrange all that. *A propos,* this concerns you,— it is from the Horse Guards; you need not read it now, though, —it is merely your gazette to the company. Your promotion, however, shall not stop there. However, the important thing I want with you is this: I wish you to start for England tomorrow; circumstances prevent my going from this for a few days. You can see L—— and W——, etc., and explain all I have to say; I shall write a few letters and some hints for your own guidance; and as Kilkee never would have head for these matters, I look to your friendship to do it for me."

Looking only to the past, as the proposal suited my already made resolve to quit Munich, I acceded at once, and assured Lord Callonby that I should be ready in an hour.

"Quite right, Lorrequer, but still I shall not need this; you cannot leave before eleven or twelve o'clock,—in fact, I have another service to exact at your hands before we part with you. Meanwhile, try and get some sleep; you are not likely to know anything of a bed before you reach the Clarendon."

So saying, he hurried me from the room, and as he closed the door, I heard him muttering his satisfaction that already, so far, all had been well arranged.

CHAPTER LVI.

CONCLUSION.

SLEEP came on me without my feeling it, and amid all the distracting cares and pressing thoughts that embarrassed me. I only awoke when the roll of the *calèche* sounded beneath my window, and warned me that I must be stirring and ready for the road.

"Since it is to be thus," thought I, "it is much better that this opportunity should occur of my getting away at once, and thus obviate the unpleasantness of any future meeting with Lady Jane, and the thousand conjectures that my departure, so sudden and unannounced, might give rise to. So be it; and I have now only one hope more,—that the terms we last parted on may prevent her appearing at the breakfast-table." With these words I entered the room where the Callonbys were assembled.

"This is too provoking really, Mr. Lorrequer," said Lady Callonby, with her sweetest smile and most civil manner; "quite too bad to lose you now that you have just joined us."

"Come, no tampering with our party," said Lord Callonby; "my friend here must not be seduced by honeyed words and soft speeches from the high-road that leads to honors and distinctions. Now for your instructions." Here his Lordship entered into a very deep discussion as to the conditions upon which his support might be expected and relied upon, which Kilkee from time to time interrupted by certain quizzing allusions to the low price he put upon his services, and suggested that a mission for myself should certainly enter into the compact.

At length breakfast was over, and Lord Callonby said: "Now make your adieux, and let me see you for a moment in Sir Guy's room; we have a little discussion there, in which your assistance is wanting." I accordingly took my farewell of Lady Callonby, and approached to do so to Lady Jane; but, much to my surprise, she made me a very distant salute, and said, in her coldest tone, "I hope you may have a pleasant journey." Before I had recovered my surprise at this movement, Kilkee came forward and offered to accompany me a few miles of the road. I accepted readily the kind offer, and once more bowing to the ladies, withdrew. "And thus it is," thought I, "that I leave all my long-dreamed-of happiness, and such is the end of many a long day's ardent expectation." When I entered my uncle's room, my temper was certainly not in a mood most fit for further trials, though it was doomed to meet them.

"Harry, my boy, we are in a great want of you here, and as time presses, we must state our case very briefly. You are aware, Sir Guy tells me, that your cousin Guy has been received among us as the suitor of my eldest daughter. It has been an old compact between us to unite our families by ties still stronger than our very ancient friendship, and this match has been accordingly looked to by us both with much anxiety. Now, although on our parts I think no obstacle intervenes, yet I am sorry to say there appear difficulties in other quarters. In fact, certain stories have reached Lady Jane's ears concerning your cousin which have greatly prejudiced her against him, and we have reason to think most unfairly; for we have succeeded in tracing some of the offences in question, not to Guy, but to a Mr. Morewood, who, it seems, has personated your cousin upon more than one occasion, and not a little to his disadvantage. Now, we wish you to sift these matters to the bottom, by your going to Paris as soon as you can venture to leave London. Find out this man, and, if possible, make all straight. If money is wanting, he must of course have it; but bear one thing in mind, that any possible step which may remove this unhappy impression from my daughter's mind will be of infinite service, and never forgotten by us. Kilkee, too, has taken some dislike to Guy. You have only, however, to talk to him on the matter, and he is sure to pay attention to you."

"And, Harry," said my uncle, "tell Guy I am much displeased that he is not here; I expected him to leave Paris with me, but some absurd wager at the Jockey Club detained him."

"Another thing, Harry, you may as well mention to your cousin,—that Sir Guy has complied with every suggestion that he formerly threw out; he will understand the allusion."

"Oh, yes!" said my uncle. "Tell him roundly he shall have

Elton Hall. I have fitted up Marsden for myself, so no difficulty lies in that quarter."

"You may add, if you like, that my present position with the Government enables me to offer him a speedy prospect of a regiment, and that I think he had better not leave the army."

"And say that by next post Hamercloth's bond for the six thousand shall be paid off, and let him send me a note of any other large sum he owes."

"And above all things, no more delays. I must leave this for England inevitably, and as the ladies will probably prefer wintering in Italy—"

"Oh! certainly," said my uncle; "the wedding must take place at once."

"I scarcely can ask you to come to us on the occasion, though I need not say how greatly we should all feel gratified if you could do so," said my lord.

While this cross-fire went on from both sides, I looked from one to the other of the speakers. My first impression was that, having perceived and disliked my attention to Lady Jane, they adopted this *mauvaise plaisanterie* as a kind of smart lesson for my future guidance. My next impression was that they were really in earnest, but about the very stupidest pair of old gentlemen that ever wore hair-powder.

"And this is all?" said I, drawing a long breath, and inwardly uttering a short prayer for patience.

"Why, I believe I have mentioned everything," said Lord Callonby, "except that if anything occurs to yourself that offers a prospect of forwarding this affair, we leave you a *carte blanche* to adopt it."

"Of course, then," said I, "I am to understand that as no other difficulties lie in the way than those your Lordship has mentioned, the feelings of the parties—their affections—are mutual?"

"Oh! of course; your cousin, I suppose, has made himself agreeable. He is a good-looking fellow, and, in fact, I am not aware why they should not like each other, eh, Sir Guy?"

"To be sure; and the Elton estates run half the shire with your Gloucestershire property. Never was there a more suitable match."

"Then only one point remains, and that being complied with, you may reckon upon my services,—nay, more; I promise you success. Lady Jane's own consent must be previously assured to me; without this, I must positively decline moving a step in the matter; that once obtained, freely and without constraint, I pledged myself to do all you require."

"Quite fair, Harry; I perfectly approve of your scruples." So saying, his Lordship rose and left the room.

"Well, Harry, and yourself,—what is to be done for *you?* Has Callonby offered you anything yet?"

"Yes, sir, his Lordship has most kindly offered me the under-secretaryship in Ireland; but I have resolved on declining it, though I shall not at present say so, lest he should feel any delicacy in employing me upon the present occasion."

"Why, is the boy deranged? Decline it! What have you got in the world that you should refuse such an appointment?"

The color mounted to my cheeks, my temples burned, and what I should have replied to this taunt I know not, for passion had completely mastered me. When Lord Callonby again entered the room, his usually calm and pale face was agitated and flushed, and his manner tremulous and hurried. For an instant he was silent; then, turning towards my uncle, he took his hand affectionately and said,—

"My good old friend, I am deeply, deeply grieved; but we must abandon this scheme. I have just seen my daughter, and from the few words which we have had together, I find that her dislike to the match is invincible, and, in fact, she has obtained my promise never again to allude to it. If I were willing to constrain the feelings of my child, you yourself would not permit it. So here let us forget that we ever hoped for, ever calculated on, a plan in which both our hearts were so deeply interested."

These words, few as they were, were spoken with deep feeling, and for the first time I looked upon the speaker with sincere regard. They were both silent for some minutes. Sir Guy, who was himself much agitated, spoke first.

"So be it then, Callonby, and thus do I relinquish one— perhaps the only—cheering prospect my advanced age held out to me. I have long wished to have your daughter for my niece, and since I have known her, the wish has increased tenfold."

"It was the chosen dream of all my anticipations," said Lord Callonby; "and now Jane's affections only— But let it pass."

"And is there then really no remedy? Can nothing be thought of?"

"Nothing."

"I am not quite so sure, my lord," said I, tremulously.

"No, no, Lorrequer; you are a ready witted fellow, I know, but this passes even *your* ingenuity. Besides, I have given her my word."

"Even so."

"Why, what do you mean? Speak out, man," said Sir Guy. "I'll give you ten thousand pounds on the spot if you suggest a means of overcoming this difficulty."

"Perhaps you might not accede afterwards."

"I pledge myself to it."

"And I too," said Lord Callonby, "if no unfair stratagem be resorted to towards my daughter. If she only give her free and willing consent, I agree."

"Then you must bid higher, uncle; ten thousand won't do, for the bargain is well worth the money."

"Name your price, boy, and keep your word."

"Agreed, then. Holding my uncle to his promise, I pledge myself that his nephew shall be the husband of Lady Jane Callonby. And now, my lord, write Harry, *vice* Guy, in the contract, and I am certain my uncle is too faithful to his plighted word, and too true to his promise, not to say it shall be."

The suddenness of this rash declaration absolutely stunned them both; and then, recovering at the same moment, their eyes met.

"Fairly caught, Guy!" said Lord Callonby. "A bold stroke, if it only succeed."

"And it shall, by G—," said my uncle; "Elton is yours, Harry. And with seven thousand a year, and *my* nephew to boot, Callonby won't refuse you."

There are moments in life in which conviction will follow a bold *coup de main* that never would have ensued from the slow process of reasoning. Luckily for me, this was one of those happy intervals. Lord Callonby, catching my uncle's enthusiasm, seized me by the hand and said,—

"With her consent, Lorrequer, you may count upon mine; and faith, if truth must be told, I always preferred you to the other!"

What my uncle added, I waited not to listen to, but with one bound sprang from the room, dashed upstairs to Lady Callonby's drawing-room, looked rapidly around to see if *she* were there, and then, without paying the slightest attention to the questions of Lady Callonby and her youngest daughter, was turning to leave the room, when my eye caught the flutter of a cashmere shawl in the garden beneath. In an instant the window was torn open, I stood upon the sill, and though the fall was some twenty feet, with one spring I took it, and before the ladies had recovered from their first surprise at my unaccountable conduct, put the finishing stroke to their amazement by throwing my arms around Lady Jane and clasping her to my heart.

I cannot remember by what process I explained the change that had taken place in my fortunes. I have some very vague recollection of vows of eternal love being mingled with praises of my worthy uncle; and the state of my affections and finances were jumbled up together, but still sufficiently intelligible to satisfy my beloved Jane that this time, at least, I made love with something more than *my own* consent to support me. Before we had walked half round the garden she had promised to be mine, and Harry Lorrequer, who rose that morning with nothing but despair and darkness before him, was now the happiest of men.

Dear reader, I have little more to confess. Lord Callonby's politics were fortunately deemed of more moment than maidenly scruples, and the treasury benches more respected than the trousseau. Our wedding was therefore settled for the following week. Meanwhile every day seemed to teem with its own meed of good fortune. My good uncle, under whose patronage, forty odd years before, Colonel Kamworth had obtained his commission, undertook to effect the reconciliation between him and the Wallers, who now only waited for our wedding before they set out for Hydrabad Cottage, that snug receptacle of curry and Madeira, Jack confessing that he would rather listen to the siege of Java by that fireside than hear an account of Waterloo from the lips of the Great Duke himself.

I wrote to Trevanion to invite him over to Munich for the ceremony, and the same post which informed me that he was *en route* to join us, brought also a letter from my eccentric friend O'Leary, which, his name having so often occurred in these "Confessions," I am tempted to read aloud,—the more so as its contents are no secret, Kilkee having insisted upon reading it to a committee of the whole family assembled after dinner.

DEAR LORREQUER,—The trial is over, and I am acquitted, but still in Sainte-Pélagie; for as the Government were determined to cut my head off if guilty, so the mob resolved to murder me if innocent. A pleasant situation this! Before the trial I was the most popular man in Paris, my face was in every print-shop, plaster busts of me, with a great organ behind the ear, in all the thoroughfares, and my autograph selling at six-and-twenty sous, and a lock of my hair at five francs. Now that it is proved I did not murder the minister at war (who is in excellent health and spirits), the popular feeling against me is very violent, and I am looked upon as an impostor who had obtained his notoriety under false pretences, and Vernet, who had begun my picture for a Judas, has left off in disgust. Your friend Trevanion is a trump; he procured a Tipperary gentleman to run away with Mrs. Ram, and they were married at Frankfort on Tuesday last. By the by, what an escape you had of Emily! She was only quizzing you all the time. She is engaged to be married to Tom O'Flaherty, who is here now. Emily's imitation of you, with the hat a little on one side and a handkerchief flourishing away in one hand, is capital; but when she kneels down and says, "Dearest Emily," etc., you'd swear it was yourself. [Here the laughter of the auditory prevented Kilkee proceeding, who, to my utter confusion, resumed after a little :] Don't be losing your time making up to Lord Callonby's daughter [here came another burst of laughter] ; they say here you have not a chance, and, moreover, she's a downright flirt. ["It is your turn now, Jane," said Kilkee, scarcely able to proceed.] Besides that, her father's a pompous old Tory, that won't give a sixpence with her; and the old curmudgeon your uncle has as much idea of providing for you as he has of dying. [This last sally absolutely convulsed all parties.] To be sure, Kilkee's a fool, but he is no use to you. ["Begad, I thought I was going to escape," said the individual alluded to; "but your friend O'Leary cuts on every side of him."]

The letter, after some very grave reflections upon the hopelessness of my pursuit, concluded with a kind pledge to meet me soon and become my travelling companion. "Meanwhile," added the writer, "I must cross over to London and look after my new work, which is to come out soon, under the title of 'The Loiterings of Arthur O'Leary.' "

This elegant epistle formed the subject of much laughter and conversation amongst us long after it was concluded, and little triumph could be claimed by any party, where nearly all were so roughly handled. So passed the last evening I spent in Munich. The next morning I was married.